Praise for <u>Take Five</u>

"Entertaining as a manic zoo. . . . Reading through the brilliant surface requires that you busy another part of your mind with deciphering what is happening, yet another with keeping track. Once you start learning that knack, the scripting of incidents leaves Mel Brooks looking like a hack's apprentice. No man has ever found a crazier way to write a book about the Christian faith."

—Hugh Kenner, *National Review*

"The story of a public life force who loses, one by one, his five senses, and pratfalls brutally through a dark comic night of the soul. Here's an unpredictably tough and funny affirmation of life as it comes."

—*Library Journal*

"It's *funny,* laugh-out-loud funny . . . even if Mano-vian humor continues to be off-limits for those unsettled by sex-jokes, Jesus jokes, ethnic jokes, or scatology. . . . If you're not easily offended, you'll be easily, repeatedly blasted into fits of shamefaced laughter."

—*Kirkus*

"*Take Five* is funny, provocative, and spirited."

—*Saturday Review*

Books by D. Keith Mano

Take Five

The Bridge

The Proselytizer

The Death and Life of Harry Goth

War is Heaven!

Horn

Bishop's Progress

Topless

The Fergus Dialogues

TakeFive
D. Keith Mano

Dalkey Archive Press

Library of Congress Cataloging-in-Publication Data:

Mano, D. Keith.
      Take five : a novel / by D. Keith Mano. — 1st Dalkey Archive ed.
            p.   cm.
      ISBN 1-56478-193-3 (alk. paper)
      1. Motion picture producers and directors—Fiction.   2. Senses and
sensation—Fiction.   3. Gluttony—Fiction.   I. Title.
PS3563.A56T3   1998
813'.54—dc21
                                                            98-8065
                                                              CIP

This publication is partially supported by grants from the Lannan
Foundation, the National Endowment for the Arts, a federal agency, and the
Illinois Arts Council, a state agency.

Dalkey Archive Press
Illinois State University
Campus Box 4241
Normal, IL 61790-4241

visit our website: www.cas.ilstu.edu/english/dalkey/dalkey.html

Printed on permanent/durable acid-free paper and bound in the United
States of America.

Preface

Ishmael Reed, for the back cover of his novel *Mumbo Jumbo,* listed blurbs consisting of nasty things reviewers had said about his past work. Since we are conditioned to believe that a blurb will tell us how wonderful a book is and therefore tend to look for whose name is attached to it rather than what is said, for a long time after I had read the book I didn't notice what the blurbs said, nor apparently did anyone else.

For D. Keith Mano's *Take Five,* one could derive a list almost as noteworthy. "At times as hard to read as *Finnegan's Wake,*" said the reviewer for the *American Spectator,* while managing to put in that nonexistent apostrophe in the title of Joyce's tome. The reviewer for *America* said it "is a relief to close *Take Five,*" and the critic at the *Wall Street Journal* "found it an unrelenting grind to read." (That others felt differently, you can see by the blurbs used for this edition of the book.) Even when the critics conceded, grudgingly, that there is greatness here, they still launched into an attack. And most were quick to point out that, though the novel, they assumed, is intended to be Christian, it would alienate both Christians and nonbelievers: the former because of its language and the behavior of its crude hero Simon Lynxx, and the latter because it is also "Christian."

I will add yet another group that would overlook the book: given its experimental form and indulgence in flamboyant language, the novel should have been embraced by the Coover-Barth-Gass-Hawkes-Pynchon-Barthelme critics and fans, but I know of almost no one who has ever heard of, never mind read, this book. In his earlier novels, ones far more commercially successful than this one turned out to be, there was not much hint that Mano belonged in the above-named group. So, *Take Five* managed to miss almost everyone, even those who might have been sympathetic to it, though its potential for popularity (a book that is paginated backwards!) was limited from the start, and it's questionable whether in 1982 an association with Coover, Barth & Co. would have done anything to help because we were just then beginning America's romance with the minimalists, life in the trailer parks, and two-syllable words. No, the book was doomed from the start, and Doubleday, its publisher (what an unlikely match to begin with!), must have felt the same, given the poor quality of paper and small print it used in its edition—"Let's cut our losses and run!"

The contemporary writer of whom Mano most reminds me is William Gaddis, whose critical reputation was at low-ebb at just about the time *Take Five* came out. Although one or two reviewers paired Mano with Coover and Barth, no one mentioned Gaddis. Like Gaddis, Mano creates, in the densest of prose, a world that is completely its own, tightly packed, erudite, swift, but attention-demanding. In other words, just what a novel should be. And like Gaddis, he creates a microcosm of American madness, not in the glib, moral-thumping method of a Tom Wolfe, but from the ground up, so that by the novel's end you feel that you have just visited and lived in another country or world, only to emerge from it with a clear eye on America: religion, family, greed, racism, anti-Semitism, scams, and the endless search for wealth and fame.

At the same time, there is one other author of whom I was reminded while reading the reviews of *Take Five* and seeing the critics' bewilderment, not only at the mix of obscenity and Christianity, but at the idea of salvation and grace, subjects that the author and book take seriously. The other author is Flannery O'Connor who, though different in almost every other way, is also *serious* about such things as grace and salvation. Like Mano, she created grotesques who—even though they mouth self-serving Christian beliefs—move from states of depravity to that of salvation, which itself also looks grotesque, if not depraved. For those raised to take the Bible seriously, the acts of intervening grace are, well, understandable; for those not so raised or who have since abandoned such beliefs, O'Connor is only a black humorist and satirist. For the believers, O'Connor shows the Old Testament God of wrath and precociousness; for the nonbeliever, she shows the deformities of the Bible-thumping South. And for Mano, though his God may be of the New Testament order, we have salvation coming out of the most improbable circumstances, something along the lines of Graham Greene's sacrilegious (Greene's books were on the Catholic Church's Index of banned books) idea of salvation through the experience of being lost and without hope. As I have indicated above, mix all of these together—an unconventional form, a novel that cannot go a page or two without offending Christian propriety, and a clear belief that this moral monster named Simon Lynxx is (possibly) saved—and you have a book guaranteed to alienate almost everyone.

Take Five is not what you would call a well-made novel. It belongs to the tradition of Homer, Cervantes, Sterne, and Fielding, or what once was popularly known as the "American romance" (Melville and Hawthorne), as opposed to the tightly composed British "novel." One critic complained that if Simon saw, heard, thought, or remembered anything, the reader too would see, hear, think, etc. The novel is indeed episodic, similar to the wild van ride that Simon takes his companions on early in the book: sharp turns, sudden jolts, lurches forward and sideways. The connective tissue of it all is the budding sociopathic Simon, rambling and ranting, an encyclopedic mind that embraces and permanently records all that it attaches itself to. And while having called it episodic, I will also say it is highly structured around Simon's decline and fall—his loss of all five senses, his taste lost because he mistakenly sprinkles stolen gasoline on his salad instead of olive oil and then manages to set his mouth on fire—and entrance into eternity. Like all episodic works, this one wanders and drifts, and Simon is the perfect vehicle for this wandering and drifting. A better editor might have required Mano to head his chapters in the way that eighteenth-century novels are: "In which our hero . . ." In Simon's case, this might be "In which our hero remembers the first time a girl dropped her drawers for him" or "In which our hero sees his mother naked." Characters drop in and out, some never to be heard from again, and they also tend to be types, as is the picaresque Simon himself (Falstaff, Gargantua, Ahab), bigger than life and yet forever butting his head against the limitations it imposes upon his insatiable appetites ("I want" is Simon's favorite phrase). And like an eighteenth-century novel, in this mock version of it we have the conventions of a picaresque hero, the surprising truth about his parentage, true love, a novel-ending marriage, and even the arrival of money (though not too much of it) for our hero.

But everywhere we have Simon, of the old-line Van Lynxx family whose mansion in Queens is, in the present of the novel, surrounded by the projects, and no longer the Lynxx's, now a historical landmark owned by the city, though Simon treats it as though it were his country retreat. Once gloriously rich, the family and its money are gone. Even Simon's parents only half-benefitted from the wealth, and so his father had to "work," hosting the "Lynxx Good Morning Show," a 1950s notion that every wholesome family likes to wake up to sounds and words of the perfect American family slapping itself on its back. But the show, like its host and family, is a con, the Lynxxes being the archetypal dysfunctional family rather than the good-natured fantasy portrayed on the radio. And Simon does not fall far from the dying apple tree of his family: con-man par excellence in search of money, money, and more money for his ill-fated directorial film career. The search for financial backing (at one point he goes black-face to pretend he is African-American in order to get money from the National Artists Minority Incentive Fund) for his current epic project, *Jesus 2001,* is what propels Simon through *Take Five.*

Although verbal wit and the inexhaustible Simon carry the novel, there are also scenes that will forever implant themselves in your memory. In one of Simon's attempts to scam money to make *Jesus 2001,* he agrees to "entertain" a woman that a hoped-for backer for his film insists he court. In a penthouse apartment on Sutton Place between 56th and 57th in New York, Simon enters a labyrinthine, macabre menagerie wherein he must dance for and woo a seventy-year-old-plus woman who has transformed her apartment (which apparently spans an entire block) into a Spanish Civil War tableaux, including a Barcelona café (as well as forty café-goers) where Simon first encounters this woman (whom Simon must pretend is in her thirties), a Spanish countryside (grass, hills, sun), and finally a chapel wherein Simon must feign death, as Mrs. Amistead weeps over his coffin. Aided by a teleprompter that provides his dialogue for the bizarre, scripted evening, Simon plays his role brilliantly (until he takes pity on the weeping woman and speaks to her from his coffin), having found a world that perfectly disgusts him ("This is like establishing residence in someone's masturbation fantasy") but in which he perfectly belongs, a world that only money could buy or invent. Rather than descending into the underground for this demonic episode, Mano has his character ascend on one of the wealthiest streets in New York, and you will never again walk on one of those streets without wondering what really is going on above you.

A final word about Simon. Some reviewers objected to his flamboyant, thundering, bombastic, nonstop, machine-gun-like diction. The objection was that nobody talks this way. At least, nobody in realistic fiction talks this way, which is of course the frame of reference for such naive critical judgments. But then nobody talks like Hamlet, except Hamlet. Perhaps the more accurate point to make is that nobody in "real life" talks the way that characters in realistic fiction do, though critics are so convinced of the opposite that they do not notice. So, Simon speaks the way that Simon speaks. If his speech seems improbable and stretched, then imagine an actor such as Richard Dreyfuss uttering the lines, as well as performing Simon's physical gymnastics. And Simon's speech is not far removed from that of the third-person narrator's, so close at times that they might be interchangeable. Simon drives this novel, including the narrative viewpoint. Simon's voice is indeed nonstop: as he himself admits, he has no filtering device between thought and speech, and the narrator gets swept along in the gush. This is Simon's world through and through, and no one else, including the narrator, will long forget this fact.

We are now nearing the end of the millennium, and here comes this bigger-than-life novel once more, with the hope that it will find the readership now that has escaped it for more than fifteen years.

JOHN O'BRIEN
1998

This book is for Bill Buckley:

who through an almost-decade, has given me sonship, refuge, ultra-liberal encouragement, present tense prose style, much Bach, ocean near-misses and —above all—a contact high from his irrepressible Christian cheerfulness.

And as they led him away,
they laid hold upon one
Simon, a Cyrenian, coming
out of the country . . .
    —St. Luke, 23:26

TAKE FIVE

V

7

Emptying. Airmail: the garbage parts flutter and glide and plummet, thrown out in a sweet, athletic arc. They drop through morning sunlight into shade. The bag pulls its ripcord: disintegrates. Cans' flat bottoms wink sun back, flash-flash, end over end: C and C Cola, Cerveza Rheingold, Raid (do not incinerate), Café Bustelo and Spam. One 25-watt bulb that sizzles like a small maraca. Eggshells, crusts, fat-absorbent Bounty towels: all orts of breakfast. Bill-less, an old Mets cap brakes its fall, the vacant cranium taking in air. Garbage hits the historic roof below, bonging off original hand-hewn shingles, circa 1640. Things round roll, faking yawn noises with their hollowness, down/into an aluminum gutter, circa 1976. Con Ed bills, second-language homework, sheets of *La Prensa* descend in pendulum jerks, tick-tock, tick-tock. Then, persuaded by a breeze, they flock southeast, away from the roof of Van Lynxx Manor, over the rose garden, over the cemetery, over the thickset, grouchy chapel, over the disheveled orchard, toward Hollis and Forest Hills. Tap-tap: garbage can edge on twelfth-floor balcony rail. An afterthought brown apple gets pitched from the low-rent altitude, fine arm action and follow-through, hooking leftward, sharp slider. It hits the ancient chimney, bounces, bursts to mouthfuls, which bounce, burst and are gone.

Under the roof Simon Lynxx wakes, wants. He has been wanting. The garbage noise mumbles away. Nude, Simon drowses, screening outtakes of dreams just filmed. He chews. BLT on rye to go: draw one: burger rare, no onion. Bagels with a smear. His soft inner cheek flesh tastes good: no tongue lives in such jeopardy. Simon wants. The morning erection raises its pith-helmeted head: it shivers, responsive as a tuning fork. Simon sublimates—food to sex to food to sex—interpenetrable categories, mouth- or lap-dissolved. He rolls over: to slap a big palm on Martha Washington's kapok-padded bosom, mussing it/them. Her wax cheek is scored by his three-day stubble. Simon stretches the seventy-five inches of him. Ankles, knees, groin crack. His hairless chest, paps too fat, has taken up the exercise, tiny calisthenics across its skin. Simon wants. The erection, rude, badly brought up, points. Shoulder and biceps close, Martha's face is vised in his armpit. With the noise of wooden dowels, her head—scrawk!—pops off.

Van Lynxx Manor crouches in a high-rise abyss.

ADULTS $2.00

CHILDREN 75¢

OPEN 9–5 WEEKDAYS

SUNDAY 12–3

The apartment buildings are berthed on either side, eighteen stories high, cheap seats—*mirra! mirra!*—for small groundskeeping business in Van Lynxx Garden. Now uncoordinated radios hail each other overhead. Breakfast sounds break. Windows are opened to Indian summer, sun by appointment only, hours 7 to 11 A.M. The Van Lynxx landholding reaches one hundred twenty yards back on a forty-yard frontage, worth eight bucks the square foot. A green wooden fence, contraceptive, surrounds it: three nasty strands of high-volt wire atop. At night they give off tiny meteor cremations, working out on moths and the odd fly. They buzz. A warning that history is precious and tough on defense.

40 × 120 yards, last parcel of the immense Israel Van Lynxx patroonship that once stretched northeastward along surveyors' lines which, in a modern era, were to be asphalted as Northern and Francis Lewis boulevards. Despite an occasional land riot, the Van Lynxx grant was upheld by bribeable British governors after 1664. Then, on September 2, 1776, General Howe requisitioned Van Lynxx Manor as an officers' R and R to celebrate the recent Brooklyn Heights success. Joost Van Lynxx, his wife and one son bedded down in their stable for a six-month duration: two hundred yards east, left at Bayside Avenue, on the present site of Fat Jim's Three Hour Dry Cleaning. Colonel Sir Carter Cole engaged a prostitute with Tory leanings named Mary Washington to provide leisure benefits. She slept here, yes: and there: and there. Her Tory leanings leaned pretty much to the prone. Mary "Martha" Washington had the French pox. She did more to discomfit Howe's officer corps than George himself in that bleak, long year of our not-yet republic.

The last Van Lynxx snores, he guzzles sleep, in his childhood bedroom again. Flash, flash: what you see here is a dream montage: his subconscious, sorry, uses pre-1940 film technique and a cheap back lot. Simon working at Filiades' Famous Cinema Diner. Burgers, wide as manhole covering, shoveled up. Draw one to the twentieth power. French fries hauled out in their fish-seine-sized wire basket. And "Service!" says Bettina Lynxx. No: Bettinas, all of them. At an infinite counter, upcurved—the rapid multiplication of barbershop mirror reflecting barbershop mirror—on an infinite stool, sit mothers who must be fed: in short order. Aldo, father, all hands at the steam table, signals a shared male fear. "Service!" says Bettina Lynxx. She had sent Simon upstairs, to this very bedroom, without dinner, without lunch, sometimes without meals he hadn't even intended to eat: weighed and found wanting by the calorie. Simon's stomach guffaws now, *mea culpa,* in retrospect, spect, spect. Lying here he had heard silverware: knew the clunk or clink of fork load and fork·unload. The progressive hollowness of a glassful, less full, just glass. Through a lapse in the old floor, smart-ass aromas came up to stack themselves, parfait-layered, under his slant-roof ceiling. Little Simon wanted: and ate pillow a lot. The Bettinas lean toward him: they teeter, they teeter: aargh, NO TIPPING ALLOWED. "Service here!" And two times an infinite number of empty-sock-shaped breasts, hole-in-toe for nipple—so parsimonious they starved his first few months—lounge on the counter ahead. "Dugs," he says aloud in his sleep. Back then, Simon has been told, he lost three ounces a week. As if his baby substance were nursing her.

Nnnn-gaaah. Simon has heard his own snoring: self-conscious even when not conscious at all. It's the sound of an old, acquired fear: Bettina shoving after his three-year-old heels with her terrible Hoovermatic. An insucked roar: the bag like some nude lung: long, hungry upper lip mustached with irate bristles. Vacu-u-um: u's ululated, diphthonggging, Bettina's Royal Academy diction. Simon wants to bite off his panic. Lips are harvested in sleep: teeth, night poachers, strip-mine chapped flesh. The skin there is glisteny: tough as burn scars. He preferred Aldo's erratic and dangerous left hook. Whoppo! it was over. A man's way—a fear you could *use* in later life—not a stupid neurotic quirk, worthless except when your analyst went dry. Nnnn-gaaah: he snores in fear and fears snoring. "The vacu-u-um, Simon. The vacu-u-um. It's coming for you." U.

Christ. Christ help him. And Simon's associative mind zooms in c.u. on the film again. *Jesus 2001:* his unfinished counter-epic: now The Cheapest Story Ever Told. Clap! Scene 34, Take 15, "The Walk on Water." Watch Jesus, method-acted by Bernie Cohen, sink glub-bub, into Central Park Lake. Cut! Missed the two-by-four laid on cement blocks just an inch below pond level. Cohen wading, dog-paddling, not a Messiah to follow, his spirit-gummy beard afloat six yards behind. Cut. Cash, cash: miracles are performed in unconstant dollars these days. Check out this very tentative budget. Jesus resurrected by adrenaline and holy fibrillator: $5,000. Jesus feeding (damn show-off) the 4,000: say $10 per non-union extra head. And the "Great Ascension" scene—harnessed rocket pack plus not-too-special effects—$10,000 at least. Money, Simon wants. He will kidney-punch Martha's headless, legless torso. Bankrupt

Simon has only one scene canned: seventy-five feet of "The Immaculate Conception." A surgeon prepped sterile, if not immaculate, transplanting chromosomes into Mary's blessed egg. At Lenox Hill Hospital, no less. Couldn't even afford Mount Sinai.

Simon coasts, alee on the fogged shore of awareness and behind a velvet museum rope. "Martha Washington's Room" it says outside the door-open door. Here he can pick up a distant, yet clearly pedantic voice: BBC intonations, so precise, so how-now-brown-cowed, that they bore themselves to pear-shaped yawns. Also he hears the unappreciative jive of black small children. Simon replies noncommittally: yup-yup, tongue struck like a dead match on palate, anything you say, right, sure. His erection seconds it, yup-yupping. The canopy above Martha's bed flaps to drafts. Climbing in at 3 A.M. last night, Simon the second-story man, has left a dormer window open. Underneath the big four-poster, a trundle bed cringes, afraid. Betty lamps, meant for whale oil, describe L shapes on the wall. Look to the right, please: a chest once owned by John Hancock and an oaken desk equipped with quill and inkpot and seal. Over on your left, notice the veneered late Louis XIV commode, with marquetry of brass, tortoiseshell and green-stained bone. On it: a large tulip bowl and jug. Also the Bible box, open, void, lined with Elizabethan wallpaper. Down front: two gilt armchairs in the style of Adam. And between them: uh—well—a gorilla suit, in the style of very pre-Adam. Late Americana, this: the chest brown-black, color of UPS trucks, hard as a Roman breastplate, brown-black gorilla legs, dyed goat hair, with a shine on the seat: Simon's most recent punk culture persona, worn at public appearances, which appearance he has sometimes even made alone. Rhubarb and drone: heckle. Nearer: Simon can distinguish a few words now. Yes, he'd know that voice anywhere. It's Uncle Arthur and his perfect vowels.

"Now. What say, boys and girls? Who can guess what this odd-seeming device might be? Up. Down. And hup. Down." Clack. Clack. Laughing. A cool yammer of inattention. "Whoosh, hard work that must have been, eh? A churn. A butter churn. Colonial women made butter with a churn. From milk. Sturdy sorts they were." Muffled wise-guying. "Yes. I suppose I do talk 'funky,' as you say. I'm British. A redcoat. And I think you talk funky too. Eh, please. Don't touch the fire extinguisher. Miss Williams? Would you exert a little authority? Not possible? I see. A regular Borstal-type, is he? Well. Listen, chap, it's quite simple, you know. We're not moving on until you take your hand off the nozzle." A street vulgarism. Laughter. "I'm glad your nozzle is. Good show. All right, then, single file along the corridor. Indian file I believe you call it. Or Native American file. Here. D'you see, up there? On the nail. That's the very hat worn by Israel Van Lynxx more than four hundred years ago. There's a hole in the crown. Does everyone see the hole? An Iroquois arrow made that hole. Now see, look at this—I've got an ice-cream stick on my shoe. Filthy thing. Who brought that in?" Laughter. "Down the hall, eyes right. This, children, is our most special room. The very room Martha Washington slept in. Don't lean on—agh!"

Miss Williams has screamed.

"She got some pecker."

"Man, if'n thas Martha, George was a real weird cat."

Oh well, Simon on stage again. He blinks. Past his jack-in-the-box erection, Simon can see fifteen black schoolchildren, white teacher, Uncle Arthur. White teacher mortified, but also somewhat myopic. She hooks glasses on: re-mortified then by her own curiosity. The velvet rope bellies down under kid pressure. Uncle Arthur has formed a labial and some nice fricatives but they do not develop. Simon is making his exit beneath the sheet. A hand comes out, rummages blindly, nabs Martha's wax head, hauls it under with him. Mouths gawk, silent, children are engrossed for the first time this morning. American history never so picturesque: Simon an exciting visual aid.

"My God."

"Ah, yes. The room is temporarily closed for alterations. Miss Williams, if you'd just step back—"

"My God. My God." Miss Williams goes over her bosom with forefingers, a fast hunt-and-peck typist. "That man had no clothes on. And he was aroused."

"Some pecker. That was a white dude with some umongous pecker."

"A repair person, Miss Williams. Back, children. There's no dealing with labor unions today. Back, children. Downstairs again. This room is closed for alterations."

"Lookit! Lookit! He took her head clean off. She gonna go down on him."

"I'll report this to the Landmarks Commission."

"Landmark? It really wasn't that impressive, Miss Williams. What say we take the children downstairs?"

Miss Williams, heroic, in front of the fifth grade. She bowdlerizes vision with pocketbook, with both palms. Futile: there's no business like show business and Simon yocks it up. Stage fright has given him a soft-on, but one forefinger, understudying the role, will pogo around beneath the sheet. Applause: encore, encore: Simon, naked, has class 5C in his pocket. Some heinous pantomiming with Martha's head and the finger. Miss Williams, whose sex life consists entirely of a crush on Albert Shanker, has made the big mistake: she calls Simon pervert, freak. Martha's head comes out, a curtain call, hand-puppeted by her dowel. Simon dubs the voice, "Excuse him, countrymen, his flong has grown limp in the service of his country." And Simon breaks wind, force five, a tough act to follow.

"Shee-it, he fotted."

"This is an outrage."

"I do wish you wouldn't draw attention to it, Miss Williams."

"That man was. Nude." The children laugh. It's a funny word, after all. Nood.

"Beah-asss."

"Shall we remove the children? Downstairs to the kitchen, I think. Mrs. P will show them how to dip candles. Back, please. Back."

"I have never—I have never—"

"This is not the time for regrets, Miss Williams. A sheltered life has much to recommend it. Get the little, get them down the hall."

"Look what it's doing now."

"You're encouraging it, I'm afraid. If you'll just peel their little fingers off the jamb, I'll step inside and have some pointed words with that gentleman."

Nocked. The latch tongue licks into its slot. Uncle Arthur does the shallow-breathing exercise, a device of his meditations. He is both glad and afraid: he hasn't seen Simon in twenty-eight months. Through the white, sparse crew cut his scalp heats pink, slow as an electric heating coil: excited here, the difference between flush and blush. Simon's sheet is still, a straight cloth line from perpendicular feet to head. Uncle Arthur waits it out. He is an Episcopal priest, retired: evil doesn't offend him: he rather enjoys the well-appointed sin. A short man, five foot five. Belly hangs over the beltline: elbows of some old woman on a windowsill. His arms are mobbed with woolly hair: light freckles there now outnumbered in a once good neighborhood by dark age spots. From the kitchen downstairs he can hear Miss Williams sobbing. Then Mrs. P: gruff, baritone, severe. Mrs. P is excellent with hysterical women. A kind of vocation for her: he has seen Mrs. P slap them cross-eyed.

"Simon. Is that you? I know it's you."

"Aaaaarh."

Uncle Arthur starts, taken aback: he has heard Simon's roar again. The sound discomposes him: it is terrific and, well, American. Uncle Arthur comes from a nation of modulated voices. The gorilla suit has not escaped attention. It stinks more powerfully than the animal it isn't. Open like an unused sandwich sign now: the chest front monstrously overdeveloped: pectorals, abdominals, nipples, navel. Below, one pair of brown-black plastic ape feet, each formed around a Converse sneaker, size eighteen. The toes have been splintered, some absolutely flat with lunatic rubber fringes around: Simon has walked, danced, skipped, scuffed, run them shineless. No longer smart, as two years ago they had been, when Simon and his staff appeared on a *New York* magazine cover: "Director Lynxx in his Mighty Joe Young finery: Art as Venereal

Disease." Arthur has sat: on one gilt armchair in the style of Adam. Feet dangle: Adam, apparently, a taller man.

"Simon, come out. You can come out now. The damage is done. You've made your point. We've all been shocked quite bonkers."

"Aaaaarh."

"I do wish you wouldn't make that eccentric noise. Please. We didn't expect you. It's been over two years now. I've tried to make contact. This has been rather a sharp surprise. As usual, I might add. But— Simon? Simon? I'm happy to see you."

No, take that back. The head has molted out, then the chest. Simon's flesh is wan, even surface to surface with the wan sheet. Uncle Arthur looks up, down, away—but, for the present, there will be no more nudity than that. Simon's black, matted hair sidewinds down in fat and Gorgon ropes past the nape. To make his eyes water, he will yank at it. The violence of this self-attack has perturbed Uncle Arthur. At rest, Simon is handsome as public monuments, the more-than-life-sized art of a 19th Century city hall. Long, fluted nose. A high forehead. The snide and arrogant thin mouth. Arthur could pick out souvenirs of dead Bettina there, but it can't be so. He knows that: still, the resemblance has always intrigued him. Simon can't see his mother in Arthur's face: his vision is 150/200, reading left to right. Simon has opened the mouth. A commonplace facial act, yet aggressive in him. The teeth are stained, chisel-big, incisive. Also unnatural, blank: there are no fillings. This seems somehow ugly: we have come to accept fillings in teeth. Simon has never required a dentist: his twenty-eight years of plaque tough by now as epoxy resin. He paint-scrapes the raw lower lip: it bleeds. He shoves in ragged cuticles: and they bleed. Red: time to stop. On tape recordings his yawn, played in reverse, might pass for a tiger's cough. Something ricochets off the roof: it bounces in diminishing amplitude—bonk, bonk, bonk-bonk, bbbbonk—to the gutter.

"Niggers. Christ, just what the proctologist ordered. Two dozen pickaninnies before I got the cat litter out of my eyes. What is this now, some affirmative action peep show? Hanh? And Miss Dry Hole out there in the critics' circle, 'He was aroused . . .' She should see me aroused. I'm a three-legged stool. I repeal menopauses. You could hang a swing set on it, little children play under its gentle shade— Hanh? I didn't hear you?"

"It's no wonder, Simon. Listening has never been your forte. Wait. Sssh." Uncle Arthur with both palms up, guiding the voice in and down. "Simon. They're just below us. Walls have ears. I don't believe it's good form to say nigger in this year of our Lord."

"Listen, you religious exclusion clause, I call a spade a spade. Nigger still means something, it has resonance. Collard greens, Washington's Birthday slave sales, the communal good fellowship of a lynching—it's history, dammit. Black? What's black? Black is a marketing device, a logo like GE or IBM, not a race. How else will those little rolling eight balls relate t'life? It's a service I perform at great personal inconvenience and some risk depending on the neighborhood. I'm an end t'the age of euphemism. People need t'get dumped on, it's an upper in the sickle-celled bloodstream. Everybody wants their own bigot—one anyway—it's part of the American heritage. Wait. This—hanh? Wait—" Simon blows cool on his fingertips: about to make the mental tumblers jibe. "Wait. A turnstile out there. That's what folded my schwantz in half last night. A turnstile. Clickety-click, this way t'the ingress. Uncle, you are blood of my blood. Bent chromosomes show. A swindler. It's miraculous: the cheating of the five thousand. How much d'we gross per jigaboo?"

"Per—"

"Alertness!" Simon claps. "Hup. Awake. I think your tea bag has been dipped once too often. This is money we're talking about. More than money: film footage. How much d'we charge?"

"Oh. Well, now . . . Actually, it's two dollars for an adult, seventy-five cents for children. Of course, the schools receive a special discount."

"They do? They did. What're we running here, a business or a wedding shower? This is my ancestral home." Simon has made an abacus in the air: he slides beads along. "Okay. In an average week, what's our gate?"

"Depends on the season. Seven or eight hundred, I suppose. Mrs. P does the books—"

"Aaaarh. The little con artists. They're working my pocket with string and a piece of bubble gum. Buck for the kids. A buck twenty-five. This is history. Education. A million-dollar time deposit. Snapshots of the nation ass-up on a bearskin rug. Get 'em through the offspring. We gotta be quick about it, the baby boom is over." Simon pulls his hair out, into handlebars. Then he steers his face left/right. "And it never even entered my radio-opaque head—me, the Sol Hurok of swanky frauds. This is the best damned show in Queens. Queens, my God. The artistic moth closet of New York. Here they line up at the box office if two men dig a sewer on Northern Boulevard: for these semi-suburban yo-yos it's the Trans-Lux East. You could run for sixteen weeks in Queens with just a backhoe and two wop sandhogs. Make 'em pay. Hang on their udders. No shots from the free-throw line. What about advertising?"

"Simon, I really must explain something."

"I don't want explanations, I want answers. Advertising. Huh? Hanh? Jesus, one look at you and I know why they say God save the Queen."

"Well, it's listed in *Cue*, I believe. And last month the Long Island section of the *Daily News*—"

"You call that promotion? Christ, the holy coat rack—*Cue* magazine. A dog lifting his leg on every hydrant from here to Long Island City gets better coverage. At least other dogs know him. I'm talking mega-bucks now. Pay attention. Let's see." Simon picks his nose: a whole finger joint gone. "I'll make personal appearances in native costume, the last patroon. Billboards. Radio jingles. Skywriting, my name up in smoke. Yah. And a colonial torture room under the kitchen. Adults only. Torture rooms draw big with the S and M crowd. Mrs. P can wear a spiked leather bra, if she doesn't already. Yah. Yah. Red-hot pincers, a thumbscrew big enough for your hand—"

"This is sheer insanity. The Dutch didn't torture people—"

"A little retraining, they can learn. Anyway, you with a green card from yesterday, how d'you know about American history? The brain drain needed Liquid Plumber when you came over. And to think I was gonna raffle this place off by the square foot. Look, how much did this real Ethan Allen furniture run you? What's the overhead, the depreciation? We'll have t'put on some help. Colonial barmaids with their knockers scroonched together, ready to pop out like cakes of soap in the tub. A bar. Hunh. That's it: The Lynxx Club. We convert to a topless disco joint at night. The State Liquor Authority has its price." Simon is rapping his forehead. "Uncle, you're in the film business now, a full and very silent partner. No more ham and swiss hold the mayo f'me. Shazam! This calls for a dance. Stand back, I'm about t'offend your senses with my huge and implausible nakedness."

"Oh God."

Simon unsheeted. He is *there* suddenly: six foot three and hairless, except for smoldering dark pubes and pen-sketchy patches, greaves, down the long shin line. Uncle Arthur can't ignore him: Simon seen reflected in the mirror, as Medusas are most safely looked at. Unpleasant, yet somehow fascinating: like meeting the man who will replace you at work after fifty years. Youth: white flesh: Simon superabounds in it. And he does his New York famous dance, hard-shoeing, a shuffle-off-to-Buffalo and all points west. D'jah. D'jaddah-jah. Jah! He twirls his slack, big privates as Clayton, Jackson and Durante used to swing their synchronizing canes. Through its joists the ancient and priggish floor expresses censure: creaking. D'jah. D'jah. D'jaddah-jah. Jah! His feet splatter and a two-three-four. He smacks his belly: it blurs: fat, pound-foolish. Simon is smirking, his cannibal teeth all out, in the moronic grin of dancers: their concentration on a hidden upbeat. Simon ka-thonks his rib cage: he hurts himself willfully. The skin begins to report handprints, invisible writing coaxed out by flame. And one last d'jah, jah-jah-jah, d'ahhhhh! Then he has stopped: the body some time later. His belly excuses itself. Simon's physique, taut, is superb. Uncle Arthur has been holding his eyeballs, with thumb and forefinger, in.

"Is it over now?"

"Over? Man, this is pawn to king four, just the grandmaster opening."

"Simon, please. I'm afraid it's out of the question."

"What you need is a wide-screen mentality. Some healthy megalo-mania. Sure, sure, I know: kale has to cross palms, ears have to be blown in. But look, I've got an executive staff, including my very own lady of the Hebrew inclination t'open the old Bay of Fundy. It'll be tasteful, I promise. This won't be like coughing with a hernia. We'll hold *Son et Lumière* shows in the cemetery once a week." Simon is affable: he can be. He scratches: his blood has come up abruptly, full of itches. "Listen, I'll always be indebted. Story based on an original rip-off by Rev. Arthur Gordon. I'll donate t'the Episcopal mission in Outer Luau. You'll never regret it. Everything's big in me. Lust, hunger, thirst, greed, gratitude, they're all the same size: eighteen triple E."

"I don't own the Manor anymore."

"I— Hanh? Huh?"

"I don't own the Manor anymore."

"I didn't hear you." Simon's right hand has rushed to his testicles: if your house were burning, what would you save first?

"I said, I don't own—"

"I heard you, but— I. Didn't. Hear. You. I have refused to hear you."

"No. You must. I tried and tried to raise you on the phone. My letters kept coming back addressee unknown. I didn't want to do it, but we couldn't pay the taxes. Bettina didn't provide for that. I—we donated Lynxx Manor to the Landmarks Commission." Arthur is covering his ears. He expects primal scream therapy.

And it comes: then once again. Arthur can hear it best through his diaphragm.

"I thought you might say that."

"Aaaarh. You pick-purse. You fingersmith. You—you *tick*. My house, my—he donated my house. I put in time here. I was the Birdbrain of Alcatraz. A nineteen-year rap and schmecks in the head for good behavior. I own this place. I. I. I. Me. I earned it. They sandblasted the skin off my soul here. I had to live with that pair of delirium tremens. I was the bataka they hit each other with. Not you. Me. My mother and her make-a-fag kit. It's a wonder I can find my own crank in a dark room. There was a kid once, he still lives here. Someplace. Someplace. A kid who lisped and planted vegetables and dug innocent holes. He was my only friend. And now I have to lay out two bucks t'see him on visiting days. Hanh? Aaarh. He do-na-ted it. You could've sold it, you dumb G.I. Joe doll. You coulda got a quarter mill for the land alone."

"Simon." Simon has sat on the bed. Veins jam and drum: in his neck they bop the theme from "Dragnet" out. Arthur pushes down with both hands: he pumps for quiet: someone rocking a car hood. "Simon—"

"My home. My home. I shinnied up the drainworks last night like Plastic Man. Not easy, by the way, for someone who's been on mentho-lated ganja since Saddy night. First I glitch both my shins on that Early

American footlocker there. Then, what do I find in my bed? A wax broad. Statuary rape. Blessed St. Fruitless Frit—I almost bepissed myself with fear. How'd you like t'put your leg over Howdy Doody in the middle of the night? Here, where I useta listen to Captain Midnight and Sky King. Where I patrolled Mig Alley alone. Where Jane Russell came t'kiss me good night. My things. What happened t'them? My train set without the train? My swell scale model of the *Missouri?* My first condom in its frame? Sheila Chiavoli's stuffed and feelproof bra? Even my handprints on the ceiling, painted over. Ko-rec-typed off. Gone. He gave me away. Do-na-ted. Oh, I'll take care of you. A quarter million dollars and the stuff of my authorized biography. You'll pay. I want whole blood. I want your bone ash. I want everything you have. Stand up, it's frisk time."

"Don't you dare come near me." But Simon, distracted by a historical him, has been rubbing teeth with the sheet: it's his only oral hygiene. "Listen. Please be reasonable. I couldn't sell, you must realize that. It was stipulated in her will. We had leaks. The sewer was blocked. The furnace gave out. She provided nothing for maintenance. Believe me, Simon, I had no other option. The city put a hundred thousand dollars into repair work and refurnishing." Simon says "Aaaah." A sound of farewells. It's reflexive: large round figures bring it on. "I didn't want to come here. I don't understand America. I most certainly don't understand you. Bettina left you over three hundred thousand dollars. What've you done with it?"

"Done with it? Whaddya think I did with it? Does St. Simeon Stylites have hemorrhoids? I spent it. What's three hundred grand in the barracuda tank? Out where I've been living they ask you to deposit that for the next three minutes." His arms bat out of hell: mad, grabbing. "Closeup of fangs, molars, saber teeth. Half time and the Texas Belles form a giant alimentary canal. Cut to an amoeba's food vacuole, closing: gulp. Killer whales the size of an inflated tennis court. See poor Simon, the piranhas have a few bones to pick with him. Dissolve: a skeleton floating in someone's mouth-shaped Hollywood swimming pool. Crow bait, that's what I am. Three hundred thousand: did you ever see a moray eel with *payess?* Shylock the shark. They're after me. I want money, Arthur. I saw those eighteen-story book ends outside. I want the Sicilian Low Bid Co. t'build high-rise coon cages on every square centimeter of this land. I want cucarachas wall to wall, and lead-paint potato chips. I want rats gnawing off babies' toes. Elevator doors that open on sixteen stories of nothing, fire escapes that crack off like fortune cookies. Yield. Red light: stop, stop. I'm a desperate man."

"It's not possible, Simon." Silence. "I'm sorry, I truly am."

"Uuuh. Y'got a cigarette?"

"No. No, I don't. Why didn't you contact me? This might have been avoided."

"Hanh. Huh. Flippo, Simon: gonna land upside down without a roll bar again. Ever since *Clap* they been following my blood-baited wake. Hanh. Dorsal fins cutting through the water. Move. Think. Nibbles at the old flesh rudder. One seafood special coming up, hold the tartar sauce. Money. Money. Right now I couldn't get enough backing t'take my own picture in a Forty-second Street photomat machine."

Simon has collared his breastplate. It clacks, tock-hollow and echoey. There's a pocket or holster behind the left nipple. Simon works out one bent Camel and a match pad. He opens the carapace on its leather hinges, steps inside, then doors it shut around: another day at the office. Contrasts entertain Uncle Arthur. A missing Lynxx: hirsute gorilla back with white homo sapient buttocks just beneath. Simon kindles the cigarette, but its spine has been cracked. He will snap it in half: make two butts and chain-light them. He smokes a while in tandem. The goatskin trousers depress Simon: shinnying, he has holed them again at the crotch. Parts of him eviscerate down. Simon tucks in here and there. The crushed feet hurt: no room for growth at the toes. Time to smith out a new persona.

"Have you come to stay?" Uncle Arthur stands. He would like to embrace Simon, but the chest is defensive, a pillbox. "There's room in the attic. Most of your possessions are still there, except for the pornographic items. Mrs. P chucked them out."

"My childhood album? I had photos that'd be worth a gold steamer rug now. Pre-depression nudies, where they airbrushed out a woman's armpit."

"Well, I'd like to offer you this place, but I'm afraid it's Martha Washington's bedroom, you know."

"Come again? Martha who? I had Martha Anagnos in here once. She puked her shortcake up on some Owsley surplus acid. That's the only Martha, you antiquarian flack. Martha Washington worked another neighborhood. Huh? Y'think you can modify history like it was a chopped-down '54 Plymouth?" Simon has a double-bore inhale. It returns through wide nostrils. "But I suppose the little Afro-Saxons don't know John Hancock from Muhammad Shabazz."

"Yes. We touch things up a bit here. Frankly, I don't know John Hancock from Muhammad Shabazz myself."

"I want it."

"What?"

"Your money. Lend me a thousand. You must have something packratted away. Huh? Hanh?"

"Simon. We're just caretakers here. We have living quarters off the kitchen. All we receive is a very modest stipend."

"How about twenty bucks? I'm a reasonable man."

"I'm short just now. I bought a new tire yesterday."

"How about eggs? I want six eggs, their cheeks up. Eight sides of toast. Bacon crisp. Orange juice."

"Fine. Mrs. P can manage that, I'm sure."

"Mrs. P. Is she still getting testosterone shots? How's her goatee coming along?"

"Simon, try to be tactful. Mrs. P has been—"

"Look. My van is parked outside. I got three people in there t'feed. By now they're eating each other. Pack me a box lunch for them. Nothing too attractive. Nothing I might eat myself."

"Then you're not staying?" Simon shrugs. The whole torso has gone up. "I'll tell Mrs. P to make breakfast." Uncle Arthur is at the door: hesitant there. "It's good to see you, Simon. I meant that when I said it."

"Never mind the water ballet. Get."

Uncle Arthur has got. Simon tweezes a nostril hair out: just one. He's short in that department: they are used as a kind of organic snuff. The sneeze irrigates his vision. Simon's contact lenses are ready: their plastic carrier is shaped like a two-seat outhouse, seats up. He sucks them: sour balls dissolved to the thin edge of taste. Surface tension on each pupil snags them up: the lenses jump from his fingertip, in. For a moment Simon's viewpoint is bathyspheric. He peers through thicknesses of his morning mouth, saliva analyzed at seven different magnifications. The eyes ache. They are brown, small, venal-seeming: much abused. Simon has never shown favoritism: he treats them as he would a thumb or a heel. He'd like to feel things with them. Already the left eye has had two nasty corneal scars: one, question-mark-shaped, that drifts, a cynical interrogation, ahead of all his seeing. Simon will reap another hair. The sneeze clears his vision. And both ears shut. Pop. Pop.

He grapples fingers on the window ledge and is surprised. His home has lost power. There are few resources left, so valuable for the creative artist, of hatred and blood fear. Simon feels deprived. Just below, the flagstone patio that tapped out Bettina's relentless Morse code: sharp high heels. He had never once seen her barefoot. The garden around it has been civilized by his uncle in a British manner. So Clive must have treated India. No fossil remnant of Simon's scatter-shot yet productive vegetable patch. The hedge has undergone topiary hairdressing: a dozen leafed chalices, empty. Beyond these, Van Lynxx Cemetery and the frog-like chapel. He can't place his mother's grave: a discreet dropped handkerchief of marble—BGL. But Aldo's monument can still oppress the dour dead. Ten feet long in bronze, "The Spirit of Radio," flying on its back, a heavenly hook slide home, safe! Two thunderbolt fasces in the upraised hand—salvage from some demolished AT&T building where it had gone under a pseudonym: "The Spirit of Long Distance."

ALDO LYNXX
1905–1960
"Ho-hum, ho-hay
Let's sing together
It's a lovely day."

HE WAS OUR MORNING

And Simon brays to the high-rise seating. "The birds are up / the dawn light winks / leave your troubles on the pillow / and su-hing with Lynxx."

Through a too-formative decade Aldo's bass voice, resilient and tough as saddle tack, had big-brothered Simon—from 5 A.M. to 9 A.M., six days per week—over WPPG's ninety-mile radius. "The Lynxx Good Morning Show" was a child's treasury of libel. The kids on school bus #78 preferred it to Uncle Milty and the "Texaco Star Theater." "Eat your Amish Farm, Simon. Ho-ho, that's my son, Simon. Say—do you have kids? Sure you do. In the Lynxx home we eat Amish Farm Wheat Germ, it gives us that old country get up and go." Father was asleep when Simon came home from school at three o'clock: Aldo's well-phrased snores made the afternoon seem anachronistic. At eight o'clock, Cox and Box, they would pass each other in bathrobes walking along the upstairs hall. Aldo had the irritable jollity of a black minstrel playing post-Civil War New Orleans. "Bettina, that's the better half, she wouldn't use anything but Bull's Wax on her kitchen floor. My son, Simon, gosh, you know what an eight-year-old brings in on his shoes. Ho-ho." "Daddy, ih-it's not true, I didn't bring anything in on my shoes. And I nn-never eat that Amish junk. You-you don't either. The kids on the bus're making fun of me." "That's show-biz, punk. Why don't you go see where your mother is, maybe she dropped dead." Simon's father autographed eight-by-ten glossies of himself taken by a frat brother in 1925—before the baked potato jowls had evolved and the small stone balconies under each eye: "Love and a good, good morning, your Aldo." Aldo and Bettina were street-dressed at the same time no more than twice a year. Always one in pajamas or one in a nightgown: as though they lived on opposite sides of the planet.

Aldo and Bettina shifted blame: for Simon, their child. They suspected him of diplomatic coalitions against father, against mother: Simon the involuntary Switzerland, recruited by strange axes and ententes cordiales. Bettina and Aldo, between them, had managed to debase even that American cliché: boy-and-his-dog. Simon doesn't recall the exact location now. Von Ribbentrop's carefully unmarked grave must lie orchard left, probably near the arthritic wild pear tree. Von Ribbentrop, a skinny and paranoid German shepherd, slavered like pots of frozen ravioli when they boil over: he had learned to look rabid, it was his most effective strategy. The first time Big Elio, bully of 154th Street, came at them, Simon said, "Sic 'im, Rib," and Von Ribbentrop charged. His master. So vicious that he unpegged Simon's left cuff: and Big Elio had to separate dog and dog owner with a stickball bat. Von Ribbentrop was not in favor of strenuous games. Whenever Simon picked up a stick to throw some fetch, Von Ribbentrop would bite him in the raised armpit. Now and then, if a tree were too far off, Rib would lift a leg on Simon: peeing into sneaker eyelets. Worse, Von Ribbentrop was a stoolie. He led Aldo to Simon by the most recondite spoors. At night when Simon—who had neither the rhythm nor the spermatic wherewithal—practiced practicing self-abuse, his best friend, the prude, would bark and whine until Bettina came to pound shame on Simon's door. But, one midnight, as Aldo went for a cold one, Von Ribbentrop sicked him in the scrotum. Next morning there was turned earth behind Van Lynxx Chapel. Next morning after that, a lazy and unrewarding gerbil, called Rover, moved in.

Aldo, at least, would hit: it was being-male-together: an instance of respect, some parental responsibility taken. Have you decked your child today? In his ninth July, while captaining Aldo's furious 10-h.p. tractor, Simon had lawn-mowed a dead rat. Aldo, raking just behind, got rodent in the mouth. The kick hurt Simon: it also fractured Aldo's large large toe. And next day, released from Parsons Hospital, Aldo had said, "Just a minute, son." Teetering, in some jeopardy on new crutches, he kicked Simon again. "That's just a reminder. I've still got one good foot, you little fruit." Simon thought it a caring: such effort put out. He was, he knew, an unattractive child: fat, bashful, with all the deliberation and stop-go of a motorcade. Myopia, unprescribed for, caused Simon to fuzz reaction time. An overlarge frenum, useless flesh beneath his tongue, tied off l's and r's and t's: this snipped brusquely years later by an army surgeon while Pvt. Lynxx was saying "Aaaah." And now he can speak. Aaah, he can *speak*.

Simon has bent to lace his gorilla feet. On the window frame he can make out penknife marks: little Simon growing. These are self-cut calibrations, for Aldo wouldn't measure him—he considered Simon's new height insubordinative. Simon touches his four-foot-six self, poor sap. Then he will rise slowly, along the bar graph of his adolescence: an arrogant jump at age fourteen, three full inches. And, how about that, he has grown since the last notch, eight years ago. Simon pounds his hollow chest: the timbre is mnemonic. He reaches up, pounds for the attic hatch, wallpapered over now, where Bettina had kept her precious Christmas things brought from England in excelsior. Ornaments that synopsized the complete oeuvre of Dickens—fragile Mr. Pickwick and Barnaby Rudge. Simon had lost a Christmas for breaking off Oliver Twist's head: rip, gone from the calendar. Bettina had taken their tree down. And returned it to Hal's Used Car Lot, used also. She was a step-up transformer of fury. Held at the wrong angle, Bettina could give deep moral paper cuts. Her face was painted with Van Eyck detail, unkissable: making love to her must have been like a game of electric jackstraws —buzzzz, foul. And, home from Bettina's funeral, four years ago, Simon had gone first to the attic. With satisfaction he stomped David Copperfield and Dombey and Little Dorrit to brilliant dust for nineteen don't-touch Christmases.

Simon is eating thread. A square mocha-colored spool wound over cardboard. Visual metaphors are the name of his game and this could be, will be, a Barricini miniature, good. The Manor has stirred in memories of combative eating: his anthropoid hams are weak: they give. He must chew: he might even swallow. He has subsisted on similes, emblems before this—an eraser, a sponge, wallpaper glue—and without harm: he has ecumenical digestion. In the 1950's Aldo, threatened by TV with its tight-squeeze 16-inch screen, would crash-diet often: Simon the crash. "Eat up, you spoiled brat. People in Armenia are starving. Eat your food, dammit." And, from Armenia across the table, a fork would tilt at him, chipping off one side of Simon's meat loaf, as Simon, riposte, chipped the other off. Tines meshed at mid-loaf. Bettina never dined with Aldo and Simon. She ate some different sort of food. What, Simon couldn't guess: cloth-spun viands maybe, sweet taffeta and rich brocade. Though he often saw Bettina nude, not once did he see the inside of her mouth. Bettina thought mastication off-color and not suitable for children. Now the tulip bowl decoys him over. Momentarily Simon will examine his own face, glazed, above a Fragonard swing scene. The majolica finish is so reflective it seems beneath water. He dabs a finger in, for liquid to wash his thread eye-snack down, but the bowl is dry.

Simon, predator, is out: now in the hall where night-shift father passed day-shift child. A long museum case shows its stuff there: arrowhead, musketry. The silken shoes of some colonial lady walker: their fabric decayed to thin layers, fine as Greek pastry. Simon wouldn't mind tasting: his stomach puts in a requisition. Voort Van Lynxx's cane: Pieter Van Lynxx's meerschaum: Meindert Van Lynxx's snuffbox: apocryphal baggage. The Van Lynxxes accumulated just cash: a Calvinist sign of election in God's double-entry bookkeeping. Each generation sold off the one before: honor thy father and convert him to working capital. Simon sees a stuffed spider monkey on the case. He doesn't understand its provenance. Uh-oh, not stuffed: duck. The monkey tosses a half walnut shell at Simon, spitty from cheek insides. The serious, excitable face has made a thoughtful moue. It seems pleased by Simon's gorilla apparatus: emulation, the highest—and in this case largest—form of flattery. But body scents won't check out. The monkey leaps. Gracile fingertips catch on an oaken beam: its powerful bushy tail whisks problems of balance away. Near the staircase an open casement frames windfall Spanish garbage coming down. Simon hears footsteps overhead: someone policing up the roof. A long push broom's business end appears. The monkey grabs it, chins there four times, then exits roofward, small *deus* returning to its *machina*.

Downstairs: Simon's hand will buff the spiral banister. What? Some revisionist historian has misplaced his childhood. Only the ancient fireplace is still there: little Simon's recess: wide enough to spin a bullock in. They've struck Bettina's modern kitchen set. Dishwasher, stove, double freezer: absent and unbank-accounted for. The slow, ruminant garbage disposal, disposed of. Counters, closets, drop fluorescent ceiling have been crowbarred off. How she had loved Formica, America's inner asphalt: Bettina covered bureaus, coffee table, even his bike seat with it. On the original 1640 oak siding now: fine-print museum explanations. Above a spinning wheel. Above curling irons, candle molds, warming pans: above the sturdy hinged pot hooks. And near the secret cupboard (which Grandpa Hiram built to hide his Prohibition still), a piece of prime liberal guile: STATION ON THE UNDERGROUND RAILWAY. Simon has to howl at that one. Grandpa and his grandpas loathed Negroes. If this was a fugitive-slave stopover, hadda be on the Southbound side.

God, even a "Souvenir Center"—for Simon to ransack. A booth near the turnstile stocked in a stock manner with bayberry candles and incense and those cedarwood ashtrays thrown up by every American natural freak from Ausable Chasm to Crater Lake. Grandpa Hiram's old pinhole camera view has been offset on postcards, 25¢ each: Van Lynxx Manor, aloof and diffident, in stubble cornfields circa 1910. The fifty-odd Model T's have been retouched up and out. Hiram was a used-car dealer almost before the first cars had been used at all. He had deleted Van from Van Lynxx six hours after the Germans hung their first hard left through Belgium. Van Lynxx sounded rather too Teutonic for the time and might have been found in restraint of trade. Simon strips three rock-candy clusters from their stringing, 75¢ each, a 750 percent markup. His vision fine-tunes itself at once: glucose. And there it is.

His mother's cupping equipment. That takes him back: right down Memory Rut. Bettina thought young Simon was too logy with blood. Sick, well, it didn't matter: she would make neat and painless incisions just over his kidney. It was their Thursday-night ritual: something they could do together. And, damn it, he felt refreshed if not sanguine, after. While Bettina worked her vacuum pump treadle, Simon could sense the over-stolid blood going out, percolative, into round bell glasses. He will remember her best as hooks and pricks and tweezers. Bettina's fingernails were so long she couldn't accomplish a fist. In three or four months, her razor-edge toenails, like Counts of Monte Cristo, would scrape their way out from any imprisoning slipper tip. And her arms were made up—

566

a line of blue eye shadow from shoulder, through elbow junction, to wrist. He thinks it over once again: was his mother mainlining? Simon can't believe this, though, just after her death, he found a hypodermic in the toilet tank. Heroin is supposed to make one euphoric—otherwise why bother, right?—and if Bettina was an addict, she was the nastiest, least serene addict around: on what must have been a very expensive low. Simon fiddles with the rubber tube: so long his exterior vein: he taps the treadle. REVOLUTIONARY MEDICAL INSTRUMENT, it has the *bicho* to say.

Aldo feared Bettina Gordon: and detested his own fear. She had been Weather Girl on "The Lynxx Good Morning Show": a touch of "Third Programme" toff and the standard fog jokes. Three months gone, having induced pregnancy by holing her diaphragm with a paper punch, she sent this sheet of copy across Studio B to, ho-ho, Aldo. "Check my weather update for 6:45. The temperature is 74 degrees, the humidity is a delightful 32 percent and in six months I will give birth to Aldo Lynxx's bastard child. He likes to shoot his gism, dontcha know, but he doesn't like to swab up afterward. It's a beautiful morning, ladies, I see my lawyer at ten." Aldo gagged into the cough box and wrote back, "I'll meet you at City Hall on Friday. That is, if you pass the Wassermann, you filthy, lime-sucking slut." Bettina passed: and, a week after the ceremony, she passed the fetus with no discomfort while making number one.

To establish his precedence, Aldo crocked her a good one on their three-day honeymoon in Atlantic City. To establish hers, Bettina did a stunt-man crash against the hotel bureau. She wore bridgework: Aldo didn't know this. In the bathroom Bettina threw her four front teeth out a window and slit gum tissue until it bled the way bad color printing will. Aldo, the jolly radio man, was mortified: doubly mortified when his weekend-old wife went to work at WPPG that next Monday morning, gapped like a hockey forward, a five-hour promo for Aldo's brutality. Three seasons with the Isle of Wight Rep. had taught her to color in a realistic matte bruise. She kept plaster of Paris for casts under her bed. And, a trouper, she wasn't above the real thing. Simon can remember five fractures. To preserve her cold taffy brittleness, she avoided calcium. Her pain threshold reached the transom. Simon had seen her roast a palm on the electric stove element, seen her take away its spiraling shape in blisters, smelled his mother char beside him, while Bettina completed a full sentence, her voice not even edged higher by the shock. Bettina could look like the M in an S and M duet when she wanted to black-and-bluemail Aldo's public self. As time went by, Aldo learned gentleness, and, compiling fourteen years' anger, he broke—new wine in an old brown paper bag.

Simon has taken a plug of Apple chewing tobacco from his shaggy pants. He bites it off: an inch-by-two-inch chaw. At once he salivates powerfully, spits toward a cedarwood ashtray: souvenir of Bayside made by Taiwanese. Nothing has been burned in the fireplace these last three years. Simon huddles under the ingle-less nook. Larry and he had filmed *Hearth* here, second of his award-winning short features. Avid flames that sawed energetically to Sven Svenson's square dance violin. The lubricious gasification of wood. Logs, seared through at their center, were folded over and seared again, folded over and seared again, a handkerchief gradually made compact. Then one ember, c.u., spangled with racing sparks—fade carefully to the New York skyline at 4 A.M., spark-lit windows going out. He has the *Times* review down pat. "The slow motion, the editing are superbly conceived. Simon Lynxx is a master of the succinct cinematic metaphor. *Hearth* stands with Lynxx's *Diner* as two of the most perfect film moments this decade has seen. It seems incredible to me that a director so young could have such a profound sense of torrid life and expectant death." Simon spits. The stone is chill: a history in carbon of three hundred years' burning. Vacant, sweet, it is like a pipe beautifully broken in.

"Simon. Yoo-hoo. On the patio."

Simon steps out. His eyes will become smaller yet, slyer yet, in sunlight. There is a glass-and-wrought-iron table on Van Lynxx terrace. The full quart of orange juice seems frosted in opaque Tupperware. He burps the top off. Mouth in partitions, the chaw segregated, he hums: a tone of pure want. Left heel rises: it does the same in front of a urinal. Eating, drinking his face can appear infantile and lovely. He kills the quart. Liquid is heard: down his throat, to stomach: merely a container-container transshipment. He doesn't taste: a smell that subs for taste has risen in the back of his throat. *Arriba! Arriba!* Praise for his magnificent drinking from the high-rise balconies. Simon gives a finger, gets one back: both good-natured. The table is within a stone's or a mango's throw of the lower balconies. Shielded by a green umbrella, which has been tilted west, against the prevailing garbage.

BB's have come down and air-gun pellets. Arrows, water bombs, pub darts: once a Molotov cocktail on the rocks in Van Lynxx Garden. They chatter or ping against oak, knock chips from the tombstones, cloud stained glass in Van Lynxx Chapel: their momenta mostly worn out by wind resistance. A barbarian descent, so it is indicated on late Roman Empire maps, progress southward, gravity perhaps the law behind civilization's collapse. No respect for three hundred years' Americana in this present generation, whose own chronicles are silverfish and lousy superintendent service and boilers that crack open, seed pods are no more predictable, between December 10 and Christmas. Eleven weeks ago, Uncle Arthur, walking out to stake tomato plants, found a compressed black man at ease on Mrs. P's aluminum beach lounge. Feet punched through blue fabric, he sat like Rodin's thinker, but the head was set on kneecaps, as if his torso had been edited out. The chair legs splayed like a young colt's first walking. Six vertebrae poked up nude, scarlet, drained of their nerve transmission fluid: they had been hammered out of his back between the shoulder blades. On one roof, eighteen stories above, homicide detectives found a sort of pirate plank. The fist was thoughtfully deep in his crushed jaw mechanism. The lips made an O, that first step a lulu, watch it.

"Aaahgood," Simon's lips O, too. Citric acid has leached through his chap-sore flesh.

"Yes. Still the lusty eater, I see." Uncle Arthur is amused. "It comes back to me now. Your lip and teeth marks on everything in our fridge. Milk bottle. Mrs. P's trifle. Butter. I think you were fourteen that summer in Cornwall. Enthusiastic but not quite sanitary."

"Yah. Sanitary. What about the holy lipsticked chalice? How many people spit back in? Hanh? Drink this in remembrance of the deacon's chancred mouth. Communion? Contagion. And some hopeful priest dabbing around with his snoot cloth: Father Germless and the magic siffwipe." Simon blows off air. "Great. This place is looking more and more like West Berlin. Barbed wire now. An entire undeveloping nation up there. I could be ringside in Madison Square Garden, waiting to get tonked by a beer can. There's gotta be a way we can turn this AAA guidebook entry into an income producer. A Red Apple, maybe. Couple of bodegas and a numbers drop. Where's breakfast? If they liked me drinking juice, wait 'til they see me with a fried egg in each hand."

"Coming. Coming. Sit down." Uncle Arthur pushes a chair. "Mrs. P was—how do you say it?—a bit turned off by your sterling one-man act. I'm afraid she's not so fond of you as I am. I do hope you'll try charm."

"I do hep yawl try charm." Simon spits: saturation bombing of an ant commune between the flagstones. "I can see my mother's face in you. That look of cold suppositories going in."

"You do try to be unpleasant. It's rather a good show, I'd forgotten. Aldo had the same way with words. I must confess, I never knew what Bettina saw in him."

"My mother had THIS SIDE UP, USE NO HOOKS stenciled all over her. I don't know how they conceived me, by parcel post maybe. And deep down inside, under that Tang dynasty makeup, she had a heart of solid Pyrex. Mind you, I don't wanna play favorites, I despised Aldo, and that's no idle conversation starter. Being Aldo's son was like following the elephant act with a spoon: you get upstaged somewhat. But I had to feel for him. Bettina had the both of us nude and on parade for a short-arm inspection night and day: she used a cigar snip on our La Coronas." Simon has sat. There's a good house, SRO, on the balconies. His gorilla outfit has drawn well. "Listen, let's reminisce on somebody else's time, hanh? These flashbacks give me gas."

"Bettina had quite serious problems. Someday I'll tell you about them, you might be more sympathetic." Uncle Arthur asks for an invitation: gets none. "Well, someday. Ah, yes. It strikes me, Simon, that you're not happy."

"Me? I'm ecstatic. Busby Berkeley handles my choreography. Does it matter that the Zionist movement has my name down right after Bormann, M.? They've donated my body to Women's American ORT. I need shekels, rijksdaalders, pesos, marks: a quarter million would hold me to Christmas. One film, one four-reeler, and I can fill the toilet tank with Piper Heidsieck. I've got this concept—"

"The last one had to do with gonorrhea, I believe."

"Gone or here? I love the way you say that: like it was a little fairy child. Do people confess their sins t'you? Hunh? Can you understand them when they do? Father, forgive me, I get a tingly burning pain when I make water. Father, forgive me, my catchpole has moss on it. The sound you just heard was my probe falling off." Simon has leaned across the table. His hands are urgent, eyes half closed: he plays his own voice by ear. Uncle Arthur is apprehensive: Simon must be fed. "All I want is my tall mast and some fat krondt to steer it into. I sing of dark places, where the footing is uncertain. I've slipped myself in with shoehorns, gone in headfirst with a rope and pitons, left a trail of fleshcrumbs behind me. I've seen light at the end of the tunnel: towns, shopping centers, integrated neighborhoods. I've had the pestle disease four times in three years: lucky I'm covered by workmen's compensation. All it did was put a head on my beer, that old subcutaneous thrill, like a second circumcision. I want it, whether it sags or gapes or falls apart in my greedy hands. Is that wrong, Father? Sure and it can't be. Do I overreach myself?"

"Ah. If I understood you." Uncle Arthur clears his throat. "Yes. It is. You do."

"Hanh." Simon shrugs. "Guess there's something t'be said for singlemindedness. They wrote 'Concentrates Well' on my first-grade report. I need a maggot, does Mrs. P still smoke those brown bridge cables?"

"When you came to England, oh?" Simon has put his hand on Uncle Arthur's arm. Uncle Arthur would like it to be a check mark of affection, but Simon is merely interested in the deep nap there. He cards and yanks the white hair. Uncle Arthur is in pain: ignores it. "You seemed shy then. You didn't say much."

"I had this doohickus under my tongue, made me sound like a swish. Every time I said 'Herro there,' some hi-guy tried t'transplant my root. Another thing Bettina and Aldo didn't believe in. Doctors f'me. I was the only kid in Bayside without a vaccination mark. I felt disadvantaged. I used to poke myself with dirty needles. Aldo got his prostate massaged twice weekly by a kraut female doctor who wore boots and jodhpurs and did her internship at Ravensbrück. But poor Simon? Oh, no." He impersonates the voice: and Arthur can hear Aldo. "'So, jerk. If they all got vaccinations, who you gonna catch it from?' I never had a lollipop. Rorropop was all I could say. I've got a lot t'make up for." Simon sticks it out. The tongue reaches to his chin: seems prehensile. The taste buds are big and discrete. "Now—aah—it's so long I can eat nautch in another room without getting up. Huh? Where's my breakfast?"

"Coming."

"Coming, he says. I have the patience of a two-day-old child." Simon spits. "Listen, you still a priest or is there a new scam in town?"

"I'm retired. I—actually I've been having a go at meditation. At my age it's time to cast loose. What say?" But Simon has not interrupted. This surprises Arthur: a word in widthwise. "I supply now and then. I write. I've been doing some articles on women in the priesthood. They're ordaining women, had you heard? I'm not in favor of it."

"Um. Ms. Christ?" Simon isn't talking to Arthur. "With twelve disciples: all female and very frontal-nude. Get the women's lib and the raincoat claque in one swell foop. Yah, has its possibilities. Do you dare, Simon?—that's the question. A bunch of Sadducees, maybe a JDL local, try to gangpop her in Times Square and—a miracle—everyone goes so limp they couldn't get their snails out with an escargot fork. Hanh? Do I dare? No, I don't think I do." Simon spits. "As you might have guessed, my interest in your vocation was purely selfish. See, I'm making this film, *Jesus 2001*, which could be *Godfather II* and my salvation, or a turkey so grosso y'could fly it in Macy's parade—one gust of wind and twelve clowns get carried over the Verrazano Bridge. What I have in mind is a New Testament according to ITT. Solid-state scripture, works in a drawer. Mary, Joseph, Pilate, Judas the Carrot, all your favorite storybook people in a new form—"

"Simon—"

"Now, before you get out the long spoon—let me preface my little song and dance by saying that I respect Jesus Christ. This is gonna be a snazzy production, not some traveling salesman's joke done in sixteen millimeter with two broads and a water bed. Bring the kiddies—it'll play with that thyroid Easter Pageant at the Radio City Music Hall. What I need is some advice, a religious eye. Hanh? Have I got your attention? What there is of it? Let me dribble this upcourt and see if I get a traveling foul. I've been reading the New Testament—an experience—and not because it's the first thing longer than a Chinese menu that I've read in five years, though that was part of it." Simon spits. "If he lived now, instead of back then when nobody had decent plumbing, Jesus'd be the master technician. Ford, Edison, Andy Warhol. I'd like t'do that. Raise the dead—which my last screening audience was, I think." Simon spits. "And I can, that's the point. He's the Director, capital D. The Gospel is *film*. Hanh? Right? I have something in mind like Truffaut's *Day for Night*, but without the frog mannerisms. Get it? Huh? Or am I talking to a piece of wallboard? The director is in and of the film. Maker and performer. That's all predestination means—somebody wrote a six-page treatment beforehand. Miracles, revelation, all it takes is money and good staff work."

"I see. Like the Magus."

"The old Bergman film? Nah. I hate that Swedish meatball. Dust-flecked columns of sunlight in the primeval forest. He should be shooting ferns for *National Geographic*. Swedes come on free and sincere—meanwhile they're trading with Hitler behind your back. The gross national product is hypocrisy and nudist volleyball." Simon spits. "This is gonna be American as a knock-down pitch. Jesus the entrepreneur. Irving Thalberg. Louis B. Mayer. Or maybe it's God who's directing, though that's a little hard t'cast. It'd be a comment on film and faith: on the way we perceive illusion and reality. That's what's wrong with your communion service, it's stagey, stuck in the three-walled room. There should be a screen behind the altar. Hunh? I see by the callus on your face that you're less than sympathetic. Listen, I'm not trying to be blasphemous. I've got no opinions whatever. It's just a matter of *making*. If they can get Superman t'unscrew the earth like a light bulb, I can get Jesus across the Sea of Galilee without galoshes. It's not all clear in my mind yet. Hey. Wait. Maybe by 2001, what with wonder funguses and artificial sweetbreads, maybe the miracle is *dying*. Hunh? I like that. I can work it in." Simon is suddenly earnest. "How d'you like it so far? It's rough, I know, but—" He spits. "Not much, huh? Simon coming down over New Jersey in a blaze of helium and plywood."

"If you'd like my honest opinion—"

"Don't tell me. I know: I should write it on very erasable bond. I don't wanna hear. God, I'm depressed. Food! Where is she? Maybe the old bloach ran off and joined the ROTC."

A vodka bottle comes down: label-less, it passes through grades of visibility against the just-ironed September sky. Simon associates: his contact lenses lost in water. Empty but weighted: fat glass bottom wrenches thin neck around, unwieldy as a thrown hammer. It lands intact between rose bushes and—and Mrs. P is standing on the terrace. She has a Tiparillo in her mouth: her head cranes to get upwind of the smoke. Some old cricket or rounders accident has given her a trick knee: Ace bandaging trusses it up. She puts the tray down—clack! with negligence. Simon's gorilla suit has offended her. Mrs. P is tall, ropy, slim, gray: her face has been wrinkled ever since Simon can remember, but the wrinkling is affirmative and taut: fine leather pursed up. She must be sixty-five, he thinks: yes, and good for another three decades. Simon has stood, not an act of defiance or politeness, but to control the food. There is one plate for Uncle Arthur, one plate for him: two sunny-sides each. Simon will transfer Uncle Arthur's breakfast, cuffing the slithery eggs up, as bears fish.

"Ay—you there." Mrs. P has gone for Simon's wrist.

"It's quite all right, Margaret. I meant to fast this morning."

"Arthur, don't try to chivvy me. You're protecting him."

"Mrs. P. Mmm. Age cannot wither you nor custom stale your infinite—jelly. Hanh? I don't see the jelly." The sugar bowl holds five lumps. Simon pours black coffee into it. "How y'been, foster mother, second string in my Oedipus complex? Remember when I cried, nuzzling into your Irish wool lap? Remember? Your neighbor, the lady with two navels, caught me hanging like Harold Lloyd from her bathroom windowsill. You came t'my defense. And you told me my urges were normal and not t'worry, ducks." Simon will eat with his fingers: there is a seasoning in the flesh. "Got another of those dumbwaiter ropes you're smoking?"

"Bloody ape. Disgusting."

"Say that again. What'd you fry this in, some polyunsaturate Du Pont left out of the napalm? You can't fool a short-order cook. Give me butter, fat, the stuff of cerebral hemorrhages. And look at that: the sacred British toast rack. Everybody in God's great zoo wants nice, warm toast, only the British hang it out t'dry like nappies on the washline. Hanh. Sure enough, hard as zwieback." Simon is not always audible. His lids are half open, flickery, some dreaming dog's eyes. A sort of cobra dance entices his spine. Simon sways, chewing: an exoskeletal digestion.

"Arthur. I warn you, I won't have him here. I'm quite capable of poisoning him."

"Tell the British Museum there that I'm leaving."

"Simon is leaving." Does Simon detect regret in Arthur's tone? "He has a film to—well, film."

"Bettina's child. Rotten seed." Mrs. P picks up an empty beer can. "Filthy wogs. I loathe this country. Nothing but convicts and tarts. What did he do this morning? Miss Williams was perfectly incoherent."

"I believe Simon was having carnal knowledge of Martha Washington."

"Best I've ever had, a kind of Eurasian slant. Nothing like your wax ladies for compliance." Mrs. P has set her Tiparillo in the ashtray. Simon makes a pre-emptive strike: appropriates it. He spits. "I suppose no blandishments, no winsome folderol, would get me another four hen sperm, buns up, with sides."

"Just what is he meant to be wearing?"

"It seems a sort of disguise. Why don't you ask him, Margaret?"

"No, thank you. I'm not at all interested."

"Hah, you think I relish wearing this cuspidor? Last January my nipples stuck to it, like your fingers to an ice cube. They hadda pour hot water inside me. I howled like Tarzan. Kree-gah. Bundolo, kill. And on July Fourth I break out in eczema, it's Diaperenesville." Simon has leaned back. Food will make him expansive. He pulls at the artificial belly button and a streamer unreels: UMBILICAL CORD. Simon spits. The chaw is tacky with yolk: he can't get distance. "Heck, this isn't the real me. I'm a farm boy. Gosh. I used to plant corn out back there before it became San Juan Hill. Row after row: I talked to the ears. It woulda made you cry. Lonely, shortsighted, spastic. I had a great future as an autistic child."

"One might ask then—" Uncle Arthur stacks forearms on breast. "Why?"

"The line I'm in, friend, you don't send up flares, the search planes'll never find you. I'm going against Consuela the Chanteuse—she got a mustache graft in Denmark. And Antonio, who has two Chink attendants wheel him t'cocktail parties on a stretcher table. And Jerry, the jolly giant: he paints himself green every morning. In my league, be yourself and it follows like the night the day, they'll bury you next t'the Unknown Hooker." Simon spits. "Kyryl. Hanh, heard of him? He's bigger than Picasso ever was. Painting, films, sculpture and on the side he *makes* people, *creates* them. It's like being baptized by St. John the Damp himself. Like having a Halston label sewn into your head. A Kyryl original. Cost Sam the Ice Man fifty grand for Kyryl t'design his freon suit. You gotta get recognized. Otherwise, might as well print your social security number on a business card and let it go at that. I need bankrolling, I gotta generate a little Eleven O'Clock News. See my picture in *New York* magazine when *Clap* came out? That was the monkey suit. Talent and looks mean nothing. If you're not a fag or a Jew, y'gotta keep moving, y'gotta be your own Trendex rating. People say t'me, I can't remember the face, but the chest is familiar."

"Stupid perverts, that's what."

"I'm not so certain, Margaret. I find it fascinating. We can't just discount this phenomenon." Mrs. P has cleared the table.

"Wait a minute, Goneril. I want a dozen eggs and a loaf—let's see. Cereal, coffee, orange juice and milk. Enough for three meager servings." Simon spits. "To go: and hold the snide comments."

"Ruddy fat chance of that."

"Look, Monty Python. You're squatting on my property and don't forget it. Big Spender here gave away my birthright, the least I deserve is a mess of porridge. I see all those quarters you've rung up on that nifty shine-counter inside."

"I did promise him, Margaret."

"I will not."

"Please. He is, after all, my nephew. And the sooner we satisfy him, the sooner he'll leave. Am I correct, Simon?"

"Correct. This is a holdup. Mmph—and while you're at it, throw in some jelly and peanut butter. Paper products are needed: we've had a group encounter with the runs. And none of your British bog tissue, I'd rather wipe myself with an emery board. The only thing you English still export is piles. What else now? Smokes. Sugar. Soap. Vaseline. I'll come in and look around myself."

"You bloody well won't, mate. You won't set a foot in my clean kitchen."

"Then lay it on, Mrs. Ty-D-bol. I've got responsibilities, mouths t'feed. I'm the world's great teat." Simon is up. "Ten minutes, then I hook up a Wats line t'your pantry."

"This is an outrage."

"Listen. Most people have t'get mugged in Central Park. Lucky f'you I deliver."

Simon has gone: once more up the garden path. Uncle Arthur heels, obedient: he must run to keep up. Mrs. P is troubled. She knows that Arthur can be intrigued by the specially unregenerate, their guest room occupied over twenty years by bigamists in transit, addicts, petty thieves and one rapist who had scheduled Mrs. P as a kind of sexual intermezzo. Overhead there is Monday-morning business afoot: large families off the starting block. Sun has been upstaged by the eighteen-story roofline of 39-07 Van Lynxx Place: light is curtain-raised slowly up the wall of 39-11. Between Uncle Arthur's Yellow Tea and Charlotte Armstrong rose bushes, Simon has noticed raw earth. He kneels, drawn down, a pagan reverence. His forefinger unzips the scabby, dry surface: moisture just underneath. Simon has prospected here before. From age seven to twelve Simon dug wherever he stood for more than ten minutes. He could pothole fresh asphalt: mimicking, in one night, the freeze-thaw action of an entire year: highway departments were confounded. Simon kept a trowel in his back jeans pocket, but, the purist, he preferred to use hands, seesawing recalcitrant rocks out: each a difficult breech birth. For him it had the compulsiveness of pinball machines and crocheted horse-tails. He could doze, wrist at work, a test-pattern hum high in his nose: Simon's kind of sheep-counting. Fifteen years ago it was his best, per-haps only, talent. Simon left holes wherever he went, a creeping barrage over semi-suburban Queens.

"Do be careful, I have croci planted there."

"Wonk not, I've got the hands of a grass surgeon. I could graft air on a bubble." But Simon's digging is dilettante now: he can't get into the dance. A shallow nest has been scratched out. Simon lays his hand there: knuckles earthward, as if testing for fever in the ground. "Ha. Ha!"

"What is it now?"

"A couple grand, I want it." Simon is up: Uncle Arthur has stepped back. "Don't move, I have you surrounded. No rabbinical excuses now—my company is singing 'Arrivederci, Simon.' If Hagar the Horrible doesn't sack a fat caravan by next Friday, he'll be leading his own shadow into battle. I owe my two fags about six grand apiece, they're waving their limp wrists goodbye. My tires have all the grip of a charlotte russe. I need gas. And film. Film. Film."

"But, Simon—"

"Don't 'But, Simon' me. All those years at the parish checkout counter. Indulgences. Tithe pigs. Bingo. Laundered money for the gibbering souls in limbo. Promotional considerations paid for by God. You've socked it away, I know. I know. What expenses have you had? No children, thank the blessed St. Peterless. A few shillings t'the RSPCA. Mulch and manure in the spring. Hand it over. And you call yourself a Christian."

"Indulgences? Limbo?" Arthur laughs. "I think you've got the wrong sect."

"Never mind the comparative theology. Where is it?"

"What?"

"Your nest egg, friend. I wanna poach it." Simon whispers. The large brown-yellow teeth rake over his damaged lower lip. "This is the one chance in your arteriosclerotic life t'help genius. I'm opportunity. I'm the new man. Hanh? What've you got? Five thousand? Two? One? What?" Uncle Arthur swallows.

"Two, more or less."

"Aha! Dollars? Pounds?"

"Dollars. But, Simon, it's all that stands between me and the workhouse."

"I want it." Simon's fingers have cupped. They play piano scales from underneath. "Cough it up, you old parlor worm. The March of Dimes ends here. At me."

"No. No, Simon." Uncle Arthur has thought of Mrs. P: and two fears balance. "Somehow I don't think you'll reimburse me."

"Lo! This is the voice of our wounded Saviour, hanging by his palms like Spider Man. Come unto me, ye that travail and are heavy laden, and I'll dinch your gonads. Hanh? Huh? You'll let that money inflate itself t'swamp gas in some five percent and a free toaster savings bank, while I'm getting shell-shocked on the Golan Heights?"

"But it's all I have. That and some insurance."

"Hah, the clot thickens. Beneficiary?"

"Well. Mrs. P, of course. But it's a pittance. Scarcely enough to cover my funeral expenses."

"Mrs. P, of course. The housekeeper. What about Mr. L, the nephew? Isn't blood thicker than Mop & Glo? Anyway, who says we haveta bury you? They're looking for clean landfill all over Queens." Simon has spat.

"I'm a Gordon, remember, the last one. I'm your gift t'the world. I'm life. Life. I ring with life. The two grand, I want it today."

"Simon. Surely you can't be serious."

"Tomorrow at noon then. That's my final offer."

"I can't—oh!" Simon has Uncle Arthur by the wrist: deftly, as one lifts a phonograph arm.

"Tick-tick. Pulse about one-twenty, going up. Only someone near death or a virgin having her *chocha* pop-topped gets that high. The Magic Fingers bed is running down and there're no more quarters t'put in."

"Simon, you terrify me."

"Great. I'll cure you of life like it was the hiccups. How old are you anyway?"

"S-seventy-one."

"Some nerve. Don't you know when t'leave a party gracefully?" Simon has let the wrist drop: Uncle Arthur holds it to his ear. "Think of me. You come down with a coronary infarction tomorrow and where am I? Short two grand, is where. Robbed. Jesus calls: for the harvest is plentiful, but the harvesters are cheap."

"Simon, this is cruel. You'll hurt my feelings."

"Your feelings? I'll corn-row your arm hairs. The money. Huh? Where is it?"

"We have a joint account. You'd need Mrs. P's signature."

"Wonderful. Where's the laugh track? I'm more likely t'get the Venus de Milo's autograph." Simon spits. "Okay. I catch on quick: swing your partner, it's the old jew-down. I'll give collateral, I'll throw in my Arriflex 35."

"Eh? Your what?"

"It's a camera, you down-dressed corpse. It's worth twice that."

"Then, if I may ask, why don't you sell it?"

"Oh, good thinking. That wins the porcelain hairnet. If I hocked my equipment I'd have just enough cash t'buy it all back. How'm I going to film *Jesus 2001*? With a Brownie Instamatic? My van, furnished, is worth a hundred fifty grand. You want me t'plotz away my capital?"

"Now, please don't get angry—" Uncle Arthur has both hands up: mediators. "Ah. Why not get a job, Simon?"

"Because—you self-righteous fonk—I do work. Every man, woman and man-woman in my company works. I hash their lymph nodes if they don't."

"Sorry. I didn't realize. Where?"

"Over a griddle, dammit. Scramble two. Side of french. Elmer's glue on a shingle t'go. Get it, hanh?" Simon spits. Uncle Arthur will sidestep: he has sandals on. "I'm a short-order cook at Filiades' Famous Cinema

Diner. That's what I'm reduced to. Antonioni making mushroom omelets."

"*The* diner?" Simon is alert.

"Didja see it? Didja see *Diner?*"

"At the Museum of Art. Last April."

"What'd you think? Huh? Well, huh? Here I am, Simon the eight-year-old presenting a cobbler's bench he made in shop class. Huh?"

"I don't know very much about cinema—"

"Spare me the prefaces. I accept your ignorance. Get t'the point."

"I loved it. And I was proud." Uncle Arthur smiles. "Everyone applauded at the end."

"Did they? Did they?" One by one Simon milks the long, tobacco-oranged fingers of his left hand. "It's a song. A little *Iliad.*"

"Yes." Uncle Arthur will say it, though he senses the risk. "You probably are a genius. And a damned fool. I also managed to see *The Clap That Took Over the World.* How ever could you make such an empty, vulgar, scurrilous—"

"I won't listen! I won't listen!" And Simon runs.

But the Spirit of Radio will stop him. This is a resonant memorial: Simon salutes it. Place of interment and place of death, neat as a convenience food. Aldo had expired just here, bear-hugging a snowman down. Simon replays it, slo-mo: Aldo out, across the terrace, through the rose garden, his breath going up in blank thought-balloons. Simon never knew that last insult or argument, not to be answered on Bettina's fragile skeleton. Aldo wore only a short-sleeved shirt. Simon could act it out now: Aldo's terrific lumber, the shins that swatted his pants legs audibly. It was a large snowman: a large father: a perfect match. Aldo's left hook pasted the moronic white skull a good one. The snow head exploded: and the human head. A stroke so massive, Dr. Wallace told them, it was as if the brain had been booby-trapped. Simon's snowman began to melt slightly at the chest: a final access of Aldo's body heat. Simon nods. He has always admired Aldo's rough exit. It seems manly. It would film well.

The spider monkey is there. It has been embellishing a headstone: WILHEMINA VAN LYNXX, 1823–1824, precociously dead. The monkey covers its mouth, a mime of shame. Van Lynxx Cemetery is cliquish. Four dozen graves: men and women segregated left/right, a kind of Orthodox synagogue for the dead. There are only ten headstones to the left—Van Lynxxes have been great users of women. On that last day, Bettina, the unuseful one, had dressed carefully first, for she was susceptible to chills. A scarf. A sweater. Aldo's anorak. Gum boots. She had stood where Simon now squats. Aldo died standing, *Homo erectus* to the end. Young Simon had wanted him down, prone: the dead have their protocol. This upright anger had distressed and threatened him. He had wept into scarf and anorak and sweater. "He'll keep, child. It's ten degrees. Let's try to remember him this way. He was an active man." Apparently the composition, man and snowman in headlock, had pleased Bettina. Indeed, she later buried Aldo feet downward, for a running head start at the final trump. "Come inside. I have a cake in the oven. I'll let you lick out the frosting bowl." Even now Simon is grateful. Bettina had spared him, not her sorrow, but her fierce exultation.

"Penny for your thoughts, Simon." There is no answer: Simon eats grass. "In one sense, I never got to know Bettina well. We didn't share a childhood. By the time she was nine or ten, I'd taken up residence in London. There were twelve years between us, you see. I'd come up to Hertfordshire on weekends, though certainly not as often as I should have. Youth is impatient. She would kiss my hands, curtsey. White gloves she always wore, yes. What I remember best—isn't it odd?—were her childish tea parties. Perhaps half a dozen girls round a garden table, just beyond our gazebo. But even when she was just six she kept those girls to the mark. My gracious, they sat straight as sticks. And when she went inside, they would collapse, laughing and giggling. Relieved, I suspect. One incident remains fixed in my mind. A girl spilled something—tea, I imagine—and Bettina struck her across the face. Not hard, but a perfect slap, nonetheless: rather like a textbook lawn tennis stroke. She was much the prettiest girl there. You realize my mother was well into her forties when Bettina was born. My father must have been not quite sixty. These things affect children. Of course, she was weak physically, but it was more than that—it was an attitude. Living with the old, in a way it stunted her. Made her round-shouldered, so to speak. In the mind." Simon performs on a blade of grass: small kazoo sounds. "She had—"

"Run it down the soil pipe, huh? Huh, Arthur?"

"Well you needn't be so bolshy about it. I just thought you might want to know."

"Childish tea parties. Hanh. That's like doing 'This Is Your Life' with Caligula. Mother was something out of a Coney Island horror ride. She played potsy with my giblets. I won't have anyone dirtying her memory." He spits. "Jesus, look at that monitor lizard, will ya? What you'd call your basic BMT entrance architecture."

A brochure rack (TAKE ONE) hangs beneath this sign:

The Chapel of
Sta. Maria Composta
Carried to These Shores
From Its site on the Estate of
Cosimo Alberti in Florence
by
Phineas Van Lynxx in 1878

Van Lynxx Chapel, begun by Girolamo Alberti in 1125, towers between the high rises, low and uncertain as cats brought to a strange room. Simon doesn't believe in history: he hasn't seen it. The marble entrance steps that might once have taken a Medici's tread are, in his foreshortened record, only remarkable for stoop-ball games: young Simon vs. Mouse Gentile. The chapel had been sacked four times, twice each by Guelph and Ghibelline. Its structure, rebuilt, then re-rebuilt, is Renaissance eclectic: Byzantine dome: Lombard Romanesque vaults of cut stone laid in courses: modest Gothic rose window defensed by a 1976 convex steel catcher's mask. The bronze doors, a 14th Century addition, have been attributed to a C+ student of Lorenzo Ghiberti. In their archway, between Sts. Mark and Matthew, some anonymous cloth guild executive, a spiritual parvenu, stretches forth his stone hand, presenting now bits of thrown and rotten papaya to God's greater glory.

Phineas Van Lynxx had made the grand tour in 1877. While at Florence he gave his hand to the beautiful Theresa Alberti, who returned it after commenting somewhat archly on Phineas' Jaycee ring. The Albertis were noble, but brilliantly insolvent: they wrote out IOU's with a distinguished and ornate calligraphy. Phineas was on the rise: he had invested in a machine that, when one struck the appropriate keys, printed neat letters on paper. Theresa considered this vulgar and faddish, even, *repellente*, profitable. Since Phineas could not have Theresa, he bought the family lares and penates instead. The deed, drawn up in a splendid hand by brother Cosimo, stipulated that Albertis in perpetuity would be allowed to worship at Sta. Maria Composta. The deed, however, did not mention outright removal—Albertis retained their right, and still do—though they find it somewhat inconvenient to make eight o'clock mass in Bayside, Queens. Stone on stone, reredos and candlestick and lead roof, Phineas labeled the parts of Sta. Maria Composta like a model airplane kit. The original stained glass and the altar fittings were priceless. Simon thumps for entrance on a bronze bas-relief: Jesus following his terrible cross toward Golgotha-in-Flushing. The spider monkey applauds: it cherishes those who make loud noise.

"Simply fine inside. The one place you can't hear José Feliciano and the Tijuana whatnots. Soundproof as the grave itself. I spend several hours daily at the altar. There's not a more perfect place for meditation."

St. Peter, blinded by five hundred years' erosion, holds a stone crook and a glossy black-gold fleur-de-lis in his hand: THIS PROPERTY IS PROTECTED BY THE YANKEE BURGLAR ALARM CO. Simon shoulders a bronze door open: Sta. Maria Composta begins to klaxon, ahooga-hoo, ahooga-hoo. Uncle Arthur inserts a key beneath St. Peter's worn left sandal: silence. Simon stares in: he is thinking of film locations. Darkness and a precipice of silence will make him giddy. There is a neutral smell: incense: pure burning. Simon can see only a fluent blue-red-yellow mosaic: light coming through the rose window gels. Red lozenges especially fool his perspective: the chapel might be endless or two-dimensional. He swipes just in front of his face to touch the far wall. Sunlight has been doused by a cloud. The colors run: they seem to lie, subtly deflected, in water. Simon's false chest slumps and he supposes for a moment that some sort of horizontal gravity is drawing him down, ahead. Simon steps out. He is in a hurry: he doesn't close the door.

"Shall we go in?"

"Aaarh! No—tell me I didn't see what I just didn't see." Simon staggers, doubled over, gut-shot. "No. It can't be."

"What? What?"

"In there. The big gold candlesticks. The chalice. The tapestries. I didn't see them."

"Ah, yes. It was part of the agreement. We donated them to the Met—"

"Jesus' feces! They've rolled you, you blind fark. All gone. All gone. Mother help me—to some kultur head start program for the ghetto splibs. No! No! No!" And, in time to this—thump, thump, thump on bronze. Simon could cry. "They were worth thousands and thousands."

"Yes. Don't you see, it was hopeless for that very reason. No insurance firm would cover us. We'd have needed security guards day and night. It was only a matter of time. Someone would have stolen them."

"Me. *Me.* Why'ncha let me steal them? You Mortimer Snerd, you could've hocked them at Parke-Bernet. Blessed Mary's stainless-steel ovaries. Gold—d'you know what gold is worth? Christ! I'm fishing nickels out of the upholstery and he squanders a union president's expense account. I want t'die."

"They belonged together, Simon. It was a superb collection."

"Scrap metal. That's all, scrap metal. A bunch of dagos trying t'get inta heaven by palming some expensive baksheesh. The footage! The footage! I could've turned this stone outhouse into *Grand Hotel!*" Simon comes at Arthur. "I'll—I'll—I'll—"

Mmmm-thwack! Mad parabolas whir past his cheek. A knife hums, running down, stuck in the wooden signboard. Simon is surprised to fear. But just for a moment. Simon never fears long. By now he has worked the knife out. It lounges in his hand: perfectly weighted, a superior tool. Simon crouches. An old man has made his entrance from behind the hedgerow. He might as well be nude: just a scant burlap loincloth and laceless Keds. The bare skin has been etched with prinky, illegible tattoos. He looks blue: it's like printing gone down on a deflated balloon. Five foot tall, but Simon judges that he was once a fuller-bodied man. The head seems boiled away, all skull: the hair, not crew-cut, but rather singed to an unkempt gray ash. Yet the lips are sumptuous: above crazy, overlapping, brown teeth. The monkey leaps onto his shoulder, up footholds of blue sinew. Simon is angry: on such occasions he would prefer to get the first punch, the first stab, in. It sets a certain tone.

"Yes, well. Simon, allow me to introduce Alf—"

"He doesn't need a name. He's a dead man. I want his tripes."

"Alf's been living with us as watchman and Johannes factotum. He's— ah, an old friend of Mrs. P's."

"He's also a cadaver. C'mere, Igor, I wanna edit your tattoos." Cunning, knife out, Simon crab-steps forward, still at a crouch. At a crouch still, Alf crab-steps back, hand out, cunning. The coated, white tongue of a sneaker flops.

"'Ere, guv'nor, you in the ipe suit, give us the sticker back." Simon slashes down, an experiment, but the severe Cockney accent has diverted him. He likes its off-pitch music. "Use never was in dainger, teddy boy. I can frow 'at in me sleep, 'cept I never sleeps."

"That's right. He never does, you know." Uncle Arthur's manner is strained conversational: the way we talk when undressing in front of someone not known well. Simon does not trouble him, but Uncle Arthur has seen Alf's prosaic, dispassionate savagery. "At least, I've never known him to sleep. Our Alf outprowls the prowlers."

"Oooo. I gives 'em a ripe poke when they gets a leg froo the wire. I make 'em waltz, I do. They don't catch me out, nor little Friday 'ere." The spider monkey has chuted down Alf's spine. "I lived ten years wiv the Feegees, back when they was eatin' long pig, notcher TV flippin' dinners. No nig-nogs never done me what for. Les 'ave the sticker, Chauncey."

Alf beckons. He gives Simon the British version of obscenity— forefinger not middle finger—and it won't lose in translation. Hot feral noises, perhaps a sort of badger's hiss, chug in his throat. Simon is engrossed, disgusted, so heedful: ah, he'd like to take Alf places. Hollywood. Cannes. A find, this: an authentic. Even Kyryl, the identity maker, would be jealous of them now. Alf is the mammal itself: near him Simon's gorilla rig seems stagey and forced. Alf's nipples woo Simon: they are blue and kernel-hard. The right hand comes out. It has been scarred: the scars are scarred: as though Alf held glossy worms. And in his presence Simon can dream: alone here with his ancestors. Then—for some reason it will seem necessary—Simon surrenders the knife blade-first. They recognize each other. Alf leers: Alf is táking. No, Alf. Abruptly, eyes shut, Simon slices down. The palm, sleek with many injuries, will just escape. It flaunts its integrity: waving, uncut, see. Friday squeals. Simon has hurled Alf's knife away, high over Van Lynxx Chapel. But he is shocked, nonetheless: he has never wanted, so cheaply, so without warning or honor, to exact blood before.

"Oooo. Don't you never try an' cut me 'ands. This ain't skin no more. Bloody tar-paulins they are." Simon's teeth clack: he has bitten his tongue on purpose. "An' don't never shut yer eyes, mate." Alf fingers: so one snags the last olive from a jar. "I nip 'em raht out like 'at."

"Now, the two of you. Simon—back off."

"He-he threw a knife at me."

"Got me narked, 'e does. That Simon Lynxx? That your nevoo, Arthur?" Alf laughs. "'E shut his eyes, the blighter. Don't want t'see poor Alf's blood. Oooo, 's war. Me an' 'im."

"You little—" Simon wants to speak. There is a chain drive of language somewhere, but Simon can't find its movement. He, the mover of words.

"Oooo. 'S war. Now!"

Friday races, a bad-hop ground ball, at Simon's ankle and shin. Simon has guessed, even while he bends, parrying, that this is a coordinated effort, meant to bring him within step-stool reach. Alf runs up Simon, Ked on knee, steps kicked into the smooth breastplate. His torso closes around Simon's head like a chloroformed rag. Alf smells of used air. The contact lenses tiddlywink off: they flit up/under lids. Alf's stomach presses against his mouth: rigid, printed, a lot of nonsense words. The old man is strong. Simon can't bite: his lips are bruised to a humiliating kiss. Friday threshes Simon's hair: lanky fingers pick to his scalp and claw there. Simon must try to breathe. The tobacco chaw disintegrates, sucked into his throat. Alf is after his eyes, his tongue, his nose, his ears. Uncle Arthur has caught the loincloth. Alf's buttocks pop out: childish things: slim and white and unwritten upon.

Simon has gone down. In plastic, in character, he is tortoised: he can't rise. Yet, with his bench-press-350 arms, he will lift Alf up. And hold him above. He has put the old man off: this time, for now. And then, from Van Lynxx Manor, six Japanese tourists appear, chaperoned through the rose garden by Mrs. P. Simon can't see them: his eyes are shut so powerfully they chip off sparks. The Japanese squat to focus Nikons: an oriental light reading is called out. Mrs. P has Alf by the nape. It's not her strength, but rather something habitual, known in the touch. Alf rolls off, laughing. He won't censor his nakedness: his private parts are lively, big, without the blue body language. Japanese record an American scene, slick, slick, sh-slick. Alf breaks for Sta. Maria Composta. Friday, rearguard, has already stationed himself at the bronze door. And, inside, Alf's laughter is on reverb, is amplified, around the Romanesque vaults.

Simon has stood. Vision is jumpy: an old Edison print. The left lens saws around its orbit rim. Eye pain has made Simon incline forward. The Japanese respond politely: they bow too. Simon hears, "Sank you, sank you." They export Datsuns: we, madness: some balance of payments there. From one balcony a sweet trumpet has begun to play taps. Applause above. Simon, nauseated, bent like a hook and ladder truck, answers his public. A wave. Dents, slick, shallow, have been punched into his gorilla suit, where once the muscular breasts stood out.

6

The van is handsome, spruce, certainly a male. LYNXX PRODUC-
TIONS, it says, MOBILE UNIT #1. And only. Simon, cradling several
breakfasts in a carton, has been moved to creator love again. Oh, this is a
marvelous thing. Custom-made by the Peterbilt Co.: worth ninety thousand dollars unequipped. The van is tiger yellow, striped with black, as
mackerel tabby cats are striped. All of thirty-four feet long, from prog-
nathous bumper jaw to the mudguards showing heels behind. Simon
removes a decoy parking ticket from the windshield and his big PRESS
card. Two sawhorses walk a beat, one in front, one behind: POLICE
LINE DO NOT CROSS. And, overhead, thieving cables reach up to bilk
a city streetlamp.

Simon grooms the van. He whispers: he mums the word. He makes it
his confidant. Wiper arcs have swept out two pupils in the windshield
grime. Some clown has bent a sideview mirror 180°. It reflects, irrele-
vantly, what will be. Simon folds it in: holds a retrospective. The driver's
cab seems feline and alert, listening behind. Jesus, the tires demoralize
him. They are treadless, each sole smooth and dusty as blackboards: next
time he cuts rubber will be the last. A September leaf has been inhaled
by the radiator grill. Fastidious, gentle, Simon will nose-pick at it. Small
shocks touch off galvanic twitching in his thumb and finger. Some short
circuit from the pilfered city.

Simon lugs breakfasts around back. A red 1956 Buick, its grill like
whale baleen, slumps against the curb behind. One sun visor, down, says
CLERGY. Fifteen uniformed private school girls, their knees white and
scaly above blue shin socks, enter the front yard of Van Lynxx Manor.
Simon counts them, so many servings here. He has a sharp eye for money
in Protestant females. FYI, here are some rules of thumbing. 1) The rich
like to suck their hair. 2) They have round ears. 3) Their breasts are separate, pointy, small: limited-issue porcelains. 4) They are restless: their

bodies waste energy. An eyebrow will jerk up. Shoulders shrug a lot. They rise suddenly on tiptoe, as if to see over their wealth. 5) Their nails are bitten and short. 6) They are sometimes striking, but never beautiful, spoiled by just one poor feature: a bulbed nose, a weak eye muscle, teeth that social climb atop each other. Also, good fortune's occupational hazard: at least one horse-bite scar. Simon eats bread and them. They are his legal tenderness: he wants, he wants. He'd like to block-book them: all fifteen ass up over a low yacht rail. Five flights above, from a high-rise balcony, two Puerto Rican boys advertise the length of their genitals: in Spanish and, would you believe it, in centimeters. Everything going metric these days. Simon has 21.5 himself. The girls catcall back: they have taken Spanish 3. Simon is annoyed. They are provocative, lewd. The younger generation gets it all on a linen serviette. Adolescent Simon had to suffer for his shamelessness. A paper airplane comes down, strafing. And, quite irrationally, he will be jealous here.

Two short, one long, one short: Simon soccer-heads the van's rolltop metal rear door with his pate. The concussions are hurtful: satisfactory for that. A report of uncoordinated walking inside. Clack, cla-clang-ingggg: the door races up with a roller derby noise. Rose Fischer is standing barefoot. Her ears are not round: nor her breasts Hummel-ware: the butch-cut hair will not reach her mouth. Rose yawns. She is Simon's associate producer: the irresolute suffix, -ish, applies to Rose: fortyish, blondish, shrewdish. Greed and ambition have kept her in, ish, shape. Breadwinner Simon hands the carton up. There is an anklet of dirt above her foot: and a string hammock of varicose veins inside the right calf. Simon slidders his hand up her thin shank: beneath a frayed nightgown. Rose's kneecap feels like the snub end of a baseball bat. With cursory effort, she will put her heel in his face and push off. Someone has laughed down from the low-rent project. Simon swings up, pure armstrength, on the steel handgrips.

"Faaugh! This place smells like the milk train t'Birkenau." Don't believe him: for Simon there are no bad odors. Only interesting and less interesting odors. He shouts. "Up! Up! I don't pay you t'cronk out on my time. Work, work—that's what I don't pay you for. Up! What's this, a rule-book job action?" Simon has the gorilla torso off. "Here, you shiksa manqué, try t'knock my knockers out again. Somebody stepped on the Neanderthal man last night."

"Jerk. I told you to be careful. I told you it was on its last legs. Both tits this time—how did that happen?"

"I met this swell bint last night, all arms and elbows she was, like a Jersey mosquito. Clitoris the size of a Volkswagen. She tried t'crack me open like a lobster claw. Unnh—scratch my back. Higher, left. Ahhh, warm, warmer, tepid. Up. That's it—use your nails, imagine you're coming. Don! Larry!"

"Take it easy, Simon. Larry's pretty saddle-sore. I think it's the ulcer, he was up and down all night."

"Runs, Lar?" Simon shakes the upper bunk. "How's it going, Mr. Softee? A case of the touristers?"

"Ummm." Larry has an eye mask on. He feels for Simon's face. "I'm bleeding again, Sy. My stool is black."

"You fags, everything has to be color-coordinated." But Simon is concerned. "I brought a quart of milk. Huh? That's good for you, isn't it? Have some milk, you'll feel like Buster Crabbe."

"Uh. Okay. Give me a minute."

"It's no wonder." Rose is hanging Simon's other half up. "The diet we live on. Pizza and water last night. I ordered a sausage pizza and then Don only had two-fifty. Gino the jolly pieman was pissed. He picked off all the sausages and half the cheese, too. And it gets claustrophobic in here, we're on each other's nerves all day long."

"Make believe it's a game, like Dungeons and Drag-queens. Make believe you're Anne Frank and Bayside is South Gestapo. A little imagination. Put some lights on, why doncha, while the Con Ed is still paying for it."

"Ah. First—there's something I have to tell you."

"Good news? Huh? Hanh? Herman Wolff wants me t'direct the book of Deuteronomy?"

"No."

"Then don't tell me, you manic depressor. I want good news. I get discouraged easily."

"I see."

"What do you see?"

"Your uncle won't sell the Manor. All that big talk yesterday. Condominiums. Fifty dollars a square foot. Just where do we go from here?"

"Wait a minute, hunh? Before you pull the chain on my power-diving career. Uncle A loved the concept. He even wants a walk-on part, maybe God. But it'll take time—some city bureaucrat has turned the place into Hubert's Dinosaurland." Simon kisses her. Rose is a surprise: she responds with enthusiasm. But, on second thought, her kiss seems a kind of scenery. "It's in the bag, Rose-hips. All I have t'do is find where they hid the bag. A little patience, you crepe hanger, that's all. Make me some breakfast, I haven't eaten since yesterday." Simon strips nude. "Pizza, huh? I don't suppose you saved any f'me?"

Cameras examine his nakedness: the above-mentioned Arriflex, the Mitchell BNC, the Auricon Super-1200. Microphones dangle in a special arbor from the ceiling. Simon has learned to duck beneath them. He steps up on the ColorTran hydraulic dolly. Lengths of film, tails to pin on a donkey, trail down the wall near his collapsible editing table. Simon snaps on the Movieola, runs twenty frames of *Jesus 2001* through, is pleased, snaps off. Tripods and boom arms and stanchions are clamped, rifles in a gun rack, above Larry's upper bunk, above the two bunks opposite. Also: six Bardwell and McAlister 10-KW spotlights, three baby kegs, two tiny Macs, diffusers, dimmers, snoots, flags, dots, slates, gobos, cookies, barn doors, blimps, hi-hats, spiders, scrims. Simon loves the terminology. He hasn't used all these things yet, but he has used all their names. Even depreciated, there has to be seventy thousand dollars in equipment here. Simon will jerk the ceiling light on. Don cries out. A circular curtain can be pulled around the john: IT IS NOT ALLOWED TO FLUSH IN THE STATION. Simon dumps water from a five-gallon bottle into the canvas sink. He birdbathes himself, splattering.

"Out of the pool, you Fanny Farmer." Simon has cupped water in both hands. Release: a bomb-bay door over Don's face.

"Goddam! Raht in my e-ah hole." Don smacks his own head.

"Only place you're still intacta. By my two fruits ye shall know me. Rose. Split some shells quick, scrambled rare with milk. Sugar on mine." Simon coughs: tests himself for rupture. "Come on, Donald Dork. You wrote off three days last week with the false menses. It's Monday morning. You go on duty at Hair Apparent in forty-five minutes. Up. Mrs. Mankiewicz has t'get her head resoled, so she can go sit on a park bench. Up. It's fourteen weeks to unemployment insurance." Don has thrown a leg over the lower bunk rail. Simon hands him fifteen feet of rubber hose. "There's a '56 Buick right behind us. I think it's my uncle's. Go do your special thing."

"No *sir*. I ain't suckin' gas 'fore m'coffee. No way."

"Listen, Hopalong Casualty, you will go down on the Panhandle Pipeline if I so desire. It's your turn. I honked eight gallons outa that Mercedes with the DPL plates yesterday."

"Man. Oh, *man*. This scene pukes. I'm tellin' you, Simon—me an' Larry can't fetch much more'n your cow pies." Don is up. "I heard about your uncle. It's in the bag, my ass. That there's a public building. I read the sign last night. A landmark—"

"Shut up!"

"You don't—"

"Shut *up!*" Simon has gathered the flesh of Don's right pap in his hand. "One negative word more, fruit fly, and I'll break your Mark Eden bust developer."

"Don't hurt him, Sy." Larry flips one corner of his eye mask up. "Don, do what he says. Please. I can't stand this bickering." Simon has let go.

"Shee-it." Don stomps a stenciled cowboy boot on.

"Yeah. And watch your bunkhouse language, Lyndon. There's a lady present."

"Nobody cares—I'm gonna go blind someday suckin' that stuff." Don adjusts his Stetson. The business is drawn out: it refurbishes his self-respect. The van door careers up. "Puke. This scene pukes."

"Simon." Rose has closed the door: drop-dissolve on act one of Simon's nakedness. She collects his flywheeling hands. "Before you start your Hitler-at-the-Sports-Palace routine—much as I enjoy it—please turn around. I want you to meet my sister-in-law, Minnie Fischer, and her son, Robert."

"What? Who? I've been boarded!"

Simon caught with his pants down again. What happened to the famous eye for detail? Torsos have risen, one upper, one lower, in the starboard bunk beds. Yes, that must be nephew Robert on top. A rickety boy: the scars of domineering horn-rimmed glasses, deep and raw, enfilade his bent nose bridge. Robert can't see well at all. His squint is so intense it seems abusive, brash. Acne has splurged on his face. Robert wets his lower lip, again, again. Simon is gratified: our best champions are those that fear us. Underneath Robert: a very brown woman. Rose's contemporary, give, take probably, three or four years, but clean and buxom to a virtue. Minnie Fischer has one discreet hand over her eyes. The other hand grasps her splendid left breast, as we grasp sturdy things—walls, bar rails, bathtub handles—for reassurance in time of wild unbalance. Her hair has been convened in two honey-blond braids. Thick: they have a pull strength of 3,200 foot-pounds each. Simon has stepped forward. Robert will press a hand against his mouth. The thumb nuzzles, but is refused sanctuary inside. Simon gives his private parts a good flopping. They sound like lips smacked. Nudity here a form of one-upmanship.

"Yoo-hoo. I'm not peeking. Pleased to meet you, Mr. Lynxx. Hurry, stick some pants on."

"Yoo-hoo? Yoo-hoo? What is this, a motorized kibbutz?" Simon has been threatened: he covers the breakfast carton. "My eggs. My orange juice. My bread. Don't set another place. Oh, mother—they come t'me like I was running a Grossinger's singles weekend. Never again. Never again. Rose. Rosie. C'mere, you off-artist. I wanna word or two, step over t'the conversation pit."

"Yes, Simon?" Rose grins.

"What is this? What? What? The exodus from Egypt?"

"Excuse. Can I have a look now? Are you decent?"

"Decent? Of course I'm decent. I'm stark naked. This morning forty Black Panther cubs gave me a complete physical. Why should you miss out? Have a look."

"I'm bashful, Mr. Lynxx. I missed the Woodstock generation by ten years."

"Open your eyes, dammit. My body is beautiful. Fathers bring their young sons t'see it. This is America, your heritage. Purple mountains.

Amber grain. Women dream of me: I'm the guy who killed Mr. Right. Hanh? Hanh? Let's have some eye-service, you pompous knish."

"Mom—l-let's go. I'm sorry." Robert has turned to the wall. Rose will breechcloth Simon with a towel. He dashes it off.

"I want them out. They have mouths. And teeth. The fat one eats like a roach, I can tell. Out, out. Dietary laws not observed." Larry is moaning. "Jesus, what is this—an invalid coach?"

"Sy. Don't roar. My temples throb."

"Rose, I want an explanation."

"Ah—Minnie has decided to run away and join the circus." Rose laughs: it is uncommon for her. "Or—to be more precise—Robert has decided to run away and Minnie wanted to make sure he wore his rubbers. It wasn't my idea." Simon is down on all fours. There are three pieces of matched luggage under Minnie's bunk.

"Omigod, she brought her trousseau. Out. She goes out. And Cradle Cap, up there, the son." Simon can't bear to be ignored. He yanks Minnie's hand down. She blinks: the smile can charm. Her face is a sound oval: youthful, taut. She has a healthy crust. Someone who deals with ultra-violet often.

"Forgive, Mr. Lynxx, I should have taken a look-see. I know people live elbow to elbow in a communal mix-up." Minnie presents her hand. "You have a very nice shape. I wish Robert had such a physique. It must be a great satisfaction to you."

"Never mind the dog hockey, you *farmisht* stowaway—" But Simon has been sidetracked. Minnie's cleavage is gorging itself: Simon, caveman, would like to house himself there: hold. "Rose. Psst, Rose." Rose has been jigging a skillet over the electric hot plate. "Rose. Time. Insult break. Hey, Rose?"

"Yes, Dr. Mengele? Left or right?"

"Is this Daddy Warbucks in drag? Can we render some fat? Huh?" Simon stirs eggs. "Rose, I love you—next you'll be in the big time, kidnapping poodles on Sutton Place. Those suitcases are real leather, you can see animal juices oozing out. And nobody gets that brown without a swimming pool and two live-in maids. What's her husband do?"

"He's in bushes. Big Westchester bushes."

"Bushes?"

"Little trees—"

"I know what a bush is, Rose. Ha-ha. Don't go glandular on me now. I mean—" It's milking time: Simon can hear cowbells. Home from the pasture. "Bushes. Is that a good line of business? Is Mr. Yoo-hoo big in the bush game? Hanh? Somehow I don't remember seeing Amalgamated Bush on the New York Stock Exchange."

"Why don't you ask Minnie?"

"Yah—"

"Mr. Lynxx, hear me out." Minnie stands: this is a chancy exercise. Odd metallic sounds—clunks—accompany it. Her nightgown is maxi-length: the material rustles and says "Sssh." Minnie has a speech by heart. Her palms shape themselves for prayer. "I can understand you're flabbergasted, also surprised. But Rose has spoken so highly of you. Right off, I thought: Minnie, this is a crazy business, leaving Sol high and dry, with not even clean socks. And Robert, my son . . . Wait. Wait. I don't make myself clear, I have *shpilkes* when your mouth is open. Wait. We all want to make a contribution to the arts and crafts. At our local high school we had Alvin Ailey. But what I mean—"

"Did Rose tell you what she contributes? Huh? Hanh?" Simon has appropriated Rose's left breast. He is negligent, brusque: he makes a Senate committee hearing out of negligence, brusqueness. Rose doesn't resist: she yawns.

"Ah, you mean—" Simon has taken a giant step toward Minnie. In reverse the nightgown unrustles, says "Hsss."

"You know what I mean."

"Yes. Yes. Don't say. Little pitchers have ears." Simon will lick his thumb: he fingerpaints Minnie's arm with spit. "Ah—it's my time of month, Mr. Lynxx."

"Just touch the hem of my garment, baby."

"Your gommint?"

"Mom—"

"Shut up, Dildo. I'm trying to make your mother. Watch. Learn. Remember for the next time they have show-and-tell in school."

"Mr. Lynxx, please. Give me a chance to get my sea legs here."

Minnie has lifted her nightgown hem: escape in mind. Her feet wear spats of suntan. Simon kicks open his green canvas director's chair: MR. LYNXX. Minnie is up for a demanding role: Simon's demands. Robert has found glasses: they abridge his face. Robert's presence titillates Simon, incest by proxy, something new. From behind, Rose hands Simon a cup of coffee. Sensuously, leisurely, Rose scratches his left breast. A statement. Minnie understands. Robert understands. And Simon understands: this is some devious revenge ploy, a brother-in-law cuckolded for unknown Westchester slights. Simon is being used. You don't fool around with Rose. And Simon knows again: he has been lucky for too long.

"How old is Pull Toy up there?"

"Robert was sixteen last July."

"Yeah? Is he paper-trained yet? How come his head is so small?"

"Robert is six and seven-eighths head size. Also he gets a hundred thirty-four in the IQ. Tell Mr. Lynxx—" Minnie shoos at her son with both hands. "Go on, Robert."

"What, Ma?"

"About his movie films. Tell."

"I—"

"He's shy, Mr. Lynxx. But, take my word for it, he's such a fan of yours, you wouldn't believe. Robert. My little Robert. What can I do?" Minnie shakes her head. "Our home life has squished him out of shape. Robert's father is a good man, but a domineer. Sol wants a dentist in the family, his heart is set on it. He's had pyorrhea for years."

"A prick." Rose serves Simon. "A first-class prick. His teeth are falling out because they hate his head. Larry? Breakfast?"

"Just a glass of milk. Warm."

"Gimme his plate." Simon makes a quick clam of Melmac-ware: egg is abducted. "So, Goiter, you're a fan, huh? Let's hear. I needle-pop praise."

"Ahhh." Robert swallows. "Y-your *Di-iner*. And *Hearth*. I saw, I saw them."

"Great, huh?" Robert nods. "Powerful, brilliant, inventive, moving?" Robert nods. "What you'd call classics of the genre?" Robert nods. "Just my luck, a deaf-mute fan. I guess it could be worse, he could have a stiff neck, too."

"Robert stutters a little, Mr. Lynxx. He's ashamed to talk."

"Shut up, Time of Month." Simon jerks a thumb at the Golden Reel awards. They hang, wampum, on leather thongs. Just beneath: Larry's single reel for Best Cinematography, Short Subject. "What is it, Cold Sore? You wanna direct?" Robert nods. "Show Daddy the bush maven a thing or two about art? Aaarh. You and every high school senior that doesn't rent a seeing-eye dog." Robert swallows. "How's the old mouth action, huh, Histoid? Ready t'give me a tongue diapering? No? But you will, you will." Simon eats. He shows Robert a high-angle shot of mastication: egg flowers bloom, burst.

"Mr. Lynxx. You shouldn't bully him. Flies you catch with sugar. He's already got a big inferiority. He comes out with hives."

"What's this, a ventriloquist? How come when I ask him a question, you talk? Hanh? Robert. You, up there. You, Enteritis. You like t'work?"

"Yu-es."

"I don't mean clapping the slate. I mean dishwashing. Hot water. Brillo splinters. Your fingertips wrinkled like tripe." Simon has Robert's hand. "Soft as semolina. I want t'see big cracks on the knuckles. You haven't lived 'til you've tried t'scrape day-old cornflakes off a soup spoon. Sound good, Fistula?"

"All. Right."

"Then get up. You're sleeping in my bunk, Schlemiel. Where the golden Aryan body lays its dolichocephalic head t'rest."

"He's fine, Mr. Lynxx. What he likes, he works for. Only one little complaint. Rose gave me the word—if you would be careful with the anti-Semitic remarks, I—" Simon glares.

"Listen, Kreplach, here every day is *Kristallnacht*. The B'nai B'rith's got my wattles in a Waring Blender. I might as well have a mezuzah concession in Teheran. Trust me, two weeks here and you'll be goose-stepping in the Judengasse."

"He talks like an SS-er, Rose. How can you stand it?"

"I like to watch people commit suicide. But you should see him dance *Hava Nagilah* for the producers."

"Da-da. De-*dah*-da, da-da!" Simon dances. Rose has taken his arm. The van lurches to their circling. Minnie, absentminded, claps along. "Where your treasure is, lat me tal you, there my heart is also." Rose punches him in the gut: hard. It is allowed.

"I don't understand."

"Min, love, let me explain. Remember *Jaws?* You thought that was a mechanical shark—uh-uh, it was Simon. This is the biggest mouth in the East. What does he care for Jews, blacks, homosexuals, women? Not a thing. Simon is the one totally unbigoted person I've ever known—he treats everyone like a Polish joke. If you have a pimple, he'll mention it. If you have one leg, he'll ask you to run a forty-yard dash." Rose gooses Simon. "Also it helps to be six-three and crazy. I've seen him knock a Puerto Rican heavyweight all the way over a compact car with one punch. Nobody, but nobody, can out-insult Simon Lynxx. He's an institution. You'd be surprised how polite even the famous and the infamous can be when they get near him. As Simon says—"

"I don't have many friends, but my enemies are very careful."

"This is a terrible way to live."

"Hanh—no one asked you t'move in lox, shticks and bagels. What's Sol doing now? Who's stuffing his derma? How'll he explain t'the schwartzer cleaning lady? What about a fourth at Mah-Jongg?" Simon has confiscated Minnie's pocketbook.

"Mr. Lynxx—"

"Hanh, fat as a barrage balloon." Simon palpates the pocketbook. "This is what happens in a commune, Man-Tan. From those according t'their ability, t'me according t'my need—which, by the way, is bottomless." He has shaken out her purse: two twenties and a five. "Is this all? I've been short-changed, you big sofa snake."

"I—we left in a quick hurry."

"Yah? So how come you managed t'pack enough clothing for a weekend in Southampton? Does Clearasil up there have a paper route? Hanh? Well, I'm not greedy, one bush in the hand is worth two in Scarsdale." Simon upends the pocketbook. "Great, we could open a garage sale, if we had a garage. What's this thing?"

"It's personal, please. My leg shaver."

"I can get five bucks for that."

"No—"

"Don't worry, we'll find you a spic lover. He'll comb your shins out. And what have we here, an electric water pick? Three dollars, down at a place I know on Canal Street, you won't be eating anyway. Let's see the engagement ring."

"No—"

"Yes." Minnie's hand is heavy, but not a dead weight: it shivers. Simon will mime a jeweler's loupe. "Two carats. Couldn't bushman the Jew do better? This is worth about three square yards of zoysia grass."

"Ow. Mr. Lynxx, no. That's of great sentimental value."

"Sentimental? What about Sol? Right now he's eating pork and fry rice TV dinners. Pull. You're not trying."

"Ow. It won't come. My hand is swollen up. Stop—you're pushing me lopsided."

"Try, Minnie. Try. Inhale your finger."

"I can't. I can't."

"We'll slim you down, don't worry. In a month you'll need t'get your hat reblocked. Living with me is living in a Finnish sauna. Open up—" Minnie gapes for him. "Not one gold filling. Even your mouth is marked down." Minnie has begun to hyperventilate: her eyes are under glassine wrap.

"Don't scare her too much." Rose has been laughing.

"Can she cook at least?"

"No. She's useless. She's been sunbathing for twenty years."

"Robert. Son. It's all right. Don't worry about your mother. She's happy if you are."

"I-I'm not happy, Ma."

"Get your step-ins on, Scrofula. We start work in half an hour. Let's bag-ass outa here, I'm bored with terrorizing you people."

Don runs the door up. Retching has been heard outside. The two NYPD sawhorses lunge aboard, shoulder to shoulder: they fence each other in. Don hikes up. His ribs are apparent, but he is fleshy, epicene across the kidney line. Don spits: spits again. The rubber hose whips in: airborne it says "ssss" and coils, a bola, around Simon's ankles. These men have fought often: Simon will allow Don one edgeless weapon. The outcome is foreseen: an explanatory rib crusher, Don's feet off the floor, just enough breath left for capitulation. Don has been grateful for these losses: it's easier to understand submission in physical terms. Rose has a cup of orange juice for him. Don teases out his left sideburn: it puffs to a small muttonchop. His beard of one night is dark, but the face appears frail, prefab: its seams show. Dimples have broken his chin's spirit. In outline it could be a large script W.

"What happened, Horse Pox? Did the tank blow first?"

"Come on outside, Simon. Just come on."

"Spare me the glitsy macho. How much didja get?"

"Six-seven, I reckon. That there Buick ain't goin' from here t'the corner. But we need oil and transmission fluid. And them tires ain't gonna last, the way you drive."

"I know. I know. I know. I know."

In blue jeans now, the seat chalky and unsound with wear, Simon goes up a folding ladder. His glass skylight will lift off. Beneath a stopped cloud, the high rises seem to slide ahead with no effort, their motion pneumatic, glib. Bop-pop the roof buckles under his bare feet. Simon can see Friday. The monkey is marvelously still, tail caught around. It sits on a dormer ridge. Oh, Simon would like to stop. There is a camera platform over the van's brow. Simon jumps up on it. He reaches to the streetlamp socket. His cable is frayed and full of leaks. As every morning, it spatters a keen shock. Simon is charged, conductive. Pins and needles stick through him. He can't feel. His hair comes up, phototropic, taking a fix on the sun. He can smell ozone, its clean odor, around his head. Simon's lips are numbed.

Red light and Simon, a moving violation, goes through. He makes wide, long, unnecessarily elaborate turns with the van. Centrifugation, its male hug at his shoulders, is comradely. The van shows off for Simon: air-cushion suspension fills potholes in. Digital clock, dials, microphone, switches: the van has a Batmobile dashboard. Green-yellow-red indicators call off fullness, sufficiency, bail-out time. Jesus, there's a lot of red/yellow. The dashboard doubles as a lighting and sound-mix console. Plug-in jacks suck like hummingbirds: underneath, coils of wire bask, reptilian. Where the rearview mirror should be there's a twelve-inch closed-circuit TV screen: without it the van would be blind and obstreperous in reverse. Simon triangulates northeast through shortcut side streets toward Queens Boulevard. Above, useless now, nostalgic, the TV screen dwells on what is behind and past. Simon uses the horn a lot, mouth open: its wilderness call is dubbed into his throat. Simon hunches forward. He has sensed the engine in his stomach—ka-pop, ka-pop.

"We're backfiring. Listen t'that. My little baby has colic: I'll be walking the floor all night. Pop—see, every time I noodge the accelerator. Hey, you, Fish Nor Foul—what didja suck back there, the damn crankcase?"

"Sheesh. You figger a '56 Buick runs on hah-test?"

"Is my face red. We must sound like a flatulent buffalo. My Peterbilt is backfiring. Backfiring. Man, that shows class—like racing stripes on a hearse." Simon had begun to commiserate: short of breath. "My swell, high-compression, thirty-six-thousand-dollar heart is occluding. I feel it. I feel it. Look, on the TV, we're laying down smoke like a squid. Pop. Pop. Might as well enjoy it. Die! Croak! We're killing emphysemiacs. Asthma victims're retching blood. We're leaving little ad hoc cancers wherever we go. Pollute. Pollute. I'm American. I'm making acid rain. See, a medallion cab just disappeared. Aagh. I'm hurting. What you've made here, you Texas fagele, is a Rolls-Royce farm pickup."

"Simon. Next time *you* suck, what say?"

"Don." Simon has tripped the power brake. Don does a two-step forward, enforced obeisance. "What say I give you all five and a Spaldeen hi-bounce up the old Hershey Highway?"

"Both of you. Don't start. Just don't start."

Larry sits copilot, one starlet leg planked across the other. Simon's right hand, warm, wide as a mustard plaster, has come down on Larry's inner thigh. The thigh feels glassy and frictionless: might as well be the green silk kimono lying open around it. No contest, Larry is the most beautiful man Simon has ever known. His fine head, feminine not effeminate, tilts up: someone shaving an Adam's apple. His hair is Minx Blonde #85, but natural, and marcelled with the zigzaggy waves in fashion four decades ago. Simon has thought: he could be Leslie Howard's kid sister. Larry is sipping milk, one arm around his stomach, about to swing himself onto a dance floor. Simon has done that: danced Larry. And Larry has followed Simon's manpowerful leading.

"Lar. Syrup Tits. How much blank footage we got in stock?"

"Oh. About enough to make me a celluloid waist chain." Larry sips. "We can't even *think* of the Bethlehem scene yet. And I'm in no condition—my hand-held shots would look like home movies of the Hungarian uprising. It's here, just under my breastbone. Burr, burr, burr, like a hand drill. Then it hurts right around to my kidneys. Dull and achy. I can't sleep unless I'm just full to bursting with bread and milk. God, if I vomit blood again—"

"Don't talk about it. Don't talk about it. Mother, I'll never forget that night. My sneaker soles clotted t'the floor. You'll be okay—"

"Gopher dung. That's real easy f'you t'say. Lar's gonna be well when he gets out of this boxcar, not one minute before. Every producer in New York, even Mr. Herman Wolff himself, admires Larry's work. An' you—you got him traipsin' around like some carny sideshow. This is no life for nobody. You're holding him back. Lar could pull down a hunnert grand between now and next September." Don is behind Larry. He massages the eloquent neck. Larry has closed his eyes. "If you cared one square foot of jimson weed, you'd hock this piece of crap. It's capital shot to hell in a handcart. We could rent everything we—" Simon tight-corners, whap! over curbstone, a peevish maneuver. Don and Larry are separated. Don hustles for balance. Simon has cut in on them: his waltz now.

"No! This is mine. Mine. I buried my mother in a coffee urn t'buy it. Get out and walk, you road apple." Simon throws a switch. The dashboard appears to side with him. "Go on, get out. Pull up your pants leg and hitch a ride." Simon smacks the horn. Its neigh low-bridges a pedestrian. "Put on your nutria jockstrap and go cruise the bird circuit. Go, go on, you radio-dispatched froot loop. Maybe you'll score a champagne trick and he'll pour Prince Matchabelli up your *culo*."

"Sy. Donny."

"They hate you, Simon. From Wolff on down. You gonna make *Jesus 2001* on what Niko pays you for hamburgers? Huh? You're so smart with that manure tongue of yours."

"Hide your male children. Button up your Doctor Dentons, Don the chicken hawk is here. Listen, rim-shot, if Wolff could find Limpland on a map he'd nuke it. And as for Texas goy fags, f'cleanliness they're ranked right next t'pig's knuckles in Leviticus."

"I—"

"Shut up, Donny. In a minute he'll hit you."

"It's ileostomy time, Don. No rear door: the queen's nightmare. Oh, pack up your troubles in the old hip bag and smile, smile, smile."

"Stop it, Sy." Larry assists Simon. Hand in hand they examine Larry's inner thigh. "Next time I won't let you in my bunk when it thunders."

"For you, Lar-Swan." Simon smiles. "Only for you."

They had come East together, Larry and Don, on the same Greyhound bus: from Austin and Houston respectively. Somewhere north of Little Rock, Larry's head nodded down, gradual, ineluctable as the slanting twilight outside. Don, his heart half panicked, routed by such loveliness, so innocently given, caught Larry's forehead between neck and shoulder. It rested there, a shot put before release, through Arkansas and half the wedge of Tennessee. For hours Don watched over Larry's head, pink scalp under shimmering blond hair, a cub animal just newly pelted. He fell in love pate downward: his stomach tense, a backup shock absorber system for the bus. Don's bladder was inflamed: his left arm turned off its circulation. There was a red scar where Larry's temple had sealed Don's cheek. Now and again, childlike, Larry's hands would gnarl, as if in a bad dream. Don wanted to console those hands. An odor of lilac charmed him. Larry awoke, apologetic, grateful for his two-hundred-mile imposition. And unaware: or so Don thought. But it was a practiced stratagem: Larry had tested seat partners before with his insinuating, sunset head.

As wooer, Don chose a gruff, see-here drawl. He was hoarse for two weeks after they hit New York. Larry had a regional accent, too: locutions from some neutral fish-glittery land of sex. It was hard to judge: offhand Don guessed Los Angeles. So he told Larry about that birth defect, Texas, and how it enforced macho as it enforced marijuana laws. The herd-instinct rush at maleness: Daddy will show you how to wee-wee standing up. Don's arms were hirsute, almost furred, but, because of a selective skin sterility, there were places inhospitable to hair. Don called these things scars and gave each a Texas pedigree: Brahma bull, oil-well rig, rattlesnake, Bowie knife. In fact, Don had been a high school textbook salesman, just six months after dropping out of high school. Larry accepted Marlboros and Dynamints and the scars. He had a labor-saving face: it listened for him. When, on the Jersey Turnpike, Larry said without emphasis that he came from Austin, Don knew that he was under sentence. Larry would be cleverer, tougher, more resolute: not to mention more attractive, more talented. Throughout their doctor-patient courtship and uncommon-law marriage Don would always be in the waiting room, appointment only.

For nine years they have lived as man and man. For three Simon has studied their companionship. It irks him, not that they are homosexual: to Simon, lust is a function of imagining. There have been warm nights in his van when, made easygoing perhaps by darkness, perhaps by pot, perhaps by a high-carbohydrate meal, Simon has let one or the other service him. No, it isn't that. Nor is it that Larry could have done better, though in a half-spiteful, half-jealous way Simon has been Don's rival. But these two have memories now, anniversaries, as any couple would, precious and resilient. August 4, when the bus opened its door at gate #27, Port Authority. A ring for Larry one year. The cat that was theirs and died. Graduation from Clytemnestra Beauty School. One or two infidelities, now more cohesive than divisive. It doesn't happen often, but here and there, when they eat an apple together, when Larry takes in shirts or pants for Don, Simon is exasperated, brought to the edge of a childish and destructive fury. Because he hasn't that: nine years of trust, though invert, though unequal, given. So much cocksure domesticity: a household even on the road: and things known, secure at night.

She came to him in a roofless, high aisle of corn. His first guest there: he wasn't an adroit host. Simon never knew her age. Eleven, twelve: he himself had just passed ten. She and the corn wore silken tassels back over each ear. Simon, in ankle-high black sneakers, seemed doltish of leg. She stood barefoot and her toes were marvelously adept. She made twigs and stones spell, draw: she built with them. At first Simon thought there might be something wrong with her face: it smiled, it frowned, it pouted: was aghast, asleep, ecstatic. A silent rendition of something. She gave her name: Berry, for Bernadette, and would he care to see? What? he almost said. Yes. Sure, yes. Uh-huh.

Berry set her purse down. Then, in a contrapposto stance, she hiked the thin pink dress up. Baby fat on her chest impersonated puberty. Then, deep breath, she lay back on the dress, arching upward, one bent elbow high, knees under, Marilyn Monroe against red velvet. Snap, change. Belly down, brows in surprise, peeking over left shoulder: to line up a target through her buttocks gunsight. Snap, change. On the back, legs veed, a corn leaf trailing between them. Snap, change. On all fours. Snap, change. Dozing, thumb in mouth, bottom high and unguarded.

Simon was febrile: the August sun trounced him. He totted up the parts of her as if it were a sum: put down one navel, carry two breasts. There seemed to be a repertoire: fifteen minutes by the Mickey Mouse watch she wore. And, when this was accomplished, Berry gave out a working girl's five o'clock sigh. She had sweated. The dress came down: the purse came up. Berry kissed Simon so long on his left sideburn.

After that he waited barefoot for her in the corn. Even at night, with the two-finger typing of katydids around him. Berry made her personal appearances at random: a Tuesday, a Friday. Once Simon joined her in nakedness. But the ceremony, it seemed, wasn't shareable. Berry had a great deal to get through: spread eagle, wrestler's bridge, squat, lotus position, push-up. He stood there, somewhat better breasted, knock-kneed to shelter his private self. The second time he presented an offering of vegetables: sultry peppers, some green beans, his most perfect cucumber. Berry accepted, the laborer is worthy of her hire. When she kissed him goodbye, her lips worked out in preparation, as if getting up a whistle. He loved her: oh, he was poisoned with love. Thinking of her, Simon would go into jerky spasms, some systemic venom at work. He didn't even know where Berry lived. They didn't talk: she had business to finish and Simon's bound tongue made him shy. Mid-September, when the last of his crop was in, she disappeared.

Simon can remember. It happened on his way home from Vito's Shoe Remake. Five pairs of Bettina's ice-pick heels had pierced through the brown paper bag: it seemed a floating mine. "Rich kid, you got twennyfi' cents?" Big Elio's gang pulled him over as he crossed Fortieth Road. "Huh? Berry Dugan's gonna drop her pants for twennyfi' cents." And, yes, there she was: Berry on a brick stoop, snapping her green purse open/shut. Even at twenty yards he could hear the brass clasp tick. A sign read SEAN DUGAN, PHOTOGRAPHIC STUDIES. Simon said, "No." It wasn't resistance, they had already taken seventy-five cents. Simon said, "No." Berry counted the change: then fitted her purse through the front-door mail slot. Elio, Mouse, Goose Gallagher and Fat Hooch followed Berry toward the garage. Simon nipped at one of Bettina's heels. Was this his fault? Had peppers and cucumbers made her turn pro? For weeks he limped, some psychosomatic groin pull. He drives now, still able to wonder what Elio got extra for six bits. Simon can generalize from a single instance. And he hasn't put devotion on the market since.

Whispering: Don has an earful of it. Then Larry listens, laughs aloud. Simon is prepared to resent the shut, smooth egos near him. Push: he accelerates. The rearview TV screen funnels a Queens Boulevard future into an endless Queens Boulevard past: the van its hourglass neck. Larry has brought Don to him by the waist. He nips Don's fingernails short. The van has pulled up. Simon will have some attention, please.

"Hey, look. Look at that, Lar."

"What?"

"The crucifixion. The holy smoke. The spirit goes out of Him and it doesn't meet Federal Clean Air standards. Whaddya think?"

"Shee-it. What's the use thinkin'? We got no film."

"Get out, Lar. Up and at 'em."

"I'm in my robe. I'll get dog stuff on my slippers."

"Out. Out. Out."

Simon has the low, svelte breakfront of a factory in mind: DXX Plastics Co. Windowless, of aluminum and strange, unquarried marble: it wears the evasive, modern look that people with wraparound sunglasses provoke. DXX has been constructed in the T square of seven-story ragamuffin warehousing. The warehouses are dead: their weathered red-gray brick, chic in suburban fireplaces, would be worth more now than the structures themselves. Water has pooled on the roof of DXX, and sunlight mirrored up from it will toss scintillating, fleet whitecaps onto each warehouse wall. Simon likes this. Brickwork, anyway, can simulate the texture of canvas stage flats: pastel salmons and beiges. A dormant smokestack muzzle, ten blocks away, has been rearranged by perspective to appear part of the roof edge. LENTINI & SON, EST. 1907. No one est. in 1907 can be called a son. And making its way straight for this facetious legend, seven windows that have been marked,

SHAFT,

SHAFT,

SHAFT,

SHAFT,

SHAFT,

SHAFT, and

SHAFT.

Then, suddenly, the pastels do it, a scrim drops over his eye. There is a banking railroad curve. Once it swerved against some paradigmatic New Mexican skyline: the Sangre de Cristo mountain range, a backdrop push-pinned to his bedroom wall. It had taken him months, on and off, to build: the track bed was sculpted, stripped down, shifted, built up again. He had hypothesized a certain time of day, dawn, and a methodical breeze that would erode sand in methodical ways. Simon made sleepers, rails, cacti, tumbleweeds. In some jackrabbit's name he dug a burrow. And, canted, negotiating this turn, the empty skull of an Atcheson-Topeka-Santa Fe diesel: engineless, destinationless, freightless, because Aldo thought train sets effete. As in Renaissance painting there was one P.O.V. from which the perspective seemed exact. Simon would pillow his head, left eye closed. For a single instant the engine front was kinetic, frightening: the earth shook. It was enough: it had probably made him a director. Simon would love to do that now: to have even that much, a child's, right of final approval.

"From down here?" Larry salutes: a sunshade for his vision. "The angle's very steep. It doesn't give me much working room. . . . Unless we could set up in one of those warehouse windows."

"But the texture: it's jam on Wonder Bread. Yah. Yeah. Annh!" Simon stomps a manhole cover: bonk! Is the city hollow? "What we do, we overpaint the sign to 1997. LENTINI & SON—get it—all Lentini needed was the Holy Ghost and, bang, he's a Mafia trinity. And don't you love SHAFT, SHAFT, SHAFT right under SON, poor Jesus getting the fat end of a swamp root? Then the smokestack—it must smoke sometimes—with that schmaltzy Esther Williams water effect. Hey, can you believe this DXX thing? It looks like the face of that robot in *The Day the Earth Stood Still*."

"Well. . . . The light is old already. The colors must have been nicer an hour ago. But how do we get up there?"

"We don't. Press the erase button on everything I just said. Actually, it amazes me how I can come up with so much rug shampoo on short notice. Listen—" His hand has flipped up Larry's silk collar. "I just wanted t'get away from Mr. Sardonicus in there. Lar. Lar. Lar. Don't pull out on me now, huh? I'll get a backer, there's gotta be some rich idiot left who I haven't insulted yet. I'll come out smelling like an Airwick. I always have, haven't I? Hanh?"

"Oh—you know me. It takes a bomb to get me moving." Don slaps the horn.

"It's almost ten o'clock, dammit. Quit fartin' out there."

"We better get in, Sy, that nasty PR on the forklift is looking daggers at me."

"Probably, hah, wants t'pick you up."

Wolf whistle from the Hi-Lo. This is not ironic. At ten yards Larry might well be a woman. To play it safe, men half stand when he enters a room. The cab rungs are steep. Gallant, possessive, Simon hands Larry up. The forklift man is, yes, envious. And Simon is, yes, proud. Ah, it was wizard work that long, fast night of *Hearth*. Their faces were seared: skin split, or seemed to, like mudpacks. Then, belly-prone, rib cage against rib cage, they had learned respect for each other. The eye that imagines and the eye that brings to form. Simon could select one spark, one flame, tottering like an umbrella ant down the log. Larry would locate it, find its best profile: a cameo part. They hardly spoke. Simon used a poker: here and here and here. No retake allowed: set, cast, props were consuming themselves. Economical effort, just fifty feet edited from each thousand. They brought a performance out of the fire, awkward, stage-frightened ingenue that it was. They made it a star.

"You. Semi-colon. Didja call Carmen last night?"

"Yuh. I jewed her down t'three hunnert. It's two hunnert extra if Mary Magdalene goes bare-ass."

"That wetback. Just shaking hands with her y'need a penicillin shot." Simon chews cable. It's black, warm, soft: it has the qualities of licorice: another edible metaphor. "Five hundred. I oughta call the Consumer Fraud Department. She's got tits on her like the flaps on a manila envelope. A dog-eared chest. How much for the left one, plus some of her horse latitudes? Do I get a rebate?"

"What the hell difference does it make? We can't pay her nothin' anyhow."

"Tell you what, Don. You go down to Eighth Avenue, say to some *Six Guys in a Barn* double feature, starring Johnny Wang—I'll set you up in the men's room with a Naugahyde dance belt and a money changer. Even give you your own stall. I'll let you have fifteen percent and all the Republican Congressmen you can eat."

"Go fuck yourself."

"Well, that caulks it. Grab the wheel, Larry." Simon is up: unbalanced, on war footing. He lambastes Don: backwash with the right hand across Don's ear. The van yaws. Don has gone on defense, squatted, hands over face: elbows flap-flap over sensitive rib-place: charade language for a chicken. Simon sits: in control again. "I warned you once today about that cesspool mouth. If you wanna do the dozens on me, hire yourself a writer. I hate boring profanity."

"It's on its way, Simon. Sometime soon, I'm gonna bushwack you."

"Bushwack. Imagine. He can't even use his own down-home jargon without he sounds like a Tom Mix and Tony one-reeler. Texas, where the men piss Agent Orange and the women get hot flashes at thirteen. Bushwacking is a form of outdoor self-abuse. That's why they call it the Lone Star State. Beat it. Go tell Rose we're almost there." The inner van door has clacked shut.

"You're a big bully, Sy."

"I know. But, gee whiz, he's such a dish drainer. Gay, my plank. I never met a gay who was. That includes you. Pooves have their period twice a day. I need cheerful people around me. Never a discouraging word. Pennies from heaven. Jesus, I'm ready for the house of constant shrieks."

"Now he'll sulk all day at work. He yanks hair when he gets like this. Then I have to cover up for him."

"Hey, Angel Swish." Simon makes eyes. "Smile."

"Oh."

"What's the matter?"

"Oh. You know, I'd just like to be famous and rich before I lose my beauty. I'll be thirty-three in March. For years now I've wanted an expensive habit—like cocaine—but . . ." Larry shrugs.

"Hold on, Monkey Nates. D'you see me wearing a Kyryl original? Do I drink Ambassador 12? I gave you twenty grand for *Clap*. Out of my own marsupial's pocket. The Internal Robbery Service never saw a dime." Simon has turned left: eeerk. Red light on STEERING FLUID. "By the way, what happened to it?"

"Well, Sy . . . you know. I was sick. And there was Don's mother. It just flies. They charge you for breathing these days."

"Right. Ten-four, you're coming in loud and cheap. It's sitting in some Yehuda money market fund, getting plump as an altered tomcat. Huh? Hanh?"

"Hi, Rose."

"Do I interrupt?"

"No. Usually Lar can change the subject by himself. But he appreciates your help."

"Got to lie down, Sy."

"Um." Simon chews cable. "Lar. Wait. It's good what we're doing, huh? You have faith in the script?"

"Script? Did you finish it?"

"Ah, correction. Concept. The concept, you have faith in it?"

"Yes."

"Yes? Sure you can afford all that conviction in your voice? I mean, it won't lower your blood sugar, will it?"

"I'm here, Sy. I'm still here." Larry has opened the door. "Got to lie down." Tick of a blown kiss. Tock of the door latch.

"There he goes, friends—Scrooge McFairy. But, Jesus, he's beautiful."

Rose has sat. If it weren't for the engine, Simon would hear her knees: a small celery noise in each when flexed. Rose crepitates. Her actions are checked off, with an aural period, one by one. Bracelet chink: ball-pen click: stapler crunch. Rose has seven degrees of tsk. Also, she's the only woman Simon has ever met who can blink audibly. Now there are file clerk rubber fingers over each thumb. She has sneakers, so old you might call them gym shoes, on. The hem of her blue skirt is seceding, loose: a ramshackle roof gutter. Larry has designed her hair. It's short, the curling tight as mouton. (Don makes women ugly, a protracted revenge.) Rose is part-time stock clerk at Harvey's Wholesale Plumbing. On the job application, where it asked, "Does obscene language offend you?" she wrote, "None of that shit, you male chauvinist cocksuckers." Rose is half out the cab window. With advice from a sideview mirror, she plates lipstick on: kiss, kiss. Snick: tube in case. Rose jerks her face: keeps it on the go. At rest, skin pores might give away her age. The Pony Express-sized pocketbook has been basted with masking tape. Simon knows there is a quarter ream of paper inside, some screenplay, he suspects, written on company time: Harvey's or his. He has never caught her at it. Simon doesn't trust Rose, but she is quick and efficient.

"Where will the van be?"

"Aaaah. Good question. Let me think. Aaah. Gotta see Sollivan the collapsible Jew late this afternoon. Don'll pick you up. If he doesn't, we'll park by the Manor again." Rose has one hand out. Simon snaps a five-dollar bill. "First. For Immediate Release, what's the promo on Blivit back there and her son who flunked the Fresh Air Fund?"

"Just do me a favor. Make her sweat."

"The lampshade treatment?" Rose snags her allowance. "Hanh?"

"I had something more—mmm, more primal in mind."

"Ahhh—done. The old pastry tube is on alert. Some set of headlights she has."

"I wonder if my husband will be grateful. It's the one considerate thing I've ever done for Sam. His brother Sol, the big bush, is on our school board. You should see the respect he gets in temple. They tip their yarmulkes. Shall we say he spoke unkindly of my morals when I left town. A bastard. He collects oriental art, Buddhas mostly. That's his biggest one in there."

"I'll milk her daily double. I'll know her from a hole in the wall." Simon dips his hand under Rose's cockeyed skirt hem. "Don't worry. I'll turn Sol's topsoil for you."

"Listen. It's late. I've gone over pages nine to thirteen. The visual stuff is pretty good, but the Mary-Joseph dialogue needs massive surgery. Why is it you can't write like you talk?"

"Ah. See—"

"Never mind. I finally dug up a Howard Johnson's that's willing to turn Mary and Joseph away. Anyhow, I think so. The manager does community theater, he's gung ho for it, but he's a little leery—he has to call the central office first. I just pray Howard hasn't seen *Clap*." Ball-point switched off. "Also Marsha will lend us the baby. Free—if we keep it for the whole weekend. She's going to a rock festival. It's a girl, so we don't take the diapers off."

"Why not? All things are possible with God."

"Simon. Money. Soon." Rose kisses him: a warning. "Charm goes just so far. Your smile would impress me more with a hundred-dollar bill between the teeth."

"Uh-huh. What's in your handbag, Rose? The Staten Island phone book?"

"Some notes."

"You and Don." The van stops. "I'm not casting Judas Iscariot just yet."

"Don't worry." Rose is on the top rung, going down. "It's been a long time since I saw thirty pieces of silver."

"Cannibals, that's all they are. Teeth. Teeth. Teeth." Tap. Tap. Tap. On the inner van door. "Come in. Come out."

Robert there. He hasn't got his van legs yet. By the steering wheel (left/right), by the brake (front/back), Simon juggles him as once he played that game—what did they call it?—you know, with the tilting maze and the little steel ball. Drop! A seat has been achieved for Robert the Ball. Now, thinking about primal things, Simon has drafted an erection from the Selective Service down below. His pants leg will fight it: some bean seed sprouting in too-packed earth. Robert's shirt is open. Simon sees bluish nipples and a cheap lavaliere of chest hair between them. Robert is thin. His lips are the color and texture of rare London broil. Simon has no respect for acne: his own glandular change was volcanic: characterized by three or four spots per month, each harder, larger than a multivitamin pill. They ached like new contusions. Robert is memorizing nomenclature on the dimmer board. He has been impressed. Simon is impressed. Simon expects nothing less: the van is, after all, impressive. Robert's hands make and remake their acquaintance politely in his lap. Eyes are away, afraid. Simon whacks Robert on his left knee. Robert has gone over sideways. His funny bone rings on the door handle.

"Aaarh. Welcome to the one and only motorized sound stage in Videoville. I know just how you feel, Anthrax. Big marquee bulbs da-ditting across the sky. Fame. Fortune. Also alimony. The graduated income tax. Paparazzi taking flash shots while you're on the john. Plant a forest in Israel as one of our most distinguished Jewish-American citizens. Great. Great. Your chicken tracks someday in front of Grauman's Chinese Theatre. Excited, huh?"

"Yuh-yes."

"Yuh-yes? Afraid of me? Scrotum all knitted up like a lichee nut?" Simon isn't unfriendly. "Good. Fear of me is a pupil reflex, if you don't blink, you must be blind. Hanh. I'm so big I'm a goddam caricature of myself."

"Y-you're just wha. Wha. I expected."

"Oh. Rose must've sent you the prospectus." Don has come through the inner door.

"Lar can't work today."

"Keen. More of what we laughably call man-hours gone with the wind." Simon pulls over. "Here, you drive. Gotta get in uniform, Robert and me have a day's work ahead. No—stay just where you are, Rubella. Don is afraid t'be alone, he takes advantage of himself. Uh—what was your mother's name again?"

"M-ah. Minnie."

"Minnie. Got it. No short stops while I'm taking a dump."

The cab door has a safety chain: WE ARE NOT RESPONSIBLE FOR STOLEN PROPERTY. CHECKOUT TIME, ONE P.M. in five languages. Rippp: Simon rides the metal shoe along its track: locked.

Mmm-ahhhmmm. There's a song of raunch and must under his breath: his strident song of eating rescored for chamber duet. Simon wants. Minnie has been standing: her imperial-gallon back, a full six hands across, is faced toward him. Simon body-punches out of his shirt. He tends to bolt sex: a stand-up meal. The skylighting is oblique, peculiar: Minnie's shadow, shadows, all four of them, pinwheel underfoot. The braids lounge cross-legged on her back. Minnie's heels are round, wood-carved, the second-smallest size of bocce ball. She has been working the push broom with stumblebum heaves, one foot on it, rather as though it were a spade. The maxi nightgown attends on her, officious and much more successful at sweeping. Don hangs a right: Minnie hangs a stage-left, four quick steps. "Oh-oh-oh-oh." She decides to get low, recentering balance. Simon has the jeans off. He shakes out his privates: some ferret unleashed, given a scent to home in on. WE ARE NOT RESPONSIBLE FOR STOLEN PROPERTY. Simon has come up behind Minnie. He ropes her. There is no slack in the embrace: she has taken up his full circumference. Simon licks her nape. The good taste of vitamin D there.

"Minnie. Mmm-aaahr. Time to punch in for work. The little hand is on raunch and the big hand is right here. Ohhh—" Simon rousts her left breast out of torpor. His mouth and nostrils come open just a bit. It's the vacant face of animals, head up, testing urine scents through their Jacobson's gland, extinct in man, but somehow remembered in Simon. The half smell, half taste of female booty. "You just crossed the equator. We have a sacrament here. It's called the Laying On of Hands. Mine." Minnie has seen his naked thigh.

"You're wearing nothing again, Mr. Lynxx."

"The better to cover you, grandma. I am such stuff as wet dreams are made of. Put the broom down, I brought my own connecting rod. Hurry, I hate suspense, we'll do the foreplay later."

"So soon? I tried for ten minutes to get out of bed in this roller coaster and every time comes a crazy turn, wham—now you want I should start from go again? My son, Robert, is—"

"I locked the door. What he doesn't know he can't tell his analyst ten years from now."

"Excuse. There's another person here, Mr. Lynxx. It's not my habit to talk on a party line."

"Lar? Gosh. He's like your gynecologist. The last time he saw a nude woman he put a quarter in—thought she was some sort of op art jukebox. Anyhow he's got an eye mask on." Simon twirls his partner: face to face now. "Minnie, it has to happen. When you go to Nathan's you have a nice frank. When you go to Moscow, you see Lenin in his vacuum bottle. You may not want a frank, Lenin you could maybe care less about, but it's the custom, so you do it. It's the thin tissue of politeness and social grace that keeps civilization going. In my van, I'm the custom. It's got to be. Don't resist. Resistance gives me hypertrophy."

They stand, swaying, broomstick between, two commuters on the IRT. Oh, Simon wants. Minnie has a pleasant, large-caliber face. Her eyebrows are thick. Simon squeezes the lobe of one ear: it's fat as a grape. Simon kisses Minnie. She giggles into his throat, the giggle a gargle there. Simon gets help from Don: a left-hand turn. He banks her sideways into the lower bunk. Simon lies felled across Minnie. The bunk gives in its bracketing: sounds of an old wharf, storm-driven. Larry's hand has reached down from above. It slaps on the bunkside.

"Stop shaking, I'll vomit."

"Mmm-aaarh." Simon lunches on her throat. Minnie has deep skin creases there: as though her neck were some telescoping device, only half extended now. He plays with a friendly tab of proud flesh. Minnie is serene. No fear, hmmm: passion not very apparent either. For spite he will give her a level-two hickey. She tastes of cider: she tastes crisp. Simon isn't used to such health in a bed partner. His usual women are mushroom folk, white and saprophytic. "Minnie. Come on, admit it. You find me attractive."

"A little color you could use." Minnie pinches one cheek, then the other. Simon's contact lenses rise on a teardrop swell of pain.

"I'm a macrobiotic diet. On the black market they'd lay out thousands for this. Whole sheep embryos. Calves cooked in amniotic fluid. Brains, livers, vital glands. This isn't just another swat in the dark, it's a hormone injection. Relax." Minnie has been tickled: the close breath of his talk, not the text: she giggles. "Great. Hey, listen, one night with me and you get three credits in Life Experience at any junior college."

"What's going on down there?"

"That, Minnie, is my hand. Right now it's tiptoeing up, along the erotic zone of your inner thigh, though, uh, hampered somewhat by this stern sheet you've got on."

"My erotic zone is also my tickly zone." She cuts off his hand at the gap. "Mr. Lynxx, I have to give my little speech before you get all in a spritz." Simon disputes her grasp, but Minnie is strong: knows how to use her weight. "My husband, Sol—"

"I won't listen." Simon thuds his van wall. "No guilt. No. The Judeo-Christian ethic ends here. This is a free city. A Papal State of lust."

"Yes, but what Sol—"

"So. I laugh at Sol. Sol never treated you right. Who wants t'make it with a ginkgo? Hanh, feel down there. Feel. Big as a pugil stick. Right now blood is filling the erectile cells: they're working away like little Nibelungs. God, I'm magnificent."

"But, Mr. Lynxx. That's just it. I don't want you should have a letdown."

"Your monthly is nothing. To me it's estrus."

"It's not my—"

"Shaddup. I wanna get laid."

Minnie has to giggle. It makes her short of breath. Simon is irked. He recognizes a female gambit: the laugh-him-to-flaccid approach. Simon executes a mighty one-armed push-up. His left hand throws nightgowning headward. Minnie is decapitated. She will fight out from under her own skirts, but too late. Simon's hand has made a thrust up/between her thighs. And right on target.

The target goes B-bonggg!

"Aaarh! What in—" His forefinger knuckle has begun to bleed. Simon sits up, he butts the underspringwork of Larry's bunk.

"Sy. Have a heart."

"What? What is this thing? What? What? The Iron Maiden of Nuremberg? Aaargh, get it off. I almost broke my hand."

"Mr. Lynxx. I was trying to tell you. Sol—"

Simon blinks. Can it be? Yes, a bas-relief of pubic hair in solid bronze. Minnie's sculpted, stylized mons veneris is huge, also green with old corrosion. He hits it: Jesus, the first time he's ever bonged a woman. Simon knows fine craftsmanship when he sees it. Sturdy riveting leads up: at the waistline Minnie's tanned flesh laps over. Across a pseudo-abdomen, around her sunburst navel, signs of the zodiac radiate out. The casting is superb, intricate, and aged with verdigris. Simon can't believe it. Minnie can: she paid two hundred dollars for this item in the back room of Glenchester Antiques. And just above the crotch, in Gothic lettering, CAVEAT EMPTOR.

"What's this bogus plumbing? Off with it. Off. Off. It's me's supposed to have the hard-on. Unnngh." Simon pries at her waistband. Minnie yells, pinched: no give. Simon peers down. Heavy grillwork, a knight's visor, is on guard in the crotch. "It's got teeth. Mother, I've finally seen one with teeth."

"Mr. Lynxx. I know you're disappointed. My husband is a jealous man—"

"I'll get that bushmaster. Wait. Wait. Don't panic. We'll spring your canned goods yet. Aha!" The keyhole, a flask-shaped silhouette, lies over her right hip. "Aha! Where's the key? Ow."

"On a string around Sol's neck. Your fingernail—did you break—"

"String? I'll stringle—ahh, strangle him with it, I'll do a nose job on his ears, they won't know him from one of his own hydrangeas. Nobody, nobody pulls this on me. I want. I want. Doesn't anyone understand that?"

"Sy—a little quiet, please. Can't you do it without shrieking?"

"We've run into some technical difficulties down here, you feeble

queer. Nothing much, I'm just in bed with a panzer division, that's all."
Simon pounds overhead.

"Ow. Ow. Stop."

"That screwdriver in the rack. Hand it down. The big one."

"Oi, God. Mr. Lynxx—"

"What for? What are you doing down there?"

"I'm unscrewing a woman, what the hell d'you think I'm doing?"

"Mr. Lynxx, please. It isn't time to press my panic button."

"Hang on, Minnie. I'll have you outa that bronze *calzone* in a jiff." The
screwdriver is handed down. "All right, you giant clam, give it up."

"My skin, you giving me a black-and-blue—"

"We may lose a little here and there, but this'll be my finest hour.
Childe Simon to the dark tower came. Inhale. Big. Bigger."

"I am. I am. To get into this I'm always inhaled." Simon crowbars
under the waistband. Green rust flakes off. "One-two-three-uhhh!"

"Owww! Mr. Lynxx, stop. You're doing an appendix on me."

"Well, Jesus, your beaver's got a dam around it."

"Sy—the whole bed is coming apart."

"Shut up and get me a hacksaw blade."

"No sawing! No sawing! You'll murder me. You're like a madman ox."

"The keyhole. A little finesse. The hand is faster than the eye." Simon
toggles the screwdriver in. "Kee-rist, will you look at this lock. Musta
come off the Bastille. Uh-mmm. How did Tony Curtis do it in *Houdini?*
Over! Flip it over. We'll turn your flank, Hup!"

"I'm turning. With this weight I'm like a roly-poly."

"Ye gods. She's got the Liberty Bell for a behind."

The buttocks have been scoured bright with sitting. Their size is exaggerated: a mask of tragedy left, a mask of comedy right. Simon can see
his white skin reflected. He slides the screwdriver in/along her spine.
Simon goes into a three-point stance, wrenches up, great leverage. Minnie shouts. Crack! Simon's head sprongs Larry's coccyx through the
mattress above. His screwdriver shaft is bent. Minnie can feel Simon's
aimless thuds: they relax her through the bronze. Dah. Dah. Dee-dedah.
Dedah. Dedah. A tune scored for hammer and tongs. Simon blows sweat
off his chest.

"No use. It's strictly a Brink's job. I'd be better off making it with the
Great Barrier Reef."

"You're a nice boy, Mr. Lynxx. Come lie beside me. I'll give you a
hug."

And Simon, tired, does.

5

"Telenex Data's breaking!"

"Eh—Millie, flip the camera switch. Get all my screens going."

"They're fi'six minutes late. Shee-it, man, we're gonna be murdered."

"Ahh—there is me. Me, Niko. Niko himself on the film screen. Look—there's you, Ball Peen."

"Niko, stop admirin' yourself. We all seen it a million times. I need setups at twenty-eight and twenty-nine."

"See, up there. I make the chicken Salad Supreme. Niko himself."

Filiades' Famous Cinema Restaurant, a dining car shunted to some improbable spur line in Long Island City, takes Telenex Data Systems on, all aboooard. The counter is eighty feet long. It has a castered track above for rapid service. Simon at seat #1, griddle end, spins empty plates down to Sledge at #50, testing, testing, one-two-three. The track gives out a skateboard thrum. There are fifteen tables for Millie and Lois and Joyce. Also, a wide window ledge for the stand-ups. And, on four walls, twice on the ceiling, six loops of Simon's *Diner* play and replay themselves. A filmed burger deluxe rockets left to right along the track, rocketing repeated six times, and Filiades' restaurant seems to carousel counterclockwise with it. Customers stumble in, as you stumble climbing a stalled escalator's first small steps, reflex expectations gone. Niko is at #25, traffic control, alert for the best bit, that close-up of his face in craftsmanlike, sweet concentration, packing spoon, napkin, saltines with a soup-to-go. It is his fame and his dignity. Alone, he has wept to see this. Niko owns three dozen prints of *Diner*, plays it annually between a Donald Duck and a Buster Keaton at his daughter's birthday party.

"Eh—last call. Last call for shorts. Take him from the top. Simon!"

"Gotta have prongs. Ten rounds of sixty-millimeter pig meat. My triglyceride box is low. Niko, come down and tie up my hairnet. Tokyo Rose here's too short t'reach."

"Lay off that Jap stuff, Simon. I'm black."

"So was Al Jolson."

"Bendya head, big boy."

"These tomatoes didn't make it through the weekend, Niko. A cat's afterbirth'd look better."

"Cut 'em up fancy. Make 'em stars."

"I wouldn't eat here if you paid me."

"You wouldn't eat here I could make a profit. Ball Peen!"

"Lessee. Short on Dr. Scholl's and bread dice."

"Sledge!"

"Om."

"That means okay in TM. He only speaks one word so he calls it a mantra. You goin' inside me, man?"

"Always, always. Get in the flow, B.P. Don't hog the ball. Hit the open man. Sledge! Stick a fork in that new kid when you get a chance, Robert's his name. B.P., give me decent English subtitles on those spic orders for a change, huh? I can't make a *coño* sandwich."

"Yeah. Yeah. Hey, lissen. 'Tis the cause, it is the cause my soul. And smooth as momma-mental alabaster—'"

"Off the airwaves, you stage mutha. The color line forms at the rear. Call 'em! Call 'em! Burgers going on."

Simon, in his neutral corner, is off the ropes, neck loose, each shoulder shrugged up, one-two, one-two. The wooden duckboard cree-acks under his feet, lettuce from last Friday coming up between its slats like grass through an urban sidewalk. He cardsharps burger patties in a patience layout across the 6' × 4' griddle. Bacon strips cringe away from the metal. Thick, thick, thick—three to each hand—Simon guts eggs. Sizzling applauds. Ham and onions and green pepper: the matrices of westerns. Simon deals bread into his five quadruple toasters. Ah, the smells: heat has amplified them. Saliva will come. But Simon isn't in the game yet: this is subtle wand-work, art: a weekend break can throw your timing off. Left foot taps, a metronome to conduct his rhythm back.

"Call burgers rare!"

"8 De."   "20 cheese." "30." "16   "35 De and 37 with bloody cheese."

"Xerox at 9 and 19."   "Lois is naked, 18 with wop." "40 and 42 and 44."

"Center, ah,   gets a De, three yellow, one wop." "7 wop."

Millie has, ah, "Bad breath on   "One De in the end zone."

worms at 8."   that 16 I called."   "15 De."   "Cheese 27."

            "Got it, next. And call louder. Gimme the odd balls."

"Center frog sides light." "One   "Two cackles   "Gacto 24."

"Poach Joyce twice."   cowboy to ride doggie style, 25."

"Kraut a pig for Niko."   on wheat, 36."   "Melted rye, 19,

    "BLT center." "Gacto 38."   "Golda Meir with the monthlies."

        "Give that melted   hot and smeared, 41." "Des-demona."

"Joyce wants a Midol, sorry."   "Gacto 12."   "Make up
an Italian repeater."   "Jackson   "Scramble your mind, dammit."
     "Filiades special turds, 26." "31 wop."   one Irish "Slab ass
     light on the Filiades."   on white." two cackles, 29."
"Des-demonah!"   "Cowboy without "Frog sticks, ten sets
"Rares ready   his horse."   at center."   "Shrimps, 30."
clear the track and call medium. Sing it!"

The plates take off: accurate, two or three rotations per foot, as though from some rifled barrel. Rice pudding and Jell-O pick up vibrations from the El track overhead. Simon lets them go backhand, blind, longest first: #50 (the end zone), #44, #42, #40. He's cold. His #37 slows one station short, and Niko whirls the casters, a Scottish curler "sooping" his teammate's stone along. Mediums come off. Simon doesn't use a spatula: along his right forefinger there is a callus—it has no feeling—with the sheen of vinyl. At night he lays this finger aside of his nose and dreams eating. Darkness: the projectors draw leader through, starting again. DINER "un Film de Simon Lynxx." The VP of King Knitwear holds his six-year-old son up to watch. Simon loves an audience and responds. Now he's hitting, hitting. At #41 the Golda Meir (bagel) with its smear of cream cheese stops on a dime. Then Millie's eight, one after another, to the service station, #25. Ah, he could hit track center in his sleep. "Arriba! Arriba!" There is a claque at Simon's end. He has been asked for autographs. The vernacular is his and the system. A legend two blocks south of legendless Queens Boulevard.

"Nothbound! Nothbound."   "3 black,   "One   "Om,   "Draws at
"Sledge!   "Ice Tommy, 4,   7 mulatto   curdled   om,   1, 6, 9, 11, 14."
You're   a pig's dong."   "A   2 hi yella,"   cum, 5."   om."   "10 wants a
long, I gotta   "Filet of   dishcloth   "King Knit's   chamber pot."
draw in my shoe   sole, 39."   here."   breaking   "13 wants
dammit."   "Circumcise   "Robert!"   now."   Italian shingles."
"Arriba!"   a hard boiled   "Desdemona to subdue   "Goulash, sell
"Some Hellman's   spare."   "A   in any honest   "Shit on   my goulash."
KY on my hair   liver   suit."   "We lost   the track,   "Robert!
food salad."   "Push   comes to   a soup   hold it!"   Robert!"
          "Castrate   me   19."   overboard.   "Two nates
"Mash   this   one   "I need eggs,   Also a   "One   on an
one   Italian   ice   plates, cups,   customer's   Spanish   army cot, 5."
Irish   special."   tea."   I'm losing my   shirt!"   Doily, 37."   "Bricks
root."   "Omm,   edge here!"   "Milk   "I need to go."
          omm,   "πανα-   Shake   a mop."
          omm."   για   here."
          μου!"

Robert Fischer backs from the kitchen. Steam has forced his acne: a hothouse crop. The clamor, its run-on shouts, have fuddled him. Robert's pelvis is out front to basket-catch a heavy stack of plates. Sledge butts him against three coffee boilers. The convex reflection there caricatures his nose: he could easily imagine that his sweat was tears. Near Millie's station, in this four-foot aisle, he touches a woman's buttocks for the first time, apologizes to them. His ankles stutter and the stack of plates is insecure, lordosis in its spine. Ball Peen at the steam table appropriates them all. Robert can see Simon twenty feet away. He has never witnessed such coordination. Simon's hands smoke with grease: they have the rugged, savage action of farm machinery. There's a hamburger between Simon's lips, this and the black, skull-tight hairnet impose a Hottentot profile on him. King Knit is all in: fidgety workers stand two deep behind each seat. Simon sucks a long rubber hose: it hangs from his personal quart of Coke above. Suddenly the walls mirror: this very drinking has been repeated on the film screens, again, again, again, again. Filiades' diner is a faceted paste jewel. Robert hears his name in Simon's mouth, roar above the roar. He runs from it. He passes Ball Peen, Millie, Niko, head down, duck-walking, as if the counter were a trench lip under fire.

```
"Robert!    "Plaid squares    "Gacto, 15."    "BLT on     "Whose     "Send
I'm 86,      with syrup, 11."   "I'm going      whiskey."   pig is this  a frog
Robert!"                        "Eat it          raw." "High-Time  here?"   sides, 8."
    "Poosh goulash  yourself."                    Staples     "Put        "Cow's
    please."  "40, a             "I'm          breaking wind   deep
"Simon you   Jew                outa            now."        up his      throat
sent empty   Sleeping bag."    the              "Millie's    tail,       43."
dog roll."   "Broke my         flow."           short on     schmucks."  "Help. Niko,
  "Gimme the finger-           "Desde-plasma."   "Omm!"      I'm short
  Filiades   nail on—"          Moh-            "Robert!"  "A      "Hard on
  Special, 19."   "Raw          Nahh." "Raw      raw boil    everything."
  "Raw, 21, 28."   at 34."       10."            16."        at 39."
```
"Stop eating you locusts! I'm empty! I'm empty! I'm empty!"

Simon slants off-tackle, shoulder down, along the narrow aisle: past Ball Peen, past Lois, who lifts his crotch. He has had her once, but can't remember when or where. Niko's blue pen writes a line across his chest, heading north. Robert is sobbing in the kitchen. Niko's uncles, George and Ari, cooks, have cursed vigorous Greek at him. An egg lies broken in the egg bowl: white and yolk grout intact shells together. Tomato slices have spilled on the floor. Simon pushes him, and Robert glides away, tomato seeds slick as ball bearings under one heel. Arms full—Ari and George behind him, arms full—Simon is back to save the westerns, but his melted cheese looks like a black, smoking Astrodome. He lets it burn off with the home fries and three charred burgers. Niko is pushing two-handed knife thrusts through a shrimp salad. The High-Time Staple people are restive, yelling: lunch hours have run down. Joyce has covered for Niko: the register punches ring out. Simon's hand is a palette: no time for utensils now. Butter, mayo, cream cheese, mustard applied with right fore, middle, ring, pinky fingers. Turgid, black smoke from the broiler comes up under his shirt, exits at neckline: six minute-steaks below going on a quarter hour each. Screens recapitulate the clever, comic speeded-up section of *Diner*. Simon roars, ashamed. Too late—thick, thick, thick—he's out of the flow.

Hot grease strums, bing! The sound of a department store elevator: pain translated from feeling to hearing, from inner arm to inner ear. He has heard/felt that burn before. Now Simon daydreams: the annual Swell Fellow picnics at Alley Pond Park. Thick, thick, thick. He reseals the hollow egg shells, in his garbage chute they seem flawless. What you need is the same wrist action that mumblety-peg stars use. This was Aldo's trick: more or less the one item of ancestral lore passed on to Simon. That, and certain secret ways with noodle salad: also how to inflate hamburgers with air and bread before they set: how to rehabilitate old, hard ears of corn. They worked the picnics together: in rich hickory smoke that made them squint and smirk. Aldo's grill was redoubtable, a 55-gallon drum hacksawed lengthwise. Little Simon fielded burgers, mitting them in toasty rolls. All errors belonged to father and son. On those afternoons Aldo seemed paternal, not some voice ricocheted off a dispassionate ionosphere. Hot franks and potato salad: beans, clams, steaks, chicken legs. "Got a little helper, huh?" some Swell Fellow would say. Aldo's skin ran, like pork chops giving up their first fat to the flame. Bettina kept a distance. Even so, smoke carried their explicit masculinity downwind at her. She would eat nothing: their meat was a conspiracy. Bettina drank beer and showed her underwear, asquat on the edge of picnic tables. It was the only time that Aldo believed Simon might come to good.

"Griddle's off."

"Been off all day. Bad news, man. They run it up. Customers fifty, us nothin'."

"It was the little boy so new and scared and Santos getting sick on Monday again. Eh—he's gonna get one in the eye tomorrow."

"Took his pants down, that's what."

"Please, B.P., I'm begging now. Don't give Simon the knife. You know how he can get. He's an artist."

"Artist? He just throwed the meat around. Empty buns comin' down all day. One hadda eggshell in it. Just a eggshell. This's been comin' a long time. He choked in the clutch."

Tick. Niko turns the projector system off. Eyes that have practiced ignoring distraction feel out of work. Robert sits, listless, on the floor, one arm hugged around a stool's trunk. Thirty-five-millimeter flickering stays on his vision. The darkened room will seem a still-shot now. Simon has uncoiled the net from his head: roughneck hair springs out. He's irritable and ready to mess someone. Three raw hamburger patties flop from the ceiling: hurled there in a spasm of exasperation. Simon eats. Sledge is cross-legged atop the counter, catching up on his TM. "Om," he says. This suggests yawning to the impressionable brain. Niko yawns: Robert yawns. In their street clothes, Lois and Joyce yawn. Quarter to three: the diner's business lasts only from coffee break to executive lunch, five days a week. Niko is worried: he holds both twists of his mustache up, arch-supporting an uneasy smile. Simon is his pet and drawing card. Also, Niko wants to play St. Peter, 2001.

"Never was a silk could move. Bein' white is all pump fake and no shot. Bad hands. Bad rhythm."

Ball Peen is a black Korean. Pre-pubic boys have his slightness: just sixty-one inches tall, with slanted, cunning epicanthi. He is dark enough, but this darkness seems the sort of blackface a VC guerrilla might affect. Ball Peen would rather not be so complexely ethnic. His beard is piebald and restricted to Fu Manchu portions of his face. These things embarrass him. Ball Peen has changed into a dashiki. He wears dark glasses so opaque they have caused an atmospheric inversion in his mind. He breathes as one would standing behind a bus: carefully and at long intervals. Sledge, Ball Peen's kid brother, is a Korean black, taller than Simon, with crimped hair close-shaven and Negroid lips. These things embarrass him. Sledge is the color of a golden palomino. He has changed into a kimono. Ball Peen and Sledge are the children of a large black U. S. Army technical sergeant and a small South Korean laundress. In front of the convex coffee boiler Ball Peen teases his reluctant Afro up. It tends to oriental flatness: he has his hair body-waved at a uni-race barbershop every two weeks or so. It seems high-strung, charged with static electricity: it becomes oblong when he passes metal.

"Calls himself a cook. Sent me down a peanut butter and jelly with lettuce on it. Man couldn't boil water if you—"

"That does it, Tojo. Say goodbye t'that air mass you call a head. Yaaah! Here comes instant conk."

"No. Not that. Don't!" The aisle's straight and narrow path has hemmed Ball Peen in. Simon upholds a quart can of water. "Sledge! Help! He's gonna do it again." Ball Peen tries to climb out/across the counter, but Simon has him by the belt and water is in cold pursuit. Like a Bromo Seltzer, effervescing slightly, Ball Peen's Afro dissolves flat. The comb has dropped off, nothing to get its teeth into. Ball Peen has gone from sixty-one to fifty-six inches in height.

"Come on, Bruce Lee. I thought all you coolies Kung Fu kicked in your mothers' wombs." Simon devises a hammerlock: screws it down. "You couldn't fight your way out of a won ton."

"Leggo. You gonna bigot me, bigot me right. Sledge got all Mommy's yellow. Lay off."

"Say, 'Simon, you are the world's number one short-order man.' Annh. Say it."

"You're bendin' my shades—"

"Say it."

"You the number one. The best." Niko and Millie laugh. "Now why didja have t'do that? Huh? Huh? Shit, man, I just had my hair frazzed out, cost thirty-five bucks, and I ain't got my hot comb here. How'm I gonna go out?" Ball Peen tousles his supine hair with a dishcloth: currying, teasing. "Sledge, you big Chink, some brother you are. How come you let him do that all the time?"

"Om!"

"Om. Man, I'm sick of all that ommming. Om, what?"

"Om no fool. He got me by twennifi' pounds, you jerk-ass nigger." Ball Peen lobs a handful of wet, pithless tea bags at his brother. Sledge and Simon laugh. Ball Peen resents this sound: it's the laughter that big men share. Discrimination of yet another sort.

"Eh—Simon, he's just let off a little steam." Niko sponges water. "So, we have a bad day. Robert, cheer up. Give us a big smile for the camera. Tomorrow you're part of Filiades' team. Don't let Simon get you. I know Simon. He's like a son to me, big heart all the way. Sssst—say something nice to Robert, Simon. He's down in the mouth."

"Sst somebody else. The little commfu left me making gasburgers. He wants t'be a big director. He couldn't direct air through a baffle plate."

"Eh—a director? That reminds me, how's *Jesus 201* going along?"

"*Jesus 201*. Great. You make it sound like a freshman course in faith healing. 2001, Niko. 2001. You're eighteen hundred years short, and about five thousand dollars, which reminds *me*. I'm ready to cancel your subscription."

"Simon." Niko flourishes an indefinite hand gesture, half safe, half out. "Five thousand. It's a lotta bucks. I gotta sell my stock at a big loss."

"Niko, the pile driver. Greek arts practiced here: he'll bend over forward t'help you. Look, you'll get five percent of net, whaddya want, something safe like Cleveland City Bonds? And lay off the bouzouki serenade. I know where you park that old Volkswagen of yours at night: in the trunk of your big, fat Cadillac."

"Well, if we could come to some—eh, agreement—about St. Peter—"

"What? With that Ellis Island mustache? With that gut? You been hitting the bhang again, Niko? Peter's supposed to be a rock, not some middle-aged chamois rag from Charley's car wash. You had all of four lines in *Clap* and I had to do twelve retakes. You moved like you were walking on 3-in-One oil. Now what I visualize, see, there's this telethon scene where Jesus lays hands on a spastic—"

"Nuts. Niko doesn't pay five grand to be a spastic. That I could be for free."

"True. True."

"Sy—hey, lissen. Come on, man, it's the least you can do, bustin' up my 'fro like that." Simon blows air, impatient. "I worked this out last night." Ball Peen has been at the American Academy for seven years. His height and his features aren't easily cast. Now Ball Peen has posed himself, sideways on, left hand out to jab, as if Shakespeare were an assailant. "Her father loved me, oft invited me / still quessioned me the story of my life—"

"Christ, wake a handkerchief head up at 5 A.M. and he'll recite *Othello*. Hanh, y'don't think there were ganges back in Shakespeare's time, do you? Huh? We invented you blank dominoes so people'd buy expensive Fichet locks for their doors."

"Lissen. Lissen." Simon strums his lower lip.

"Abbajabba-dub jub, forsooth. You couldn't do iambic pentameter on a hollow log. Anyhow, the broad who plays your Desdemona'll have t'wear shoes on her knees."

"Okay. So fugget Shakespeare. You got a part f'me in *Jesus 2001?*"

"So solly, they didn't have Head Start programs in Bethlehem."

"Why, man? I studied the trade. What's wrong with me?"

"Nothing that four tons of Porcelana wouldn't cure. Call again when I'm doing *Porgy and Bess in Yokohama*. Niko, where's my doggie bag? I've got an important appointment at National Artists this afternoon."

"Right here. Nice T-bones. Nice noodle salad. A big thing of goulash. I treat you good."

"At one-seventy-five a week you should. I put this salmonella outlet on the map. When I came here there were grease bubbles the size of lima beans floating in the coffee."

"Eh, Niko's food was—"

"And keep the goulash. It's been on the steam table looking like something a sea gull wouldn't dive for since Labor Day."

"Sy—me an' Sledge, we worked up a comedy routine. Good topical stuff. Sledge—"

"Gotta go. Come on, Trachoma—"

"It was a joke, all what I said—"

"*N'importe. N'importe.*"

"You're the best. Number one." The door closes. "Shit, he's pissed at me. Now I ain't never gonna get my big screen break."

Robert has to run. Simon is in a knavish mood: it elongates his stride. For sixteen months Ball Peen and he have teamworked the counter service together. This should entail a certain professional courtesy. Simon takes pride in his craft: Ball Peen's criticism has offended him. It's a violation of their food-brotherhood. Robert heads Simon, cranes back to look at his face, falls behind. Does this three times. He wants to learn Simon's expressions by heart, what they mean. But it's too early for Robert: he can't discriminate quite yet. Simon has stepped into the gutter. Long Island City streets are still cobblestoned, an indication that people don't sleep here. It brings back photos of a Pompeiian bakery in his Latin II text: loaves carbonized and hard on their carbonized tray. His shoes have metal taps. Simon tests for hollowness where he walks: he would like his coming and going to be preceded. The gritty, companionable snap-snap that a cobblestone sparks off is like sand on a vaudeville stage. And he begins to dance.

Eyes get that lounge lizard drowse. Lips draw up. The pristine, big teeth nip air. His shoulders are sinuous and feminine. Simon dances without shame: foolishly, abandonedly. "Djah. Djah. Aaaah-ah, djah. And a jah, jah, djah." The doggie bag partners him: now submissive, now the male. Robert, up on the sidewalk, has disassociated himself. He is mortified: he would rather see Simon nude here. But this is also a lesson, part of the apprenticeship: to become an audience for exhibitionism and particularly for Simon, Mr. Exhibit A himself. Around them, factory buildings give off arid heat and the noise of traffic accidents. High-Time Staple has a machine with this real jim-jam sound. It stamps out steel cases—Bap! Bap!—but alternately, waiting for raw material, there's a particular tackle-acketytack! Simon counterpoints, not for the first time. This machine has been on his dance card before: he is its dreamboat: together they could win the Harvest Moon Ball. Shouts from King Knitwear across the street. Simon extemporizes an encore for his USO tour fans. Tackle-acketytack! around fireplug and lamppost. The camp Gene Kelly of a street where no one lives.

"Good. That was good. I enjoyed that." They walk. Simon scuff-taps at cobblestoning. Robert has his elbow.

"I-aah. At Niko's. I didn't. Know where th-things. Where you kept them. And all the noise. It confused, fused me."

"Food is war. And love. Tar baby can't dig that. Errol Flynn and his last platoon. Banzai! One for all, all for one. But not for him—that nonoccurrence. What can you expect from a race brought up on fatback and pine cones? Barbecues, banquets, buffalo roasts. They reconstitute civilization. Meat: it's ritual and romance. Jesus handed out flesh and blood, he knew what he was doing. The five thousand he fed, that was the first Rotarian picnic. It's the West. Empire. Nuclear fission. The assembly line. Loofah gloves. Acrylic lacquer. Panel trucks. Greatness! Now you take earthquake, plague, war. They produce heroes. Aaaah, but famine. On an empty stomach there are no heroes, Squint. Uh-uh. I've studied the literature. Courage is gastric."

"I—"

"Take my father. A walking bile duct. Poison sumac comes up on his grave. But behind a charcoal grill, with franks splitting open and smoke in his face—Peter Churchmouse. He'd kiss everyone. Kids, dogs, three-hundred-pound volunteer firemen with hair on their kidneys. Sing 'O Sole Mio' and 'Bye-bye Blackbird.' He'd glad-hand you up t'the elbow. It was ceremony. The sweet song of molar on molar. I could cry. Sharing." Simon reconsiders. "Not that he'd ever share with me, the big praying mantis. At our table he was Captain Forkthrower—zonk, and his harpoon was in my mess. Once he broke the damned plate in half." Simon laughs: this is a lie. "No, Dewlap. It's men in groups, that's where joy hangs out. Women don't have it. I get heartburn when I eat with women. They're closet Frenchmen. Gourmet food, 'gourmet' is another word for dinky servings. They won't pick up food in their hands. An open mouth and an open fly: it's the same to them. Gross. Vulgar. Civilization started dying the day we let women share our tables. Eating, Jesus, I love it. That's why I made *Diner*. Do you hear/see the rhythm in *Diner?* It's peristaltic. It has Homer's huge, pounding meter. Diomedes of the great war cry. And *Hearth*. Digestive, too. Consumption. Life and death and love."

"I—I see."

"Sure you do, Glaucoma."

"I'm not stupid. I. Just look, look that way." Robert thinks it over. "My mother, she picks things up in her hands."

"Yah. I like your mother. At the moment she's having a little trouble with her gearbox. Heard of hard-shell Baptists before, but a hard-shell Jew—"

"What about *Clap?*"

"Hey, Croup, whyn'cha take a flying *fongool* t'Gotswanaland? Huh?"

"I. Ah. Just asked."

"In this organization we don't ask. We just listen. To me. What's that? I didn't see that before."

The construction site is ambitious: more than a half block square. Simon rushes down the side street toward it. Six hundred derelict apartment-house doors form a palisade. The doors remember old identities: 3E, 6H, 7B. They parade in a straight line, unhinged, crazy, along the sidewalk. Some have beady peepholes or distinguished glass eyes that stare back. They are pastel-colored: salmon, beige, maroon, robin's-egg blue. There are worn spots where the rapping of decades has been aimed. Above, a crane—its Erector set structure proving and reproving the law of right triangles—slants up, trawling in the sky with two tires for bait. Simon, a voyeur, kneels at the keyhole of 17J. "Jos. Steinberger." The excavation is deep. Spiral ramps, wide as an avenue, guide-tour the eye down. Holes call to Simon. There is archaeology in all things. A squad of dump trucks expose backsides to him, rubber mudguards union-suit their rear wheels, as if these were generative parts. Simon knows the yellow clay. He has dug in this part of Queens before.

"Got to get in. Got to get in." Simon bangs on 2F. "Look at that De Chirico perspective. The ghost of a million entrances and exits. It's an Avon lady's nightmare. Wild. Hold this."

"There's no one working?"

"Crane operators' strike. They want time and a half on their coffee breaks. Aaaah!" Simon has a running start. He vaults, hangs, flips his right leg over the door top. "Wow. The world's biggest transom. Gimme my dinner. Okay. Now your hand."

"Pup. Pup. Please, no—"

"Hurry up, Papule. This thing's compacting my reproductives."

"I don't—ohhh!"

"Alley-oops. Uhhh. Use the feet, dammit, you're a dead weight." Robert's face and neck seem flayed to the muscle, but bloodless. His eyes pop. The hand in Simon's has given up. Robert's feet kick impolitely at 2F. Simon, doggie bag between teeth, has leaned down. His left hand scruffs Robert up: kittens are lifted in this manner. For several moments they face each other, as though on an unbiased seesaw. Then, Geronimo, Simon pushes off.

"I'm sc-uh. Aired."

"Jump. I'll catch you." Robert lets go. Ungently, with one hip, Simon breaks his fall.

"Why are we here?"

"It's what's called a location, Pink-eye. You wanna direct, cultivate a sense of place. Like they say all the world's a stage, but some places *locate*. Get what I mean? Look at this. Could be a chasm. A bomb crater. The entrance t'Baron Rothschild's wine cellar. I gotta do something here. Golgotha! Yah. Jesus carrying his cross *down*hill."

Alert sunlight spots mica in the clay. Bits wink on and off. With its articulate scorpion arm, a backhoe stands guard over the shifty, not-to-be-trusted earth. Simon has started down the avenue. Brickwork from a superannuated building lies about. Unsewn-up arteries of old pipe poke through the soil. Simon comes to a stop: his nostrils widen. Heavy-duty-tire tread marks have hardened on the ramp. An open equation teases him: $X = ?$, where X is heavy-duty tread marking. He lifts one pants leg. There it is, the green clocking along his ankle: same pattern as the tread track. He shows Robert: Robert doesn't make the connection. Simon shakes his head: once again astounded by himself. Consciously he had never noticed that clocking before. This reassures him. Simon's associative talents, especially his visual talents, are remarkable. At center the excavation impedes sunlight: shadow contrast jars the eye. They are forty feet below the wall of doors, going down. Going up, a full dump truck hesitates, stopped at the instant when time ran out on collective bargain-

ing. It hunches: the metal shield over its cab very like some triceratops'
bone headplate. A panda, in bondage, is held for ransom on the grillwork. "Baby John" it says underneath.

"Baby John. Right now he's making engine noises—brrr-uhhumm—just
like Daddy. Pushing his Tonka toys through the cat box, wearing his
Tonka hard hat. Shooting his cap gun at imaginary picket-line crossers.
Bless him." Simon tickles the panda. "Daddy's home now with a twelve-
day beard. Caulking the leaky gutters, watching 'Let's Make a Deal,'
cleaning the Smith & Wesson. Worried because some uppity spook has
moved in down the street. Had a six-pack with his Cheerios this morning. Ah, America." Simon runs, feet floppy, down the steep ramp. Robert
decides to follow. He's leery of watchdogs, misdemeanors: will Rebozo
Construction forgive them their trespasses?

"What's that?" Simon is down. He digs, but cautiously, professorially.
A faucet has been unearthed. COLD.

"French tickler, circa 1910. The relic of a hard people. You're looking
at Mole Man. Dig, dig, dig, dig, dig, dig. I used t'love that, when I was
your age. There are surprises in the earth. Once I found a cannonball
just off Bell Boulevard. What d'you do, Wet Cell?"

"D-do?"

"Hey, were you born or were you blister-packaged? I mean, you know,
do. Like the rest of us. For fun."

"Read. I write. Pup. Poems."

"Lonely, huh? It's no wonder. Your face looks like an old piece of linoleum: tack heads, bobby pins, paper clips coming through." Simon tries
to touch. Robert weaves: down/left, away. "Psst. Hey. Pull the taffy a
lot, huh? Hanh? Been spronging the magic wanger, Froggy?"

"What?"

"Masturbate, Whitefish. Twist the fine tuning. Huh? You can tell old
Sy. Old Sy loves grisly items."

"I don't—"

"Now, Robert, we'll never get along at this rate. I expect candor. You
don't do it? All God's creatures do it. Dandelions blow their seed in a
strong wind. Little girls take horseback riding lessons. Baboons rub
against the cage bars. An Irish setter humped off on my left knee only
last week."

"I don't know how."

"What? What?" Simon goes for him. Robert runs, but without conviction: he will let himself be caught. Simon applies a loose half nelson.
"Don't know how? Really? Christ, it's like meeting a Togo Islander, light
a match and he runs away. Robert, take it from me, you're missing the
cruise ship. It's skyrockets. Roman candles. The stars and stripes forever
spelled out in Catherine wheels. Do some investigating: they must give a
course somewhere. Try the New School for Social Research." Simon

unties the half nelson. "I know how it is. Tough to get the facts, man. First time I brought it off was in the shower. Eureka, I said, what have we here? Trouble was, I thought that's the only place you could do it. Something about hot, soapy water. It was a logical deduction: after all the neighborhood punks said a cold shower would do the opposite. Man, at your age my skin was alla time wrinkled up like a prune."

The ground is level now: they have reached bottom. Two dozen bulky square columns loiter around: each with a fright wig of rusted steel reinforcing rods atop. Simon thinks: it could just as well be a ruin. His shoes stick: the water table is just below. Sections of cement-lined piping loll in an open trench. Wooden molds, mostly circular, wait for cement. At center he sees one 20 × 20 concrete slab, dry land. A moat of brown-yellow water defends it. Simon can imagine horses, carts, body servants, concubines led down to some Scythian king's tomb. It's dank and chilly. The autumn has progressed, foot by foot, with their descent.

"Mr. Lynxx?"

"Uh?"

"Don and Larry? Are. Are they . . . ?"

"They are. Yup. Right out of *Grimm's Fairy Tales*. So bent they meet themselves coming and going. Coupla fruits of the loom. If the world depopulates, they'll get sued for contributory negligence." Simon has one eyebrow up: he senses a confidence, would like to lever it out. "Fascinate you, huh? First real queens, gosh. *L'Chaim*. Today you are a ball-point pen."

"No—well . . ."

"Worried about it, though? Sex, that is. Dream of female groins, bearded and fierce like Rasputin?"

"I. I."

"I. I. Oh. Uh. Ah. Um. Stop stuttering. You give me a tic. It's like every other frame was edited out of your body." Simon long-jumps the moat. He opens his doggie bag, a picnicker, on the concrete slab. "So you turn out queer, there's lotsa room for advancement in that line of work: they've got a strong union local."

"I—"

"Jump over."

"My father—"

"Jump." Doubt aborts his takeoff. One sneaker sinks in/over its ankle top. Simon finds this entertaining. "Your father what? Go on."

"Uck. It's dirty."

"Nah. It's good Queens mud. Organic as fresh PCB's. You were saying about your father—"

"My father. Don't. Look, don't tell my mom about this. God, I'm ssss—wet." Bubbles blow out at the sneaker lace holes. "Once I was camping in a tent. With, with a friend of mine. It was, ah, hot. So, I mean, so w-we took our clothes off. My, my father shined a flashlight in. Herbie, he was oh, older than me and he had, you know."

"A pink nightstick. Gotcha. Go on."

"Uh. But we were s-sleeping. We weren't doing any, a thing. At all. I don't even *know* what homos do. He kicked my friend. Made him go home." Robert supports his chin. "My father is, is. A pig. He wunt let me for, forget it. Be, because I don't date girls. Because. Ah, I don't catch footballs. I'm. I'm allergic to his ssh, shitty bushes. I'm gonna kill him."

"Uh-uh. Take it from one who has hated not wisely but too well. Fathers are a worse rock-in-the-shoe when dead. Anyway y'don't want patricide on your secret rap sheet. Nah. Listen t'old Sy, the ace bunk flyer. If you like nubile males—run up your jolly roger and grapple to."

"You. But you hate homos."

"Child, I hate only two things in life: poverty and boredom. And that's really one thing, anyhow. Life is pleasure. The more ways you twist your pipe cleaner, the more pipes you'll get into." Simon lies prone: the cold slab anesthetizes his back. A small cyclonic wind does odd jobs around the construction hole. Simon stares up: he has a way of getting to the bottom of things. He can see only a dirt cliff horizon and the blue sky. "When it's dark, I don't care what kinda service contract I have. Long as it's service. But—and this is wisdom, so pay attention—y'can't con the street trade. Repeat. You'll get exactly what you're worth on the free market. It's supply and demand. I knew a guy once, he had one leg shorter than the other. Man, he could trip the light fantastic on a flight of stairs, but somehow they always held the senior prom on a flat surface. Tough noogies. He went steady for a while with a paraplegic girl, but it wasn't his cush, hiking her wheelchair up all those curbstones. He wanted beauty, grace, romance. Figured, hell, if he couldn't pull the ball, he'd hit to right. So he came out, as the gays say. Wore a see-through T-shirt, painted his nipples with Kustom Khrome and swung his buns around a lot. Know what happened?"

"What?"

"Well, he found out they don't hold the Gay Ball on a flight of stairs either. See fags together: it's the good-looking ones with the good-looking ones. Rich with rich. Homecoming queen and all-star fullback so t'speak. He was a bench warmer in two genders. Yah. He committed suicide three years ago."

"Oh."

"What was left? Sheep? Persian cats? A lifetime spent touring military hospitals?"

"That's not a funny story."

"Did I say, 'Stop me if you've heard this one'? Sad, sure. But it isn't only looks, if that's what you had in mind. I said market value. Money and power. The best cure for a scabland complexion is t'rub it with

thousand-dollar bills. But, believe me, kid—and this isn't just one of my
gangtool verbal assaults—believe me, you've got it cut out for you. Work.
Rob the disabled. Hold up eye banks. Work. It won't be a three-inch
putt."

"Are . . . do you—"

"When the breeze blows funny, I tack, I tack. Generally, though, a
straight line is the shortest distance between two holes f'me. What's this,
the world's great navel?"

A large manhole cover has been set into the slab. There are three-inch-
wide openings around the circumference. Simon looks through: darkness
there, but cold, blown-upward, will quick-dry his contact lens. Simon
tries an ear. Distant water rushes so effortlessly, evenly—ssssss—it might
as well be silence. The nose. Hmmmmm, a cavern smell, toadstooly,
sweet, neutral. Simon turns on his back, the emptiness below disquiets
him. Overhead, slow clouds make an entrance stage right. With no other
point of perspective the slab might seem like a raft on calm water. Simon
sticks his forefinger up, perhaps to catch the rotating earth's brass ring.
He is mellow. Simon enjoys having a disciple. He empties the doggie
bag. He is moved to swell fellowship.

"Have some steak, huh?"

"No. No, thanks."

"Here, come on."

"No."

"Dammit, I'm sharing with you. Eat, it's an act of love."

"But I'm not hungry."

"Jews. Tell me, how many bars have you put out of business? Warm,
friendly places where men meet. A neighborhood goes dark after six
when the kikes move in. Don't drink in public, it costs too much. A bottle
s⌐hnapps on the kitchen windowsill. Why pay extra for good comrade-
ship? Kosher food, my cooch. That's just an excuse to miss the weenie
roast. Unsociable. Women and Jews kill a meal." Simon rips steak off.
Dirt has mixed with his food. He doesn't mind that. Robert cries. "Um—
you're wetting your acne."

"You in, insult everybody."

"It's exercise, Sepsis. It's the U.S. prime stamp of a great associative
mind. Name-calling, listen to Falstaff, name-calling is metaphor-making,
and the history of the metaphor is the history of art. See a face, see an
image. Be quick, quick, quick. Poke-check their soft places before they
poke-check yours. Do I care if you're a Jew, a black, an anthropophagus
with head beneath your shoulders? I'm defining things. I'm naming you.
Don't believe those liberal-left bumper stickers—all men are brethren.
Bah. There's no art in it." He hurts Robert's elbow. "Y'wanna last in this
DMZ, then learn t'kill. But without anger. Without passion. Passion and
anger leave you open." Simon lies back. "I'm a genius. And six-three and

strong. I'm so virile I've got herpes III and IV. Women a block away turn t'tapioca if the wind is right. And still I've gotta struggle. What chance d'you have? I'm doing a favor, Robert. Hey. Huh. Make a metaphor."

"Leave me alone."

"Look!" Simon kicks Robert. He holds up his steak bone. It has a Y shape. Thongs of meat hang from it. "Make a metaphor."

"A meta—"

"Quick, quick, quick."

"The. The letter Y."

"Flunk. Zero. A slingshot. A puppeteer's finger board. A zipper coming down. Two roads converging in a yellow wood. An ostrich footprint. A dowsing rod. The buttocks cleft of a woman just over her coccyx. Mind. Mind. The mind. The mind!"

Simon roars down. It is deep there, beneath the manhole cover. An echo may come back. But by then they, Simon and Robert, will be gone.

4

"No. You can't, you can't, Mr. Lynxx—"

"I can, I can, Miss O'Neill."

"No, Mr. Sollivan is in conference, he—"

"Yah—I know what that means, he's laying vile hands on himself again."

"You can't go in, he—"

"I'm going! I'm going! See me go. Gone!"

Miss O'Neill, an old woman, rises—awkward and knee-sprung when off her prosthetic swivel chair—but, darn it, Simon is past the desk again, third time this month.

NORTON SOLLIVAN
V.P., Public Relations
National Artists
Domestic Productions

Oak Con-Tact paper has come away from the steel door. Overhead there is a horseshoe, cupped, hollow, but expecting luck, as a vagrant expects dimes. The lock has been broken: Simon snapped its tongue off last July. He has put his moose's shoulder to the door. It gives—and the sofa and the end table stacked behind it—into Norty's 30 × 30 office. Miss O'Neill taps her intercom button, dash-dash-dash, Morse code for: It's Him Again.

"Norty, baby!"

"Moses Christ, not you."

Norty is a regular blade: polished cotton shirt and chambray tie to go with his pinstripe polyester brush poplin gabardine three-piece suit. The third and lower piece relaxes, one empty pants leg hiked up on Norty's desk. Except for white sweat socks he is nude from the waist down. Norty's genitals seem decorative: a four-in-hand tie between the white cotton shirttails. Also, they are inexplicably purple, luminous, the way Portuguese men-of-war are. Norty has covered up: his knees smack together, violently modest, as people catch thrown things in an unprepared lap. And what's this? Simon is curious. A large, new kettle has been boiling on Norty's single-ring coffeemaker. Steam chugs up.

"Have I come at a bad time? Hanh?"

"Get out. Just get out of my sight."

"Whatcha doon? Playing Autobridge again? I told you an' I told you, not on the rug, it'll foul the Electrolux." Simon heads, galley west, for the kettle. "What's cookin'? Huh? Hanh? A little matzoh ball soup? Can I have some?"

"Get out. Get out and shut the damned door behind you. Miss O'Neill sees me like this, she'll pop her hysterectomy scar."

"Hey, you're really upset." Simon slams the door. "This isn't the Norty I know. Where's the usual interfaith blessing, the old neat's-foot oil? No bromides f'me today?"

"Hah. That phone number you gave me from the little black notebook. Eh, Mr. Disaster?" Simon frowns. "Don't hand me your babe-in-the-woods look. El Dorado 6-7441, my fingers should fall off from dialing it. Did you maybe get it from an exterminator?"

"Wait. El Dorado 6. El Dorado 6. Don't tell me." Norty has begun stirring his kettle with a souvenir Samurai sword. Simon thinks: it isn't easy, he lives by the Bell System. Norty's privates seem drunk and disorderly. He has shaved there for some reason: stubby five o'clock shadow on the magenta pubes. Six pairs of underwear stump around, short-legged, in the kettle. "I hate to tell you, Norty: they already invented the washing machine."

"I warn you, smart-ass, don't crack wise with me." The steaming sword is out. Simon steps back. "I'm through with your goyish monkeyshines."

"What? What? What'd I do now?"

"Look—this you don't understand, but try. I'm a married man, schmuck. I have a wife and two children with bright, gentle faces. They look up to me." Norty stabs a pair of shorts through the placket: holds it aloft. "Boiling water kills them, doesn't it? God, I've never seen any such repulsive things. I put one on a plate and had a good look through my son's kiddy microscope. Aaagh. I almost lost my dinner. Two years in the Army, can you believe, two years rummaging every piece of poor-white trash and its old aunt—I thought only schwartzers get crabs. Everything, but everything, you touch is a catastrophe, Lynxx. Was it such a big thing? I ask to get my rig lifted a little. Out of respect to my wife: I hate to bother her, she does a lot of charitable work. I ask could you recommend something clean and young. You know I can't afford tsuris at home. And what happens, you give me a phone number I should spray

Black Flag on. The day I met you, Lynxx, my good angel was on jury duty." Norty has stopped stirring. They both peer into the kettle, forehead to forehead. "Die, you sons of bitches." Simon jabs a finger in the water.

"You got 'em. It's Nagasaki in there. I just saw a troopship go down with all pincers aboard. But I can't understand this, Norty. Honest. Marabeth is so hygienic her bush squeaks."

"Marabeth? Don't putz around. Her name is Denise."

"Jesus. Jesus, you won't believe it. This is a terrible misunderstanding, Norty. You got the second team. Denise is Marabeth's roommate. She plays this-little-piggy with the Latvian superintendent so they get an extra garbage pickup. You gotta ask, Norty. You gotta ask. I said Marabeth. M. Marabeth. Not D, Denise. Remember? Good God, it's not my fault you got a pig for your poker."

"Is this a fact?"

"A fact. I swear before whatever god you're worshipping this month. Brunette. Bangs, right? Big girl. Forty-two-inch shoulder blades and a 28-inch bust. Right? Right? Woozy as a club fighter in bed, clinches the minute the bell rings. Right? Jesus, Denise's had more strange men in her than a rented bowling shoe."

"Shit." Norty lifts his shirttail. "Crabs from a Latvian super. They couldn't even have a decent pedigree. See? How can I face anyone in bed? I look like an eggplant. Purple. I asked my druggist for a first-rate antiseptic. He hands me this stuff, gentian violet. He doesn't tell me a tattoo comes off easier. I gave myself a dozen hard-ons scrubbing with Lava soap."

"You could say it was a birthmark."

"Not funny. A laugh doesn't occur to me somehow. This is a holocaust, Simon."

Norty trudges off. He is five-nine, but a horse. His calves are articulated, hard: each seems to have three new apples in it. Above the waist Norty spreads. He can hit: they have had it out once or twice and hurt each other. Simon knows the glossy, hairless, bollard-sized caps of his shoulders. Norty has bent to search through underwear in an open suitcase. His buttocks pinch shut, so tight they go pale along the crease. And, on one cheek, a childishly written scar: B+. Carlo Bucchioni had scrawled that with a soldering iron: his four sons born, it would seem, each to hold one of Norty's four limbs immobile. For three days Norty had managed the only Jewish numbers operation in Red Hook. As Norty tells it, "Simon. He said to me, 'Kike, do I spell it all out—Buc-chi-o-ni—or just an initial and the sign of the holy mother?' What would you say? I was already sucking one tooth like it was a cough lozenge and blowing blood bubbles out of my nose. I said, 'Just an initial, Mr. Bucchioni, and the holy mother. And don't be mad, I'm gonna piss on your nice floor.'" It was a defeat. Norty joined the Army that next day. He hasn't been across the Brooklyn Bridge since.

Simon is Vishnu, the many-handed god, at Norty's desk. He rips off six pre-Castros, screening tickets, an unlisted phone number or two, and the nude stills from John Frankenschlegel's *American Hubcap*. Drawers drum in and out: it's a percussion section he has presided over before. Simon culls the soft-centered chocolates from a Lady Godiva box. He reads the INCOMING and the OUTGOING. With Norty's letter opener he pie slices a large disc of hashish. Simon drinks from the English Leather bottle filled with Jack Daniel's. This is SOP. Norty watches him, resigned, a second pile of underwear in embrace. He cracks his nose, which is broad and four times broken: loaded with clucking shards of cartilage. Norty's blond hair, mod, wild atop, has been cleverly shaved at the sides. With a hat on he can regress, nostalgic, to the sock-hop fifties.

"Adele is afflicted, Sy. I'm certain of it. Now and then she gets a far-off look in her eyes: the way people do when they have an itch they can't get at. It breaks my heart to cause her suffering and embarrassment. But she's such a little lady, what can I do? I've never yet heard her go wee-wee. Yesterday I mentioned bedbugs, as a sort of trial balloon. Naturally, brought up the way she was by Herman, Adele pretends not to hear. This could be my swan song, Simon. Adele could get the wrong impression of me." Simon is speechless: chocolate has pasted tongue against palate. "If you could stop the highwayman act for a minute—give these a wring-out. The mattress is brand-new, a Posturepedic B-52 bomber, four hundred dollars, custom-made for Adele's back condition. How could I throw it out?"

"Uh. Got some bad news, Norty. They're not in the mattress." Simon, leaning half out of a fortieth-story window, strangles underwear. Hands on Sixty-eighth and Third come up to test for 200° rain. "They're on Adele's thatch, take it from a man who knows. It's like Levittown for crabs now. They're out pushing their little lawn mowers, watering the marigolds, waving to the next-door neighbor."

"Madonna. I'm a corpse. Only thank God she's farsighted. I pretended to fall yesterday. I told Adele I pulled a groin muscle, it would be difficult to have relations. She accepted my word, though I'm not so sure she knows what a groin is. But now I can't play in the doubles tournament at North Ridge. Shit, I must be getting old. These things don't have a funny side anymore. My children are reproaching me. I can see it in their eyes. When once we practice to deceive, oh what a tangled web we weave."

Norty has hung clothes from a bronze star of David above his desk to a bronze cross on the far wall. Simon is anxious: he wants news from the Coast. Modern chairs squat as houseflies do, when the shadow of your hand passes over them. Spotlighting crosses and recrosses. On the long right wall there are eight-foot blow-ups of Norty, world traveler. Imitation oak panels can be slid like clothes-closet doors to conceal one, two, six, any combination of blow-ups. Norty, at thirteen, holding the bar mitzvah scrolls: a shaft of God light, catered by I. W. Singer Son, Occasions, bounces off his white silk yarmulke. Slide, cancel. Norty in special audience with Pope Paul. Slide, cancel. Norty on the turret of a tank ("Best, Moshe"): a sign just behind the turret, SUEZ 25 KM. Slide, cancel. Norty with four IRA leaders, hunkered down, muzzles at attention in a Belfast alley. Slide, cancel. Norty walking toward the Washington Monument with Martin Luther King. Slide, cancel. Norty on a podium just alongside George Wallace. Slide, cancel. A full-length mirror for his female guests. Norty has stopped now to comb his decade-bridging hair in front of it.

For seventeen months Pvt. Norton Solomon had run the 109th "Roaring Weasel" Regiment based near Kalmuk, Georgia. This was his first enduring romance with power, and absolute authority corrupted him at least a lot. The draftees had respect for his strength, his comparative age, his Brooklyn wiseness: these qualities, in turn, were reinforced by the enigmatic B+ on Norty's left buttock. Military life seemed to improve his luck. Five weeks and six days after Norty's arrival he owned a cathouse called the Long Arms Inn. It took one forty-eight-hour poker game with three Kalmuk aldermen. The Long Arms was based on Route 311, ten miles north of the camp gate. Norty had two-fer passes for those he favored, private or noncom. He also operated his own PX: Southern Comfort and hash and pills and furloughs. He had a bookie franchise tapped in direct to Atlanta and could cover bets on anything that wasn't absolutely inert. The officers were circumspect with Norty. Norty had a friend in high places: Pvt. Simon Lynxx, six years younger and teachable.

They recognized each other at first sight: two guys on the take and make. Mutual distrust was an exciting bond: it brought out the best in both. Simon had been on base eight weeks before Norty and his buttock arrived. After a short, rave-review opening in the enlisted men's mess kitchen, Simon—who had signed up for Army Pictorial—was promoted. He made stuffed grape leaves, chicken niçoise, veal marsala for the officers' mess and a dress or two for Mrs. Col. Kakistos. Mr. Col. Kakistos, the base commander, was an underconfident man, who had once dumbfounded his superiors and himself by being very brave in Korea. Col. Kakistos' thumb would sneak over the plate edge to supervise difficult fork loads. He spoke and wrote an archaic, verb-first kind of English. Col. Kakistos was dislocated and slovenly: he failed his own inspection each morning. But at this time the extra catgut no longer had Simon's tongue and nineteen years' backlog of verbal flash was let out.

Col. Kakistos employed him as a valet and pre-stenographer: Simon prepared second drafts that preceded first drafts, mostly for the desk of operations officer Capt. Augustus Van Voort III—an unslovenly and super-located West Point nuisance. Col. Kakistos came to depend on Pvt. Lynxx, who supplied him with useful base gossip: all edited and press-released by Pvt. Solomon.

In return Simon administered the black-thumbtack concession. Example: at 1830 hours, July 17, Capt. McCoy orders a twenty-mile hike in full gear. At 1930 hours, one black thumbtack appears, courtesy of Pvt. Solomon, over Capt. McCoy's mail slot. By 0500 hours, July 18, Simon has laced Capt. McCoy's coffee with sodium amytal. At 0715 hours, during the first fall-out, Capt. McCoy goes into coma, a rotted log held to his cheek for security. At 0720 hours you will hear Sgt. Raft kicking him. Gen. Harbort slept through four regimental reviews, boosted upright under one armpit by an aide-de-camp. Maj. Distall had confiscated some of Pvt. Solomon's betting slips. Every time Maj. Distall bedded his wife a black thumbtack would dot the i in Distall. (Pvt. Solomon observed M.O. patterns very carefully: after relations Mrs. Distall would set her washed contraceptive foam injector to dry on the bathroom windowsill.) Maj. Distall was spectacularly allergic to shellfish. Simon shredded crab meat into his morning omelet. Within an hour nickel-sized hives would form on Maj. Distall's crotch. The coincidence was striking. It struck Maj. Distall. He sent his wife, in dishonor, to a venereal disease clinic near Macon. For seven months, before Pvt. Solomon relented, Mrs. Distall was on penicillin and the Major cut holes in his pants pockets. Simon also ministered to Mrs. Kakistos sexually: this without a black thumbtack. The Colonel was impotent, heavily salt-petered, for most of Simon's hitch. He confided in Simon: Simon was sympathetic and procured strong "aphrodisiacs," which, by some misfortune, were available only during Mrs. Kakistos' periods. It was a gladsome time for Simon and Norty. Ah, they often reminisce.

"Norto, buddy?"

"Uh."

"I hateta bug you during the peak hours of your misery, but—aaah. What happened in L.A., huh? Didja see Golden?" Silence. Simon has moved a panel. George Wallace elbows in front of Martin Luther King. "Look, you can talk while you suffer, can't you? Huh? Norto, don't make me recite the pledge allegiance for it. I'm ready for a plot in Marble City."

"Wring these out."

"Look. Cheer up. Adele's so dry they'll die of thirst. Just happens I've gotta few crises of my own." Silence. "God. One thing I can't stand, it's someone who only thinks of himself. So you've got the dengue, so? I've had worse things and I never complained." Norty has stopped stirring.

"What? What's that?"

"What's what?"

"This dengue thing? What is it?" Norty looks at his crotch.

"How do I know? Am I responsible for everything I say? Huh? I think it's the only disease that sounds worse than it is. I think. Dengue. Dengue. I go big for words like that." Simon has dropped an impertinent hand on Norty's left shoulder. "Have a heart. Golden? Golden? You know, the man who looks like a Rock Cornish game frog."

"Golden is Golden." Norty shrugs: Simon's hand goes up with it.

"Hey, Norto. Spare me the Mosaic sententiousness. Nu? You're not your father the I-Cash-Clothes man with a pushcart in Red Hook." Silence. "Yah, I can guess what happened. You got out there in Cloud Cuckoo Land and you forgot all about me, huh?"

"Shut up. Shut it."

"Ow. Fine. Uncle." Norty has clouted Simon, a short left above the solar plexus. Now he has Simon's shirtfront in one fist. He screws the material counterclockwise. Lines of stress run up/into each armpit. Simon's navel makes a guest appearance. Off balance, Simon back-pedals, showing some agility and more tact.

"You better catch on, *dreck*. You *are* responsible for what you say. I'm supposed to be the ax man here, Mr. Cast Iron—yet, time after time, like a greenhorn, I hang my meat out on the IND track for you. My wife says, why? Herman says, why? Lieb and Gluck think I've got no chalk on my pool cue. Mention your name and, it's like magic, I lose another friend. You, Lynxx, you are stupid and ungrateful."

"Okay. Okay. I'm stupid. I'm ungrateful. Try to be forgiving, I haven't had your advantages. I didn't get a soldering iron on my tookus at an early age. I still haveta learn." Norty lets him go. "I'm just a wacky kid. I wanna be famous. I wanna be rich. I wanna be able t'hire and fire people, just like you. Is that so much t'ask? Huh? What did Golden say?"

"Light me a cigar, prick." Simon sets two in his mouth. Norty's desk lighter is a praying porcelain angel. The halo has a flint in it. Simon lets out an expansive, double-harness puff. "I could retch. Eighth Avenue insects. What kind of woman is that, I ask you? A fur stole, probably mongoose skin, now I think of it. Between her knockers an emerald the size of your toenail. Also crabs in the downstairs. I took her to Four Seasons. I showed her the highspots. I could have done better for ten bucks and a fifteen percent tip in some Forty-second Street rap parlor."

"Golden. Golden. We're digressing." Simon has put a cigar in Norty's mouth.

"All right, listen to me. I did my best by you. I waited until I had the check in my hand. Two hundred grand. Two hundred grand would make Jack the Ripper mellow. Plus I bought him dinner at one of those places where the cigarette girl has her tits squeezing out like toothpaste. I gave him three of my pre-Castros. He was receptive, believe me. Château Margaux 1959 with the filet mignon. If I said, 'Let's go have a gall bladder operation for dessert,' he would have said, 'Sure, why not?'"

"I don't like this." Simon has sat. Hands hurry together, slick with sweat. "I hear the condolence card tones already. Sounds like you're preparing me for the death of a friend. But I don't have any friends, except you. Jesus, I'm in the twilight of a career that had no afternoon."

"Quiet." Norty attaches underwear to a jury-rigged clothesline with paper clips. "I mentioned your screenplay. Your treatment, I should say —and, excuse me, you could use a new typewriter ribbon. Also your shoeprint on page three isn't impressive to a man of Golden's stature. But . . . he's still listening, he's happy. 'Who is this Simon Lynxx?' he asks me. I come right out with *Diner* and *Hearth*, the awards, I praise you to the fake terrazzo ceiling. 'Full-lengthers he's done?' Golden asks me. Sure, I say. He's made one so far. *Clap*, it's called. 'Oh,' says Golden, 'was that with Lauren Bacall?' No, I say, that was the stage play *Applause*."

"Gee, Norty. Why dja have to tell him?"

"Please. You're dealing with Joe Golden—an Einstein he isn't, but six Einsteins he can hire." Norty has sat beside Simon on the sofa. "So I took a deep breath—no, first I ordered him a double Metaxa—then I say, 'Mr. Golden, this is a brilliant film, a hilarious film. This is about a man who gets the clap and, just because of it, he becomes President of the United States.' Golden looks at me, like maybe I passed gas under the table and he was downwind. 'Wait—Mr. Golden—it's not a filth picture: it's an incisive political satire. The hero is a fufnik. Nobody thinks he can put his own socks on. But he catches the clap—get this—from a dirty toilet seat. First man in history who really got clap from a toilet seat. Ha-ha, isn't that something?' A face like bulletproof glass is looking at me. For anybody else I would have said, huh-huh, huh-haw-ha, that's all folks, and asked him about his golf scores. But I persevere: I kicked the chair out from under me, I might as well strangle. 'Mr. Golden, his wife doesn't believe it—she thinks this henpecker has a mistress. She gets new respect. His friends are impressed. He's impressed. The local Republican committee is impressed.' Now Golden shows interest. He leans forward. 'Is this Nixon?' he asks. 'Is it the truth?' 'No,' I have to say, 'it's a fantasy.' In Hollywood, Simon, this is a worse word than clap. Fantasy. For fantasy you don't even need someone in the box office. The Edsel was a fantasy. But I persist. I tell him the story. The great ending where Smith says 'Amstan' on his deathbed, then cut to his potty chair going into the furnace—which even Orson Welles himself told me was superb parody. You know I loved *Clap*, Simon. You know that."

"Yah-yah. I know. Go on."

"So Golden leans forward and he says, 'Do me a big favor. When this friend of yours—what's his name?' 'Simon Lynxx, two exes,' I say. 'Right. When your friend is in L.A. next, give me a ring.'"

"Yes? Yes? Yes?"

" 'So I can catch a plane out until he goes away!' "

"Mother." Simon's hands squeak. "Mother. That isn't what you'd call a vote of confidence, is it? Mother. Did you bring up *Jesus 2001?*"

"Yes. He didn't want to hear. *Clap* was a kamikaze film, Simon. I couldn't lie, he'd find out. I loved it, you know that, but it wasn't family. Everything is family or action or maybe horror these days. And it should be family horror."

"Norty. I'm in big trouble. I'm scared. Lizard tongues are flicking out at me. Swop! and Simon is gone, some fat iguana's lunch."

"Neither a borrower nor a lender be—"

"Jesus. There are other lines in Shakespeare or haven't you heard? Listen, after eight years, you chief petty officer, even I catch on: I'd have more luck applying for a Liberty Loan." Nonetheless Simon has cupped Norty's bare left knee. "Look. This morning I had two new mouths t'feed: a four-hundred-pound yenta and her son. I need sixteen teats. My two agfays are considering white flight. My tires are all radial and no rubber. If I met a payroll it wouldn't recognize me. I'm on the rims, Norto."

"Sell the van, Sy. I've told you—I can get a hundred twenty grand for it, furnished."

"No! No! No!" Simon has doubled over. There's a polished marble ashtray, once a baptismal font, on the coffee table. He glares into it: can see the several colors of his face, but not the outline. It swims. "Help me, Norty. A job—something."

"Three weeks ago I made you an offer. That blaxploitation film treatment. We need someone to translate from the original dub-a-jub."

"I hate writing, you know that. I can't sit still in one place. I keep thinking I'm dead: I haveta feel myself all over f'signs of life-as-we-know-it."

"Sy? Is there a choice?"

"Okay, how much was it? Refresh me."

"Fifteen hundred on top. I could probably get you two thousand if I wangled. And three grand on satisfactory presentation."

"Two thousand. For six weeks I'll be like strapped into one of those boat chairs trying to land a deep-water turkey. And I suppose with some methadone junkie leaning over my shoulder t'do color while I do the play-by-play. Two thousand. I could cry. Film alone runs me a hundred twenty bucks for a four-hundred-foot load. About four minutes' worth. With the actors I have, I'll need fifteen retakes. With good actors I couldn't afford film."

"Me you don't have to tell, I'm in the business. Too bad you're not black. N.A. has just this last two months opened a minority incentive program down on the second floor. Harold Gluck is in charge, with matching grants from the International Arts Council. You could make another *Jaws* for the money they're pissing out, so long as it's the Great Black Shark."

"And they talk about skin flicks." But the information has been stored: Simon is processing it. He snatches a foot-high bronze statue of St. Sebastian from the coffee table. Simon sprongs the murderous arrows: they play different notes, B C D A-flat, according to their length and angle of entry. "Norto. I'm gonna test your memory—"

"Don't break that. A dear friend gave it to me."

"Scrapbook time. Remember when you asked me t'lift those Vietnam transfer orders from Captain Van Voort's room?" Sprong C. "Remember when your name was Sol-o-mon?" B-A-D sprownged. "I was in Van Voort's closet for two days because of that stupid sprung lock, afraid t'bang, trying t'look like a suit bag. Remember?" Three-fingered chord. "I couldn't sit down. I peed in Van Voort's dress helmet. Two days. Everything I cooked after that smelled of camphor balls. Guard duty for being AWOL when I didn't even leave the base. Hanh? For you." Simon plays a scale.

"Remember who got you off guard duty?" The statue is confiscated. "And who, besides me, was headed for Da Nang?"

"Norto—"

"Sure, sure I'm grateful. But that was a long time ago. We were dumb kids. We all did stupid things."

"Stupid? For me, maybe. You left Kalmuk with at least sixty untaxable grand in your pocket."

"Well, I was thrifty."

"So was Captain Kidd. And when you dislocated your ankle? I carried you all the way back t'camp on my shoulders. Six miles. And all you said was 'Faster, faster, we'll miss the ninth race at Gulfstream.'"

"I know. How could I forget? But these are hard times, Simon. What can I do?"

"Wolff. You can do Wolff for me." Simon has felt Norty's reaction: nine on the human Richter scale. His sofa sings. This is a killing frost, this name. Norty has gathered his scrotum in both hands.

"Aaah. Good you reminded me." Norty is up, across his office. He toggles the intercom switch. "Miss O'Neill—"

"Mr. Sollivan. He barged right in. I tried to stop him."

"It's okay. This trip he scored. Next time we'll get him. Did you arrange with the caterer?"

"Twenty-three hundred dollars with Moët. Nineteen hundred with André."

"André? Herman Wolff gargles with André. Make it twenty-three.

Over and out." Norty swivels to Simon. "Herman will call in a minute. Five o'clock on the dot, just after his four-forty-five cardiogram."

"What—huh, what's the French club soda for?"

"Listen, I shouldn't be telling you—it's a secret—I'm throwing a big shindig at Kyryl's place. On Saturday night. It's Herman's fiftieth year in film."

"See. That's it." Simon's cigar tip goes red: a warning. "Slip me in. That's all I ask. Just let me get close t'him."

"Simon. I'm not hearing. I should listen to you and I'd be back in the Army, the world's oldest private. Herman is sensitive. Two cousins died in Auschwitz. Word gets around in this city: Simon Lynxx opens his mouth and it's a one-man pogrom. I've told you a hundred times. You'll regret. The chickens will come home to roost and now it's happened, you're all over chickenshit. This is a business that runs by friendships and enemyships and right now, if they knew your name, you couldn't buy a fifth card in five-card stud. Me, I appreciate your gall. I laugh. But to Wolff you're a cossack riding into the shtetl."

"Aaahr. You and your phony blow-ups. 'Best, Moshe.' If Moshe Dayan ever saw you, it was out of his bad eye. A Jew. This room looks like the non-denominational chapel at some airport. You have a detachable foreskin for when you go to the New York Athletic Club. At least Wolff knows what I am. What are you?"

"I'm his son-in-law."

"Yeah. And his daughter is a crab crash pad."

"Could it be I'm hearing an extortion threat?"

"Would I do that?"

"Does a diuretic make you piss? No. No, you wouldn't do that, you're not desperate enough. Not yet. I've still got a month maybe." Norty is thoughtful: he puffs. "Sure. Solomon rubbed some people the wrong way. Sollivan could be anybody. I'm bigger than a name, I like to think. My lifestyle is an offense to no one. Religion interests me deeply. I believe in the big producer upstairs. I take the garbage out and all those stars give me a surprise. Right here, in the heart. But why should I put a name on it? I can appreciate my wife, who needs a maid on Shabbas to flip the TV on. I can appreciate Herlihy in the art department: I'm talking to him, I hear the rosary clacking in his pocket. Knock on wood, I might even understand the shithead Arabs and their Allah. I'm a humanist, Simon."

"Yah. That's what they call a hypocrite when he knows the dress code."

"It hurts me that you should say that." Simon has gone prone, chest down, on the sofa. Norty sword-thrusts a pair of underwear out: not yet: allow to simmer. He sits on the sofa arm, analyst and analysand. "Now it's testimonial dinner time for you, schmuck. Remember when you were

throwing Bettina's money around? Huh? Then your farts were Chanel
No. #5. The young ladies were putting one behind each ear. But now
it's not so easy, is it? I warned. I gave advice. Did Simon Lynxx, the big
director, listen to me? You and I, we know you don't mean the things
you say. We know, but everyone else is reporting to the Anti-Defamation
League and the NAACP. Simon, I admire your use of language, it's
laugh-a-minute stuff. But I've had a hard time in life—my father wasn't
number one in radioland—I know what makes success."

"Success? You're telling me about success? You married Herman
Wolff's four-foot-six-inch daughter, that's all. For power. Just so you
could go around here firing people like an antipersonnel mine."

"Adele is—"

"Adele is so frigid she thought sex went after three, four, five. Out in
Beverly Hills they called her the icewoman who never cometh. Right?
No one would touch her out there—out *there,* where they'd let Bugs
Bunny Greek them just t'meet Herman Wolff."

"Adele is—"

"Please. You forget I was there. I walked you around this very block
fifteen times before you proposed. Hanh, remember? You were crying,
Norty. 'Is it worth it, Simon?' you asked me. 'Tell me again I'm doing the
right thing.' Adele had an orgasm once by mistake and Herman hadda
send her to an internist because she thought it was a sign of cerebral
palsy. You told me yourself."

"Ah. I can't explain to you. People grow up. Just believe me, Adele is a
fine woman. I'm not worth her pinky toe."

"The wedding ring was brown. At the ceremony you had trouble getting it off your nose."

"Enough, I know you're under tension, but enough. I want to help
you. Because you're a genius who's committing suicide. Because you're
an old friend and I love you."

"Because I know enough t'give Herman angina."

"Maybe that, too. Have it your way."

"Let me come t'the party."

"God. God. He'll know it was me." Norty scratches the tough second-
growth scrub above his groin. "When Max Kravitz demonstrated in Chicago with the Black Panthers, you told him he'd be a soap cake comes
the black revolution. You could be right. But Max is Herman's bridge
partner. Also Adele looks at you like you were a pork chop. She thinks
you represent the bad element in my acquaintance. Which is true, as witness the color of my dick." Norty scratches. "Jesus. Why am I still itch-
ing like this? Maybe I should sit in the kettle for a while."

"Your dwarf orange looks hung over." It's on the coffee table: eight or
ten waxy, dark-green leaves in a four-ounce plastic box. "Needs water,
probably should be repotted."

"That so? Little Herman brought it back from Disney World for me. He always asks about his orange tree."

"Got any dirt?"

"I could swing some." Norty stomps to his desk: the carpet nap is so high, so self-assured, it slips a pair of Peds over his white sweat socks. "Miss O'Neill. Go steal a pound of dirt from Katz's palm tree—then you can call it a day. Over and out. Ah, Simon, could I ask a little favor? I don't see so good up close anymore." Norty has dredged out a pair of undershorts. "Is anything moving on this?"

"A corpse or two, that's all I see."

"You're sure?"

"Whaddya want, an autopsy report? Little death certificates signed by a little coroner?" With Norty's IRA souvenir bayonet Simon has made four incisions, one along each side of the plastic box. He upends it, taps. The orange plant comes out whole: a perfect square. "Lookit those roots. Poor thing was trying t'eat plastic. That's me: no room, no nourishment. I've gone back t'fanning for dimes in pay-phone slots. My life is a remake of *The Living Desert*." Knock: Miss O'Neill. Norty lets the sofa back dress his lower half. Simon returns with an OUTGOING tray full of soil. "You're right. I talk too much. There's no seven-second delay between brain and mouth. But get me to Wolff—I'll charm him, I'll hum lullabies, I'll be his *shabbas goy*. Please. He's the only one I haven't put a touch on yet. Please. I'll be good."

"Agh. When he calls—God protect me—I'll ask."

"No. Just let me come. I'll dress up like a busboy."

"I can't. I can't. He'd know. It'd be like I gave to the United Egyptian Appeal behind his back." Buzzing. "That's Herman now. Five o'clock, not a minute less. I'll put him on the speaker, so you can hear." Norty is arranging his tie. And, for Wolff's voice, he will put his pants on. "Herman?" Norty has set the phone in its amplifier cradle. "Hello, Herman?"

"Norty? That you there?" Herman Wolff's voice is raucous: age has smashed it. He doesn't quite trust the telephone, its capacity to transmit. Wolff speaks loud crosstown, louder to Chicago, louder yet to the Coast. Simon is alarmed. Acoustics locate the voice somewhere above him. Simon gets down on hands and knees: less of him to aim at. He crawls toward the desk.

"You're better, Herman? Adele was worried."

"Still a little snotty, but thank God I can breathe. I just got off the machine. Dr. Levitt says I made pretty pictures. The ticker is fine."

"Good. Good."

"Tell me, Norty—everything is all set for my surprise?"

"Herman, I promise, it'll be the biggest do of the year. The media is already on line around the block. Kyryl's friends are flocking. Also Cy Packman, Barbara Zell. Berto Clamande. Arnold Zantz, Sterling Whitecraft, Liv Bergman. Oh, Blythe Scott and Van Telep. RSVP's've been coming in all day. Bobby Joe Comestible wants to do a medley gratis. He owes it all to you. I've talked to Elizabeth St. Maurice. So you should be prepared, Liz'll pretend you're both going to see the rushes of *Little Willie*."

"It shouldn't look like a put-up." Simon thumbs—me, me—at Norty.

"It won't. It won't."

"Dr. Levitt says—what? He says, ten o'clock the latest. You'll make my excuses?"

"Sure, Herman."

"You'll see everyone has a good time?"

"N.A. is putting on a spread will knock your eyes out."

"Norty. Wait." Conversation in the background. "Dr. Levitt says it's all right if I have a visitor at my office. Once per week. Four o'clock, so my food is digested and I don't get a cramp." Simon waves. Norty has a finger against his lips.

"What kind of visitor, Herman? I know a nice person of the Puerto Rican faith."

"No, thanks just the same. For them I gave already at the IRS. That kind you get crabs from. Blond I prefer. I'm old-fashioned. And she would have to look legitimate."

"Okay. On the *zaftig* side?"

"I wouldn't mind." Conversation in the background. "Also, Dr. Levitt reminds me, she should be gentle. In my condition I don't need to be hanging from a chandelier and getting my heinie whipped."

"No. No."

"Last month I went to this Japanese massage parlor. The swank of swank. Fifteen bucks for a cup tea. I thought it was a place of ill repute. This beautiful chopstick comes out. She's wearing a bra and some kind of Chink diaper. Very attractive, though my taste doesn't ordinarily run that way. She asks me, 'Hard or soft massage?' This left me in confusion. So I said—what would you say?—I said hard. I thought this was maybe the code word for a blow job. Norty—this ten-gallon can of soy sauce, she walked all over my back. She fractured every bone in my body. I wanted to cry, such pain I had. Three days I couldn't come to the office. When I got home my cardiogram read like the old parachute jump at Coney Island. I've got to be careful, Norty."

"God, Herman. What a terrible experience for you."

"I wasn't doing this—believe me—when I was your age. With two lovely children you have. That's the truth, Norty. I'm from a different generation. But since Carlotta left for the other world—I get lonely now and then. I wouldn't want Adele to know. This is between you and me. Yes?"

"A man is a man, Herman." Norty signals. "By the way, I have a fan of yours here. He would like to express his admiration for *Gorgonwyck*."

"Is that so?"

"Just listen." Simon shakes his head: no, no, no. The face is blurred: long hair whips him on both cheeks. Simon hasn't seen *Gorgonwyck*.

"I'll put him on the speaker."

"Aaaah. Mr. Wolff. You, in person. God, I can't believe it. To me, even in the same room, your voice would come via satellite." Norty kneads the air: more, more. Hyperbole is asked for. "Gosh. I haven't missed one of your flicks since *Little Miss Muff* in 1931. And that includes *Adagio for Three English Horns,* a breakthrough film, which deserved more recognition. It was *nouvelle vague* twenty years before the frogs knew their *vague* from their vague. And, as for *Gorgonwyck*—I . . . I just can't say enough." This is true. Simon garrotes himself. He can remember only three stills from the N.A. lobby. "The red carpet scene had to be—I may sound a bit incoherent, but it's because my respect for you comes in on the up side of idolatry—the red carpet scene was a universal simile. Yes. Blood, the female cycle, stoplights, stopping—" Norty rolls on the floor. He has wet underwear in his mouth. "A gloss on our sick and murderous age. A gloss, Mr. Wolff, a gloss. When the camera pans slowly over Gorgonwyck for the last time—by the way, the blue-grays, my Lord, your frames have the texture of eggshell, rough yet fragile, we—ah, we know that Shanda will never come back. And when the old idiot limps across the field—against the marvelously geometric pattern of hedgerows—the Renaissance perspective counterpoints his disability in a human, moving, yet in a bravura way. Your sense of—"

"A piece *schlock!*" The machine's surrogate voice has broken: too many decibels for its woofer. Simon is in body arrest: killed. Trinkets of fame on Norty's desk hum. "Nobody could like *Gorgonwyck* that much, except someone with his hand out. Who's the con man I'm talking to, Norty? I hate it when you put me on the speaker. I don't know where my voice is going. It's like I'm trying to find my pants in the dark."

"Herman. Mmm." Norty uses a Kleenex. Laughing has dredged his sinuses. "This is an admirer. Genuine. Don't worry."

"I worry. What's he after me for? Money?"

"Nothing. Honest, Herman. Would I do that to you?" Simon has a felt-tip pen. He writes PARTY! on the back of his hand.

"I can hear him breathing in there. What piece of my flesh does he want?"

"Frankly, Herman—he'd just like to meet you. A man in your position has to expect that. I thought we could invite him to the Fiftieth."

"Who is it? I have a nasty guess. It's that *Mein Kampfer* Army pal of yours, the one that makes films through a toilet seat."

"Herman—"

"It is, I knew. The Wehrmacht son of a bitch, what's his name?"

"Herman, your heart, don't get excited—"

"Simon Lynxx is his name, Mr. Wolff. And I'd sure like t'meet you someday."

"Shut up! Don't speak in my ear. This is what happens when I'm on the machine—I talk to someone whose mouth is ovens and soap cakes."

"Reports of my suicide are highly exaggerated, Mr. Wolff—mostly by me."

"Shut up!"

"He's just an asshole kid, Herman. A jerk. He doesn't think sometimes when he talks, but it's only for yocks. Would I be his friend—"

"You would make friends with Arafat, Norty. I'd like it better if you had one honest enemy. A man with so many friends has to be a shyster."

"Herman, for God's sake." Norty kicks Simon: this has gotten out of hand. "You want me to antagonize people? I'm in public relations."

"So's a whore."

"Herman: you hurt my feelings."

"Can I come t'the party, huh, Mr. Wolff?"

"Is he still there? Backing he wants, Norty. I've heard he's all over town with his face where his behind should be. To make an anti-Semit picture about Jesus. I'll give him backing. Right now the garbage lid comes down. A blackball so big he couldn't even film a chest X ray."

"Don't do that, Mr. Wolff. Oh, please don't do that." Simon addresses the ceiling. "I'll dance for you, Mr. Wolff. I'll sing, I'll be a clown, be a clown. I'm reformed, I'm a new person. Norty will tell you I'm on my knees here. I'm—"

"Shut up!"

"I'll throw him out, Herman. He won't bother you again. I was taken in by my good nature."

"Wait. Can he really dance?"

"I don't know, Herman—"

"I can. I can. I'll dance the hora for you right—"

"Shut up, Mr. Nothing-in-the-Film-Industry. How tall is he?"

"Six-two."

"Six-three."

"Shut up. Aryan-looking, I suppose?" Norty looks.

"A real WASP face, Herman."

"How old?"

"Twenty—"

"Seven."

"Blond?"

"Dark. Scarecrow hair. What's in mind, Herman?"

"He could get a trim, use some Brylcream and grease it down. I'm thinking of that other problem we have. At ten tonight."

"Oh. I forgot. Jesus, my mind. It's the fourth Monday."

"Can he flamenco?"

"Can I? Can I? I can! Listen." Simon—d'jah!—is up on the desk. Sudden, Andalusian heels clack against its black walnut surface, just three inches from the speaker. Thonk! Wolff's phone has fallen. Norty shoves Simon off.

"Herman? Are you all right? Jerk, couldn't you use the blotter? Herman?"

"My eardrum is gone. I'm seeing stars."

"He's a lunatic. Why don't we send Lance again? The prick doesn't deserve."

"With Lance she's bored. I get that feeling from Les. It's her only pleasure. Eichmann there has acting experience? He can cold-read?"

"He's nodding yes."

"So give him a try."

"If you say so, but—"

"Schmuck—are you listening? Eh? Where are you?"

"I'm here, Mr. Wolff. Still on my knees."

"You're dirt. I could walk all over you."

"Right, Mr. Wolff."

"Shut up. I'm going to give you one last chance. You will act like a gentleman, right?"

"Right."

"Perfect manners, the way your mother brought you up. Don't forget, I'll hear a report from everything you do."

"Sure. Sure. You're dealing with a chastened man. And if I do good— can I come to the party?"

"I promise nothing. Nothing. Norty, give him the poop. Dr. Levitt is very concerned. This minute he has his hand on my pulse."

"I will. Sure."

"My best to Adele and the kids."

"Take care, Herman."

They don't speak: abashed, abased together. Time they found work for the hands. Norty pops his crushed nose once or twice: something to do. The room reports sound differently now, as will a theater without any audience. Simon's ears click: has he come down from an altitude? Norty steps back out of the pinstripe polyester brush poplin gabardine slacks. Simon has taken a half gallon milk carton from the small refrigerator. Norty and he drink it off: alternate gulps, lips on the same spot: fear has made them intimate again. With Norty's sword Simon slices the empty milk carton in half. Norty touches his toes, remains bent and vulnerable: the face gets red. Little Herman's orange plant has been moved into its new apartment. Dirt is landscaped around: an over-meticulous act.

"Water this three times a week. Huh, Norto? Leaves'll probably look wilted for a while. The shock."

"That was almost it: you almost foxed my box. Simon, let me tell you, Herman Wolff is a dangerous man. I know. He was friends once with Meyer Lansky. With Batista. I know. And Kyryl. And Kyryl. I can't tell you about it, but—trust me—I know. I know too much. He raises one finger: Adele, the kids and my poodle walk out. My checks start bouncing like Ping-Pong balls. You heard what he said, 'Two lovely children you have.' I'm just a hired father. I've got nothing. Zero."

"Calm down. So there were a few gaposis moments—it came out all right in the end. Gosh, Norto. I don't mind licking a buttock or two. I have no principles. He gave me a job, didn't he? Huh? What is it anyway? Huh? What do I do?" Norty has handed Simon a card. "Mrs. Edward Armistead, River Towers. 405 East Fifty-sixth Street, Penthouse. Nice address. What is this? Who is she?"

"Go there, tonight at ten o'clock sharp. One minute late and I'll put you where that orange tree was. Just say 'Barcelona' to the doorman. Shave close. Take a bath. When you get upstairs, Les—he's the butler—he'll tell you what to do." Norty has come near. He lays one hand flat on Simon's cheek: slowly, under pressure, the face turns away. "No hijinks this time. It's your last chance, Simon. Do everything Les says. Everything. And, God help you, don't laugh."

"I get it. Just another pretty gigolo. Do I get paid? Huh? Hanh?"

"I think there's some remittance."

"You don't know?"

"No. And I don't want to. I've been arranging these junkets for five years now. Twice a month, second and fourth Monday nights. The participants don't talk. You don't talk. Right?"

"Right. I get it: as of this minute I'm a Harry Langdon short." Simon does some test sign language: soil falls off his hands. "Gee, this is kinda kinky. Fun. Like breaking a piñata full of snakes. Ah—this Mrs. Armistead. What's her preference? Do I flamenco on her kootzle? Does she stick my wand in an empty light socket?" Norty shrugs. "An older woman, huh? They marinate them pretty good over on Sutton Place, last longer than dill pickles. What's she look like?"

"I've never had that pleasure. She's a recluse. A person of deep sorrows. Herman has known her for a long time. I think she was his one great love. That's between you and me. Mention it, I'll deny. All I know, they met while he was with the Abraham Lincoln Brigade."

"The. Holy. Wait. That's the Spanish Civil War, isn't it? How old is she?"

"Seventy-one, two. Something."

"Jesus. And still at it? Her slot must be like Mammoth Cave: guides, tourists, bats hanging from the roof. Jesus. Seventy-two."

"Careful, mister. Leave that wonderful associative mind at home."

Slide, cancel. Pope Paul cuts in front of George Wallace. "Herman is very sensitive about Mrs. Armistead. He's a romantic. In my experience most killers are."

"Jesus. She better get on top. I don't wanna break her hip."

Simon sucks his thumb. He can taste soil.

3

Simon says, "Barcelona."

"No kidding?" The doorman is surprised. "You don't look the type."

"Whoa. Gee. Haw. Hold on. That remark piques me. Why—what should I look like?"

"Come this way. It's already ten-oh-two by my watch." Simon is step and step, rushing: from behind they might be one entry in a three-legged race. The doorman's livery is baroque: purple, with epaulets the color and width of a cream napoleon.

"Slow down. Wait."

"This way."

"Hey, Cap, I'm new t'this line a work. I mean, I'd appreciate any interesting sidelights y'could give me. Filler. Background material. On-site inspection is difficult, especially if the site is underneath you already."

"None of my business."

"Would five bucks correct this speech impediment of yours?"

"Five bucks. Shit, you should see the Christmas bonus I get."

"Oh, well. Maybe forewarned is limp-armed."

They turn left and quickly past a double bank of closed-circuit TV sets. Kyryl would indulge the op art possibilities here: vacant elevators watched, vacant apartment hallways, vacant alleys, not what you'd call prime-time viewing. The lobby corridor is over-immense. Its walls reach toward him: they seem insubstantial: from some old scene dock. Drafts butt out behind twelve-foot-high tapestries: like an inexperienced actor trying to find the curtain break. There are at least six suits of armor: uninhabited outer men. Wind, thwarted, blows off steam—eee-aiissh. The doorman has stopped to press a button. Simon gravedigs in the marble cigarette urn. It has been raked by a River Towers grounds crewman, neat as sand traps at Winged Foot. Simon will inhume his Beechnut tobacco chaw there.

Buzz.

"Les? Gentleman here by the name of—uh?"

"Simon Lynxx."

"Simon Lynxx. Uh-huh." The doorman hangs up. "All right. You're okay."

"Ah. Might I ask? What's this Mrs. Armistead look like? Does she smell of Arpège or formaldehyde?"

"Never met the lady. She doesn't come down much, has trouble with her legs. Uses one of those big walking braces, so I hear."

"Great. Great. She just calls out her orders, like to Chicken Delight. And here comes Simon, the giant drumstick. What keeps her going, the blood of little Jewish orphans?" Simon gets off a spitless swallow. "Wolff. I'll make you pay for this. Mother. A big metal walking brace: does she take it t'bed with her? Jeez, Simon. I guess that's what they mean by a dowager's hump."

"You finished shooting off your mouth?"

"I hope that's not all I can shoot off tonight."

"You guys. I thought you were supposed to keep a tight lip. That last guy, Lance, I never got a word out of him. Made five trips. What happened to him?"

"They kicked him upstairs. He's working at Grant's Tomb."

"Big joke. You ready?"

"What—what's that?"

"An elevator, whaddya think it is?"

The doorman has drawn a clumsy arras back. You can't blame Simon: there's nothing, an eight-by-eight black square of it, behind. The glass elevator door is so clear, so self-denying, that he can make it out only after much eye appeal. They hear dial tones approaching. Light sways down: it examines cracked concrete in the elevator shaft. Then a plastiglass cube settles, keeps settling, jouncy, behind the door. Art deco bulbs are arranged along each wall seam, as they are arranged around a makeup mirror. The door is opened. Fun-loving drafts jump Simon. They blow up one sleeve of his only suit jacket and out through the hole under its armpit. From below they balloon the shiny, dark blue trousers that had fitted Aldo during his best diets. Simon steps into glare. The plastiglass floor gives under his weight, resilient: it makes the cranky but unresponsive noise of a disturbed sleeper. Between his feet Simon can see shaft bottom. That's enough: that's not enough. Simon steps back out.

"Are—aren't you coming with me?"

"Why? Penthouse, thirty-second floor. It's the only stop, you can't miss it."

"That thing, that self-service Baggie, I just bent the floor. It's not safe. It's like some ten-year-old's tree house."

"What d'you go, two-twenty, two-thirty?"

"About."

"Well. Don't jump around too much. I think the elevator inspector gets a payoff."

"Oh, thanks. Man, I'd rather go over Niagara Falls in a Fleet Enema bottle. Listen, these other guys. I mean, after you send them up, do they come down with little puncture marks in the neck? Do they have a high, squeaky voice?"

"Dunno, I go off at midnight." Buzzing. "They're impatient. Better get in."

"Wolff. I'll kill him."

The elevator starts: a fitful yank that appears to stretch its transparent walls, as soap bubbles are born, ellipsoid, struggling into their natural shape. Simon sings. Simon whistles. Simon does not dance. The elevator is lethargic, five floors per minute. Cables drop on its roof, slither off. Concrete passes: there are no ways out in the shaft wall. Light is so brilliant it discourages a careful or interested seeing. Then, abruptly, it goes out. The dial tone rings off—though, for several seconds, his habituated ear will continue to supply it. Simon can feel the elevator dodging up and down: stopped, there is still give in its cables. With no motor noise now, Simon hears the plastiglass put in a currish protest. His heels are dangerous, sharp. Simon sits, then lies spread-eagle, face down, distributing his weight. There's nothing to see. Fingers press the floor. Flatness: that's his only sensual reference and it isn't much to go on. He remembers dead man's floats. Suddenly a light flashes on at shaft bottom, twenty-five stories below. Simon seems to fall free: the suspension, the suspense is terrifying. He shouts, "Jesus, shit! No!" Simon twists sideways, a half gainer: the human body wants to protect its head. His heart swats at him. But the elevator has started. Lights, one after another, blip on. He is insulated by brightness again. The elevator door unlocks.

"You may rise from the floor, Mr. Lynxx. I do hope you're not intoxicated."

"God, a seaplane with wheels is safer than that thing, God." Simon comes on loud. He has been unnerved: rare. He repeats himself: rare also. "I'd rather go over Niagara Falls in a Fleet Enema bottle."

"Keep your voice down, please."

Simon thinks, Jesus, another old grad from the Abraham Lincoln Brigade. Les is at least seventy, tall. He seems dressed for marriage: a cranberry-trimmed navy blazer, white trousers, white silk scarf. Only the beret is informal, not in keeping. Les's nostrils are pinched, as if by some suffocating hand, more decorative than functional. His fine nose suggests that the whole concept of *smelling*, the unfortunate word itself, are beneath scrutiny. Its bridge has been hemstitched with very red capillaries, blood right there, palpable: and tinier veins, the strands in printed money are not more diffident, web his long cheeks. Les is used to a sophisticated balance of service and power. And he has discomfort: Simon can see that. Les stands erect, almost eye and eye with Simon, but this erectness has been maintained by a careful, heroic weighing out of bone-deep aches. He is shot through with arthritis. The last joints of Les's fingers go off at an angle. When he shakes hands—necessary, but not winsome, ritual—the joints work inside Simon's palm like a beer-can opener. Simon gives pain: his standard hello to authority.

"Howjadoo?"

"I see." Les takes back his re-bent hand. "I see, Mr. Lynxx."

"You're the butler, Les."

"That is correct."

"Tell ya, Les. As one servant to another, this setup takes the prow out of my prowess. Look at it: you can't crank up a decent hard-on without knocking over someone's priceless Ming vase. Between you and me, that's why the rich love perversion. Even their women go around in drag. For perversion you need secrecy, handcrafted hardware, a full-time wardrobe department, and money, money, money. Kitsch, that's what. Perversion is just another kinda interior decoration: you want your sex t'match the De Kooning and the Kandinsky and the Eames chair. Another inanimate object. This is my Rothko and this is my Chagall and this is my latest fetish. I had it flown in from Rome. Me, I prefer middle-class fookie. I like t'stick my enob into something damp and real, like a gaucho pie."

"I'm sorry you're displeased." Les has rolled up a frown. "Well, perhaps I should phone Mr. Wolff."

"No. Ah, no. No. No. Me, displeased? Where'd you get that idea? I'm just an employee: the Man Power people sent me over t'do some piece-work, that's all. Just think of me as a handy utensil: a screwdriver, an egg whisk, a three-way pocketknife."

"Right. Then we understand each other. Allow me to apologize for the secrecy, Mr. Lynxx. No doubt it seems, shall we say, a cloak-and-dagger operation. But there is someone inside whom we all admire deeply. This is an evening she looks forward to. At Mrs. Armistead's age there aren't many pleasures available. We don't want her disappointed or embarrassed. In fact, she must not—must not—be disappointed or embarrassed."

"Sure. I'll be firm, yet gentle. A regular two-ply tissue."

"Gentle? Yes, gentle is a good word. And discreet, I trust." Les studies Simon: has him display: front, profile, rear, three-quarters. He reaches up, jerks long hair roughly back. His roughness is not deliberate: the result of age, of fluky coordination. "Please follow me. Mr. Wolff said you would consent to have your hair cut."

"I would?" Les stops: he turns. Simon can hear his pelvis snap like a knuckle. "I would. I would."

"We received your photograph and measurements just two hours ago. You'll be patient, I hope—our preparations are just a bit primitive."

Les has unlocked a door: EMPLOYEES ONLY. The corridor beyond it goes on and on, possibly that full block from Fifty-sixth Street to Fifty-seventh Street. Simon would like to pull out and pass: Les doesn't walk: he pushes his feet along. Metatarsal bones have calcified and no shoe-horn can help him: his shiny formal pumps have been crushed to mules at the heel. There are small rooms on either side: voices within sound agitated, newsy, foreign. Guitars are tuned and one wind instrument, could be a sax. Simon full-stops. Four white butterflies have startled him. They eddy in place, up and down. Simon goes on, staring back. A net appears from one of the doors: swipe, they are gone. "Les. Hey, Les. You wouldn't believe this, I just saw a man catching butterflies. Honest." No answer and two women costumed as Spanish peasants swish past him, past Les, the backs of their dresses unzipped to bra straps. Then it comes, clear, unmistakable: the baaing of sheep. Simon says, but not aloud, "Christ, y'gotta draw the line somewhere. Wolff or no Wolff, I'm not making it with some horny ewe. No lint on my wontz." The corridor ells finally. Through a window Simon can see river and dignified dowager finials on the Fifty-ninth Street bridge. But an opening-night ambiance has gotten to him. It's a show. Simon will be up for the performance. And anyhow he has always loved expensive eccentricity. Les stops in front of a door marked * RAMON *.

"After you, Mr. Lynxx." Simon steps in. A costume rack: RAMON. A prop trunk: RAMON. A tackle box full of makeup: RAMON.

"Victoria, this will be our Ramón. Simon, Victoria. Victoria, Simon."

"He's heavy."

"You're no hip flask yourself, sister."

"Les, he said—"

"Simon has a sharp tongue, Victoria, but let's not worry about it. I have Mr. Wolff's assurance and that has always been sufficient. Sit at the table, Simon."

"I don't know—" Victoria is unsure. Her glasses are hazed: the fallout from a dozen face-powderings. She wears a smock: breasts and gut make it seem pre-maternal. She cups dark brown base in her left hand: a palette for her right. Les has been judging.

"Yes. He is rather on the brawny side. I'm afraid we'll split a seam or two. The face is handsome enough, though. I like the face. I don't think she'll be disappointed. You'll need to take off some hair. I'll send Gerard down." Les has a pocket watch out. "Our time is short. We can't keep her up much past two o'clock."

"Jesus, I take an elevator and I'm in out-of-town rep. There better not be cameras. If I find myself playing in some quarter-a-glim peep show on Seventh Avenue, I'll—"

"Your voice, Simon. Try to modulate it. How is your vision?"

"Uh. Good. I wear contacts."

"Let's check, just to be on the safe side. Try reading this." An eye chart has been pushpinned to the far wall. "From where you are now."

"E. ABCH. VXZRS. UTMIWJK."

"Fine. Fifth line."

"SU. That little thing is a P. TR—"

"Fine. Fine." Simon watches Les in the mirror. Les, from behind, has put a hand on each of Simon's shoulders. The hands are light. "I'm trusting you now. I was your age once. I realize that a young man might find material for satire here. Don't laugh. Don't send it up. Don't betray revulsion. It will be a test of your character." Arthritis has distorted Les's face. The mirror reversal is extreme: almost a different man. "Things you've said. They're defense mechanisms, perfectly natural. You're uncertain of yourself here. At heart, though, you're a good person."

"Gee, Les. Wouldja appear at my next parole hearing?"

"Besides, it will be worth your time, I promise."

And now—heeere's Simon! He has entered stage left, aloof. Sparks are struck: the traveling spot has hit rhinestones on his black toreador's suit. Simon scintillates: he's gorgeous. The orchestra phrases a vamp for him. Applause, whistling, forks on wineglasses say together, "*Sí! Sí! Sí!*" And Simon begins to dance. He stares down/over his right shoulder. The spine makes itself rigid: a backbone. Simon can feel his hair, pomaded flat, the wet look, a chill clench from forehead to nape. He is now six shades darker than he was. His nutcracker teeth take advantage: the smile is fierce, insolent, Castilian. In each high-held hand castanets chatter without sound: without sound his heels ra-ta-tat on the padded stage floor. Just overhead a loudspeaker dubs flamenco noises in. Simon goes along with the grand illusion. He enjoys it: oh, he enjoys it.

"Ramón! Ramón! Olé!"

A woman's voice: his cue. Simon glances out, front and center: belligerent, impassive: *Ramón,* in fact. Can this be? His eyes hurry: they accommodate themselves to spotlight wash. The café is huge: the café is real. There must be thirty—no, take that back—forty people sitting at two dozen circular tables. A balcony overhangs this Sutton Place *cantina:* another twenty people up there. Just under the balcony Simon can make out what Les and Victoria have told him to look for: a wide Teleprompter screen. KEEP DANCING, it tells him. A rose has been thrown at Simon's feet. Women wear mantillas: some young men have uniforms on. Waiters slide in and out, supple at the hips. Simon has gotten up a nice sweat. The orchestra doubles its beat. Simon tastes makeup. He hasn't danced flamenco in ten years: he still isn't dancing it. With great effort his heels approximate the loudspeaker ra-ta-tat. Calf muscles are in a go—no-go countdown alert: the shoes of some banana-footed other Ramón have hurt him. But KEEP DANCING, it says. Simon will: as if he were just a strange hi-fi component.

Rrr-ppp. Pop. Pop. Uh-oh, something has given along Simon's left inner thigh. His crotch detects a breeze. The orchestra has geared up for its coda: Simon's tongue is fat, white with panting. He whirls, castanets down, castanets up. His right armpit detects a breeze. The loudspeaker has no mercy, ratata-tata-tatratata-tat-tat: his heels will blister tomorrow. Applause and one more rose. It's over. GO TO TABLE #12. The traveling spot takes over, maître-d's him there. Female hands touch at Simon, as if for a blessing, when he crosses the café floor. And Simon is gracious: he nods, he smiles, he winks. The room is smoke-filled but Simon can smell nothing and there are no cigarettes. At table #12, a lovely woman, her dark hair built high, some sort of ornate comb driven through it, has risen to accept him. She kisses Simon. Her fingernails scrawl on his neck, yet her lips, he can tell, are circumspect, careful of the makeup. Simon wants more, but she seats him, all business. The woman whispers fluent Spanish into Simon's monolingual ear. PRE-TEND TO TALK, on the Teleprompter. Simon leans in close.

"*No se habla* here. The only greaser word I know is *puta*." Crack, under the table: no feeling: her shoe tip has frozen the water on his knee. "Aaah-oh. Shees, the universal language." The dark woman smiles: she digs a little with her comb. But her left hand has settled on his open-air groin.

"Don't fuck around, buster. You do and I'll pull your dick off. I've got a four-year-old daughter to feed." She locates one testicle: squeezes. Like a hard, slick onion in stew it scoots away. "Smile. That was nothing. Have some champagne. You're at a party. Laugh it up." Simon holds his left kidney, laughing.

LET YOUR GLANCE WANDER TO THE FOUNTAIN. Simon's eyes take off: they hang-glide for several seconds, touch down near the fountain. A woman sits alone at her table. Simon can't discern the features. She toys with a full wineglass, as if dusting it off. Their eyes catch, hold. She is made nervous: her wineglass goes over, clonk! But, huh?, when she picks it up, the glass is still full: red rioja painted on. Simon looks away: lead us not into temptation to laugh and lose a sperm bulb. Three guitarists have followed Simon's act: no one pays much attention. The dark woman has started to kiss Simon's neck. SEEM IMPATIENT WITH HER. Seem, my dingus, Simon will chock her a good elbow in the rib cage. She inhales, whooping, angry and windless, but ad-libs are not allowed. Someone has come up behind Simon, that light hand again. A waiter: it's Les. He leans down.

"Excellent so far, Simon. You dance spiritedly."

"Yeah? I feel like I just passed a kidney stone. I thought that sixteenth tarantella was a bit de trop." Simon pronounces the p.

"Ah—you seem to have developed a few embarrassing holes."

"No kidding. Who used this outfit last, someone from the Donner Pass party? And listen—I gotta put in a complaint about the seating arrangements in this joint. If I'd known Wicked Wanda here was coming I'da worn a jock and a bronze cup."

"Let's not worry. Please look toward the fountain. Fine. Point discreetly." Simon does. "You'll find a pencil and a piece of paper in your right-hand jacket pocket." Simon does: the pencil has no point. The paper reads, "I find you entrancing, may I join you?" Les nods. "Now pretend to write. Good. Put the note on my tray."

Les pushes his feet off. The dark woman begins to speak in an all-vulgar Spanish. IGNORE HER. Les has traversed the *cantina* floor. Simon sees him in conversation near the fountain. Two men appear: they ask for his autograph. Simon writes with his dummy pencil. Les has returned: there is another note on the tray. "I should be delighted." STAND UP. The dark woman slaps a proprietary hand on Simon's wrist. THROW HER ASIDE. Simon does better than that: he pinches her left breast. The woman says, "Shit!" tweezed right out of character. A glass crashes on the floor. CROSS THE ROOM. People murmur. The orchestra plays a cover-up tune.

Her face has been eaten. Each wrinkle is savage: a notch made, year by year: to remember things by. KISS HER HAND. SIT. They've set a second Teleprompter, just twenty inches wide, behind her chair. Simon kisses. Blond hair has been manufactured for Mrs. Armistead: the wig will slide, come up short, top-heavy, whenever she nods. Simon has taken his seat. She was beautiful once, he knows that. The nose, for instance, is still fine, a survivor: when they were plush her large cheekbones must have been delightful, now they tell only skeletal backstairs gossip. Mrs. Armistead has smiled. A black beauty mark, swamped by the counterswell of two wrinkles, bounces off. It will roll across the table.

She speaks lame Spanish: some compliment apparently. Simon has no answer. Wolff, he is thinking: that one shiksa every Jew must love, the more unattainable, the better. Simon likes Mrs. Armistead. Simon recognizes great presence when he floats past it. Though the teeth are not real, he enjoys her smile: it covets nothing. Les is right. She must not be disappointed or embarrassed. He makes the commitment: he will be Ramón and why not? He has only to accept this high-budget mirage: and mirage-making, after all, is his special brokerage. Mrs. Armistead taps her filled-in bosom. She waits. She is excited, bashful. Simon can see her walking brace, a length of suburban fence, near the fountain. Eh, what? Yes: the Teleprompter. I SPEAK ENGLISH. I WAS EDUCATED AT CAMBRIDGE. And Simon pads his part: gracious, modulated. One or two women have known this: he can be a kind, attentive wooer. "Forgive my silence. A thousand pardons. I was stunned by your beauty. I speak English, as you see. I was educated at Cambridge."

"You were? I am surprised."

"A café dancer who is educated? But I come from what they call a good family. My father is a rich man."

"Yes? And he approves of this—your dancing?"

"I have not seen my father in five years. I am a Republican. We are on the eve of a new Spain. My father, he is the old Spain. It cannot be. It cannot be." Simon reads. "My name is Ramón Echeverría. And may I ask yours?"

"Elsie. Elsie Carruthers."

"You are American, I think." TOUCH HER HAND LIGHTLY. Simon takes direction well. Touch. Mrs. Armistead withdraws, but he can sense a hesitation.

"You mustn't, Ramón."

"I'm sorry. Again I ask your forgiveness. I have been stupid and rash." Mrs. Armistead examines her hand. She can believe that it is lithe and forty years her junior.

"No. It's not your fault. We Americans, you know, we are a strange people. We lack passion. I am here for—well, we call it a last fling. I'm to be married in Philadelphia. My fiancé is waiting. I've made him impatient, perhaps angry. But I've led such a sheltered life. I wanted to be alone—to see Europe. And have it see me." There is a racket: chairs are overturned, some glass breaks. The dark woman on her way out. "She is unhappy. Is she your girl?"

"My girl?" Simon shrugs. "Yes, she thinks so. But she demands too much. She wants me to be friends with my father. There is a great deal of money involved, you see. This troubles her."

"You are so young." Her voice is not meant, was never meant, for such large rooms. The orchestra has masked it. Simon looks up. I'M WELL PAST THIRTY. IN PHILADELPHIA I AM AN OLD WOMAN ALREADY. AND I DON'T KNOW WHERE MY LIFE HAS GONE. EXCUSE ME. I'M ASHAMED. I SHOULDN'T BE TALKING LIKE THIS.

"Old? You are beautiful. And foolish. Elsie, in just a few moments I must dance for my supper again. Tomorrow is Sunday. Will you come for a picnic with me? I will show you the real Barcelona. Our countryside."

"I couldn't." They come up, graceful and intense, her hands. They hush at her lips. "I couldn't. It—you understand—it wouldn't be fair to Ernest."

"Nonsense. My sister will come with us. A chaperone. Even an American from Philadelphia would find that proper."

480

"I want to! I want to!" Her fist bangs: each a hard, neat stroke on the
table. Her face, its indignation, amuses Simon.
"Then do. Where are you staying?"
"At Mrs. Alcott's. Near the Hotel Falcón."
"I know it. I will meet you outside. Can you ride a bicycle?"
"Oh, yes."
"Don't disappoint me." STAND. KISS HER HAND AGAIN.
"That's just it, you see. I'm afraid of that. I'm afraid I will disappoint
you."
The traveling spot has opened. It picks out Simon. It pesters him:
it urges him away. The applause is insistent, he must dance again, but
there is time for him to say, "I'm not afraid."

"Victoria, put some makeup on his chest. Do we have the flowers? Yes.
I'm pleased, Simon. She was humming, that's a very good sign. Very
good. I think she's happy."
"Who's this Spanish fly I'm playing? Did she really know him?"
"Ah, the past. Is it ever real?" Les sighs. "Let me give you the run-
down, we haven't much time. You'll find what you have to say on the
picnic hamper lid. Don't rush your lines." Victoria has handed Simon a
bouquet of wildflowers: they are fresh and alien. "Whatever you do,
don't try and make her stand up. It could be disastrous. Now—in about
two minutes—I'm going to open this sliding hatch, and you . . . Victoria,
you're slipping, you've forgotten his cross."
"Sorry, Les. Here, lean over." The cross is heavy, at least a pound:
Simon will have to carry it. "Be careful when you bend. Those slacks
were made for a 'normal.' You could stand to lose some weight."
"One more dig, Sitzbein, and you stand t'lose a tit."
"Sssssh, both of you. There." A red light blinks. "The shepherd is on.
One thousand, two thousand, three thousand, four—" Les tolls off fifteen.
"I'm afraid you'll have to get down on your knees here. Creep forward
about ten yards. Keep your head below the stone fence. Then rise slowly,
as if you were coming out of a slight depression. Understand?"
"I'm in a slight depression already. Yeah, I understand."
Simon gets down. The flowers are held, retriever-style, carefully, in his
mouth. Simon tries to goose Victoria, not a sexually remunerative act:
the crotch of her pantihose has settled to kneecap height. The panel
slides up. "Now. Keep low." Les gives a helpful slew-footed shove and—
Mother Mary God—Simon sees broad daylight just after 12 A.M. "Wolff,"
he says, "Wolff, you could terrify me." Thirty-two stories above Fifty-
sixth Street, Simon is in an open pasture: an open pasture forty yards
square. He crawls at a crawl through foot-high Tartanturf. There are real
crickets in it. Overhead, blue sky has been simulated by Cinerama tech-
niques: a 1936-model sun strokes him. He has found the stone wall,

breached here and there by fifty years' artificial neglect. Just behind it, Simon can hear the small talk of running streams.

Half up, three-quarters, then full: Simon has come out of his slight depression. There is a rivulet, two yards wide, beyond the stone fence. Bettina recalled: she took young Simon to see jungle panoramas at the Natural History Museum. Now he's on exhibit. Times change. Soil gives under his step. Some ants, willing to suspend disbelief, have thrown up anthills here. Simon is in a valley: it extends southeastward, following its stream, by trompe l'oeil perspective, up/into the wall, to a theoretical Mediterranean Sea. Breezes are fanned out of the north, from painted Catalonian hills. They bring back his own Sangre de Cristo Mountains on the bedroom wall. Mrs. Armistead waves at him, mostly from the elbow, her shoulder movement constrained by an old bursitis. Simon waves back. Mrs. Armistead has a straw hat on: defense against Wolff's brilliant, ultraviolet-deficient, sun. She is sitting. The white frock has been draped around her: she might as well be legless. Wineglasses, bread, cheese attend on the large picnic hamper. Simon figures out a safe rock path across the rivulet. Cold water splashes him. Six sheep cross further downstream: a shepherd, blanket over one shoulder, yells some Spanish encouragement to romance. His dog barks on cue. White butterflies, extras, jitter. Simon kneels. He presents the bouquet.

"Lovely. Lovely." Mrs. Armistead aims the bouquet at her nose: near-miss. It reflects—purple, blue, yellow, green—from her flake-white, panchromatic cheek. "I can't tell you how happy I am. I've been here a month and this is the first time I've seen the real Spain."

"I'm glad." Simon cold-reads the hamper lid. "Tourists can be worse than an occupying army. We take advantage of them, or so we think. They take advantage of us, or so they think. A pickpockets' convention: no one can prosper. You Americans—the most of you—suppose that cultural exchange is like a blood transfusion, so many pesetas a pint." SIT CLOSER NOW. Mrs. Armistead reacts to his new propinquity. Her feet move: something under the drapery after all.

"Ah, Ramón. Ah? Where is your sister?"

"Up there." He points. Three bicycles slant against the rock wall. "She wants to sketch the shepherd. I think she is a very talented artist. My father doesn't like that: he would prefer an important marriage alliance."

"Will she be back soon?" LAUGH.

"Are you afraid?" EAT. Simon overplays. He can't get his lines in for bread. But Mrs. Armistead is pleased: she favors exuberance. This will be a good Ramón. "Do I—hm . . ." Simon drinks. "Do I threaten you?"

"A little bit. But don't let it go to your head. Most new things threaten me. What—?" TAKE OFF HER HAT. "What are you doing?"

"This hat. That silly, big brim. You do not fool me: it is for hiding. There." The sun of technology makes her squint. Simon can see Mrs.

Armistead's pupils sphincter: they furl themselves. Her embarrassment is coy and full of grace. "The rich. They hate light. My poor mother does. Brown hands and face are the sign of a peasant. But parasols will not shade them from what is coming."

"Will there be war, Ramón?"

"There is always war. Quiet war. Loud war." Simon hacks the cheese. "It is time for a loud war."

"How can you be so sure?"

"It's easy. I am going to start one. I and a few friends. Here, eat."

"No. No. I'm full with the day. I wish I were free as that shepherd. But it's no use. I have money. Money. Money. You knew I was rich."

"It's rather obvious, don't you think?" Simon chugalugs fine Málaga from the bottle: there are no stage directions for this. "Aaah, good. But money doesn't make you beautiful. You—you are beautiful, yourself."

"Ernest Armistead thinks of my money— What? What—what? What good are these?" Simon starts, scared. She is a crone. The face has shrunk: spiteful: on the skids and mean. Mrs. Ernest Armistead harries her bouquet. Head after head, flowers are sent to the block. One of her fingers has bled. "I don't smell wolf. Why? Why?"

"Why—?" But none of this has been scripted: all new material. Simon is on his own. He tries to improvise along. "Ah, why should you? I'm not a wolf."

"The smell. Gone. I want it back. But no, he said I couldn't have it anymore. He took it away from me. I never liked him. A nasty little dwarf. All he cares about is money and that stupid Brooklyn."

"Ah-uh."

"Brooklyn. *Brooklyn.* Can you imagine?"

"I—I certainly can't." Simon finger-follows the text: no Brooklyn, no dwarf.

"He said I couldn't have both. Not this and the flowers. And my beautiful perfume. No. No." Her voice is grating: ill-behaved. "The son of a bitch. But they have their uses, don't they? Like toilet paper. Oh, they make themselves so useful."

"They? They sure do." Even extempore they do. "I guess."

"Are you strong?"

"Um—" There it is. She's back on book. Thank however you say God in Spanish. "Strong? Me? Damn right I am." A blasphemy clashes with the Catholic, strict hills of Spain. Simon is apprehensive: he will apologize, my regrets, to the sliding hatch. But Mrs. Armistead is serene again. "I've eaten well all my life. I can lift a horse. And dancing is good for the body."

"I haven't much time left, Ramón. I've delayed my return too long." On the mark so far, "Too long." Simon turns a page. KISS HER TENDERLY. He upchucks a wad of cheese.

"I—ahm. May I try to make you stay just a little longer?" He has her far shoulder. She doesn't resist their coming nearness. Simon has closed his eyes. Her décolletage fires off a round of strong perfume.

"Ramón. Your sister."

"She will be busy for a while. These artists, you know. Elsie, don't deny me this. It is innocent. It is a way of remembering. These are fragile times. Some things must be fixed in the mind. Your lips."

Simon has encountered them. And, you know, it's not unpleasant. They are soft: they are quite moist: they feed with diligence inside his own much larger lips. When she comes to him, shoulder cartilage crackles with her need. Mrs. Armistead's grip is staunch: it will not be compromised. He has never known this kind, this degree of desperation. And, as best he can, good sport Simon gives her relief.

Darkness has come: at 1 A.M., fashionably late. Would you believe it, they're real, real cobblestones. Simon does a quick set on them: tap, tapatap, tap-tap. He feels tired: must be a kind of stationary jet lag. Across the large-as-traffic boulevard, up/toward Barcelona's moon, house roofs overlap each other in a canny, 3-D perspective. Ah, how we Americans can make: it's enough to turn one patriotic. A rogue crowd of workers has passed on cue, rabble-rousing north toward the Plaza de Cataluña. Red/white flares sway down. One window of the Hotel Falcón lies defenestrated, struck by a real cobblestone. Her balcony is just overhead: Simon waits there, in the wings. His breath pushes out. The air force uniform was meant for a one-seater pilot: rip. Its cap shifts around on his oil slick of hair. The workers send back a long, syndical-anarchic shout and, on some other plane of his hearing, guns fire, ragged, far away in this apartment house world.

Simon cries, "Wolff." Fighters come in low: their stereophonic sneeer passes from left to right. Simon has aimed a fist at the tenting heaven. It's curved and facile as some planetarium sky. "Wolff. For what this little *tsatske* cost, Jew, I coulda got Cary Grant t'do a nude scene." The sign now blinks: CLIMB, off, CLIMB, off, CLIMB. Simon legs up on a trash-can rim. Rotted Mediterranean fruit and a dead paella inside. "Christ. Spic garbage flown in fresh every morning. Ahh-up. Careful now, klutz. Break your neck and they'll have to export the body."

His way has been made straight. There are handholds. The vine could take a 500-pound pull. Another mob passes and Simon, halfway up, swings behind the pediment in honor of this keen facsimile. Figures start to scuffle. Someone drops, picturesquely dead. Cement is shot from the cornice above him: Simon-be-nimble over the balcony rail. His pants tear, mimicking a flatulence. He sits: ah, he salutes this hoax. How Simon has loathed that word "phony," favorite of gum-cracking office girls. The real is the imaginative failed. The phony is a failure of imaginative style.

Bombs crump and his seat shakes with Sensu-round. Wind has begun to blow, a New York wind: walls of the Hotel Falcón ripple, then belly out. Simon says, "Wolff." It is an endearment. "Who's there?" she answers before he has come there. The fear in Mrs. Armistead's voice does not approximate. Once more, fortnightly, she has been taken in by it all. Simon walks. Luminous masking tape has been stuck down, a blaze mark through the french doors to her four-poster bed. Mrs. Armistead is bolstered up. Simon waits, a military silhouette. It would be bitumen dark, but for the Teleprompter that says again, WHO'S THERE?

"Ramón."

"You can't come in. You can't come in here. This is my bedroom."

"I must, Elsie. I must tell you something."

"Don't betray my trust." GO TO THE BED. TAKE HER HAND. It quivers in his. Simon is made curious by the hand: he has never been this close to bone before.

"I'm not betraying it, Elsie. I've come to tell you that there is war and that I love you."

"Oh, God. It is not allowed." The Teleprompter prints out LAUGH. That's just as well: Simon already has.

"What is not allowed? My love? The war?"

"Both, Ramón."

"No. Both are good." LIE BESIDE HER. "The war is good because our people will triumph. My love is good because you and I, Elsie, we are meant for each other."

"Ramón, I'm shaking. I want to make love." Oboy. Simon checks out his groin: no dice. But the understanding Teleprompter says,

I WON'T ASK THAT OF YOU. WE WILL HAVE OUR TIME.

"What is it, what you are wearing, Ramón?"

"I am a pilot in our air force. I fly at first daylight. The planes are not much good. Elsie—" There is an explosion: they hug: they Sensu-round each other.

"Ramón, I'm so perplexed. You've ripped me out of myself. I'm naked. I love you, too." And, in the darkness, her voice is youthful, lush. He, in darkness, resents the decades that have passed.

"I must go. The airfield is outside Barcelona and already the streets are wild. Stay indoors today. I've spoken to friends—you will be safe." She gives his lower lip a bite, and, though Simon can feel her plate shake in its Poligrip, he, unprompted, smiles.

"That was good, Mr. Lynxx. Very good. You surprised me."

"Oh. Did I really?" The leather flying helmet helps Simon to a skull-clean, Wasp Man aspect. He snaps goggles into place. The silk scarf around his neck jumps in a 100-m.p.h. propeller slipstream, taking off by itself. He fast draws a .45 automatic from the shoulder harness. Simon models on another sort of runway: his fur-lined boots clop. "Say, is this costume for rent? It's got a kinda 1930's arriviste chic."

"I think perhaps Mrs. A has surprised you. She can do that."

"Dunno what you mean. This is like establishing residence in someone's masturbation fantasy."

"Well. It's no good. I won't try to penetrate your defenses. Pay attention now—directions are clearly printed on the instrument panel. They're simple enough. There isn't much to do."

"Yah." A man waves. "Where's the American Express office? I wanna see if this month's *Saturday Evening Post* came."

"Go. It's clear. She's in the viewing booth. And please—please fasten your safety belt."

Simon crosses the tarmac, very aware of his pilot self: a hero complete with high-priced options. Ground crewmen salute. The sergeant has an aerial map: he boosts Simon wing-up, hands cat-cradled under one boot. The canopy is shot into place: tripped shut. Simon turns greenish, an undersea look. The propeller appears at rest ahead of him, stilled by stroboscopic effect. RELEASE BRAKE. Simon does: men rush to jerk the wheel chocks out. Mother God of whiplash, Simon is hurtling and incredulous and airborne just in time down the Cineramic runway. Sun at six o'clock low waters both his eyes. The city has been miniaturized beneath. Simon plays. A world will answer to his touch, port or starboard. He heads east and, as predicted, the Mediterranean comes into view, a dawn-glare cutting edge. Simon tries to touch the illusion, to find the limit: he pulls back and earth is above him, a perfect Immelmann turn. He can't get out: Simon has been caught in film.

Crack-crack-crack. His seat leaps: Simon is canted to one side. Wind blitzes through a flak hole in the Plexiglas. Liquid, it must be fuel, has splashed down his neck. Buildings, streets, trees reaffirm themselves: Jesus, he's gonna splat out somewhere in upper East Side Spain. Sparks explode across his instrument panel. Simon hits the stick, in authentic terror now, but he can't pull up. Sections of tail snap away: they go down, edge over edge, like flipped baseball cards. Simon has battled with the canopy, slamming, wrenching, but it won't come off. Five, four, three, two, one—a woman screams for him.

"Well, there's no use complaining. I told you to fasten the seat belt. Now you'll have a nasty lump."

"At least you could've given me a queen-sized coffin. Some corpse, I've gotta keep my knees bent like a toad. Whatever happened to death with dignity?"

"You look just like yourself, Simon." Les laughs.

"Oh, brother. Something tells me you've used that line before. Christ, death depresses the hell out of me. Can't she just take the pledge at Necrophiliacs Anonymous?"

"Sssh. You're supposed to be dead."

"My fingers passed away ten minutes ago. Let me stop holding this damned ice bag, hanh? I've got the grip of a Nupercained fag."

"She'll touch your hands. Mr. Wolff is a stickler for realism. You were sweating, ah—in a most lifelike manner."

"Sweat? You're just lucky I didn't find the damned airsick bag. What a metaphor for my career—eeee, thump, going down. Jesus, no wonder they lost the war. I felt like an asteroid in one of those electronic Atari games. That's the last time I go on a charter flight."

"All right. I'll take that. Place your hands over your chest and drape the cross just so. It's almost over. You need only lie still now."

"I don't like it. If she comes in here with a wooden stake and a mallet, I'm bailing out, realism or no realism."

"Ssssh. She's coming. Don't move."

Simon kills time in the coffin. It's uncomfortable, going bowlegged to your maker. His dress uniform has ridden up/over both shins. The coffin lid impends, substantial: Simon imagines himself as the bait in some lethal spring trap. Overhead, Jesus slumps on his cross. The chapel is modest. Daylight has been strained through red-blue glass. Somewhere monks chant. He can hear a blind man's noise, tack-tack, tack-tack. Eyes left, Simon squeezes off a glance. Mrs. Armistead is inching across the small nave, just behind her metal brace. Simon holds his breath. Now she has knelt at a prayer rail. The wig slips forward, almost in with him.

"O Lord God, forgive me—I have not been a religious woman. It escapes me, I can only remember the silly prayers of my childhood. Have mercy: I come to you now on my knees. Be good to him. Protect him. Take him to you." Mrs. Armistead rises. This has cost her: pain is charged to his account. Knuckles become chalky at the coffin's edge. And a beauty mark pops off onto Simon's chest. "Ramón. Ramón." She has taken his hand. "I loved you. I loved you. I loved you." Her head tilts back: the wig follows some time later. Simon can see dewlaps strung beneath her chin. Anguished, she cries out. Old tears arrive. And Simon is moved. He deplores her suffering: it seems cruel, maniacal, senseless—worse than that, boring. In his bumpkin way, Simon would like to console. He reaches out: he touches her hand.

"God damn!" she shouts. "It is *not* a game! It is not a game!" In reprisal some switch has been hit. Easily, powerfully, the coffin lid battens down. He can't force it: fingers have been pinned, cold, to his chest. Simon is afraid, lights out. Rich fabric muffles his cry: no sound can get through. The coffin begins to move, bumping, along a track: it turns once, it turns again. Perhaps he is upside down. Simon sucks for air. Fine silk, neutral, enters his nose and mouth. Simon is going to die.

2

Simon's biological clock is mainsprung. The sun arc-lamps his third—or will it be his fourth?—morning today. Frail rain falls. Vandam Street has taken the early autumn leaves to itself: each shines like a still-wet decal. Aromas are leavened out of porous concrete. Simon has been walking all night: to Manhattan's bow and then back aft to the Fifty-ninth Street bridge, down its tedious, stair-circling Queens-side tower. His left shoe is without a sole tip now. Five toes pat the rough, chill cement, yet New York is no more valid than Barcelona forty years, forty blocks, ago. Simon doesn't want to draw conclusions, or even beginnings, from that. He walks, the empty Jack Daniel's quart at his mouth: he blows a lone tugboat sound from its hollow neck. Oooom. Oooom. Good booze wasted once again. His heavy-duty metabolism, the cholesterol-fat brain, seven and seven-eighths in depth, have matched intoxication surge for surge. He tries to stagger: to playact it. His feet dally at each step, ankles unlatched, as if he were crushing cigarette butts out, the way pianists will rub fingers on some already struck key: useless musically: a trick of cheap peacockishness. Ah, it's Simon's great burden in life: he's never had a cheap drunk yet.

Possessive, built to expect compliance, the coffin wouldn't give him up. Wolff's orders, Simon has guessed: Let Mr. Brown Shirt have a little scare. Remembering it: the scalp feels itchy, loose: a toupee of skin. Ten minutes, six hundred separate seconds: so much dead reckoning. He pulled muscles. His toad feet kicked and kicked. Oh, there are awful, instinctive contractions when a body knows that its vitalness is on ration, running short. He breathed in the dusty silk: nondescript smells, smells of air exhausted through a vacuum-cleaner bag. He was near faintness then: cold-cocked by horror. His madeup face had come off on the coffin lid: Simon saw it recorded there, mouth open in fright, a negative him. Only later, past Fourteenth Street, heading south, had he identified Les's slim envelope. A party favor, a souvenir from Spain: twenty-five brittle hundred-dollar bills.

ssssSSSS. At the corner he hears it, bicycle tires susurrant on a wet sidewalk. Simon jerks back to save himself: a wrist will be grazed by sharp brick. But there's nothing. Around the corner, in its deep, grated well, steam rushes from a Chinese laundry vent. Associate, associate: metaphor-making can inflict real pain. Simon drops his bottle behind the grate. Smash-kisss: a gas grenade. He licks his slit skin. Tongue there imagines her perfume. He'd like to know that, why he had touched Mrs. Armistead's hand, that most of all. It irks him: it was an uncharacteristic, over-earnest response. Simon is fast, but he has never yet been spontaneous.

The van waits, a car length down from HAIR APPARENT. Vapor exits from its small stack: Simon's substance leaking out. Home, confronted with the gear of his life, he feels exasperate and mean. JORGE, DUKE OF ASTORIA, has played connect-the-lynxx-spots with a spray-paint can. And one fender has been grazed. Simon taps the code: friend. Larry, in silk bathrobe and fuzzed blue slippers, their toes cut out, boosts the van door up. His legs are beautiful, legs of a swimmer seen darting past, more stroke line than limb. Shaved, too: Simon has a quick feel, leaping in. There are strange odors, feminine: they dispossess him. And—what's this?—now each bunk bed wears a pink sleeping-car curtain.

"Where were you, Sy? Where were you last night?"

"Have you looked outside—huh, Juicy Fruit? Someone painted the Sistine Chapel on us while you were asleep. Christ, what a CETA job: they must've put up scaffolding and a MEN AT WORK sign."

"What? Who?"

"The damned Duke of Astoria, who else? He's gotta be eleven feet tall. Take a look, they played tic-tac-toe all over me with green Polyglycoat. We're now driving a subway car or the world's biggest Rorschach test. But you—you use earplugs the size of a crank dong. You'd sleep through a radical cystoscopy."

"Don't yell."

"I'll yell. Jesus, if we weren't parked in front of a hydrant I'd call the police. My fender—aaarh!" Simon pitches his shirt against a curtain. "And, since you ask, I've been peddling my pound of ground chuck in a senior citizens' home all night, just to keep you in L'eggs and latex. What—what's all this filigree anyhow? You've turned my nifty barracks-like home into downtown Flitsville."

"Sy—enough." Larry has sat on the bunk edge. Face snuggles into palms. Simon is careful now: gotta suave the situation.

"Jesus, don't cry. I can't stand to see a daisy weep."

"You, you don't know what it was like last night. We got three flats, just one after another. The spare had a hole so big I could wear it on my

thumb." Simon comes close. This is Aldo's legacy: he doesn't trust a
disembodied voice. "I was rolling tires up and down Francis Lewis Boulevard, sixteen horrid blocks to the Gulf station on Cross Island. The tires
were wet and kaka and *so* stupid. I can't do heavy work, Sy, you know
that. My art is going."

"Easy. Easy." Simon is beside him: thigh to thigh. "Take a day off."

"I did. I am. But that's not all. I tried to get water at your house last
night. Well, it was the most terrible moment of my life. I went up to the
door and this little old man pops out. So grotesque. Tattooed and almost
naked except for some sort of washrag over his thing. 'Good evening,' I
said. I mean, what else could I say? And without even answering he took
out a knife—it must have been a foot long—and just cut my bathrobe belt
in half. Look at it, will you? Then he poked me in the buns all the way
down your front path, *all* the way. I couldn't run in my slippers. It was
nightmarish, you should have heard me shriek. I thought your uncle was
a priest, not some tiny lunatic." Simon won't laugh: he can't afford to.
"It's no use. I love you, Sy, and we have good memories, but I've got to
move on. My stomach is peeling off like old wallpaper. I feel it. After
that scene I was on the can all night. Everything went right through me,
instant replay."

"I can't wait to see the rushes."

"It isn't funny, Sy."

"I know. I know. Hold on, I'm the man of a thousand faces. Tell me if
I look any different." Simon turns away: an impersonator on stage. He
fusses with his hair. "Mmm?"

"Ah. Well, you've got a lot of money in your mouth."

"Damn, you recognized me. Improves my profile, doesn't it?"

"Yes. Oh, they're hundreds."

"Those are for you." He packs two in a bathrobe pocket. "Don't tell
that steroid, Don. Have a ball on me. Go buy yourself a shot glass and a
fifth of Kaopectate."

"Where did you get it? She must've been a rich old lady. Or, ah, man.
Hmmm?"

"Believe me, you wouldn't believe me if I told you. It wasn't too bad—
once I squeezed inta the iron lung."

"Your hair's all gone."

"Yah. Haven't been able t'pull down a pillar all day."

"You look clean and cute, like one of those sexy cadets. I bet you
broke her heart."

"Well, her pacemaker gained an hour: it's on Central Standard Time
now." Larry laughs. They hug. "That's the femme I know and love. Get
your pants on, we'll buy tires and oil and food. We'll have an all-
American barbecue tonight. Steaks thick as my fungo bat."

"You're without scruples."

"Wombat Eyes, just don't forget who's keeping you in the manner to which—after much hardship and strife—you've had t'become accustomed."

"Yoo-hoo, Mr. Lynxx. Can I make an appearance?"

"Great, just what I need: it's the wailing wall."

Minnie's wide feet plunk down: the feet alone. They seem brown children: they get playful toeholds on each other. A cord is pulled: the lower bunk comes open like some Punch and Judy show. Minnie waves unspecifically: the way parade queens will, hurrying past on a float. Her hair is a questionable achievement. It goes up now, tiara-shaped, as gin rummy hands are held. Two dense strands gift-wrap it in place: a natural bow. Minnie smiles, but chocolate has blacked out one front tooth. The suitcases are empty. Simon adds up her wardrobe: five outfits here, four there, another five slumped on his Movieola. An evening dress bells down from the fresnel rack. Minnie is pleased: she waits for praise.

"So, give me an honest opinion. Is he a Van Cliburn with the hair or isn't he? Right off the bat he got my tint color."

"Wonderful. You look like a six-card flush." Simon has crossed the van. He raps her hip for good luck: bong, bong. "Still got a diving bell for an ass, I see. Found the manufacturer's handbook yet?"

"You've had a drink or two, Mr. Lynxx."

"Larry, run us up t'Fortieth and Skillman. Harvey the Tire King's place." Simon has torn a pink curtain down.

"No—"

"This is my home, you stainless-steel bialy—not suburban Larchmont. And you've got one day, twenty-four hours, t'give me the key t'the city or it's out—you and that bionic behind of yours. Also Balloon Juice, the son. Where is he? I wanna intimidate him."

"He's at work, Mr. Lynxx. Bright and early. Just between us, he's extremely impressed with you. In the flesh you're even bigger than life. He told me last night—how you two boys had a serious man-to-man talk." She plies his arm. "He needs a Big Brother. I tried to hire one for him, but they told me it's only for orphans. His father is always undermining."

"Minnie, did you pick up that note I just left on your call-board or not? Your rent is overdue. And something tells me—mind you, it's probably just a groundless suspicion—something tells me you've been pulling a murphy on the landlord. I mean, how d'you take a dump with that breeches buoy on? Huh? Hanh? Intravenously?"

"I'm not very regular, Mr. Lynxx."

"Regular? Regular? What—do you save it up like a Christmas Club?"

"Look, I'll get the key. Tomorrow I'll get. You're a first-class man, Mr. Lynxx, a sledgehammer of a man. Any girl would be happy to give you a one-night stand or even a two. Just be nice to Robert and—" Minnie starts untying her nightgown front.

"Thanks. I don't accept fixed assets on deposit. Tomorrow. And, dammit, stop cross-dressing my van."

Larry is a prim steerer: the van seems to mince. Simon has sat, taciturn: he'd rather not work today. Above, the closed-circuit TV covers their rear. A block-long past has flashed before/behind Simon's eyes. He will take five, arms logged across his stomach. Blood gets turned off: hands ring and prickle, feeling vibration only. There is a V of brown Ramón makeup on his chest: it aims at the sternum, as if Simon had been sunning in open-necked shirts. A guitar string, tiredness, plucks itself in his left calf. Pupils have lost their good irrigation: his contacts are beached. Listlessly, Simon starts himself up. He plugs an electric razor into the dashboard. A square of tobacco is snapped off. Simon shaves over the wad, stretching out his cheek with it: convenient.

"Uh. We film the 'Journey to Bethlehem' scene t'morrow."

"Are you sure? Where? Not Sheep Meadow again, not without a permit. I won't run with all that heavy equipment again. Last time we had to leave a boom behind and I fell over that stupid extension cord. Right on my tailbone."

"What I'd like—how's this clutch you?—I'd like t'make some subway station into a mass-transit crèche. Have the Three Wise Men get off a D train. There's a donkey, coupla sheep—the usual Catholic zoo—and straw spread all over the platform. Mary with one Milk Dud out. Guardian Angels with red berets all around. Something about those stations. Bare bulbs. The platform edge, it's a stage apron. You ever watch from an express—little tableaux, that's what they are. And when the poles pass superfast they flicker like frames from *The Great Train Robbery*. I always wanted t'arrange a happening down there. Dress all the stations from South Ferry to Van Cortlandt and move the audience on trains."

"Kinky, nice. I'll buy one—mail it in a plain brown wrapper. You've got some head, Sy. That's just what they're like. The very thing."

"Listen, Faunlet, if I had power and rhino—Christ, what this country needs is a cabinet post for fantasy." The van stops: red light. "But back to the pit house of dank reality. Ah—this afternoon, if you feel up to it, whyncha have a look at my ancestral estate? It's not Universal City, but then we're not exactly Bergman and Nykvist, are we? Yet? Don't make that Camptown face, huh? I need support, not a labor-management fault-finding panel. Look, the setup isn't so bad, if we break it into discrete locations and keep them clean. There's the chapel, God's dark discomfort station, we can use it for the temple. The cemetery: well, Gethsemane or Golgotha. The orchard out back: hey, that's not a bad counterpoint—those tacky high rises against a pastoral scene. Give some Spanish omelet a month's supply of D-con, and he'll let us zoom it from his balcony. I know, I know, just stop pouting, hanh? I'm not all grokked up about it either, but we won't haveta give the whole City Council a walk-on if we wanna use it."

"Sy, I'm sorry, there's not the littlest chance you'll catch me near that nasty uncle of yours. I won't come within hailing distance."

"That wasn't my uncle, Candy Pull, that was his pet ape."

"Ape? No, I saw the monkey. The monkey was much smaller and it certainly didn't have a knife."

"That was the pet ape's pet ape."

"Huh?"

"Alf's the security guard: he keeps people from feeling too secure. Don't worry, I'll take care of Alf and Uncle Arthur."

"See, there's Suzy Grant."

She crosses: her privilege: the green light has conferred it, and she doesn't/won't look both ways. Offhand he'd say the 70 percent bracket: already Simon has footed her physical balance sheet up. Long cheekbones: solid credit rating there: a facial deformation evolved in the rich: from looking down at people maybe. He'd know as much from just her skull remains: *Homo dives*. The nose is shorter than her cheek line, which upcurves to seat a deep-lipped, always wet mouth. The straight brunette hair hasn't been done. Here and there a strand is damp where she has caught it to suck. One ear can be seen. She has a plaid skirt on, loafers, a white blouse: the sturdy, simple things that wealth can affect and afford. Her legs are long: made articulate by high heels they would be superb. Languidly, Simon wants. He is curious to see her negotiate the curb. And she goes up with a strong, field-hockey-trained elegance. Women give it all away on the stairs.

"Prime squanch. Suzy who?"

"Grant. You know, Jack 'Baron' Grant's daughter. He owns the whole Texas-Delta pipeline, both ends. I met them at Gordon Kanzinsky's. Grant put up the cash for *Firefly*."

"What? What? Why didn't you say so? Follow her, you silly fap. Turn left, turn! Action stations, thank God I shaved. Where's the audio case?"

"Sy—not the audio case. You smashed my Rangertone last time."

"Head her. Not so fast, give her some play. I knew I smelled something. Money. Big money. I'll chop it out like peat."

Minnie has one hand up, but Simon, a monologist, won't allow questions from the floor. His rehearsal face is plausible and sincere. Minnie has been taken in: thinks Simon is speaking to her. "Jesus, Jesus, Jesus. What have I done now? I just can't believe this. Will you forgive me?" Minnie will forgive: Simon ignores her absolution. "Your poor leg. God, that must have hurt. What a jerk, I just didn't see you coming." Simon has hauled his audio case out: so heavy it growls, crunching grit on the van floor. "I'm a director, you see. I was preoccupied with my new film— not that that's any excuse." Simon swan-dives into a grimy buckskin shirt: comes up for air through the neck. A brush has been dipped in Quik-Set epoxy resin. Simon will butter one edge of the case with it. "What can I do? How can I ever make amends? I feel terrible." He addresses this to Minnie: he practices eye contact and honesty. "Please, let me buy you a drink, dinner? Don't say no. It's the very least I can do."

"Sure, Mr. Lynxx. I wouldn't even mind going Dutch." Minnie ducks. What now? Simon huffing and puffing and blowing her hairdo down.

"Hanh? Huh? How's my breath?"

"Like a gin mill."

"What's this gunk?"

"My hair set. No!" Simon has sprayed aerosol into his mouth. Hmmmm: doesn't taste bad. Larry has turned left again. Simon humps the audio case up front.

"Where is she?"

"There."

"Pull ahead, to the corner. Quick—give me a résumé—what does she like? Straight sex? French? Swedish? Round the world?"

"I've only met her once."

"Hurry up, dammit. Hobbies, politics, favorite brand of vaginal foam—something."

"She skis, I think. Ah. Ah. Yes, she wants to act."

"Ha! Bull's-eye. My ball is stuck in Bonus When Lit. Mary Magdalene —we'll just cut the sandal-fetish scene."

"She's at some snotty girls' college."

"Yeah? But what's she doing in Sunnyside? This is a nouveau poor slum. You sure that's her?"

"I—I think."

"Think? Think, he says. Listen, you strange curtsey, I don't waste my good looks and the proceeds of my imagination on just anyone. This is a time-and-motion study. There's gotta be some profit when I deduct overhead."

"It's her."

"It better be, or I'll go after your polyps with my hors d'oeuvre fork. Pull over. Here. Right here. How do I look, huh?"

"Your eyes are red and puffy. Fix your cowlick. Sy, be careful—not too hard—Zaza Gulbenkian is still on crutches."

"Serves her right. All I asked was she should put her mother in a nursing home, so we could sell the old upper plate's Dakota pad. Was that too much, huh? But no: the selfish klootch wouldn't do it. Okay. Wish me good luck and break a leg. Hers. Three, two—wait. What's her name again?"

"Suzy Grant."

"Grant. Grant. Unconditional surrender. Got it. Banzai!"

Simon lists. Full, which it is, his audio case can weigh more than forty pounds. Countdown: they're half a block apart and closing. Her walk seems destination-less, unheeding. A victim, that's what: Simon knows one when he sees one. Her shoulders are rangy and boyish. With small breasts: good: the rich don't go in for ornate, large settings. Simon notes pedestrian traffic around the newsstand. He changes hands: he'll smart-bomb her in the passing lane. A guide dog lies, dog-tired, on its private four square feet of shag rug. Simon has slowed, has stopped. She puts coins in: he can hear the clank. They know each other, this girl, this blind man. They are cordial: she must pass him often. Simon, for a moment, doubts. Could be Mr. Pipeline has cut her off. But now, right on time, she heads outside, away from the newsstand. He'll have her cold against parked cars. Simon, a fire-and-forget warhead, corrects for speed, for trajectory. Her knees are athletic: game-playing knees: one has been scarred. A horse bite probably and that, for better or worse, commits him. Ten feet. Five. Stand by to ram: one. Simon has averted his look. It's vulgar, in poor taste, to aim when you clout someone with a forty-pound metal case.

"Shit—oh! Shit—ohhh! You—unnng."

"My God. Oh, my God. My God, God. Are you all right? Christ, this is terrible. God-o-God!"

"Unnnng. Ah-unnng."

A shin splint: one of life's four or five most exquisite, trivial pains. She has been folded in half. Limber, Simon thinks: she can touch her toes. Long hair closes over the face: a white nape is left to his mercy. Simon checks out the dewcup of one ear. He sees translucent, amber wax and wouldn't mind having a taste. Her hands flock around knee and calf but won't touch: don't try to move the patient. Simon, meanwhile, is sneak-previewing her cleavage: where the material has bulged out between blouse buttons. A gold cross just inside. Datum received: better curse in some other faith.

"You. Uh-uh-uh. Please let it stop." She comes erect, but pain has frostbitten through her shank. Sensation goes and, with it, balance. Simon is glad to steady her. For a moment, made impolite by pain, she will clutch his not-properly-introduced arm. Then helplessness irks her: she pushes off.

"Allah—I'm a clumsy fool. I can't tell you how sorry I am. Look, let me give you a hand."

"I'll manage for myself, thanks. I can walk— Oh, no. What? What's on there? Get it off." Her leg has moved for the first time. But pantihose, two inches of it, is glued flat to Simon's case. Material stretches out: but the Quik-Set epoxy will quikly hold. "Get it off. Get it off me. No—don't touch there. What is it, why won't it come off? Oh, God."

"I can't understand this. Why do things like this always happen t'me?"

Simon smacks one open palm. "Look, what can I do? I'm afraid I'll rip your stocking. Moses and Aaron, this comes of being so preoccupied, thinking about my new film. I'm a director, you know. The pressure. I wouldn't wish it on a basset hound." Simon pulls, but with simulated force. "Crikey, it's stuck on like a process server. And you're bleeding. Look at that." Look, indeed. Simon admires it: one of his best cheap shots. "I wanna die. Just die. Die."

"Please. Won't it come off? Stop, that hurts. Uh, uh, uh. I can't put any weight on my toes."

"Wait, don't yank. You'll rip it. Here. Let's not panic. Strong minds will prevail. What say we back over to that car? So you can rest. When I lift the case, just sort of shuffle backwards."

She accepts this auto-suggestion. Together they fetch and carry, slide-limp, slide-limp, to a green Oldsmobile. One bent arm will L-bracket her against its fender. The head is pitched back: the Adam's cute apple valves saliva down: a sun-taking pose. Pain has etiolated her skin. The mouth is to be valued and Simon does: a sea creature's lips, wide and soft and chapped slightly raw: the price she will always pay for their moistness. Her teeth gnaw. After a blink two tears are made: they lounge, self-contained as drops of mercury, on her upper-middle-class cheeks. Simon gives a free, no obligation, estimate of her legs: good, even table grade. Blood has come through pantihose. The scrape is ugly and irregular: TEAR ALONG DOTTED LINE. Quick H & R Block audit: rings, none: no jewelry of the sort one remembers men by. Her plaid skirt is held together by a five-inch safety pin. It's plated gold at best. Simon checks the blouse label: Lord & Taylor: okay, but not what you'd call conclusive.

"Is this—pardon the question—is this a stocking?"

"Pantihose. Please hurry: I feel ill. I want to go home. Now."

"Guess you couldn't sort of shrug them off—"

"Here? In the street? No, I couldn't. God, you must be insane."

"No. But see—if I pull hard here—" She has leaned forward. A tear flops out and, on its tide, a contact lens.

"Shit. I think I've—yes, yes, dammit. I've lost a contact lens. Can you see? I think it fell by the tire. Be careful with your big feet, don't step on it. God, and I haven't renewed my insurance."

"Relax. You're in capable hands. I wear them, too. See." Simon holds a lid up and—blip—artfully pops one of his own. "Nuts. Nuts. Now I've done it."

"What?" There is mucus, a nice pearl, under her nose. "What?"

"Boy, aren't we a pair? You know what I just did? I popped my own. Now nobody move." Simon goes down, knees together, as women in mini-skirts bend over. Their two lenses have overlapped on the pavement.

Simon holds them, sunny-side up, against the Sunnyside sky. "Was yours tinted, I hope?"

"No."

"Mine neither. How can we tell them apart?"

"Oh, for heaven's sake." She has bammed the car hood. "Well." Bam. "Well." Bam. "Put it in your eye."

"Not so easy. Which one? Trial and error, that wouldn't be hygienic. I had conjunctivitis last week. Eyes are your most precious possession. Look, what I have in mind, let me call a cab and take you home. Wait—don't say no. Think of how lousy I feel. This is a disaster. And let me buy you dinner tonight, soon's I finish filming. Eight o'clock?"

"Sorry. I don't go out with strangers. And I live right over there."

"You do? How lucky." But Simon is dejected. A sullen five-story building: CHECKS CASHED at the storefront level. Two chipped cement Atlases hold up the door lintel: they look undependable, sly: you can't get decent servants anymore. A broken third-floor pane has been patched with cardboard and shipping tape. VERSAILLES ARMS it says, laughably. A mongoloid child is squatting on one sill, face watersick and out of proportion, surprised, surprised, surprised by—never used to—cars passing below. A building on very fixed income.

"Just rip it off. Please. It doesn't matter."

"Darn. I promise you—a dozen pair, the best. I'll have one of my go-fers deliver them personally."

"Don't talk so much. Rip it."

"Hang on. Here goes nothing."

Her eyes are squelched shut: cute. Simon edges the audio case away. An inch: a half inch more. Her shin is small, not wider than his forearm: blood has bound the pantihose to it. Simon puts one hand behind her calf. It bunches, the muscle ashamed to be caught slack, and this fleet contraction turns him on. "Up. Up," she says: a groan, not a preposition. Simon means to be tender, but the material has shameless elasticity: it will give six inches. And, in no time, Simon is impatient. He bats her leg around. "Up! Up!" The pantihose shreds, harsh in its coming off as a weekold Band-Aid. New blood. Released, she tries to walk at once, but bone soreness has paralyzed her leg below the knee. Simon balusters his arm beneath her elbow. She is little: she can't jerk him off. There are sparkly hairs above her wrist. The armpit, his hand has slid up to it, is hot, moist with pain's special sweat.

"I can manage."

"Don't be proud. I know my place-mat-sized face must seem loathsome t'you right now. But I'm really a great guy. Please lemme help you upstairs."

"I can manage. I can. Manage."

Her lips finish: licked and sealed. Sheeze, now Simon has another worry. The rich are never, never this attractive: pure loveliness is gauche, darling, *so* overdone. Take that upper lip. Her upper lip is a prodigy: it has more surface than her lower lip, unheard of in women. It fans up: he can't remember a mouth with such aptitude for sensual sharps and flats. At this moment they, Simon and she, each have one eye squinted, both the left. Simon hams up his squint: he'd like her to see humor in their situation. She resists: already she has unhitched herself from his arm. And, as she moves away, pantihose threads fly out from her shin: a spider web burst by some rowdy wasp. The hole runs from instep to knee. Simon will follow. Pieces clank in his audio case: uh-oh, damage again. The front stoop is difficult, yet—even limping—her hand tucks skirt in/against one buttock. No free shows going up: the rich are stingy that way. Training. Training. Simon still has reservations, but this is certainly a better sign. He waits just behind. A cement funeral urn, empty, on the railing: it is five feet high, deep enough even for his great last residue of ash. Now she has unlocked the street door. In her dark lobby, Simon speed-reads a mailbox row, Grant, Grant, Grant, Grant, Grant—no puck in the net: shutout: big 0.

"Stop following me. Please."

"Can't help it—my Christian upbringing. When I was so-high, they put me on the altar guild."

"Oh? Really? The altar guild? How precocious."

"Hell, you should see me snuff a candle. That kinda thing—well, it sticks with you. Do unto others—I feel responsible f'you. Heck, I am responsible." Simon has let the audio case down. "A walk-up? Well, at least you won't have t'tip the elevator man come Christmastime. What floor?"

"That is my business."

"Oh, how wrong you are. Look at that leg. You're walking like a lame excuse. I mean, on you it's very becoming, but—hey, listen, I don't blame you, we've just met. You don't know what kinda post-hole digger you're stuck with. But you gotta first-chop surprise coming. Oh, yes. I don't cop out, my little quiche lorraine. When I make a mess, I roll up my bell-bottoms and swab it up. Come now. What floor?" His intensity and a shin guard of ache defeat her. Lips unseal themselves, seal. They let a sigh pass. They say,

"Fifth."

"Fifth. Is your mind in neutral? Fifth? You can't, can't hike it up five flights."

"I can."

"Discussion period is over. I'm carrying you up."

"No. Don't touch me."

"It comes with your Blue Cross policy. You've got extended coverage—me. Ahh—gotcha. Up. Hey, no hitting. No hitting."

"Put me down, you great ox."

"Go limp, for God's sake. I'm listing. Yes, your finger was in my giant nostril. Use brown soap and it won't fall off."

"Would you at least not move your hand on my hips like that?"

"Sorry, just getting some purchase."

"Thank you." No girdle: filed and noted. Her buttocks are larger than you'd think: unexpected prize money.

"Hand, please. Hand. Hold our lenses. Careful. Good girl. In case you wondered: this store-door delivery is being provided by Simon Lynxx— the complete service man. Two exes on Lynxx. Perhaps you've heard the name." Silence. "Charmed to make your acquaintance as well. Don't be scared, I may be a bit batchy, but I'm strong." Simon starts to climb. "Hey. This is pleasant. You're light as a cutpurse's touch. Haven't— haven't I met you before somewhere?"

"I don't think so. This is my first broken shin."

"Hard to believe. I have a great eye for faces and you, my tiny side order of spaetzle, you have a great face. That, by the way, isn't just shameless flattery. Faces. They're an occupational occupation with us directors. We directors. We directors? Wait. Aanhh. It comes to me: Gordon Kanzinsky's pad. Am I right?"

"Would you please not grip my knee so tightly? I can't feel my toes."

"You say please a lot. You're very polite." She lounges, untractable and hammocked. Arms, in a crisscross over her chest, imitate another bustline. Elbows are B cup 42's: breasts beneath them are 32, 33 at the outside. She'd be more secure with one arm around his neck, but that might be mistaken for an intimacy. "There. Four flights t'go. Pretty smooth, huh? I ride like a Mercedes-Benz."

"I just hope you haven't fractured anything."

"A bone bruise, that's all. I've got it down to a science. I mean, don't worry, ten days and you'll be able t'ski good as ever. Well as ever."

"Is that so? Interesting."

"I ski, too. Davos. Sugarcube. Vail. Aspirin. Maybe I've seen you there: we might've shared a mogul together. Two down, three left."

"I can make it from here."

"Out of the question. I finish what I start. I'm the gentleman of the moving industry, haven't you heard my commercials on the radio?"

"I think you're a lunatic. And there's alcohol on your breath."

"Just pray some cop doesn't pull us over. We were shooting a crowd scene yesterday. Hellish, like putting smithereens back into their original smither. Whoa. Pant. Gasp. This should be an event in the decathlon. You a film fan? Direction. It's like playing chess with three kings, just that much more t'get checkmated. Locations, plot, dialogue, imagery, camera angles. And actors. I hate actors. Yesterday my Mary Magdalene quit. Uh—as you may have guessed—it's a religious film. I feel deeply about these things."

"I'm sure. And what is your film called? *The Altar Guild?*"

"Ha-ha. No. *The Three Commandments:* it's low-budget. I've gotta dig up a new Magdalene by tomorrow. Four, we're on the homestretch now. These halls're dark: d'you live here by preference? I mean this place'd even exacerbate good things. It's a shame you don't act. With those lips, people'd pay five bucks just t'see you eat an avocado. As they say, I could get you in films, kid. Aargh. Where are we? Seems like you've put on weight since I met you."

"5D. Over there. Let me down."

5D is a bummer: two dim, overcast rooms. Dampness has egged on the sour and mattressy smell of wood rot. It's an old, high-ceilinged apartment. The kind, Simon reflects, that might lead you to think that some taller species, now long extinct, was common in New York four decades ago. Such rooms never seem furnished: to seem furnished they'd need chairs and tables six feet up. Simon has made a debit-side face. Maybe the Texas-Delta pipeline doesn't *go* anywhere. She limps left, toward her kitchen—and without so much as an apology for the below-his-subsistence-level living quarters. Simon is ticked off: how to explain this complacent poverty? After all, he has invested time and foot-pounds, not to mention the clanking in his audio case. Disappointment will bring on hunger. Simon snaps a Frito of paint from her wall. Crunchy: no wonder little black children like them. A shy roach goes on the lam under her refrigerator. The refrigerator starts up: whrmmm: maybe he was the chief engineer. Worn linoleum has recorded walking-years: from stove to sink to table: housework in an isosceles triangle. Wall over the stove is furry with grease and dirt. Simon keeps an eye, his right, on her: guileless, lovely at the sink. Rich hair, brown as a polished Steinway, will nag her cheek: she scolds it aside. One shoe off, then the other. New shortness has made her seem more lush: SOME SETTLING MAY OCCUR IN TRANSPORT. Well, just so it shouldn't be a total loss, Simon wants.

"What you need is a stiff one. Where's the liquor closet?"

"I don't drink."

"Not even some lady brew like maraschino anisette de menthe? Something so sweet bees commit suicide in it?"

"Mr. Lynxx—"

"No cooking sherry? How d'you make veal piccata?"

"Mr. Lynxx—"

"Simon."

"Simon. As soon as we ascertain which lens is which—I'm going to say goodbye." She has stoppered the sink. Her hair cavorts: goes too far this time. A rubber band is available. She ties it off: tourniquets it: a rough ponytail. The ears appeal to Simon: things small and intricate that you might find on a goldsmith's bench. They are pierced, but she has no earrings on.

"Cute. Wholesome, is what. You look like a truck-stop princess with your hair that way. The queen of CB radio." No answer. "You won't believe this—but when we first met I thought you were a platinum blonde. No kidding. It was only on the way up I realized that your hair was brown. I mean, you're so damned beautiful, I couldn't even *see* you. I was like a rabbit caught in the glare of someone's headlight." No answer. She has washed their lenses off. "Hey, dummy. I'm appreciating you. Say something. Say: Thank you, Simon."

"Very good." She applauds. "You're very good. Just don't get any on the floor."

"Have a heart, huh? I know I've come into your life kinda sudden—like a cliff diver in Acapulco, splash!—but it was an accident. Could happen t'anyone with a forty-pound case and the reflexes of a house plant. Smile. Heck, I'll make it up t'you. We'll dance. We'll sing. We'll eat à la carte. We'll—"

"We'll say goodbye."

"That's not fair. Give me time, I haven't had the chance t'make a really bad impression yet. Hanh—I see by your neck you're supposed t'be a Christian. Some Christian. Some happy warrior. Meek, mild, forgiving: saintly. Oh, one was a doctor, and one was a priest and one got her shin bent and creased—"

"You're forgiven. Just shut up." She has made a sign of the cross. Simon examines this gesture with some natural skepticism. It doesn't appear ironic. "Now, do you want to test lenses first or should I?"

"You better. Better I should get your germs. My germs are terrible. They work out with weights. They have little lats."

"Oh. I hate these things." A lens is at ready on her forefinger tip: like an octopus sucker, round. The tip shudders, loss of optic nerve, as it zeros in. Two, one, contact. She stares at Simon: rheumy, the good right eye shut. "No. I don't think this is mine." She tweaks the lens out. "Here. No, wait— Use. Ah." Simon has slam-jammed it in. His eye-disrespect makes her squint.

"Nope. Yours. Pardon the intimacy. I've never gotten into a woman's contact lens before. I feel like a transvestite."

"But it can't be. It can't be. You're just saying that. You want to confuse me."

"One libel after another. I walk up five flights and I'm in the McCarthy era. Go on—you're so smart—try the other one."

"God. Do I have to? If you knew how I loathe—" And this time her pupil can't watch: it flinches to one side. The lens is off-centered: it squibs up/under her lid. "Ohhh. Shit. Get me a mirror. Get me a mirror. There's one in my bag."

"This way. This way. No, you can't exit through the icebox. Right: calm down. That's a girl. Simon, the big eye man, is here. Chin up now: in both senses of the word." Eye pain has induced a hyperventilation: her breasts swell, dispell: each itself like a small air sac. In this at least she will trust him. "Big coward. Roll your lid up. Say 'Ahhh.' Make a nice orb for me. Come on, you poltroon, I'm losing patience. Women. Up. Up. There's the little freshman beanie. I see him. Steady now. Goal!" The lens has hop-skipped on. She sees: she sighs. Simon kisses her upthrust, vulnerable mouth. Those lips, rich, deep as never-tilled prairie soil, the Central Plains of her, take him down and down and—kranggg! A howling slap. His left ear revs up, thrumming: some rotary engine.

"You cheap son of a bitch."

"I saw that. You hesitated. There's a chance for me. It wasn't an instinctive thing. You don't hate me."

"I do. Oh, I do. And I didn't hesitate. I just wanted to hit you harder. I was winding up, you big lout. Go on. Get out of my house. I'll call the police on you."

"I can't. You've got my lens."

"I don't—"

"Take a look." She blinks. "Open your eye. That'd help."

"It's. It's. Oh, now I'm crying again. I can't see a thing. My eye hurts. My leg hurts. My head hurts."

"Damn, we've got the same vision. Compatible, that's what: we're both half blind. Ha! D'you have a strawberry birthmark? Huh? Hanh?"

"Keep away from me."

But Simon is dancing. Da-d'jah, da-de-dah and a jah. It frightens: it engrosses. And this isn't a performance: this isn't even for her: pleasure— sensual and private—has taken Simon as its protégé. She has never seen anyone make himself/herself so resplendently grotesque: on purpose. The dance is a voucher of Simon's irrefutable self-assurance: were she that sort, she might be jealous. Oh, he pouts: he shouts: he flouts. The kitchen floor will dither as Simon begins a great flamingo-legged strut. His face is hot Halloween: eyebrows wig and wag: Cab Calloway teeth come out. Below, someone clangs the plumbing with a heavy spoon. Simon bucks and wings—one wave, one hand-juddery salute—then off/through her living room: to dance out his keen appraisal of the furniture. Sofa: lumpish, old, badly couched. Table: it wears a build-up shoe, a brick, under one leg. Easy chair: weak arms spread out as if to say, Sooo big. There's a fish tank, high and dry. The TV has no picture tube. On it, ceremonial portraits of Mr. and Mrs. Grant. Simon does a turn for their benefit: ah-ja, ah-ja. Ja. Ja. Ja. They look loaded, but formal photographs have given him the runaround before. A modest bookcase: Bible, concordance, St. Augustine, Bonhoeffer, Merton, Tillich, Law. Pipes clang again: Simon tries to work their rhythm in. He has acquitted her of poverty. Now it seems some kind of affectation: only the rich can afford to be poor.

"What is this? What? Do you want money: is that it? I have two five-dollar bills in my purse." She sits, but on the sofa edge, her legs locked under: set for a drag-race start. "You won't go. I can see that. You'll be here forever."

"No, ma'am. Da—d'jah. I'll go. I'm a très busy man. But first—when do I see you again? How's about tomorrow night? Hanh? I'm holding your peace and quiet ransom for a definite commitment." He sits in the armchair: prooing! A sharp spring comes through. "What have we here? A home hemorrhoidectomy?" He shoves the spring back. "What kinda line of business you in? Huh? And, if so, whyncha at the office doing it? I mean, y'must haveta work at least three hours a week t'keep yourself in such style."

"Uh, I'm in . . . clerical—clerical work. Part-time. Look, are you sure this isn't my lens?"

"Yup. We have the same magnification, but a different shape. I can feel yours putting a cervical collar on my cornea." He pops it out. "Mine are big as high-hat cymbals. You could bang them together and seven trumpeters'd come in on cue. Big and beady. Not almond-shaped like yours and soft as purple bolsters."

"I give up. I can't feel any difference. Here." They trade. Simon's hand will intimidate her. His thumb pad is chunky, a fat pincushion. Nicotine on the fingertips and, on the back, brown makeup base. A hand for waylaying.

"I see from your bookshelf that you're serious about the faith of Christ crucified." Time for Simon to witness: to detox his image. "I like that in women. My Uncle Arthur is a priest."

"Yes. And it isn't my custom to have strange men in here."

"Strange? Strange, little Dew Point? After what we've been through? We've shared more pain than Siamese twins connected at the retina. That's friendship at least." He leers. Then his face will rest: off-duty, it is handsome: she has to give him that.

"Look, Simon. Let me appeal—this is a good one—let me appeal to your better nature. I've been under heavy pressure for the last few months—"

"Yah? Hah? What's up? Tell me. There's nothing I relish more than someone else's misery. Tell me. Go on. A boyfriend? He's married? He's about to be deported? He's only potent in a tutu and ballet slippers?"

"No. No, but that's another thing. I'm taking a vacation from men. The entire species. I'm trying to get my head together."

"Look, the guy was a jerk. A real summer repeat. He didn't deserve you. I know the type. Probably, when he dies, someone else's life'll pass before his eyes."

"Wait. Wait. Simon, let me be frank— I . . . Well, I don't think I can stand very much more of you." Her hand pokes at the coffee table: is called back. "You're a very interesting person. And ha-ha funny. It's just I'm not a good audience right now. And the noise level: I feel I'm sitting too close to the orchestra."

"Me, I'm a counter-irritant. Just think how silent the silence'll be when I'm gone. Ah—Mom and Dad look like substantial bourgeois folk. It's nice here and all—no offense—but how come your couch needs twelve weeks with a good chiropractor? I mean, just nosy. Dad and you—the Electra complex not what it used t'be?"

"Dad and I are fine. I just don't believe in sponging. I'm twenty-eight and—"

"No. I don't believe it." He really doesn't. "Twenty-eight? You don't look a day past the Roman Polanski limit."

"Thank you. I've been on my own a long time. I like it. This happens to be all I can afford right now. It's enough."

"Tomorrow night?"

"I don't think so."

"Why? Let's guess. Twenty-eight and unmarried. Ah, so—you prefer women. Look, it's okay with me. I'll pick you up in a Mother Hubbard. No, you pick me up. I can pass. I'll order a glass of white wine with ice when we get there and then I'll go freshen up for half an hour."

"That mouth of yours. It's horrid. So many big teeth. Why are they brown?"

"I chew tobacco."

"Yes. Of course. I should have guessed." Her hand jerks down again.

"Go on—take a butt. I won't think you're a flatbacker for it. You've been playing prisoner's base with that cigarette box since we sat down. Let your hand come a long way, baby. Gimme one, too."

"Oh, dammit: yes. I'm not supposed to have one until three o'clock. But: yes. And please, when you finish, it's time to go." Simon at your service. The match blurts alive just a half inch from her face. "God, you scare me. Your hands and legs, they never stop."

"Listen, Cherry Tomato, when they're building settlements all over your left bank, well, y'tend t'get a little brash and hyperactive. I'm running. I'm running. I wake up sometimes with both fists clenched: it hurts me t'open them." Simon has his first inhale: it consumes one-third of the Marlboro. "Nonetheless and all considering, I'm one of the nicest tomb-robbers you'll ever come across. What I need, I need someone t'spring my great maleness from the violent ward. Jane Eyre and Rochester—you know. Tame him: cut off his hand and blind one eye if you haveta, but

make him a useful citizen. Hell, where's your feminine instinct? Don't
you wanna domesticate me?"

"It hadn't crossed my mind."

"Who was this churl, anyway? Is? The one with the tutu. Where'd you
meet him: at some inter-denominational mixer in a Unitarian church
basement?" She laughs: not at what he has said: an inside joke. Simon
hates that, being left out: he crashes inside jokes. "I'm right? I'm
wrong?"

"There's no man. Or woman. Give it up, my friend. You could never understand."

"Try me. I'm pretty cunning. A genius, in fact. Right now I'm not too
flush: happens a Sanhedrin of Jewish torpedoes just booked passage f'me
on the *Andrea Doria*. But great men—like rare spices—smell best after
they've been crushed." Then, *moderato cantabile*. "Please. Trust me. I
can understand."

"No. Worse, you'd laugh. And I'm not up to that right now."

Her legs rise, fold in, an undercarriage going up: deer-slim ankles accept the weight. His smoking, even that is a grandstand play. Simon will
send big, rubbery smoke hoops at her: unsigned copies of his big, rubbery mouth. She will give him no attention back. Sinuses are turgid.
Once or twice she will snort: her whole body takes the rifle-kick of it. By
this time Simon has watched her in poses enough, under enough stress,
to know that this is someone who will never not be beautiful. It delights
him. He'd like to see her eat, sleep, climb trees, run or pratfall: see her
bald, sunburned, with glasses on or in great pain. Yet she dashes his
spirit: sad. Simon doesn't much care for sad people. This sadness, on the
other hand, seems large and eccentric, and he will make a concession for
large and eccentric things: one lodge brother to another, you might say.
The nose is short, as if in deference to that brassy upper lip below. Her
chin has a chamfered dimple. Front teeth overlap: perfect, though they
flaunt an imperfection. Few women are cute and beautiful at once, the
words exclude each other. And yet she is lonely: it comes off her like
fumes. Lonely: but beautiful women are lonely by hard and conscious
effort. He permits himself to be intrigued.

"Can I ask a personal question?"

"I suppose. I may not answer."

"Where's the head?"

"Oh—couldn't you go in a restaurant or something?"

"Jesus, some Christian. I'll lift the seat. This it? Yes? What a crabby
face—cheer up, just because I use your john, doesn't mean y'have t'get a
rabbit test."

"Go. Go. I'm sorry."

"I should hope."

Her bathroom is close: the humidity of some recent showering has been preserved inside. Simon wrenches one faucet on: the noise will cover for his U-2 reconnaissance. A bathroom, in Simon's experience, can be a rich, concise biography. But he won't find Grant, Suzy, here. Too clean: not even that ubiquitous stalagmite of toothpaste beneath the brush holder. A cat box, pristine, unclawed, waits just under her sink. Two combs: the single evidence of cosmetic repair. Simon has check-listed her medicine cabinet for firm coital evidence: no punch-out card of contraceptive pills: no douche: no Vaseline. Her shower curtain has been jerked shut around the tub. Aimless now, Simon blaps it aside. Hanh. What? A priest's collar and a drip-dry black dickey hang from the shower head. Simon has been cuckolded: damn, always the last to know. He fires out at her bathroom door, both elbows up: an expert pass block.

"You didn't flush—"

"I'll flush, you four-flusher. Religious, my flong. You're living in Greater Gomorrah here with a priest. Oh, what a nifty setup: one end sins for you, the other end forgives. Just hit the backspace key and, type, it's self-corrected. Cheap, convenient: the Freddie Laker of sin he must be. Those books—they're all his, right? Right? And that mortician's outfit in the bog? Father, forgive me, I know not how t'do it." Simon assumes a pose: disappointed, severe. "And t'think I trusted you."

"I don't have to listen—"

"Just a minute. I'm looking for Friar Tuck's cigar butts."

"I can't—." She laughs: the sound is bogus. "I can't believe this. What right have you—?"

"Well, and what about me? What about eager, honest, stupid Simon? Imagine the melted-out feeling I got—no man, she says, no woman—and then I come across that formal wear in the shower. My organ bank defaulted right there. Hanh. Huh? Go on. Try t'explain. I wanna hear this."

"I don't have to explain anything."

"Brassy, aren't we? Oh, there's no substance, no heart left in this permissive society: it's like a BHT diet, all additive and no food."

"Listen. Shut up. I'll tell you." She has signaled him to the armchair. Simon sits: in judgment and used!

"It better be good. Damn spring just got me in the old cowabunga."

"That stuff in there. You probably won't believe this—and I probably wish you wouldn't—but . . ."

"But . . . Yah?"

"But . . ." She hums. She is uncertain. Then the upper lip unfolds, out: a smile so vivacious that, despite his resolution, Simon has to answer it. As yawns answer yawns: deep in the cortex. "I've known this guy since I was three. Our families shared the same driveway. Out in Jersey: we went to kindergarten, elementary, high school together. He has a parish in Boston now. And a wife, also from the old neighborhood, and two children. He went to Union: he still has a lot of friends here in the city. When he comes down, about twice a year, he stays at my pad, place." She has lit another cigarette. "He left his equipment here last July. I'll be damned if I'll get up the postage to send it back. So: satisfied now? I should've let you think the worst of me. But that's not my nature. I don't tease."

"Ummm. A likely story. Cost you a cigarette to get it straight without laughing: I saw that. Hell, whadda I care? Women go big for guys in uniform. Sex: I guess that's what they mean by 'the modern tithe.' Ah, well. Don't worry. I can stand the competition."

"Oh, can you?"

"I can. But I guess you think—given the length of our engagement— you think I've got no right t'be jealous. Well, maybe I have some news for you." His voice is *adagio* now, but still *cantabile*. "You may not realize this, Suzy, but I've had my eye on you for a long time."

"Suzy?"

"Uh-huh. Surprised? You may wonder how I know your name."

"You don't know my name. My name is Merry."

"Jesus, that queer. I knew it. Aaargh! I'll punch holes in his enema bag, that's what I'll do. God. Expect him t'tell the difference between two women: I must be outa my globe. Aaargh!" Simon has mugged himself: clouting, strangling: his money or his life. "Time? What time is it? Nearly noon. A whole morning leaked away. Heh—" Simon poker-faced: he raises her a smile: then folds. "I trust your shin is feeling better. Merry, was it?"

"Merry Allen."

"Yes, a pleasant name. Not too apt, but—" Simon molds a box out of the air, puts air things in it. Packing to go. "Well. My sincere apologies—"

"Wait. You. I. I see it now. You thought I was someone else. All that rigmarole. Dancing around. My eye—" Merry flings her pillow down. "You son of a bitch."

"No. It wasn't like that. Not exactly. Sure you don't have anything t'drink? Doesn't Father Whatsis leave any consecrated dregs around? Well. You haveta understand my position. I'm on an ice floe, Merry, and my particular cake is getting smaller every day. The power of compound subtraction. I'm desperate. Believe me. Otherwise I'd never have hit you in—in—"

"My God. He did it on purpose. He *aimed*."

"Well." Simon is clinical. "Y'gotta admit it's one hell of an audience warmer."

"Sick. That's what you are. Sick and dangerous."

"Gee. I hate people who hold a grudge. Listen, Merry, I think you're a first edition. No bull: at least a ninety-six on my peter meter. Business is business, but, who knows—if my schedule wasn't so pucker-tight—maybe I'd have whacked you one out of sheer good-naturedness and lust. Instead of sheer, heinous greed. Uh. Daddy, I take it, doesn't own an oil pipeline?"

"Is that what Suzy's father owns, you sadistic bastard?"

"So I was led t'believe by a usually reliable source whose grapes I will harvest in about half an hour."

"What does this Suzy look like?"

"How do I know? She must be really something, though. After all, he mistook her for you."

"Oh, aren't we smooth? Too bad we didn't do our homework."

"No, what it was— I should've trusted my nose. I've been in this zone of fire long enough." He thinks back. "When I saw you crossing the street, my first reaction was: great slice of head cheese, but not big money. Not old money. I mean, just look at you. Legs and arms all scrunched up. The cigarette. Your shoulders, they're rounded, probably because that charming thirty-three-inch bust has been preying on your mind since sixth-grade gym class. Now real money—there's a kinda self-confidence that comes with real money—in the second generation anyhow. So I'm flat-chested, so what, Daddy'll buy me some breasts. Oh, your father's comfortable enough, I'd guess sixty, seventy-five grand, professional money. Doctor, lawyer, CPA. Right?"

"Lawyer."

"Um. Tell you the truth, I'm down t'the tobacco threads in my pocket. I mean, panhandlers on Houston Street snub me: they're afraid I'll drive off their regular clientele. This film. Ah, Dad wouldn't be interested in—"

"He thinks films are degenerate."

"Ah, recognition at last. Well, we try our best." Simon up: urged on by the insistent spring. "Gotta keep moving. Gotta make the supeenee pushers work."

"So tomorrow night is off?" This is addressed, through smoke, to her high ceiling. She has lit another cigarette.

"Tomorrow night?"

"Oh, just go."

"Hold on. Sure. Right. God knows I owe you that much at least. And a dozen pantihose. But, now I think of it, tomorrow night—" Simon plucks his tongue: tick-tick. "How about we—"

"Thanks anyhow, I don't need your charity."

"Well, there's this big problem. Sooner or later we have to face it."

"Do we? And what's that?"

"Merry . . . shall we be candid, you and me? Right now you're this far"—Simon presents thumb and forefinger: not much daylight between them—"this far from falling in love with me."

"You—you've got the almighty gall—"

452

"Uh-uh. Uh-uh. Let's be honest." Simon zooms in: his body, its closeness, exhausts her. "Ten minutes after I leave, you'll start lighting the
filter ends of your cigarettes. You'll blow kisses into the closet. I recognize all the symptoms and, Muslin Eyes, I've had this territory for a long
time."

"I could laugh. He thinks he's irresistible."

"Hey, ding-a-ling, that's the whole point. I do. And I am. If I didn't, I
wouldn't be. I'm Homo Robustus. All teeth and opposable thumbs: take,
take, eat, eat. Selfishness is compelling. Be gross, be violent, be cruel—
yah, and be gentle now and then for a change-up. Women love it. You'd
love it."

"I'm not listening. For your sake. I'm embarrassed for you."

"Also, I've got compunctions, there's something wrong with you. I
smell sickness. I bet cats and dogs avoid you. You're on the rebound from
someone or something and it's a four-wall shot." He drops just one kiss on
her forehead. "You're ripe. I don't wanna hurt you."

"That's a hot one."

"Any more—God—than I have already."

"You won't hurt me, mister." She can't say it to his eyes. "I'll bust your
chops before you bust mine."

"Wow. That was brave." He laughs. He tugs her ponytail. "Suppose
we make it tomorrow night."

"No."

"That's sensible."

"I'm working nights." He has to lean in: her voice is humiliated, low.
"How about the zoo? Central Park, by the polar bear cage. In the afternoon."

"Afternoons are rough. Daylight is running short. Can't make it 'til
Friday. Two, two-thirty. It's a date. I should be outa film by then."

"I may not be there."

"Nor me. In either case we'll understand. Unless, of course, we both
don't show up—and then we'll always wonder. Ha? Who goes?" Someone
has knocked. Little, testy raps: doled out. "I'll get it."

"No. Let me."

"Too late." Simon has opened and—speak of the Devil—there's a priest
at Merry's door. "Hey, it's the Boston shuttle himself. Come in, Father,
come in. Sure and your laundry's ready. No starch in the collar."

"Sir?"

"Don't mind me, I've just been making Merry."

"Sir?"

"Tim—" Her limp to the door is meant as a distraction, but no one,
nothing, upstages Simon Lynxx. "Tim—this kind man helped me home
when I fell."

"Lying to a man of the dark cloth: shame. That'll run you one Hail

Mary and fifteen wind sprints. Truth is, Tim: I hit her in the prayer bone with a forty-pound equipment case. Don't make her kneel t'kiss your ring. Or anything else."

"Merry. Just what is this?"

Just what it is, is Simon going down the stairs. They boom: there will be repercussions: in her doorknob, in Tim's hand on the wall. And a whoop, a bellow, a roar that, megaphoned by five flights of hollow stairwell, is shout therapy on loan to the world. Five levels up, a silent woman has opened her mouth: to assume some of it.

1

It's Lawrence of Bayside: Simon in his Sunday-best burnoose. The Van Lynxx Chapel doors, fourteen feet high, are opened out. Before them, for them, Simon affects a trig and maiden air, lots of flung sleeve: Peter O'Tooleing around. He loves to mum in thin, loose dress: his skin, humid and slippery, feels extra-nude beneath. He can recall Bettina's puff-a-billy vaporizer and the sheet tent she strung up for a naked, nose-stopped five-year-old. Simon is beat. Remember, he hasn't slept in thirty-three hours, not since sex-ed period yesterday for Miss Williams' fifth-grade class. Now, as though they were a daily comic strip, Simon will reread the twelve bronze door panels done in bas-relief. It all comes back to him: Genesis, Chapter 22: Abraham and his son, Isaac, in death's ready-room. Whistle. Time out. Coach Yahweh wants to make a substitution: Abraham in foul trouble. Lower right, panel #12, a ram well-done to stay is on the grill: sheep not separated from scapegoats here: sweet leg of lamb in God's unvegetarian nostril. Simon is hungry. And—fumpf!—behind him, beyond the Spirit of Radio, beyond the rose garden, on the terrace, tiger-striped flames do a fire drill around Aldo's previously mentioned barbecue: black smoke, five stories high, is sorting Spanish laundry above. It has been opened to him, but Simon raps anyhow—tonk-tonk—on tons of resmeltable bronze: three thousand dollars' worth (okay, two-fifty, knocked down for a quick sale) at scrap-metal rates. Simon would rather not go in—Van Lynxx Chapel is dark, two hours ahead, on its private Daylight Wasting Time—but Uncle Arthur must be found and sweet songs sung to him.

Simon has dabbed in the empty font. He can't see well. Old blink images, Polaroids snapped just outside, superimpose their form on blackout. Reverent, he signs himself with the sign, an X, of homework incorrectly done. Pirouette, pirouette again: sandal leather chirps: the burnoose hem harem dances around his feet. Djah, Allah-d'jah: a chic sheik. Last sunlight, seven o'clock low, passes behind the red/blue rose window: then cloud, then light, then cloud. Simon free-associates: a tavern maybe, lit with shifting color from some ancient jukebox front. Purblind, he has read the center aisle, pew by pew, with one hand. Turn left now by a chunky, ornate bishop's chair. Each wooden arm snarls: each a leopard head, crest of the Albani clan. Simon has sat, episcopal and tired. Just overhead a crimson ombre candle shivers in the chill. He has hacked off a fresh plug of tobacco. Saliva thaws bitter molasses out. Thoughtful in his fashion, Simon uses the reserve chalice: a bright spittoon. And Uncle Arthur's ciborium is within grab. Simon chews a communion wafer: chews three, four, five: try eating just one. They neglect to taste. And as they dissolve on his mouth roof, transubstantiated to calories, Simon will drop off. The head dodders up twice. He will backstroke against the undertow of sleep, vie with it, this mock-up for boring death, and go down, mmmmm, a third time.

Death: Bettina's. She lay, not fragile then—frail, a frail—nourishment, its needle track, hooked up to one arm. Dry teeth pulled in/at her lip. Finger on finger, hands were sewn up across the nightgown chest. A hobo tumor, free-lancing, had made mulligan stew of her stale womb. "Ma. It's me, Simon," he said. Bettina would recognize her son: would recognize, as well, the three-day coward's bender he'd been on. Simon had driven, a guilt trip, eight hundred miles to see her off. Bettina murmured: the sound was beyond his hearing's grasp: a trick. Simon leaned to listen, breathless, leery of death's old smell: and, with those dry teeth, Bettina had bitten his earlobe: bitten, held. The pain was pure: and obdurate and final in a dour way. Simon's brow nicked against her wedding ring. A prodigal act: it spent all the glucose stoked through her blood in half that day. Simon would beg. "Please, please," but not aloud. He didn't want the shrewish nurse to see him this way, so. (Imagine the dialogue. "Visiting hours are over, Mr. Lynxx." "Yes, well, I seem to be stuck.") He kissed Bettina's yellow hand. Now her breath was regular, ominous, nearly a snore. Had she, God, gone to sleep? Had she put him carefully someplace where she might, like her bifocal glasses, find him handy in the morning? Or would she draw him down deathways, a discipline, a learning experience such as parents think it their business to provide? With one hand Simon pushed off on Bettina's head. The lobe snuck out. It bled. Bettina slept at peace: and, in the night, was dead.

It's not so much death: madness taunts him. A mirror in the fun house will break out sweats: also a record played at too few r.p.m.: and foreigners, their nonsense speech: and passion, religious or national or true romantic. Simon is alert to insanity in himself, as women born of DES-taking mothers watch, though they cannot see, their endangered cervices. The time he put in with Bettina after Aldo's grenade-like end has, retrospectively, some tones of Havelock Ellis: "B.L., aged 55, a widow, and her son, S.L., resided for fifteen years in the Borough of Q." B.L. brought men to Q. Men who looked led on and unsure. They came in service station dress: with toolboxes and vacuums and encyclopedias: in hard hat and uniform cap and Sam Browne belt. They reminded S.L. of a second-grade reader called *What Daddies Do*. It might have been the same quick-change stud. S.L. would watch his ceiling, while, next door, bedsprings clonged and small cash—clack—fell as pockets fell. Then bitchy tussle sounds. Then B.L.'s fist on the wall between. "Get your hands off me, you bastard. I'm a mother. My child is in there." Once, at age seventeen, her child yelled out, "Don't mind me, I'll go walk the dog." But sounds of male feet passed his room no matter what. Two kinds. The angry feet were louder: they had taken time to prod their work boots on again. The meek ones tiptoed by: and picked up pre-Revolutionary splinters through a sock. Then B.L.'s European scratching on his door. "It's all right Simon, I've sent the big lout packing. Would you like some cocoa and a brownie, dear?"

Bettina's hair went black with age. Her tresses—she was the only woman he knew who had *short* tresses—might have been penciled in. A substance like graphite, smeary, lubricious came off them. Bettina's face was lewd zinc-white. She wore it well—someone in a private No play—though the smile, by contrast, was the dingy smile of clowns. And, yes, her arms seemed peculiarly round: that suspicious line of blue makeup, from wrist to elbow fold, it gave an artist's chiaroscuro there. But then Bettina would sometimes stain one cheekbone mauve or green. After all, he has thought, Bettina was before her time. Now Simon sees his mother in those op art women he has known: *fin d'un autre siècle*. Their names are impersonal: a sort of Linnaean system: genus and attribute. These have been his companions: Velveeta Cheese, Beta Scan, Dinah-Glas, Stoned Wheat, Miracle-Whip, Econoline Van: and his favorite, Vinyl Chloride. They are garish as first-day covers from the post office of some emerging Central African nation, whose only export is philately. Yet limp: flags flown indoors. Simon is derisive toward them. While he wears a gorilla suit.

Bettina was charming when, once or twice each month, she stole. A spotty, orgastic flush rose on shoulders, on nape. She lost her accent: she spoke New York American: she could say shit. Also she was gay. Afterward Bettina would exhibit loot on Simon's bed: the pettiest larceny: dollar novelties, candy, clasps and hooks to hold together or up things that she didn't own. And she shoplifted from Simon. He learned to play hard on Christmas Day: half of Bettina's presents would be gone by Twelfth Night. On Thanksgiving and Easter she went to Daddy Freeman's Orphan Home: to redistribute her Indian giving there. The orphans called Bettina Wonderful White Lady. Simon knew better than that. Fridays she would cajole her son into playing casino for money again. Friday night the sixteen bits of his allowance would arrive, slap-shotted, under Simon's door. "Simon. I cheated. You know how Mummy is." Oh, he did. Simon has always been honest in small transactions. It seems a periapt against insanity.

On consignment, one week and one day after that pleasant surprise, her husband's death, Bettina bought a lubberly St. Bernard dog. She called him Aldo. Aldo's skull was bigger than a square five-gallon can. The eyes were bloody and whiteshot. Bettina made Aldo wear a choke collar with six D cell batteries in it. Whenever he barked, whenever he said Ahem, fifteen-volt shocks zapped out: current so vigorous it stood both ears up and gave him a painful erection. Aldo came to have the paranoid, bootless gaze of innocent men being booked in foreign police stations. Pretty soon he went, not rabid, just mad: he ate whole potted plants—geraniums, wandering Jews—and even some soil. Bettina returned Aldo to the pet-shop owner, who returned him further, still on consignment, to his maker. Bettina would play her husband's tape library, the complete "Lynxx Good Morning Show," eight thousand hours, at random and with spite. On July 4, for instance: "Ho-ho, looks like six inches of fluff stuff by tonight. Yes sir, our good Mayor Wagner has issued a snow emergency. The LIRR will be delayed, so, Mom, if you want the pasta to be chewy don't drop it in 'til you hear hubby stomping on the WELCOME mat. Ho-ho, gotta get back and build an igloo with my five-year-old." Deliverymen synchronized their watches by Aldo's mad time, reported the score last night from Ebbets Field, shopped A&P for a sale at 1956 constant dollars. It was morning all day long. Not sentiment or a '50's hankering: a posthumous humiliation. Aldo foolish and out of date as airmail.

Simon has read her poetry. Ten-page sonnets, sinuous and self-concentered as a fingerprint. Plus one ream-length epic: Homer's *Odyssey* redone: in which wise Odysseus stands for the female orgasm, trekking home to satisfaction despite Circe, Polyphemus, Scylla, Charybdis and all those men who just turn over when they've shot their glob. Bettina wrote after she stole: wrote nude, high heels excepted, the bedroom door open, on a chair seat no wider than bicycle saddles are, one candle-drip buttock hanging down from either side. Then, for ten or twelve hours she slept. Simon would come in eyes up, up and away—as you approach a hot fire with more wood: to shift the bedspread over her. Bettina's lips smacked: not tasting, rather the way llamas do before they spit in your face. He can remember those long, dark hairs—swords at salute over bride and groom after some military wedding—that roofed across her spinal groove. Skinny, bone-bare, Jesus, he knows what they mean by *stark* naked. "Thank you," she would say the next morning. And click off a seditious wink. Simon can guess where it came from, his metaphor-maker's eye. Now and then, in her poetry, there are chance images, most often visual, of an apt and nasty power. That, plus verbal marksmanship from Aldo. Simon will imagine their chromosomes—Aldo's, Bettina's—many-arm wrestling, gene at gene's throat, each too stubborn to be recessive, in the egg that was him. Any other womb, he thinks, would have miscarried such discord.

"Break."

Mmm. Is that her, she?

"Break it now, Lord."

Mmm. Simon, not too buoyant, has surfaced. Up. His vision is starry: the wet-eyelash seeing of swimmers. He spits tobacco juice. His saliva has set up, clotted: he chews it off. Opposite, in the north wall, five small windows narrate Pentecost. Apostles on fire, each with a blue lit gas jet above. The stained-glass landscape behind them is green/brown as old terrarium sides: designed for a blazing Florentine noon. Simon has held his breath: to concentrate hearing. And. Wait. He can pick out a minimal life noise. Then:

"Break my neck, Lord."

In a cultured, unemphatic voice. Hers.

"Now. Now. Break. It now."

Simon on the qui vive. For a moment stained glare will poke his eyes out. But he perseveres: persecutes the sound through an Italian immigrant dimness. There: by a shallow side altar: look. Uncle Arthur has been kneeling: all this time. His neck, his shoulders cramp: half in reverence, half in the hard requirement of a misfitting sciatic nerve. Simon, snubbed, takes offense: such lead-lined privacy seems to ring his uncle around: Arthur here a wholly owned subsidiary. Simon will fidget. He hates to be last on the bill: even a double bill. Religion and its early matinee idol, Jesus, irk him: they have the last great theater chain: in God he antitrusts. And, worse yet, Arthur's savage adoration appears manic: maybe a heritable trait. His tense rest is absolute: constant as theorems about linear space. Simon doesn't understand stillness: it is, to him, not viable. Simon can terrify himself: so can you. Stare at a mirror, eyes open full. Then grimace—anger's grimace or fear's or delight's—and hold. Our gestures are brief and porous: they let meaning out: and only face, indeterminate face, will gaze back. Madness is the language, physical and spoken, of eventuality abstracted from its agreed-on, work-lamp sense. A sense that, for Simon, must move and yell and—

"Break! Break my neck!"

Well, give the poor man what he wants. Rude, anyhow, in company, to talk with tongues. One wide sleeve up: another. Simon, on desert feet, has snuck into the theater of Arthur's meditation. Now have at it: strangle him back to life. Arthur is both choked and amazed: God never so Johnny-on-the-spot before.

"Mayg I ash whoog's—?"

"It's God, you old tureen. Me. Come t'cure you of your holy fantods."

"Oh, Simon. Haahhh. I presumed it was one of the local hobblede-hoys." There has been weeping: Simon can see the salt remains. Abruptly, a ricochet of disgust, he drives Arthur back/down. "Ah! Oh. I can't—I'm not young, Simon. Don't do things like that. I might have injured myself."

"Just look at him, on his knees, seeing eye t'fly with God again. Crying. Not me, friend. You won't catch me getting senile. Praying t'Jesus when I wanna pass water. When the prostate gives up, so do I: we made a suicide pact." Simon is incensed by it: age. "Barbie and Ken go t'the complete care home. Set comes with little wheelchair and little false teeth and little adult incontinent pads. Also a little year's supply of prune juice. Hear Ken's bladder gravel rattle. Press Barbie's stomach and her bowels take a bow in the therapy pool. That's what we need: a kit that'll teach Sis how t'diaper Daddy. Calling Scully-Walton! Hanh. Hah. Jesus, you and your 'Break my neck, God.' You scared me leakless, you old creaker. I hate it: it's mental backfill. Who d'you think you're talking to in here, anyhow?"

"God. Yes. Him."

"Thasso? Really? What's the area code?"

"Actually, Simon, it's toll-free. An 800 number."

"Christianity: Hartz Once-a-Week Wormer, that's what it is. Hanh. Jesus. Admit it—go on, you dastard—ech-shully death scares you half t'death. And the other half you can manage on your own. Right? Right? Well, I've got news: there used t'be a heaven, but they rezoned it for light industry. Anyhow, what's wrong with the earth? The earth. Soil. Holes. I'd rather rise again as ragweed, or a big Hubbard squash." Uncle Arthur has stood: in thought. Simon is too exercised, shouting: it puzzles Arthur: a mechanism in gear, engaged: what? "Christ, you should've seen yourself. You were stiff as a nun getting her first pap smear. It's not natural. The joints wanna swing and sway—"

"And what is—hello, the chalice is gone."

"Over there. Though, God knows, I should melt it down for phone slugs."

"Simon." Uncle Arthur sloshes the chalice. "This was empty before. You haven't been—ah, expectorating?"

"Sure. That's my spit of the very new covenant. Give it t'your congregation. They'll see God, believe me. And their breakfast."

"You are wonderfully gross. Mark my words, something will come of it. Now, if you'll excuse me—"

"Time out. Retake. Wait. Don't waddle away mad. Rats, and I had such good intentions when I came in here. Hey, I apologize. I really do. Forgive me. Huh?" Arthur laughs. "You do? I bet y'don't even listen t'me is why. Christ, what a waste of rancor. C'mon let's get outa this stone humidor: it puts me in a monsoon low. Look, what I meant t'tell you, I've got a neat-o surprise: a real Van Lynxx barbecue. I bought sirloins, ten of them. Real meat, not those poker chips you call God."

"A barbecue? Here?"

"Where else? We're a hunter people. Here the remains of my kin lie side by side with the marrow-split bone of cow and pig and whatever animal pastrami comes from. Here. Step outside. See, I salvaged Aldo's old fifty-five-gallon drum from the cellar. It was standing in as a mouse's bassinet. Grease on it older than I am: 1950's grease. We didn't use Wesson Oil back then, we used Vitalis." Follow Simon's forefinger: black smoke, now a seven-story stepped mast of it, backs away from the wind. "Wait'll you taste my meat. Tender as a labia majoris. Don't say I'm not a fun guy t'know."

"Simon. I— Did Mrs. P—?"

"Nah. Old Lip Fern wasn't in. I made like an earwig up the drainpipe again. Look how it's bent. You better get that fixed before I break my mother's helper some night."

"Who? Those people—"

"That's my staff, they comfort me."

"But what—?"

"Meat, Arthur, meat. We're gonna have a donkey roast. That quintessential American event: the back yard cook-out. Steaks, chops, ribs—I mean, what other profligate people'd spend two grand or whatever for a microwave oven and then eat outside? Huh? Shades of Pathfinder welcomed t'the hogan, haunch of venison over one bloody shoulder. It's our heritage. The Chinese let their mole hairs grow, we eat meat where flies can traipse all over it. Don't make that *Debret's Peerage* face at me. Whaddyou Fauntleroys know? Forty-two people chasing a fox an' y'don't even eat it. Listen. Listen. Wait'll you taste Simon's own garden salad: cabbage, red and white. Walnuts and bread crumbs and fresh spinach and feta cheese. Also lots of low-tar pot."

"But this is city property." Simon has gone ahead: through the cemetery now. Arms are held, a scarecrow, out and wide. The burnoose is his kind of garment. Grand gestures are impelled.

"Oh, by the by. As a special non-centennial tribute: Lynxx Features has chosen this very location for its new full-length film. We start cranking tomorrow ayem."

"But you mustn't." Uncle Arthur has spoken into a sleeve: Simon can feel breath up his arm. "I couldn't authorize that. This is city land now. A historic site."

"Yeah, *my* history. Christ, you'd charge Jefferson t'take a drip in Monticello. Look, I toldja: this is a religious flick. Joseph, Mary, Peter. Paunchy Pilate. The whole block association. You'll love it." Simon has redeemed his Arab arm. "So Jesus is lead guitar with a group called the

Gadarene Swine. So? So who's a fundamentalist these days? When you lapse into the public domain, you really lapse."

"What? I didn't quite hear you."

"Missed! Hah!" Tomatoes break: each flat as a dumdum bullet on the rose garden walk. "Back to the Puerto Rican League, you putty arm. Orlando Cepeda! Roberto Clemente!" To Arthur, an aside: "Bet you didn't think I spoke Spanish. Minnie Minoso! Luis Apariccio! That's telling 'em." Simon and the weather have pulled in a shirt-sleeve crowd: maybe two, maybe three hundred watchers. The tomato man has yelled. Smoke, Romeo-like, is climbing his balcony rail. He fans with a dish towel: to protect an underaged spider plant. "Jeez, I only wish my films would gross this well."

"Don't incite them. Please."

"Who, me?" Simon has stooped. With a lady push, he chucks the burnoose up. And again, for his west-side audience: a full gringo moon. There is the countdown silence that tells surprise. Then indignation: big rounds of it. "Yah, and Chiquita Banana t'you, too, *madre*. That got 'em: never seen so much white flesh before."

"Oh, Lord." But where there's smoke, there's cooking: Simon has reached the terrace.

"Friends and vassals, I wantcha t'meet my uncle. Arthur Gordon. He's a priest—blood is thicker than usual. But let's turn a deaf eye t'that. Not because we love God or because we're open-minded, but because we need him. Simple, ugly self-interest, something we all understand." Simon's eyes dazzle. "Hot. Hot. I'm a salamander. Ahrr, I can smell him, Aldo. Standing here, ablaze and gassy as a retro rocket. Hunh. Great fire. What'd you use, Abiosis, gasoline?"

"Yuh. I siphoned some-some into the old sssalad oil can you had."

"Uncle. This is Robert, my train-bearer and general suck-around. I'm teaching him how t'offend people. Go on, Robert, say something rancid t'Uncle Arthur."

"Pleased to meet you, sir." And the pleasure is returned.

"Marvelous. You really left him up in dry dock, didn't you? I've half a mind to rescind your scholarship." Simon has splashed out some sleeve. "And, on the ground here, looking like a felled laundry hamper, is Minnie, Robert's mother by a previous miscalculation. Minnie uses Rustoleum on her crotch."

"Oh." Arthur nods. "How do you do?"

"Do? Doodle. I'm very confuzz. You? Hello. Low." Minnie has been holding a reefer the size of monarch butterfly cocoons in one nostril. She will try to stand: will fall twice. The sound of garbage cans thrown over at 5 A.M. Robert is upset. He drafts a tentative move to help her: but won't.

"This is Larry Nim, my cameraman. The cowboy with his hand up

Larry's thigh is Don Ressler, my production manager. Yes, since you asked, Don and Larry are queer. They take more in the rear than a Toyota hatch-back. But you know all about that: you went to seminary, didn't you? And—over by the hollyhock tree, indistinguishable from it—with runs in her legs—is Rose, my producer. And Minnie's sister-in-law. Did I leave anybody out?" A tomato comes down: sop! "Right. Glad you reminded me. I need a big wooden bowl for salad. Larry, get Uncle a seat. Robert, break the breads out. Wait'll you see: pumpernickel, sour-dough, Irish soda, white so enriched it has t'find a tax shelter. Where's the hickory? Rose, shuck corn. Now. Now. I'm gonna show you how t'tenderize meat."

Simon, yes, punts steaks. Up, great hang-time. They slap on flagston-ing, down. Zonked, with the sound of locust electricity in her head, Min-nie will cringe and cringe again: his onslaughter taken by proxy. It is, to her, literal as a massacre. Simon's bare kicking foot has gone pink. Min-nie tries to pull on her joint, but the thing isn't there: oi, she has been holding her nose tip between thumb and finger for God knows how long. It won't come off. Simon has uprooted rocks, one a home-plate-sized ten-pounder. Simon will thrash the meat: his rock two-handed high, Moses busting tablets on Mount Sinai. Minnie has hallucinated a monkey now. The hallucination goes hup-two-three up Don's leg. Don grins unsurely: Friday grins unsurely. Don doesn't dig satire. He lint-brushes with one finger, as though for dandruff there. And, sheet, Friday has defecated in-side his shirt collar. Don goes for him, turning, but, nuts, his shoulder has turned, too. Don executes a circle and Friday, jump, is gone into the rose trellis. Larry just can't get over it: he laughs in a new and masculine way. Simon has thrown six ant-and-dirted steaks on the grill. Grease huz-zahs. Mrs. P has appeared at the terrace gate. Alf is behind her: in Arthur's third-best suit. Clothed he looks, arriving, as if he had just set out.

"Arthur. Arthur, what the bloody—" Suit jacket and shirt drop, decid-uous, from Alf. The knife is between teeth: as dogs fetch. "Can't go out for one minute, can I? Dead right I can't, not for one minute. Will you look?"

"That's *him!*" Larry will point Alf out. "He slit my bathrobe belt in half. Him, keep him away. Simon!"

"Mrs. P. Aaaah!" Simon all of a welcome. He shakes her hand red. "Pardon my salivation. Food. Meat. Yank your very stock footage up and read Alf for a while—"

"Get oft me, you big bastard."

"Hey, close your endocrines. I bring tribute."

"Out of my yard. I've had it up to here with you and your swaddie crew."

"Okay, gang, pick up the fire and let's go."

"Please, Margaret—" Arthur mediating, advocating: and hungry now.
"I do think we might give Simon the benefit."

"Yah. Here I dragged the family totem out." Simon's lip is stiff:
chapped by flame. "Look—I made a kill. I'm sharing. *I'm* sharing. Gimme
a hickey of peace, also go find that big wooden bowl Bettina had."

"You been progging around in my kitchen, have you? Eh?" Arthur has
a snub, haired arm up and around Mrs. P. Fingers scout the ungiving
place at her nape.

"Margaret. I think Simon means well."

"You're daft, Arthur. He's a cheeky sod and a pirate, is what. Just look
at him, got up like Ali Baba. He's out for the main chance, can't you
see?" But, time-being, Arthur can't. Smoke has interceded.

"Simon—" Don at the terrace gate now. "These folk don't want us
here. I'm goin' back t'the van, some damn monkey made doo down my
neck."

"Tough, Don. Monkey see, monkey doo."

"Mr. Wrestler, please. Don't go." Arthur performs a beckoning: elaborate: as if it were an invocation. "Alf. What say we try to discipline Friday just a bit? I know how you feel, Mr. Wrestler. Friday made his toilet
on my English muffin yesterday. Wonderful things, your English muffins.
I wish we had them in England. Heh. Ah, now don't those steaks smell
good? We'll have an American barbecue—"

"Shut up, Arthur. I can't bear that jollying farf of yours. It's so bloody
pastoral."

"Is it, Margaret? Oh, well—" But he has captured her anger for himself: he prizes it: safe with him.

"Well, it's your look-out. He'll scarper off with something, mark what I
say. And it's you and I will have to answer: we'll be out on the streets
without a shilling. Don't smirk there. I'm watching you, Simon."

"Watch! I love being watched. Oh, a watcher." Simon trusses himself,
sleeves and hems together. "Rose, go check-see if the corn water's boiling. Robert, get plates and forks. Food. Life. Love. I'm being watched!"

Bap. B'bap-bah. Bong-going now on the half a fifty-five-gallon drum.
Heat can't quite catch his fast palms. Bah: bip-a-bap. The garden hose
grazes at Don's neck. Larry has brought him soap. Simon levers the grate
up. Hickory is strewn in. Boh-bap: boh-bap. Boh. He has been a buff,
loitering, sick with love, near the Thirty-sixth Street Hook and Ladder
Co. Simon knows his old flame, fire: its lineage: mom and dad, first
cousin, generation back, ahead. The light a tenement windowsill gives
off: the tarry, intestinal burning on a pier. Bim. Bim-bah. B'bap. Alf is
down to his loincloth. Doodle-pad tattooing has taken Robert by surprise. Simon turns steak bare-handed. Through heat waves Van Lynxx
Chapel will seem an image seen in water. Third time: the impractical

burnoose sleeves flare up. Simon pats them out against his chest. He smells scorch, scorched.

"Beautiful grain." Rose strokes the salad bowl. Pot has made her wood-romantic.

"Put it over there."

"I don't like the old lady. She has a beard."

"Um. Sear. Sizzle. Sear."

"How much did you get?"

"Uh?"

"Money."

"Enough."

"Where from?"

"An advance on my severance pay. Everything set for tomorrow?"

"We're doing it here?"

"Um. Sssssss."

"What a come-down."

"Ssssss."

"I'd watch Larry. I think he's got other plans. You know. Not happy with the firm."

"And you?"

"I wanna get banged. This good shit makes me horny."

"All in God's time."

Rose has nested against his arm. There's a red parenthesis on each side of her nose bridge. Always: Simon can't figure it: Rose doesn't wear glasses. Her hair is thin and sad: the elbow, balding, of a raccoon coat. For three years Simon has watched it wear away. They met in an elevator at the McSorly Rehearsal Studios on Eighth and Forty-eighth. Simon had been improvising scenes from *Clap*. Rose, on bush parole from Westchester County, was understudying Ophelia for a showcase production of *Hamlet* at Lun Far's Cantonese Restaurant. Lun Far wrote his own fortune cookies and did all-Oriental Shakespeare on the side. Rose was somewhat older than the Korean Polonius, but Lun Far, to whom Caucasians were ageless, had apprenticed her anyway. It cost Rose seventy bucks per week, paid in advance, for the privilege of hoping that Ginger Fong would break a yellow knee.

Past M to B, going down. McSorly's elevator used its own flow chart. It often recast whole productions: sending a chorus line to the Ibsen rehearsal on 8 and Norwegian starlets to a Scott Joplin revival on 5. This time it stayed at B: as though convinced, after a twenty-year argument, by persuasive gravity. The basement exit was impassable: fifteen full ash cans there. Simon faked weakness in the matter of ash-can lifting. Actually he had new slacks on, not ash color, and could sense sexual freebies headed his way. They improvised fine love on an amputee sofa, staked out long before as the property line—strong smells make good neighbors

—of two competitive tomcats. This sofa had worked out a tentative living arrangement, almost a hotel-room ambiance, with two limbless chairs and a similarly underpinned end table. The linoleum looked angry-risen-river brown. There was a snug, island sense of cresting flood water, chair leg high, stopped just in time.

Her response had been gratifying: is yet. Simon can run her body off in straight sets. He has heard wild groupie crowds yelling through her climax-hoarse voice. Rose admires his physique: an unabashed, hard-hat male praise: she will even, now and then, wolf-whistle. Simon and Rose have worked together, learned together. Failed, that most of all, to-gether: to those who share a paranoia intimateness will come most easily. Back then, back at McSorly's B, Simon was applying slash-burn methods to Bettina's last will and testiness. Rose foremanned the con-struction of the van after Simon, made restless by blueprint detail and postponement, had gone off after more immediate ways to spend. Rose bought wholesale, haggled, took kickbacks and was as competent in her management of his affairs as she was slipshod in dress. Slipshod to ab-surdity: once, stripping her down, Simon found a bra on, yes, backward. Despite his thug's language, despite drunkenness and extra-van sexual distance events, she has been scrupulously true: to the point of washing socks so stiff with foot business that they could stand alone: hard as shoe trees. It can't last, he tells himself: she's saving up for mutiny. Who, after all, after three alternate-side-of-the-street-parked years, could blame her? And yet Simon has never had to perform for Rose: only with her can he step offstage. Simon wouldn't let on, but at forty-three, meager and just a bit unclean, dirt charcoal rubbings on elbow, on Achilles ten-don, Rose Fischer is still the best lay he has ever had.

"What good're you? I ask. My husband made barbecues, that's why I left him. Every Sunday. If it rained he was out there with rubbers and a black umbrella. I swear that's why I left him. And guess wha-guess what? Here I am in the big, sophisticated city, getting clinker soot in my eyes. Brilliant director, hasn't got two nickels he could rub together. Short-order cook, that's all."

"Stand back. Asbestos Man's on fire again. Out. Out. Out."

"Screw me, Simon."

"I've got guests. Later." Rose has given him a perfunctory feel. He, perfunctory, bumps into it. And, for the first time since, he has a thought of what's-her-name, Merry.

"Screw me. I'm your only friend."

"I screw my enemies, not my friends."

"You must get laid a lot, Simon. You must get laid a lot these days."

"That's an exit line, Rose."

"Yes. All right. It is."

Having gone too far, she goes, too. Her feet are tropical—Simon can

remember their wet liniment warmth in the large of his back at night—
and now moist sneaker prints fade after her across the cool terrace stone.
Rose has a lichen-green sweater on, coarse-knitted as chain mail is:
Don's tank-top undershirt will look through it: white patches here and
there. The sort of outfit, Simon thinks, that a newsstand owner might
wear. To his left, planted in Mrs. P's tulip bed by her metal center of
gravity, Minnie has been grasping poolside handholds from the air.
Scraawk, through her muumuu. A goose-pimpling noise: of shovels when
they hit rock. Minnie has thumbed Rose down. She would like to hitch a
hike up. Rose, instead, gives out another joint. Robert, Minnie's agent,
will turn the offer down. Simon is interested. Robert sideswipes Rose
onto a soft shoulder of the terrace. She will resist, snappish: but not with
the kin authority that an aunt should have. Now Robert—Simon
says "Oh?"—has grasped Rose high on her arm. Even feeling-no-pain,
Rose feels: leaves. Remarkable: in forty hours the relationship of an aunt
and a nephew has become outmoded. Simon takes it personally. In his
presence all things change. Robert has sat beside his mother: has
terrified Minnie. Her vision slurs. She will keep looking from the sky to
him. From the sky to him, as if Robert had not sat: fallen.

And now to coin a salad. Avocado, onion, radish: green olive and
black pepper: black olive and green pepper: ham and salami and two
handfuls of bristled anchovy: cheese. Simon shears through red cabbage.
The rawest of raw vegetables: it can make an empty stomach ping.
Tastes enlist on his brilliant tongue. Don and Larry dance, well-versed in
each other, at ease. Mrs. P disapproves: i.e., she looks more British. She
has sat very upright, to snub all languorous inclinations and reclinations
in the big chaise longue. Uncle Arthur squats near her left shin: on a
New York *Post*. Minnie has closed the fierce foreigner's eyes of her son.
He is beautiful now: a danger to her heart. Simon drinks wine. Un-
paired, he would almost like to sulk. Alf, Simon can see, is on the prowl.
Rose, made tolerant by narcotic, allows her own capture. Alf, just between the two of them, has begun teasing his loincloth up. A why-not?
shrug from Rose: tattoos down there, too? Three yellow plastic snakes
jump out of Alf's groin. Rose is delighted. Alf says his laugh, "Ow. Ow.
Ow." A Jiffy Bag tight with water has plocked down on Van Lynxx mansion roof. Behind Simon, the gutter spout clears its throat just once.

Listen to a wood fire: you can hear sea gulls cawing far away. Now
Larry has pre-empted Simon's food-fond hand. They slow-dance near the
barbecue. Simon is possessive and proud: Larry will be loyal: his.
"*Maricón! Maricón!*" yelled down from an antagonistic high rise. Simon
leads: he slips on/off Larry's seal-smooth abdomen. They make a regal
pair. Don and Rose enter the dance-off against them. Their movement is
a ritual attack: they conspire as beaters would around some quarry.
Spanish rhythm counterpoints soft rock from Don's Sony portable. Then

Rose has cut in: Larry will hedge his bets awhile with her. Simon, attending the salad again, has sprayed oil on from one of two square, identical cans. He's glad: he tone-controls his meal. Egg cracked: then garlic ground into the bowl's wood. Ups-a-daisy, he tosses it with ladling hands. Robert has asked Mrs. P to dance. She will refuse but is propitiated somewhat by his boy's courtesy. This has not been missed: smart move: maybe, Simon thinks, Robert will be a Jew and an asset after all.

They push Minnie up, Rose and Don and Robert: each at a part of her: specializing. The effort looks patriotic: another flag on another Suribachi. Her muumuu bags wind and is driven ahead: arms now back against the drift. Minnie will walk half a step or two behind her own feet. Watching, Simon smiles: Minnie can amuse him. But an instinct says, Be careful now. Better not show it: Minnie is Rose's special victim—ooh. Friday, way down there, seems some kind of lanky rat. Minnie has been scared: she founders. Awkward and bottom-heavy, sure of falling, further in arrears of her feet than ever before, she will come down all over Alf. It feels like an assault to him. One arm has earmuffed over his head. Hearing is full of squawk-box battle-station static and—and the knife swipes out. Simon has already started running, but too late. The murder will come. In panic, cornered by her large arm, Alf stabs Minnie. The thrust is homicidal: meant to gut her. His knife gashes her muumuu abdomen. And, slanggg! snaps off at the handle.

"Wot! Wot! Wot! I busted it onner gut. Look ere—me sticker's broke in fack. Unnatcheral is wot it is."

Alf has seen God: enough. Enough: he lays the scrimshawed haft at her feet: just so you place offerings before a pre-cast idol. Embarrassed—poddon me—Minnie looks at her stomach. What was that? Slanggg? Could such a noise have come from her: a rivet giving down below? Simon, nerve-sprung, laughs. But this is troubling, nonetheless. Alf, he knows now, will kill: in a reflex. He can remember the breast-broken gorilla front. Mrs. P dismisses Alf with no more than a crossing guard's bored wave. Friday has the long blade: he holds it hara-kiri high. Eight o'clock: a floodlight gets the drop on them. Minnie, as if this announced her new act, hootchy-kootches to Simon, misjudges by five good feet and plays a carom off Aldo's barbecue, which will answer her hidden hard goods in their native tongue: ca-bash. Simon and Minnie hug, Robert, with a wooden spoon, starts to shovel dirt.

"Mr. Lynxx, I can tell. You've got meat under your arms. Hoog—such a he-man smell. I'm biting. Bite. Bite."

"Hey. Stop. My arm isn't pareve."

"Mime under the influ. Enza. Hmm. Mmm. So this is what I'm told reefer madness. Isn't it? No. People look like silverware. I need my sunglasses. Ohhh, sorry. Oh. I stepped on your toe. No, that's my toe. I wondered why it hurt. Hurrrt. What a snappy salad. I could dangle my feet in it. Can I be of help, Mr. Lynxx?"

"Just try standing on your own. It'd free up my left arm."

"I think—uh-oh. Uh. Oh. Mr. Robert Fischer is ashamed of me. His father socked him once for smoking just a Kent. Now look. Will you? Sitting sober as a rabbi. His eyes are like a police siren. Annnn-oooh. Annnn-ooooh. He's growing up and I could fall head over tookus in love for him. Mr. Lynxx, I'm eating those steaks and they aren't even in my mouth. With this stuff I could diet all day long."

"Ha." Simon laughs. It's a great pleasure, a satisfaction, we have all known it: introducing another to new and evil things.

"Larry. Oh. It's my head. A woman could get pointers from him. He's so lovely, my tongue comes out, I want to lick. I'm learning, Mr. Lynxx. I haven't learned since Momma told me not to swim after meals. And that was good advice, you get a cramp. The tree is waving. Hello. Hello. Oooh, we talked last night, just a couple girls. A regular klatsch. Mmm."

"You. Hands off my salad."

"Woof. Tastes to me from gasoline. Burr-burr. Listen: my tongue has a busy signal in it." Minnie handcuffs Simon behind the back. Now she's lifting him: one whole inch. "We. We'll make a sex soon. Soon. Am I singing? Soon. My key is on the way, Mr. Postman. Rose thinks I'm afraid. She's right. I'm so afraid I want to tinkle. Inkle. I'm making pebbles out of my mouth like a frog." Simon laughs again. "Is that your uncle for real? I thought you were so famous, you don't need relatives. Why does he wear black—a priest. Minnie, Mr. Lynxx told you. My memory is up ahead of me, I can't catch it. Yoo-hoo, Mr. Lynxx's uncle. Come talk to us."

"Yes? Can I be of any assistance here? Ah, the salad looks just super. I'm glad you came, Simon. Mrs. P and I don't have what you'd call a wide circle of acquaintances—oops." Minnie has pressed kisses on him: not pressed, ironed. "Really—you shouldn't, dear. I'm an old man. Quite past it."

"Mr. Lynxx, your uncle is cute, like a little Rumpelstiltskin. I could just see him in leotards."

"Please. Ha." Minnie has measured his inseam. "Please. I'm rather ticklish."

"Does it come off?"

"What?"

"The ringtoss around your neck."

"Yes, it does. If you'll—just wait. Well, now you've snapped the stud off. I heard it—no, I'll look in the morning." Simon laughs. "You're so, mmm-forthright, Minnie. Whatever did you do to Alf? He was absolutely routed. I've never seen it done before."

"Did I do? Who?"

"I see. You've been snorting marijuana. Is it nice?"

"Better than a whole box Loft's nut mix. My eyes are all over my head. Ho, I should play bingo now, I could do a hundred boards." Minnie sings Arthur away: America the Beautiful. Her voice, in her ears, is magnificent and strong. She cries for love of country. "Poddon. It just slipped out. Like a bubble. Bloop, it was there. So tell me about your nephew. His parents, where are they?" Simon lights up a cigarette. "Oh-oh, I put my tootsie in it. You don't have to say: an orphan. I knew. I knew. This isn't recent, I hope: there's a lone-wolf feeling all around him. No one to brush his hair in the morning. You should be his father. Do you give a good piece advice, now and then?"

"Can't say I've been much use, not really." Simon hooks his chaw out: forefinger digging in there. They look aside: polite. "My nephew is rather a special case. A test case for me. I want very much to understand him. It seems, you know, important. He's so strenuous. But I'm afraid Simon doesn't care for me. I'm not his cup of tea. The religious thing. It comes between us."

"I make brownies for the synagogue. You should taste. Mmm. So what do you do? Is it hard work, to be a gentile's rabbi?"

"Odd you should ask. I'm retired: sort of a gapeseed, a daydreamer, you know. Now. It's difficult to explain: especially to one of such a different—and quite marvelous, I might add—such a different religious background. How should I say? Well, Minnie, I suppose I'm trying to make myself a clean receptacle for God. Sublet myself, unfurnished, to Him. You know? But I'm along in years now and somewhat inclined to nap of an afternoon. A young man with energy, yes, and with real sins, not the dim half-remembered ones I have left. That's what you need. Simon here, I fancy he'd make us a marvelous saint. Eh, Simon? He has the physique for it. The passion. And the appetites, if you know what I mean."

"My son thinks this is Cecil D. Be Mille. A genius."

"Your son, Minnie, is a positive charmer. A gentleman. Mrs. P was quite taken with him."

"I'm happy. I brought him up not to slam-bang the screen door. Oh—something just gave a hop down there. If I throw up just go on with whatever you're doing. Once I had a Kahlúa with milk, it almost killed me." She belches. "Better. Robert, he's my joy. He's so thrilled to be making real films tomorrow."

"The movie, yes." Uncle Arthur has a cabbage shred. "Whuh. Very strong. Bit of an acrid taste. Simon—I did want to talk about that, your film."

"No talk."

"But we must." Uncle Arthur puts an arm up. "I'm not my own man here."

"Corn!" Simon has ducked the arm, the issue. He rushes in. "Corn! Rose, as usual, you're letting my cobs go soft."

The old kitchen is dark: in some particular, good way: as if history had caked it like a prime, long-laid-down Bordeaux. Simon touch-types on the wall: heading toward and around the staircase: to Mrs. P's small, modern kitchen just under that. And then stops: is still. There are harsh black-lung breath noises: noises that canvas rubbed on canvas will make. Simon is apprehensive: two figures toil against each other. His first instincts are official: break it up: this looks like a misdemeanor, though who is misdemeaning whom, he cannot say. But now his eyes have resolved darkness: he sees them fairly well. It's, God, Alf. Alf with a hand up Mrs. P's dress. Very up. Her underwear is sensual as a display ad: yellow, striped, bikini: not serviceable at all. The buttock cheeks hatch out: one, then its sister: they are admirably firm for her age. And a black garter belt no less. Alf falters: passion has made him unlandworthy. Mrs. P will give support, will hold him up and away, yet also to her. Alf— Simon hasn't a good angle—seems at her breast. The suckling, anyhow, is luscious. She is being drunk like winesacks. Simon can't credit what he has seen. By conditioning he expects the worst of people, but this worst he has never even bothered to expect. He backs. Out of the kitchen, out onto the terrace. Simon feels, well, second-bested: the shocker in shock. Enormities of this kind are his sales talk: his maker's mark. Simon, Christ, Simon has been outgrossed.

The high-rise wall is lit, its windows on at random now. Metaphor: a computer card punched out. And what if you processed it, the cryptic information there? As good a truth as any: better than most. Alf has unsettled him: lust sputtering, flywheeling on to senility's light blue verge. Can it be that Simon will want, want, want even then? People think greed is a frolic: little do they know the responsibility of it: the price of lewd liberty is ever-watchfulness. Don and Rose collude. Their forefingers countermarch through the dirt of an azalea bed. Simon lights up. He loves to do that. A male, lonely moment: match struck, held at the end of your squint, neck down, then—shake—out. Private. More gratification there than in smoking itself. Larry and Friday stalk each other, Aldo's barren fig tree in between. Friday has picked up Larry's sandal, also Larry's oblique, swan-arch manner. Larry is enjoying himself. Simon assigns corn to Robert. Above Van Lynxx Chapel the ambitious searchlight from some supermarket opening pokes up, a tornado of merchandising light. Simon has his back to the fire.

"Minnie tells me you've got plans for her." Uncle Arthur has smiled: but he's uneasy. " 'Improper' plans, I'd say."

"Oi. Me and my big trap. I say, Minnie, it's your brain thinking, but also it's my mouth talking. I'm all the time sssshing myself, but it doesn't stop. I'm on automatic, Mr. Lynxx. Ssssssh."

"Well?" Arthur the priest.

"Why not?" Simon inverts steaks. "Should my French connection drop off because you've been caponed by the Holy Ghost? Hanh? Listen, I've seen things—in there, in my own house, and not five minutes ago—a gerontological porn peep classic." Arthur reacts: perhaps he can guess. "I'd tell you, but you'd think it was one of my hyperbolic fantasies. And anyway, I say *skoal*. Even the old models have an emission device. Look —why's everyone pick on me? Because I'm not shaft-shrunk about life? Because I play pin-the-tail without my blindfold? Minnie'll get what she wants. And better than she ever had it."

"Right-o. No need to invent a tantrum, Simon. It isn't necessary. I'm not making a judgment. I was merely concerned—Minnie, after all, has a child here—you might compromise her. Surely, with so many others to hand, you—"

"Sssssh. See, I'm sssshing."

"You—" Simon holds his fork low: in the style of Alf. "What's that little covered-dish belly full of? Huh? God gas? Doesn't the steak make you drool? Hah, Tartuffe? What's your morning erection for? So you can use your stomach like a sundial? Shame—fishing a confession out of this poor, retarded plate of schnecken. Tell me, my child, does he do this or do this or this?" And Simon thinks, Why am I seeing Merry now? Oh, that other tight-ass priest: Tim. "I'd love t'be you. With all that impacted repression, I'd come five times getting it slammed in a car door."

"Sssshing."

"No, he's right enough. I am that: repressed or temperate, it's a matter of semantics, isn't it? But not hypocritical. You see, this is the terrible, chancy balance of faith. I'd like to talk sometime, Simon. I could learn from you and you—but you wouldn't, I daresay. You find me a threat of some sort. How furious you became in the chapel. It's a compliment actually."

"Your uncle told me—am I talking?—you had such a childhood I wouldn't wish it on a schnauzer."

"I had no childhood. I was born with my second teeth and pubic hair. Found floating in a plastic commode down the Gowanus Canal. Who likes rare? Rares! Rares!"

"Stop him!" Larry has been foot-winked by a monkey. "He's got my other sandal. Simon, he's stripping me. It's obscene."

"Robert? Rare!" Simon stocks a paper plate: steak, corn, salad, sourdough bread. Robert is distracted: his mind akimbo. "Rare? Red and wet as wounds? Good. Put hair on your palms. Huh—anything else you want? Wine? You can still taste the Cesar Chavez toe jelly in it, but it does the trick. Eat. Go on."

"Simon."

"I said, eat. Aaarh. Open up." Simon will feed. "Good, huh? Taste the hickory?" Robert nods. "Say I'm a sweet cook."

"Y-you're great."

"Wait'll you try the salad."

"Simon."

"Don't talk. You're not smart enough t'do two things at once."

"Please. Huh. Lis-listen to me. I've gotta tell you. Don and Auntie Rose, they're up—up to something. I think th-uh, they're trying to make Larry leave you. Auntie Rose is the worst."

"Yuh. I suppose." Simon scrapes his butt out: barefoot: he can feel it, but so? Where there's pain there's life. "Take some advice, Bobbo. Keep all your options ajar. Rose may look like someone who's been in a mud-pack since 1953, but she's with a Yiddisha-kopf, very schmardt. Rose could manage to dial an obscene call collect. I come on like Nelson Eddy in *Naughty Marietta*, but right now I've got all the prospects of a spat manufacturer. Believe me, an usherette could do more f'you in films."

"But—"

"Forget it. I appreciate the loyalty. These days if a yo-yo comes back t'me, I'm touched. This business, it's a morgop. That, for you anagram lovers, is pogrom in reverse. I'm living in a one-room ghetto: me. The Yeshiva Cossacks ride too fast and they go right through. WASPTOWN: Population One. It's suicide, I know. But mine, not yours. At least you're the right faith. Even the MGM lion has t'go t'shul." Robert laughs. Simon has backed to the barbecue. "Rares! Don! Rose! Leave off plotting my death and eat. Rare? Come'n get it." Uncle Arthur is in an argument. He stands near the terrace gate.

"*Nein. Non. Nyet.* This is a private party. Van Lynxx Manor is closed to the public now. Closed. D'you understand? *Fermé.*" Two women nod, agreeable, yet undeterred. They wear clothes you could wash in a hotel sink. Their faces, Simon wonders about it, are manifestly the faces of people who have never spoken English. Language shapes the mouth: try talking German through a knothole. Or Japanese with your tongue out.

"Cut! Cut! We welcome guests here. Come in." Simon seizes the women: a tablet-chair arm around each. "I'm Simon. The last Van Lynxx. Mosta the people who've slept here've slept with me. I'll give you an autograph, which is more, I bet, than you got at the Lincoln Memorial." They nod. "No spik, heh? All noddy, no Englishy? How you ladies like I fram you with my biggie caulking gun? Oh, good. No more crack, no more draft. Likee? All weatherize. Likee suck my exhaust pipe, too? Yes. Go peck-peck on my cuttlebone?" They nod, enthusiastic. "Such very nice ladies. We make whoopee. Me on top, you on bottom. Big bang-bang. So sorry you look like a pair of distemper shots, yes? Don! Bring that bench over. I just gained three inches in translation."

Mrs. P has built up corn ears: thin end on fat end, a log cabin saddle-notched. Robert eats: Simon is really pleased to see that. Alf has edged back through the french doors: out. He is respectful, awed. Since his loss to Minnie he seems smaller: four foot fourteen, instead of five foot two. Alf has his pajamas on. The pattern mimics his tattooing: tiny skiers herringbone across a blue snowfield. It's dark now. They all appear to be at center stage. Uncle Arthur trips a switch: the electric fence wires are on sentry-go. Above, someone has begun to play taps. The desolate rhythm is varied: a somber jazz riff. Hands clap. Simon can see no one up there, but match heads will flicker on again, again. They look like threats to him. He is master of a colonial enclave in some unwelcoming, misdeveloped land. Simon—male, lonely—lights his cigarette.

"Eat! Eat! All is forgiven, written off. I rip up your IOU's. This is my body, you won't need salt. Eat. I love you all." Simon tastes his salad. It's bitter, badly dressed: he can't understand. Simon squirts more olive oil. The square can tonks a record of its hollowness. Could it be? Robert said. One can was. With show-off dexterity Simon squirts, bull's-eye, to his mouth. And to the cigarette.

Fumpf!

Rose shrieks. Simon, Christ, has retched an arching tongue of flame. It gases: it roars. Liquid fire spews from his open, yawing mouth. The terrace, for one moment, is torchlit: and they scream. Simon, flamboyant, burns alive: his face is bloating there. He mustn't inhale: he mustn't inhale. Simon vomits yellow blaze down—graaaugh!—and the salad oil can goes off. A vicious, hard explosion: shreds of it knife and, ardent, coil. His salad catches: napkins, paper plates. He is a pyromaniac and wild. The high rises are tamed. Arthur hasn't a prayer: Robert cries. Fire spits: it drools. Then Simon is out. Snuffed. A few flame-trails, blue, trickle down his burnoose front. Simon, smeller of cooked meat, smells himself: seared. He has fallen on both knees. Minnie will rush to him. Pain fishhooks him: he can't throw its barb out. Larry has covered his eyes. Simon is grotesque: brows gone: lips swollen and dark. He sways. He is conscious still and doesn't want to be. A taste of powder, of moth wings, only that, has dressed his mouth.

IV

6

"Sheet, when's he gone haul tail outa that bunk up there?"

"Don. I'm putting a sssssh finger on your lips. In his condition, sleep is from God a natural healer."

And, with that, Bettina comes on: guest-hosting the dream talk show again. No wonder his nights aren't syndicated. Her base makeup will smell marshmallowy: like new Pennsy Pinkie rubber balls. And applause: some nervy brass, but you'd expect that of Bettina: she has a claque even in his dreams. Nothing for it: just have to screen this thing through. Now what? Bettina has been treadling on the vacuum pump. Why did he blood-let her? The cup is down below, in a guidebook Freudian place, no doubt: Simon won't look, he's too embarrassed for his dull-sloganeer subconscious mind. Cripes, imagine: dream sequences in his dreams: can they blame him for snoring? Simon watches blood get sipped up the plastic tube: inch-long red/brown shuttle buses, each with its driver, each with its iodine stench. He's very small, foreshortened, nude. "Whew, child. I'm working like a Coloured." Not a Colored. He hears spelling in her accent. The pump has a manometer. They both check it: 999.9 rolls up to 000.0. "I feel better now," but Bettina won't listen. The Flushing Hospital room has made a turn: walls swivel—nice lens work there—from oblong to diamond shape. Bettina takes a suction stop. In a veil. In a large rain hat. In a see-thru umbrella. No, in an oxygen tent. Curse his uncelluloid dreams: not one of them worth opening in a Thruway tollbooth: well, could be worse, he could have to finance this screaming pterodactyl. "But, Mother," little Simon says, "that's my air." Something has cracked off the roof of his mouth. Flesh. Bettina lights up. Omigod, what now? Yes: little Simon has a fuse: he's peeing sparks. Bettina holds her ears: Jesus, another bomb. Smoke, gray, luminous as black-and-white TV, rises from his small discharge. It stinks: it purveys smut. He will never love combustion again—gaah, chaw. Can't get a big tobacco wad out. Some crust. He pictures, doesn't taste, the chalky coat—remember it?—of that obsolete miracle, sulfa drugs. "I feel better now," Simon perhaps has said.

"Buh-nuh? What the ding-dong d'he say?"

"Shhh. He's talking in his dreams. Uh-uh-uh: such a young man for this to happen. I can't look at his lips. For me a cold sore is five days in bed."

Since his appendectomy Simon has been, as we all are, held accountable: at least to that grown-ups' obligation, pain. It is, perhaps, the most emphatic loss of trust, though there are other trusts left, which, in turn, will fail. Pain, a firetrap of it, inexorable, that would not, at age five, be kissed or—Watch! See, Simon!—distracted away. Bettina brought Denise, her mink stole, to Flushing Hospital: this had always been his *outré* sickness wear. In it, in mid-June, he seemed some improbable juvenile from a Chekhov notebook. Ah, how many fevers had Denise sweated out of him: how many Bettina smells had he sweated out of it/her? Perfume: throat and ear and cleavage perfume: the boo-saying, sharp aromas of her armpit. Denise could suffocate a cold: could heat up the sexton-like repair squads in his immune system. And those ten hospital days had processed him: moved him on, if not up. Disinfectant smell: exotic not-mine feces smell. The gargle, heard first-hand, first-ear, of a man dying: very like the sucking children draw from empty ice-cream-soda glasses. That watch pocket sewn in his hitherto integral body. Into his *skin*: rough on the finger as seams done with the Christmas leathercraft kit. Soon after Simon and Van Lynxx Manor had to renegotiate their understanding. So many objects there: they would press eyestrain on him, compared to the olive-white hospital plaster and its few Dick and Jane hospital cracks. He had caught on—at age five, perception enough—that suffering is a spare place and will not lend its toys.

"Nine ayem awready. He's been sacked out theah since Tuesday night. We pissed all Wensday an' Thursday away, now theah's a real New York fug outside. Least he could do is show up at Niko's."

"He's reconvalescing, Don. He has trouble even getting a mouthful of yogurt down."

Aldo brought mazes to the hospital. They were draftsmanlike products, set out on graph paper: SIMON WINS A DIME at the goal. But Simon never won: Aldo, the ten-cent Minotaur, would not be tracked down. Even Dr. MacMillen, with his large large intestinal experience, gave up on one. Whether out of ineptitude or small economy Aldo's mazes didn't arrive. Still, it was as much attention, in consecutive minutes of caring, as his five-year-old father had provided him with. The nursing staff tuned in on Aldo: he would broadcast a hearty morning plug for each of them. "Nurse Jones. Gosh, she's pretty. Thinking of her makes me wish I'd saved up my own appendix. Nurse Hazel Jones lives in Maspeth and she makes jewelry from old medical instruments. Hazel, you take good care of my little boy. And now, for Nurse Jones, 'The Tennessee Waltz.' Save the next waltz for me, Hazel." It was chivalrous of Aldo. And cheaper than leaving a tip.

"I he-ahh. Nnnn. Nnnn."

"See—now he's awake from your big mouth. Another hour he could have had."

They'd rather not watch: he hurts again. Simon can see the upper lip: it crests, burst like popcorn, below his cheek ridge. Mornings are bad: at night the mouth skins over, sets. Simon will have to shatter each lip again. He practices on a syllable: another. "El, em, en, oh, pee." He hears the skin give, split and chip, age-dried rubber bands. Pain isn't a consideration: pain solaces him: sensation of some sort. But the funny wetness: the liquid that comes from lip fissures: this is distasteful to him. Not blood—blood he could accept—the juice instead of mending burns. Is it lymph? Is that the word? Colorless: an unhealthy-looking healer. Simon's tongue has been shod. When the tip dabs at his palate, it's as if two glove hands touched. A glossy, thin lacquer on both. Were he to die, Simon imagines, his mouth would outstay the other flesh: preserved. Now they are all in attendance at his levee: Don, Minnie, Rose, Lar. Simon has flipped legs over the bunk edge. When he takes a crack at swallowing, their throats bow and scrape. The van has turned left: it will choreograph them. Simon breathes. Sinuses are a flue for his mouth: the reek of campfires, rained on and out, has come up. Larry sucks, nurses—mmm—on Simon's right big toe. Simon doesn't note this fancy footwork. Simon is trying not to yawn. Once before, in the naive and forgetful night, a yawn nearly ripped him apart.

"How's the bod, Sy?"

"Vuh—" Simon has a charade for them: lipsticking. Minnie catches on.

"Right here, Mr. Lynxx. Vaseline. Medicine chest in the jar." They wait. Simon will do a painstaking-away lube job on his oral tissue. "Hurt? Does it still hurt?"

"Mmmm." His lips work out: smile, pucker, frown, smirk. "Hurts me more t'remember, ow, remember what else's been dipped in that jar." He talks small-mouthedly: as ventriloquists do. But loud and clear.

"Please, Mr. Lynxx. You should go see a top ear, eye, nose and throat."

"Uh-uh. I have a minor medical plan. It only covers me for Pittsburgh, but the premiums're very reasonable."

"Well, y'know, that ain't no joke. Sheet, what if Lar has another bad attack? What if one of us all gets bunged up on the job? It's goddam stupid is what."

"Lissen, Fecula, t'get workmen's comp y'gotta work first. Last steady job you had was pumping dark chocolate in an oil-rig bunkhouse. Say aaargh, Simon." He has plucked up his tongue with thumb and forefinger. It seems prickly, arid to their touch: like dried okra. "I'm all right. Feels like I've been eating toasted Modess for a week, but could be worse. Did I do much damage t'my cover-boy bloom?" No one will answer. "Huh? Don't all comfort me at once. I look like the hairy prow of a tugboat, don't I?"

"Well, yuh—" Don is sickened. His reaction appears honest: not spiteful. It could worry Simon. "You look like some white Nigra with them fat lips."

"I got the scouting report on you, Don-boy. Woompf, you wanted my whole head to go up like a flammable nightie. Yeah, remove hat before striking. Cauterized like a seven-and-seven-eighths-inch wart." Simon heaves off/down: he is unsteady. "Geez. Wish I could see the outtakes on that one. Must've been a great act: the human can of Sterno. And for his next trick Simon the Singe will weld a boiler with one belch. See a doctor. Oh, sure. Don't you all hope. Well, forget it. I know your machine-washable loyalty. A day in the burn ward and I'd be reading get-well cards from every last one of you—stamp canceled somewhere in Downtown Skulk. Hanh. Gone and postage due."

"Simon, that isn't fair." Rose has unbuckled curlers from her hair. The hair, in solitary all night, drops straight down: unrepentant, bodiless as a psyche. "Can you eat?"

"Orange juice. No, juice'll sting worse than battery acid. Some milk."

"Hell. That's the last quart, Rose. See he don't take all of it. Rest of us, Simon, we like a little milk in our coffee, mornings. I mean less'n you got money enough t'buy another. We spent that thousand of yours on film. What we do—"

"Shaddap, Lord of the Fly. I'll pull your retail outlet off."

"Now wait, fast-mouth. It's half-ration time. Some-us around here gotta be responsible. We can't all afford t'be big ar-teests. Some-us like t'eat, too."

"Don. Why is it, when I'm around you I feel buried t'the neck in an anthill? I'll—wait. What day is this and why?"

"Friday, the twenty-seventh."

"Safe. Wolff's party is tomorrow night. Jesus, for a minute there, I thought I'd slept through it. Oh, I better croon. I better be Metternich and Talleyrand. I better be the whole conniving Congress of Vienna. Uhmmm. On second thought I better just learn t'walk on my hands and knees, and look like a plate of chicken fat."

"Drink." Rose has shut his hand on a jelly glass.

"Drink. Yes. If I can remember how. Hold your nose, here comes yak-breath."

This is, suddenly, a child's small performance. Brought out of bed to sing: to recite the poem: to walk upright, aimed at grown-up shepherding arms. Simon stands, big and boyish: in butt-split jockey underwear:

still, yet, that moment's consequence has dressed him. The left hand will bib his nude front. Bulky, he has moved as though in overcoats. And Simon drinks: drinks what? Milk is misspent from one corner of his not-usual mouth. His heart riots. He is afraid, sad. Metallic perhaps, non-committal: a taste, if you could call it that, of water in some alien town. To them he appears stripped down again. Under-evolved. There is only an after-smell: of day-old empty milk containers. His van has stopped now. Simon chugs the rest: breathing while he drinks, sniffing down and into his own throat. Simon has been subtracted from. He digs the glass rim against his forehead. He means to leave a mark there.

"Hurt, Sy?" Larry cauliflowers, cups one ear: as if pain were a low tone that could be pre-amped. "What is it?"

"Nothing. I mean—*nothing*. Snake eyes. Boxcars. I crapped out. Oh, nuts. Nuts. No taste: my mouth is like a socked-in airport." Simon beats his nape. "Is it gonna stop? Huh? Or is it gonna be Ash Wednesday in there forever? Lar, I'm trying t'make it happen up top, in my head: make myself remember what milk tastes like. But it's all sight gags. Cows and curds and wheys. White. Tell me—go on—what does milk taste like? Tell me."

"Well, Sy. You know. *A la Recherche de Tastes Perdu.* You could write seven volumes."

"I do get something—just Geiger-counter blips—through the nose. But it's all different, like seeing with one eyeball in a drunk tank. Hearsay. I don't trust it. Ever drive along a highway and all at once you smell coffee perking? Good coffee. Then go another hundred yards and it's just a mashed skunk? Oh, mother. Mother." He sits. "Christ, somebody scraped my gusto with a palate knife. Well, maybe I'll eat broccoli now. I never liked the taste of broccoli. Or Styrofoam or pool-table felt or oilcloth. I could even eat food stamps. Gee, a brave new world of bland has opened up before me."

"Maybe it'll heal."

"Are you out of your ballcock? Lookit my tongue. Smokey the Bear should be standing on it with half a dozen homeless rabbits and a deer."

"Hell." Don laughs: nervy. "If you're gonna eat cardboard, maybe we can put this here operation on a paying basis for once."

"Shame, Don. What a thing to be saying. Mr. Lynxx, a doctor could—"

"Jesus. Which is worse: a Texas mince who wants me t'recycle garbage or idiot advice from Look-Ma-No-Cavity with her soldered groin? Minnie, my star boarder, what can a doctor do, except run up a *cordon bleu* bill? What? Gimme taste bud transplants from a dead gourmet? As long as I can still ravage people, I'll be satisfied."

"Such a stubborn. Won't take yes for an answer. And your uncle, Mr. Lynxx. He thought at first this was a bolt lightning. He was here three times yesterday. Please give him a phone first thing."

"Probably thinks I was struck down by God on the road t'Great Neck. I wouldn't give him the satisfaction. Let's get this thing moving—wait. Hey, this thing *is* moving. If we're all here, who's driving?"

"My own son, Robert."

"Robert? Does he have a license?"

"A permit."

"He'll do real good." Don passes it off: but not credibly. "He got the hang first thing."

"I'll undescend your testicles, you—" Uhh-up Simon has Don in the air again: shirt material saws under each armpit. "He's gotta look like Rootie-Kazootie up there in the driver's seat. He's legal in cow college towns, not here. All we need is one of New York's worst t'flag us down. Christ, we haven't paid insurance since 1976."

"We? You. You're the one—ow. Come on. Ow. Lay off." Simon has Don by the sideburns now. They are a useful bit and bridle for his head. Simon will put Don through some paces. "Stop. I was just mouthing off. Stop. Aw, please. Please. Please."

"Voilà!" Simon shows a tuft to Don. "I'm gonna pluck out your macho hair by hair. The boss is back."

"I'm bleeding. Look. I'm bleeding."

"Tell the other girls y'cut yourself with your Fisher-Price shaving kit. Don, if y'don't like it, get. This is a local, we make all the stops."

"I'll just do that. You wait and see. Hell, you're loco. Know that? Loco."

"Let's not banter words, Don. I'm homicidal. Now get up front where you belong. God, a century plant does more work than you do."

"Okay. So you're stronger'n I am. So? Ain't exactly a news flash, is it?" Don's look has caught some irony. But the eyes are surface tense with water: of hair roots yanked and smarting, of peer humiliation. And there is trivial displacement activity. His thigh, the site of holsters, has been slapped: hatless, a hat brim has been bent down. Don appeals for complicity from Rose: she will not assign it. Larry has pulled the john curtain around his tender ambivalence. "Okay. But mark what I tell you. Not that nobody here doesn't know it already. This film, Simon, it's a cow-chip fantsy you roped us all into. You ain't got cash enough t'shoot past page twenty-five and you never will get it. And that's no matter how many times you beat the shit out of me. Simon? You hear?"

"Uh-huh. When you get up front, ship the junior arsonist back here t'me." Simon is preoccupied: he has a plaything: a different face. Simon clowns at the mirror. He has been disfigured: yet, you know, it's an interesting disfigurement. The blemished mouth will give Simon new opportunities for insolence and threat. Anyhow, as they say in showbiz: Use it. An actor prepares.

"Something else for breakfast?" Rose there.

"Uh. Got an Enfamil sandwich? Nuh—f'get it, too much work swallow-ing. Besides, everything tastes like the ear grease on an old telephone receiver."

"Lay off Don, huh?"

"He loves it." But Rose is smart. Don can do him damage: equipment, prints, the van itself. "Okay. Okay. I'll hangfire for a while."

"Anyhow there's something in what he said."

"Money. Money. Money." Simon rehearses an intimidation: is grat-ified. "I'll say one thing for Dallas Ex-Lax: he's right-on about my face. There are some towns in Alabama where I couldn't marry the sheriff's daughter. Abba-dabba. Jub-jub." Simon twiddles his lip. "Shine, Baas? I do 'em up good. Hold it. Hold it. Goddam." He has gouged Rose's shoulder: thumb almost beneath her clavicle: a simile for the mind's abrupt clench. "Money. Wait. The hyena brain has not been burned beyond recognition. Rose, tell me? Have I got the unmitigated, cracksman-like nerve t'carry it off? Have I? Tell me."

"Probably. Is there something particular you have in mind?"

"Gotta do it. Gotta. It's the breeder reactor of all scams. Oh, Simon, Simon: I love you. Pull this sting off and they'll beg forgiveness at Mensa. Oh, man. Oh, whatta hot lick. Ha! Oh, ha! The Gordon Liddy Medal, with clusters of blank tape. Gotta do it. For laughs, if nothing else. And, man, do I need a laugh. Though, if I laughed right this min-ute, I think my lower lip would splinter off like a frozen taco. Who was it Norty said at NA? Come on, Simon. Hens. Roosters. Cluck. Gluck. Harold Gluck. I'd be the invisible man. Sure. All I need is a nice luggage tan. Pull out the makeup trunk, Rose. Hurry, hurry. Lar? You, in the con-fessional there. D'we still have those Afro wigs from Clap?"

"Somewhere, I think. Is it very important? I'm indisposed now."

"Indisposed. Bull dinkey. You're indisposed t'seeing Don get frappéed. Stop reading your Marvel Comic in there and help me. Now. Now. It sho nuff is important. Yassuh. Ah, the firebug. Robert, get over here. Closer."

"Mr. Lynxx." Minnie is at their intersection. "Robert knows. Believe me, he's heartsick with blaming. That's why he was behind the wheel: he didn't want to be in here when you woke up. He knows. He should have put that can gasoline in a safe place."

"His hindsight is marvelous. Instead he let me make myself a Molotov salad. We shoulda stacked up sandbags t'eat that thing."

"How-how are you?"

"Just fine. Look." Simon opens: gives Robert a visual tongue-lashing. "Feels like the ashtray at an all-night poker game, but fine: just fine, thanks. Hell, I'll never taste a woman's Mekong Delta again, but, mox nix, who cares?" Robert has turned away. "Look, dammit. They used Easy-Off on my mouth."

"God. God. I'm sorry."

"Wouldja feel better if I hit you?"

"Yes." Robert has taken his glasses off: there was no hesitation. "I'm ready."

"Don't, Mr. Lynxx. Hit me, not him."

"Christ, this must sound like the Masochists' Desert Classic."

"It's just. We spent a fortune on his orthodontistry."

"Wonderful. I've got the Triangle Shirtwaist fire in my mouth and she's worried about his bite."

"Please. Forgive."

"I'm not a forgiving man, Minnie—it's a schwantz for a schwantz, as Moses said in the locker room—but I'm in mid-fraud right now, which means that DOA here, your precious *schmegeggy*, gets a stay of persecution." Simon is down. The makeup trunk, three by four, also three deep, opens into a five-step front stoop of shelves. "Where is it? That pubic scalp?" Simon slings mustaches up: they come down, slowed, rotating: like pollinose seeds. He has a black goatee by its chin. "Now: all's we need is thirty quarts of Morocco binding and I'm coon-for-a-day, limited edition. Take those dark brown sticks: the 9A's and 9B's. I'm gonna look a bit like run laundry in places, but . . ." Simon has voided his underwear. He sits, head forward, talking at the mirror face: intimately: convict to visitor. "Quick, Gas Pocket, I'm gonna teach you about makeup." Simon scribbles 9A on each shoulder, on nape. 9B on feet, with an arrow indicating UP. "See. Easy. Like a paint-by-numbers set. Color me ethnic. And don't waste: I've got the square footage of a WPA mural. Rub hard with your fingers. Minnie, you. Help. Many hands make work dark. Go on, Rose. Talk. Know what, Rose? Your face looks better reflected. Maybe you should get into your clothes backward. Go on, tell me. And no bad news, I'm a sick man. I'll relapse all over you."

"Just secretarial business."

"So. Secrete."

"The weather report for Saturday is good. Do we film?"

"We do."

"Can you manage it?"

"I'm fine. All I needed was a high-daddy embezzlement: it's got me wired like a copilot."

"Well. I'd watch it today. You don't look right to me."

"Blow on your fingers, Lip Service, you're giving me duck bumps. How can a kid that age have circulatory problems? Sorry. You were saying, Rose?"

"Let's go over my checklist. Number One—"

"Here they are." Larry has both Afros: one in either hand. They, his hands, seem muffed for the cold. "A male and a female."

"Jesus. Don't let them breed. How can you tell, did you lift their tails?

Ah, give me whichever one matches the goatee best. Sorry again, Rose. Number One—"

"Number One. Your uncle is upset. Decidedly so. We rented the goat and the mule yesterday. We had to leave them in his chapel overnight."

"*My* chapel." Simon banks his contact lenses in. One has missed the rim. His head will shake—no, no, no, no—until they settle. "So? What's the sweat? Someone—I just got the candidate—will have to shovel dung in a dim religious light."

"Also—tremendous discord over this—the mule ate Mrs. P's begonias. I promised restitution."

"Not much I hope."

"Also the mule tends to buck. We face the prospect of having Our Holy Mother drop-kicked into another state. I merely warn you."

"Okay. Okay. Whaddya want for twenty-five bucks? Trigger?" Simon pelts face and neck with Albolene. Skin seems iced over. Rose can follow the forty-watt bulb, its swaying, in his cheek. "Did you get straw and plywood for the manger?"

"Excelsior was the best we could do. And the mule ate about six pounds of it before Don could stop him. This caused a black, weedy diarrhea all day long. Most unappetizing."

"Teach him, the big glutton. Ja-may-cah. I'll show you an unheard-of eye-land. And would you like a free bamboozle? Olivier? How did he do Othello? Long, floaty, flipperish fingers. Yah."

"I won't ask why you're doing this. I'm sure you have vile reasons."

"I do. I do. Ma-til-dah. She take-ah my moh-ney and she go to Venz-wehla." Simon chicken-pocks himself with 9A and 9B. When making up others, he may tend to paint: caricature. But he is expert, the acknowledged master, of his own face. "I'd really like a sheep. A sheep is your best biblical creature."

"Frankly, Simon. We have trouble enough with two kinds of shit."

"Couple cats, then. Something cheap. Wait. This is the year 2000 plus. So why're we sticking so close to the original screenplay? How about poodles for sheep? Ah. Ah. The monkey. If we could get the Illustrated Man to sign him over. Have Friday nursing on the Madonna's other faucet. Like it? Huh. No? No."

"Moving right along. Let's see—" Robert is at Simon's feet: at his feet with a stick of 9B. Robert's lips kiss in distaste. Simon does not approve: there's too much to learn in life. His own curiosity has overruled squeamishness again and again. Robert's shirt slips out. Below his beltline, chipmunk hole under tree root, Simon can see the approach to Robert's buttock slot. It seems vulnerable. And vulnerable, as well, those amber droplets of the eyeglass arms behind each ear. Simon, an illegal guardian, slicks Robert's froward hair flat with Albolene and dark brown. Choke. Choke again. The van staggers: it misses.

"What's wrong with my rolling stock?"

"I-I th-think. She. She can't."

"Say it, Fishmeal. You've got more sentence fragments than a parole board. Christ, just listening t'you gives me Parkinson's disease."

"The fuel line, she can't draw it up. Been like that since yesterday. May-maybe it's clogged."

"Don's been sucking dirty tank bottoms again. Another bill. How does a darktown do-wah's palms go? Little pinkish finger pads? Yah. Worn down to the honky in all of us. What next, Rose?"

"I've called Tallulah and John. All set there. Maybelline wants to help with continuity or whatever. I presume, from her eagerness, that she's still carrying a torch for you."

"So's her husband. And I know just where he'd like to shove it. What I don't need is t'be reheated like yesterday's pot roast. God, it's shameful, some people just never learn t'share. Keep me out of temptation's ice-sheeted way tomorrow."

"I've heard that one before."

"Yah. Get thee behind me Satan, I wanna do it doggie style." Rose laughs.

"Impossible. You're impossible."

"Well—" Simon has to grin: we're all suckers for praise. "Improbable, anyway."

"Listen, though. Cassius is in Toronto doing an industrial. He's out. Who'll be the reporter?"

"Roland."

"He likes money."

"Nah. Don't worry. I got him a free ride on the Orient Express last week. She stuffed a necklace of twenty solid-silver ben-wah balls up his Bowl Power. Then yanked like she was starting an outboard motor just as he came. He'll do it. And—"

"And—?"

"Hold on. I've just thought of a stab so demonic it frightens even me."

"What?"

"You don't really wanna know, d'you?"

"No. You're right. I really don't."

"Jesus, could those black Lum and Abners carry it off?" The goatee is held over his nose. Simon inhales through it: a respirator. "I'm getting in deep here. Mother, if the actuaries ever learn about this one, it'll lower the national life expectancy in males. Well. Yes. No. Yes. Indecision. Yes. Yes. Call Ball Peen and Sledge."

"Both?"

"Both. Be sure they're here by three tomorrow. Hint at celebrity, star-light, whatever. They'll come. Write that one down in mauve marker pen, it's important. You can tell them when you call Niko t'say I'm still smoked tongue. Or Robert can tell them. Minnie, don't forget to paint my maypole. I can't play this part without a black swizzle stick. I'm a method actor."

"Mr. Lynxx—I."

"Do. And don't give me a hard-on, we can't afford another two pounds of makeup." 9B stings on Simon's thigh. Robert: an oblique reprisal from him. Simon waits. "You made your point, Orgone. I'll pass it on. But not again."

They're alarming, Simon's too-perfect teeth: brilliant, suddenly re-honed: flesh hooks. He is black-on-brown now: a subtle shade: under-painted, thick as Rembrandt canvasses. Minnie will say, "Ohhh," all admiration. The goatee and two caterpillar eyebrows have been spirit-gummed on. With a Q-Tip Simon packs brown cotton up/into each nostril. The nose is flared and African. He'll have to breathe through his mouth, but that seems an altogether appropriate habit. Blacks, Simon can remember, flash their oral inner equipment. He practices making the fat tongue fatter: more conspicuous. What else? Simon pinches a gold cap on his left canine tooth: ah, the crowning touch. Larry has netted Simon's hair. He lodges the Afro wig in place. Simon can't take his reflection. He has to laugh. There's a rubber cannibal-king bone sewn into the wig. DOGGIE stamped on it.

"Scare yourself, Sy?"

"No. It's the stupid bone. It's ridiculous. Ha. Makes me look like a spear carrier from *Bwana Devil*."

"Let me snip it off."

"Nah. On second thought that's just the Kingfish Stevens touch I want. Anyhow, who'd laugh at a six-three, two-hundred-thirty-pound soot? I know: a six-eight, three-hundred-pound soot. Careful, Simon."

"Mr. Lynxx, I don't know you from Adam."

"Do I smell different, Minnie? Like smoked foot soles? Could you find me in a dark spud cellar? Why d'I have this sudden urge t'eat fried possum?"

"All right, Sambo." Rose nips yellow off her pencil. "Now that you're through admiring yourself—"

"Who's through?" Simon has backed to the mirror. "What a half-assed job. He tie-dyed my behind. Shape up, Mold. With that kinda workmanship, you'll never get a corner office in this organization."

"Well I—I sure started at the bottom."

"Jesus, I think that was a joke. It's a sad day in Sloatsburg when I play straight man to an intellectual cedar chest. Lar. Over here. Smooth my whoopee cushions out. Rub hard." Simon has begun to color stomach: the stick screws around in his navel.

"What exactly are we shooting tomorrow? Nine through the top of thirteen?"

"I guess. We can't lease the holy infant until next weekend, right? Isn't that what you told me?" Rose nods. "So—the entrance t'Bethlehem. The interview with Wide World of Sports. I have half a mind t'sketch in a natural childbirth scene. Hell, Mary screamed, didn't she? Ha: funny. Suppose she says, 'And He told me He took precautions. Immaculate, my foot.' Ha. Funny. Or 'That's the last time I use the damned rhythm method.' Ha. Write those down. Minnie, get my green dashiki and the attaché case. It's on the rack. No, to your left. Over further. Where's the makeup spray? Is this my last stick of 9A? Rats. Better save it for a quick touch-up of the tarbrush." His half-browned rear dissatisfies. "I look like I've been sunbathing with a truss on. Ah, well—"

Simon is splashed green. He strides across the van: his new persona on its shimmy and shakedown cruise. Minnie, fooled, amazed, smacks one hand across her mouth. A brown palmprint is left there. Simon kicks his train: swipes at cloth: causes a bright flourish in it: the movement of Elizabethan royalty on stage. He has collected a modest first-aid kit: Albolene, eyeliner, brushes, spirit gum. In the dashiki pocket his hand will come up with half a plug of chewing tobacco. Wizened, hard. Yet delicious to the eye: shiny, with its dry molasses layers, as a lump of cannel coal. Simon grinds the plug in his hand. He can't chew safely now: teeth and tongue no longer discriminate. Simon tends to eat inner cheek flesh. Applause from Larry, from Rose: dark glasses have clinched his anonymity. They won't question the intent. Frankly, they're just glad to be rid of him.

"Where are we now? Sperm Count, go get a fix on our position. Rose, I'll be back by three or four. Got me a little Mau-Mauing t'do." Simon sings. "My head, she's turning around. I left my leetle love in Kingston Town. Kings-ton Town. What is it, Minnie? Huh, woman? Can't you see I'm busy being arrogant and high-toned?"

"Here. For you. A token of my esteem."

Minnie watches: all clear: Robert has snapped the cab door shut behind him. To cover, stage business, Minnie will finger the life line in Simon's right hand. The line has no staying power: deep and succinct: a chisel gouge on wallboard. Simon is curious. What next? Next a big, ornate key, its head in the shape of blow-cheeked winds on some 17th Century map, has been set over his palmistry. Minnie smiles. Green sweats off bronze. Simon is stirred: a wad of sentiment, a wad of lust shove at each other in his throat. Simon combs Minnie's long hair down. She has begun to bash her shy forehead against his African chest. At Minnie's nape Simon can feel a blush form: distinct to the touch as warmth coming up in old apartment radiators.

"Minnie. I'm moved. In fact my Krafft is Ebing."

"For when you get back. A relaxer. Maybe to make you feel your old self."

"At best I expected chicken soup."

"I cook terrible, Mr. Lynxx. Except frozen pizza."

"Believe me, I appreciate this. If it wouldn't ruin my makeup, I'd give you a large kiss. But Robert. Ah, Robert: let this remain a big secret between us. Bettina—my mother, I mean—used to tell me a fairy tale. Every month or so. Y'see, once upon a time this little boy, very much like me, lived with his mother in a deep, dark Ingmar Bergman forest. That mother, Minnie, loved her little boy beyond all telling—in fact she loved him as much as Bettina loved me. Very much as. They were poor. This was before the forest was parceled off as a Hideout in the Poconos at fifteen grand per lot. But I digress, maybe because I feel pain and embarrassment coming on. Anyhow—and here Bettina would poke my chest with her finger, I shouldn't miss the analogy—once upon another time this wicked witch promised the little boy he would have anything he wanted: a six-figure salary after taxes, a second home in Gstaad, a Lotus sports car, Hayley Mills, headlines in *Variety,* if he would just kill his mother and bring the pieces in a picnic hamper t'the wicked witch. So, guess what? Finger still on my bony six-year-old's chest. Well, that little boy up and did it. And he ran, with the picnic hamper, through the forest, all excitement: he couldn't wait t'be Bernie Kornfeld. And—guess what again? That little boy, who was very much like me, he tripped over a root and fell. And his mother's head rolled out over the dark forest floor. And it said, this sententious head, guess what it said, Minnie?"

"I'm at a loss to guess, Mr. Lynxx."

"The head said, 'Did you hurt yourself, my son?' "

"That's an awful story, Mr. Lynxx."

"Minnie. My mother was a nationally ranked bitch."

"Yo, Simon."

"What is it, Robert?"

"We're on Queens Boulevard, almost to the Breyer's Ice Cream factory."

"Okay. Rose, my sandals. Robert, tell Don to stop by the Barclay's Bank on Bridge Plaza North. I'll cab it in from there."

"Mr. Lynxx, did she really tell you that?"

"Uh-huh. Now look at me. I haveta go around in disguise. Mothers have more power than a Democratic party whip. Even nice mothers. Remember that, Minnie."

"I will, Mr. Lynxx." The van has stopped.

"Time t'hit the silk. When I get back we'll do some collective farming, you and I."

Simon has come out in installments. The rear sliding door teases up. A gypsy cab is startled, braked. Late-to-work people consider him. And Simon is considerable. He bucks down, tongue fat and prominent behind the merciless teeth. A Masai prince now, here, in Queensboro Plaza. With his attaché case.

5

"You can sit down, Mr.—"

"Simpson. I per-fer t'stand."

"Well. All right. Fine. If you could just lean out of my light. You're a big man, Mr. Simpson. You cast a substantial shadow. The first name is—"

"My peepul call me Sledge."

"Your people. By that do you mean family?"

"I got no fambly. Peepul as in 'Let my peepul go.'"

"I understand. Yes. Sledge Simpson. And this film you're interested in. Have you some kind of working title yet?"

"*Jesus 3X.*"

"*Jesus 3X.*"

"For father, son and holy ghost. The entire *mey-nage à trois.*"

"Does it have—could you take just one step back? Thanks. *Jesus 3X.* Does it have a religious theme?"

"Yah. Man, it's the gospel according to me. M.E. Me."

Hi-ho, it's fun to be black and big. Simon has hupped one green-insolent thigh onto the desk. Six pencils roll: then logjam. The blotter is moved: it makes L-shaped room now. Simon lamps a lot of jelly-roll tongue and a watcha-gonna-do-about-it? look. Harold Gluck does nothing. Harold Gluck is puny: he seems to need a covering letter to justify his presence. Skin the shade of toes callusing: a blown-kiss mouth, so small, so tight that he can only smoke panatelas in comfort. Dark eyeglass frames cinch-belt his face: square as the Lone Ranger's mask. Hair has been gummed back: a surprise airborne drop on guerrilla baldness at his pate. Under the Arrow shirt, each shoulder appears hung on its clavicle end by a linchpin hammered into place. Simon is confident. It'll be standard-shift easy to intimidate Gluck. For starters, just watch the laminated portrait of Mrs. Gluck. Simon traces her bustline with his thumb: lazy rape. In disagreeable moments, and this is one, a sort of third eyelid will coast down over Harold Gluck's gaze: murky, studied glaucoma. Simon feels power. But Harold Gluck isn't director of National Artists Minority Incentive Fund for nothing. Harold Gluck is director of National Artists Minority Incentive Fund because he has an artificial leg.

"That chair. It's really quite comfortable. Why don't you just—?"

"No sir. No. Sir. All my life I been foxed on by burro-crat types. I know what this cheer desk means, man. It mean I'm black and you white and I gotta stay over this side. No sir. I feel better if we kinda share it."

"Interesting. Very sociological. Yes. I presume that *Jesus 3X* is a recasting of the gospel story."

"Right-on. A *re*-casting. Matthew, Mark, Luke and John gonna look like the Harlem Globetrotters coming downcourt on a fast break. Does that per-plex you?"

"Not in the least. I have no preconceived opinions. The New Testament, thank God, is out of my jurisdiction. Now, Mr. Simpson—"

But, sizzzz—static—Simon has tuned his hearing off. Huh, will he ever forget Norty Sollivan, downstairs, just half an hour ago? They had circled each other in the revolving door: enter Simon, exit Norty. Simon made an abrupt lunge, great acceleration, swinging his partner, and Norty was redirected, by centrifugal insistence, back/toward the National Artists' lobby. Where Simon had taken him out of orbit, one elbow caught: celery grabbed from a not-so-lazy Susan.

"How 'bout ten, man? I need a pop f'my habit."

"Hey, guy—always ready to pitch in, but you hit me just wrong. It's Friday. I don't score the old paycheck 'til three P.M." Simon went full face then: point-blank black. The disguise had held. "Anyhow—these are bad times, let me tell you. I'm overqualified for my job. One fuck-up, and, bang, I'm selling pretzels in front of St. Patrick's Cathedral."

"Lessee the wallet, honky."

"Look, fella. Don't touch. I work out at Jerome Mackey's. You may be big, but I can bench-press three hundred."

"Now ain't that just disgustin'."

"This place is loaded with special cops. All I have to do is shout."

"I am. Like disgusted."

"I'm not exactly taken with you either."

"Man, there's a crab walkin' in your eyebrow. Lookit."

"What?" Pupils wheeled up to see: all blindman white there. "You wouldn't be kidding me, would you? Huh, fella? I've got an important lunch date. Which eyebrow?"

"Shee-it. Wunt touch your money with a rubber on."

"Wait. Which one? Don't go yet. Wait. Jesus. First he mugs me, then he can't even give me a little advice. New York. I hate this city."

Norty did a well-I-couldn't-care-less shrug and revolved back out/onto Third Avenue. But, once there, he shook fists at God, struck his own head six terrific swats with the New York *Post* and revolved 30 r.p.m. speed, back into NA. Simon had been watching. Invisible, able to cloud men's minds so they cannot see him, Simon the Shadow knows. And laughs. Hanh, he must try this again sometime. At the 25–40 elevator bank Norty waited, talking to his shoes. Ding, a young secretary came out. Norty saluted, chivalrous, New York *Post* carefully across one temple, and rode up to boil his eyebrows.

"Mr. Simpson— Ah? I'm glad you find this amusing."

"Huh? No. Pologies. My mind gone fly-fishing. Images. Symbols. Couple big visual meta-fours just come in on the airwaves. Y'know how it is."

"I'm afraid not. I have been spared, to my profound relief, any desire or aptitude whatever for creativity." Gluck stinks just then: of medicine, of nose drops swallowed down. Offensive: Simon will back away. Is this the filtering brown cotton in his nostrils? He can't be sure: smell received or smell generated within? "We'll need some data on your artistic background."

"My flicks, huh?"

"That would help."

"Ah. See. *Black Freud*, 1974. *Black Marilyn*, 1975. *Black Marilyn* won best picture at the Tobago Film Festival. 1976, *Black Buck Nixon*. I couldn't get that one released in a Trailways baggage room up here. You wunt find Sledge Simpson at the Trans-Lux, but I gotta wear dark glasses in Tobago."

"You do? Sunny down there, is it? Well. Well, yes. Those are impressive credentials. I think. Yes. Anyhow, Mr. Simpson: you understand that NAMIF isn't interested in a Ken Russell or a Frances Ford Coppola. Now. *Jesus 3X*. Can you give me a rough estimate of your budget needs?"

"Rough?" Simon's tongue has settled, ovoid: as some reptile would engorge a whole egg. "Quarter million. Can't take less. Even then I gotta use forceps and a jack t'pull it out."

"Frankly, that's highish. There are, as you can imagine, many applicants. It isn't our usual policy to put up the whole nut. We like to spread the risk around, in a manner of speaking. What other sources could you come up with?"

"Hum. Other sources? You count welfare?"

"I see. Bad as that, eh?"

"Man. This ain't *Deep Nostril* we talkin' about. I gonna need more than six tits an' a clean sheet. *Jesus 3X* is a major minority flick."

"Right. I don't dispute that. We'll do our best: after all that's what we're in business for. Don't drop that paperweight. It's a memento. Our committee meets on the first Wednesday of each month. I'll need a treatment to send around to my colleagues."

"Treatment? Treatment?"

"Just ten pages or so."

"Treatment? I'll give you a treatment." Thock! Simon clops his open palm down on the desk top: first-rate noise. Harold Gluck has a fending, swift hand up. His artificial leg kicks wood in the desk well. Also thock! They are both surprised. But Simon thinks he can sense weakness, loud and clear. Simon is mistaken. "Don't break you white man's wind on me. I sing songs up here—with my eyeballs. An' in a im-provsatory manner. Free form. Words? Shit, Sledge Simpson don't pucker his natural response with no script. English was invented by the teachers' union, them bigots. Save your treatment stuff for *Gidget Gets an Abortion*. I'm a creeative artist."

"Ah, but we do need something concrete. You may not like it, Mr. Simpson. I may not like it. Actually—no offense meant—I have better things to do than read ten pages of the gospel according to even such a reliable exegete as yourself. But money is tight these days."

"You ever make a film, Cohen?"

"Gluck."

"That's what I said. You ever make a film, 'cept around your bathtub?"

"No, as I indicated before, I have neither creative talent nor creative ambition." Gluck lets out a conciliatory smile: yes, the teeth are fake. "Face up to it, Mr. Simpson. You'll just have to manufacture something. For appearance' sake, if for no other reason."

"Um. I got a reel of *Black Marilyn* in there. Powerful, rich as a ounce of uncut scag. Make your soul jive and boogie."

"No. We haven't any projection equipment available." The bluff has gone through. "Here. In any case, you'll have to fill out this simple form. Just biographical material. Use my pen." Simon swipes at the legal sheet: he doesn't think. And, look out, five 9A brown fingerprints have come off on it. Five more. Then a thumb and a forefinger. Simon's persona rubbing away. He crushes the paper down.

"Lord. Oh, Lord. Agin. I get this all the time. Right up the clarinet hole." Simon laughs: Simon shakes his head. The sweet, sad irony of oppressed people. "Evry time. The man got to stick you with a pen and a piece of paper."

"What now, Mr. Simpson?"

"What now?" Simon has disclosed teeth: a murderer's row of them. "What now? That what you askin' me?"

"If it isn't an inconvenience."

"Shit. I can't read nor write. That's what now." Gluck is silent. Simon has unfurled a hand for show: as if it were defective, somehow not prehensile, and couldn't hold pens. "You feel good now? You shamed me good enough yet? Huh?"

"I—"

"Why'd I go an' say that? Why'd I let you worm it outa me? Lissen, Cohen. You better not tell nobody that. Treatment. Treatment, he says. Whyn't you just cut my balls off? Take that there letter opener. Do it. Go on. Yeah! Oh, yeah!" Simon applauds: still more impressive noise. He's into it, Sledge Simpson. He believes it all, even the parts he hasn't thought of yet. "An' I ain't stupid, I see you figurin' I'm stupid. I got dyslexia, you know what that is?"

"I do."

"They thought I's a mental retard in school. Cause I make little letter d's steada little letter b's."

"I assure you—"

"Big eyeglasses. All you Jews born with big eyeglasses, so to read the fine print. An' how come there's no brother sittin' behind that desk? How come it's another white Jew? Oh, man, I get so tired. You see some new film out. *Black Snatch* starrin' Black Peter an' Black John with music by Black King Cole. Boss, you say. Brothers out doin' something. Yeah. An' unnerneath—all the time—unnerneath it say: Pro-duced by Moses Goldberg and the Zionist National Bank."

"Take it easy, Mr. Simpson. Your secret is safe. Pardon me." Harold Gluck has blown his nose: a single Kleenex from Gluck's pocket pack of twelve. Simon is still hot, indignant for his new self, but the patient extraction, this thoughtful, neat blowing, they disturb him.

"Know where I was born? Lynch, Mississippi. An' it were'n named after no man called Lynch. Population sign on U.S. 96 say seventy-five and the Klan yoosta write 'mi-nus one' evry time old Uncle Remus die with his foot in some rich man's skunk trap. I's number sixteen: ten brothers an' five sisters. Time I was born Mizz Simpson' womb was like Motha Hubbard's cubhad. No nurshment. I couldn't walk 'til I's seven. My legs was bent like pork ribs. An' they hurt: in the bone. My brother, Ray, he made me a little wood cart so I could pull myself between the cotton rows. We hadda pick—"

"Whoa. Please. We've all had our little setbacks in life. It's better not to dwell on them." Harold Gluck has pushed a Luden's honey cough drop in: not much clearance at the lip. "NAMIF doesn't consider suffering to be a prerequisite: just three references and a short treatment."

"Setbacks? I wear my big setback right here. On my face." Simon pinches skin: gingerly, gingerly. "There's nobody care about your color."

"True. But I do have what one would call, I believe, a Jewish nose." The cough drop smashes. Gluck has turned in profile. "A textbook example, don't you think?"

"That. Shit, that's a union card in New York." Simon is angry and too involved. It defeats his cunning.

"Well, why don't you take your dark glasses, Mr. Simpson, and walk around Tobago for a bit?"

"Lissen, Cohen."

"Gluck, Gluck, Gluck." Harold Gluck has shoved himself up: hands on desk edge. "Enough. I'm bored. Very quickly: In 1956 I left Hungary, where I had been living comfortably in Kobanya Prison. Sixteen years for distributing a leaflet unfriendly to the People's Republic. Twice each week, while the supply lasted, an AVH strongman would remove one of my teeth." Gluck makes his upper plate shoot out: return: a small cash register drawer. "I also received very stimulating shock treatments. And scopolamine: two shots a day for six weeks. For variety I was also wrapped in sodden blankets. Forty-eight, seventy-two, ninety-six hours at a go. When the blankets dried, my skin was so brittle that it split and cracked. Cardinal Mindszenty was a ward mate of mine in Kobanya—but you wouldn't know about him. Then, after five years and a month, I was released by the '56 uprising. In time to see my seventeen-year-old brother machine-gunned. My first wife died of pneumonia while we waited in an Austrian DP camp. For six months after escaping we lived pretty much on mushrooms and an occasional cat."

"We never had mushrooms in—"

"Oh, shut up. My turn on the violin, Mr. Simpson. I was wounded at the border. An inconsequential thing, a flesh wound. Unfortunately it became gangrenous." Harold Gluck tugs his pants leg: as if signaling some trained animal out. He walks. Simon can hear the sound of unoiled leather harness. "They cut it off just above my knee."

"I—"

"As for reading and writing. Well, I started learning English when I was twenty-three. Now then, Mr. Simpson. Would you like me to fill this sheet out for you?"

"If—" Simon tugs his Afro forelock. "If it wunt be an inconvenience."

"I'm sick of it. This eternal game of Queen for a Day. I don't mean to disparage your bad luck. One's own hardship has a special poignance. Please sit. Thank you. Once upon a time men were valued for their achievements. Now, if you've had both elbows blown off, you can lecture at any junior college in America. Or ten years' imprisonment for espionage: why, you can live off the cocktail-party hors d'oeuvres alone. To be candid, I'm sick of being lionized for my misfortune. This is Harold Gluck. You know Harold, lost a shin in the Hungarian uprising. I'd like to forget it." Harold Gluck takes another application form. "If I may, though: one or two stylistic comments, Mr. Simpson. From one who knows. There are ever so many people who picked cotton. Why not say you picked something else: pockets, noses? And you are—it's too obvious —in a state of repulsive good health. Get run over by a car, Mr. Simpson.

No, better yet, a jeep. Then you can blame the military-industrial complex." Harold Gluck laughs: through the tight mouth it comes out a tweet. "After all, you want to be on the 'Today' show when *Jesus 3X* opens in a Trailways baggage room."

"I got a rusty nail at home. Maybe I could give myself lockjaw."

"Ha. Good. We understand each other." Harold Gluck writes: NAME —Simpson, Sledge. "This is just a p.r. gimmick and a nice tax write-off for NA. You tape some gibberish about *Jesus 3X* and I'll have my secretary type it out. We might finagle, oh—fifty grand at the outside. I promise nothing. It's done pretty much at random. Black of the Month Club, we call it. I couldn't care less who got the money."

"Fifty's all right. Ahem." Simon swallows down: a wedge of greed. Hands rub together: his own gestures will begin to surface now. Simon has love for Harold Gluck.

"We'll need references. Can you find someone who has a good word to say about you? Perhaps some notable figure in Toboggan—Tobagan—film circles?"

"Ah—"

"Is there a Tobagan Film Festival?"

"Could be. Could be. I never been in Tobago myself."

"As I suspected. You're a splendid and—I must say—energetic fraud, Mr. Simpson. A credit to the race. Of frauds. If I asked you for identification, could you produce some?"

"Um. Happen to leave it in my other dashiki. But Monday—"

"No matter. No matter. Don't inconvenience the real Mr. Simpson. He'll probably need his driver's license. To tell the truth, Mr. Sampson—"

"Simpson."

"That's what I said. To tell the truth—I'm not even Jewish."

"That so? I'm not even anti-Semitic."

"Gluck is a useful name. Could be almost anything. It's German Catholic actually. The Jewish nose was produced in Kobanya, by a truncheon. You won't blow my cover?"

"Your secret is safe. Actually, I'm—" Simon stops there. "I'm surprised."

"You're right. It is a union card. And I *am* anti-Semitic. Now. How about those references?"

"Well. I know Norty Sollivan."

"Dear me. I wouldn't mention that prick around here. If we all had dysentery, Norty Sollivan couldn't push a toilet-paper requisition through NA. Well, no rush. Mull it over for a day or so. Someone must like you, Mr. Simpson." Simon is up, thoughtful, pacing: on a conscientious eight-foot-long patrol near the chair. His dashiki, emerald-gold, will undulate in many small, fleet ripples: the motion and color of a southern green snake lashing through grass. This has fascinated Gluck.

He holds one finger up: as though trying to catch his own attention. Simon is unsure: has he been signaled? Then, snap, Gluck's wide-beam glasses fall off. "Not now, dammit. Stop. Sit down, please. Quickly. Please."

"Uh?"

"No. Too late. Hurry, it's coming. Mr. Simpson—the door. Lock it. Lock it."

"B'why?" Gluck's words stammer. Simon can monitor dread in them.

"Now. Do it now. Lock up. Up." Gluck trips the intercom key: he has to convey his finger there. "Sally, don't disturb us. No phone. No, not him either. Half—half hour." Simon is back from the door. "My pen, Mr. Simpson. Take it."

"I tole you, man. I can't write."

"Take it." Simon is appalled: what lewdness. Gluck has hiked up one pants leg. He starts to amputate his artificial limb. It's a thing of stressed metal bands and fabric, like tough, gnawn turkey drumsticks. Simon will look elsewhere: the way children do when elders strip. "Flashing color in your dashiki. Kicked it off. Happens to me with a picket fence, venetian blinds. I'm epileptic. It's coming now."

"Hole on. Don't do nothin' rash. I just ain't male nurse material."

"Please—"

"You got a registered coward here,-man. I faint at the sight of skin. Lemme call a doctor."

"Don't. It would probably cost me my job. People like a history of misfortune, but present troubles tend to irritate them." Gluck has cleared the desk for action. He hops to Simon. "Take my leg. I don't want it broken."

"No. Uh-ahh. Ummm." Simon with an artificial leg under his arm: as if someone had stepped through him. The shiny, black loafer kicks up. "Wait. What am I supposed to do with this, this—?"

"Just shove it in the umbrella stand." Gluck has lain, three-quarters spread eagle, on his desk top. The teeth are out now: they bite a memo pad. Gluck is dwindling down. "That taste, like I've had artichokes to eat. Oh, here it comes. Here it—aaah—here."

"Lissen. I'm very sensitive to other people's suffering. I try t'leave whenever I can."

"Hold me, Mr. Simpson. Hold on for dear life: I won't remember anything afterward. Just walk out. I'll need to nap. Give me a call next week, remind me of this. Don't be scared, you're strong. It's quick."

"Man-o-man. I wish I was in Tobago, wherever that is."

"The pen. On my tongue. Keep it down. Aaah."

A weird, long shudder plows Harold Gluck. The stump has risen, shaking its wind-sock pants leg out. Simon, queasy, disciplines it: bullet snub-end shoved down. Crest-break, faster: spasms build in frequency and zest. Gluck seems to be coming together: drawn rigid by an inner purse string. It mimics the orgasm: most of all Simon will find that repellent. He wrestles the disease-strong torso flat. And then—punch, punch, punch —Gluck's right fist has connected on Simon's ear. The concussions are robust: Simon is almost out on his feet. One contact lens has snuck up/under his lid: he can't see. Simon snorts smells in: they are antiseptic, neuter. Hearing hums monotones. His skin is pinned and needled. Again, Gluck's fist gets through his guard: six, seven. Simon is losing: he has to clinch. No time here for politeness, for those conventions that regulate handshake and kiss. Gluck is dangerous: wild as a charged fire hose. Simon will need all his weight. He climbs, a husband, a lover, on the thrashing stomach. Thigh over thigh, Simon rides Harold Gluck: rides him down.

Descent from an upright posture is threatening, uncivil: it disturbs the pedestrian world. Also, Simon isn't well-dressed enough to fall. To fall— on Madison Avenue in New York—you need at least a jacket and tie: anything short of that is vagrancy. This thought alone will keep Simon erect. Oh, he has taken his lumps: three: above the eye, behind the ear, beneath the fake Afro scalp. He shuts down one nostril and bloody-brown cotton is fired, recoil-less, from his nose. Gluck probably broke it: the bridge. Simon can smell wet, salted internal damage there. Chromatic pains ring under his skull: a series, bong-bing-b-bong: some suburban door chime. Simon wants to get prone and nude soon: he can't recuperate in clothing. A cab has turned, another. Simon hangs out the usual, peremptory gesture: service. But it has slipped his mind: peremptory is menacing when you're Mr. Sledge Simpson. The cabs go OFF DUTY for a racist half-block. Simon has put his attaché case down. He holds on: to the rim of a wire-mesh trash basket: it is like steering, like bus drivers at their large-diameter horizontal wheel. The trash basket doesn't appear very full now.

"Gluck. Jesus. Getting gang-banged by his own body."

Simon envies Harold Gluck that wild, athletic fit. He, Simon, has never been enthralled so. He respects concentration. This, he has always supposed, is the postulate of great art and its special negotiation with a human mind: fierce, blunt, generous, killing, whole. *Nota bene*: he can be, capital R, Romantic. Gluck's arms were rigid: they seemed to sing, the way taut rigging does in high wind. His legs spread, crotch thrust out/up on indurate buttocks. Simon can't recall having such quick and thorough intimacy with another man. It was a moment that one must feel responsible for, protective of, parent to. Simon pushes up: he is nauseated. What about playing Christ as epileptic? Christ, it's a thought. Or as addict: after each miracle, the virtue gone out: symptoms then of vehement withdrawal. Simon has begun to walk, acrophobic, afraid that he may see his feet from way up here. The day, along residential Sixty-seventh Street, is brilliant and correct. In it he will be a non-participant. That spirit bubble, the inner ear, adjusts for equilibrium. A stride of ill repute: alcoholic and ungainly. He can't carry it off. He comes down hard on a brownstone stoop in simpler, more compatible shadow. And for some time—for, say, fifteen minutes—Simon will be very sick.

It shames him. He has a fever rush that can be smelled: dry warmth, of electric baseboard registers burning off their dust. A gel has been slipped in/over the sun. Pink-salmon varnishes his sight: color of closed eyelids looking toward glare. Both ears have a bad connection: they fry fat. Then his vision has come up, on powerful dimmers, overcompensating. Sixty-seventh Street is strobe-lit. Simon ducks his head down/between open knees: the body, like a wagon train, circling for defense. But then his feet drop through pavement: again: uhh, once again. He has to keep an eye on them: confront the illusion with common sense. His right hand won't go up. He watches: he bullies it. Weakness has the drop on him: he isn't used to that: it can make him sheepish. Simon tries deep breathing and his pulse gets on a high horse. The beachcomber wind concerts itself here and there: child cyclones form: their poor vacua fish up paper and leaves. An old lady has crossed the street to avoid him. He must get up: he's lowering the social tone.

Simon has noticed it: Central Park, to the left and beyond Fifth Avenue. Proneness is acceptable there. And perhaps he'd like to dig for a while: that might be recreative. Feet mooch, the step of people in loose and heel-less shoes. Simon will walk conservatively: right beneath his head, to keep it on. A water truck has overtaken him. The truck fingers, poking for small change under cars. Its gush is in his ears already. An artificial humidity has risen: there's more smell than he can house. Stomach shoots juice out: a practice drill for emergencies. But health is just around the corner: is around it now. Some sort of woman: any sort. He never does see her face, but that deep-in-my-pelvis walk will serve. The transaction of their presences, from sighting to her disappearance eastward and behind him, will take no more than six or seven seconds: no more, enough, to make Simon well. The response, of course, is slavish: like erections on hanged men. He shows off much tongue. His saunter gets tuned up: wheel aligned. He is male: one pole in some magnetic equation. Simon has no ulterior intent: the energy, nonetheless, is available, PDQ. Simon comes out into sunlight on Fifth Avenue: healed. His own hormone treatment.

A honky honks at him. Simon—what did you expect?—has crossed against the wise, well-meaning red. It arouses: blackness does: it gives implicit license. God, the day in/day out grind of being white and Protestant. There is a bleary incubus, a haze, over Central Park. Leaves have autumn rust spots on them. In a fast-dealing gust they shuffle, they click: hard, enameled. He feels sudden and new, on bail from the rare indignity of illness. Simon noble-savages north over bathroom-tile pavement. White walkers defer: black make a comradely but asymptotic approach. Simon has come up with some first-class babareebah head movements. You know, Congo cats must see more, heads jiving around all the time. Now Simon sees a brother. This, he can tell right off, it's stored in his secondhand racial memory, this has to be what they/we call an Uncle Tom: gray suit, wire-rim glasses, Phi Bete key flippety-flop on the thigh. Simon is embarrassed for his just chosen people.

"Hi theah, niggah." The black is unhappy. His walk, organized at first, cracks into discursive, flat steps: stops full.

"Pardon me, sir—"

"I say: Hi theah, niggah. A kinda how-dee-do mung bruthers."

"Sir—"

"Suh. Suh. Suh. Oh, man: you is sure uh bad-ass dude. Like some Ku Kluxed train portuh. Yassuh an' massuh. An' ol' Mr. Bojangles, he *dance*. Sheet, thuh Twennieth Century Limited doan run no moah. They done *limited* it. Them white man threads, uh dress-up chim-pan-*zee* can't look moah almos' human than that. What you, uh Brooks Brother? Real black man let de wind blow in." Simon has upped his dashiki skirt. "Keep thuh parts procreative. Gib 'em air. White man suit be worse than weahin' uh rubbah jock."

"If you think going around in costume, like some stage Nigerian, makes you any more authentic, I can—aaah." Simon has rested his shut fist on the black man's chest. Just, um, rested it there. 9A brown knuckle spots come off on the linen shirtfront.

"This heah make me o-thentic. Doan matter whut you weah. Go in thuh men's room foh uh piss, some silk's still gone hand you uh dime t'shine his shoes."

"I'm a radiologist. I have a profession—"

"Pro-fesshun. Haw. You thinks you jes' uh whitey they lef' in thuh oben too long."

"Take your hand away, now."

"Umm."

"All right. If it comes to that, all right. You're bigger than I am, but I'll fight. I had a bladder operation two months ago, but I'll fight. Glasses and all, I'll fight." The black unhorses his jacket; appears ready, at least. "Oh no. You've put some kind of shit on me."

"Trouble wif white shirts—"

"This is an outrage. We'll never reach parity." The black has his vest-pocket handkerchief out. It's phony: two triangles of cloth on a plastic card. But that will just rub it in. "Look at this. Look at this. God damn you." Uh-oh: a well-developed sense of property. Now he *will* fight, bladder and all: not for dignity, for Pierre Cardin. Simon is gone. One step onto a park bench: step two, over the granite wall and up/under low shrubs: into Central Park.

"Keep thuh faith, baby."

"Come back, you fascist. Look at this. Dirty, dirty black hands. Oh, we'll never reach parity. I've told her that a hundred times. Never. Well, let her try to wash this off. Let her just try. Never. We'll never—"

Simon has to frog-walk, low. He barges, crashing. The undergrowth is rank, in two senses of that word: a) it's lush, very dense, b) it also stinks from male urine. Ripeness is—faugh—all. Branches switch his face. They scalp him: the Afro is gone, treed. He will look, when he reaches up for it, like a nest robber. Something about this thicket is artificial, urban. The branches, for instance, seem slack and ropy: items you'd associate, not with nature, but with an overloaded six-way plug. The forest floor appears to have, well, *accumulated*: as detritus might accumulate, after fifteen years, beneath a large appliance. And, at the heart of darkness, there it is. Simon stands erect: Simon says, Hello. The condom bush, I presume. Limp, milked, let-out rubbers decorate seventy or eighty twigs. The bush, a hawthorn, is otherwise long sterile. Tent caterpillar slums from April stretch on it: color and texture of old, torn nylons. Earth all around has been buffed nude by human friction. Simon finds it meaningful: at last (he knew there was one) the graveyard of forgotten copulations. A place for true believers, a shrine. Such punctilious loyalty to the act. Collectors have this sort of passion. It could be his theme song: anything worth doing is worth running right into the ground.

Simon needs to display. He has hitched the dashiki front up. Urine blasts out a foamy bowl, p.s.i. enough to unearth small roots, knock fat acorns aside. Simon, His Mark. And looking up (one commonly does it at a urinal, one disowns the act: it's *down there*) Simon can watch penthouses of 6 East Sixty-seventh and 1 East Sixty-eighth. Do they watch him? Legible Fifth Avenue voices come through: he's in earshot, in eyeshot. Coitus here would be a raspberry blown at civilization: the place has outlaw bravado: like getting screwed behind doors half ajar. Simon is raunchy: the ambiance has worked on him. Alone, in such a place, Simon has often made time with himself: "Hi there, Big Boy." His body, aroused by this reckless gall, yet bashful, skittish yet, would shiver a protest: "I'll run. I'll scream. They're right next door. They'll save me." But they never did. Simon is an easy lay for himself. Their mating, mind and body, is of giants, enormous: trees sway: animals duck belowground. Aaaah. Then, Um? A stupid branch has pinked his buttock. Simon swats it away. Um: he has another think coming: the branch is honed, steel. The branch is a knife. And his attaché case has been taken: no longer attached. Never a dull moment. Simon, caught with his pants up, is being mugged.

"Ay-hem. Doan nobuddy git nuvvus now, speshully him what has that there mean shiv up mah ass. I's jes' shakin' the las' drop off'n mah egg roll afore we pro-ceeds wif thuh pro-ceedin's. This sho is uh barrass-ment. Mah mammy allus say, Put yo clean unnerpants on, nebber can tell when you gone get tapped wif yo pork hangin' out."

"Shut it. Shut-shut. Shut it, man. Man, just shut up. You hear me? Huh? Huh—you hear? See what he's got in that suitcase, Hossmeat."

"Don't say my name, Piggy."

"Shit. Ain't your real name. Your real name George Foster. Ge-orge. Huh, George."

"Fuck you, Julius Jones what live on 139th Street." Simon laughs. Great: he's being mugged by Amos and Andy. The man was right: they'll never reach parity.

"Off that, dude. Off it. Off. Don't laugh. Shit, don't laugh at me. Shit. What's he got, Hoss?"

"Ain't nothin' in this dumb bag. Just some ladies' makeup stuff. Maybe he's a queen. He got a kinda dress on."

"Right. Right-right. Oh, man. I feel this knife in my hand. I feel it. It's a *weapon*. Sweet. Sweet. Hey, dude. You, dude. You got a wallet? Out it. Now. Man, now."

"Mister. This here's one real crazed junkie. He got a monster habit. I don't want him to cut you, mister. He ain't wrapped too tight. You better do just what he say. You better be real swift."

Simon will discount that news release. Pig, a/k/a Julius Jones, doesn't live up to his advance press. He's twelve or thirteen at the upside: just young enough to be dangerous by mistake. Tall: five foot ten: pituitary all in an uproar. He has grown out of his ankles. They appear rickety as a tenement fire escape. Simon has the urge to blow at him. Pig affects a jumbo, dry dandelion for hair: his Afro is reddish, teased up, mostly air: you could read newsprint through it. He will blink. He will sponsor man-neristic facial tics. His smile is out of context. Pig specializes in the abrupt. Yet his pupils are too precise for heroin. Simon is art-critical. The word repetitions, the jerkiness, they seem stylized: outtakes from an old Brando performance. And Hossmeat is pure parody. Five foot one: Ping-Pong-eyed: a mouth that pronounces O: the face of someone hung yes-terday. Hossmeat would love to call it off: a do-over. His blue sweatshirt says YALE. He has to keep rediscovering his hands in either sleeve. Simon is their lion: the trophy of some New York male initiation. But they have flushed peril out: they know it. Simon won't be a pushover and, for that reason, he might die on this comely September afternoon: the accident of their fear. Still, Simon can't run. He'd get maybe five yards through the extension-cord jungle in his spilling, awkward cos-tume. And he doesn't particularly want an out. The scene is cinematic: it engrosses him. Anyway, given his cash position, Simon can't afford to be sniped.

"You li'l cats is mos' *foul*. Done scare me down to one inch long. Yas-suh. This sure is thuh earliest Hallerween in yeahs."

"Man. Oh, man. Don't run no wise changes on me. Watch, dude. Go on, watch. Watch it, man. Huh. It's sharp, sharp. It's sharp. Dude ain't so smart-ass, this is stickin' in his gut."

"Now, what I jes' caint rhyme: how come you nice culled boys rollin' on a bruthuh black man? Lordy, you shud be out pullin' thuh ortho-pedic shoes off poor, ole Jew ladies. Rapin' fine, white co-eds up at CCNY. Thas ah fack. It's expected of you. It's yo eth-nick sponsibility, li'l Mr. Hossmeat."

"Sheet, I's only ten. How'm I gonna bang up no ofay broad? I can't even get my own self off, nohow I try."

"Hoss. Man, Hoss. Don't talk to that mother. That mother's dead. That mother got me mad. Shit mad. Shit-oh, shit. Mad. I'm gonna come down on that dancer there. Hey, dude? What your business, dude?"

"Me. Li'l me? Ahm onny thuh hebbyest pimp up on Lenux Ave, is what. Got me uh slick red Caddy-lac and uh Blackglamuh coat and sho nuff eight blond vanillas wukkin' in mah stable. I get paid for moh or-gasms than enny man in Hollem. Them chicks, I put uh meter down buhtween they legs. Tick, tick, tick. Sebenty-fi' cents uh mile, you *ride*. Mah bottom woman, she sco' two hunnert uh 'our, clean."

"What he say, Pig? He sure don't talk like no American cat. You a gator, mister? You from Alabama or some nigger place like that?"

"Listen, Mr. Big Pimp Dude. Big Pimp Dude got big stash. Toss it down, man. Now. Huh? Huh. There. Right there. I'm sick, man. Sick of the *time* it's takin'. Sick."

"Mah. Mah. Jes' how you gone see straight t'kill me, you head jerkin' and boogyin' round like that?"

"Don't jive me, man. Now." Simon has smiled. It's a clean affront.

"I doan pay t'get fucked, Mr. Pig. People, they pay me."

And Piggy has thrust home. The knife tossed underhand at Simon. A balletic exercise, abstract, full of ghetto *sprezzatura*. Simon jerks up: on parade and at attention. The dashiki has been hit.

"Oh, yeah. It's singin', Hoss. Hoss, I can hear it. Music, man: that is sweet music. Oh, yeah. Next one is skin. Skin. Skin. Mr. Big Pimp Dude."

"Well, suh. Seems you done gib me uh extra fly, jes' wheah it ain't con-venient 'less I piss throo mah belly button. You bloods sure got spirit. Doan mind at all committin' su-cide on this heah fine aftuhnoon. Say what you come on along t'my spot Saddy night. Ah set you up in uh legit bizness, rollin' drunks in thuh park. Co-mission and bennyfits and two weeks' paid vacation time."

"Hoss, this is bad. Like he don't hear me. Like the man is deaf. No way. Can't go on like this, no way. No *way*." Piggy is in idle. They throb, head and arms and thighs, held just out of gear. Pig will look cool at murder. But style may cost him efficiency. Simon has high hopes of that. "Hoss, I gotta do this cat. I gotta do him. Man, the thing's comin' up on me. Hard. It's *hard*."

"Don't cut him all up, Pig. 'Member las' time, 'member that? Cat's blood whoosh all over."

"No. No, I gotta do. I have *got* to do it. The man's been hasslin' me. Get up close behind him, Hoss. In, in. I got to work. Shit, here it is. See it. See. See, now!"

The knife has been cast out again. Simon is all profile. Another cast: negligent, to get the range. Pig might be throwing birdseed at him. Simon has effaced himself in the condom bush: is embellished by it. Time's up. Now Pig must stab or lose face. Simon can sniff Pig's fear: a cave smell. Hossmeat is to one side. He will be a diversion, "Yah, yo, yah." He reminds Simon of little Friday. His teeth, on their own initiative, clack. Hossmeat makes rabbinical, small hand-washings. Simon is ready and at ease. The exhilaration of it. And, relief: Pig has aimed below. He means just to instruct: a submortal nick out of Simon's thigh. The stroke extends, graceful, somewhat self-indulgent and—glom—as you hook a mosquito, slapping down, Simon has Pig's knife hand in his.

"He gomme! He gomme! Owshit! Grab on his legs, Hoss. Get his legs from out."

"How'm I gonna do that? How'm I gonna do it?"

"You two nigger chits pay 'tention now here. This's one fierce Bogart you messed up wif. Sledge, he gone giv you uh lessum now, first grade. In how t'git yo asses whumped on. Real easy like."

Up: Simon declares Pig a winnah: right arm way overhead. Tick t'tack: gristle, sprained, rips in Pig's shoulder housing. They, Simon and Pig, Pig on tiptoe, hang down from the knife. Simon has let his thumb hump-slide up/along the blade. For one burlesque moment (every fight between men has at least one: farce is a type of savageness) they appear to ballroom-dance. Simon, more male, leads: thigh vs. thigh: left hand up with Pig's right hand: right hand down with Pig's left hand: long, flat porch-glider steps. Simon is concentrated: in his thumb, thumb, thumb-power—filling, power-full. The blade has started to fold sideward: to jackknife: at an unwise, unmeant-for angle. The break is heard in their forearms: spang: they get its vibes. Then Pig has said, "Oh shit. *Shit.*" His astonishment will honor Simon. And Hoss, foolhardy, yet you have to give him credit, has done a submarine roll. Now he is on foot, standing under/inside the dashiki, cheek to bigger cheek with Simon's spacious nakedness. Very tropical in there, green. Hoss beats, bulls: bites. It will dispirit him: that feeling of there-is-so-much-to-do-here. Simon has only been tickled, pink—not brown—around his buttocks. He won't make reference to the event: it's beneath him. Now his right hand, Pig's left tagging along, has come up and upppp. The hand is in Pig's Afro: some heavy social grooming goes on: an ape-to-ape intimateness. Pig has sobbed. The Afro, his liver-heart-testes, has been made fun of. And Pig can remember that magnet half-instant when human faces pull close—urgent, curious, unreserved—pull to the point at which positive and negative must fulfill a promise: when some girl has caught her mouth on his. He doesn't believe it (this-is-impossible-we-are-two-men) and, disbelieving, he is taken easily. Simon soul-kisses Pig. A snide rape: a smirked thing done.

"Mutha-fuck." Pig drools spit out: Simon's. "Mutha-fuck snake faggot kist me."

"Oh, tasty-fine. Yessuh. An' that jes' a mouf-ful, what to come. Cause wheah you headin', mah good man, theah ain' no ass cherries. Uh-*huh*. Li'l boy like you jes' sweet punk honey foh thuh trusties up at Attica. Oh, they gonna hab you doin' push-ups on uh hard thing. Bettuh squidge some pork fat on yo' butterscotch be-hind. Foh sure." Simon has shoved Pig away/down. Pig rolls. "Bettuh stot getting sleek, Pussy. Bettuh stot *oilin'*. Cause you so dumb you couldn't boost birdshit fum uh empty parrot cage. Pig man, you gone do some *long* time soon."

"Run, Hoss! Run!"

"Hey! Hole up!" Hoss yelling through green. "Hep me!"

"He done gone, li'l man. He done split like a Liberian tanker." Shrubbery stools on Pig: jostled, it will attest to his departure and general ENE heading. Simon is big with child: and at term. The pregnantness under his dashiki has dropped. Simon delivers Hossmeat, a difficult confinement. "Eeeny, meeny, moe. Done grooped me a niggah by thuh toe. Hossmeat, you have been eloped on. Julius Jones is gone wif my dollah nine-ty fake real mole-hide briefcase, an' lef' you to ennertain the guests."

"Piggy! Piggy!" Simon has Hossmeat by the AL in YALE. Just YE there. "Piggy! Piggy!" Simon clutches. The shirt is taken in across its chest: seems to fit. "Piggy! Piggy!"

"Aw, shuddup."

"Mister, please, mister, don't boogie me. I too small down there. My mam she can't neber take my temperature, what I don't yell out."

"Shuddup."

"Don't do me, mister-sir. I'm gonna cry now. An' I'm all wet right into my sneaker foot. I kin hear it squoosh."

"Shuddup."

"Don't boogie me and I tell you that crazy popper's real name, ain't no Julius Jones. Then you call the raise, you drop a dime on him. Teach him a—"

"Hole still."

"I'm holdin'. I'm holdin'! It's my body don't care what trouble I get in. It's my body all by itself bein' disrespectful and smart-ass."

"Now ain't dat a lessum to us all? I learn it fore I get kicked off'n mah mammy's teat." Simon is reflective. He'd very much care to taste that discrepant, that other-than-his, saliva: Piggy's. But he can't. An experience, a gift of tongues: taken from him. "Allus wuk alone, li'l Hossmeat. You truss nobuddy futher'n you kin poke cane up uh woodchuck's hindy hole. Heah?"

"Mister-sir, I hear. But I don't alla time peep what you sayin'. You talk like my grammaw if her teeth is out."

"I's talkin' good Nigger English, if you shet dat rubber raft mouf an' you lissen. Sledge gone tell you huh story, famus black man done tole me."

"Ow. Ow. Don't pull my hair so tight like that. Make my face go right up in th'air. I hearin' you."

"Hum. Oncet pon huh time, theah's two foul thiefs gone rob a butchuh store. Well-suh, these two bad cases, one night they whock uh big hole in thuh butchuh store wall. Yup, right intuh dat freezuh place, wheah thuh hebby meat is hung up. You listnin' down theah, Burr-head?"

"Hebby . . . heavy meat. In the freezer place. If I lissen real sharp, you gone bring the Man down on me? Piggy gave me some sweet pluck t'drink, it's not my idea. All I want is mebbe we off a rich Jew kid's bike down here. I don't want t'off no black man what is seven feet tall. That is Nut City, man. Pig, he's not hooked up right. He been snortin' blow make him think he's Mr. Big Bad News. I don't handle no blow. All's it do is make me sneeze."

"Hesh up. I'n innerested in you petty losseny wif bruthuh Pig."

"He ain' my brothuh is what, he's my cousin."

"Shu-hut—"

"—Up. Yessir. You go on with that real fine butcher story."

"Umm. Well, dat fust thief, he stick one hand in. He feel around—" Simon makes a parenthetic grope: left hand out. "Aha. Sho nuff, uh fat an' juicy steak right theah. But thuh butcher man, oh—he is *wise*. He been waitin' an' waitin' an' waitin'. He got uh grey big cleaver thing all shoppened up. And, and—and WHOOMP!" Hossmeat has died. Simon props him up again, as you would a bridge table: smack, smack, the knee hinges knocked straight. "Whoomp, I say. He cut dat thief's han' clean off."

"Clean. Offffff. Fffff." Hossmeat can't stop making f's. They slush down to inarticulate breath.

"Yeah. An' dat numbah one thief, he get uh kind of thotful look on his face. Like he was sayin', 'My, my, an' wud you eber, an' how 'bout dat now?' So dis cheer number two thief, he say, he say, 'How's it goin' in theah? Theah enny steaks aroun'?' An' you know whut dat numbah one thief say den?"

"I sure hope he don't say whoomp. That first whoomp make me see little stars in my head."

"He doan say whoomp."

"What he say?"

"He say, 'Well, I got mine. Now you reach in an' git yours.'" Simon has bent over: eye and eye with Hossmeat. It's a rhetorical stare. "Membah dat. In crime they's onny limi-ted potnuships. Limited to *me*."

"That a swift story."

"Wuk alone. Ain' fair t'no fren, leavin' tem-tay-shun wheah he kin bang his shins on it in thuh dark. Doan truss yo own mam. Sure doan truss whut ol' Sledge tell you. An' see you lay off folk wif color. Mr. Face, he laugh his white head off, he long t'see us dumb coons muggin' and croakin' an' scag jonesin' us-selfs. Less coons thuh bettuh. It is his amusement. Doan gib honky no 'musement. You is black, Hossmeat. Far's I kin tell, jes' between you an' me an' dat condom tree, ain' much else you is but black. I wunt gib ol' snot foh you future in dis cheer mean town. You is a marked-out cat. People, they git shot up wif penny-cillin, they doan wan' t'catch thuh blackness fum you. It is uh terminal dis-ease. But you go t'shit in dis place, you see it be black shit. Dark an' sweet an' strong. Theah is some honah in dat, uh man kin live wif. An' one thin' futhuh—"

"Yuh?"

"Evvy chance you has, take uh piss in some white man's coffee." Simon is stirred. He could weep: his contact lenses weigh anchor. Now Simon has jammed Hossmeat face-first into his tall stomach: for some ambiguous nourishment. All this should not be overrated. It isn't the child: it's the mise-en-scène. In Simon there has always been a readiness to accept character and situation, to play, to direct, to fetch from himself the most sensuous performance: a readiness that has kept him from being resolute, even resolutely egocentric. It is inconvenient: it has harassed his ambition. "I lay some foul wisdom on top of you. Is whut."

"Yup. A-huh. It sure is that."

"Know whut-all Ah'm gone do now?"

"Guess you gone stomp on me somepin' pretty fierce."

"Num. No. It is yo lucky day. Ah am gone take this here ten-dollah bill an' poke it right down intuh yo sneakuh heel." Simon has knelt. Thin and unsocked, the Achilles tendon is distinct to him. Simon will touch it more than his business requires. Slight, slender toughness: the hairspring of sudden getaways. It will be used. Simon can feel nervousness thrilling in it. "Like so. Den, li'l Hossmeat, Ah'm gone fetch you one mutha ub uh kick. It gone hurt, but you ain' neber yet earnt no ten dollahs so fas'. An' if you divvy up wif dat soul cousin ub yours—him whut still is layin' footprints throo thuh bush—I got to be very dis-satisfied wif you."

"Yes-sir, I won't. An' thank you."

"Ah's doin' all this, Hoss, cause you 'mind me ub uh snippety li'l weevil what I knew long time ago. No bigger'n uh Milky Way bar he was. I jes' wish some-un back then gib me uh whop in thuh be-hine like whut you got comin' now. Save me uh lot ub mis'ry an' gy-ration. You ready?"

"Yes-sir."

"Enny ques-shuns?"

"No. Well."

"Well?"

"Well—"

"What well? Go on."

"Well. When I was down there, under your dress—"

"Dashiki."

"Uh-huh. How come your ass cheeks is all white?"

"Ah is a mulatto."

"Oh."

"You like me?"

"Yes-sir."

"Cause I got hole on yo neck bone or foh real?"

"For real." Hossmeat can smile: it's a white crocus, lovely. Smiling has gotten him out of errands and discipline: through the fifth grade: past monitors and security guards and chthonic superintendents. Simon, so smiled upon, will second-guess himself. This high counsel, was it misinformation? Something of a liberty, after all: to give advice in racial drag.

"So long, Hossmeat. Hunker on down. I send you out intuh the world."

"You give it to me good."

"On thuh mark, set. Ummphh!"

Contact. Simon gets all of it, a bozo kick—Christ—not the smartest move with sandals on. Aldo is remembered. The right big toe gives out a slapstick sound: tock. That cliché of punishment, this-will-hurt-me-more-than-it-does-you, does. Hossmeat has gone up, comfortable, sitting in the air: like jet pilots ejected. Yet his feet do their stuff before gravity has done its. My, Hossmeat knows how to motor. The condom bush, beaten around, becomes deciduous. Simon can picture those leathery, fresh-grown Achilles tendons, snip-snop, snip-snopping. Just now Simon has a mellow idea of fatherhood. The tribal song and dance bucket-brigaded down from generation to generation, small hands under big thighs. His own big thigh is sore: and one shin, where Hossmeat browsed on it. Walking, Simon has to compensate for a charley horse. And connections are made here: 1) briefcase gone, 2) shin splint, 3) Central Park. Don't tell me. Yes, whoogemacallit with the long cheekbones and that mouth meant for scavenging over coral reefs. By the polar bear cage. What day was it, when? It's today and almost now.

"Two o'clock. A slanty kind of clam she was, yes. Use dogs. Native beaters. Track her wet sasquatch through the magic thicket. Good sport. Long as it isn't out of my way. Long as it isn't out of my way. Much."

And does it enter his mind: Will she be there? It does not. They have always been. Even when Simon wasn't on hand to verify this phenomenon: female thereness. Like a hypothetical tree in the philosopher's forest—unheard, unwatched—they fell anyway, oh they fell. Simon breaks cover, out. An asphalt path is heating up. Gum wads, inert and cold-blooded things through the night, have come alive in the sun. They snap at his heel. Simon, heading zoo-wards, is crass, is nouveau riche in blackness. He has a boogaloo walk by this time: it pairs off well with his babareebahing head. Pleasant, you know, a sort of systemic chiropractry: though not the most direct route between two points. White women take evasive action: they give themselves the cold, muddy shoulder of the path when he passes. To black women Simon will shout. "Sistah!" Understand: the black female has never lured Simon. Not bigotry, an aesthetic and practical determination rather. Black women too regularly have pickax-handle shanks: their insteps don't arch: ankles right-angle. It's all that walking barefoot with leg irons on. But now he is open-minded. White Simon in a black bed has had to be polite and non-colonial: diplomatic emissions. A nuisance, ambassadorial sex. But just at this thought-pause Simon will spy squirrels having intercourse: it might be like that for the black him: a perky venture, unpolitical and blithe. It is in his makeup now.

Cursive cirrus has been handwritten overhead: as one scrawls with a side of chalk. Then look down: he can collate three or four granite outcrops and dead-reckon their interrelationship beneath the clothing soil. I am a camera: a snazzy Arriflex. Simon tries to click his hooded tongue: no dice: life without tsk-tsks. There is a sick, bad-candy stink of dog feces: the house odor of Central Park. And a wild-card smell, leaf smoke. It is the twinge of new school shoes: it is that strange first dusk on un-Daylight Saving Time: it is summer-stored-clothes stench in the subway. Simon, free, associates. He is unsuperintended. Peer pressure has blown off. None of your I'm-Simon-Lynxx-I-direct-you-know-films. Note with what ease and address, a few moments ago, he said Shit. The sun has kept its long jab out, but Simon is insouciant. Skin won't burn on his now-dark nose bridge. Blacks have a rep that, if unappealing, must save time over the long haul. Man, promiscuity aside, nothing is *expected* of blacks. Simon can feel for them. Empathy is at best a peccadillo virtue not to be taken in trade for compassion—but worthwhile nonetheless. And her name, right, was Merry Something.

Rrrrrrppp—off—off—off—rrrp. Pop. Pop. Pop. They've—who's they? Black Simon suddenly knows They—they've sicked a police scooter on him. It nags his left hamstring: it sheep-dogs him. Simon will go quietly, but the officer doesn't seem bona fide: too large for his machine, like someone who has saddled up a goat. Simon stands Caucasian, erect: arrhythmic: the rebahs gone out of him. Through his Plexiglas visor the policeman's face is magnified: mostly nose, as are faces seen through an apartment-door peephole or reflected by bathroom faucets. Feet drag, outriggers: they could be some training-wheel attachment. Tires are ovoid, pushed flat on one side by the weight of municipal authority. A red pillow is under him: it appears domestic, not-in-keeping. Simon meanwhile has sucked his burnt-belligerent lips down. Engine noise will ask for special consideration, rrrrp-ppp. Both gloves are off: they pray together, hard gauntlets, on the pommel. But silence to start with. A lot of well-phrased silence. Policemen never have to dance or sing: or laugh at your little pleasantries. Attention attends on them. They are spoiled: more disdainful than fainéant, gorgeous women. And, in spite of himself, Simon will speak first.

"Officer?"

"Cool it, Shaft."

"What's that?"

"Cool it, Shaft."

"I don't get your drif'. Sorry."

"Look. You and me, we understand each other. Real fine. You're disturbing the peace, Muhammad. *My* peace. Your face is a drip-drip in my toilet bowl. It makes me irritable. Clubbings come to mind."

"I'm just walkin' here, quiet's a soot flake."

"We know, Kareem. You're a sterling citizen. Listen, I'm tired. Something disagreed with me at lunch. I don't need any of your fat lip. Take some good advice, huh?"

"Yes-sir?"

"Cool it."

"Yes-sir. I certainly will."

"Smart boy. That's what I call a smart boy. A little slow, but smart."

The scooter, obedience-trained, is on point: low, tense, wakeful. And off: given its head. Sparks grindstone from one scuffing steel shoe tip. Simon has been outraged. To his mind comes a revenge of acronyms: NAACP, CORE, ACLU, SDS, ADA, hell, UNESCO. And because the asphalt is so licit, so city-franchised, he will cut away from it up/onto a knoll, a grandstand for playfields below. Simon is out of proportion: shrill and in libraries. The pulse can be heard, a vulgarity: his walking should play at drive-ins, that big. He must not be allowed. Ghost towns are made by his breath: he sweats rivers overfull. Simon has gone to earth: has sat. On a construction site across town somewhere, TNT exploding—thooomp!—overstates his sitting down. Yes, and SNCC.

"Lead me! Lead me! I'm going on a fly!" Women work out below. Two of them: both braless and in thigh-split track shorts. They get off precise, spiral, breast-cancer-making passes: they harm each other, full of contrary hormones. "Post pattern on three. Hut! Hut!" They have a squaw profile: it's the sweatbands. Perspiration has guttered leg hair.

One with basketball knee pads on: one elastic-bandaged for a groin pull, though women, Simon would presume, have inner thighs, not groins. At the big toe of his knoll, their personal effects. A towel. A track suit. An Adidas bag. Wallets. Watches. Tape. "Buttonhook. Hit me! Hit me!" The sun has been cradled in Simon's lap: warm as a just-incontinent six-month-old. He will finger himself down there. Not a Chink's chance: anger has first call on surplus blood, has pumped it behind the retinas. Merry would hit the spot right now. Certain kinds of psychic repair are given only by the female.

Weathering newspaper, gray as rag, lichenous, has stuck to the Manhattan stone. After a moment Simon will dig, but his knoll is shallow-pated. Soil flashes: bottle glass and mica and pop-tops in it. The earth here can cut him. Anyhow, he hasn't perseverance enough. Digging is a meditative discipline: mystics' work. And, see, his two women are gone. Their pass patterns have been down and out and all away from him. The watch is on: the wallet has been secured. He can hear their thrown bruises: sounds of a pumpkin beaten on. His mere vandal presence has discommoded them. Now Simon stands: he goes up. Coarse grass, street-wise vegetation that has had to hustle for its place, gives off the sourness of corrupt success: success at any price. Hi: there is a figure just behind his knoll. Her legs are out: hands reach kneecap low: she might just be finishing a sit-up. Simon walks toward. An old woman: he has already thought of Mrs. Armistead. The yellow sun-hat brim bends, accommodating breeze. But for one Ped, both legs are consigned whole to sunlight. She spoons plain yogurt up. Her book is thumbed by illiterate wind. Simon near now: he puts her in eclipse. And, God, terror. Where he comes from terror, terrify, terrorize, terrible, are nickel-and-dime hyperbole: why, darling, it just terrifies me. But this woman has seen big Simon Black and she is in *terror*: she will rehabilitate the word for him. Legs bunch: they buck. Unpliant joints, hurried beyond their flexibility, can be heard out loud. Yogurt spews. Simon will smile, but the smile has no face value: she has fallen sidelong, twisting: *Christina's World.* Her purse is underneath: held close as recovered fumbles are.

"Not again. No! No don't, no don't, no don't. No—God, not me—"

"What? What?"

"No! Not again. I can't. No. No." And the sound gets going, "Noooooooh!"

"Lady, look. Look, please. Please, for Christ's sake, look. I'm cooling it, I'm coo-ling it!"

Cats stink up the place. A manic, alienated smell: a smell of madness long shut away from fact or love. The lion house is sullen and moist as night fever. People there get chintzy with breath: they appear withdrawn into themselves: rib-caged. The stink—thick bass organ chords of it, a left hand that won't give up—seems to hint at contagion. Fingers have been taken in. No one wants to touch. Yet they are made somehow contiguous by the smell. A great stench can muddle human territoriality. It has the monotone, irking power of shrilled noise: noisome. Lion house visitors breathe orally, from a sneer: you breathe so in the harvesttime of fear or anger. But—hahhhhhh—Simon will gobble air. He feels protected: the smell grants him anonymity. And hunger: he will salivate. Someone who has just been introduced to the dark, game-bag pleasure of kidneys and sweetbreads and tripe.

A male lion walks single file alone. In the stubborn arithmetic of imprisonment: figure 8 + figure 8 + figure 8. He will double-time, suddenly eager, at each bow-tie loop of the 8. This turning—cage front, cage rear—is now his life's one hopeful event. Someday perhaps he will turn to find the yellow veldt again. And run, lion: run. A niggardly behind, Simon thinks, for such assassin's brawn. Like most of us, lions show to best advantage from the front. Spine and lion loin are saddleclothed with worn-thin flesh: a bald square foot, gum-shiny, on his left flank. Fur tufts dress the chicken-wire mesh where left turn after left turn has been made. He looks transvestite: wigged out in mane: a lioness impersonator. Simon smells. He can sort *lion* out. Hunh, hunh: noise of an air brake catching. The lion has pulled up. He will stop to sniff at a blobby cairn of his own excrement. One more sniff: who-is-this, wait-don't-tell-me? Simon anthropomorphizes: thoughtfulness on that broad face: some doubt, some boredom. The lion inhales: reinforces his lion identity: we use mirrors instead. Then, mane down, he tracks forward, following the repetitious spoor of his never-gained-on self. Well, Simon muses, just about everyone is into Consciousness these days.

His namesake, with the one x, sits next door. A most unsatisfactory animal: not finished, sort of. The tail tails off: motel-door chains are longer and they have more élan.

LYNX RUFUS

HABITAT:

WOODED OR BRUSHY LAND, FROM

NOVA SCOTIA TO GULF OF MEXICO,

WEST THROUGH MISSISSIPPI VALLEY.

CLOSELY RELATED SPECIES IN ABUN-

DANCE IN EAST. IN PENNSYLVANIA

NEARLY EXTIRPATED DUE TO HIGH

BOUNTY.

Um: and not doing well in the Garment District either. "Hey, Rufus."

But for quick-heaving sides, this lynx specimen is marvelously inert: on a wildcat strike, may be. The clearie marble eyes are intense, yet distracted. Simon has come across that stare before: people on standby at a midnight airport gaze so and those who wait beside hospital beds for the dying to bring it off. "Hey, Rufus. You is some wasted-out cat." Simon flags one hand through the resolute line of sight: disregard at any level will irk him. "Rufus. You on speed or somethin'?" He can't imagine daily life with such a mad, Mack Sennett pulse rate. Simon has leaned over the bar: chicken wire clangs: he'll put his fingertips where his mouth is. No reaction: playing to an empty house again. Amongst cats, lynx smell is cheap Christmas-gift cologne, high-pitched: a penny whistle scent. Simon shakes out one armpit. But Lynxx smell is a still, small voice: it can't be orchestrated here at all.

HABITAT: it says, just that. Another cage. Two claw-torn tree trunks are catty-corner six feet above. And a still-higher-up shelf at the rear left. Simon rubbernecks around. Now he's up/on the restraining rail. Tap-tap: nobody home. Tenantless, but with souvenirs yet of being once lived in: some memento scent, some compromise between lion and lynx, pertains there. A hose has been glubbering water out: turds float, bowel movement, in its stream. But no, nothing: a rare specimen indeed from the heart of darkest Africa—HABITAT: VACANTNESS. Simon would like to get in. Question: is an animal cage with men in it empty? Simon has picked up yellow forget-me-not buds of popcorn. He feeds them in.

"Chick-chick. Hey, chick-chick. Nice popcorn. Chick-chick."

What we have here—all this chick-chicking—is some bo-diddly black mischief. A father-horse has appeared just beside Simon. He perspires: ridden to lather. He wears a five-year-old boy on his neck: is overdressed in him. Bifocal arcs of sweat have come out on each eyeglass lens. His head is hang-dogged: little knees blinder. The child has reined in, downshifting on clumps of black hair. He will break his animal: a thriftless, arrogant rider. And Simon has had flashes from the past. Up on Aldo: his buxom, scenic-lookout tall shoulders. One cold compress hand against the paternal forehead as they watched Macy's Thanksgiving-countdown-to-retail-Christmas parade. Aldo had a starter button: a gumdrop brown mole at his nape. Often trimmed by careless barbers: excuse enough for Aldo not to tip. It would save him a bundle through the years. Aldo tended to forget his equestrian son. Once he had gone through the kitchen doorway with Simon on high. A horseshoe nailed there, ill luck for Simon, had nailed him—thick—between four-year-old eyes. Simon hung down, half conscious, a knapsack. One quick thought before the semi-coma started: how would he survive to adulthood with such child-slaughtering parents?

"Chick, chick, chick. Eeeh, chick-chick."

"Can you see it, Jer?" Father shrugs Jer higher up.

"Uh-huh."

"Wait a minute." Father cranes. The mist has opaqued his view. "Says. Uh. Habitat. That's all. Just habitat."

"Chick-chick-chick. The sign is gone. Chicken leopard."

"That so?" Eyebrows rise: he speaks up. "It's a chicken leopard, Jer." Eyebrows back in place. "Boy, my shoulder sure gets stiff. Zoos are great: open a kid's mind. But wish they'd design these cages so children could see. Hey! Careful, Jer. My jacket." Jer rides high. One vest pocket in service as a stirrup.

"I don't see. I don't see it." Father touches Simon.

"Where is the damn thing?"

"Up on the shelf. See. Just moved."

"It's up on the shelf. It just moved, Jer. God, these things stink."

"I don't see. I don't see."

"Jesus, Jer. Are you blind? Use your eyes."

"Chick-chick-chick." Father has been watching Simon.

"If I may ask, why do you make that sound?"

"Use to hunt them."

"Jer, hear that? This nice man used to hunt chicken leopards."

"He's black."

"Oh, God." Father sucks lower lip in. "I'm sorry. He's only five."

"Uh. I am black."

"Where was that? Where did you hunt?"

"Nigeria."

"In Nigeria. Fascinating. You'd think—now wouldn't you—that they could afford to put that shelf a little lower down."

"I don't see."

"Jer, look—for God's sake." In a whisper. "Kids are jerks, that's the truth. Their minds are someplace else. He loses his shoes every morning. Lost one already today. Just walking along. I look down, he's got one bare foot. Lost it two blocks back. You'd think he'd notice. That's why I've got to carry him. Least I can see his feet all the time."

"In Nigeria we don't have that problem."

"Oh. Train the kids good, huh?"

"No shoes."

"Oh." Lower lip in again. "We Americans are jerks. I was sorry that I had no shoes, until I met a man who had no feet."

"Ex-cuse me?" Simon has looked down at his sandals.

"It's just a saying. Just a jerky American saying. Ahh—why do they call it a chicken leopard? Eats them, I suppose. Chickens."

"Uh-uh. Makes tracks like a big chicken. Three toes. Eats mealies. Destroy my father's cornfield."

"I'll be damned."

"Daddy. There's nothing there. I want to see the seals."

"Just listen to him."

"Wait. Maybe I make him go for my hand." Simon swings over the rail.

"Don't do that. Please. No. I'd feel awful if it got you."

"Don't worry." Simon pushes a hand in, luring emptiness. "Tell me when he moves."

"Wait. I can't see him. I can't see him." Father is readily scared. Simon pulls them in: ten people have come over to catch his act. They follow father's apprehensive, head-wild looking. Simon has relaxed against the cage. He pokes at an empty water pan. His shoulder is through. Still a long way to go.

"What is it?"

"Chicken leopard. He used to hunt them in Nigeria."

"Small animal?"

"Where?"

"Up on the shelf."

"I wanna go see the seals."

"Shut up, Jer. Please, huh?"

"He shouldn't be doing that."

"I told him. I told him."

"What is it?"

"Chicken leopard."

"What?"

"Some kind of leopard."

"I see its tail. On the tree trunk."

"No, that's part of an old push broom. It's up on the shelf. See?"

"Habitat? Is that an animal?"

"Probably just fed him." Simon has given up. He rolls across the bar. "They sleep a lot. Especially when full of corn."

"Well, thank you for trying. Jerry and I appreciate it."

"Any time. What was that, I was sorry because I had no feet—?"

"No. Forget it. A jerky thing."

"Yes. Goodbye. Or, as we say in Nigeria—ubbawomblaglub."

"Yes? And ubbawomblaglub to you, too. Goodbye."

"What did he say?"

"Ubba—I've forgotten it already. It means goodbye. In Swahili, I guess."

"No, about the animal."

"They sleep a lot."

"They what?"

"Sleep a lot."

"I'll say. Most of these damned things sleep a lot. And make a stink. Piss away your tax dollar."

"What is it?"

"Just a stupid chicken leopard. Up on the shelf somewhere, stinking. You seen one, you seen them all. Might as well leave them in Africa, along with you-know-who."

"Did you see it, little boy?"

"No. Can we go to the seals, Daddy?"

"Christ, Jer. You bug me sometimes. I swear, he has an attention span this big. Get down. Slide off me. That was a fascinating man. A professional chicken leopard hunter. He told us some hair-raising stories, didn't he, Jer? Here in New York you forget how people still live off the land. Get down, Jer. I want to see this thing for myself."

THE ZOO ENCOUNTER

A Real-Life Short Feature

(Final Shooting Script)

FADE IN

1. INTERIOR—LION CAGE AT THE CENTRAL PARK ZOO
Cage bars out-of-focus, foreground. Camera will not move. A lioness is pacing. We see golden flanks pass through the frame. Pass again. (Hold this take for fifteen seconds.)

2. EXTERIOR—THE POLAR BEAR CAGE. MERRY
Cage bars out-of-focus, foreground. Same angle. (Match bars with 1. above.) Camera will not move. POV is inverted from 1. We are inside the polar bear cage. Merry is pacing. We see her golden blouse pass through the frame. Pass again. (Hold for ten seconds.)

3. LONG SHOT, THEN ZOOM—SIMON
Five-second pan. Camera can't find Simon. Search, search. Then zoom: an Italian-ice cart. Simon has taken cover behind it. Repair work is being done: Simon presses the loose beard back on: tugs his Afro wig down, in place. The cart has begun to move. Simon will move with it, still down,

stoop-walking. The Italian-ice man is annoyed. He pushes faster. But Simon keeps up. Both are running now.

4. LONG SHOT, THEN ZOOM—
MERRY SIMON'S POV
Splashing foreground. Merry seen across the busy seal pool. She will pretend to read a paperback. She paces, impatient, agitated. Turn, look up. Zoom: expectation, disappointment. Repeat. (During this take, the camera begins to dolly left-right. Then faster. Then very fast. Simon's POV from behind the moving Italian-ice cart.)

5. CU—MERRY
Rack fade: over Merry's shoulder, then tight focus on the polar bear cage behind her. Bears seem middle-class, self-satisfied. Fur the color of dog piss on city snow.

6. MCU—SIMON
Track Simon walking toward the polar bear cage. Camera will concentrate on his legs. No more boogaloo or babareebah. Now Simon has the footsore, bowlegging gait that black athletes affect just before they run a 9.5 hundred-yard dash.

7. MCU—MERRY
Merry is poised, posed. A long cigarette out. She lights up with accurate and careful grace. A nonchalant inhale. Then gagging. Tears. She has lit the filter end. Rips filter end off. She will light the now-ragged cigarette again. But her movements are perfunctory: grace gone. She holds the cigarette behind her back. As adolescent boys would in the high school washroom. We see a shadow rise over her skirt: Simon's shadow. Cut to:

8. SIMON—MERRY'S POV
Simon is head-on, very near. Rack
fade: to the active zoo scene behind
him. Simon's face has blurred. The
human eye is a particularist. It will
edit out irrelevant material: for
Merry, black men in green dashikis
are irrelevant.

9. CU—BOOK
The camera scans her paperback.
Merry has been reading a blank page.

10. MCU—SIMON
Simon, the Transparent Man: a voyeur. He is aroused. Ignorance here
is intimacy: she might as well be
nude. Camera in tight, on the dashiki
front. We note some tumescence
there: an erection pulling itself together. Merry is vulnerable. Simon
wants.

11. ASSORTED LIBRARY SHOTS
A) Lion roaring. B) Water buffalo
charging. C) Rhinoceros mounting
rhinoceros. D) (If available) Rhett
Butler lugging Scarlett up the red-
carpeted staircase. 96 frames: 72: 48:
24.

12. EXTREME CU—MERRY
She is beautiful. (Soft focus: use
gauze on optical glass.) Bring
"Merry's Theme" up. Wind on her
hair. Camera pulls back: it will pan
slowly, lovingly down/along her slim
figure. Double take: there is a gawky,
full bandage on the left shin.

13. SAME—BUT MCU. SIMON AND
MERRY
Simon is too close. He has invaded
her personal space. Merry is ill at
ease. She has sensed a pickup move.
Merry turns away, to the polar bear
cage. Pan camera, then zoom in. We
track her glance. A polar bear is

tearing rotted fish apart. Pull back.
Merry has turned away in disgust. To
Simon, who is even closer now. Away
again: again in disgust.

14. EXTREME LONG SHOT—MAN.
MERRY'S POV
Tall, dark, brawny: an arrogant
walker. (Use stand-in.) Camera has
first noticed him sixty feet away:
beyond the seal pool. Face indistinct.
It could be Simon.

15. MCU—MERRY AND SIMON
The cigarette is scuffed out. Merry
pulls a hairbrush from her bag. The
bookmark has fallen. She picks it up,
while brushing hurriedly. Then, nervous, she will draw hair back over one
bare ear. As a pulley catches rope.
What else? She would like to pick
her nose. Some hesitation here. Side
glance at Simon. He smiles. Snap decision: this is only a black man after
all: social graces do not apply here.
Forefinger winkles into her nose.

16. LONG SHOT, ZOOM—MAN,
BALLOON, PIGEON
Camera in tight on the arrogant
walker. It isn't Simon. Walker jostles
small child. Child's red helium balloon is set loose. It rises. Camera will
follow it up: Merry's hope gone.
Balloon against sky. Hold. Pigeon
flutters across frame. Track pigeon
overhead, toward polar bear cage.

17. EXTREME CU, SLO-MO—MER-
RY'S SHOULDER
Sound match: polar bear crashing
into pool: pigeon dung flopping on
Merry's shoulder.

18. HEAD SHOT—MERRY
Lips move: shit, shit, shit. Sound
match: a child's tricycle horn. Bleep-

bleep-bleep will censor Merry's language.
19. MCU–SIMON
   He slouches toward Merry. Up-angle
   camera. Simon is big. He looms.
20. INSERT: LIBRARY SHOT
   Godzilla ravaging downtown Tokyo.
   A Japanese woman shrieks.

"Birds, eh. A huge pain in the snout, as my father, now regrettably
dead, used once to say. They are equipped with top-notch bombsight
and very so little compunction." Nod, nod: Babu-English Simon grins it.
up, nod.
   "Just isn't my day, that's all. That's all." Merry has spat Kleenex wet.
Her mouth is applause and curtain calls: soft with a lot of give. Tissue
moist, moist lip tissues pressed against it. Her saliva trading has been innocent, intent: very suggestive for that. The green dashiki crests, surges.
Simon awash in it, dog-paddling, many arms: near. Too near: alarm.
Merry thinks: this foreigner, do they spit on Kleenexes, the nubile women
of his land, when lust has come over them? Has she signaled desire by
mistake? Her virtue lost, mistranslated, as though it were some slight se-
mantic point? Merry gives ground: gives pavement rather. Bungggg: the
cage rail against her lower spine. She has been menstruating: tears are
available. Merry will wipe pigeon off her bought-for-the-zoo golden
blouse.
   "From watching at you—pardon—I am coming to the conclusion, I am
concluding that you also are lonely, too."
   "No. Just waiting for a friend."
   "Ah. I, however, am being lonely all the time."
   "That's too bad."
   "He? A he?"
   "What?"
   "Is it a he you are getting stood down by?"
   "Yes. No—he hasn't stood me, ah—down, as you put it. He'll be here
soon."
   "Oh. But if such a damn fine woman was waiting for myself—oh, you
bet. I would be here before you could say Jack Robinson. Eh? Have I
got that correct? Tom Robinson? English is my sore point and my joy.
John Robinson?"
   "Jack Robinson is correct. Though a bit outdated."
   "Good. Ah, yes. So he is coming? But—pardon again—I am watching at
you for an hour and he hasn't shown a face."
   "It can't be that long. An hour? Are you certain?"
   "Perhaps we could stroll to the kaffe. Would you participate with me

in an ice-cream cone? I am partial to ice creams. With chocolate sprin-
kling. We could—"

"Many thanks, no." She has ducked: a curtsey of the head.

"I am brand-new with the UN Building. Junior undersecretary of
Zambia: a responsible position and a great kudos, as you can suppose.
The name is Mugobou. Peter, in America. I have anglicized myself. Very
soon I get my diplomatic plates and can park, willy-nilly, in front of hy-
drants. Big, big advantage here in the Large Apple—especially for someone who has a car, which I am now negotiating at with a reputable Jew
named Crazy Sid the Dealer." One more dashiki surge: après le déluge,
Simon. Merry, downstream, is lapped at. The paperback up/between
them: an intellectual defense. "Ah, you are reading Mr. Thomas Merton.
A whiz-bang pundit, so I am recalled. He had, they tell me, one frightful
to-do with an electric fan. Shocking, oh." Simon Babu giggles. "It is good
homework to get off punts in English, you see. Keeps one in tip-top
shape with the vernacular."

"I see. Well, perhaps you know another colloquial phrase: coming-on-
too-strong."

"Oh, dear. Is it B.O.? And I am using Five Day Deodorant Pads one
after the other."

"No. It means, I'd appreciate it if you didn't stand right on top of me."

"Roger. Oh, yes—indeed. I have heard that white women in New York
will thumb their snoots at a black man. Now I see it is alas so true."

"Don't go sensitive on me. It has nothing to do with your blackness. It
has to do with your hereness. Back off, friend. I thought you were a dip-
lomat."

"Is this entirely satisfactory? I am at arm's length now."

"Thank you."

"Please show patience. I am not yet in the swing of things. New York
has had me by the long hairs, you bet. First day here, and I am given a
Grade A ripping off. I went to see your well-known Harlem. No sooner
am I out of the taxi-car when a person of Spanish extraction I think has
two knives at my neck. Two. One for cutting, the other for poking me at
his leisure. Look. This is the hole he put in my best outfit. I am still, by
the way, haggling with your World's Most Experienced Airline for the
complete loss of my luggage. But that is beside the gist. Let me tell you,
I was one frightened Zambian. I am forced to surrender my wallet and
my nice pukka shell necklace. Also much of my self-possession. Luckily
not the six ounces of hash brought in through diplomatic pouch for trade
with the natives. But big joke on him: I had mostly Zambian quids then.
Worth about four cents a thousand at your criminal exchange rate. Still,
it was some baptism of water, be assured of that."

"I apologize for New York."

"Oh, wait. The worst is yet to be disclosed. This was just my day number one along the Great White Way. Day number two is also a staggering blow to foreign relations. I am taking a taxi-car ride to see the world-renowned Triborough Bridge, when—out of a clear blue sea—the driver says, 'This trip will cost you fifty bucks, nigger. Put it in the little tray and get your black ass out.' Well, I am no Simple Simon, plus I am big enough to lick his chops but good. Right there on the little tick-tick machine is reading out only three bucks and some small coin. Naturally, I refuse point-blink. 'Okay, nigger,' he says to me, 'then I am taking you to the police station. I tell them you pulled a gun on me. They will beat you all over with—' What was again the implement he referred to? Garden hoses, yes. Apparently the black people of New York are often beaten to a plop by garden hoses. Heedless to say, this does not sound like beer and skittles to me. So I am—"

"Hold on. You had a gun?"

"Heavens to Benny, no. Oh, no. But, curse the day my mother disgorged me, there is sure enough a very heinous .45-caliber pistol behind the back seat. Empty of all bullets, yes, but sufficient evidence for a kangaroo jury."

"Why didn't you just get out?"

"Dear, dear lady—I tried. But, clack, down came the little iron bars that hold the back door closed. I cannot, for the death of me, pull that lock button up. The driver is laughing and I am caught red-fingered with a gun. Furthermore, the window will not come down far enough to push out a postcard, not to hope a large-sized deadly weapon. And we are now on our way, lickety-split, to where the garden hoses are being kept. A real bad press for me in the New York *Times*, People and Places section. My civil service rating will go down to 3Q. Next post is surely Sri Lanka, sorting mail. So, what to do? Indeed. What to do is kick in fifty bucks. Two days giving my regards to Broadway and twice already I have paid through the ear."

"That's incredible. That really happened? I've seen those metal bars in a lot of cabs, but—"

"Can I presume to tell you a confidential secret?"

"Don't. I don't think I want to hear it."

"I think you are one hell of a snazzy chick, right-o. Could you please give me the runaround of New York? A Cook's trip as you say. The Statue of Freedom. Mr. Fulton's Fish Market. Even, perhaps, the Shuttle. So far all I have known of New York is one diplomatic cocktail do and this, the famous Bronx Zoo."

"Bronx? This isn't the Bronx Zoo."

"It isn't? Aieee. And I have taken six dozen Polaroid snaps yesterday. What is this place? I am depressed."

"This is the Central Park Zoo. I'm sure no one in Zambia will know the difference. Excuse me—it's been nice chatting—I have to go."

"But your friend?"

"Him? We have an American expression. He should drop dead."

"Ah, that expression we have in Zambia, too."

"I'm sure. Yes. Well—ciao." But—give that man a free ride—Mr. Mugobou has caught the bronze ring on her handbag strap. Merry is off-stride, spun at him: a case of white backlash.

"Please do listen, please. In a foreign land one is always looking a bit foolhardy. I haven't yet got my idioms down pit-a-pat. But back home, goodness, I am quite the gay Lothario. You are so sightly a woman. Oh yes: when I was seven and knee-high to a grasscutter, I fell head over feet in love with a white woman such as you. On a Coca-Cola sign. She seemed to me like the peak of Mount Kilimanjaro. Now colonialism has run its race and there is still Coca-Cola to shake a stick at, but, bah, only black women on the signs."

"Touching. Very. Look, I'm sure you're very nice. In Zambia. Maybe it's jet lag, but in New York you're pretty much of a creep."

"Come. Come." A laying on of big hands: on small shoulders. The purse has slid to elbow bend. Tender bulges, tree-frog soft, swell, then subside, then swell at her throat. Merry for the defense: in a tai-chi position. "Come with me. We will paint the town blue."

"Take-your-hands-off-me."

"This is persuasion, not force. In Zambia we touch a great deal."

"I'll count to three. Then I'll scream."

"It is foolish. I have diplomatic immunity."

"One—"

"You don't like black men."

"Two—that's right, buster—three. Hellllp! Hellllp!"

"My God, you crazed bint. Merry. Merry. It's me. Me-Simon."

"Wha-who?"

"Me. The guy who splinted your shin."

"Si—"

"All right, biggie. Back against the cage. Back. Back, I mean business." The parkie, though gunless, is trigger-happy. If called on, he will use a large key ring for brass knuckles: it is around his right fist. "Back and easy. Back. What'd he do, lady? Huh? He got a knife? Goddam animals are outside the cages. What'd he try?"

"Simon?"

"Merry."

"Simon."

"What's going on here? You want the cops, lady?"

"Oh, mind your own business. Go feed the lions or something."

"Hey, lady. Hey, look. Who screamed, you or me?"

"I did. Does it say that somewhere? No peddling, no bicycling, no screaming. I screamed. Now I've stopped. You can go."

"All right, okay. To each his own. Say—you ever hear about the boy who cried wolf?"

"Oh—don't give me aphorisms."

A crowd has come by: citizens arrested. They are let down: done out of a scene: piss on their small parade. Rumors will form, grown like salt crystal from a crooked seed.

The park attendant.

Him.

Sure, him.

He made a racial slur, I heard it.

Nigger fag, he said.

And spade something.

She broke it up.

She's a plainclotheswoman.

Yes? You wouldn't think.

A gun in her purse.

I saw it, gave them second thoughts.

I bet.

And she, Merry, in plainest clothes, is not well lit: a faded dupe of her master print: the Technicolor washing out. Cheek vessels have scrimped on their blood. By now this is standard for Simon and Merry, their abrupt meeting. Simon seems most at home with her this way: i.e., with her in shock. And Simon has put out his fetching, just-one-of-the-boys expression: unfortunately invisible and pointless under all that Mugobou. Wait: Merry has packed it in, has left. Her hurt look is an efficient display: much adroitness: Simon digs expertise and flair. Head back/up, eyes gunsighting along the spectacular cheekbones. Each haunch swings So long, Charlie. She is, well, browned off at him. Simon has to follow. He feels liable for Merry: with hundred-proof Simon, Merry is near beer, in over her head. A true sportsman (you don't have to tell him, he knows) would throw this one back. But first, first let her love him somewhat more decisively.

"That's right, buster. That's right, buster. Europeans only need apply. Hah. Huh. Liberalism is fine: fine until some black funt wants t'set up a Job Corps in your underwear."

"Bastard. Leave me alone."

"Mer-ry. Huh? Don't go away onnacounta one little covert operation."

"Please stop following me. I want no part of you."

"Careful." A discrepancy in the pavement has tripped her. "You can't be indignant and see where you're going at the same time."

"I said, keep away from me."

"Aw. Here you've been waiting a whole hour and now you don't even wanna talk. I just can't unnerstand women."

"Get away! People are staring."

"I would, too. Shriek like that in any zoo and, sooner or later, you'll get a press gallery."

"I'm not shrieking. God, that ridiculous getup. No. Stay back."

"Slow down then. Us blacks like to shuffle along, nice and easy. Huh—what's your grievance, I don't plug in?"

"Damn it, there are things a gentleman doesn't do."

"Such as?"

"You—you stood there and let me pick my nose."

"So? Should I have offered t'help?"

"You humiliated me. You haven't a shred of decency. You stink, that's what. I despise you."

"Let's sit down. Come on. Y'look like a guy with morning sickness. What I'll do, I'll embarrass myself too. I'll quick-brush my hair. And light the wrong end of my cigarette. And pretend t'read a blank page of Thomas Merton. And pirouette gracefully on one foot, whenever I think you're coming."

"Oh. I asked for this. I thought you'd stand me up. I was prepared for that. I thought that would be the worst."

"There is no imagining the worst."

"You're the worst."

"I'm also unimaginable. Sit. If you walk away now, you'll spend a week thinking of all the sharp and evil things y'could've said t'me. Sit: give yourself a minute. Y'may be able t'say it all right t'my face. Satisfaction'll cover you like a warm lap robe. Sit."

"I'm crazy. I don't understand this. I'm crazy." But seated. The bench has one slat missing. It shapes them. Seen from below: a green silk ballooning aneurysm, a green plaid ballooning aneurysm: three unmiscegenated feet apart. Merry has caught her face: it was falling. "Jesus," she says. "Jesus." In a bizarre, conversational tone: a term-of-address tone. Bizarre to Simon, who says Jesus as you might say Ow.

"Let me tell you, my little spice rack. I have had one hard-ass day. Being black is like being a catheter: brings out the worst in people. Ah-hum. Don't think I could run this jig gig for more than six hours per lifetime. Probably that's why they all bungle together up in Harlem. Misery loves t'motor-pool. I mean, life—even on a Tuesday—is like talent night on Guadalcanal. Everything heightened. Know how it is after a poke of good Colombian: big and loud and luscious. Too much damn *significance*. Camera always CU on your face—so that even a thin smile makes your teeth look like Stonehenge. Fierce. Sinew-gnawing. Dangerous. Get my point, there is no normalness. Being black is like being famous in some unrewarding way. I do not care for it, no."

"You made me nervous over there. You crowded in on me. It wasn't because you were black."

"No, huh?" With his thick lower lip Simon blows out hurdy-gurdy noise. "Blubba-lubba-glub. I bet some of your best friends—"

"Please. Enough."

"—have black doormen."

"If you only knew how hard it was for me to say that— And then it was just you leering behind all that makeup." Simon throws an arm up/on the bench top, toward her. Not affection: expansiveness. "Don't."

"Don't what? Someone might see us? They'd throw you out of the country club?"

"I know what you are. I know why you're here."

"Yah? That's more than I know."

"I'm not ready for it. I can't stand the pressure. I thought I could. And —all right, I admit it—I was interested. But, thanks, I'm going to take a rain check on this one."

"Huh? You don't make much sense. Run that tape over the sound head again."

"The devil hath power to assume a pleasing shape."

"Ah, she likes my shape. This bench is giving me a shape. I've got buttocks on my buttocks. We had slit trenches in the Army built better than this."

"May I inquire? Why the elaborate disguise? I mean, so much effort— just to embarrass me."

"Ah-well. Being gorgeous is a kind of disfigurement, I guess. Hunchbacks alla time think you're staring at them, same thing. Beautiful women, if it rains they think a low-pressure system unloaded on a high-pressure system solely t'make their mascara run. In fact, Miss Self-Service Island, I've been doing my *Jazz Singer* routine since about nine A.M. For motives so gross they'd sterilize you. Hell, Mer, I didn't even remember our date, not until I saw the park."

"No. I can't believe that. You—"

"When I lie, Felt Tips, I lie big. I construct Pentagon-sized fantasies: whole cultures, customs, tribal dances. Margaret Mead could live full-time in one of my hoaxes. I don't have the patience for mere distortion and subterfuge."

"Yes. I take that back: I believe you. Lord, and I was right. You would have stood me up."

"Nah. To stand someone up, strictly speaking, you gotta remember them first. Maliciousness is involved. I just forgot."

"And you have the gall—and I inconvenienced four people to—" She hyperventilates: her breasts surfboard on the rise/fall. "Look, I'll shut my eyes and count to ten. You be gone then. Huh?"

"Merry."

"Goodbye, Simon."

"I'd love t'help you out. I would. But all of a hunger-fit I've got my tubular gland set on your jutty, baby-fattish knockers. I'll do the counting, you go. I'm morally incapable of denying myself pleasure. I try, I try, but I just can't bring it off. I'm all conditioned reflex: see, want, grab. Veni, vidi, wicky-wicky."

"You're right." She nods. "I created this for myself. Of course. You're right. I have to go."

Voice indistinct now: she recites a sentence: it has meter: lips move iambs out. Simon is turned on. He has known this power before: in auditions. Merry, she senses it, has one minute in which to please him: the casting bench. Hair has swung left/right: perhaps in receipt of a Frenchman's double kiss. Her hands play Here's the church / here's the steeple / open the doors / and see all the people. For a moment she will just look down: something spilled on her blouse front maybe. Then Merry has come to a full stop: she is inert. Merry can be still. Simon is curious about that in people, stillness: secretly he esteems it as much as he esteems great energy. They are, he would imagine, antithetical: he and she. Stark differences have their appeal: are often more compatible than compatibility. And she is tender, soft: Simon thinks of brown fur on a pancake. Perfect loveliness: too perfect, near abstraction. He'd almost rather look at her than touch, an unbusinesslike attitude. Time in: Simon has set one finger on her thigh. Merry shudders: at head and arm and neck and leg. Absolutely balanced mobiles respond so.

"Merry?"

"You're still here."

"Ah—if memory serves, you were the one exiting zoo-left."

"Yes. And I will. I'm not ready yet, though. What do they expect of me, anyhow?"

"They?"

"Oh. You know. They."

"Merry, little Medallions of Veal—listen, I need you."

"You—bullshit you need me."

"No. It's true, Merry. Cross my heart and hope for a myocardial occlusion."

"Uh-huh, sure. Tell me another one." But her pulse, on the off chance, has taken a flyer. Blood is re-stored in cheek: along long throat. "Give me one good reason why?"

"Well." Simon scratches his goatee. The spirit gum has gone to dust: salt grains of it fall on his lap. Simon clear for a landing: her ear is approached. "Mer, I need you because . . . Well, because—because I gotta take a shower in your apartment. Otherwise I haveta wait for this glop t'rot off." A kiss on the lobe.

"What? What was that?" Merry swerves: confronts him breast-on. "What happened to the big film director? Doesn't the big film director own a bathroom?"

"At present the big film director is holed up in his quarter-million-dollar film production van. Which is equipped with everything you'd need t'make *The Book of Genesis:* however, only a canvas sink. Washing, Bubble-Clit, is like having sex in a bidet. If one nipple gets erect, somebody has t'leave."

"It's out of the question. I can't—I can't bring you up again. No. How could I?"

"Because I'm black? They'll think you're block-busting? It's simple as NBC—no prob. I go in a few minutes after you do. I make TV repairman noises. Then, like a withdrawal from the sperm bank, I come out all white."

"Don't you think that's rather an imposition on me?"

"We can talk sex later."

"God. It gets worse and worse."

"Or is Father Feel up there? Using his collar for a cock ring?"

"Shut up. I have to think. Go buy me an ice. A red one."

Simon will go, athlete's-footing it, a yassuh-slow walk, to the Good Humor cart. Three in line ahead of him: he can wait. Dry ice has a quick smoke. Freezer hatches clump! and un-clump! Jaded oversweet smell of milk and sugar garbage. Simon semaphores: patience signaled to Merry: ha? Who is having her shoes spat on. An old man is spitting on her shoes. An old man is *spitting* on her shoes. This has to impress Simon: that Merry can touch off such outrage in people. He wouldn't have thought it: certainly a character plus. The man kicks leaves at her. Raincoat and fedora: dusty pants cuffs: white collar and no tie. A la mode Ellis Island, Simon thinks. Merry has turned away from him: leaves overshoe her loafers. Ellis Island is shouting at the shut door of Merry's back. Slavic words, could be Czech or Serb: whatever, a marvelous language to express deep disgust in. Simon shoplifts her cherry popsicle, change clacked into the freezer. He warns of his coming. "Hey! Hey, you!" The man has seen Simon. He takes himself off: literally or so it would appear: one hand in pants belt, one hand behind his own neck. He bounces himself. And at the zoo gate he will shake his fist ear-high, as if for luck—baby needs new shoes—in a crap game.

"Who the hell was that? Your ex? A creditor? Looked like he was wearing Brian Donlevy's old raincoat."

"Nothing. Some nut."

"Want me t'go after him? Huh? He left a trail of garlic. One good bammer—jah-whang—and it's back t'steerage."

"Please don't." Merry wipes spit off: left foot up on their bench. Simon can see color reflect from the glassy insides of her thigh.

"Wha'd he say? You haf relatives in Transylvania."

"I don't know. I don't speak whatever he was speaking."

"Weird little bridge scene, though. Does this happen often?"

"I think he was some kind of racist. He saw us together."

"Yah? Maybe. But still weird."

"You're just jealous. You don't like it if someone else is stranger than you are."

"That did cross my mentality."

"Come on. I don't want to go home alone. You can use my shower, I don't care."

"Um. Whatever."

You don't convince Simon: it looked like an old antagonism. There was that peculiar intimacy between them, almost the intimacy of kinship, made formal by long dislike. Simon is put out: he hates to miss the drift. They walk. Merry roughs loafers on asphalt. Simon looks down. It's opportunistic, unfair: to examine that vulnerable place, the top of someone's head. Her part line, ruler-drawn, exact, will amuse him. He would muss it, but. But then, apropos of nothing, Merry cries. She is a handsome and forthright crier. Open eyes fill: lids snip premeasured tear lengths off: fill, snip. It reminds him of manufacturing. She has bisected the popsicle: two cylinders. A tear on each now: wet red against the hoary pink-white surface. She seems not to have had proper notice of her crying. Maybe Simon should raise the issue. Merry deep-throats ice.

"For future reference: it's my custom t'ignore women who cry. I'm not sentimental: I'm the kind of guy who'd rape a Hobbit. Bad upbringing, I suppose. I cried once when Bambi's mother died. Remember that? And my own mother leaned over in the theater, I think it was Radio City Music Hall, though, maybe not, she leaned over and said, 'Shut up, you stupid fag. Bambi's mother never wanted him, she forgot to use her pessary.' Me, I didn't know what a pessary was then, but I looked it up that night. Not too cleverly: remember I was only seven or eight. Little misunderstanding: I thought you spelt it p-e-c-c-a-r-y. Peccary, and there it was, this hog-like animal. How or why a mother deer could use a hog escaped me. Maybe it kept men deer away. It would've kept me away. Not that my mother didn't cry. In front of mirrors: when she thought—*she* thought—she was being particularly beautiful. 'Oh, Bettina,' she'd say. 'Oh, Bettina, *Bettina*.' That kind of crying didn't count. I mean, it was so goddam depraved. Mother thought she was beautiful, even when she looked like a molded plastic suitcase. She was moved, you know. She moved herself, and—and so who cares? Yes. Bettina. What's the problem, Merry?"

"Nothing. A bad day in a bad month in a bad year. Is that true, about the peccary?"

"Perhaps. Perhaps. I've heard it told before. Hard now t'separate what's real from what the ignorant tribesmen have made of it. There was truth once: all legends have some. And there was a historical Simon

Lynxx: he existed, even the skeptics have t'agree on that. Pretty much. It is averred. I think."

"Could I trouble you to put an arm around me?"

"Well. I can't recommend it."

"I'm not ashamed to be seen with you."

"It's not that, but I do tend t'leave brown fingerprints around."

"So don't. You didn't get yourself an ice."

"Uh-uh."

"Have the other half. I just like the cool."

"No. Mouth doesn't work. I had a fire."

"What do you mean?"

"Gasoline exploded in my mouth. The old head went up like a Cape Cod lighter. Here—ook." He has furled the lower lip down: brown crumbs of scar tissue are breaded on it. "The towering inferno, that's me. Little men with axes were running around between my teeth."

"God, it's terrible. Simon, it's raw and nasty. I can see pus. Does it hurt?"

"Did. Doesn't now. But the darling taste buds of May are blasted. Food won't register. Even hot and cold. Might as well be eating the inside of a life jacket."

"What're you doing for it? No wonder, no wonder I didn't recognize you. It wasn't the makeup. Your whole mouth is swollen. What're you going to do?"

"Maybe get a skin graft. From my heel. Then I'll have my foot in my mouth all the time, not just mosta the time."

"Don't joke about it. Here. Suck the ice. Even if you can't taste, ice is good for burns."

"Is that it? Are you a nurse?"

"I wish I were. Oh, don't I wish I were."

She has crafted shapely tears again. Simon accepts the red ice. In and out, in and out, checking his wrist, not certain just when, where ice will bump mouth roof. He is depressed now: in more suitable circumstances he would probably masturbate. It's like a mother's assurance to him: it makes better. Merry will watch his sucking. Simon sees the man: the man has a boy on his neck. They stop. The double-person has intercepted Simon.

"Hey, fella. You."

"Uh?"

"There was no chicken leopard in there. I climbed up to see. I even got the attendant. That cage has been empty for a week. You made an ass out of me in front of fifteen people and my own kid."

"Simon, what does he mean?"

"That cage was empty." The man is riled: tooling up for a big deal performance. Simon, who has seen him twice, has never seen him like this before. An out-of-character mood, though, Simon can feel that. The man has a childish shoe in each hand, worn finger-puppet-wise. His anger seems to walk at Simon. It's the wrath of a new believer, one who has just met his God in drab mufti, taking the crosstown bus. "Jesus, Jesus, such a thing, does it give you pleasure? I listened. Oh, I listened to your whole line—Nigeria, corn—corn!—and that cage was empty."

"Nothing is empty. Nothing." You don't face Simon down. He can see and raise anyone's tantrum. The man will defend his double-self, little shoe heels up: a rearing pony. "I fill things. I fill. I fill them for sod webworms like you. And this is all the gratitude I get."

"That cage—"

"Shut up, white man. I did you a big favor. You and that racist Quasimodo hump you've got on your back. Now move outa my way."

"You can't just—"

"Move! Or you'll be seeing more than chicken leopards."

"Yyy—" Simon is past him, ubbawomblaglub and so long.

"Chicken leopards? What was that? Simon, don't walk so fast. What was that about?"

"A game. A sore loser."

"Everything is a game to you, isn't it?"

"Hey, Money Jugs, whaddyathink art is? Play. Play. When you stop playing, then they cancel your visa t'the magic island. You're dead. For every artist there's an opponent—real, imagined, I dunno—right across the table. He wears black and a hood. Maybe that opponent is style or one mambo-big image, one symbol waiting haunch down and dangerous in the high grass. See, that's why women are such dough-boring writers, painters, musicians. They don't know how to compete or want to: they're unopposed. They play pretty solitaire. Metaphor-making is a game, there's body contact in it. There's victory in it. Y'gotta win. Pin your vision to the mat—slap, slap, slap. And if you don't get a hard-on doing it, you're disqualified."

"You're no great artist."

"The game isn't over yet. And when it is, I'll play another."

"I don't think I like you."

"It isn't required. Anyhow, if you did, you wouldn't love me."

"Shit. All this dressing up. You hide because you don't really know who you are."

"Ho-hum. One's company, two's an encounter group. It never fails. Spare me, huh?" They are near a fenced handball court. Poing sounds chime in the steel wire. Simon has an urge. Two blacks have been playing one-wall. "Okay. You wanna see the real me?"

"Is there such a person?"

"Look, you wanna see or not? An exclusive. This is like being invited to tea and Jews at Berchtesgaden. The real me."

"It's a trick. I know. You'll open your fly or something."

"You wanna or not? Last chance."

"Oh. I'll regret it—yes."

"Coming up. Hey! Yo! Brethren!" The two blacks have been apprised of Simon. They turn. "Lay you five against my ten, plus—plus—this tender white chicken part. Lay it all I can whup both you backcourt fouls, two-on-one, twenty-one points."

"Simon—God. Stop. They'll think you're serious."

"I am, shush. Lookit her, my good men." Simon flirts for Merry: has drawn one corner of her skirt up. Merry breaks the popsicle stick on him. "Ever see such fine pale food? Thick shaving cream like that make your bristles stand up."

"I'm going. I'm going, Simon."

"Ssssst, keep it down. I'm hustling a pair of fat marks." Simon has his ten-spot out. Now he's through the wire gate. "No sweat, Cloudlet, just look foxy and grab all the side bets you can."

"Simon—"

"Sledge is the name. Am I on or am I not on?"

"Arnold. You are. And this here is Ralphie. Man, you a gone goose, what with that dashiki and no gloves. This is a mean black ball we got. Brand-new and hard."

"Love all mean black things."

"Wait on. Your white chick, she really gonta spread her legs?"

"Like a lady cellist, yes sir."

"Shit, Ralphie."

"She is. I broke her in for you folk: don' step on your peckers thinkin' about it. Up. I am set. Volley for serve."

He has them scouted: better than average, Arnold better than Ralph. Both spry-squat, with muscular calves the color of Yoo-hoo. Yet two-on-one will favor Simon, not them: they have, he has seen, a similar in-close style. They won't team up well: they've played each other too often—yow! The ball wounds Simon: hand bone is contused: he had forgotten that, like hitting a bronze doorknob. But palms will swell quickly with shocked blood and just in time. Arnold-Ralph take serve, then five straight points. Merry, anted up, has put her body on notice: one fist riding shotgun for either breast. Point five is lost on a fifteen-shot volley and by then Simon can't feel at all: his thumb pads are solid: shiny as seasoned, hard briar pipe bowls. Arnold will serve deep for point six, left corner, far: a sure ace. No. Simon Says, Take seven giant steps, fast. Green cloth has flown out, some Archipenko futurist statue, motion sculpted behind. On one forefinger, ever so gently, he picks the ball up, as you might snitch frosting from a cake. Lob sky high backward, over his shoulder. Ralph is set to kill the cripple ten feet out, but—yaaaaah!—SIMON, green and shaggy with movement in front of him. Ralph does a stage-fag wrist slap down. The ball has passed away: dead at his feet. And say goodbye to all these nice people, Simon is gangbusters, gone.

Upwind, downwind, rigged for speed. A mainsail spilling the breeze: a loose boom swept across the deck. His dashiki fills, lets out, tacks around again. "Ha! Hoom! Hoonyah! Look out! Hamm!" Noise is his doubles partner. 9A brown sweat has dripped on green. His Afro wig rotates: DOGGIE bone over one ear now. The right hand is a hanging judge: it fires killers out: each ankle-high, unreturnable, strung taut as bricklayer's line, his level best. The left hand is erratic, improvisatory, brilliant: full of strange English: hum a few bars and it can play you any tune. Ralph-Arnold fight off his pick: their bodies argue: the dashiki is a little child nagging knee and hand. They hit it: they get involved with it: a one-obstacle obstacle course, down in front, DETOUR, MEN AT WORK. Simon is death and taxes. Victory has made him appear eerie, wizard-like. He wins by thirteen, the last ten in a row. Merry will applaud, but she cannot understand. Indeed, no woman can. Arnold does: he hugs Simon off the ground.

"Oh, shit. Oh, shit. You are some nigger. Worth five bucks t'see that happen." Ralph will join the hug now: they grind heads: a skull session. Simon is giddy: delighted by triumph and by that great rocket sled, his body. "Float like a butterfly and sting like a bee. You was everywhere. I hit your ass more'n I hit the ball."

"You boys play pretty good. Too short a game though: don't use the backcourt enough."

"Yeah. Yeah. Right: he's right, Ralphie. Man, what we could do with this cat uptown. Huh? I got some people think they're pretty hot shit. You an' me, we could steal their tires off. Come on up—have a coupla beers—we gonna make you rich."

"Uh-uh, like to. But gotta plant the chick. It's seedin' time."

"Hell with the white ass. Man like you don't need that. Come on up with us."

And, you know, Simon is tempted. He'd like to run a day with these men: their health would honor him. Merry's hands have caught in the wire: they are fragile: they can't hold his. But Simon will lose face, beard particularly. Black makeup has been riding high on a perspiration slick: it won't last. Simon is tempted, but he says no.

4

The nozzle spray pecks a secretarial noise, 120 w.p.m., 120 w.p.m., on Merry's red shower cap. Simon has been a storm in here: local disturbance. Water goes down, checks by dead reckoning for its latitude/longitude, reads Northern Hemisphere and circumvolves itself clockwise, around-the-drain-wise, submissive to great ground rules of planetary swirl. Sound—hoooog—that cats make before they retch a well-knit hairball up. Simon, the champ, is beat: has had it to here (and here and here) with scrubbing: parts of him, uh, are as far away as the north forty. Muscle has been drawn out: is attenuate: no pump left. His arms—can you imagine?—feel longer: more Simon: who needs it? The right elbow bursa, its neat ring seal broken, disburses blood and lymph into/beneath skin: an extra knob there. And he's wearing elevator soles: white clam-fat blisters on each heel and toe: like hot-footing it over radiant sand: teach him to play handball in sandals on cement. Brown water teats hang from her bathroom ceiling. Brown overflow tints-in pentagon interface after pentagon interface of the floor tiling. Merry's cold cream has been mined out: plus a full can of very cold Crisco. On her toilet tank bubble-bath powder is ignited prematurely. And, a floor below, water, his erosive mountain runoff, has begun to collect in Mrs. Leopold Lieb's medicine cabinet. One third full by this time. In three hours Mrs. Lieb, heart-set on two Midol, will get—gush!—wet breasts. And cynical smart-ass razzing from a bottle of water-crazed Brioschi.

Faucet screwed off: 300 pounds of torque strength. Tonight, before she bathes, Merry will have to call Mr. Stern, the super, with his two-foot-long Stilson wrench. Thank you, thank you: Simon has taken a shower curtain bow. Hum. Busybody brown finger marks all around: on vacant hamper, medicine chest, plastic trash bin. Simon has given the place a complete internal again. Already it is more his than hers. Simon has that effect on unclaimed space: land rush, squatter's rights. He will

368

now piss, unsquatted, in her tub drain, doing what he can to flesh the room's character out: script-doctoring it. Then up/over/out. Sebaceous brown rings left behind, some one-half inch wide, by which you might adduce a drought-flood history of the tub and its age.

Streaming body, consciousness streaming . . . blop slop Creature plop from the Brown Lagoon must be inch deep out here little bubbles coming up predict one hundred percent chance of precipitation downstairs huh break her lease for her break her Bakelite cusu she calls this nose wipe a towel red red big on red she is MIA? initials I guess action certainly missing humm mirror fogged and image problems as usual lookit this a total sog already and just the great seedmaker dry wonder how many hours in a lifetime fritzed away drying off now feet feet worth drying can't get socks on wet feet unless rolled like Trojans never could get dry drove Bettina to upper-class all-British team voice you bloody slob my nipples showing through nice starched dickey could've won wet T-shirt contest aaaah do we dare? high-hat-it in there like this big blank canvas amazing proportions aaaah do we dare get back into that dashiki? Could walk by itself if I put one arm around its waist blood piss sweat makeup honorable discharges and do we see deodorant no we don't old Missing In Action too refined to perspire also no sign of hairbrush maybe sends out for bathroom supplies like Chink food holding out on me fine she's had it I will I will nude demonstration against below-standard guest facilities just flash pendulum at her tick-tock see if she can tell time God Wolff tomorrow and Bethlehem scene but first better dispose of soap pretty far gone brown and hairy rodent's miscarriage ha! Lynxx up for patented turn-around jump shot unstoppable splash! basket uh bowl two points unngh could carry my right arm home in a bassoon case second elbow growing on my elbow now pull the chain aaarhhbbbabubab-babloop to you too damn soap floated like a highway bond hah step into the john hold it under until the bastard drowns pull again die you prick he wants my foot too VERY NARROW MAN FOUND CLOGGED IN NYC SEWER SYSTEM wetter now than before okay good for her meet the permissive '80's in person "The Anatomy Lesson" very famous painting I think educational just be-bop out of here natural if that's possible . . . And Simon, under two-twenty these days dripping wet, will drip nude wet into the next room: ta-daaaah.

"You were in there long enough. I thought the wall was coming down."

"Ah-hum."

"Did you clean the tub out? Or is that a foolish question?"

"Ah-hum. Over here."

"You want my attention, is that it? Just hold on one moment."

"Great. My big entrance and Ant Man could upstage me. Hey. Merry. You got another towel at least? That cloth Sight-Saver y'gave me died in a mad carouse. Huh? I'm cold. Skin's all shrunk up like I was a giant areola."

"So, put your—oh no. Oh, no. Not that."

He is noticed now: so, on August 6, 1945, the citizens of Hiroshima noticed. Merry has almost fallen. She wipes, why?, her upper lip: an old response: dizziness of this sort associated with hay fever attacks. Back: away: crump: her coffee table has taken the rap. Chocolate cake on it, sugar bowl, scarlet napery, silverware. Cups, each from a discrete ceramic background, clack, gossip, as witnesses to some lurid accident might: overlooking, for the moment, their social difference. Simon at knife point again: what a day. She shakes it, the knife: to hold her small defensive perimeter: she expects a glib, a vaudevillian rape: one-liners, tap dancing: maybe "My Old Kentucky Home" played on her xylophone rib cage. Oh, she has seen men, their nude parts before: an arm, a globing buttock, a navel in window streetlamp-lit flash. Some sort of mental composite has been put together: fracture lines still show here and there: classical museum statuary. But this is *nakedness:* butcher-shop nudity: Rubens' nudity: white-pink, hairless, terrific: with a pool forming around its feet. His half-hard member will perform: twitch Hello! to the nice lady. And now: how much is three and three? Hop, hop, hop, hop, hop . . . ur? hop? Right: psssst, feed it a lump of sugar. But, pause: no head hair either. She puts the knife on safety: is somewhat reassured. Very few men, statistics show, rape with a red shower cap on.

"Uh, Mer. Could you put that fowling piece down? It gives me an inner falsetto."

"You. In here, you. You brought all that in here. In my own living room. That. That—"

"Something, huh? Slap a periscope on it, y'could travel under the polar ice cap. Never come up for air."

"God, you're vulgar. You're gross. You're, what's worse, you're fatuous. And I'm sick—sick—of your infantile carryings-on."

"Ah, but notice. Despite all the ladylike reactions: anger, disdain, an intramuscular injection of blush. Despite all that, the biorhythm is going bah, bah, b'dah in Dolby Sound. Eyes wide as a divided highway, reading me left/right, adding me up/down like a bar tab. No shy, oriental, fan-fluttering aversion of the glimmers, not for old MIA."

"Oh, shut up. You're never naked, not with your mouth open. I'm looking, my friend, because I don't trust you. That's all. That's all. Don't flatter yourself. What—what am I supposed to think? You went in there black, remember? Or green. Then there was this white thing, this, this— this *gorilla.* I thought you'd come in from outside. I thought you'd forced the lock, I—look, move, you're dripping on my couch."

"Well, one towel. What'd you expect, one towel? That's like prescribing two aspirin for Ghidra the Three-Headed Monster. There's thirty-four square feet of skin here. Stick a national flag in my ear, the UN would have to recognize me. They'd send little ambassadors. Hanh. You ever see a bilt like this before?" Simon telegraphs across the jungle: badda-dum, badda-dum: fist on stomach tympanum. "I'm a free city of flesh. Excursion trains make a side trip t'see me. But not only that, I mean, here I am, debauched, a lifetime of trolling my giant boathook for drowned corpses and still, admit it, I look *innocent*. A kid. A Renaissance *puto*. I should be helicoptering around the blessed Christ child's head in some cathedral triptych. The fontanelle of my soul hasn't closed yet. I'm soft. Look, huh. Huh, Merry? Gimme a review. Gimme a pass/fail mark at least. I need approbation. Huh? It's no skin off your nasal passages."

"I refuse to be drawn into this discussion."

"Hey, you absentee ballot, look—here, over here. I'm the fullness of time. I'm a sweeping generalization. Hanh. I could replace dollar diplomacy and the International Year of the Child. Watch!" The toes of one foot walk out: downstage: solo: perhaps an aside to their audience. Simon will appreciate thigh and calf. The calf flops, thumps: alive as a runner's heart and as big. Then his Arnold Schwarzenegger routine. A Sergio double biceps, a Scott three-quarter back, a mighty crab. Some deltoids. One wow of a trapezius act. Then throw her the latissimi dorsi— Flying Squirrel Man himself—plus that tiny shelf of drawers along his stomach. Simon in a pose-off against Simon. Mr. Southern Queens. The game never in doubt. "Hah. Aaah-whoo. Beautiful. If I could run in circles fast enough, I'd hump myself. And I don't even work out. Haven't done a push-up since one squalid morning-after when I woke up on the floor of the White Rose Bar. It's youth. American youth. I'm a yout. Merry? Jeez, cleared the place out again. Where'd she go?" To the kitchen: back now with a pot of boiling water. "Hey, Miss Selfless. I just gave a performance worth two tails and an ear. And you're out making high tea. Listen, trouble is, you women don't think men want t'be sex objects now and then. What I'd give t'have some hard-hat with hair on his behind whistle down at me from an I beam. For nothing. For walking. Let's have a little applause before we pull the trap and make this poor sucker disappear into the prop room downstairs."

"You have a good body, I guess."

"Good? Guess? Is 'Guernica' good? Is Buñuel good? What'd you soak your contact lenses in last night? Turtle Wax? Look." Merry will look, but she has carried something off: an illusion: Simon can perceive it. Effective: but what? There are soft vortices at mid-brow: a knot in wood. She sees him, yet does not see him. Her posture is weekend easy. The quick breathing has taken a breathing spell. Simon is curious. Then irked. Then, for the first time in her presence, he will feel nude. Worse than that: undressed. "Over here. Yo. Merry. Y'want me t'plot my position? No, huh? Nothing. Christ, I walk through a room and male cats spray t'commemorate my presence. Cold-blooded animals go inta heat.

But, for you, compared to the next guy, I'm maybe one stop up on the E train. If that. Right?"

"Oh. I suppose it'd help if you took my shower cap off."

"Aaaaargh. I knew there hadda be something. A prophylactic on my head." He has it off: holds the cap against his inner forearm: bent: Discobolus. "Better? I must've looked like a centerfold from *Latex Lovers' Monthly*. Say something appreciative."

"You're quite lovely."

"Yeah? Hanh. You mean it? I didn't force that out? You're not just being polite because I'm a guest?"

"Uh-uh."

"And I've lost six, seven pounds. Hey, have you seen better? Outside of a Bull Worker ad? In person?"

"No."

"Have you seen worse? I mean, have you seen *anything*? You give just the slightest suggestion of impacted virginity. That's a compliment, mind. I mean, y'don't come across many Teflon hymens in this year of our promiscuity. But it's as if my supercharging manhood—quite lovely, quite lovely, but—it's as if it were something you might hang umbrellas on in the lobby of a museum."

"I don't know. It's, well . . . Even naked you seem to be in costume."

"Always some half-sautéed psychosocial answer. There are no paraphrases for this. It is. I am. Don't analyze. Touch. I should be in one of those stroke and feed zoos for children. Much more educational than a baby gnu. Don't—gone. Zip. Like the Scarlet Pimpernel."

Merry, fast woman, is by him again. The cool wake from her skirt takes up his private part—3/8 inch up—puts a cuff of flesh on it, as you might shorten one trouser leg. Simon is down, weary: he should bug out, thanks for the memories and who was that masked man anyhow? They are not equal: Merry and he. It's a matter of arithmetic: in fact a matter of Lynxx's Cruel but Infallible Point System for Predicting the Success or Failure of Any Male/Female Relationship. Goes this way. Try it sometime: Simon would like that.

Attribute	Male	Female
Looks	1–5	1–10
Intelligence	1–7	1–4
Money	1–10	1–5
Success	1–10	1–5
Age (Drops one point per five years from age 20–25 on up.)	—	8–0
Personality	1–5	1–5

Hanh, all right, and what does Simon Lynxx score in this September of his life? Usual perfect 5 for looks: likewise perfect 7 for intelligence. Money, down to the underfur just now, but his non-liquid van—oh. Simon hands himself a 7. Success: we still need that bankable, boffo feature film: 7. Personality: capital F for 5. 5 plus 7 plus—uh, considering the big 7 for intelligence, doesn't add too well: abacus fingers come out. Total: six handsful and one thumb: 31 out of a possible Robert Redford 37. Poor, sadsack Merry. 9 for looks, but beyond that . . . Intelligence: not much data available: an occasional insight: hmmm, say 2.5, and he could list that under Deductions, Charitable on the 1040 form. Money: should get some input re parents health, might be a minor heiress, but if you judge by this Lower Depths apartment: 1. Success: also short on data: has afternoons off, probably cashier-waitress, otherwise she would have told him: 1. Age: 7. Personality: 1.5. No, has moments of charming pissed-offness. Make it 2.5. Add—damn decimal points, have to use half-fingers—23. Lynxx's Law: any relationship separated by a margin of more than three points will have the half-life of a rare uranium isotope. (Sidebar: Inertia Component [children, alimony fear, clean underwear—for married pairs only]: add one point to your inferior male or female for every three years: inapplicable here.) Simon has blown Merry out of the box: an eight-point lead. True, there is Lynxx's Love Factor: give your loser ten points for shared love, that chemical, unarithmetic madness. (And reduce it one point every three months of the relationship: love tends to depreciate about as fast as a pop art movement.) But Simon isn't in love, not even in love with Merry's love for him. Go then: it'd be the humane act. Or, lay her once first: it'd be the humane act. Something to press between pages. To remember: when Merry's age is worth just three or four.

But (he can designate no + − point value for this one: the trouble with systems) there is a dormant, interesting queerness. Men in old raincoats spit on her feet. The Sylvania is still picture-tubeless: wallpaper playing through it now, pretty good burlesque of daytime TV. Vacant fish tank bought with bathroom cat pan, he would suppose, at the same non-pet store. Simon, thoughtful, does ten jumping jacks for warmth: gets ten apprehensive uh-thump responses from a wide, low table. On it: white cloth and what might seem to be Christmas/birthday failures: a random life-assemblage. 1) small ceramic bowl 2) its inverse rubber mold 3) wedge of clay 4) wind chime 5) ice-cube tray with water 6) paper strip, turned over once, then set end-to-end with glue 7) a diagram of the visible spectrum 8) incense 9) a dark some-metal-or-other sphere, hardball size 10) X ray, anonymous, of the human skull 11) one roach (optional). These things, Simon can see, have been arranged, though he can't assign a wind-chime-bowl-incense-clay hierarchy. Two pillows, negatives for past kneeling pressed in them, lie near the table. And

above, on her wall, a wooden crucifix: not high enough, as people hang
such signals of their faith: within child reach. Merry is behind him. She
has two towels and a cerise silk bathrobe.

"Please put this on. Seeing you constantly nude—ah, in about two minutes the thrill will go. And I wouldn't want that."

"Funny. I never get tired of it. I wear exposure meters out."

"You did a first-rate job in there. My kid cousins don't swab the deck
like that."

"Cousins, yeah. But no kid brothers or sisters. Right?"

"How do you know so much?"

"Well. There is that cat-rubbing-against-the-table-leg narcissism about
you. Usually comes with being number one."

"You should talk."

"I should. I'm an only. Saw to that. Clawed my mother's womb t'ticker
tape coming out."

"She couldn't have any more children?"

"I guess she could. But I was a tough act t'follow for some other kid.
In fact, I'm a tough act t'follow f'me. Geez, I get tired of being me every
day."

"Think of your friends. Take milk in your coffee?"

"Okay."

"Six lumps I suppose."

"Three. Ah—it doesn't matter. I can't taste. Cheaper in the long run, I
suppose: be able to switch from Wild Turkey t'twelve-proof benzine."

"Really? Are you serious?" Simon has been working both towels behind his back: a two-handed saw. "You can't taste at all?"

"Not at present. Gonna take the cunni out of my lingus."

"Do you want cake? It's homemade."

"Uh. I didn't eat today. I better."

"Would you like a sandwich? I have some salami."

"No. The cake. I can sort of squidge it down. Chewing I get mostly
tongue sandwich. Some lip now and then. Not a varied diet. Also not an
unlimited supply."

"God."

"And what have we here? Yow-sssheeez!" Simon has picked up the
metal sphere. Things do not often surprise his strength. But this falls, a
wild sycophant of gravity: just saved by Simon's quick lap. It is improbably dense.

"Careful. You'll break the table."

"What is it? A bulldozer's testicle? I'd hate t'see the gizzard this came
out of."

"That's my black hole."

"Uh-huh. Yes. Hum. Is it? I didn't think they were detachable. You
know what I want, roll it over."

"Oh, dear. That was rather expected, wasn't it? I hope imagination wasn't seated in your tongue."

"Lay off. I'm not myself today. Being black has depressed me culturally. Move over. Lemme sit down."

His calves are damp yet: he seems to have waded across the room. Clung, red bathrobe silk will give a stilling feel: as though he had set: as though it were skin on the surface of year-old paint. Simon yawns: idle inroaring. Merry has made a presentation of food: on her coffee table. The cake is careful, fine: well-brought-up. But hunger, for Simon, has become an abstraction. And Simon is not versed in the abstract: big difference between "want" and "I am wanting." He has done phrenology on the metal sphere. Its arrogant weight insists on his groin: where weight is welcome. Something about heaviness, too, that will affect the jaw. We register lifting there. To understand Simon's fascination, hang one hand/arm by its thumb on your lower teeth: chew up and against the tension. That pressure, his ears crackle with it, is a representation of compactness, strain. But where were we? Merry has given him coffee. Simon, not alert, bolts half the cup at once. He's slipper comfortable with Merry: an indication that he doesn't care much. She appears on-duty, anxious to confer service: they all are with Simon, except those that take first-round dives, that capitulate like POW's in some one-sided and incomprehensible war. Merry means to be an earnest listener. But Simon is fed up with entertaining. He'd like to be the entertainee just once. Merry sips: there is a yelp: polite: within the allowed sound range of afternoon civility: still, a yelp. Sipping has hurt her.

"Simon." She arrests his arm. "Don't drink like that. It's boiling. I just scalded myself. Listen. You have got to see a doctor. You've lost all sensation in your mouth."

"Uh-huh. Yo, I'm in love with this lead goiter. It's self-important." Simon has balanced the sphere on his fingertips. They spread, indulging its heft: webbed with metal. His biceps muscles guess the weight: they hover, rest: a scale's arrow indication.

"Don't put me off. This can't go on. A thing like that could cause cancer."

"Right. Raa-at. Stick your tongue out and say, 'Oi, a gonif is in my pocket.' From Simon's mouth those kike specialists'd love t'put a whole new bingo room on the synagogue. The Lynxx Palate and Uvula Memorial Wing. Uh-uh, can't afford t'lose momentum. The engine dropped out years ago, but I'm still going, going, going. Probably downhill, but while I'm moving I'm alive. Motion. Motion pictures: every time you stop the reel a frame burns out. I even move in my sleep. I shred sheets with my toenails. See Simon run. The Irgun is after him, but he's keeping his precious non-kosher weenie just out of reach. Hah. Shaddup, you-whose-

cheekbones-I'd-like-to-giant-slalom-down. Be lovely. And reticent. Uh,
why—reticently—d'you call this a black hole?"

"You don't know what a black hole is?"

"Nuh. I don't go t'Disney films." Simon will score the cake slice: gouge
it open with his fingernails. A fork can injure him now. He smells.
"Good. Tell me. Huh. I'm so interested I might go inta coma."

"I–I . . . See, I begin to stutter when I talk to you. I mean—are you
just being polite, you know? Or do you really care? It'll take a minute to
explain."

"Ummm." Icing daubed under his nose. "Don't mind the chocolate
mess. It isn't my punk rock singer makeup. I find that a little snort of
what I'm chewing helps the old tastarama. Wait'll you see me eat spa-
ghetti. Go ahead, I'm inter-erupting."

"It fascinates me." She has pressed one fingertip against each temple:
I, A, i, a, various subheads ordering her explanation. "Stars—suns—they
collapse. You know that much?"

"So? Maybe. So?" Harassment: Simon is making an announcer's
(Aldo's) speed-up sign: big circle with the right hand.

"Look. I can't talk if you're going to pressure me this way. I'm not like
you, I don't have . . . diarrhea of the mouth." The word is distasteful, a
failure. Shamed, her tight knuckles brighten.

"Merry, hey. Don't use words like that. Huh? They offend me in you.
You don't have the profile or the accent for it. Or the Son of Sam nerve.
Very few people can say diarrhea with the proper light-fingeredness. I
can: that's because there isn't much discretion in my discretionary fund.
Gotta use a kinda campy, Motown sound: extra umlauts and cedillas.
Y'can't take a word like diarrhea *seriously*. See, that's why women can't
curse: they're too earnest about it. It makes them ugly: like baiting a
trap with your own finger. On the other hand I don't read Edna St. Vin-
cent Millay aloud with much success. But, umm—go on. Just some con-
structive criticism around the batting cage. Go on." Simon, laid-back,
lays back: the bathrobe will come apart. But Merry has shut her eyes.
"Go on."

"Gravity works on suns, which are huge masses of superheated gas,
and—look, I'm just going to run through this quickly—and. And. The gas
and the radiation pressures fight off gravity. But after a million million
years, when the nuclear fuel starts to get used up—when the atomic material has been fused to iron—then the sun starts to collapse of its own
great weight. Into a white dwarf usually. But even when it's a hundred
times smaller, it still has the same weight, the same volume of material.
Ah—I'm leaving things out, but that's what you wanted. It's so, well,
superpacked that a pinch of it would go through the earth, through rock,
right through and out the other side like a hot knife through butter."

"Yah."

"Yes." Merry has no ear for Simon: his tones. Yah, just yah, without a question mark. What could that mean? She needs to check his face.

"Well?"

"Christ."

"What now?"

"It's—" It's that Simon has been chewing without skill. Chocolate, in a spittle mash, pushes out: beads strung down from his left mouth edge. There has been no oral maintenance. The custodian tongue won't work. Two side teeth are blacked/browned out: a bum's disfigurement. And Merry has seen blood. She scissor-kicks up: at him: to dry-clean his face: sprung from a tight lotus position. This isn't caring, or not just that: his mouth, not right in its head, has given her the willies. Impatient, a boy going out somewhere, Simon will duck under, then away. She swallows: language enough to state her repulsion. Simon, alerted now, dish-wipes cheek, chin, lip. Oh, enchanting: an old fogy's slobber in the towel. And, dammit, blood: he has been a source of protein to himself again. It could depress anyone. Simon had thought he was chewing judiciously and well.

"So? Can't take me anywhere. This is nothing: it was eight years before I could tie a shoe."

"You can't go on like that. You've got to see a doctor. Up. Put your things on—now."

"Sit."

"No."

"Yes. And warning." His face is unpleasant. "Skull and crossbones. Dog crucified on the doorframe. Bloody cotton at the jungle crossroads. If I want t'drool, I'll drool. There's always the Jerry Lewis Telethon. Let them put me in a wheelchair, I'll do a roll-on part, anything t'stay in showbiz. You were explaining—seven white dwarfs—go on."

"All right. Have it your way. Why should I care? Stupid macho jerk: just stupid. Uh, white dwarf." She finds her place. "But there are bigger stars. More, you know, mass. Also more powerful gravity. Some explode as novas, but others compact this terrific mass into a smaller and smaller area. Say five miles across. And for the biggest stars gravity is too strong. It crushes down, faster and faster. Instantaneously, in fact. Until the star reaches no volume at all. But still immense weight. Still the weight of a sun. Can you imagine it? A star reduced to nothing, yet with the density of thousands of trillions of tons. At this point it just blips out. Pops itself through into another space-time dimension. Or something, no one is exactly sure."

"Yeah? That's true? Sounds like something a used-car salesman would make up—t'explain why your trunk is in the glove compartment."

"It's called the Schwarzchild Singularity, I think. Happens in a wink, a mini-second." She'd like to fool with the metal sphere: its weight, though, has made Simon's lap a crotch: insinuated in there. "That's just symbolic. A poor approximation, of course. But I use it to meditate. Infinite weight in an infinitely small volume. It's the ultimate Zen koan, don't you think? Better than one hand clapping or the goose in the bottle. Yet, ironically, it isn't impossible. Black holes exist in space. Their presence has been verified."

"Zen coon? What's that, some Jap with a pink Cadillac?"

"Ko-an. You don't know what a ko-an is?"

"I haven't read a book since 1959. I can't stand to sit still. I do things. I'm a functioning illiterate. But I listen: and remember: and steal from everyone. Ugh, this black hole here feels like the worst possible case of hydrocele. Coon. Quan. Huh? It's what?"

"The koan is, well, a device. A meditative exercise. If you concentrate long enough on something illogical, impossible, then you crack your dependence on reason. The mind opens up, stills itself, becomes unassertive. Is. It's an antidote to reason."

"An antidote t'reason? Who'd want that? That's like finding a cure for heartbeat. Now me, I don't reject the old head gear. Brain: it's all brain: synopses from the synapses. I believe in metaphor, and an Italian salute to your Jap quantz. All that Eastern philosophy comes from the West Coast anyhow, thought up by some LA fag who's aged-out on Locker Room. Listen, Merry: everything in the world has at least one edge—color, shape, feel—that fits against some edge of everything else. Okay, they may not be exact map overlays, but there is a joining. Gotta find the connection: no place without a door that goes someplace else with a door and so on. I mean, you're heavy into this face-slap stuff? No wonder Orientals are squint-eyed: all those concussions. A Buddhist, eh? Always amazed me how a guy who sat around fasting and meditating could get so fat."

"No, I'm a Christian. But I still consider Zen useful. Merton did. The Trinity, for instance, what's that but a koan? Three-in-one, meditate on it long enough and you break through. Not into Zen, but into faith. The—ah . . . the rejection, if you will, of reason—it's similar."

"Uh. You actually go t'church and all?"

"Yes."

"Nuts. Just my luck. Your worst lay is a churchgoing woman. Kinda broad who tends t'cough just when you're coming. 'Was it all right for you, dear?' Yeah, it was, but now I think it's broken. Depressing."

"Sorry."

"I hate it—nothing impersonal, you understand. It's just I think chicken films're less damaging t'human dignity. They want you on your knees. Hanh. Oh, yeah. Except when the beggar's bowl is passed. Then they don't want you bending over. Makes the wallet pocket tighten up."

"Uh-huh."

"Don't feel like arguing, I notice."

"Is there any sense?"

"Where's the old Jesuit fire? Don't you want t'recruit me?"

"Some reason why I should?"

"Oh. It's just I'd like t'see you in a missionary position."

"Your teeth are red."

"In tooth and claw. Sharp of you to change the subject. I'd go through your theology like a shot of Drano. I'm a walking Pentecost. Tongues, tongues, tongues." Merry is pale: she has whipped her hair back. Simon lays off. "Well, now that I've had my little say. Well—good cake. You meditate a lot?"

"Some. I try."

"On this?"

"And other things. I like the black hole concept because it's oxymoronic. Irrational, yet discovered by hard reason. That, for your information, is why Christianity is so much more complex than Zen. The Trinity may require faith, yet Christians don't deny reason. What d'you think the whole of Scholastic philosophy is?"

"I dunno. Something like a married spinster? Oxymoronic. Jeez. I don't know about the oxy part. No wonder people spit on your shoes." Simon is up. He will shop at her table. "Why this?" The spectrum, he means.

"Oh. That's one of my favorites. I invented it myself. I try to imagine a new color, one that's never been seen before. Think about it for a moment. It's an especially good exercise because the mind's eye can recall color only with difficulty anyhow. It's in the word. Think of yellow. You need the sound to bring it off, at least I do. Yet colors are very particular. Definite things. I think that's why it's so hard to picture a new one. Now smells or tastes—I'm sorry."

"That's okay. Bet you'd ask for a voice vote at a deaf-mutes' convention. Hum. A new color? I can do that. No sweat." Simon has shut his eyes.

"You need a new word. Unfortunately—for me, anyhow—phonemes have color value. The color narz, that's brownish. Nnnn sounds are brown for me. I think new color requires new language. Maybe something along the lines of a Chinese pictograph. They were very interested in that sort of thing—synesthesia—at the turn of the century. You know, Diaghilev, Cocteau, Baudelaire. The ballet. There's a character in a novel—by Huysmans, I think—who has a mouth organ he calls it. It's a liqueur chest. And each liqueur corresponds to the sound of some musical instrument. You could drink a symphony, so to speak."

"Have you thought of one? Huh, smart-ass?" Simon seeing again: his eyes crossed with effort.

"No. That's the point. The koan of it. Physiologically, I guess, the eye has seen all the colors it can. But try the same problem in terms of a black hole, of turning inside out. What's the opposite of, oh, blue?"

"The opposite? Does color have opposites?"

"These are abstractions. Experiments. There's no anti-spectrum. Or perhaps there is. But not in this dimension."

"I don't like it. A dry-hump for the head, that's what." But Merry has puzzled him: move her up from 2.5 to 3.5 under Intelligence. "Hey, Orlon Orbs, you sit in this fifth-floor basement, this intellectual lying-in hospital, all day long? You need exercise, a game of touch croquet'd be about your speed."

"Sharp of you to change the subject." Merry laughs: her performance has confused him. She will light up on the strength of it. "Want one? I haven't meditated my way out of the nicotine koan yet."

"Yah. Yah. Love it." Simon grabs. "Hanh. How's my mouth look now, still like a betel-nut chewer?"

"Smile. No, it's stopped."

"Your fishbowl is empty."

"Or it contains all fish."

"Maybe even some chicken leopards."

"Or the water is out here and we're swimming."

"Right. Sure. And all this leads you t'God?"

"No. No." She holds out one wing of her hair: a lean-to for the ear. "Well. It helps annihilate consciousness. In that sense, yes. But faith is a gift."

"My uncle is a priest."

"Yes. That's right, you told me." Her eyes are careful. "Catholic? In New York? Lynxx?"

"No, Gordon: Episcopal and retired. In Queens. Using my house as his private pork barrel. English, brother to Bettina of the famous peccary. Came over here t'cabbage my inheritance—standard Christian tactics. You'd love him. Another one who meditates. Squats all day in the family chapel, intense as an elephant-foot umbrella stand. Whatsa time?"

"Almost five, I guess."

"Just right for it. Five is an excellent time. My favorite, in fact: along with one, two, three, four, six and up, A.M. or P.M."

"What do you mean? For what?"

"Time for the horizontal dance. Time to play the old slide trombone. Sing it Simon: time to skin-dive: time t'overlap a lap, graft flesh, miter my joint. Time t'auger well, spelunk. Time t'be adrift in dark rivers, t'pump bilge. Time—time t'screw our courage t'the sticky place." Simon in front of her, very formal: knelt. Merry has crossed arms over breast, knee over knee: very formal. "I'm out of euphemisms. Merry, you with the A-cup astral projections, Merry, let's make love. It's very important t'me."

"Oh, motherlove. Here it comes. I should never have let you up here. Hoist on my own petard."

"Hoist yourself on mine instead. We can meditate. Like, how it's possible f'me t'be inside you and outside you at the same time."

"No." His fingers reconnoiter, index and fore: they're glad steppers. But it's uphill work, up and under her skirt. "Dammit. Stop, Simon: you don't want sex. You're doing this out of spite. We were talking, and I said things that surprised you. And you were in over your head, big boy. That's why you're doing this. Spite."

"No. No. I swear it, on my Saviour's pierced and fallen arches. This is just raw, childlike lust. I wanna do some single-entry bookkeeping. I wanna repot my plant. I wanna make a night deposit. I have no anterior motives. I. Want. Your. Twat."

"I don't believe it. Go on, admit. You were out of your depth back there."

"All right. I was. Lemme get in yours."

"Stop. You tickle. God, how many hands do you have?"

"Handshandshandshands."

"Ha-stop."

"Wantwantwantwant."

"Simon—"

"Feelfeelfeelfeel."

"You'll tear my blouse—" He kisses her. His seared lips have an unlikely grain: like soft candies still in their cellophane. She will hold him tight, against her: a good strategy: half embrace, half restraint.

"What's wrong now?"

"Your mouth. I'm afraid to hurt it, it feels—"

"Wait'll I start eating at the Y. You'll be able t'light a Roman chandelier: volts in your socket, watts, amperes, ohms, ahms, um. Listen, pay attention, this is all the verbal foreplay you're gonna get. I feel a hormonal surge: my prostate is swollen like the horn button on a 1922 Hispano-Suiza. Mind if I hold this breast while I'm talking? Thanks. Listen, Mer, and this is the truth—I'll get it notarized if you want—listen, I admire your bright, diseased mind. Think of the genes we could braid together. I'm not just after your warm pampas grass, I'm—"

"Ssssh—" She will gag him. Face reined against her stomach by its hair. Simon waits. This is an ambivalent closeness: he'd like to know its spirit. "Good. Calm down. Good. Please, I won't think you're a queer if we don't. No need to prove yourself. I'm sure you come with excellent references. You know, what you need—have you ever been rebirthed?"

"You mean that guru-farb where they hang you in a big developing tank like some helpless bait worm?"

"They used to do that. They do it dry on a bed now."

"That's new? I've done it with women who felt like a culvert in the dust bowl."

"Spare me. Do you know about rebirthing or not?"

"Yah. Yah. My friend, Norty Sollivan's been through it all: est, I Ching, Rolfing, rebirthing, yoga, Chinese stoop tag—you name it. He's into awareness so much he's almost asleep."

"Well, I think it'd be good for you. I feel a lot of bad—pardon—shit coming up. Particularly about your mother. I don't think you wanted to come out. You ought to go in and try again. It's an extraordinary ex—"

"Didn't want? Baby, I came out running. I chewed the cord in half and asked for seconds. I formed my own receiving line for me. Spare you? Hanh. I get Caisson disease from all that deep consciousness feather-merchantry. Bad shit coming up. Safe space. The universe supports me totally. Look, I don't wanna knit layettes for the secret fetus in me, I wanna get screwed, that's all. I wanna have my smooth stones skipped across the magic lake. Is that too much to ask? Confess, Mermaid, you like me. Huh? You came t'the zoo."

"That doesn't mean I'm ready for bed."

"No. Whaddabout the cake?"

"The cake?"

"It's big as a Morris chair. You cooked it last night because you knew I'd be here. You were gonna invite me. It's first-degree, premeditated sex."

"No." She watches the fish tank. "I can't have done that."

"You did. You did. Come on: let's make a sweat sandwich. Hanh? Let's fit like kitchen canisters. You'll enjoy, I promise. I'll chase your clit like a cat after a chipmunk."

"I can't right now." She pinches his cheek: it is not unpainful. "I'm spoken for."

"Hah! The horny monk. He's been defrocking himself in here. I knew it." Though unreasonable, this is an honest jealousy: Simon can feel cuckolded even by women he has never met. It makes Merry laugh.

"Don't understand me too easily, you big fool."

"Who then? What then? You're trying t'be mysterious."

"Uh-huh." She laughs again. "And, anyhow, I have a period."

"What? What? You have a what? On *my* time? The nerve of a panel thief she's got. A period—hanh. I've heard that woodnote before. Bet it's a phony ripcord in there. I been around, you deadbeat, I've known women who bled like hemophiliacs in the bedroom, women with eternal periods, Jurassic periods. Very convenient, you piker. She invites me up here, she shoots my valuable afternoon, and all the time she has her ovaries barking like a trained seal. I wanna rebate."

"Oh, shut up. Leave if you don't like it."

"Splendid. First she takes advantage of my innocence, then she kicks me out."

"Take advantage? Of you?"

"Listen. Whaddya think I am? Fastidious? I'm used t'bloodbaths—you shoulda read the reviews of my last film. Hah—just think of me as your doctor. Hell, I don't mind dipping my quill in red ink. What's another debt? We could still rotate your crop."

"No, we couldn't."

"Some host. I hate intransigence. There's such a thing as courtesy, you know. Thoughtfulness. A little accommodation. A really gracious woman would understand."

"No."

"What a tightwad. Whaddya got down there that's so special, huh? Tin Pan Alley? Jesus, I been on my knees longer than Jose Ferrer in *Moulin Rouge*."

"I couldn't care less."

"Hah—it came this morning, didn't it? The red badge of cowardice. But *after*. After you made the cake." Merry won't answer. "You were gonna do it. You were. You wanted me."

"I'm tired, Simon." Merry scrapes the cigarette flat. Her head will knock against a sofa pillow: ten times: neck loosening. "Is it over now?"

"Over? Three hours today, two hours on Monday. Five hours and I still haven't laid eyes on your crack of dawn. Hanh. No woman does that t'me —it's exploitation, it's below the minimum wage. Five hours. Uh-huh, friend, I don't work on spec: I get a guarantee, plus percentages. I strummed for you, I played the gold kazoo, I—I *danced*. Uh-huh, next time you see me, I'll be wearing a black hood. And I'll have a sickle. I'll come to reap."

"Forgive me if I don't show up."

"That's a plump one. You'd have to move out, get an alias. I'll slide in under the door like a draft. I'll pour out of your tap. I'll be spackle in your hairline cracks. I'll reupholster you with skin. Our navels will make a hollow sphere together. It cannot be avoided."

"Simon, do you think this is romantic? Do you think a woman wants to know she's just a sexual—thing?"

"Gee, Mer. It's always worked f'me before. The raw, tooth-grinding, ten-fingered, blind, neolithic grab. The fumbling hand. The slavering lip. The sheer, raucous sincerity of it. Women always know how they stand with me—prone. Even a hardened flute-tease like you."

"Is that what I am?"

"Yah. Yah." Simon has palmed her slim left breast. He thumbs it as he would a cheap lighter. The nipple is awake: sleep-in-its-eyes: querulous. "Well, I'll be lubed. She has a rudimentary nervous system after all. Hanh. Bet you've never had an orgasm. Except with yourself, in front of the mirror, using some vibrator thing you could break pavement with.

Orgasm, it's the only woman-nakedness. When the throat lining tears off in a raw growl, and the lips dog-smack together and the limbs are in a wild paralysis. You'd never let a man see that. You might, might, give a man pleasure. But you'd never give him *your* pleasure."

"Shut up. Just shut up."

"Oh, a hit. A palpable hit."

"Get out, why don't you?"

"I intend to, don't worry. I gotta film a rented mule t'morrow. But first, little Tuckpoint, grant me one favor. One."

"What? What?" Her goalie knees have hit together: save.

"Not that. Not yet. Up. I wanna carry you again."

"What?"

"Come on." He rousts her out, up: a good yank. "This, like this."

"Don't hurt me, please."

"I don't hurt women. Go dead. Trust. It's one of your goddam safe spaces."

Simon, yes, has swept Merry off her feet: arm around back, arm under/behind the hard kneecaps. For a while, but not for long, she will test his resolution: afraid: a new height of indignity. Right palm heel has driven his larynx in: that one judo stroke, all she can remember from three lessons given by a lesbian Thai who pinned her too regularly, with too much close élan. But Simon carries on. They tour the room: it's a thoughtful, tender proceeding. He hums: as though to make her drowse. His arms rock their cradling.

"You're insane. Simon, what is this? What is it?"

"It's a carrying." He croons: he is absorbed. "Slowly. That's good. The back. The neck. Let go. Now the thighs. I still get resistance in the thighs. Better. Fine. That's beautiful. I can feel the center of your weight now. Those five flights up. It's the way I'll remember you best. Even if we never meet again."

"You're insane."

"I am. I am. And you're leading again."

She laughs. And he. They're silly together: a foolish contagion. Simon dances Merry, waltz-time and with old grace. As one they have a taller, more specific gravity. She rests there. The red silk will swirl around them, an eidolon of fire. Merry has stilled in/against his stilling chest.

3

"Cut! Cut! Kaa-utt! There it goes again, through the bougainvillea. Bye-bye. Arrivederci. I'm a dead man. So long."

And sheeze, yes, on its thirty-yard slouch toward Bayside-Bethlehem, Francis the rent-a-mule has veered 90° left once more—through Uncle Arthur's rose bed, through Mrs. P's azalea bed, browsing now in fat juniper hedge. That scripture might not be fulfilled. Joseph and Mary, bareback, impotent, along for the ride, take their unborn and overdue Son's name: in vain, Francis has padded his part. Joseph, wearing a three-piece polyester suit, gives Simon the very high sign: lunch was inhaled today, some four-on-the-floor Mexican red. His yarmulke, though this is impossible as far as yarmulkes go, seems somehow backward. Mary, virgin, verging on mulecide, kicks all the brown flank she can get at. Her oafish, large rubberfoam pregnancy is sidesaddle under one armpit, more like Johnny Appleseed's sack. Simon has booted his script, soccer style. It goes up: many bickering, white pages: a dove released. Applause and "*Mula! Mula!*" from the balcony, balconies above. Newspaper confetti will drizzle down/on Van Lynxx Garden. In two hours of unprintable filming and language the mule has won a devoted claque. Simon megaphones palms together, up.

"Robert! Don! Someone grab that shrub addict before it bites on the electric fence. Move! Rapido! Joseph and Mary aren't grounded. Aaaargh. They told me, they told me, never work with animals or pre-pubic children. Every damn time, just like clockwork, broken clockwork —zam, into the underbrush like Ramar of the Jungle. Where's the matron with my Thorazine? I'll jugulate myself. John! Tallulah! Can't you stillbirths keep that four-footed neuter soubrette from ad-libbing?"

"That's not my fuckin' job. I'm an actress, not a fuckin' animal trainer." Tallulah/Mary, great with rubber, looks uncordial. Stanislavsky-trained, she has spent ten days commuting between St. Patrick's Cathedral and a maternity ward: to store up emotional background. But love's labor pains are lost. Francis doesn't believe in an ensemble performance.

"It *is* hard, Simon." John/Joseph, in the attic room of a good dime bag, skims his yarmulke away. "Whee. I can't find the clutch on this model."

"You know what, Mr. Simon—fuckin'—Lynxx? You can take your idiot film and jam it. Up. Sideways."

"Hey, Tallulah." Simon will forecast: non-union walkout coming. He eases off. "I advertised for someone who could use her ass."

"Oh, funny. You get up here, bigmouth. You try it. You get stink and chafe. Funny. He finds himself funny."

"Okay. Okay. I can smell dissension when I hear it. Help is coming. Cheer up, Tallulah—you've been mounted before. Who's in charge of the carrot supply? Robert! Nice carrots, Francis. Eat, you son of a mixed marriage, or it's back to hauling Borax." Sunlight, fuse-blown, goes off. "Now what? Look. Thunderheads clanking in like Rommel at El Alamein. Even the sky wants a payoff. St. Luke never mentioned this: another arty screenwriter who didn't understand film. Rose, can we run this dynamic vignette tomorrow again?"

"The lease is up on Francis at eight A.M. It'll cost another twenty-five bucks."

"Sheep pebbles t'them. Rent me a mule that can't take direction, will they? Fifteen bucks, hanh. I don't care what his SAG card says. Lar, how much film have I dribbled inta my shoe today?"

"Feet and feet. About one-third of what we have."

"Aaargh. Bettina! Aldo!" Simon calls out to Van Lynxx Cemetery. "Your child's got his frond stuck in the Vegematic again. Quick. We'll need more light. Don! Don! Edge the big bank in. Rose, help him take the scrim off."

Cable has grown out of his van, kink after storage-bent kink, runner-bean-wise: a new, hardy vegetable in Van Lynxx Garden. Cable to the Auricon Super-1200 camera on its crab dolly: cable to a light board, district manager for Don's rickety bank and seven ColorTran stands, each with one Bardwell and McAlister spot: cable to fishpole boom, to the Rangertone sound sync, to Roland's directional mike. Roland, an Action News reporter, mulch of Salem butts around his feet, has been on call beside Bethlehem Road more than two hundred minutes now, left hanging for his exclusive interview with Joseph and Mary this Christmas Eve day. Simon is depressed. Jesus' plywood and canvas crèche has been thrown up, up against Van Lynxx Chapel: NAZARETH MOTOR LODGE, SORRY FULL behind it. Schleppy work: solid as a Little Rascals clubhouse, or something Practical Pig's first brother might've built. How well, now, he can remember the extravagant production values in *Clap.* A leased, leashed goat has been grazing excelsior from Jesus' cradle/trough. Two poodles, untypecast as sheep, dog it in the manger.

Also three wise men, each a plaster Virgin Mary. They wear reverse drag. Looted last night by Don and Rose from middle-class crabgrassy Catholic Bayside, where Madonnas with infinite patience wait for a call-back from their agent in sky-blue telephone booths.

It isn't just a cliché then: the carrot/stick will do, does. See, Robert has cajoled Francis out. They're at the tape mark, ready and willful. Simon mimes slapping water on his face from her (Bettina's) cement birdbath. It is desiccant now. Simon hooks leaves out and one Rheingold can. A decoy cement sparrow has long-lighted on the rim. Simon sez, "Mommy. Mommy. My tum is hurting me." Once upon a time, Simon . . . She told him once-upon-a-time stories here, once. Bettina would character-act out exceptionally wicked trolls and witches and ogres: they all had Aldo's plausible, commercial voice. Parables of the Lynxx family. Once upon a three-year-old time he couldn't see up/into this birdbath to which no birds came. Yet cool water, its New York slicked wetness, would startle his reaching finger. Simon hangs over the void bowl. He'd like this to be done with: cataclysms, death even, would suit him fine: thunderheads concur in his mood. Anything but the present piecemeal drip-drying away. His tongue flops out: the meat of it heavy with scar crust as a slice of beef Wellington. Ah, he'd love to plant: the happy, benevolent miracle that is bulb shoots in April. Rose has bumped him: monitory, watchful, executor of his spite-fits and his caprices. He will grab-bag in her un-formfit Levi's. A quaggy buttock can fit one hand. He raises it: drops it. Recalls the soft sculpture he has seen of a giant light switch. On/off. On/off. On/up. Off.

"Hey, Rose, whyncha bend over the birdbath, huh? It'll only take a minute. Lemme give you a little booster shot. Little inoculation against me, anh?"

"Somehow, just somehow, I don't think this is the time."

"I know. Gee. But failure makes me horny. I wanna do something that doesn't require six technicians and a unit manager."

"You're the one that insisted on a mule."

"Yes, Rose. That's right, Rose. But not a mule with his own *auteur* theory of filmmaking. You shoulda had an open call for mules. You shoulda done a few dry takes. Then I'da known t'build the manger six feet deep in a weedy thicket. Lar! Lar-yo! Is there anything we can salvage? What's it look like?"

"It looks like three innings of a donkey baseball game." Larry sits, upright yet fetal, contracted, on the camera dolly. He has green cut-offs on and a fishnet shirt. He doesn't look well: the difference between litheness and scrawniness is, in large part, mental. "Getting cold, Sy. My nips have been up and down, up and down. Get a move on. Ten minutes and we'll be shooting through God's dark filter."

"Yeah. Sure. Here, take my sweater. Don! We ready? Hah? People!

Once more bravely into the furze. Tell you what—Joseph! John, I mean. Dismount, we'll try with you leading Francis. Oh, Jesus. Rose—did I see right? Did he just fall off? He's been eating toadstools again. He's wasted. John! Robert, help him up."

"I'm okay. I'm okay. Things just seem a little bigger than usual."

"I bet. Oh, mother. Did D. W. Griffith have days like this? John. Yoohoo. Bethlehem is over there, see it? In all its garish Hollywood splendor. It must look good t'you at least—with your revised and expanded vision. That wasn't a Smith Corona I saw you smoking."

"I'm all right, Simon. Don't make a federal case, I see it."

"Okay. You lead Francis. Make lady mule sounds."

"I don't think there are lady mules, Simon."

"Then try t'look like a gorse bush. You do character work. And when you get to Roland—don't cover him. Give Larry an angle." Pock! And papock! Two dead soldiers, from the Miller High Life army, have been thrown down. John, once a Marine lieutenant in Vietnam, will hit gravel: basic training. "Oh, God. It's the shell-shock victim. Robert, help Mr. Christ up again. Please."

"I'm all right. They fragged me in Da Nang. My own men. Under my own bunk."

"I know, John. That's where you spent the war. They were just trying t'wake you up. You're lucky I wasn't there. Brush him off."

"Bottles. Why do they have to do that?"

"Because they're underprivileged, John. Don't you read the New York Times? Throwing bottles is one of their underprivileges. Tallulah, hitch your gut around, you've got the holy embryo arranged like a colostomy pouch."

"Well, maybe if I had a saddle—"

"This is modern ancient Palestine, dear. Not the Ascot hunt club. What now? Rope. Robert, get that clothesline. The long piece, enough so I can throttle Francis if he reinterprets his part again. Hurry. Hurry. That cloud looks like some beds I've been under. Rose—will this affect our continuity? John getting off the mule, I mean."

"There is no continuity, Simon. For continuity to exist there has to be a start first."

"Thanks. Critical, aren't we? Who's got a fag? The smoking kind?"

Ball Peen is in the on-deck circle: serviceable: very sound-stage-struck. His performance—match scraped, match windbreaked, touched, shook out—appears nostalgic: a little homage to Raft and Bogart, great lighters. He has said, "Real." These are, memo note, real film tools. He has been saying "real" to cable, to clapboard, to reels: real reel. Simon adopts the lit Kool: gives no receipt of gratitude. There is trouble around Bethlehem: another Middle East crisis. While Robert has been noosing clothesline around Francis' neck, Francis—guess what?—Francis has been swallowing the other end. John, then John and Robert, then John and Robert and Roland try for an extraction. But Francis has found floss to suit his big teeth: has reined himself in: tight. Simon can't watch: his mind is Tap City. An advance-man wind comes like acrobats, tumbling, through the hedge. Simon will chair-arm his elbow on Ball Peen's 4'8" shoulder: again no receipt of gratitude. The dark glasses are up, pincushioned into his Afro. Ball Peen's glance, black and Korean, a joiner of continents, is shrewd-primitive. He could feel discriminated against: Francis or no Francis, professionalism here is so heavy it has the tone, he imagines, of a private and racist association. These-are-not-things-blacks-can-know. Sledge has been standing, tall as Simon, morose, mute, beside Larry's camera. Simon will now place the Kool in one nostril. He has been doing that of late. He hasn't time to oversee his strange mouth.

"Uh, Simon. I know you got major hassles here—and if it ain't the best time . . ." Ball Peen hums: a sound bridge. "I mean, what you call me'n Sledge down here for?"

"All in due course, Low Rise."

"You find a part for me? I can do it, listen. Comical-tragical-pastoral. That's Hamlet, you know. I am ready, man. I been readying for this ten years now. I won't show you up. Huh, is that it? Don't haul my chain. You got a part?"

"Could be. Could be. But, I don't know, it all depends. I have this out-of-the-basepath idea. *Eine Kleine* nightwork. Byzantine foolings. Do not disappoint me by being a man of principle."

"What? What's the catch? What I gotta do? Oh, shit. I don't like your tone of face."

"Very perceptive. You see mule-induced desperation. At this moment I'm Gary Gilmore, Short View. I have no regard for life, particularly yours. But screw the cable hookup in right and you'll get reception: groupies, cocaine on the coffee table, skywriting, northern lights spelling your name, limousines chauffeured by six-foot white men. Broad of the Week Club and each one built like an Al Capp cartoon."

"A part. That's it. Uh, now. I don't wanna seem pushy. But Sledge—I gotta put in a good word for him. He's my brother and—"

"I know, he's heavy. Yah. And it's heavies I need. All is possible with God and an absolute lack of scruple."

"Oh, sweet Jesus. Sweet, sweet Jesus. A part. A film credit. I'll kiss your white dong, Simon. I'll be a *nigger* for you."

"That's not all you'll do, Campstool. Things are grinding to a climax. *Götterdämmerung.* And woe to those who give suck in that time."

Uncle Arthur has flattened a beach chair down: to make guest room for the storm. He is unquiet. City property, his political benefice, has been taken advantage of: landmarks marked. Yet this driftless folly—filming, the illusion of illusion—might be a sermon text: it can occupy him. A)

Mules and their mad free will. B) Destiny as improvisation, compromise. C) The rough teleology of a final script. And D) editing still to come: redemption and/or judgment. We have a parable here. Uncle Arthur lets wind explore him. Mrs. P has locked Van Lynxx Manor, interdicting a topcoat and tea. Alf scouts from the roof. For one hour he has been hatching bare heels: inert there, in savage repose: predator at the water hole. Against gray shingle his Dead Sea Scroll chest, the tattooing crabbed with age, is not conspicuous. Don's light bank has gone on: brilliant, shocking: without the health of sunshine. Fifteen feet tall on telescoping, stork-knee limbs: it has straddled the garden path like a railroad signal. Now Robert jogs in: clip- and clapboard under one arm: triumphant athletes come out of a game just so. A Red Sox cap brim will withhold evidence: you can't quite note the immature, hormone-bitten face. And, on lower lip, saloon pianist fashion, the unlit half Camel butt sticks: has been stuck for three hours. A movie persona screenwritten overnight. Uncle Arthur is disappointed. In this he sees corruption of the natural child. In this Simon sees a little prick.

"Roland! I know you'd rather be home taking your parakeet's temperature right now. But let's have some Howard Cosell Jew's-harp-twang excitement in the voice. It's one more shopping day t'Christmas: children've been waiting four thousand years for their Schwinn ten-speed. And probe: get that stuff about wife swapping and open marriage in. Okay? John! I know the rope is covered with mule spit: the mule doesn't like your spit either. Try t'look colonial-ranch-style middle class: maybe Mary was unfaithful but the kid's gonna have good genes, a shoo-in for Bronx High School of Science. Right! Count down to disaster." A large throat has been cleared: nature stealing Simon's thunder. Francis will wigwag his ears. An "ooooh" is pushed up from the mezzanine seats. Wash has already been taken in. "Listen t'that. God wants a writer's credit. Everybody and his graven image tries t'throw a bop into me. Lar —ready?"

"Get back, you—you . . ." This is Robert bullying Sledge away from the camera. You? You what? Simon ponders and is amused. Wunderkind promise here: a young boor on the horizon.

"Zero! We're on." But Friday has wind-sprinted past. Glum: the light bank is out. "What now for furd's sake?" Don is swatting azaleas with a metal boom.

"That gaw-damn monkey pulled my plug."

"Can't you control your assistants, Don? Saint Pubis, whyn't I take up a fun thing, like wheelchair basketball?" The bank is on again. "Joseph! John!" Joseph/John flashes a carrot. "Good thinking, but mask it from the camera. You didn't walk all the way t'Bethlehem with a vegetable stand in your pocket. Tallulah! Please don't lean on your tumescence. That's the Christ child, not a throw pillow. Are we A-OK, friends? Speak up. This is our last shot at it. Is Roland's mike on, Rose? Right. No fluffs, people. Larry?"

"Set."

"Camera!" The machine sings. Simon will count: one thousand, two thousand: five seconds and go. "Action!"

Francis pitches ahead, recalcitrant, taken up in segments—head, neck, forequarter, gut, hindquarter, tail—like a length of freight train, but moving. Simon has himself by the scrotum: athletic moral support. The camera descends: going down, fourteenth floor, thirteenth, twelfth, faster, tenth-ninth-eighth, faster yet, seventh-th-th-third, red brick blearing, stop, at Mary's red brick shawl: a sweet color meld. Rack fade: Tallulah, ripe, one night away from changing B.C. to A.D., looks appropriate: someone God would go for, not flashy, discreet. Odd how disgruntlement can appear beatific. Track, track, track: Larry has summarized the acquiescent pack animal up/down of mule shoulder work. Francis, a slow study, is canter perfect. Now just ten mule lopes from Roland. Simon will try one breath and WASH! Lightning has blown the great fuse upstairs. Francis is in catatonia. His segments bump back against each other: whoa. The rope has gone rigid as a line drive. Joseph, intent on Roland and his step father-to-be dialogue, is brought down. Ba-baa-DOOM!: thunder. The mule will shrink: a three-orange jackpot of dung balls has puttered out behind. And, can't stay, sorry, off through Uncle Arthur's rose bed again, through Mrs. P's azalea bed again, trawling Joseph and carrot after. The Virgin yoicks, "Mother of God! No! No! No! Stop him! Help!"

"Cut! Cut! Kaaa-uttt!" Simon, alone, stampedes: rose bed, azalea bed. The mule has it, Simon, coming to him. "You funk-out! You factory-irregular horse! Hanh! A little thunder and it gets four cold feet. Hanh, call yourself a professional. I'll give you something t'be scared of, you big pussy." Simon unpacks one, tenth rib low. Francis has the kick of a mule. His backstroke is awe-full: it expresses death. Tallulah has been bucked onto Francis' neck. Her nine months' worth of padding is behind her now: bustle there: a breech birth.

"Don't! Simon, don't!"

"I'll ruin your career, Francis. I'll see you never work again. It's the zoo circuit, friend. Unnnh-hah!" Francis turns, traverses, slow as 19th Century cannon. Simon has anticipated. He's getting a kick out of this, another, another: mule shin and thigh and flank. "Take that. Go on—report me to the Teamsters Union, you—you . . . You damned Democrat!"

"Stop! Please! He'll throw me!"

"Oh, shut up. Go say a prayer t'yourself." Simon has lost interest. "That's all! Pack it up! Another shooting day shot. Stow the heavy gear over by, no—in the chapel. Quick! Jimmy those lights down before we attract every footloose megavolt in the neighborhood. I wanna die. Gimme a sharp saltine, I'll cut my throat."

Lips move: Simon, a dummy for his own voice . . . That did it. That was Herman Wolff's last chance. Oh, I tried t'be reasonable. But he paid the mule t'fold on me. Anyone could see that: a Zionist mule. I'm losing my mind. So this is insanity. Not bad: feels like an average Tuesday. Well, it's done: better t'be hung like a horse than a lamb . . . Rose and Don and Robert have him under observation. Larry follows, Simon framed in the viewfinder . . . Jeez, I'll need a couple twenties for John and Tallulah. What's this? Well, hi there. The key to Minnie's pre-cast tookus. How opportune. Time for some debt service. Soak my frustration in the old mucoid tube. Stir up a little estrogen cocktail. Wow, lightning. God's Polarity Therapy. Blow wind, crack your cheeks. Old Simon's about t'put his head under the big winepress screw. Crunch . . . Friday is in the birdbath: and will hear no evil . . . I'm scared. This could be a felony, Simon. This could carry a prison sentence. One banana peel and you'll do time, Simon. Years and years t'practice your Tantric Tennis in Leavenworth. Come on, you coward, anything worth doing is worth doing crookedly. But can I trust Ditty-bop and his Zen Coon brother? Merry. Merry, I ask you, is greed enough? Please, God, I'm doing your biography, let greed be enough. Okay, Wolff didn't take a shine t'me, I'll take two shines t'him. Only fair. It's done. It's done. I'm insane. It's done.

"Hey, Lar. I'm sorry. Jeez, right now my brain's so shrunk you could mail it out in a number ten envelope. Pack up, go put hot pasties on your nipples. This was a total meltdown. My core is exposed: people around me are getting sterile or producing infants that need two baby hats. You know I can do better than this."

"It's all right, Sy."

"Rose, um. Would you mind slipping these to Tallulah and John? With my gratitude. I'd write a check, but the last one I gave John was made by B. F. Goodrich."

"Twenty dollars each? Come on, Simon—"

"I'd do it myself, gladly, but I've gotta go peck corn with the other chickens. Listen, Rose—listen: I can't handle criticism now, I'm in my late Nixon period. One more such Pyrrhic defeat as this, and I'll start rocking like a retarded child. Huh? Can't you see the signs? I know, I know. Tallulah'll have a polyfoam miscarriage, but please—absorb abuse, deal out praise, fish some lies outa the tickler file. Stonewall. Anyhow, you're the producer, aren't you? Christ, take some personal pride in this Gertie the Dinosaur episode we're making. Give them calls for early next week. Tell them we've got a horse who studied with Lee Strasberg. Aha, tell them Grandma has an appointment with the great Wolff himself tonight. It's almost true. The better t'eat me with. That's a good girl. Rose, I couldn't manage without you. And, oh. Lemme have those two scripts. What?" Uncle Arthur is in the bend of Simon's elbow, unbending it. "What now? What part d'you want?"

"Simon, now really. This is rather too much. Not in the chapel, not all that outfit. There's certain to be damage. Put it back in your lorry."

"Chapel? I've seen soil closets that were holier. I should leave it empty so that you and God can chase down a simultaneous orgasm? Uh-uh. Besides, it's mine. My great-grandfather sacked Florence t'get it and you know how religious he was—he woulda used the shroud of Turin for a contour sheet. Lemme alone. I feel like the catcher at a driving range right now."

"Simon. I do think I've been—we've been—more than patient. I've given you your head. I wanted you to have a sporting chance. But you're riding for a fall now. Mrs. P is perfectly sulphurous. I've never seen the like. I expect she'll have the Landmarks man down here tomorrow morning. Frankly, I'm afraid you'll be had up for criminal trespass."

"Now get this, Uncle: I'll handle my women, you handle yours. Huh, she's a housekeeper, for node's sake. Not blood. I'm blood. Fire that non-flowering tuber and fly her out of here: Emery Air Freight'll take anything. Or give her some pump action in the old Sag Harbor. That's what she needs. Though, by now I suppose you'd need simulator training on a woman."

"You simply won't understand. Mrs. P and I are both in the employ of the Landmarks Commission. They have jurisdiction, not I." Uncle Arthur will now look at his own moving, reasoning hands: and, another problem, they are old. "If you'd see clear to be just a jot more tactful. The flower beds, for instance, you've given them a dreadful mucking over."

"It's almost winter, Uncle. This is hardly a Victory garden just now. There's nothing gonna come up except perennial beer cans."

"Yes. Well, the chapel is still full of manure."

"No, it isn't. I told Rose to—"

"I don't care what you told her, it's still full of manure."

"Burn incense—"

"No! I've had quite enough and more of your glib cheek. That at least. The chapel has to be cleaned. And I mean soap and water. In return, though I'm a damned fool to do it, I'll try my level best to mollify Mrs. P for a day or so."

"All right, all right. Right-right-right. Right. *Right.* Just one administrative crisis after another. If you want a job done well, do it yourself."

"I'm glad to hear that."

"Don't believe a word I say. It's just rhetoric. Robert! I've taken enough crap for today. Robert! Where's my apprentice smell-feast? Robert!" Out of the game again, rushing. Robert has been spoiled by this day's importance. His run is appealing, serious, loyal. Simon, you realize, has called him Robert again. Simon doesn't often use Robert's given name. Simon, like Adam, is a great namer of things.

"Yuh, what's up?" There are presumptions in this: I-am-necessary: they rile Simon. Knelt now, Robert has set the clipboard flat, responsive, along one thigh: a squire's attention.

"Go shove your bogus hand props, that MGM commissary act wears me thin. Get a shovel from the cellar and start forking mule balls outa God's boudoir. Like I told you day before yesterday. Christ's real estate broker is complaining. I dunno why: for someone born in a manger, alla sudden he's forgotten who his roommates were. Then you can filch some Ajax and scour it down. Go on, Chilblain." Robert is put out: he has been putting out since 7 A.M. "*Mach schnell.* What's dung is dung." The glasses are off: to face faceless Simon down.

"Shovel? Uh-uh, why me?" And Simon, articulate as ever, slaps him a good reason why. The swipe is ornate, long: badminton slow but dense. Robert has rolled with it, into the birdbath. At first he will take his myopia for stunning, for injury. The Red Sox hat and the unlit half Camel are back there. Knocked right out from under his new self-image.

"Listen, you double fault. If I say do a rim job on that chapel, you'll say Thank you and Sir and with your mouth full. What makes you think, I got hard mozzarella enough, I need an adolescent Little Caesar around here? With that Andy Capp butt stuck on your lip, huh? Answer me."

"I. My glasses."

"They're in your hand, Turgid. Now make like the honey man. I'll see you get a mention in the titles. Sanitation by Robert of Hollywood."

"You—" The comment has died, but is there, outspoken, in Robert's posture. Simon will go for him: a hand at his slack collar. The neck is loose, not well rooted in it.

"Did I recognize a threat?"

"No."

"Gonna tell Mommy?" Simon has introduced prima facie evidence: the big key to Minnie. He taps Robert with it. "Well, if you do, knock first. I may be dropping my mother load."

"Let me alone."

"I don't lump back-talk. Not unless it's very amusing. I'm in loco parentis here, know what that means?"

"No."

"It means I'm your crazy father. Get. Go. Now." Released, Robert will seem tiddly: under the, Simon's, influence. His arm is out, as though to compensate for a heavy pail in the other hand. "Well, are you satisfied, Uncle? Huh?"

"I've nothing to say to you, Simon. I'm ashamed. Goodbye."

"What's a guy have t'do, huh? I mean—make up your mind, why

dontcha? Oh, hell." Simon shrugs. The shrug is florid and unadroit: a poor acting choice. He does not feel indifferent. This last bearish cruelty to Robert was uncharacteristic: out of control: bitter: troubling. Simon is proud, after all. Until now his select violence has always been even-tempered and humorous. And to the point, not wasteful. Simon has guessed what it is: fear, his. Of ends: an end. "Ho-boy. Ho-boy, death. Elisabeth Kubler-Ross, I need you now." Rose is smiling. Robert's humiliation has gratified her. And Simon can regret that, too. "What're you so happy about?"

"Me? Who, me? I'm not happy."

"You better not be. Where are the Seoul brothers?"

"By the chapel. There."

"B.P.! Sledge! C'mere! Go away, Rose. Dust off." They come, the long and the short of it, his destiny. Some fat, sparse rain has fallen. Twilight draws a hypotenuse from one apartment roof, down. Ball Peen will yawn: the yawn is florid and unadroit. Another poor acting choice. Ball Peen has noted the scripts.

"What is it, Simon?"

"What is it? What is it? Hand me the envelope, please. Flashbulbs. Drumroll. Commercial break. In a minute you'll both be crying like Miss Teenage Eastern Hemisphere. Sssst—over this way." He directs them: well, pushes. One arm across Sledge's back: one arm across Ball Peen's back. A split-level embrace: over a period of time it'd cause chronic spinal pain. They stand in dirt. A few rose bushes confer nearby. Sledge is tea-with-milk color: freckles da-dit his nose bridge. Simon can seldom see a face so conveniently. "You and Pearl Bailey. You and Sun Yung Moon. Fame. Cash flow like a hemorrhage. Honor done t'your race. Races. Whatever." Ball Peen has dropped under/out from the embrace.

"A part? Is that—them scripts—are they?"

"Howdja like t'be Judas? The biggest kissing scene since *From Here to Eternity*. A guest pass t'that hundred-a-plate dinner in the upper room. Follow my eye. CU on a dark hand. Lithe, slinky, virtuoso. That hand tells us so much. But whose is it? Whose? Track up the arm. Dolly back. Yours! It's you dipping your very own treacherous sop in the Lord's gravy. You hanging, purple-tongued with Stella Adler acting technique, from your own short tree. You. Judas. It'll go great in redneck Mississippi drive-ins. They'll cheer."

"Man. Oh, man." Ball Peen slaps himself five: one hand congratulating the other. It's ingenuous and involuntary and young: it could give remorse. But Simon, the desperate, is remorseless now. "Judas. Now, way I see him is street-wise. Oh, yeah. Jesus Christ, he's the poverty program come to Harlem. Judas gone score some that federal funding. He don't know no better. He's been hurt. He been worked over by the system. Yeah. Judas. Yeah. Judas. An' Sledge? Um—you know."

"Sledge. Well. St. Peter, I thought. The big stone himself. Huh, Sledge? That make your cock crow thrice?"

"Wait on. He ain't too quick with lines."

"He can play it like Marcel Marceau. We'll concentrate on his, uh, sculptural aspects. A Barbara Hepworth saint. Something you could sit on, if you didn't know it was art. Solid."

"We'll do you proud, Simon. Oh, Simon, my *man*. You'll never regret it. I been waitin', waitin'. I polish my craff for this. You are black. Black. Black."

"Ha." Simon throws a flag: five yards for illegal procedure. "As in all good things there is a kicker. A clause done in print the size of bacteria. I haven't read it t'you yet." Ball Peen inhales: cheeks go in. "Don't sulk. What'd you expect from me? I can't be inconsistent this late in life."

"Simon—"

"Do I get favors, huh? Listen, when I sneeze, I gotta call Dial-A-Gesundheit. Let's not be sentimental."

"We ain't got money."

"No. Nothing so crass—or so safe—as money. Though, now you mention it, that is an arresting idea. But no. Hmmm."

"Come on. Put it to me."

"Watcha doon tonight?"

"We got us four ticts to the Buck Nougat concert. Couple chicks—"

"Uh-uh. Gone as the snows of 1969. Forget it. Put a new roll on the player piano." Ball Peen will nod: priorities reordered.

"Okay. Done. Come on, don't play me like no fish, Simon. What?"

"This. Huddle time. A little chalk talk. It's fourth and forty-five with 0:01 left on the Knute Rockne Memorial Scoreboard. Everyone down. Down. Come on, remember your tribal heritage, hunker in front of the cooking fire. Down. I'm gonna block out the biggest scene of your life." Simon has made a tabula rasa: leaves finger-whisked from one square foot of tulip bed. "Now pay close attention. Tonight at eight there's gonna be a party. At Ten Great Ferry Street. It's one and one half blocks off Greenwich Street near the river. Huge warehouse turned into an artists' loft and high-rent commune. The great and the near-great will be there. I will be there, don't ask in which category. I will be there. Yes, and you will be here. X, that's you. Same as your signature." Simon has drawn a vertical coordinate: let it stand for Greenwich Street. He furrows a horizontal across: then six or seven more. "You get off at the IRT Chambers Street stop. Here. Right? Walk one block west on Chambers Street to Greenwich. Right? Then downtown. This is Warren Street. Then Murray. Then Park. Then Barclay. Then, aha, Great Ferry. One, two, three, four, five blocks. Walk west on Great Ferry. Cross Washington Street. Ten Great Ferry is in the middle of that block. If you find yourself in the Hudson River you've walked too far. Anyhow, even you

340

couldn't miss it. The second floor, it's got a vulgar, round bay window. Sticks ten vulgar feet out over the pavement. Or just follow the stench of PCP canapés. Now. Now. Across the street there is an alley. You and your silent partner take up position there, at X. You will hear sounds of decadent laughter. You will feel left out. You will probably shiver. But you will wait. Simple, yes?"

"Ah—"

"Repeat, please."

"Chambers Street IRT. West to Greenwich. Down five blocks to Great Ferry. Then over one block."

"One and a half. You gotta cross Washington."

"Ten Great Ferry. Big window. And an alley acrossways from it. Then what? I do not like the sound, Simon."

"Wait'll you hear the substance. At eight-thirty P.M. the great producer-director Herman Wolff will arrive. He drives a matzoh-colored Cadillac: license plate HW, for Hebrew Wehicle. You will note where the car is parked. At ten o'clock P.M. Wolff will leave because his cardiogram says TILT. I will lean out the window and wave—one if by land, two if by sea—when he starts down. Mr. Wolff is even shorter than you are. Balding. He wheezes when he walks. What you will do—you will mug him as he approaches the Cadillac."

"What? No, sir. No way. You got the wrong guys."

"You will mug him. You will go through his pockets like a can of Gumout through a carburetor. Take his wallet, his watch: take his senior citizen's reduced busfare card. Shake him a lot, make his teeth hum, but do not injure him. Do, however, call him funky anti-Semitic names. Intimidate. Be a two-man National Socialist party. At which point—cavalry sounds—at which point I will come across the street and use all sorts of kung fu on you. We will rehearse the mechanics in a minute. You will then run away. I will run up credit in large denominations with Mr. Wolff. You will do this or the heavy bronze doors of showbiz close forever. I have spoken." Simon stands. Ball Peen and Sledge remain squatted.

"Simon. Be reasonable. That's crazy and dangerous."

"It accords with my mood—also crazy and dangerous. The cost of living just went up for both of you."

"Suppose the man recognizes us? We'll go to jail. He's a big wheel."

"I'll write Amnesty International and appear as a character witness at your trial."

"Nuts."

"Look, you beef-wit. Buy two sets of pantihose, two ski masks, something ingenious. Anyhow no Jew can tell one black from another."

"Simon—"

"B.P., you don't understand. Jews expect t'be mugged. It makes them feel good on Yom Kippur. It's the one liberal act they do that's unselfish. Don't deprive the poor man."

"But he's got a bad heart."

"His heart is made of fiberglass. I guarantee it."

"Suppose he leaves with someone?"

"I will see to it that he doesn't."

"Suppose there's cops?"

"This neighborhood is like North Devoid. They haven't picked up the garbage since 1926. We cannot fail."

"Can Sledge and me think this over?"

"Of course. Provided you agree first." Plack-plack: Simon clapping scripts together.

"Sledge? What you say?" Sledge laughs. "Simon, you sure it's fool-proof?"

"Would I risk your freedom and your franchise if it wasn't?"

"Yeah. Yeah. You would."

"I probably would. But this is so safe Standard & Poor's gave it a AAA rating. Say you're gonna make him eat pork. Worse, say Sephardic Jews're smarter. That'll really get him."

"Man. I'm shitting minestrone already."

"Some black. Didn't you learn basic offing in the ghetto?"

"Hey, man. You know us. We was brought up in Butte, Montana."

"Just my luck. I forgot you were a Jap wearing Grecian Formula II all over."

"This Wolff—he's real small?"

"About the size of a lawn ornament. Uh—Uncle!" Uncle Arthur turns. "Fins and atonement. Come over here. Ball Peen, Sledge, I wantcha t'meet Arthur Gordon: he's my uncle and he's just about the right size. You can practice on him."

"Simon, I want you to apologize to that boy. You broke his heart."

"I will. I will. But first my friends needta rehearse the armed robbery scene from St. Luke. 'A certain man went down from Jerusalem to Jericho, and fell among thieves, which stripped him of his raiment, and wounded him and departed, leaving him half dead.' You can let up on the half dead part. Quarter dead. Uncle, these two fine actors will use you gently. Make it big, theatrical. Curse and spit on his gabardine. Don't let the collar con you, he was trained to kill in seminary. I'll be back in a few minutes. Gotta fertilize some ova."

"Simon—"

"Simon—"

The tongue, appreciate it, takes part in running, dishes breath out. Simon cannot pant well now: he has lost a step for that. Down the garden path, low, hedgehopping, toward the patio. He buzzes Van Lynxx Manor, daredevilish. And there is/was a taste to running, mmm, taste of old blood back along the throat. Simon has recalled it. He dekes a slow rose bush: in motion again, the Wolff recklessness behind him. Like all thieves, Simon has a superstitious affection for the law: he and it, they travel in the same social set. Static electricity is wired in his shirt: arm hair has risen: ions ten-four on the same band. Friday paces his run. As humans go, Simon is diverting: rain forest alive. There: the rear door of his van is open. Don, outside, has been lifting metal tripods in. Don can only suppose, at Simon's earthmover sound, suppose that this—the lifting in—is wrong and due for punishment. He goes on defense: one tripod held out/across his chest, a medieval soldier's wooden bill. But Simon will only use him for pushing off on, hand atop Don's shoulder, and up and in. The van door, a roller coaster rounding past, even five or six female squeals to give realism, lubrication required, slides wall-length, down.

"Hey. Open her up. This here'll get wet."

"Shove it under. Take twenty. Go inna that unnumbered Swiss bank account of a chapel and light a candle f'my wick."

"Simon." The dice-roll sound of locking. "Shee-it and nuts. What's the use?"

Again: the dark has fazed him. He is restless: worse, restive: unreferenced there. Simon counts on the eye, its imagery and counsel. He does not have ideas: pure concept won't hold his mind. He punches out at the forty-watt bulb. Hit, it loops away/back on its string: wraps over his hand. Snip: lit. Inconstant illumination dims, then surges: the generator: Simon on his own power. He can see the super-rapid AC flicker: the raggedness of old silent films run on a new projector. Simon stripping off. He has her key between big eater's teeth: a grenade pin pulled. Ah, woman odor. It is his contention that, from smell, nothing else, he can guess a woman's place in her menstrual cycle: and he has often been right. Simon grabs a piece of himself: self coquettish. The van is roomier, equipment out. This has been his response to any emptiness: expansion, a quick taking up of space. Impertinent and heavy rain tunes up on the skylight: the serene, just-under-roof sound of his childhood. He gets hydrotherapy, aural, from it. Time to wait: reconstitute. These have been bad days. He can't, his spirit can't, run up many more such. Calm, to calm: banking on Minnie for that: he is over-created, over-refined: in peril. Simon rocks, back/forth, heel/toe: an infant habit. Left alone by Bettina in the crib, he learned this comfort rhythm: lullaby: baby Simon, wept out, shook his body into a self-parenting drowse. Now he will spread the bunk curtain: surgeons open muscle so. Minnie is asleep. She lies flat, undefended, on her back: a position that only the most naive sleepers can maintain. One charitable breast is bare. Tenderly, teasing his own excitement out, Simon palpates it. The nipple has come to: where-am-I?: large, slotted: a screwhead. She will pose tough questions: uh? unn? Some dream interrogation. Minnie smells mossed, moist: three days from her ovulation: a hole dug in fresh loam down to the water table.

"Minnie. Ssss. Minnie, wake up. It's America. It's free enterprise. Here. For you. A young nation moving westward: farms spring up behind me, hamlets, cities, retirement communities with shuffleboard, a place or two like Hoboken. The chaste and lazy earth will open and say yes. I'm prairie fire and furrow. I'm mountain and gold-rush town. It's manifest destiny, me. Me, Minnie. The Eagle has landed."

"Ohhhh. I've got a butcher block headache. Mr. Lynxx, you?"

"Who else talks like this? Eric Sevareid? It's the 31st of lust and your mortgage payment is due. I've come to repossess what I've never had." He sets the key in her cleavage. "I'll be gentle. I'll play over you like sun on wide morning lawns. I'll stretch and envelop. I'll be quick as death or long as dying. There will be relief: the relief that a bud knows, burst. I promise. All that, whatever I just said so well."

"Um? How's the tongue?"

"Taste it. I can't." Simon kisses her. Minnie will respond, evasive: the qualified kiss of someone who probably has morning mouth.

"Did the film shooting go okay?"

"Oh, splendid. A Four Wen Production. And we've got a new working title: *The Natural History of the Common Mule*. A Disney true-life adventure, playing at select area farms."

"Is that so? Ach, I'm exposing myself."

"Don't worry. I'm so exposed my film is white."

"You haven't—Mr. Lynxx, I don't ever see you in clothes. You're a whole nudist colony."

"Don't get up for my sake." Simon presses Minnie down.

"What time is it? Rain on the ceiling. Are we alone?"

"We're alone."

"This—" She holds the key up. "It's . . . oh."

"It's Christmas morning. Time t'unwrap." He catches a breast. "For me? You shouldn't have. What can it be? A tie? A knitted barstool? A new micro-chip f'my brain?" He has slid over her: as over a split-rail fence. "Listen, I've been in a rut so long, I'm in rut. No games people play. I'm not gonna be Aguirre, the Wrath of God t'you. No Wagnerian music. No yellow stars of David sewn into your skin. I'm tired. I'll say please and thank you. I just wanna make love, Minnie."

"I'm scared of you, Mr. Lynxx. And this is the truth."

"Min-nie. What drool. Me? Old Sy? I'm harmless as a placebo."

"A who? Pla—" But Simon has canceled her lips: a forefinger across them, sssh. Meanwhile, south of the border, he is reeling up material: handcuffed by repetitive nightgown: as much in it now as she is.

"Hey, Min. I'm really a big soft Camembert. It's the truth: Kirlian photography has shown that my aura wears a dress. Once in a while I vilify a person's race or maybe his mother. Just clean fun. People're so sensitive, I can't understand it. Huh? Lift up a bit, what're you wearing, a World War II parachute? I've been rejected so much of late, I feel like a public retraction. Just love me."

"Where's Robert?"

"Robert. Robert is editing film in the chapel. That kid, Minnie, he's like a son t'me. Sharp as a broken filling. He takes t'film direction like a duck to orange sauce. I predict an honorary degree from the Tuskegee Institute f'him. You should be proud."

"I am. I am." He kisses her again: unsatisfactorily: off-target, blubberish, the great touch lost. It comes home to Simon that his mouth must be ugly. Could get a man down. And, down, his fingers have reached bronze: her Maginot Line: *ils ne passeront pas.* "I think you're a goodheart man, Mr. Lynxx. You shouldn't hear me wrong."

"I play the string game with kittens. I sing old Edith Piaf torch songs in the shower. Uh. Let's try the key. I wanna get into someone more comfortable. Huh? No rush, but—"

"Give me your solemn word for one thing. You won't tell Rose."

"I won't tell Rose. Of course she's probably outside the van with a stethoscope. She writes anonymous letters t'herself when she masturbates. Rose likes to see disaster, bone fragments, there's a little of the Indianapolis Speedway crowd in her." Simon is kneeling: his head raises the upper bunk. "You're a good sport, Minnie. A trooper. The show must go on, come off. I'll make you happy. And no special installation fee."

"Wait, I don't want you should get your expectations too high. I'm an old woman. I'll be a big disappointment."

"Aw, don't say that. You're ripe as a mango, just gotta get the rind off. There. Boy, lookit that safety-deposit box. Who wore it last, Darth Vader? It's a wonder y'can get your backfield in motion at all."

"You won't hurt me?" The key taps: noise of a white cane coming. "I've been—at home, well. It's three months since I've had to do with. I'm nervous. My heart is flopping. Can you hear?"

"Probably it's from carrying all this weight. Just don't try going through an airport checkpoint: you'd register like an arms shipment t'El Salvador. Jesus, damn thing reminds me of a Coney Island bumper car. Relax. Relax. The Director of Emissions himself is in charge. Now how does this hoogemawhatsis fit?"

Good sport Minnie in a pose of wild and free abandon: set hard as X-Pandotite cement in it: stiffened easiness. She huffs out, breath practice for natural childbirth. The left arm is up. Minnie traveled by overnight train once: an emergency cord was right over the bunk: perhaps, she couldn't tell you, her hand is feeling for it now. Simon likes Minnie even more: he will cause her pleasure. The keyhole is above Minnie's

right hip, at one end of a metal belt. Simon sizes it up with his fingernail:
exclamation-mark shape! The lummox key is big, unhandy: corrosion
scrapes off. Must be her spare (Minnie has to have a spare), looks unused in this century. And . . . won't . . . go . . . uh. Simon is impatient.
He thonks her hip—dock, dock, anyone home? Minnie will turn sidewise
to give access, complaisant, passive. Simon pushes. He scrapes rust off.
Jiggles, levers—jams. In. Minnie has tried another terrible pose of relaxa-
tion: someone three days dead beneath an avalanche. Simon twists the
boorish bronze-cast sunburst handle. Laughter: the image has just come
to him: a sexual windup toy. There is grinding. Then friction wins out.
"Uhhh. Little bastard doesn't wanna go. Give up, you schmuck, we
got the joint surrounded. Uhhh. Do I turn to the right? Uhhh."
"Left, Mr. Lynxx."
"Left? Woop!"
"What?"
"Jesus God."
"Mr. Lynxx?"
"Je-sus God."
"What? What?"
"You won't believe this. Je-sus God." Simon coin-flips the ornate key
handle. It is fat, round as a medal, in his palm. The neck will glint where
metal has been sheared off clean. "Jesus God, coitus interruptus and I
mean but good." He pounds on the lock.
"What? Stop, it hurts. What?"
"Now let's keep our wits about us, Minnie. We have nothing to fear
but fear alone."
"What?"
"Uh. Don't drink any prune juice, I mean—"
"What? What?"
"Uh. The damn cheesy, stupid key broke off in my hand."
"What! What!"
"It's not my fault. It just broke. All I got is this fiddly little end piece."
"Help! What! Help, I'm trapped! Police!"
Can't keep a good woman down. Minnie bucks up: stronger, wow,
than epileptic Harold Gluck. Simon rises, thrown: Simon comes through
the upper bunk, springs and mattress on his head, standing there. Minnie
will dance under the nude bulb. Her nightgown has been tussled high.
Simon must remember this. She is circling, peculiarly graceful, one hand
on hip, one above it to hold her nightgown out: a bullfighter's stance.
She can't see the lock. Feet thud: his van, better than he could, shock-ab-
sorbs her fear.
"Calm down—"
"Aaah-aaaaah!"
"Did you get a warranty when you bought it?"

334

"Aaah-aaaaah!"

"Maybe they have a local service center."

"You! Klutz! Klutz! You heavy-hander, you had to use force. I'll die in here. Help! Help!"

"Ssssh. Easy-easy, ssssh." Simon has cut in. He spokes her useless wheeling. "Wait, try this. Lean to one side and I'll hit it on the other: like when a pinball is stuck. Maybe the piece'll fall out. Sssh. Come on, Minnie. Lean, put one arm on the bed. Remember, we can always get a locksmith, though I guess the last locksmith who saw one of these died in the Crusades. Have a try, come on." Minnie leans: has to, in fact. She is wind-spent: bronze doesn't go with high emotion. Simon hits, double-fisted. The first chord of Beethoven's Fifth.

"No! Stop. I—uph—can't breathe. Uph-uph. Go. Away. Go." Her skin is hectic, piebald with blood-flushing: it frightens him to see. "Jerk, you—you couldn't be patient. A bull in the china works. A crazy man."

"It's not my fault. That key was a hunnert years old."

"Look, assassin. Look, big thing. Look, *look*, what you did to me. Sol! Sol! Why did I ever come here! Sol, you were right. This is what happens to a New York City swinger." Minnie will now hit Simon often: on chest, arm, shoulder: fifty percent accuracy. She can hurt him. The flurry has a lot of weight, plus metal inertia, behind it. "You don't know how to be gentle. You. *You*. You break everything you touch."

"Well, now. That's a bit hard. Whoa! Not in the face, not in the face."

"Everything! Everything!"

"All right. It's true. I'm sorry."

"God help any woman who loves you."

"God help her. Go on, punch me some more."

Simon takes it standing up. Then, back against the ring post, bunk post, he will clinch. It reshapes: an embrace: Minnie has allowed him. She needs a breather, also a place to hang all that ballast. Minnie would cry again, but her diaphragm, held in tight custody, can't manage the extra work load. Simon rocks: Minnie picks up his crib cadence. Yet one hand, autonomous, will continue to pound the large gong that is her behind. Penitentiary noise: loud, echoed a cellblock away: and hollow.

2

Kyryl. A reader.
Reader. Kyryl.
It is written across the lintel of Ten Great Ferry: ART MUST
ANNOY. And, to that end, Kyryl's Orbit Gallery will go for a spin:
rounding, around: slow. Eighty feet in diameter, long-play: its floor sinus
passage soft underfoot: one exact r.p.m., punctilious as a second hand.
But Simon won't give you the right time of day: he backsteps, sullen and
fixed, to counter a clockwise turning. Four hundred people tick past,
queasy with Chivas and hash and rotation. Against an axis-pillar Kyryl
has stacked up *Oral Hygiene II*: his objectionable trillion-times-real-size,
off-white or convalescent-sallow SEM sculpture of human tooth plaque.
Inconvenience and distaste, his commerce, his waywithal, have grossed
two hundred million dollars for Kyryl since 1958: when first he brought
the still-notorious Bronze Room, forty tons of sculpture, to Great Ferry
Street and abrupt fame. 8:42 soon. Wolff hasn't made an entrée yet.
Simon wants to check out/through the wide bay window for his trainee
hit men, B.P. and Sledge, but there are witnesses about. New carefulness
has taken a piece of his action: his rough spontaneity. And the stupid
music jeers: desultory, yowl-like: performed by an electronic calliope
sensitive to chance cosmic ray reception at Ten Great Ferry. Dong-bah-
woool: three random Moog sounds for every random cosmic discharge:
motiveless leitmotif in the ray-permeable home, commune, museum,
manufactory of Kyryl himself.
"Simon, was it?" A lapel tag does the honor: introduces him:
EDUARDO. Eduardo is in pharmaceutical white, button line along his
left collarbone. He has a redhead's stale, cluttered skin. Nose, brow,
mouth: the features are unevident, hard-to-make-out: as though seen
through a glass freckly. Rouge: in specific, compass-drawn circles above
each cheek. A nurse's cap, a child-folded paper sailboat, waits for

freshening wind on his tight copper hair. "What was it? Simon?" Two dry martinis have had a safe-conduct from Kyryl's corduroy-and-rubber-soft bar. Eduardo, on short notice, is in love.

"Gimme. Yeah, Simon."

"I bet you're a Pisces like me."

"Where'dja get your conversation, Eduardo? From a walk-in freezer? Gimme."

"Where's your moon? In Virgo?"

"In my pants. Don't give me that high-colonic stare. Whyncha save us all trouble and take a bottle of Asti Spumanti up the back access ramp? Huh, Eduardo? Gimme."

"Not both. Not—you drank both, Simon. That wasn't very nice."

"Yes it was. Very nice. My need is greater than yours. I'm a wanted man. I've got my picture and résumé in every post office from here t'Chula Vista."

"I don't—"

"Wanna back into me, Eduardo? Wanna pull up at the old loading dock?"

"You sound very S. I'm into leather myself. I can tell from your basket that you've got a big one."

"Big? NASA tracking stations pick me up. I've been sighted off coasts. Small seaside resort towns haveta evacuate. Uh . . . This thing of Kyryl's. It's supposed to be tooth jelly?"

"Supposed to be? It is. *Oral Hygiene I* was commissioned by the American Dental Association in 1968. Isn't it horrible, yet somehow squirmy-sensuous right in the pit of your stomach? Frankly, I like Number II better than Number I."

"Never mind your diet. Hanh. Looks like maggots convening in a wound. Or a pile of corncobs from some plantation outhouse."

"Or anything at all. That's the beauty of SEM art. That's why Kyryl's still on top. Still, twenty years after the Maalox School hit New York. The others—Henry Climax and Walter Mitsui and Ben Shalom—they're kaput. Kyryl understands us. Our aspirations. We feel safer with commonplace reality, yet we want to elevate it somehow. Make it beautiful or eerie or spiritual. Art used to do that by itself. But art with a capital A has lost its credibility. It got too pompous. Telling stories is démodé now. Like they say, fiction is dead. Kyryl invented non-fiction art."

"Snore. Let's flug the an-aesthetic theory, huh? What I wanna know is, how much'd that glog of gum massage be worth t'some Jew art collector?"

"Uh. I don't want to upset you. But my mother is Jewish."

"Yeah. So how much is it worth t'her?"

"Well. SEM sculptures go for—the big ones--this . . . between sixty and eighty thousand at least."

"Eighty thousand. Hanh, what's it carved from, the world's biggest lump of cocaine? Eighty thousand. No wonder the room is turning."

"I know. I know." Eduardo has laughed: the sailboat picks up a small-craft warning: choppy water. "People are amazed. Kyryl signed a dollar bill once for charity. They auctioned it off for twelve hundred. How's that for inflation? His SEM—"

"SEM again. Listen, I don't speak homoglot. SEM is what?"

"SEM was on the cover of *Newsweek*. You really don't know?"

"Nah. I live in a pothole on Northern Boulevard. They don't deliver."

"Well, you know Kyryl developed throat cancer in 1965. They had to cut his voice box out. He was suicidesville. I think for eighteen months he didn't do anything, a man of his manic energy, too. Then Dr. Whythe happened to show him pictures taken by a scanning electron microscope. S-E-M, see? They were photographs of Kyryl's own malignant cells. The scanning mike is super-fantastic. It works like a TV camera. That's what I do here. I prepare SEM pictures to inspire Kyryl. He sent me to school for it. Pictures of ordinary things: bacteria, spit, viruses, plant rust. They're simply beautiful. Three-D and they have tremendous—tremendous—resolution. Kyryl did a whole series called 'My Cancer' in bronze. See, the scanning mike captures that special structural integrity. Note how the tooth plaque cells interweave: it's beautiful. It's reasonable. All things in nature have it. That was the beginning. Number Six and Number Eight of his Cancer Series are in the Museum of Modern Art."

"Gee. I've got this unusual discharge. It's green and fulla little germ-shaped things. What'llya gimme for it?"

"Penicillin?" Eduardo laughs. "No. We've done 'Gonococcus' already. It's seventeen feet high: in front of the North Springfield Savings and Loan Building."

"That must reassure depositors. Substantial penalty for late withdrawal."

"Mmmm—hi, Eduardo." A rickety brunette, her face fed on by decal butterflies, has rotated around to them. Simon will grab-ass her. The buttocks irritate him: sodden and gripless: a behind like breasts. The backside of his unexercised generation. "Oh, I'd know that hand anywhere. Especially there. Simon." She kisses him: the kiss is without mettle or pursuit: a kiss for her own mouth, returnable. "I didn't recognize you without the gorilla chest."

"It's in the shop getting resoled. I'm just me tonight, Pollen."

"Oh, awful—isn't it? I couldn't go anywhere without my butterflies. I mean, who would I be? How's the new film coming?" Pollen might smirk —she has heard about Francis—but smirking would use up a week's assertiveness.

"Wonderful. Wonderful. We've got fourteen feet in the can already. I've been shooting leader. I love blank, white things."

"Leader, yes? I don't understand film chat."

"*N'importe*, Polly. Hey—if y'have three or four minutes tonight, I'd like t'get my dinghy launched. Huh-ha? Little sweatshop work? Little buck-bathing in your hot seacock? Huh? Hanh? Y'remember that night at Norty's on the billiard table? You came and you came and you came. Had my thumb out and they whizzed by me like I was hitchhiking on the San Diego Freeway."

"I'd love to. But, you know, Sy—" She shakes her head: golden dust, yellow corn dextrin, has powdered them. "You know, I can't recall how. So many, many months now."

"I can retrain you in five minutes." It isn't anything as expensive as laughter: a butterfly folds wings in her dimple.

"I intend to smell evil substances tonight. I want to sleep forever. If you find me unconscious, well—do what you have to, but put the toys back where you found them when you're finished. Eduardo, sweet. I'm a little short of boring money. Is Kyryl still paying a hundred for SEM'ed womb scrapings?"

"Sure. Right now?"

"Can I trouble you? I've got to pay my Scrooge of a poodle trimmer. Sy, you don't mind if I take Eduardo away?"

"In fact, I'd appreciate it. A few more minutes with Ed, the Biopsy King, and I'd need a brain-weave. If I discover your corpse I'll do it like a paint-roller."

They are a shy four hundred. Simon knows them, the Kyryl Korps at least: he has specialized in their mean gossip: research for small black-mail. They express themselves, not verbally, but in pose and counter-pose: as fighting male bison would: a reserve that touches arrogance. Simon, gorilla suit or not, has never been modish, accepted. He can talk: talking, for these, is misapplication of force: a spoon, say, used to cut steak. They exist, palpable and often mute, yet rival tension hums between them: it might be a competition of tableaux vivantes. Two women have been brought around, near, past. They smile: and something wise or resonant is implied by mere adjacency. One has her blond hair drawn out wild on wire mesh: it flourishes, wind-shook in calm, three feet behind. The Salem Girl, this is: meant to be coming up, up out of seasonless urban living into a menthol-bucolic springtime. She was made by Kyryl, who crafts persona on the side: signed or unsigned according to price. Beside her—against her, the way a bishop will threaten red di-agonal squares—beside her is Vampira, formerly Simon's friend. Through one long December night Simon stood vigil with Vampira: to give solace after the canine teeth were yanked. Now, redone in bridgework fangs, she won't acknowledge him. Simon saw what he should not have seen.

And the film establishment has suited up for this game: formal, uncer-tain: a duty visit: conspicuous and different as men nude among topiary hedges. Liv Bergman, who has never spoken without an accent on screen, even in her native tongue. Helen Redstone, April Alka, Sue-Margaret Lane: Wolff-made starlets. Clement Pochelli, author of *Giant Slug* and *Monster Snail*. Critic Amanda Ellen Kurtz, who can (and will) ask five figures for a good review. Kalman "Chuck" Wyznyng, the Czech tennis champ. Comedians Fogarty and Brown. Lash Decay of "Meningitis," the punk rock group. Network anchorperson Doe Hoover, who got an exclusive interview and a child from Idi Amin. Editors, publicists, cameramen: they walk paired, the buddy system, in this cartoon ambiance. Commune children deploy: squat, tumble, do London-Bridge-is-falling-down. They are reticent: their miming is playless: methodical and well-practiced choreography. Simon has seen them count cosmic Moog beats out: shrill-ahhh-ing!: and shift: wah-layyyy-oon!: and shift. Most are naked: the left leg black or purple or green. They insinuate between drinkers, relate by juxtaposition and prefigurative form. Simon has kept watch on Berto Clamande: *Appoggiatura in Venice. Un Homme et Son Chat. L'Amour à la Caen.* Simon admires Clamande. He'd like to accost the brilliant French director. Anyhow, Clamande and he have certain things in common: June the Prune and Chloe Speed. Simon short-hopped Chloe on rebound from Clamande: a long weekend or three one-night stands, he can't decide which. Clamande caught the Prune, also yeast infections, on rebound from Simon. An intimacy, there: like being Estonian with someone. But Clamande, he knows, can be spiteful and liverish: Simon hasn't drunk enough yet. He aims at the bay window: ETA, one quarter hour in traffic. Walls are ductile, soft: the mucus and meat color of human internal tissue. Neon capillaries line them and pneumatic risers: these push up, pucker down. The Orbit Gallery is itself an objet d'art: *Peristalsis I:* very large intestine work. Kyryl assimilates.

Testing: a TV flood has come on, pain-white. Faces are cropped along the nose bridge: dark/light: severe as harlequin paint, as half-moons. Pageant people, phototropic, turn toward network coverage. "—Take some background stuff, the sculpture. What else? Do some of the weirder costumes. For Christ's sake, not that one. Did you shoot that one, the one in the baby carriage with no arms and legs? For Christ's sake, they'll love that in Des Moines. Huh? Bounce your light, I can't see. Is the mike jack in? Let's do an intro. Okay. Phil Norris here for 'Ready News.' We're at the Fiftieth Anniversary of Herman Wolff's, what? I'm moving? Of course I'm moving, the whole room is. Move with me. What? You didn't bring enough cable? Shit, I can't walk backward and talk at the same time—" Simon butts in/through a conversation, his seventh: arms pushed down, turnstiled, excuse me. Gudrun, Kyryl's second wife, is breast-feeding the child of her fourth husband. A young man has picked up Gudrun's other, understudy, nipple. He sucks: out of politeness, maybe. She will just nod: a blind man accepting very small change. Simon has tapped himself all over again: to locate the pencil flashlight. He executes a dry-run figure eight, close in/against his chest: beacon signal for B.P. and Sledge. But he can't quite achieve the window: its long sill, which doesn't move, has been much preferred by sitters. Alice Yawn is there, in the sonorous pleasure of self-contemplation. Simon has had her—three, four, five, who's counting?—several drowsy times. Seeing him, she will yawn. It is her communication: greeting, goodbye, innuendo, signature. The yawn blows up, perfect, O'd: could be out of a bubble wand: first-rate quivering along her jawline: excellent water at each eye. Alice's yawns drive, sharp and slow and hot, into your brain pith. One night she made every member of the "Iron Jell-O" rock band yawn at ten yards: so aroused by influence in a high place that she took Simon's hand to her crotch.

"Beautiful Alice. A-um." Simon yawn-answers civilly: has to, in fact. "Gotcha loop in t'night? Hanh? Huh. Whyn't we go see if I can untie it with my nine-inch marlinspike."

"Oh, Simon. I'm not sure. Didn't you give me a dose last time?"

"No. No. We both had it, remember? We made a swarming petri dish between us. So much clap we hadda take a bow afterward."

"Yes? I don't always believe you. Anyhow, there's so many famous people here tonight. You're—a-um—fine for a weekday."

"*Gracias*. And your lingam's no Gold Coast property either."

"There's Sonny Carbo."

"Where?"

"With Norty, see. I never miss his TV show. Oh, I want him. I've got to concentrate. I scored Jake Grossman from here to the bar. You should've seen it. He was talking and he yawned and he drooled right into his glass."

"Marvelous. You've seen more throats than a generation of strep-tococci. If I could break your law, ah, of total conservation of energy, wouldja mind leaning forward a bit? I wanna stick my head out the window. Air in here: occupation by more than four hundred egos is danger-ous and depressing. Whoop. Damn drunken floor. Sorry."

Simon gawks out: all along ta-tumming an innocent you-can't-mean-me song. The night is gross with vapor: it has been misting rain since three o'clock. Great Ferry looks overdramatic: an optical lens put on. One streetlamp has painted itself into a corner of fuzzy glare. But, hold everything, B.P. and Sledge are front and off center: spine-flat against an alley wall, trench-coated, un-at ease, missing only the WE ARE MUGGERS sign. Sickness takes Simon: he is appalled. His best work has been improvisatory, but the premise here feels thin. Ball Peen will see Simon: hssst, over there, he thumbs: the Cadillac wallowing, scow-wide, four car lengths west. Okay, good enough position: no direct light on it. Simon has returned the countersign: three flash-blips: over and way out. Sledge bends to tie one getaway shoe. A box of Good 'N Plenty, a pen, a nasal inhaler, dump from his vest pocket: clack-clack. Sound will carry on the soaked air tonight: clack-clack: Simon's bones breaking, clack.

"Oh, Mother. I'm making aaah in my pants." Simon gets carried away a bit: by the floor. "Those two, either they'll kill him or they'll ask for his autograph."

"Ah-hummmm. Muggy out, huh?"

"Muggy? No. The muggee hasn't got there yet. Ha. Ho. It's spreading to the dura mater. I'm Terminal Man."

"How's your film?"

"You mean the one over my eyes? Oh, the other one. I made a great deal. It's being distributed by a major chain. Woolworth's."

"Oh. Part for me in it? Aaah-um."

"Aaaah-um. That's just the audience reaction I'm looking for."

"I can do other things."

"Jesus, don't you diversify. There should be one or two certainties in life. Ooop, sorry. Damn floor. Listen, have you seen Wolff yet?"

"Uh-uh."

"Must be he's around someplace. Probably they're giving him plasma from a fetus ranch."

"Oh, look: Seamus Ochs. No, to the left. With that mousy tart."

"That corn borer. I wouldn't raise my head t'look at him." Interesting: watch the turntable-floor buff buff Alice Yawn's little shoe. "He called *Clap*, quote, 'About as powerful as *Macbeth* without a Macbeth.' But I got him. In the ads I put 'dot-dot-dot POWERFUL dot-dot-dot, Seamus Ochs.'"

"Well, I think he's handsome. And he's even bigger than you are."

"Where? Which is he? Which one?"

Male size: now you've got Simon's attention: can-I-take-him? The slow wheel has drawn Ochs away, but, uh-boy, Alice is right. Built like a homonym for his last name: not taller, yet the sort of Irishman who has been contoured by bar rails: chest high up and broad as ancient cooperage. Two hundred thirty, forty dray animal pounds: and no wonder people respect his opinion. Critics, he has thought, are tiny folk by-and-small, but a man that wide doesn't need to be critical. Ochs is narrating some long-story-made-short: black hair lies mortarboard-flat, a postgraduate spit-curl tassel over his left eye. And of course the mousy tart is packing it all in, is—pulse hop—Simon has clenched feet, hands, biceps, teeth—the mousy tart is Rose Fischer. With a full-length, full-breadth gown on loan from Minnie, taken in across her back by one tent-flap pleat: motel bedspreads fold down so. Why would Seamus Ochs tell Rose Fischer anything? How—when it cost Simon a night in the fraudulent Gardens of Spain to land here—how did Rose finesse her invitation?

Simon can plot out five or six mandarin-obscure betrayals. And he is irked: in a social way, in a professional way, Rose has gone over his head. Over her own head. The wheel hauls Norty past. Norty will know: he has a Ph.D. in Rumor. Simon shoves off from Alice Yawn: into the carousel swing of things.

"Hey, Norto."

"Sy. Some turnout, huh? A great tribute to a great prick. Ask for Chivas, otherwise they'll give you Clan Fishbein." Norty has been holed in the keel, Simon can tell: he respires like this only when drunk. Sober, he will spend breath, one inhale per fifteen seconds, as though his native currency—CO_2 for oxygen—were at a depressed exchange rate. "Say thanks to your old boot camp pal."

"Thanks. Herman is here already. Where?"

"How'd you know? Sssssush: keep it down. He's in the Bronze Room with Kyryl. Very private. Big K slapped something special together for the Fiftieth. Prolly a collage of human labia. Herman ducked up the side entrance. He's really shy. A little Jewboy on an Irisher block."

"Look, Norty. Before you pass out—"

"Eh, by the way, Herman was delighted. He was very pleased. Mmmm—why was he delighted? Whaddid I wanna say? Huh? Refresh my mind."

"I'd need a 50 BTU Puritron. Listen—"

"I'm pretty fog horn. Far. Gone. But, yes. Monday night. What you did for Mizz Armistead Monday night. Herman is very sentimental. Hello, dear, wanna fuck? That's nice. No answer. They don't talk." A six-year-old girl child has come, nude, between Norty and Simon. Some sound cue is needed and is given. She will reach behind knees, bend: will present her clean anus to Norty in the manner of female chimpanzees when their moment is upon them. Then—aaaah-eeo-dit!—away.

"Crize-zake. All these unbaked cheesecakers upset me. I mean, I got kids my own. If Kyryl wasn't so rich, he'd be hammering out license plates."

"Nort. Put your mind in Drive for a minute. It's Snub City here. If I approach Wolff he'll look through me like I had a glassblown head. Can you give me the green flare when he's set t'leave? I wanna make my big slide-show presentation downstairs, in the street. Where he won't feel peer pressure t'use me like a toxic waste disposal."

"Hey, Sy. You do that, he'll be pissed at you is all. Herman loves sneaking out—hi-yo—it's the Lone Shtupper."

"I've gotta take my chances. Please, Norty. Otherwise all this, it's seed spilt on Rockcrete."

"Sure. Okay. Long as he doesn't connect you with me."

"He won't. Just don't go into cerebral arrest for an hour or so, and—ah, what's Rose Fischer doing here?"

"Rose Fischer. Rose Fischer. Is she the wardrobe mistress?"

"No, she's my mistress. Scarsdale's very own Emma Bovary. I haveta dance flamenco t'get here, and she just waltzes in."

"Can't figure. S'many names. Must've been Herman. He gave me a whole stack of three-by-fives, phone and address. I just handed it t'my secretary."

"Wolff? Why Wolff?" Simon is alarmed. "I don't like this. Handwriting on the wall and it's not graffiti."

"Unless she's one of Kyryl's cadet corps."

"No. Jesus, Rose here. I could puke up a Mexican breakfast."

"Stop worrying. Come on over. I'll innaduce you to the NA crowd. Damn floor isn't doing me any good. It should rotate the same way my head does. Remind me around nine-thirty I should go stick a finger down my throat."

Norty can't get anywhere fast: son-in-lawhood sits great upon him: is propitiated: handshake, kiss, remember-me-to-I-was. Simon gazes up. The roof is revolving, too: might as well be inside a goddam one-story yo-yo. For future reference, Berto Clamande leans on the twelve-foot phonograph arm: *Disco I:* artwork within artwork, tenanted by artworks. Kyryl has said: "My object is to hold a mirror up to nature. And see another mirror there." The phonograph arm bumps along a floor groove: groove etched to play, at one r.p.m., "Bugle Boy of Company B." Now Bella Chicago closes with Simon. Simon is wisely cordial in her swarm-avid embrace. Five years ago Bella shot Coleman Garfield through the Danskinned left buttock while he was playing Hamlet—a very palpable hit—at Lincoln Center. She got one month's notoriety and three years' hard labor. Garfield went to law, indignant, not so much at the assault as at the angle of entry. He might have been magnanimous toward a gut shot or even handsome death. Everyone is prudent, warm with Bella. Simon can make out—chest to chest—a .45 profile beneath her Bonnie and/or Clyde 1920's lapel. Norto has given his speed-it-up sign. The NA splinter party is self-contained: they face interlopers down: RE-SERVED: a velvet rope of nasty fleering does it. And—look sharp, Simon —Harold Gluck is there.

"Gang. Wancha meet Simon Lynxx, old army fuck-up. Won the Golden whatsis award for Best Short Subject: y'remember. Two years running, only man t'do it. Sy, this is May Rosen. Sol Handwerker. Bill Marcus. Lois Pechter. Harold Gluck. Vi Grossberg. And Art McArthur, our token goy—we call him Arthur Bar-Arthur." Norty mistrusts: paranoia from a bottle: May Rosen is mooing: heavy laughter wrenched off. "What's the joke, May? My fly open?"

"Harold was telling us about BABBLE. Show Norton, Hal."

"Oh, hell. Really. Once is enough." Simon has shaken hands: camera tight-in on his face. No start of recognition: safe. A good one on Gluck.

"What's babble, Harold?" May Rosen has elbowed Norty: liquor kicks off the jock in her.

"Make him do it. Use your seniority."

"Come on, Harold."

"It's his private acronym: B-A-B-B-L-E: Beat A Black Before Lunch Every Day."

"Beat a black, huh?" Norty can't find what he was drinking: it's in his other hand, the purloined glass. Bill Marcus nudges Art McArthur. Norty is hated. "Own up, Hal. Tell."

"Oh, well. My doctor says I'm an A type. Working for you does that. Gotta relax, but how? Jerking off mars my complexion. Exercise takes the finish off my wooden leg. So every afternoon before lunch I beat up a black." They laugh. "Oh, yeah: now and then I lower my standards. A Puerto Rican. A Chicano. I did a Korean once, but it didn't turn me on."

"How? Huh?" Don't tell him: Simon can guess. "Whyncha let me in on this before?"

"You never asked. It's quite simple. The last disadvantaged phony in before lunch gets it good. I allow pure chance to decide: I'm a totally unprejudiced sadist. I lock the door. I take them into my confidence. 'Look, friend,' I say, 'this is embarrassing. I feel an epileptic seizure coming on. I need your help. Please. Stick this under my tongue and hold me down.'" Gluck gives May Rosen his glass. He has sprawled against Sid Handwerker, a desk. "The dumb dusky wants out. His eyes bug. He thinks epilepsy is some sort of voodoo. And maybe it's catching. But—hah and aha—he needs funding from NAMIF. I unstrap my leg, lay back so. You play the jig, Norty, hold me down. Tighter. Oh, here it comes. I'm coming. I'm coming. Ong! Ong! Ong!"

Harold Gluck again, doing his physical jerks: this is where Simon came in. A larger performance now: Gluck plays to the art gallery: more ham-fisted. Uppercut, forearm clout, good wood in Norty's crotch. Norty, smashed anyhow, will take a standing count. The holder has been held: Gluck, an organization man, keeps Norty up. And Simon, deep breath, deeper, would like to lay waste around him.

"Stop! Ha! You're killing me. Is this f'real? Ha, you gotta do it for Herman."

"Yesterday—yesterday, my friends, I had this granddaddy of all buck niggers in my office. Big. And I hit him so hard, I swear it on the crown of St. Stephen, I hit him so hard his Afro wig popped off. No, I'm serious, don't laugh. It bounced—hop, hop, hop. As they say, 'Ya hadda be there.'"

"Sumbitch." Norty is wish-I'da-thought-of-that impressed. "Sumbitch, you are a fiend, Harold. No wonder they tried t'kill you in '56."

"*Gluck.*" All at once the name is adjectival, profane. "*Gluck.*" Simon has called him out. There is a hushing, a restless intake after that name, that *Gluck*. And now Simon will come too close: his breath has warmed Gluck. On it Gluck can smell the singeing of human skin: can remember a burned Russian corpse near him in Budapest. He glares who-is-this? at Norty. "Aren't you afraid, *Gluck*? I mean, word travels uptown. Monkey mail. It's just a matter of time, *Gluck:* you'll need a wooden prosthesis f'your head."

"Oh, yes? To be sure. And what business is it of yours, my friend?"

"I can put your name on the subscription list, *Gluck*. It'll come special handling and at night. They'll wear your teeth, *Gluck*. There won't be enough of you left t'bury in a car ashtray."

"Norton. Take Harriet Beecher Stowe away. She's bleeding on me."

"Sy—hey. Cut it out. He's soused, Harold. Lay off, Sy. Just a joke: where's the great sense of humor?"

"Maybe I get tired of hearing the oh-so-flip side of New York liberalism. Maybe it's time you went back to raping small dogs, *Gluck*."

"That will be enough, I think. Someone take my jacket." Not hold-me-back-please bravado: Gluck is enthused, Simon knows that. He has known such load-off relief, such readiness, himself. Payday: and Simon can predict the mode of Gluck's fighting. Eyeball pushed through its buttonhole, in, gone: nostril split open, thumb-and-fingernail, the way you'd peel a label off. But, eye or nostril, Simon is counted in, is committed, and Norty has to soft-shoulder him aside. The uneven, kapok-puffy weight of his drunkenness clothes Simon. They are drawn ten feet away by it: an undertow. Simon hears May Rosen boo.

"What the fuck's wrong with you? Huh, what's coming down?" Norty has hit Simon biceps-center, middle knuckle out: a men-in-groups punch. The impact will stagger Norty. Simon has to adjust him vertical again. "Shit, can't take you anywhere. Wonder you don't have, have two friends y'can rub together."

"Look, I've seen Glucks before. They'll spring up in any field where cows leave a stinking flop. Norty, I promise you, I'll cut his ecknard off someday."

"All right, sure, we know. But the epilepsy thing's cute, y'gotta admit. And maybe he's making it up. Jesus, I never thought I'd hear the day, Simon Lynxx talking like Eleanor Roosevelt."

"Shut up. Maybe I've had a prescription change. After all, you think about it, what's the difference between me and a Harlem do-rag? I mean, as far as Talmud and Torah Film Productions is concerned?"

"I'll ignore that. Shit, change of prescription. You almost got a change of sex. That man is a killer. Not like you and me in some bar fight, punch for punch, and time out for a Löwenbräu. He'da left you a cripple. I just saved your sausage."

"Thanks."

"Hey. Y'don't fox me. There's something wrong."

322

"I need a hundred-proof anchovy is all. Just lemme know when Wolff
leaves."
"I'm not so sure now. You got me leery. You're kinda crazed tonight."
"Norty, for Christ's sake, you promised me."
"Okay. Okay. Hey, and what happened with your lips?"
"Nothing. I went down on a Bunsen burner. Go vomit or something.
Leave me alone for a while, I won't piss in the gorgonzola dip."
Drone: a high-tension-wire sound. Large platforms fold, drop-front-
desk-wise, out of the intestinal wall, down. Presenting, presenting . . .
Bobby Joe Comestible and his International Harvester Combine: two
backup guitarists, piano player, percussion. Comestible hollers, Ooooo-
eeee: hog idiom: he is like everyone else here, over-amplified. Strum:
Happy Anniversary to Her-mannn. Simon should be labeled HAZARD-
OUS: astigmatism, the spin-off product of rage, is dazing him: he sees
prismatically, through bent, miscolored light. This for Gluck's horse-
playful beating: this for the equivocal position he has had to assume.
His stomach does a roll call: nothing present and accounted for: he will
need to eat, though food, his old consoler, is vapid now and tastelessness
might nauseate him. Comestible has been vamping 'til ready: prelude for
a hoedown round of "Bonaparte's Retreat." His audience, in entertain-
ment also, mean with professional spite, assumes its uninflected figurine
stance/stances. Simon and the buffet table will synchronize orbit trajec-
tories: they dock. And fingers graze his arm: quick-dab: the half-furtive
snatch of Catholics who dip holy water at a church door font. Each cuticle is in blooming health: oily, fresh, gardened. Clean nails gloss. Simon
has turned, tripwire-set for a brawl. The tall and courtly man smiles:
gentle, genteel, gentile. His white hair is sparse and provisional: not
combed, just obedient. Late fifties and a jogger Simon would bet you.
Simon has scorn for joggers: the body is a convenience, as women are.
The man seems apologetic. He has touched Simon: he doesn't often,
Simon thinks, presume to touch.
"Pardon me, sir." Simon would guess south, southwest: somewhere in
the paunch between Sun and Bible Belt. And a goose-easy acquaintance
with great men.
"Yah? Uh?"
"I couldn't help overhearing that altercation. Nor what preceded it.
Babble. I was proud to hear you speak up, sir."
"You were, were you?" Simon has been zoned for heavy insults. But,
jingle, he's in the presence of money: shift. "Well, I believe in saying
what I feel. Deeply."
"Yes. I know that. I sensed it. May I shake your hand?" He may:
Simon offers: they grip, testing: a standoff. Oil of Olay squeezed from
the cuticles. "I'm George Bannister."
"Simon. Uh, Van Lynxx. Van Lynxx."

"Simon—yes, don't let me distract you from the buffet. Are you an artist?"

"Films. Director of."

"Aha. Is that so? I'm all admiration. And even more ignorance, I'm afraid. Have I seen any of your films?"

"Probably not. Most of my work's been done in Europe. Little Italy, places like that. Though I'm filming a modern life of Christ now. On location."

"In Jerusalem, that is?"

"In New York. I said on location. I didn't say on the right location. Necessity is a mother."

"Of course, a life of Christ. I can tell a Christian when I meet one. Not in the Sunday sense. A man of honor, I mean. And courage. Let me recommend the guacamole." Bannister has brushed up nuances of it: on a potato chip. Simon, the big dipper, will dig-we-must with three fingers: glop: the best is at the bottom. Bannister can't watch. "Here. How thoughtless of me. Chips have been provided. Here."

"Uh-uh, thanks. Ahh. Swallowed my throat a while back, little accident. Been living hand t'mouth since. Can't trust your hired help anymore." Finger in and up: Simon daubs guacamole, cream cheese, some orange stuff on his mouth roof: mixes his palate. Reflex action, he has to hope, will forward it collect from there. Bannister snaps his chip. A green/yellow crescent moon under each of Simon's fingernails.

"Yes. Well. What were we—you seem to understand the black man's plight. Have you worked with blacks?"

"Oh." Simon touches up his mouth with a napkin: no blood: good. "I've been one."

"Pardon?"

"It's like this, George. Once or twice a month I change the ribbon and type myself up black. Then I wander around New York like a native son. Y'can only know what another man feels by being him. As they say, walk a mile in my blue suede shoes."

"Are you serious? I know you are: it's just—the damn way I dress, have to dress—I'm a target for put-ons in a place like this."

"I'm serious."

"Godddam, that's brilliant. Have to take that back to Mortensen at the OEO. I imagine you've had some experiences."

"Y'should try it."

"I wish. I wish I could."

"And—mmm. What's your line of work?" By some mistake Simon has made a good first impression: he doesn't want to waste it.

"In a way I'm sorry you asked that." Bannister examines left hand/right hand: front/back. A first-grader's hygiene inspection.

"I'd say you were a man of means."

"In a sense, yes, that is true. Your means, though. I'm—this is embarrassing—I'm your Secretary of the Treasury."

"You're my what?"

"Yes."

"Well, considering my treasury, you must have time on your hands." Bannister laughs: deeply: a south-of-the-cotton-curtain laugh.

"I'm representing the White House at Mr. Wolff's fiftieth." Bannister can shrug: he has a charming, hopeless demeanor. "No one knows me from Adam Smith. My contribution to history is negligible compared to Herman Wolff's. Or, God, Kyryl's."

"Got a carcinoma roll?"

"What's that? A cigarette? Sure." Bannister shakes a Marlboro out. Simon is disillusioned. Never mind a gold cigarette case: not even the crush-proof pack.

"George, I like you. How's about getting your tariff lifted?"

"Come again on that one."

"Wanna get laid? It's available here at all participating dealers."

"Oh?" Bannister produces a shrewd man-to-man look. Simon has seen it before: with Norty, in Alabama roadhouses, a long time ago.

"Heard about the Bermuda Triangle, George? It's here: brunette with reddish streaks. 747 jumbo jets have been lost with all aboard. Fishing trawlers have gone in and never come out again. Strange lights are seen. Besides, she has bongs you could bowl a strike with in a crooked alley."

"Oh? Heck, yeah. I'd like that. But I couldn't. No. Might embarrass the Administration: they're all reborn down there. Reborn yesterday, if you ask me. I guess it's pretty quick and easy here. Jesus knows, I could go for a spontaneous act. You think coming out of the closet is hard, you try coming out of the Cabinet."

"George. You've used that line before. I can tell an old favorite when I hear one."

"Sure. But not for attribution. Only when I'm alone in my motel room. Which is often enough." Martinis, a tulip bed of them, have come past. Simon picks two from the tray. "No. No, thanks. I'm over my limit now."

"Well, I'll pitch for both sides." Simon ups, downs the left-hand martini. "Come on, George. Whatever you want, I can get it. Greek, French. English. It's all here. I can even get you Polish."

"Polish? That's a new one."

"That's where you have to teach the girl everything from scratch."

"Ha. Have to remember that one. But, no—thanks. Probably couldn't get it up, tell truth. The with-it generation puts me off my feed. I'd rather hear about your film. Tell me."

"My film. The cinematic tension in my film is sustained by a vigorous recurring theme. I flute it and re-flute it with a thousand Bach-like variations until a pitch of almost uncurbable, heat-rashed excitement is built up. To. In. Yes?"

"What is the theme?"

"Thought you'd never ask. The theme is: Simon needs money. Simon needs a lot of money t'make his film. You got money, George? What with cab fares an' all, a low-cost disaster loan, say a check for fifty grand—five with four o's—would be . . . whassamatter, you just sobered up, George. Where'd the reassuring Captain America smile go? Hanh? Huh. Jeez, I might've voted for you, George, but I couldn't find a coin t'flip. How's about rolling a few logs my way? Or is it all admiration f'the arts and no jojoba oil?"

"If you lived in Washington, Simon, you wouldn't bother. Down there they know: I haven't got two nickels, frankly. Alimony. The lawyer murdered me. Child support for three college-age children. I tell you, I'm living off my expense account. I would've welcomed an Abscam, but they never asked. And as for influence—"

"Please. Don't distract me from myself." Simon drinks his right hand: last time he'll bother with a good first impression.

"My Lord, you sure know how to stow it away. I can see you're a real heller. I'd trade places with you now, this minute. Me, I'm on a choke chain. Front men ahead of me. Rear men to sweep up. They write out everything I say. Back in March—you may even have read about it, only time I made page one of the Washington *Post*—I called the German mark a Fritz dollar. Caused a *verdamter* stink. They haven't trusted me since."

"You poor bedsore. Your bandage needs changing. Corpsman! Zipper, I mean you. Over here." Zipper is four foot seven and bald as lentils: female on a technicality. Tattoos of the New York subway system track down/into her navel-open décolletage. Van Cortlandt Park and Pelham on forehead: 14th St. at her appendix scar: Battery Park in depilated parts unknown.

"Hi-yuh, Sy. Still takin' slobby seconds?"

"Shut up, Dry Socket. I wantcha t'meet George Bannister. George here is Secretary of the Treasury. Zipper doesn't like men, George. And she's a homicidal pacifist. Also a lesbian: penetrable only to things cast in a rubber mold."

"Of thuh whole trez-ry? Is that thuh honestest?"

"Yes, ma'am, it is. Have I detected a southern accent?"

"No. Zipper's from Rego Park. But Mrs. Zipper broke her water in a revival of *Gone With the Wind*. Go on, Zip. Do your act."

"Well, Ah'm kinda overcome. I never yet done a cabinet membuh."

"A member is a member. A woman's grasp should exceed her reach or what's a placket for? Anyhow, George's been baying after a spontaneous act all night. Isn't that what you told me, George?"

"Yes—but . . ."

"Haht dam. Gimme two dimes, just two dimes, Mr. George." Bannister has one hand in left rear pocket: his vigilance there, too. An error: Zip works by misdirection.

"I have a nickel and— Hey! What? Ow!"

Ah, sure and it's great to watch a craftsman at work. Purrr-up! Bannister's fly has Y-ed wide open. And, a pizzicato pluck!, his treasury hangs out, distinguished as the man himself, with salt/pepper fringe of hair around. Snopppp: one deft hand move: taffy pull and noose: Zipper's famous (too large and too stiff) cardboard notice has been price-tagged on it with a strangulating #8 rubber band: CONGRAT-ULATIONS! YOU'VE BEEN ZIPPED! PRESENT THIS CARD AT EMILIO'S ROMA FOR A FREE ANTIPASTO.

"S'long now!"

"My God. My—"

Heads turn: stop: get a load of. Hold that pose: cheese. A flashbulb prints secretarial agitato: worse than the Fritz dollar thing. Zip is long gone, dodging belt-low, under martinis. Bannister has turned in-to/against the buffet table. Can't, dang, get the rubber band off. His national endowment is turning blue below: blue as her free antipasto coupon, which, double-dang, won't fit in his fly slot. From the rear pants legs are seen to rise: one red sock.

"Quick, isn't she?"

"My God. I'm ruined."

"Nah. Circulation'll come back in a day or two."

"My God, the Washington *Post*."

"Well, since you're busy, I'll be off. See ya, George."

And—d'jum-um: *d'jummmm*—the top-line act is on: Comestible has im-provised an entrance flourish. Wide, curving doors slip apart. Eight men swank-march in, in Kyryl's pink and witch-ball-mirrored livery. Keen light hits them: they form a blinding gauntlet. Which Herman Wolff now walks. He is child-short: bald but for a boa of gray, mussy hair horseshoeing around his skull. This skull, Simon will see, has been in-dented at the pate: it could hold water: a small birdbath, empty. Ap-plause, huzzahing, claque-noise. Wolff has one wrist pinched: a last pulse check. Cameras mount shoulder-up on TV men. The room, lit, is a hot compress: its floor has stopped turning. Wolff, with a kind of nice shyness, chucks both hands high above his head: unbeaten and untied. Roses fall from the ceiling: hologram-projected diamonds sparkle in mid-air. Comestible will insist that he's-a-jolly-good-fellow. That nobody can deny, and Simon won't.

Then Kyryl is there. His skin appears scraped down: the color of blood on brown paper. He is narrow, edgy, S-shaped as a sea horse: and with a sea-horse fife-thin face. Cancer has eaten off all but the essential system. Kyryl runs a fever always now. Simon, despite himself, is overawed: men who look like that are burned for warlocks: they can't have carefree intercourse with the world: they are their art. Bone-bare chest under a phospher-studded and white bathrobe: kerchief at the neck to hide his tracheal breathing tube. Wolff is unsure, a doubtful proposition, beside this subluminous ocean thing. Kyryl seems gristle-bound: compressed by sea levels above: on land he would bloat up. Two men are standing near with a ten-foot-by-six-foot canvas: muslin covers it. There is no spontaneous and genial applause. Just a single whispering voice, surprised to audibility, which will state the consensus. "Kyryl-l-l," it says. Kyryl has forced the amplifier against his cut-open throat. Hummm—stereo on stereo—from all around. Kyryl is miked into the building itself. Hummm and:

"Why doncha come up'n see me sometime, big boy?"

Kyryl's lips dub: exact: expert: the prerecorded voice of Mae West. Simon goes, Aaaaah: enchanted, afraid as children at *Snow White*. There is the sort of laughter that an awkward stage murder will push out. Simon, Magus, would pay to have Kyryl's gadget: voice amplifier and tape machine in one. Now it has buzzed, beeped. Kyryl strokes beneath his chin: an easy electric-razoring.

"Welcome. We are gathered here this night to get freaked out." Some clapping. Comestible throws in a comma chord. "And also . . . also to honor one of the great men of American film—Herman Wolff." Kyryl has touched Wolff's arm: there is paralysis now on that side. "Smile, Herman."

"Yes," says Herman Wolff.

"Now, my fellow Americans, I want to make one thing perfectly clear . . ." Nixon's stubbled, dismal monotone: Kyryl has it in his mouth: a grotesque voice-appropriation. Buzzz: channel flip. "Think of that, friends and subordinates. Half a century. Herman taught voice to Clara Bow. In fact, Herman goes back so far, he has an Edwardian casting couch. They tell Kyryl that Herman auditioned the entire chorus line for *Gold Diggers of 1849*. In depth. Is that right, Herman?" And before Herman can refute, "Ky-rii-ehhh E-lay-iii-sonnnn," a lento, nave-echoing Gregorian chant, which will end—mimicked to each distinct tongue place —with the old tobacco commercial tag, "Umbly, umbly, mmumbly, ah, sold to American!" The company has been taciturn: irritated as they are meant to be. There is a troubling paradox here: between rehearsed-smooth technique and Kyryl's eclectic, insane material. Wolff has been put in Pending: meek, vulnerable, head even: like someone whose height is to be measured now. Simon will hear, "Za-oui." Clamande is beside him, beside himself with enthusiasm. And a CBS radio newsman. And the gossip columnist Art Clay, Jr. Simon limbers his tight mouth: puckers around air: he is drunk enough now to meet Berto Clamande.

"Thank you." Applause. "Thank you."

"Herman. Kyryl has made—*made*—a precious gift for you. It appreciates in value even while we talk here." The voice is crackly, interfered with: as automobile radios are beneath a power line. "Thanks to his son-in-law, Norty Sollivan—"

"Yeah, Norty!"

"—Kyryl procured a phlegm sample from Herman's throat." Wolff will swallow: a peculiar unsensual exhibitionism in all this: he doesn't enjoy it. "We scanned the sputum with our SEM. And Kyryl has made—*made* —a painting of it with his own hand. Raise the cloth"—buzzzzzuzz—"O-ho, say can you see, by the dawn's er-lee light, what so—" Robert Merrill out of a Yankee Stadium PA system: opening day, 1977: live.

"*C'est fou. C'est insupportable.*" Clamande is ecstatic. "What a madman."

"Kyryl himself presents to Herman himself—with love and mutual admiration—*Wolffspit Fifty!*"

One human cell done in oils. It has great mass: it has carny-barker relish for indecent detail. The nucleus stares out: dull and damaged: purplish, a shiner. It was still alive then, but dying fast. Membrane has ruptured: necrotic cytoplasm contracts, as though in shame of notoriety. Yet with archeozoic courage, the cell will approximate—a last grand air—its pristine almost brick-square identity. Guy wires of protoplasm, tendon-strong, rope it to Kyryl's SEM stage. He has colored here and there: morbid stains: the eye shadow, cheek shadow of a done-up cadaver. Simon knows: this is some precursor thing, brought back from its cretaceous time: the beast hero on display in front of humans: hapless, heartsick, furious: and, for all that, most mightily dignified, a he-animal.

"Kyryl has nothing more to say. Go, Herman Wolff. Greet your subjects. And anyone who shows Herman a résumé or a three-page treatment—Kyryl will do a frozen section of his bladder wall." Buzzz-uhh. "There she goes, Miss Americahhhh—" Wolff has moved out, Bert-Parks-in-Kyryl sending him forth. Spotlights riposte and cut, quick visual repartee, over the honest basin of his skull. Simon has capped Berto Clamande's shoulder with one palm.

"*M'sieu. Ne m'touche pas.*"

"Mister Clamande. My name is Simon Lynxx. I directed *Clap.* I'd like—"

"This does not give you the right to put a hand on me."

"I wanna say, I'm a big admirer. *Un Homme et Son Chat*—"

"I'm not interested in your admiration." The CBS man is on RECORD already. Art Clay, Jr., has slapped a notebook open. "*Merci.* I accept praise only from persons of worth." Clamande is drunker than Simon: he turns away. Simon will pull down on his elbow: hard enough to raise a fifty-pound window blind. His eyes give Clamande a yellow flag: warning: slow.

"Gee. Gosh. I'm tryin' t'be nice."

"Remove your hand from me."

"Listen, Clamande. Be gracious, huh? Don't gimme chicken *merde*. I'm not a patient man."

"I will give you one second before I—"

"Give me? You'll give me? No, uh-uh. First let me give *you*. First lemme give you some names to conga by, you stalkless, strafed-out escargot. June the Prune, huh? Like that one? How about Chloe Speed?" Clamande is aware of his publicness here: the eyes disclose caution. "Oh, you recall, hanh? *Vous rememberez?* I may not be a household word like Clamande or Bon Ami, but at least I don't have meathooks and shackles and suspension chains dangling from my palatial bedroom ceiling. I don't hogtie underage girls and whip their tiny, glabrous figs with a rubber pizzle. I know at least six women you've monogrammed with a hot Gauloise tip. A little *Femme Flambée*, eh? Parley-voo S and M?"

"*M'sieu*. That is a libel."

"Fine. Hey, you, CBS. Bring that tape deck closer. This should hit Page Six of the *Daily Murdock* by t'morrow afternoon."

"My lawyers will—"

"What will? *Hein?* Sue? I'm worth $4.95 if I take the subway home tonight. But at least I don't give women 200-degree enemas with a metal turkey baster, while my Left Bank *homosexuel* friends play hard leapfrog on each other. How come you sent poor June to a private doctor, *un homme très discret*, for plastic surgery on her rotobroiled left nipple?" Clamande is afraid: simple as that: he backs. "Not so fast, Petit Guignol. And I don't have the corns t'hand a BC HAD ME T-shirt to everyone, male or female, whose duct I've french-fried."

"I am not amused by your fantasies, I—"

"Oh, fantasy, is it? All right, Mr. Fantasy, do you or do you not have one testicle the size of an Excedrin? Huh? Hah? Answer me, you blancmange."

"This—"

"Libel, huh? Well, why don't we pull those Ralph Lauren slacks off and present your *coq au vin* to an impartial jury? Hanh?" But Clamande is not there: fade and black, one of his more impressive directorial effects.

"A nation of maître d's. N'wonder they haven't won a war in three hundred years."

"Would you like to repeat those allegations, Mr.—was it Links?"

"Go read *Abattoir Management*, if you wanna get your cell discharged. Berto Clamande is a brilliant artist. Brilliant. I wouldn't say a word against him."

Ahhhh, nothing to beat the strenuous spoken life: Simon, once more, is strong: let-out across his chest, free. And another influential enemy made: the best doors closed: celebrity of a kind in that. Behind him, his own lion-cough threatful voice: the CBS man playing it all back. Kyryl's amplifier will howl, overloaded: shrill—eeeee—of a tire spinning nowhere on ice. His floor has started up, around. Unaccountably then, the room is wingtip to wingtip with a hundred green and very disoriented small parrots. Each nude child has his/her own live, bending snake. Confected swamp odors blow from the vent: wet, tall-rooted, tropic-rotten: Kyryl boxing the sense compass again. Simon can track Wolff only by checking configurations of the throng. Wolff has caused a vortex: is too short though: unseeable in its eye. Simon will step-stool up on tooth plaque: over there: yes, Wolff with, with, with: with an arm dropped across Rose Fischer's neck. And now—Bettina-Aldo-someone-Jesus—they butt heads together. The exchange, so unremarkable and careless that it is more than intimate, will bring dread up in him. Simon hips, shoulders, tough rushing yardage, toward the bay window. A cellar-door-slanted young blonde is there: privy to herself. Simon canvasses the street. And, in passing, it's an amen-like tic, not serious, he has said:

"I want your body."

"Uh. Yes. Okay."

"Hanh? You mean that, or are y'just working on your vapidity? It's okay if I try an' find your Puget Sound? Hah? Take your divot? Go on all fours in your crawl space? Hello? Anybody home? Wanna screw?"

"Fuck? I said okay, didn't I?"

"Jeez. You're all thrilled, like maybe your call number at the public library just came up." She has been sitting, several oblique lines, on the windowsill: rotation will pin Simon against her. Breast, thigh, stomach: he does a short-range forecast with one hand: fair and much warmer.

"Don't muss me, though. You gotta not muss my Princess Leia hairdo. I don't get done again 'til Tuesday. It's busy around here."

"I won't. We'll go through town like it was a whistle stop—zoom. Even the dogs on Main Street won't wake up. Is there a soft, level spot with toeholds around someplace? How about upstairs?"

"Yes."

"Ah—I'm an incurable romantic. Ah—I hope you don't think I'm being too forward. Ah—do you have a name?"

"Kyryl calls me Anny. For Android or Anonymous or something. Anny. That's my name."

"He must think a lot of you. Hold on, lemme see if my Caddy's been ticketed." Cut to outside. Now the rain is a maniac: it trip-hammers Great Ferry. B.P. and Sledge are hugging: under a large green beach umbrella. B.P. has galoshes on. "Lord help us. It's the dynamic duo. Inconspicuous as the '68 riots. Let's go, Anny. Shades of the prison house are closing in. The condemned man ate a juicy croot."

"I don't understand what you're saying. Do I have to?"

"No. No."

"Give me a hand."

"Going up. Sheeze-us!" And up. Anny has square twelve-inch platforms on. A big girl to start with: 5'10" easy. This makes her 6'10". Seven
foot if you figure in the tinfoil crown, which she must now put on. There.
Just right.

"Well? What's the matter?"

"Ah. It's just. I think you've stopped between floors. Press the emergency button, maybe the superintendent'll come."

"What're you waiting for?"

"You haven't unpacked your feet yet. They're still in the crate they
came in."

"I have to wear these. It's part of it."

"Of what?"

"Of *it*. Oh, I don't know. Let's move."

"Can you?"

Anny has to wait a moment: her transmission has stuck. Domp, uh-
domp: out of neutral. She has one hand inside his collar: this, Simon
thinks, must be how a walked dog would feel. People make way: concern for, uh-domp, their toes. Still and all Anny is quite well-shaped up
there. Long neck, ending at the *Star Wars* hairstyle: somewhat reminis-
cent of an L.A. Ram football helmet, but . . . Plump, mushroom-cap-fat
lower lip: excellent and even cute bunchy nose. The white, tenting stola,
cut from a king-size bed sheet, cannot expurgate her breasts: they draw
down, elliptic: as water drops do on window glass, just before they swell
enough to take the plunge. And her Disney cupid behind is perfect: buttocks round like—simile: come on, Simon, simile—like the double shadow
image of a cup's edge on light coffee. Simon has said his prayer: "Lord,
Lord—you who protect the brave and the stubborn—let me mount this
one without falling off on the other side."

Kyryl's third story is done in a vocational trade school mode. Sawdust
and hardware on the floor: workbenches: bare wiring, insulation, plaster-
board: many odd lengths of sawn plank, a full Cuisinaire set for some
giant learner. Flimsy plywood partitions have been knocked out/up:
they vibrate, croon back to the droning motor that turns things on their
axis one level below. Simon will walk, Anny will pick 'em up and put 'em
down, along a firetrap narrow hall. There are barrack rooms on either
side. Simon can see a single 6o-watt bulb in each: four bunks: functional steel shelving and the same factory-outlet cheap eight-drawer bureau. Walls are precinct station color: green above darker green. In one
room he watches a naked woman, leg up ballet-barre-high, paint her big
left toenail: bulb light glares on the shin: concentration has dressed her:
innocent. There is toy wreckage around. A three-year-old male child sits

on his potty chair in the hall. When they domp past, he will say, "All gone. No more." Simon nods.

"Tell it like it is, kid. Hey, Anny—where are we? In Kyryl's early Stalag period?"

"It's where we sleep. There's more an' more of us all the time."

"Handsome accommodations. Sorta like living in the penalty box at Madison Square Garden. Well, even the *Mona Lisa* has another side t'it, I guess."

"Oh. You want t'see Kyryl's mother? Kyryl likes that. For people t'see his mother."

"Uh, well. Is it far? I'm rushed. I been invited t'an aggravated assault and I don't want them t'start without me."

"We're right there. This is it. Everyone wants t'see Kyryl's mother."

"Interesting lady, huh? The apple doesn't fall far from the tree, huh?"

"Ssssh. I can't understand you, but I hear you all right. Sssssh. In here. Quiet."

Anny has cajoled the door: it gives in. The room is spacious, specious. Portly and soft alphabet blocks furnish it: chairs. Overhead an energetic mobile will shrug with the draft of their entrance: circus animal and clown and acrobat, three dozen such. Powder-blue walls: a crib hit crossfire with low pink spotlighting. The nurse gets up. She doesn't stop knitting a size 8, double E bootie. Simon could faint and t'hell with machismo: the room has made him throatsick. A pair of bronzed orthopedic shoes point out, in prima donna first position, on her dresser. Anny is beside the crib: she beckons him nearer, near. Simon would love to mask his great reluctance: he feels, tide change, all sexual interest going out. The woman, famished by age, genderless as a tortoise at first sight, is asleep in green pajamas. Her right lid can stay open: the eye, though, has long been iced over with corneal rot. One tube feeds at her elbow: another disposes down to some sort of rare Tang urine vase. She is, Simon thinks, just a strange splice in so much tubing. But he will grant the scrupulous resemblance: fish mouth: bloodied complexion: mussel-shell-rigid, tight hair. A sweet odor, a euphemism, has brought up belches in him: more than air: liquid he cannot taste.

"This is a guest." To the nurse.

"How do you do?" Tink-t'tink: an expensive music box picks "Rockabye Baby" out. "Is this your first visit?"

"Uh, yeah. I didn't know about. About. What I mean is: I usually go to a nice interment on my day off."

"Would you like to see the scrapbook?"

"Will you take a rain check f'some time after my death?"

"She's been in a coma since . . . oh, I suppose it's more than five years now. Six in April, that's right. April 4th. Lovely woman." Nurse will now step on a pedal: taped voices out. "Hear that? That's her talking. And see over there?" Home movies come up on a wall-broad screen: Mother clipping roses: on the Palisades Park Ferris wheel: hugged by JFK at Hyannisport: in some playground with her eel child.

"Anny—ssst."

"She moved this evening. Thumb and forefinger. Left hand. She must be having a dream."

"I hope I am. Jesus, this show'll send the two-headed calf and the alligator-skin boy back t'honest work. Will you make our excuses to—?"

"Hey—"

"Anny. Now. Come."

Simon is really out of it: in the corridor again. He crosses himself: pow! whap! on forehead, sternum, each breast, with a compacted and heavy right fist. Simon has superstitions after all: like maybe that death is catching. And he would not have kept his own mother so: a souvenir of herself. Anny is out now, too. She loafs high against a doorless doorpost across the hall. Simon's behavior has seemed churlish. It is the custom (she was taught this during her novitiate at Ten Great Ferry) to kiss Mrs. Kyryl goodbye. Anny might get annoyed with, sigh, this man— but that's what personae, even obscure ones like hers, are for: they take up your free time. Just *being*. Anny is. Something. She indicates the room behind: a will-this-do? with one hand. Good question: will it? The room is a mummer's storehouse. Boulder-sized papier-mâché heads: torsos even bigger than that: arm and leg sections: club feet: the fake offal from a fun-house field hospital. Porky Pig stretches, drawn and quartered, fifthed, room center. Dumbos, Snoopies, hags, hunchbacks, Winnies-the-Pooh, Mighty Mice: comedy is of nature largish, yes—but, at a certain size, it will panic and intimidate, as extravagant, prolonged laughter would. Simon goes in: he is jumpy and withdrawn, among so many hydrocephaloid, hollow crania. They stack up.

"What's this? Is this where the Sunday funnies come t'die?"

"Oh. This is where we keep the costumes an' stuff for *Terrible Circus*. I play Snow White. Well, I'm learning the part." She has directed his vision: the Snow White head lolls: three feet from chin to hairline: eyes and mouth are black, blank: fearfully unalive. "It's hot inside her, boy. I could die sometimes. I sweat and it does nothing good for my hair. Especially if I have to run. There's a running scene."

"*Terrible Circus?*"

"We tour around to insane asylums. All over. Kyryl gets off on madness. And after we perform, we let the loonies put our costumes on. You should see them. Like wow. We bring, ohhh—great big mirrors. The crazies stare at themselves. And stare. Kyryl says they're out of their heads already, so it's good for them t'get—well, you know—*into* something. They're floating around like disembodied spirits. Kyryl is very smart."

"Isn't he? Half dollars come out of his nose. Ah—couldn't we find someplace with a door?"

"Uh-uh. Not at Great Ferry. Ever. Kyryl says we have nothing to hide. I don't mind, do you?"

"No. No-no. I'd just hate t'give someone an inferiority complex. Y'll have t'use climbing irons t'shinny up mine."

Anny has gotten off her pedestal. There is a mattress, unsheeted, in one corner: Simon sits on it. Now Anny will slip a slipknot at her nape. The stola simply spills off/down: sssht: not much of a striptease. Her fine droplet breasts seem witty and sportive: like Muppets on the stage of each crossed forearm. Simon can appreciate this, sure: but it's also all so pat: impersonal. He'd prefer some blemish—a scar, cellulite, one mole thrown in for luck. That would give character and place and time. Anny cores her flawless navel with thumbnail, in: tidying up.

"Is it all right?"

"It's a goddam three-color gatefold, is what. My compliments to the layout department. Christ, you belong on a garage mechanic's calendar."

"Yes. I know. I'm beautiful. It gets boring."

"There's so much here I shoulda brought a doggie bag." Simon slaps the mattress. "Come, Miss April or whatever month you are. Before you spring a leak and I'm left with my dreams and a handful of gassy rubber."

"Uh. First. It costs sixty dollars. I gotta have that first. And tipping is allowed."

"What? What?" Simon is off the bed: angry enough to draw a technical. "I thought you liked me for myself. Sixty dollars? Sixty! How much for the live one across the hall?"

"Oh, I'm sorry. Should I put my dress on again?"

"Wait. Now wait. Don't gimme that Howard the Duck look. Jesus—whatever happened t'free love? Sixty. I'm dealing with an Armenian rug merchant all of a sudden. Sixty? Sixty, come on. I'm sure we can do some collective bargaining."

"Kyryl won't—uhhhh—you know, let us work for nothing." She yawns. "He told us when we came here, *Ars gratia* money. Or something. It's what he said."

"That water moccasin. Look. I'll give you fifteen and an orgasm. They wanted t'use my orgasm as a thrill ride at Great Adventure."

"I can't bargain. I'm not good with figures. Sixty."

"Sixty?"

"Sixty."

"Well." Don't mistake this for acquiescence: Simon has an evil idea: nothing if not vindictive. The cash comes out. One ten-dollar bill feels tacky: been using it for a nose blow.

"Thank you." Anny reaches: her first alert reaction.

"Hold on. For all this I want something special. What you gotta do, you've gotta act out my favorite fantasy."

"Well. But no spanking."

"No. No. Nothing like that. It won't hurt."

"What then?"

"Well. Ahum. This is a bit shy-making. Y'see—" Simon eats some cuticle. "I'm a big ear, eye, nose and throat man. Doctor, I mean. Park Avenue office. Beautiful young things come in for an examination and—gee. What do I get t'touch, huh? I ask you? A fat earlobe, sometimes a shapely nostril. I'm frustrated as hell. What I'd like t'do, y'know . . . I'd like to. You know."

"No. I don't know."

"I'd like t'play doctor. Before we make nice-nice. Examine you from the top of your charming futuristic head t'your little pink and peeling foot soles."

"Well." She shrugs. "I guess that's okay. As long as you leave my hair alone. And your hands are warm."

"Oh, swell. You're a sport. Just lie there and look like a patient. I'll go warm my hands."

Anny on the mattress: an intentional grounding: left hand up to net down her hair. Simon is at a corner sink. Brushes, lids, cans crowd in it. It has that random de-daub coloring of a painter's dropcloth. Secret smile: play this the way you'd play four kings, Simon: the sting here depends on high seriousness: a sixty-buck practical joke and it'll serve her right. He waits for the water to overheat itself with running up three flights. Anny is in an agreeable mood: glad to be off her foot-high feet. She has one hand against the right cheek: she nuzzles into it: crosses her own palm with a kiss. She's the type of woman, Simon would guess, whose privacy cannot be intruded on. Dr. Lynxx preps, warm and soppy fingers held up. Now for something in the nature of a medical instrument: not too ridiculous. Yes: we have several wooden paint stirrers: leverage enough to depress a cow's tongue. And one Q-Tip: miniature cotton candy: authentic: last used to swab turpentine, but . . . Simon leaves the sink. He has a diagnostic face on: a face that will announce metastasis, insane cells, death. Anny has watched him: so-so weird, these New York people. Simon ignores her eye, her personhood: the ruthless, aloof power trick of doctors and policemen. He measures off her glitter-rock body: impassive, as though he were about to park in it.

"Aren't you gonna strip?"

"Me? No. That wouldn't be ethical, would it? I never undress in the office. That'll come later." Simon whispers: a prompter. "Please call me Doctor from now on. I can't get it up if you don't."

"Oh. You have a thingamagig problem? Are you the one who did Kyryl's throat?"

"I was consulted, yes. That's why I'm here. Doctor. Say Doctor when you speak t'me. Huh? Remember?"

"Oh. Hello, Doctor. What else should I say?"

"You've got a general complaint. You need a complete checkup. You're worried. You're awed by my competence. And a bit afraid."

"I've got a general complaint, Doctor." Two beats. "I need a complete checkup, Doctor." Two beats. "I'm awed by your competence, Doctor. And a bit—"

"Don't horse around, Anny."

"Ha. Someone can't take a joke. It was just a little joke."

"Even Bob Hope doesn't pay sixty bucks for a joke. Take some pride in your ancient calling, huh?"

"I've got this general complaint, Doctor. It's all over. Just an all-over feeling. Here and there. Now here. Now there. I need a complete checkup, Doctor."

"That's fine. Just relax, Miss Jones. We'll call you Miss Jones. I prefer formality. Arms down at your sides, if you will. Relax. Yes."

"I'm—ahhh. Very relaxed. Do you make a lot of money, Doctor?"

"Mmmm-himmmmmmm."

"How much about?"

"Two hundred a year."

"Thousand? Oh, wow."

"Turn your head to the left, please."

"You married?"

"No. Miss Jones, you're here to be examined. Not I. There are other patients waiting."

"Sorry."

"Open your mouth." She will. Simon flats out her tongue with a paint stirrer. "Say ahhhh, please."

"Ahhhhh—gaakl" A soupçon of turpentine. She pugs her nose up. "Phoo. Where'd you get that. Pappp. Tastes awful."

"Some antiseptic. It won't kill you. Hmmm."

"What's the matter?"

"I see that a shoemaker did your tonsils."

"Yes, he—ppp." Simon has pinched her tongue in mid-glottal: stops it. He will turn the tongue over. "And you smoke. Some leukoplakia here."

"Nunnng—allll little."

"Head on the other side now. Thank you."

"My ears are dirty, I guess. They get waxed up all the time. Is that a sign of something?"

"Poor personal hygiene probably. Turn." Simon has posed her head with a concise jerk: the impatient puppetry of barbers. He will shut down one nostril. "Inhale. Exhale. Slight deviation of the septum. Does it give you trouble?"

"Only when I breathe."

"Yes. Could you try to be serious, Miss Jones?"

"Okay. God, you have a cold look. I get a sinus headache sometimes. I think."

"Who?"

"Who?"

"Who am I?"

"Oh, boy. Doctor. I get a sinus headache sometimes, Doctor."

"Arms up, please." Simon has begun palpating her right breast: expert and asexual finger swirls: just enough to keep the flesh in motion, stirred. The breast is simmering. Simon will now pause—part of his game plan—frown, backtrack with the forefinger: what-was-that? He dwells on an area high and close to her armpit. "Uh-oh."

"Uh-oh what?"

"Lump there. You better have your family physician check it out. In the next few days, I think. Tell him, upper nodal quadrant."

"Huh?"

"Lie down, I—"

"Huh?" Anny is no longer prone: an athletic, violent sit-up. One hand has been crotched under her arm.

"Lie back, please. The examination isn't over, Miss Jones."

"Where? Where is it, Doctor? The lump."

"Calm down."

"No." She rolls, woman overboard, to the mattress edge. "No more fuckin' fantasies. Where is it, Doctor? Where's the lump at?"

"Just under your thumb actually. I don't think it has much of a head start. Possibly it's a form of cystic mastitis. But to be certain I advise you to consult a doctor. That's a low-success area. Near the lymph nodes in your armpit."

"Lump. A lump." She touches around: but her hand is a bungler: panicked. "I can't find it, Doctor. I can't find it. Is that it? Did I feel it then?"

"Look, will you kindly lie down again? May I remind you: I'm paying for this checkup."

"I have a lump. It's happened. It's happened." This spoken to the charnel pile of comic stripped-off heads. "It's finally happened."

"Miss Jones. This is preliminary and superficial. It may be nothing. It may be benign. Is your period due?"

"No."

"Have you had a cold in the last few days? Any infection?"

"No. I've always been healthy as a cow. And now this." Simon's lips tighten: are white: are thin. "What can I do, Doctor?"

"Earn your sixty dollars. Not much else right now. I didn't get a chance to see if it adhered to the surrounding tissue. The healthy tissue, if we presume the worst. Have your doctor check to see if it puckers, contracts. He'll understand."

"Wait. Hold on. You're a doctor. You check it. You check it right here."

"Miss Jones, I—"

"Look at it again, for God's sake."

"My dear." Simon rasps his throat clear. He has been waiting for this: he proposes to enjoy it. "My dear, we are both professional people. I don't work for nothing."

"You mean—?"

"Yes, I mean."

"Christ, how much?"

"For you—I think sixty dollars would be about right."

"Oh, shit. Have a heart, huh? They make me kick back on everything here. I'll give you twenty."

"Gynecology *gratis*—"

"All right. All right, you bastard." Anny is on her feet: the six tens recovered from a platform shoe. "Here. Some ethical person you are. I oughta write to the American Doctors' Association."

"Many thanks. But first, Sugar Extract—first we have some unfinished business to get through. Time I took a package tour through your lumbar region. Lie back."

"No. Not that. Not now. Some other day. I couldn't do it with you now. I'm too upset. You wouldn't enjoy it."

"You underestimate my capacity for pleasure."

"No. No, I won't. I can't."

"What? You mean—let me read this inter-orifice memo again—you mean I'm not gonna get my baton twirled?"

"Just feel the lump, huh? See if it adheres or what." She is prone again: so desperately prone that her belly pokes up. "God, Kyryl. He punched me in the tit. That son of a bitch. I bet he did it."

"Hey. You down there. Conference time."

"Go on. Examine it."

"Miss Jones. If you're not gonna put my bone in a warm splint—then what you've done, you've paid me my own sixty bucks for this examination. Listen, Snow White, you're not dealing with Dopey the Dwarf here. I took billing and dunning in med school. In fact, it was part of the entrance exam."

"Please. Look at it. I can't take the suspense."

"Uh-uh. Sixty bucks or your flesh."

"I haven't got it."

"So what's all that white, soft stuff you just dumped on the bed? Window putty?"

"I'm dry and tight. I couldn't."

"Then go pry a clam knife in Mr. Mollusk: that amphibious thing downstairs. He can earn sixty bucks for casting his shadow in bronze." Simon is bored. He hauls up the Porky Pig head: cumbrous, weighing in at fourteen pounds: a hangover head. But its untenantedness has caught his deep attention: bit of the hermit crab in Simon: always a housing problem. To fill, to hide, to impersonate, to explore: oh, in the pig's eye. He has raised it, aiming for a black neck hole.

"Kyryl? Are you kidding. He never gives me anything. I have t'pay rent here. I'm an apprentice."

"Well, wait then. You'll be eligible for Medicare in forty years. How d'I look?"

"What? Oh, stop pissing around, for God's sake. I'm scared. I'm really scared. Can't you see that? No, you men are all the same: pricks, like my father."

"Pah!" The head stinks of scalp sweat and aged Aqua Net: a blunting scent. Anyhow, not precisely what Simon needs to replace his broken gorilla suit: wrong image. "Pah," again. Closing in: Simon is stifled. The mouth hole won't line up with his vision: blankness. He touches unresponsive, glossy pig cheeks: dead to his finger: gone the way of all papier-mâché. His hearing is down: systems off. "What? What'd you say?"

"I said, Okay. Use me, you cocksucker. Just shove it in like all you men do. But I won't pretend I'm coming."

"Aaaah. That's what I like, a pragmatist. Be. Right. There." Simon locked in head-to-head fighting with the pig: up, lift: stalemate. He pants: what a way t'go through life. And then, flash, out of the animal's lax-tongued, over-happy mouth, he has seen Kyryl and Wolff bolt past. Wolff wearing a raincoat. "Yipe. There goes my bus."

"I'm waiting. Hurry up, Doctor. I wanna get this thing done with." He has bent forward now, tugging, pullover-shirt fashion. The chicken-wire neck will tweak Simon's nose end. His eyes weep.

"My regrets. No time t'get a digital readout on your clabber. Meanwhile, take two Laetrile and buy a half-bra." Simon waving at the door. "S'long, Miss Jones, it's been fairly kinky. Keep me abreast of things."

"No! Wait! Doctor! Stop!" Anny is up. "Oh, Jesus no! Doctor! Doctor! Jesus, they'll take my goddam tit off."

And, run, that better not be the only thing comes off tonight. Down/around, down/around: three one-lane zigzaggy fire escape metal flights. Saint Siloogie, let B.P. and Sledge have the *cojones* to mug Wolff without a requisition signed in triplicate. No time left for the flashlight tip-off: well, got that idea free with a Captain Midnight Secret Decoder Ring anyhow. Just hope they have the choreography dress-rehearsed by now: don't go up on their kick or punch lines. And where is his own rough script? Cue Simon: run it once, without feeling, in the head.

ME: You two. Leave that good man alone.
B.P.: Think you're mean enough to make us, whitey?
SLEDGE: Uh. Yeah. (Various ad-libs.)
ME: I may not be. You may have me outnumbered. But, by God, I'll
try.
B.P.: Take this, honky.
SLEDGE: Yahhh! (Ad-lib kung-fu jive. Throw a Western Union
right.)
ME: (Block with left. Counter with right the way Johnny Mack
Brown used to do.)
SLEDGE: (Ad-lib groan. Profanity. Fall against car: bang hood to
make impact seem louder.)
B.P.: (Swing lead pipe, bat, something long and hard.)
ME: (Duck. Kick him in balls.)
SLEDGE: (Rush me, cursing.)
ME: (Bruce Lee monkey flip over my back.)
B.P.: (Jump me while I'm down. Pull shiv. Desperate struggle. I dig
two fingers in his eye. Much pain screaming.)
SLEDGE: (Another rush.)
ME: (The old flying dropkick.)
BOTH: (Run.)
with the jerk-ass umbrella, for hump's sake.

Instant waterlog outside: Simon takes on weight. Wind has steered
him half around: doing a good turn. He will luff into it: contact lenses
press down: hairline is beginning to recede. The rain has pricked his
face, keen as silver toothpicks. Great Ferry, remembering its past, is a
river inlet again. Runoff extravasates over the curbstone. Oh, large-
humored God, keep Wolff from getting a cardiac infarction: or pneumonia. Thunder does sheet metal work high up. But Simon can hear yelling
and some pretty mediocre anti-Semitism across the street. He roars. He
will jump up/on a Volkswagen's parked, low muzzle: and leap: and
glush! ankle-deep: Simon, shoes squelching, to the mediocre rescue.

"You little Jew! You little Jew! You little Jew!"
"I knew it. I knew it. Give me a kill. Go on."
"You little Jew! You little Jew! You little Jew!"

Wolff kneels. This is inconsiderate. Sledge, upholding him by both
raincoat lapels, has bent over: as if to look through a low microscope.
Wolff, in turn, is caught up: one pinky finger poked through Sledge's
lapel: strap-hanging on a buttonhole there. Sledge, Simon would admit,
has done himself up hideous: a victim of critical burns: face swathed in
two Ace bandages: so anonymous he can hardly see. B.P. has a glad-
pumpkin Halloween mask on: rain has knocked the wind out of his Afro.
He bystands: MC-ing it all: in charge of personal effects: wallet, pills
(red, white, yellow, yellow-blue, little red), inhaler, chapstick, comb,

watch, pen and, to his disgust, a leather truss. Wolff does not resist: his neck is lax. Pockets are inside out, hanging: corners of an empty flour sack. Sledge will stir Wolff occasionally, as though he were some regular evening chore, side-to-side, front-back: or a Ferrari gearshift. Sledge's nose has come through the Ace bandaging. Sledge is rattled: can't think of a decent ethnic slur. B.P. kicks Wolff half-footedly, in the buttock, just to do something.

"Crawl, you little Jew."

"Oh, it's coming. Seventy years and it's coming."

"You two. Leave that good man alone."

"Think you're mean enough t'make us, whitey?"

"I—"

"Fuckin' ad-lib. Fuckin' ad-lib."

"I may not be. You may have me outnumbered. But, by God, I'll try."

"Take this, honky."

"Yahhhh. Throwwwww a Wessern Union right!"

And Wolff goes along with it: an involuntary corner man for Sledge: still buttonholing him by one finger. Rippp: fabric has given out. Wolff rolls. Sledge will throw his sluggish, operetta-big right cross. Simon defends, arm up, and, in repayment, unslings an authentic specimen: sockdolager time: irked by Sledge's literal adherence to the script. Right, right in Sledge's kisser. A small metal clip has sprung off. Ace bandage begins to unravel, flailing, irrepressibly elastic, around his head. Wolff has fallen sidelong: hands in at belly: knees up: the way young children dive. Bash! Bash! Bah! That's Sledge mauling the car hood for realism: sound ineffects. B.P. is at bat now, scuffing toward Simon with loose galoshes. Simon will shriek Hai! and kick for his groin: somewhat low: kneecap: ungh, grunting, first genuine noises of the night. They both limp. But watch out, it's—

"Rush me, cursing!"

Give way, bend and one, two—har-up! Hee-up. Hee. Sledge, a wreck of bandaging, won't go over the top. His weight is uncenterable, sloppy. Simon staggering around beneath: a fireman's carry. Ace elastic has dropped across his mouth. He can barely hiss at Sledge, "Stop repeating the stage directions, you great nincompoop." Sledge will somersault down: will flip himself over Simon's shoulder. B.P. has been marking time: is apologetic: his switchblade won't come out, corroded, 1955 gang war surplus. He attacks Simon with the handle. Hai! Karate chop to B.P.'s happy-pumpkin face. Orange plastic has splintered, handing Simon eight thin paper cuts. "Oh-oh-oh, my eye. Aaaagh. Aaaagh. I'm blind." But it's don't-call-us-we'll-call-you: the whole showcase production wasted. Wolff has his face under one armpit: he curls tight on raingunned cement. Simon and B.P. and Sledge simulate a battle ruckus: fist spanked against open palm: breath-groan: ooof and aggh. The car hood gets it again, but good. Then, plash-plash-plash, swift footsteps away. Glare! Lightning has taken a police photo of the crime scene. Then, what now?, plash-plash-plash, swift footsteps back. Idiot: Simon throws the green umbrella at Sledge. Ah, some nice verisimilitude: Simon has a plastic-blooded fist. He makes up his face with it. Yet Wolff has him scared: dead, could be: twenty years to life: Simon, a Czar of disorganized crime. But the right leg will twitch out, hyperextend, when Simon touches it.

"Who is this? Who is this? Am I dead? I can't look."

"It's Simon Lynxx, Mr. Wolff. Norty's friend. They're gone, you can come out now. Mr. Wolff? It's safe. Are you all right?"

"Put me on my feet." Wolff is tottery. Rain snare-drums the bald head. "Wait." Wolff has pinched water from his eyebrows. "Wait. I know you."

"Simon Lynxx. The poor jerk who made *Clap*. Norty's friend from the Army."

"Ah-ha."

"Yes."

"I remember. The loudmouth anti-Semite."

"Right. I mean, no. Not really."

"It's okay. Boy-oh-boy, I won't forget. Fifty years in film and I get this for my trouble. You're bleeding."

"No. Nothing serious. I think it's their blood mostly. You should get out of the rain, Mr. Wolff."

"Yes. But first a big hug. Thank you. Thank you. Though I walk through the valley of death, I shall fear no evil."

Wolff embraces Simon at hip height. Behind, thumb and forefinger reach out to sneak a pulse check. Rain has filled the shallow pool in Wolff's concave pate. Penitent, jubilant, foolish, Simon will dab at it. A rich and secret odor comes up. Herman Wolff has befouled himself.

1

Simon handles a foot. The examination table is davenport wide and low: is Wolff's bed as well. Some have slept in a coffin: Herman Wolff sleeps in a state of diagnostic suspense. Fibrillator, oxygen tank, intravenous rack, EKG machine, EEG machine, vascular occlusion device, even pajamas that fasten down the back: his annual checkup daily: semper apparatus in this East Side penthouse bedroom. EKG contacts have already been stuck on his shirt-open chest: separate, yet in electrical cahoots. Simon will—sssh-up—foam shaving cream over the right ankle pit. Wolff's heart has a listening post there, beneath that soft flesh dent. Gray skin on the feet: moccasin-tough calluses: toenail large as a Tonka Toy windshield. Grown-up feet. How they interest and repel small children: crossed on a hassock, say. Hard and forbidden places they have gone: there is an extra, inescapable walking that will come with adulthood: the young know it. Wolff croons what might be a Yiddish folk tune or just a nonpartisan, general bitching. The voice is skillful and winsome: also self-compassionate: Wolff wants to lull his plaintiff-timid body calm. Blup: the last suction dart-head plugged in/on. By this time Simon has gotten chummy with Wolff's fecal smell: a real breath-holder at first: now less conspicuous than dust on spectacles. Wolff hasn't noticed. And, hum, it isn't the sort of thing you'd call someone's attention to.

"Uh. Is that okay, Mr. Wolff? I'm a little apprehensive. I built a transistor radio in high school shop class, it played three bars of 'Love Me Tender' then it just melted all over the workbench. One minute solid state, the next a dish of baked Alaska. I mean, you look endangered, Mr. Wolff. Or—no offense, um—you look like the switchboard at a transient hotel."

"Don't worry. A first-rate job. Professional. A pre-medder couldn't do so good. I appreciate. Believe me, I appreciate. One of my valves could use a new washer. Deep breath, Herman. Big, deep breath. Ooop! I overdid." A contact has plipped up: six inches high: jitterbugging on its wire. Simon is reminded of the Eisenhopper Aldo gave him for his seventh birthday. "Smack it down again. Don't be afraid to shove. I need new stickers, the workout I've given them. A broken cigar has more suck left. Which also I had to give up, smoking." The nipple is hard as a pellet. Simon feels around: second bosom tonight: nothing but work, work, work. The coincidence beguiles him, and laughter, expurgated, will come out nasally: a frog in his nose. "What was that? Sniffling? A cold you have, I hope to God not."

"No. I just inhaled wrong."

"I catch colds over a telephone call. The Vichy government had more resistance. Last year I got Hong Kong flu from a dirty ten-dollar bill. A-hum. Ahhhh-um." Wolff has breathed. "I bet he's thinking, the old hypochondriac. It's true. I admit. If I didn't have my health to worry about, I'd go crazy bored. It's someone I can talk to. And how are you today? Not so good. How's by yourself? Don't laugh, even hypochondriacs can have a real disease."

"Gosh, Mr. Wolff. Ten films a year, how can you be bored?" Simon is listening to himself: language censored like mail from a theater of doubtful war.

"Ach, you shell-gamer kids, from what do you know? After fifty in the business, it's all a big remake. Do you think now, putting your coat on? One arm in, what next? Hunch up the shoulder? Do you think? No. It's on, who can even remember doing it? Power. Money. What about the gas pains? I'm standing at a urinal in Regine's, and this pusher kid starts dancing. Look, he says, I could be John Travolta Number Two, Mr. Wolff. I should look at him and wet my shoe? But he's got me: for me to squeeze a good piss out takes five minutes and a gift certificate from God. Then, while I'm zipping up, he starts doing impersonations. Female, yet: Bette Davis, Marlene Dietrich. He's got two wigs in his jacket. My hand is wet and he has his agent shaking it. I can't go anyplace and who can afford to stay home? Receipts I gotta get for the government. My income the welfare state has already said farewell to. I have an accountant, he's so stupid I think he's a secret Irish Catholic. Expenses. I live on the kindness of waiters. From them, for a dollar, I always buy their pen, so I can make a one into a four and it looks legit. Eights are terrible. Never have a dinner costs eight something, an eight is an eight. Seven you can work a nine out of. Five you can screw into a six. Three is nice. Three makes an eight if you're careful. But eight, eight is a dud. You're stuck with an eight. This is my best advice after fifty years: steer away from the figure eight. And, with all that fididdling, my accountant still hands the government five hundred grand on April 15, so they can fund Spanish-speaking teachers for Spanish kids. God forbid they should learn American. For thirty years and your cardiovascular setup, I'll sign it all over right now, the whole chicken-shoot, and *mazel* to you. Look, give the blue button a punch. I want to see maybe I died by now."

"Blue . . . Blue. Blue. Here."

"Hold up. Wait. Ahhh. Ahhhh. One, two deep breaths more. I can't get over yet—this close I came to being in cold blood. Those black dick-suckers. Black, I'll call them that, they want me to. You ask me, black is more insulting. Negro had a distinguished tone. Some Italian tenor, sings Puccini. I'm not prejudiced. I make one *Black Jack in Harlem* film every year. I put up for an all-black *Godzilla* once. They need work. Six, maybe seven blacks in America can act, but—so?—four, maybe five people in a black audience can watch—they come out even. Those bonzos. Just let me send an all-points out on them, they'll have star billing in a snuff film, and a fat piece of the gross. No. No. Don't agitate, Herman. Revenge is sweet, but it could also blow a hose. Flip the blue. I'm shutting up."

The EKG does paperwork: a graph of Herman Wolff, his ups and downs. Wolff is still now: a veteran observer of himself. He will deploy biofeedback technique: producing alpha waves and an occasional stately theta. What does this suggest: table, laid-out body, demure crossed swords of overhead light? Yes, Aldo dead. Simon, a ten-year-old, lit his father's wake. The funeral director, from some progressive school of grief therapy, let those bereaved participate: busy hands. Bettina did hair with comb and spray Adorn: gave Aldo the mid-line part he had always thought faggish. And Simon sat, tech man, at his own light console: pink and yellow and white dimmed from One to Ten. Not a great career credit: APPRENTICE, HARPER'S FUNERAL HOME: but his first break in showbiz, nonetheless.

"Red button."

"Red. Got it."

The wires stir: input, heartfelt, coming through. Wolff has a hairy chest: though greens and tees are landscaped clear for the EKG. His diamond pinky ring—overlooked by B.P. and Sledge, ineptness wherever you go—will flash like a mirror in outfield bleacher seats. Simon is, confess it, reverent: greatness knee-jerks him around. Shake the hand that shook the hand that shook the foot of Herman Wolff. His carrion mouth goes from numbness to *being* numb: refined distinction here: he can feel not feeling: it isn't much of an improvement. There are brown-yellow, Yankee bean soup streaks on the paper-covered examination table, under Wolff's belt-loose, great man's behind.

"Blue, again."

Simon downshifts. The machine is reliable, of a moneyed competence: it will purr and acquiesce. Wolff's Sedan de Ville had that same cocksure tact, I-will-get-you-there, when Simon drove it. He recalls, recalls. Each event a little Station of the Cross. Wolff would walk solo past his vain and judgmental Jamaican doorman. Then, near the elevator, he had run at Simon with such aggressive need that it had seemed an assault. What came next? Oh—Simon toting Wolff, child on hip. Wolff hung from a steel elevator rail, against the ropes: Simon his trainer and towel man. Who would have thought it? Herman Wolff and Simon Lynxx reeling, elbow bend bent in elbow bend, intimate as lost booze hounds. Don't tell him crime doesn't pay. They are a club now: with secrets, rites, dues paid. They have their own long history.

"All right, stop. White button. No, on top the blue. Let's see my ticker tape, I'm getting a clot already from suspense. Tear it off. Find, if you can, my bifocalers. A red case on the night table." Wolff is propped up, Roman-eater style. "Pour me a VSOP. If it's bad news, I'll need it. If it's okay, I can drink my good health. For yourself, too: you deserve. I use that Marilyn Monroe glass, fill it up to her shiksa nose. If we see mole-hills being made out of mountains—maybe a suspicious zag-zig—you can give me a lift over to Mount Sinai. Of course, I could pull four aces on the EKG and, next minute, drop quick like a hooker's pants. This, you should know, is exactly what happened to my wife. A clean bill and she went down the way my stocks do—bang—in Dr. Levitt's reception room. Going out, no less. Levitt says, 'Ridiculous. This woman is in perfect health.' Am I gonna argue? In perfect health, but also a corpse. Flat dead across the old copies *National Geographic*. With the human heart who can tell from last Tuesday? It's a fickle organ. I miss Carlotta. Forty years' marriage, she could tell me, 'Take out the garbage, Cecil B. De Mille.' A hotsy-totsy adventure with some blonde from the chorus was excitement then. I had to play hide-and-seek. Carlotta would hit if she found out. No tears. No big threats. No yelling. Just a bop to make my eyes go crossed. A lady. Now I'm free and everyone with two boobs and a snapper wants marriage. To them I'm a walking alimony. Three months' honeymoon and all of a sudden I'm doing mental cruelty, so long, my lawyers will give a ring."

"Here, Mr. Wolff." And inside the red case, what have we? We have one ticket stub, one paper clip, one thermometer, one I AM A JEWISH CARDIAC PATIENT medal, one ammonia capsule, one—ick—it won't come off Simon's finger. Pull with the right hand. Pull off the right hand with the left hand. Pull off the left hand with—a great W. C. Fields rou-tine. Furry, black: one false mustache, no questions asked. He sticks it to a table leg. Simon, movie fan, is engaged by this evidence of Wolff, the private person. Scotch tape has been securing both bifocal lenses. On the nose bridge there is an accumulation of that peculiar green gunk: chemi-cal salts made from human sweat and plated metal. Wolff will be pas-sive: doctored. He allows Simon to jigger each eyeglass arm on its ear. In. Place. So.

"Good. Let's have a cold read what those tree-swingers did to my

pump. Okay here. Okay and okay." Wolff scans this one-page treatment
of himself, forefinger pantographing along, up/down, left/right. "Okay.
Ech: not so hot: but it's a usual, I've seen it before. This peak isn't the
Matterhorn, still not so awful you remember I was shaking with fear. So
—Mr. Bandage Head, Mr. Mummy's Curse—you didn't fail my heart. A
skoal is in order. To my health. To yours: the hero. *Abi gezind.*" Wolff
will drink: Marilyn's smile is cleared. "Aaaah. I can feel my hands.
Warm. The capillaries are opening for rush hour. Come, take a look at
my Dow Jones. By now I'm more fluent in EKG than in English."

"Could I? If that wouldn't be an invasion of privacy, Mr. Wolff."
Simon has it down, just about: a tasteful fawning note.

"Invasion? My life he saved, he wants to know if it's Emily Post to
have a look. Enough nonsense. See, this is where comes the thin ice. My
leaky quarter. Dr. Levitt says to his stethoscope it sounds like a dry
power steering. I could go—bloooom!—a water-main break. He advises
open heart, but at my age they could find a bankrupt pawnshop in there.
Let God decide when I should call it a life. In 1971 I had a heart attack,
on the john. Now I don't push anymore, it isn't worth it, being regular. I
was in critical: a five-alarmer attack. Let me recommend it to you."

"Recommend?"

"Wow. Some short shrift you made on that glass VSOP. To me it has a
taste from crushed ants. The way a goy can drink—this I've noticed and
don't come down on me for a bigot talk—a goy will have one for the road
and it's his own party, he's got no place to go. I can admire it. A Jew
would fall through the seat of his pants. And please. Give the one-man
Special Forces team a big refill: you earned it. I heard those black
coconut-bangers squeal. It was Carnegie Hall. There's scotch, you prefer." Wolff has sat up. His feet troll, playful. EKG contacts, at their
harvest season now, drop off him. Gillette Foamy is dry: it has scaled on
breast and ankle. "Recommend? you say with a question mark. Well, if I
was again a twenty-year-old momser, I'd start up this private service:
Herman Wolff, Personalized Heart Attacks. Look, someone you love, he's
aggravating too much: airport-quick deals, a big sale on something he
hasn't bought yet, tension. Dexedrine up: Placidyl down. So you come to
me, strictly off the record. From me you get a coronary contract out on
him. My boys drop something in his black coffee: pop, he wakes up in
Montefiore, with a doctor who's got a face looks like the holiday death
toll. We fox up an EKG: you could drive from Burbank to Anaheim on
it. His heart is making cloverleafs and exit ramps. Bottom line, a month
flat on his tookus: even climbing to the bedpan is risky. A warning. The
carcass is giving two weeks' notice. The next big deal is strictly export—
to another world, where the customs duty is a killer. Lay off the frieds
and the salt. Later work out on an Exercycle, getting nowhere at 20
m.p.h. Me, it made a new Herman Wolff. What did I need, ball-busting

my people fifteen hours a day? For ball-busting you can always delegate. Believe me, it's a much-sought-after job." Wolff laughs. A cordial, mild trill. "Now it's bed early. A dumb detective to read. Never on the set. There's a knock in the engine and who can afford that kind of valve job? Hey. I have a stethoscope, you wanna tune in on it?"

"Well—"

"Of course not. A young Hotspur like you. What could you care, I'm doing my autopsy in advance, an obsessed old man? How's the punching hand?"

"Fine. Sore a bit. Surface cuts. Ah, could I have the EKG sheet, Mr. Wolff? A kind of—"

"*Memento mori?* Sure, keep. It's not my best, I've done better. But, sure."

"Should I leave? It's after midnight."

"No. No. I need the talking. You may have guessed by now." Wolff whews: big exhale. "I'm all fitutzed. Well, give your opinion, what were they after? You little Jew. You little Jew. Again and again, the same one-liner. I'm not so short." Another easy laugh. "I'll never forget. Mr. Jumbo size: his face is wrapped like maybe a gout of the head he had. Humm. On one hand, a pro bowl operation. On the other hand, an act that could use work, a practice run. Wham! I'm grabbed. I'm doing a breaststroke in the air. This is it, I think, three columns in the New York *Times*, contributions to the Will Rogers Fund, please. Forest Lawn has an urn ready and a plastic dustpan. Then, no: kidnap, I'm thinking, that's it. So —into the urn anyway. Norty wouldn't spend to pull me out of a locker at Penn Station. He probably won't spend for the urn. A cigar box I'll get or a Hefty bag. But, you know, it was—I had—there's a German word, *Fingerspitzengefühl* . . . a feeling, an intuition. Tell me, is there a leak in my brain, too? I keep thinking, this is a film scene. I've watched enough of them. All this time I'm expecting someone to yell, 'Cut, print!' Little Jew. Little Jew. It was like they ran out of material. Also, now I remember: one, the pumpkin, he had an umbrella, he shouldn't catch a chill waiting to dislocate my neck."

"Gee." Simon would rather not encourage it: this *Fingerspitzen-whatsis.* "I don't know. I mean, how can you be sure they were waiting? And for you?"

"Is that impossible? As a surprise party, it wasn't so surprising. Anyone could get a wind of it. My car was right there: H.W. But a heist? The watch was Timex, the top-line model, but still a Timex. Not one of those fancy press-a-button red-number things, they don't tell time, you have to ask them. The wallet: so, seven dollars, my license to drive, my HIP card . . . What else? A photo of Norty with the kids: this is not legal tender, believe me. The Labor Department should hand Herman Wolff a violation. For that kind of work, not even a minimum wage. And yet, look, my

ring they left. But that I don't wonder. Mr. Brobdingnagger has his eyes
bandaged over to a pinhole squint. The other, his pumpkin mask is slipping around to one ear. They're so disguised they need a seeing-eye. Little Jew. Tell me, in that rain, how do they know I'm not a little Catholic
bishop? Unless. It's got to be they're waiting. And for Herman Wolff."

"Well. Let me toss this out. Suppose they were pissed at the take:
seven dollars and Norty. That would piss me. Jew—it could've been a
general term. The way people say, oh, that even a WASP like J. P. Mor-
gan, oh, jewed somebody down."

"Hmmm. Then why little Jew? Why not cheap Jew—" Wolff does a
walk-through in his mind. "No, I remember. The Jewing starts even before they're in my pocket. Why? Who? Actors I've edited out of a film?
People left off the guest list?"

"How about two black muggers with a broad-based anti-Semitism?
Just that. Nothing personal. No ulterior shtick."

"Of course, it's possible. The schwartzers have a crummy time. They
live like termites in a concrete bunker. I'm not without sympathy, but
where do they think the word 'ghetto' comes from—Martin Luther King?
I've also in my day done a holdup or two. For need. Did you ever eat a
cocker spaniel?"

"Ah, no. Though, in some Chinese restaurants, you never can tell."

"I have. And I've saved over for sandwiches the next week. But—heh!"
A laugh: Simon hasn't heard this one before: the quick sound, he can
surmise, with which Herman Wolff disposes of a thing: it isn't attractive.
"But. If I get a number on those motherfucks—excuse my English—if
. . . it'll be the end. And it'll be the end my way. There's enough crowd-
ing in the courts already."

"Shouldn't we call the police?"

"Pah. What? Now hear this, be on the lookout for a man wearing Ace
bandages all over his head? A waste of time from Tiffany's, elegant. No,
don't worry. I'll call the police." Wolff sips. "Tomorrow I'll take some
police to lunch. A lieutenant, a captain, they moonlight being crooks.
This is nicer, the personalized touch. Would I want Mr. Pumpkin in Attica for three years? What about the wife and kids? As a child, my father
used to say, 'Ten good swats or miss Izzy's birthday party, which?' I took
the ten. So. I'll have a hot copper wire poked up their piss holes, maybe
jiggle it around a bit—and we're even, no hard feelings. What gives me a
shocker is you, that you should be risking a cut-up for me. Who knew
they had knives or not?"

"Well." Thought you'd never ask, Herman. St. Simon the Plausible has
it all by heart. "I hate to admit this, but . . . I didn't know it was you
down there, Mr. Wolff. I saw someone getting taken off from upstairs,
from Kyryl's window." Simon has a drink: not much of one: hot copper
wire talk will serve to concentrate the mind. "I'm far from superstitious,

but it is quirky how fate does business. This girl—I was blueball crazy. One of Kyryl's androgynes, I don't even know her name. I think he clones them from the window at Bloomingdale's. Maybe it was a man: who can tell? Kyryl's women could masturbate themselves pregnant anyhow." Wolff is being amused: Kyryl and Wolff, where do they interface? "So . . . I had this sublet agreement on her body, with witnesses, notary, cash up front, I'm ready t'move in and she calls a TV time-out on the one-foot line. No score. Suddenly sex might break her lip gloss or something. I was pissed off. Hey, ordinarily I wouldn't've gone gung ho like that. Ordinarily I'm cautious. Especially about my teeth. Lose your two front teeth and the old IQ goes down forty points. Or so people think. Try saying something profound without your two first-row seats. But tonight—guess I was in a Paris Island mood and you happened to be the beneficiary. I'm glad of that. Very glad. There's no one I respect more, as a man, as an artist. You gotta understand, though, it was a dice-roll thing. Hell, I'm no hero."

"To me you are. And I don't forget such things. But Kyryl—what did you think about *Wolffspit Fifty?*"

"Not much of a likeness."

"To say the least. I felt up there like I cut a motorboat fart on national hookup. But this is Kyryl's way—so intimate with you he's not there at all. I visit his place, I make sure the toilet flushes, if I'm not careful, my turds will be doing a special on 'Saturday Night Live.' Kyryl. No one graduated in his class. No one. And I've seen them all, my hero friend."

"This is just my POV, Mr. Wolff. But Kyryl—he gave you the dago scroogie up there tonight. An airy canary, that's all it was. Sure, I know he does that t'everyone, and they've gotta suck it up 'til the straw goes honk. But not you, you don't."

"Ahhh." Wolff has dressy brows: a muttonchop over each eye. Wetted, they didn't appear so: now, drying, they've come open: a pair of resurrection plants. Wolff will lift them: it is between-friends, confiding. "Kyryl and me, we go back. Like you and my son-in-law, it's too late now for a finicky appetite in friends. What I want to know is how Norton got hold of my piece of living phlegm. I'm not so senile, I don't notice when somebody has an arm down my throat."

"Uh. Norty made summa cum in swift ones. You ask me, some anonymous donor hawked that oyster up. Artificial expectoration, sort of."

"Yah. The same crossed my mind with hobnail boots on. If I needed another fibrillation, I'd ask what he was like in the services. But forget it. I know these barroom loyalties, I wouldn't ask you should snitch on him." Simon is disappointed: he has no such scruple: Norto might kill him, but he'd understand. "I can't kvetch. He's given me two fine grandchildren, my future is insured, a double indemnity. Thank God, they take after my side. His sperm was a tracer bullet, hollow like his head. I lost my own flesh-and-blood son, did you know?"

"I didn't."

"A suicide."

"Jesus. That's awful."

"At age thirteen, yet. Something I can't put a finger on to this day. The pain—the pain is over, it's a long time. I'm not in pain. But, answer me, at thirteen who is so serious-minded to take a suicide?" Wolff will smile: it's father-simple. "I like to think he was a mature boy for his age."

"Do you know anything? I mean, why? Did he leave a note?"

"From camp I made him write a three-pager twice each week. This was his getting back: from death, not even a postcard. Ach—I know—he had headaches."

"Migraine?"

"I could say yes to that. And I have, don't worry. It's easier, migraines. People understand this—pain. But—nu?—I was his biggest headache." Wolff drinks: he has Marilyn down by the throat now. "But not so big. Not so big as that: it couldn't be. It couldn't be. Sure, I expected of him. I was sometimes strict. Is that a wrong thing? He knew I loved him: did this make it better or worse? No. And no again. I won't take all that responsibility. I can't. Carlotta said so, I shouldn't. And I believe her, she never lied to me. The suicide—it's a peculiar Jewish way of clearing things up. We dwell too much. We can see every side of the issue. This is tiring. It's not fear of life, no. I reject that. I won't hear it. Not my Joseph. It's disgust with the thinking process. Not suicide, you know what I mean—menticide. If there is such a word. The brain should just shut up on its harping for a while. He was too fair-minded. He got sick of judging and weighing. Me. Me, he weighed and judged. And others, yes, but after all I was the father. And I'm not easy to put in the scale. I'm too big, I'm too small: I'm a problem. Norty, your friend, he would like to be a son replacement. So he tries to act like Herman Wolff: in the A&P he's putting together a big package deal. You don't impress Leonardo with a fingerpaint. That schmuck, he can't understand—a man doesn't want his son to be himself. Better, he wants, if he's any man at all. Not better in money. Not in Liz Smith or Rona Barrett. But in the heart. Why else did I work, but so my son should have free time for his heart? I'm not deep. Who, on the run, has time for deepness? No, I'm telling you wrong, my hero. I never was, I never could be: I'm a second-rater. A first-class second-rater. But Joe was deep. And out there the rip-tide of it took him away. He thought—I felt his hurt in this, *felt*—he thought I didn't understand him. I didn't. I didn't *want* to. I loved it that way. This child of mystery who was mine. I expected not to understand him, I hoped for it. What? Did I want a Norty Sollivan, tell me? Someone I could see through like eyeglasses? Norty, he knows one thing: he knows better than to hurt my daughter. That day comes, what's left of him you couldn't bait a hook with. She's happy, then I'm happy. I've learned . . . No, I always knew. We were a moment ago talking about money and power. There's one thing counts in this world: blood. The family. I let Norton be family, so long he shouldn't bring a disease home." Why does Simon want to rub his eyebrow? Wolff is silent. His forefinger, inquisitive, will flick at brown and human-alluvial soil: soiling. "What? What? What's this?"

"Ah—"

"Is this shit?"

"Ah—"

"Tell me. Don't hang your mouth open like a moron boxer dog. I asked—is this shit?"

"It's shit, Mr. Wolff."

"It's shit. It's my shit." To leap: the verb made transitive here: his body, that failed in-house operation, is an object: thrown down. "Look, I've been sitting in my own kack, the filth of it. Look, niggers, niggers. Nig-gers! They did this to me." Swatches, pink, are color-tuning, high: on throat and cheek, on temple side: Wolff, at seventy-plus, has blushed. "God, I should wear a diaper suit. It happens. It can happen. They-scared-the-shit-out-of-me. Listen, you, this better not be in Earl Wilson tomorrow." Simon has an answer to that: no answer. He turns aside: a boy, hurt. "Wait. I'm sorry. I didn't mean. I'm just—what? What's the matter with me, is it time for the nursing home? I'm not a coward. It isn't true. I was in Spain fifteen months, I didn't mess my pants. Not even in the farmhouse, not even there, when they came to search. Ach—no wonder it's burning back there. Please, Simon. Give me ten minutes for a shower. Make yourself another shot. Go—down the hall, left-hand door, my living room. Go—it must stink in here. The heart he's worried about. I should take a reading on my asshole instead. Go. Carry your glass and mine."

"Maybe I should—"

"Please. Can't you see when a man is embarrassed? Do what I say."

Slam-dunk: Simon, alone in the living room, goes up and up to score. Physical now: frightened wacky by his huge and absolute success. Again: a full palmprint on the ceiling. Man to man, triple-teamed, keyed on, elbowed, they—*they*—can't contain him. He will go, deadly, to the boards: and rebound. He has rebounded. Simon must find, there should be, someplace—a mirror. Ah, yes. His reflection pokes fun: all teeth, all eyeball, all whore's hello. The chemical bond between face and sense, sound and meaning, is frail as sanity. Like when you repeat a word and he will: carcass, carcass, carcass, carcass, carcass, carcass, carcass, carcass, carcass, carcass: until it has no more significance or intelligent weight than a photon's mad trail. Simon is doing his dance: da-dja, dja, oh, daah—who's afraid of the big bad, big bad, d'ja? "I do believe that is shit, Mr. Wolff. Not to put it coarsely, Mr. Wolff, this is what we in the profession call shit. You're sitting in your own shit, Herman." Next door a shower kicks over, throttles down, accelerates from o to 55 in no time, pulling out. Then, d'ja? The room solicits his consideration: a discreet, a woman's, request. And, for some reason, Simon has been subdued.

It's a room in which the *Lusitania* still floats: and will float: immune. Sssssh, Simon: a hissing shames his rash athletic lark. Well-I'll-be: Simon is: there are six gas jets overhead: each has been scooped in a cut-glass tulip mantel: two high on the long walls, one apiece on the short. This light, more iridescence than illumination, has given bother to his lazy, modern eyes: eyes familiar with the point-blank pupil-closing of raw electric shine. He waits for a lens adjustment. Opposite, in the black marble fireplace—Simon will walk over, drawn—he can see a parlor stove. It swells out, round: torpedo-nosing. The bulge is elegant and delicate: a puzzle of dollhouse-small isinglass windows in wrought-iron mesh. Simon, flame-lover, has to look. Coal burns inside with its conniving, quiet jelly-glow: plasma, not that scatterbrained, on-the-hop blaze of wood. Red can slow him down. Isinglass panes, from coal bed up, take on scarlet, scarlet-orange, orange, orange-yellow, yellow: it will retrace, in his memory, the rose window of Van Lynxx Chapel at dawn. He feels only contact warmth. The room is colored, not lit. It dates from another age when night was still queen of evil, powerful and inconveniencing—as night has been for all but our latest half century. In Wolff's room the compromise time is remembered: when darkness would yield some part of its primeval right: not all: not yet to be a bulb-tricked, synthetic afternoon.

Simon will judge the room, will canvass it: from birth he has lived with and in antiquity, don't forget. Wolff's green carpet, ten by twelve, is diagrammatic: walking, a household frequency, has made it nap-bare in that worn path and this. Burn scarring around the bronze ashstand: CHICAGO EXPOSITION, 1893. A sun bleach beneath the windowsill. Yet there is inaccuracy: four deep sofa-leg dents where now no one can sit. And the main room entrance was someplace else, then, whenever: see, this foot-scuff line heads toward a doorless wall here. Dun linoleum (beyond the rug) is authentic, of proper age, but not of proper place: note kitchen stove prints and a rusty spot that under-sink water ticked off. The furniture is humble mahogany veneer: splintering: nail polish on a corpse. These are true, they have lived together: three straight-back chairs, alike only in their resolute uncomfortableness: a rocker: an end table with wick-down/out kerosene lamp: a griffin-foot chiffonier. It is inconsiderate furniture: body-disciplining stuff. Even the rocker will give no more than four inches forward/back, as though movement in excess were unrefined. A bookcase has dense calf- and morocco-bound volumes, gull-track Hebrew printing on them, alongside and at odds with the profane: *Thus Spake Zarathustra, Youth's Encounter, Imaginary Conversations, Chansons de Bilitis, Das Kapital:* and an edition—letter M gone— of the *American Cyclopedia.* Simon, 1980's man, will immigrate back in time: is reluctant to do so. And on the rocker arm, some woman's thrown shawl: a careful reconstruction of untidiness.

New York *Herald,* late edition: August 15, 1913:

CANAL AT PANAMA OPEN
FIRST VESSEL THROUGH

Simon rubs the paper stock: a day old, he'd hazard: if not hot, then lukewarm off its press. Simon isn't much surprised: this same travel courier, Wolff, has taken him to Barcelona, 1936. A full jar of Lydia Pinkham's Vegetable Compound on the chiffonier. Glossy small change: not one cent over 1912. The mass-made Ingersoll watch still keeps time: but not as Herman Wolff has kept it. Six fresh-cut roses in their crystal bowl. Item for further consideration: are they anachronisms: or rather an endorsement of the perennial in life? Simon stands back. Mauve wallpaper with gold striping. A single ornament hung: *Stag* lithographed *At Bay.* Genial red chintz curtains: why 'chintzy' in the language? Each window has shutters of slatted wood that can—Simon tries—telescope to one quarter their width. Near the exit: a hat rack of elkhorn, one alpaca skullcap gored on it. And below, three steamer trunks that—like Simon—don't know whether they're coming or going: but are prepared.

The photograph album is wing spread out: on a kind of music stand: as if to be sung from. Simon will flip/skim through. All periods have their exclusive physiognomy: these seem a clean and upright people: born unretouched. Men especially provoke Simon: they stare let's-step-outside at him: him, the tentative future of their nation. A non-verbal encounter can vex Simon: he speaks to value and define: for that reason he has no picture of Aldo or Bettina. The faces here are militant, bluff: obstinate in a jaunty, hat-cocked way: photographs not taken: given. Simon recognizes even the infant Wolff, sheepskin-clothed, bald once again. Wolff in jumpy time lapse: at three, five, seven, ten, thirteen. On the photographer's pony, crop held wrong end up: pony's head just drab blurrr, shutter speed too slow for an unrehearsed neigh. Adolescent Wolff beside the Williamsburg Bridge rail: his hands pray a fake dive, cutting up. And there is Wolff II: at least one year older, could be more: preview of Herman, his coming attractions. Same honest toucan-beak nose: same eyebrows most-likely-to-succeed. Simon will find them embraced, Wolff and Wolff II: a composite prison mug shot: Wolff II in profile, Wolff face-ahead. And again, on some unidentified Brooklyn street, they play at workingmen: vast sledgehammers held croquet mallet low. They smirk, but there is a competition, a statement in the pose.

Wolff and Wolff II, by drawing up, have filled their biceps: small men yet spiky, potent, hard. Wolff's back has curved, has arced through the wall poster behind:

OM OUR FACTORY
O YOUR HEAD
AWES
$3.00 HAT
OADWAY
KLYN

Father is done in brilliantine: his head shines: a glaring example of the style. Tense paper collar: tie knot obese and gaudy, like a painted turtle shell: pocket-watch-strung vest with white edging: ivory lion-crest cane: bowler hat held on wrist the way a falcon might be held. His waxy mustache, longhorn-pointed, hooks up: one hand ready, when this photo bosh is over, to screw it tight again. Caught me in time, just leaving: important business. Which business will not, overleaf, include the woman. Mrs. Wolff has been wadded down/into flouncy shirtwaist and then-fashionable (also crippling) hobble skirt. A Caesar salad hat, not that different from her rowdy brown hair. Mrs. Wolff's face hasn't yet been baked: face of Wolff and Wolff II: it looks more feasible on them. The camera, Simon would suppose, is a male stare to Mrs. Wolff: she seems afraid for her unappetizing virtue. Not as afraid, though, as father-grand-father, the rabbi. For him a camera is Gog come to fulfill: eyes have shut against apocalypse. Behind, there are a daffodil, a tulip, a hyacinth in that same crystal bowl, but he has dressed for ever-wily winter. Beard pushes through the burdensome black caftan: a busted horsehair mattress. Plain rope around his waist. One sidelock hangs, one—now-where-did-that-go?—is up/under the fox-fur hat. Simon can whiff domestic trouble here: plain rope and brilliantine. But it's not his place to pry.

Ho. And ha? Simon is stumped. A serious continuity problem over there: the modern chairs. They are hospital-screened off: out of place: not down to date. Twin brown recliners with great orthopedic aptitude, motor-run. Yet, look—queer, no?—both are positioned foot-above-head. And, between, a *fershluggina* barn sale: the mahogany veneer table has been messed with junk. E.g.: What is he bid for one pair of sole-split high button shoes? Or this fine corset (MRS. W. P. RUTHERFORD, MFG.)? How about a samovar? Some wax fruit? Licorice. Cigarettes (TOLSTOY BRAND: black tobacco, cardboard mouthpiece). A—gick—envelope full of human hair locks. ANTISEPTILENE. QUINLAN'S HAIR TONIC. MRS. WINSLOW'S SOOTHING SYRUP FOR CHILDREN TEETH-ING. Torah scrolls the heft of an iron rolling pin. Macassar oil for, uh, your antimacassar. Pickles in a wooden tub of brine. Cigars (GEN-ERAL SHERIDAN). And we have also a box of—no, yes—yes, a box of horse dung: that does it for close inspection. Simon has to think this one over. Jars, more than thirty, unlabeled, of: ointment, polish, fat, soap, jelly, grease, oil, perfume, powder, sauce, cream, general ooze. And a lidded quart pot. Simon, once bitten, unlids. Cold matzoh ball soup. He cracks a hand in/through the old woman skin on top. He will eat, apple style: this was a favorite taste. What can it be like? Never to ask again, Please pass the salt.

"Uph?"

"So, I caught you noshing." Wolff in blue terry cloth: the bathrobe is dilapidated, secondhand from himself. Monogram letters ask HOW?: rhetorical questioning. He has childish slipper socks on: tiger feet. Once again, his cathedral-ceiling eyebrows have closed in.

"I couldn't resist."

"Sure. I can understand. Even an anti-Semite. Before she leaves on Tuesday-Friday my housekeeper makes from the old home recipe. It's cheaper being Chinese, believe me. In a restaurant for kosher food they charge like it was flown in from the book of Exodus. And you can't get butter for the bread. I'll heat it up, you want."

"No. I couldn't really appreciate it. Coupla days ago I burned my mouth to slag. See?" But Simon can't tap Wolff for sympathy. Wolff is closeted with himself: a private audience. He sits sidewise, on one buttock. The rocker, visibly shaken, will complain: it ekes—eeeks—movement out.

"Tum-tum. The plotz is now getting thicker. A little bird flew by in the shower there. Oh, yes. Those two persons of baboon extraction . . . I may yet have a surprise ending for them. I may." Wolff will deliberate: three inches forward, three inches back. "But. But this I'd like to know for sure: did I give up? It isn't crystal clear in my mind. Was I still struggling or was the death wish coming up for air? They say the Jews at Auschwitz, that they walked, shrugging, right to the gas chamber place. Could that be true? And, if true, does it constitute a suicide? First degree or third degree? A self-manslaughter charge? In the law, I have it on the best authority—not that I'm one drop religious, a BLT doesn't make me scream *trayf*, and no one in his right mind should go through life without a lobster thermidor—but in the law a child is not blamed for suicide. He isn't yet of age. They recited the mourner's blessing for Joseph, no questions asked. It was important to Carlotta. Me, I was KO'd and didn't know my head from second base. But—but!—a surprise ending for our friends, the Two Inkspots. With style: some James Bond gizmo. Maybe I should hire a screenwriter, you think?" Simon is casual: so casual he can't move. "Oh, yes. Surprise. No one seated during the last ten minutes."

"How? Did you recognize them?"

"Recognize? I couldn't tell one jig from another if they wore numbers. I notice they're black, that's it."

"Then how?"

"We'll see. Could be I'm jumping to a conclusion."

"No. Tell me. I'm dying t'know."

"Wait. You'll see in a day or so." There is no threat: no irony. Simon breathes. "And I promise, if it should turn out I'm right, you'll be in on the kill."

"Okay, in on the kill. Right." Simon, the Third Inkspot, has sat down: straight-backed. "So. Well. I was snooping around, I hope you don't mind. It's really something here, the newspaper and all, Mr. Wolff."

"Herman. Say Herman. You're to blame I'm still alive and kicking, for which Norty and about seven hundred other people would wish on you a small cancer."

"Herman. Herman. I'll try it, but I don't guarantee immediate results. It's hard for me—just . . . Hell, I'm talking t'Herman Wolff." Simon thumbs himself in the chest: little me. "But, you know, I look at this room and it doesn't seem so unthinkable. No Oscars around. No autographed portrait photos with Ike on the golf course. Love to Herman, from Bubbles Catchdork—that kind of L.A. silt. The furniture is—it's a home. I'm getting at this in a remarkably unoriginal way."

"Sure." Wolff bangs his rocker arm. "Why not? This isn't from the prop department. Genuine. My home on Siegel Street, Williamsburg, Brooklyn, New York. All—almost all—direct from out of storage. Sixty, seventy years old. Some even eighty: the ashstand. And it could last another hundred. Not expensive: Hearn's best bargain stuff. But *made*. With a capital M. You were looking through the album?"

"Yeah."

"So. What'd you think?"

"Think?"

"Give me your impression. As an innocent bypasser. Take those five people—pack them in a four-room railroad flat, of which you're now in the parlor. Not much gelt. Use the imagination."

"Tsuris."

"Go on. You can ask questions. I like being asked questions. I'm the expert on my own life."

"It did strike me that . . . Well, the old gentleman and your dad, they didn't use the same haberdasher."

"Ha. You're not whistling Dixie."

"What did your father do? For a living?"

"You're not the only one. Whole police departments wanted to know that. My father was before his time." Wolff has been cued up: roll it. "He was Meyer Lansky without Miami Beach. A numbers maven before there was any numbers game in town. A rumrunner before Prohibition. A heroin pusher, but there was no heroin around." Wolff is animated: the authoritative edition: and glad of rogue genes. "He was too early. A frustrated man. He foresaw organized crime the way Andrew Carnegie foresaw steel conglomeration. The nation wasn't ready for him. In other words, my father was a small-time crook. He tried hard not to be a greenhorn, he ended up being a tinhorn. He did arrange to get killed in a flashy goy manner. Found—June 6, 1921—rubbed out in a Stutz Bearcat. Before even anyone knew the word 'rubbed out.' My father may have been the first man ever rubbed out. We were eating second-day stale bread soup from the Ravitch bread bakery on Graham Avenue, and my father could afford two bullets in a Stutz Bearcat. It was an American death. But I'll say this—no Irish kids from Devoe Street ever pissed on Herman Wolff. That much my father did for me."

"The rabbi was your mother's father?"

"Yes. From Kiev. For safety he sent my mother and an old aunt here just before the 1905 pogrom. In 1912 my father paid for his passage to New York. He was flush then from forging gutta percha checks or something. It was a big mistake, at least my father thought so. Grandpa was not an image-improver, not for an aspiring American hood. My father went down to meet the barge from Ellis Island—took one look at the old man with fox-fur hat and payess—then he turned around and went home again. He told my mother, there must be a snafu, her father never showed up. The old man was three days lost in New York before a Russian immigrant carpenter read the address and took him here. I mean there. Grandpa had to move into our bed, which meant that Sam, my brother, got the closet. I shared the bed until I was twelve. In the middle of the night he would turn over, and I would dream I was going down for the third time. His beard flipped over me. He slept in his overcoat for fast departures. Sometimes I'd pull up the covers and grab beard instead. He would yell murder and make a commentary on the Zohar—don't ask me what that is. A holy man, but he snored like I was getting a Vibro-Massage. I loved him."

"Sam looks a lot like you. Where is he now?"

"A knife you turn in me. My great sadness. My other great sadness. Sam? I haven't a clue. He left home when he was fifteen. Since, I haven't seen hide or hair. He's alive, he's dead, I don't know. It was the first tragedy of my life. By giving a glance at Sam I could tell what Herman would look like in three years. We were carbon copies. And close. Never a jealous moment. After he left I didn't grow another inch. But then, I ask, why didn't he try to find me? I want him to be alive so there's hope, yet sometimes it's better to think he's dead: that would explain how he could go through life without me. I don't blame him for leaving. He had it to here with the fights. My father beat my mother up. If my grandfather tried to protect, he got it good instead. My mother was never healthy. Her legs gave her trouble, and for a working woman legs are the most important part. Today maybe they could diagnose phlebitis and a cure, but then it was just a nuisance to my father. When Sam left I inherited his bed in the closet between here and the kitchen. The smell of wet boots on a rainy night. It's the kitchen I should have here—and maybe I'll put it together one day. Then, especially in wintertime, it was the kitchen that people lived in. My coal stove over there. A parlor stove we could afford to light up only on special days. But in the kitchen, that was the engine of a railroad flat. You could always get warm there. I came in cold, I made love to the water boiler. A big bear hug."

"Gee. I don't know if I'd be so nostalgic, given the circumstances. That wasn't exactly the Brady Bunch you were living with."

"No. No, but it was me. I knew little Herman Wolff. I knew who I was then. I didn't have to wait for the reviews. And sure—when I was your age I worked like a coolie to put distance between me and a lousy childhood. But look, who escapes his past anyway? More Jews I know waste more energy trying. My father, for the prime example. He actually practiced talking like an Irishman. You are what you were. Face it. Roots. I was doing a Kunta Kinte act long before it was the rage. I preserve them. I built this room right after Joseph died. They're all gone now, even Carlotta, and I'm on my way out. Kyryl is lucky, he still has a mother."

"Lucky? I met Mrs. Kyryl tonight. Her premises have been vacated. She just lays there like a remaindered cookbook. Even the overseas operator couldn't get through. Jeez, if that was my mother, I'd crimp her cord and have Mel Torme sing 'Auld Lang Syne.'"

"No. How can you say such a thing?" Wolff is alarmed: his dismay appears honest. "A human life. His mother. You don't mean that?"

"But she's just laying there, getting intravenous Gatorade. She can't—"

"To your own mother? No, you couldn't do that, could you?" It sounds reproving: it is not a question. Simon, leery now, won't answer. "Huh? Are you supporting euthanasia?"

"Well. How many years in a coma? What's the sense? For what he's got, a taxidermist would be cheaper."

"It. It." Wolff masters his distaste. "Okay. We see different. It's like religion, no sense arguing. So, tell me about yourself. I would like to know how comes about such a tough guy, also an anti-Semit. There may be a connection."

"I'm not anti-Semitic, Mr. Wolff. Herman. That's the third time you've called me that. I don't think it's fair. All you have to go on is—is the hundreds and hundreds of anti-Semitic remarks I've made. Gosh, I mean. That's just circumstantial evidence." Simon has sat forward: in the dock. "How can I explain? Would you believe, I just talk. Tact was an elective in my high school, I took rug hooking instead. I insult people so they remember me: the space rates're cheaper. Those stick figures at Great Ferry, they go around disguised as themselves. Insults, costumes: everybody has his favorite audition tape. But I don't *mean* anything by it. If I meant it, I'd haveta care. And I'm too young for that kinda serious involvement."

"Foo. Admit. The film business is run by a large percentage Jews. You feel discriminated on. A white nigger."

"Ah. Not. No."

"The terrible things you say. I hear from everyone. Shame on you, Simon." Wolff crosses legs: a peekaboo from dark, bosky pubic hair. Simon's glance will flinch away. "A self-destroyer. I've run into your kind fifty times. You want a stone in your throat. So far you haven't come across the man to do it. But you will."

"Are you the man, Mr. Wolff?"

"I tell you—I thought about it once, to be honest. But with all self-destroyers, it's the same. Secretly you'd be happy. I didn't want you should have the pleasure."

"No. No, I wouldn't. I wouldn't be happy." Simon has shaken his head: so fast his jowls also say no: double, double negative. "I don't want t'be self-destroyed. I don't want a big stone in my throat. I want money and power and fame and the love of painted women, just like the next megalomaniac."

"You want to die."

"No. Stop saying that. It's crazy. I don't."

"Believe me, I can tell the signs. Who was Mr. Lynxx? What line of work? He's alive?"

"My father? Dead. A long time now. He was a radio disc jockey. He had the 'Lynxx Good Morning Show' back in the '50's. He replaced commuting husbands in bed. The housecoat and curler set used his voice like a Stim-Vibe."

"Ah. Ah? That Lynxx. Albert, was it?"

"Aldo."

"My wife listened, a regular."

"Oh? She did? I'm sure Aldo didn't replace you."

"Who knows? Don't be so cute-ass. She was a woman. Aldo Lynxx must've raked it in, huh?" Simon performs the disappearing handkerchief trick. Watch closely: pack silk into one crushed palm: nothing up my sleeves: presto: gone. "He didn't leave you money? Or he left to your mother? She's still alive?"

"Dead, too. The money's gone. I spent it on *Clap*, my feature film. A blockbuster that was: like a drug rehabilitation center moving inta Forest Hills. It cleared whole neighborhoods out. All I have now is the family mansion. I'd sell that off, but my mother left it to my uncle, and he left it t'the Park Department or somebody. It dates from the 17th Century. My bedroom is a national treasure."

"You would have sold the family place? Fah. It scrapes me out inside. I just can't understand that. Siegel Street I would have moved stick by stick to where I could be near it. But it was a savings bank branch, all glass and metal, by the time I had a nest egg enough."

"Swell, Herman. For you masochism is the chef's special. I'm an S. My childhood was a one-man massacre: me. In the morning Bettina and Aldo would center-jump t'see who'd give me the daily trauma. It was hard f'them. I was an only child, there wasn't that much t'go around. Bettina wanted t'leave me sexless as a Miss Muffet's Tuffet. With her in charge, I could've cross-fertilized myself. Olympic cheek tests were beyond me. I mean—*naked* I would've been a transvestite. Now Aldo, he had no definite agenda, which was why he usually lost. He just wanted t'take me down a peg or two. Mind now, from birth, I had about five pegs total going for me."

"Still. We don't reject our beginnings. This is the heart of a man's life."

"Herman. Why don't you ask your brother, Sam the Missing? Ask him about Siegel Street."

"Sam? He was young. He was fifteen when he left, I told you that. What did he know?"

"Right. Me and Sam. I don't owe table scraps t'my past. You may not like the handiwork, but you're looking at a self-made person."

"No one is self-made. It's all environment: for good, for bad." Wolff will point: a man choosing volunteers. "You. You wanted love. If not love, attention. You're still trying to make an impression on Mom and Dad. In this industry Jews are Big Daddy. So you throw a tantrum: blue in the face. You talk wise. You want us to punish you."

"Gee. Sounds kinda prefab, Herman, all due respect. Psychoanalysis like that I can get for a nickel and my correct weight besides."

"Well. Freud I'm not. No. I could give you the punishment you want, but I'll do better yet. I'll make you really hate me."

"You couldn't do that."

"Ha. Sure I could. In fact, I will. It's easy. Okay." Wolff smiles. "How much for the film? For a fair shot, how much would you need? Money."

"Aaah-ah."

"Don't try to jew me up and down. Give an honest figure."

"God. I mean. A quarter million at least, but—"

"I'll arrange five hundred thousand."

"I—" Simon is white. His face goes flat, harelipped, like a child's pressing against window glass. He could throw up. And Wolff knows it: nods in recognition: the dreadful fear of fulfillment.

"Not no strings. I'll keep an eye on budget. On the schedule. Think of it as help."

"Mr. Wolff. God. God. Thank you. You'll never regret—"

"I'm regretting already. Listen, one condition. This attention business has to stop. I saw *Clap*—it was silly dreck, we know that. I also saw the shorts. You can be good. You have a brilliant cameraman—what's his name?—and you use him well. But shock, shock, shock. You have to learn about America. It can't be shocked, not since 1956 or so. The only thing shocks an American today is his heating-oil bill. So. Don't push. Bring good people together. Make with confidence. Make an R film I can release. A PG I know better than to ask."

"Her . . ." voice crack ". . . mann." Simon, bolt upright, has bolted up now: on his remote feet. He needs to do: gratitude a charade: first sylla-ble—arms out, Frankenstein lurch, lift, carry, squeeze—sounds like tug, dug, mug . . . *hug*.

"Don't touch me. Away. Fooff."

"This. You can't know. Twice I've sold my blood on Forty-second Street t'pay actors off." And Wolff will think, What's wrong with the mouth?, noticing at last. Simon has that anguish-smile—blown up, puffy, spread apart—of a boxer with his mouthpiece in. Wolff misgives: big men should not look vulnerable, look so.

"Back off. Sit."

"I wanna touch you. Can't I? I'm not good with words. I'm too good that is—inflation. They're like Weimar marks, not much purchasing power left. Hyperbole is my mailing address."

"Sit. With you gratitude means only breakage. Go back. I want to ask a serious question."

"Okay. Okay." Simon has backed, sat. His banana hand snags hair: a sheaf will pull out.

"Tell me, Brontosaur—you believe in God perhaps?"

"Now I do. I'm in the same room with him."

"Terrible. Shut up. What were you born? A Roman?"

"Oh? Oh, Catholic you mean. No. I'm Protestant, I guess."

"That's like a reformed Jew."

"Maybe. Well—I think they were reforming different things."

"You believe in it?"

"Ah, depends what you mean by belief."

"No?"

"No."

"Could be I'm laboring under a mistake. This film of yours—Norty gave me a thumbnail—it's about Jesus Christ? No?"

"Yes. In a sense."

"Sense? It's not an uplift religious picture?"

"There are, oh, some satirical elements, what you'd call. I suppose."

"Hah. Another *Jesus Christ Superschmuck* I need like a busted inlay. That one caused crop failure in the heartlands. People want still to believe. When the blood runs down from Jesus on his cross and Ben Hur's family is cleared up from the leprosy, I weep every time. And Jesus by me is Daffy Duck. But it's a good story. It makes people feel blessed on."

"There's a considerable atheist segment these days, Herman. It's a misdemeanor to say amen in school."

"Did you hear yet of an atheist U.S. President? It's not a platform you run on in America. But, besides the point, listen to what I'm saying: to make a film you should believe."

"I see. And when you make *Black Jack Comes to Coontown* you have a heavy spiritual commitment, is that right?"

"Difference. I don't make films anymore. I arrange them. An artist I don't pretend to be by putting Diana Ross in an adult Western. You're the artist. So what do you believe in, boychik?"

"Hey, Herman—I'm easy. If you don't like the story line just say so. I'll make whatever you want. *Beau Geste* with a scuba scene. *Star Wars* where Luke Skywalker dies of Hodgkin's disease. Nothing's so trite I can't plagiarize it."

"I don't horn in on creative people. I have too much respect."

"Sounds like you're horning in right now, Herman. And be my guest."

"Pay attention, Jew-stomper. Don't get my goat. This is a one-time opportunity to make yourself. It's not just a film. In the movie game, how many at-bats do you get? Already you're o-for-one with men on base. I'm passing out good advice. Do something you care about, not a big lampoon all the time."

"Gosh. I care about myself, Herman, that's about it. A ground swell of public interest in me has not come rolling through the breakwater yet."

"Self. You couldn't manage better than that?"

"I'm being honest. What is this, huh? If I can't bring out the ethnic vote I don't get on the ticket? No money?"

"We're having a quarrel."

"No, we're not. We're best of friends."

"Herman." Wolff has taken himself aside: a word in his own ear. "Herman, don't get involved. This Hitler, again and again he'll march through Skokie."

"No, he won't. Uh-uh. He'll learn to keep his mouth shut."

"Promise only you'll think it over. A story from inside. Something that means to the blue-collar man. Where the self by mistake meets the human in a dark alley. Wrestle with it. Have a showdown. And tomorrow I'll speak to Kyryl."

"Kyryl?" Simon is on guard: quickly unsure. "Why Kyryl?"

"A lot of businesses we go fifty-fifty on. You'll get. You'll get. Meantime you'll think. There's no rush."

"I'll think."

"We have to like each other. Right now we don't even understand."

Wolff croons some more: befriending his insecure heart. Aromatic com-
bustive smells putter around. With a taper of *Daily News* Wolff will lift
flame from gas mantel to kerosene lamp. "Do me a favor. Go sit in the
recliner chair, the one by the wall. Okay?"

"Okay. Okay. You're the boss." Simon is silly: police horses disperse
his mind. Pulled it off: a larceny, grand. Many grand. Walking, he wants
to tiptoe high, tongue out, mouth buffoon wide, as people do who have
gone head to head with violent death and made it away again. The
recliner is obsequious, a body servant: joints and wheels jiggle perfect
recompense for his spine: Simon can't distinguish sitter from sat-on: he
drifts.

"When I was six years old, seven—this was the bogeyman: gas. A
devil, a revengeful God. I don't know how many my classmates in school
it got. We would whisper. 'It's the gas. The gas.' Suicides took wife and
children along, on the family plan. Gas or the influenza."

"Where does the gas come from?"

"A container butane. But let me set the stage. It's fall: late September
like now. After Labor Day, before a Labor Day there was, the old straw
rug that made me hotfoot it across the parlor went into storage. And we
brought out the green. A two-rug family, the cream de la cream."

"You can't go home again. There's a man from the collection agency
waiting. That's what I hear."

"Bah, with the right equipment you can go anywhere. This isn't Bog-
danovich crap nostalgia. This is a science, with chemicals. You should
see some of the things I've done. What am I saying? You saw Barcelona
at Mrs. Armistead's place. A quarter million that set me back—what did
you think?"

"What did I think? In that runabout coffin of yours, I thought I was
cold meat, goom-bye. Next stop the crematorium at Restful Hills and no
charge for export crating. A little pile of ash: I'd be easy t'buy clothes
for." Wolff will laugh. "I didn't need a laxative after that."

"Ha. We had a Ramón once, Chico Gómez was his name. Les, the butler, he wasn't right on tap to open the coffin lid. Gómez went whatever is
crazy in Spanish from claustrophobia. I had to peel off bills to give him a
month in Vermont for some outdoor reassertiveness training. He still
can't call from a closed telephone booth. He's very religious now, wears a
spic picture of Jesus in color and three dimensions around his neck. But
not you, huh?"

"They let me out too soon, I guess. Uh—this rummage sale on the table
here—"

"Hold it. I'm getting something from the kitchen icebox, wait."

"I'll take a cold one, while you're up. Forget the glass." But Wolff, a
wall away, can't hear. This isn't good for Simon: to be alone with quiet
guilt. He likes his sins to be loud and gallery-hung: he must confess:

pride there. "You're short for your height, Herman. And easy to rob—
ssssh. Tinker with the machine, Simon. Tinker. Tinker. Before you end
up with your eleventh finger in a cast." All buttons squeezed, down: the
chair, supple as his own hand, cups him like water: headrest up, footrest
up: Simon shaped into a hammock U. Triple time then: one hip down,
reverse, armrest out, back in, tilt left, tilt right and—damn: he's talking
again. "You're short for your height, Herman. And. Easy. To. Rob."

"What was that you said?" Can't keep Wolff from the door. "I didn't
hear."

"Just childish prattle. Don't give it a moment's thought."

"Elsie Carruthers she was, now Elsie Armistead. It's forty years later
and still she has her boathook in me. Ach. I think this is enough for both
of us, even with all that truck-horse weight on you." Wolff has seen
gaslight through—what could it be?—a large nose-drop bottle. He shakes-
before-using. Gubble-up: the rubber bulb pinched: air balls carom in it.
"I was saying? Martin, yes. Martin Gallagher. She still calls me that, my
name in the Lincoln Brigade. Like father, like son, trying to be a pasteboard Irishman. But then—Simon, you should have known her in Barcelona, a princess, a queen. Mind like a Trac II. You see her now with
fluid on the noggin, a turnip. But back then, in front of her, in her *presence*, I never got a sentence out in one piece. A stammerer. Franco himself could never do that to me. And this is Herman Wolff, the hard heart,
never in over budget. Even now my pulse goes up, ninety, a hundred.
Ramón—" Wolff has screwed the bottle cap off. "Hah. Her big romance
he was, her big false step. I never got a hand on her: it would fall off, I
thought, if I touched even an arm."

"Uh. Yeah."

"You've had a similar experience yet? You're in love?"

"When the bathroom mirror's working."

"Women, I mean, you big honyock. A nice girl."

"They're all nice, Herman. They make my patent pend. But women
don't hold the attention, somehow. For brains they have a sort of large,
articulated ovary. They pall on me, like eating butter straight."

"A woman hater, too. I blame your mother for that."

"Well, I never saw Mrs. Armistead in Barcelona. I wasn't lucky like
you. She seemed pretty alert—also kinda raunchy, for her age and all."

"No. That wasn't Elsie, it was this, the tetradiethylamide acid. She was
using it."

"The tetra-who?"

"Tet for short. Déjà vu in a glass, Kyryl says. Here." Wolff has come
very close. He will hold the nose-drop bottle in an alcoholic's way: protective, semi-sexual, avid. "Sit around. No, all around without totaling
the chair. Put your head where your feet are. This will be an experience

that only twelve or fifteen people have had. Good boy. Head down. I'm going to give you nose drops like a daddy."

"Time out. Are you licensed t'dispense that? I mean—"

"Trust me, Lifesaver, it's good for the inner soul. How much is your weight?"

"Two-fifteen, two-ten. I haven't eaten right since they made burnt norton in my mouth."

"What a load. But four drops each nostril should be enough."

Head down, he's inclined to imagine. As nose-stopped children do: what would it be like to live on the ceiling, to reach up for lamps, to step across door lintels, high thresholds really now, room from room. Wolff has bent down: bifocals set for close work. Ublub: the dropper is full and held up like a match in darkness. Tet seems transparent, but, at bottle center, smudgy iodine-orange murk has come to light. Simon is charmed again by that other person, our upside-down face. Wolff smiles: lower teeth get top billing. His mouth appears to see, Cyclopean. And Simon has thought: how conditional human beauty is: humanness is. We could learn to love this, the chin above, the brows below. Wolff will be gentle: unlike Bettina, who sheathed the dropper deep in Simon's nose and then, point-blank-blam, shot. Wolff closes one nostril kindly: drop, two, three, four.

"It smarts. Nemmmm."

"Don't blow out."

"What'll happen, doctor?"

"You'll see."

"Will I be able t'play the nose harp after this?"

"Shush. Other nostril."

"Ow."

"Stay quiet. In the eye is dangerous. Drip-drop. Drip-drop. Now breathe through the nose only. Gentle."

"Wooooh. Hum. Wooooh."

He has Simon by the nose: tight as an alligator clip. And—what ho? ha!—suddenly each Wolff finger will give a character profile in smell: temperament and talent and what-I-had-for-breakfast last. Blumberg, the windbag snob of a right thumb: Cohn and Feldman, working middle fingers, both heavily wifed. He'd know them anywhere-ere-aiiiiir!—it ohhhpens out, a fortress gate, wide-lens countryside beyond: people with curious accents and habits and tawdry junk for the tourist, him, he who will roadster out in it. And pick up speed: people/odors break against his radiator grill. There is four-dimensionality in them. Simon can smell around, behind. They are layered like mille-feuille. Aromas invert: they do impersonations: they give off a shadow: they age and die. Glistening, instructive labels stuck to them. The whole experience is didactic and over-produced: variety gluts his market. Simon will turn aside. The plastic chair cover is his first-grade oilcloth lunch mat, Mrs. Zito and Mrs. Sand and Nancy Louvis, who lost her eraser stub in one earhole and was an example forever. Simon pinches shut his nose, but there is busywork inside: resident smells: of interesting mucus and pollen specks and blood-exchange in the membrane. He exhales, too informed: dipsomaniacal with it. Creak-ummmmm-up: Wolff is in the second recliner chair.

"Yaaa-um. Whooo."

"Relax."

"Relax? I don't wanna even breathe in. My left armpit just spoke French t'me."

"Don't let it fluster you. You'll get stomach sick. Pick and select, be fussy."

"Ohhhh. Is it starch? I just remembered a girl down my block, Catholic, lace-hanky Irish, from Our Lady of Perpetual Motion or something. One tit developed in the first grade and the other four years later. She had two distinct puberties, and when she was on the rag her mother ironed it. Plus breath like Brewer's yeast. Ack. I'm kissing her and I don't want to."

"Zero in on one at a time. Here. Take this." Simon is given a spatted shoe: some mildew on the instep. "Now put that thing like earphones . . . here, I'll help you. Set it on your temples. I'm also attached by wire. Let your mind follow me. I'll give you a tour. We'll start in the closet, which is my bedroom. You'll enjoy, you'll be surprised. A humid night in Brooklyn—sometimes you smell the ocean, but mostly the stink out of Newtown Creek . . ."

. . . Shabbes end for little Simon: now half awake, now half asleep. In his dark closet/bedroom, there are shoes below and clothing hung just overnose: each item a journal entry for that peculiar people, the Wolffs. It is moist tonight and extra gossipy: rain has come. Father's shoes, sixteen pair—hidden on rent day from Mr. Harrison, landlord—fragrant with Dr. Mallow's Dry Acid Powder for the Elegant Foot. They stand, wooden-tree-ankled, like men in a row behind some dissembler's curtain: anonymous and furtive: men who are all his father at one time or the next. Her shoes, Mother's, wrenched limp with long close guardianship of tumid feet, smelling from inferior polish—nearer black paint—that will run on a wet day: to ink-in between each bare toe. Simon's own canvasy sneakers: resoled by mistake or mischief this afternoon with fresh asphalt, then clacking gravel crust. And Grandfather's shoes, blood-sweet, sawdusty: one whole hour kosher-killed last Thursday discussing texts with Kalmchak, the intelligent ex-Kiev butcher, for general enlightenment and end-of-tongue, three cents, a rabbi special. What one cent means to little Simon now: there is no small change. The aromas kibitz:

they call out and josh one another. Simon listens, smells. He doesn't want to sleep. There is still a taste, a stub of *menukkas Shabbes* left.

Which Sabbath peace his father will gut open soon. Drunk *against* things: against the front door, against the hall table, against the suddenly, spitefully exitless walls. Against him, Simon. Father noise: noise louder, for a child, a son, than popcorn chewed with earplugs in: and as head-private as that. Or, worse, sober: back from some mysterious fourth-rate crime. Too old, the child knows, to be what he still is: a punk. Ting-ting-ting: kitchen sound: into its rusty pan the now middle-aged ice block drips them further toward insolvency. And tick-tick: living-room sound: the gas meter, a second implacable creditor, counts. Screeee of an ungreased, empty-and-heading-home pushcart on Siegel Street. These sounds are in his nose: why should they change nature and lodge up there? Simon will turn on the short cot. His mother's long housework dress has grazed him: in a deft take-off of her loving but somewhat vague brush-caress. Kasha smells on it. And stuffed carp. The virile tang of black bread and calf's-foot jelly for homemade kvass. Kvass that made Simon Haaaaah! breath out and proved his immaturity once again. A hand stinks still from horse dung, major humiliation: gathered on Siegel Street in full sight of everyone, everyone being cute Leah Berg, for Mother's windowsill garden. If truth were told, though Simon wouldn't tell it, not a foul odor: cereal-nutty, more like. Verses from the end-of-Shabbes hymn potter around in his mind. Simon will murmur Hebrew.

At the close of the day of rest,

to sham Grandfather's disappointing girlish treble. Only enormous men, visa and letters patent stamped by God himself, could bless, could vindicate with such an irksome soprano voice.

Deliver thy people
Send us Elijah.

And, of course, he has been sent, you can't deceive a child: Grandfather himself: Elijah-Elisha: right here in Williamsburg: yes, even with that glass-cracking voice. So he doesn't yet make she-bears rend and devour shitmouth Irish children on Devoe Street, to the number of forty-plus: a sordid miracle that would have given Simon rich delight. Play with the payess: go on, Simon, horsey reins: it is allowed. They hairspring up: austere and devout, yet long-suffering with a grandchild. Simon is surprised at their silken, gallant feel. And Grandfather's nose: most certainly a Jewish nose (such articles do exist and should), but Simon—either one—has imprinted himself on it: like some infant leopard on spots: it seems suitable, fine. Touch his small sack of earth from the Holy Land or his old tallith with balding zizith fringe, carried in safety

through pogroms. He is magic, primeval: a season that hauls itself
around again, again. Why else would he refuse to touch her, his own
daughter, when she has become unclean with monthly blood? His eyes
are slow-lidded, micaceous, yellow: Qumran scrolls, too precious and
fragile to unroll. There is not much said between them: the loss in translation can tire and frustrate an old man. One deals with exquisite seman-
tic distinctions: the other with licorice and return bottles found. One,
improbably wise, yet afraid of their dumbwaiter when it will stumble up
tonight, its rope wet as though retrieved from seas. The other, improbably foolish, memorizing a brother who, he knows, will soon leave here.
But now and then, casually, One would say to Other, "Snoresh nishama."
Which, Simon has heard, means "root of the soul." And that, when a free
moment should arise, not before, he should discover it in himself.

Also, this One, this grandfather, is unimpeachably a Jew: clear-cut,
the real McCoy. It's not hard to tell, outward evidence aside: he has
been hit with stones, with gangrenous fruit, with (in winter) iceballs,
and even with a chamber pot full of serious business from sixty feet up.
When walking beside this authentic Hebrew person Simon is, for once,
sheeny-kike-hebe. No more that neighborhood racial puzzler: a "white"
Jew: given fake passport by his hoodlum father, who can, at will, look
exactly, nastily like that Prince Alberted fop on the American Brand
Cigar box lid. Irish kids whistle Sam and Simon through, all-clear: it
demeans, it isn't right. Some thrill of fear should go with being Jewish.
To cross certain streets, terrible Devoe for one, is to enter a psychotic
land where crucifixion and arrow martyrdom are dwelt on from in-
fanthood up. Simon feels unearnest, delinquent, poor in spirit, next to his
tooth-broken and contused Jewish hero friends: and they do not trust
him. They, after all, have gone beyond Siegel Street and McKibben and
Moore and have become, by mere ambulation, killers of Christ:
punched, kidney-kicked, spat on for it: a cathartic contract, clean in
one's mind. Simon, instead—and Sam and Ma and Elijah-Elisha—are
beaten for being Jewish at home: by Father, the American Brand. More
convenient, steps saved, but not conducive, you know, to a strong ethnic
identity. And this is why young Simon misses Sam, left by now. And this
is why young Simon misses any sibling whatever now. To have, as at the
scene of an implausible accident, some witness who will corroborate
their lives.

His blown bubble will gravitate up: pendulous, wary as a pregnant
woman on stairs: gondola of extra soap swaying just underneath. Past
one floor (base hit): past two and three (rounding second, third): past
four, Mr. Chulnik's window (all the way, out of here, home run, roar).
Sam, whose game this is, would have play-by-played it so. The airshaft
can't be much wider than a baseball bat held at child's arm's length.
Here, on December 1, his mother will screw their winter icebox—fruit

crate with tarpaulin cover—into its bracket ledge. Simon is awaiting her call now. He has Sam's work duds on: droopy: torn: cuff over the shoe: it's rent day. Time for their poor routine: the Wolffs are a good buck-fifty out this month. Bubble up: one floor: single: pop: man on first. It's dusky at noon in the close airshaft, but bubbles will float true there. A modest angled skylight has been set six stories up: of stained (with grime) glass and zoo-cage iron bars. Into any Williamsburg airshaft unspeakable things are made to drop: memorabilia of sexual passion and homicide, wet garbage sleaze, once or twice a fetus or something nearer ripeness than that. Simon can't see below, and there is no access in: the windows are one foot by three tall: Sam could only get head and shoulder frame-through. But a stench heaves up, imperial in its way, as though tides had gone out from the seabed that gripped all human corruption at once. Bubble up: pop: out. Yet Simon prefers this to the front window, the action window. He cannot process much data now: the street events that persist, thoughtlessly, without Sam. An ambulance last night, drawn by nurse-white horses, fast enough to cause more business for itself: spark-light flinted up from galloping and the cobblestones. Is there any body, any slight burnt corpse left from a spark? Once, younger still, he had prowled the street for it: none. Bubble up: pop: two down. Simon is in a slump. Bubble up: pop: side out: Sam's turn at bat. Simon will suck the pipe stem: suck soap in. Why can't he taste it? "Simeon!" His call: one minute to show time: he pulls, head and shoulder, in.

Mr. William Henry Harrison, landlord, has gone to his complimentary box seat. Simon and Mom play a stock farce vignette: her arms plead out: his lie around her whopping hips, but one elbow cutely up: to parade the split in his, in Sam's, blue cotton working shirt. Mr. Harrison nods: he has seen it all in rep before and probably better acted to boot: good enough for a one-week extension, no more than that. Simon, in shame, stares away: out the parlor window where, on this September day, he can see seven floors of wash hung, tenement to tenement, mast to mast, a most incredibly rigged ship. Gusts come. The laundry will tack, north-northwest: Williamsburg, with it, is giddy, drunk: three hundred sheets to the wind. And sheets seen through a bedroom door. Her bureau there, his stage: wigs rest, waxy and hard, each on its manikin-head stand. He will talk for them of a rain-dull afternoon, his own, all-female, puppet show. What? Sixty-three, Mr. Harrison. Seven times nine is sixty-three. Finger spool in his hair: a buck-fifty worth of tousling: hard enough to make tears come. And who was ninth President of the U.S.A.? Mr. William Henry Harrison, Mr. William Henry Harrison. Laugh. And where is Des Moines? Iowa, Mr. Harrison. And where is Topeka? Kansas, Mr. Harrison. A tough one, ready? And where is your father? Out working, Mr. Harrison. Laugh: the mean nose moves, shifty and crayfish-jointed. Why does he loathe this man? Fear, surely: this man might put their parlor out onto Siegel Street where all Brooklyn could watch the Wolffs at home. Yet it isn't that: the nose. In his abdomen, in his young but finished racial sense. That fine, thin, delicate: that, yes, *goy* nose. It's repressed: fit but for smallest, snivelly breaths. Effete with interbreeding and deep genetic disease. The recliner chair has squirmed loud under him. Simon wants to spit: a health precaution, not really an affront: he wants—oh, he wants—spit . . .

". . . Mmmmm. Am I—who? Herman?"

"Herman's here—no, stay down. Stay. Getting up quick is a big mistake. The first two, three times you'll fall asleep at the end, don't ask me why, but this is our test experience. I think the mind is disturbed. Afraid. It wants to give the structure of a dream, which at least it can understand. A tolerance, a confidence you have to develop, I guess."

"Whooo. I'm in Madison Square Garden, Doc. Whoo. He hit me with the ring post, it was a lucky punch."

"Groggy like that you'll be. But by tomorrow it'll clear off. Me, I don't even get hung over anymore. Now, listen: your nose will run a couple days, maybe a little blood, too, if you blow hard, but it's nothing to be worried about. So? Well?"

"So. Well. Jesus."

"How was it? Tell me."

"I'm still on the disabled list, pow. Where were we? Which one of us is you, Herman? And why? Christ, I've eaten some strange grains in my life, but that trip belongs in the National Air and Space Museum. I wish I had it on acetate. Christ, I can't remember my own life that well."

"Hah. Don't I know? I could feel you, like an ESP-er. And until this, Bufferin was a drug scene for me. At first I thought, this one—with all his anti-Semit feelings—he's going to fight it. But you didn't. You went along. You don't get afraid, I see that. And someday soon we'll go out your way. We'll sniff around the Lynxx place. There must be wonderful things left in an old house like that. Even the walls, the floors. In fact—if we're going to be partners—I'm insisting on it."

"Fine by me." Simon inhales: the air will go peremptorily down: from nose right to red vein: no devious metabolic transfer, no middlemen in for their cut: he has been opened up. Wolff yawns: jubilant even at 5 A.M. This night he has stupefied someone. We love to influence another life: it's human enough. And, at mid-forehead, in his sea creature primordial third eye, Simon has felt a new sensitiveness: a somehow welcome pain: as when you breathe in on bright below-zero days. His nostril hair is crystalline and stiff. He can't quite settle on an attitude. When the great are at ease with us, when they give you a hitch to Siegel Street, it's tough to separate gratitude and low indebtedness and anger and suspicion-fear. He inhales: thorax split wide, visible, naked, again.

"Better now?"

"Where'd you get that Sine-off, Herman?"

"I shouldn't tell. This also doesn't belong in *National Enquirer.*" Wolff's hair has been shaped by the headrest: a little shelf around his skull. "Kyryl, who else? He makes. It happened like so. Five years back a crazy Swiss chemist came to him with Formula 201. It worked like a dream, but there were certain side effects. One person in three became very myopic all of a sudden. The other two, they tended to weep uncontrollably for about six months. But the idea—Kyryl knows an idea. He set up a professional lab, with twenty assistants, at Ten Great Ferry. It was all hush-hush like the Manhattan Project. And this, what you just had, is it. Formula 955. Now he's trying to get a big merchandising package wrapped up. One or two—well, one—little side effect to get wrinkled out, and he's a millionaire for the five hundredth time over. Can you imagine the possibilities? Never mind street drug sales. Never mind the pusher trade. A little money in FDA hands, and he's got a breakthrough tool for psychoanalysis. Talk about transference on the couch. For the first time a past can be shared. It'll change the world. How many schmucks have said, 'I know how you feel,' which they don't and couldn't care anyhow. You can live Henry Kissinger. You can live Raquel Welch. You could live a Charles Manson. The past of a man is reference material now. Live, not portions-of-this-program-were-previously-taped. The past will be in one common pool, and mankind will never be the same again."

"Gee. That's carrying socialism a bit far, isn't it? Kyryl, huh? I didn't think he was into pharmaceuticals."

"What Kyryl's not into doesn't have windows or a door. By the way, don't drink for a while after. It isn't the safest combination. But, admit—go on, *kveller*—an experience, no?"

"An experience."

"Do you see about Siegel Street?"

"Yeah. But it can't all be reruns. You can't live on old Late, Late Show movies. Being Herman Wolff right now isn't a bent asparagus exactly."

"Pah. I'm uncomfortable. Maybe the trouble is I don't know how to spend money. A Cadillac I got. Some imagination, huh? And women: they want into my pants, but for the American Express card, not my pecker. With one nickel in my pocket I knew what to do. Here." Wolff is offering Simon two sticks of licorice: from a cut-glass jar.

"Not right now."

"Tastes good. Even today."

"Herman. I'll know what t'do with money."

"God help us, you get a little success. You'll go through people like free pretzels in a bar."

"People want to be gone through, Herman."

"No. It's the system. There is in people—well . . . See this. Look."

Wolff has lowered his head: as if to butt. Skin shines in the bald dent. "Touch it. You can sit up now, but don't stand. Touch it." Simon runs his finger around: child finger around a chocolate icing bowl. The surface is deceptive: he can sense give, tenderness beneath Wolff's scalp. "I'm soft up there. Anybody gives you five hundred grand is already soft in the head. But. You know how I come by this? Fifty years ago I was making ends meet with construction work. A girder fell. One side hit me, slam. The man who was working with me—this is on the seventeenth floor of the Sheffield Building in Chicago, which is gone now like I should be— the man with me, it knocked him off. Across the back, crash. This is the last thing I remember. He's falling. Does he shriek? Does he curse God? No, all the way down he's yelling, 'Watch out! Watch out! Look out!' Imagine, so he shouldn't hit someone else and knock them off, too. In the hospital for twelve weeks, I couldn't get over it. I still can't. A man dying who is more worried for other men. This is where we are God-like. Where we are people. Money and power and fame. Excuse me, but fuck it."

"You're a romantic, Herman. The guy was probably in shock, ever think of that? Probably he didn't even know what he was saying. Or maybe he was a lousy conversationalist. Hah. Now me, I could tell a lotta fortunes between the seventeenth floor and blap!"

"So. Still the cynic." Wolff has shrugged. "Listen to me—one last time. I've had it all. Your muscle, your big sex, your energy. And luck. It could go like this. A finger snap."

"I've heard. People die. I still want."

"What do you want?"

"Everything."

"A prick. You'll talk behind my back. Oh, yes—you'll tell them how you *yentzed* big Herman Wolff out of five hundred grand. I'll hear about it. I know it's coming." Wolff has grabbed Simon's wrist. "Don't do it. Not for me. You diminish yourself."

"Look." Simon extends the other hand, his right. "Look, shake."

"Yes? And what is this supposed to mean?"

"It means I'll try not to."

"I'll shake. I suppose it's the best I can expect."

"The best." Simon blows his nose. "Mmmmph. Like I have a head cold. Can't smell at all."

"Oh. Well, that's the Tet. This is the one side effect I was talking about. It'll last a month, six weeks. You won't be able to smell."

"What?" Simon shoots up: a sudden growing: the chair, shocked, searches for his body shape. "What?"

"Careful. You fall on me, they won't be able to find the body for a week."

"Herman. Hold on. Take it slow. Did I—you mean I won't be able t'smell anything at all?"

"No."

"For Christ's sake. I can't taste as it is. Didn't I tell you that? Didn't I? Jesus, what'll I do now?"

"Calm down. A month at most if you don't use Tet again. Me, I haven't had a smell in two years and who could care less? The city is a garbage pit anyhow."

"Oh, shit. Oh, shit. Oh, God—shit . . ."

"What?"

Simon breathes. Air goes into him, characterless, like

III

Lucky

A Screen Treatment

by
Van Lynxx
Simon ~~#####~~

1

The Cast:

                              Fifteen
        Luke "Lucky" Striker. ~~Thirteen~~ years old.
   Let's be frank -- he's fat.
Overweight.^ Lucky has a club foot. Also, a piece of flesh

under his tongue -- a frenum -- that impedes his speech.
   He'd be a wallflower, but he can't afford a wall.
Lucky is friendless, lonesome.^ ~~He~~ Spends his time planting
        vegetables   and two green fingers.
corn and ~~tomatoes~~; he has a green thumb~~.~~^ Lucky has another
                              to play
talent -- he has self-taught himself^the clarinet. Lucky
     phee-nom
is a ~~phenom~~ with the licorice stick. A young Benny Goodman.
                    repulsive.
Lucky should not be ~~ugly~~ Awkward, bashful -- yes. But with
                    Jackie Coogan
an~~otherwise~~ attractive, ~~boyish~~ face. Innocent sexually. He's

so shy, he wouldn't even play with himself -- for fear he'd

be turned down. We like ~~this~~.Lucky.

        Al   A mean
   ~~Hank~~ Striker, Lucky's dad. ~~Hank ugly~~
        The size of a two-door freezer.
son-of-a-bitch.^ Big, with a beer belly
that'd get him turned away at an abortion clinic. Al
~~you could tell the same thing all three ways but he hasn't had it that way~~

has a great patter, he's an~~otherwise~~ auctioneer~~.~~ When he works.
   Al   most of
But ~~Hank~~ spends^his time playing semi-pro baseball,
                              thirty-five
barnstorming around West Virginia. Even at ~~thirty-five~~
Al   still   pro
~~Hank~~ thinks he can^make the pros. A ~~heavy~~ drinker.
  pro Face like a floating   shoe-tongued
A ~~heavy~~ brawler.^ crap game. Club-footed,^Lucky makes him
        Al   vegetables
sick. ~~He~~ thinks music and ~~cold vegetables~~ are faggy.

Betsy   *LUCKY'S*   Betsy

~~Molly~~ Striker, ~~████~~'s mother. ~~Molly~~ looks like a   A1

cracked Southern Belle.   mint julep

~~wood up artsooemee~~   She had ^pretentions before ~~shit~~

          a panned-out

knocked her up. She's ^~~washed out~~ river now.

    hair is   She wears a wig made of something like dog fur

Her ~~███████~~ going. ∧ But despite her scrawny body, she's

    unemployed   with an electric vibrator ^

an ~~██████~~ nymphomaniac.   She masturbates twice a day, ^

so powerful it blows fuses.   clit set

The rest of the time she goes to church. Has her ~~██~~ on

         orgasms by

Rev. Cutter. Bored to ^~~orgasms by~~ Lucky. Long bony

      Stark white make-up.

arms, long fingernails. ∧ Has to take ^in mending to

buy see-through underwear in case she's hit by a pick-up

~~make ends meet a black the Dubois who gets and kicked in~~

truck. Loves to sew up men's crotches. A Blanched Dubois.

~~her face at the beach~~

        Thin, handsome, ascetic-seeming. Wears

   Rev. Hannibal Cutter. ∧ ~~█████████████████████████~~

black in the shower.   gallstone

~~█████~~   A fire and ~~brimstone~~ preacher. Rules the town

~~██~~

like a patriarch. Rev. Cutter is a widower. He has one

                  for taking kick-

daughter. He lost a parish in the big city ^~~████████~~

backs from a pimp for orphanage referrals, ~~████████~~

~~XXXXXHXXWXXXHXXXHXX~~ ∧ The old hypocrite has been holed-up in

        Greasy, probably puts STP

the hills ever since. ∧ ~~█████████~~ on his hair.

Moose-deep   Svengali eyes; hasn't blinked

~~████~~ ^voice. ~~████████████~~   since 1923.

Prays against A1 who thinks Jesus is faggy.

~~██~~ A ~~young~~

John Carradine type.

Merry Cutter, the Rev.'s ~~daughter~~ daughter. A knock-out.
but joyful   Happy breasts that say Hello!
demure, reserved, ^Great legs. Eyes you could skinny-dip in.^
                    seventeen   Slanty cheekbones. Upturned sensual mouth.
Merry is ~~seventeen~~ years old.^ Every boy in town has the hots

for her. She gives them the cold shower. Sings in the
            Genuinely   Yet wise
choir.^ ~~Very~~ religious. ~~Smart~~ and cool. She knows why
                He knows she knows.
Daddy is up in the hills.^ Rev. Cutter is strict with Merry,
                He distrusts really Christian people.
but a little afraid of her.^ A perfect minister's daughter.
            unaffected. ~~█████████████~~
but mature and ~~████████████████████████~~ Merry reads a lot

and loves music. A loner. Ostracized because of her beauty.

As Lucky is ostracized because of his awkwardness.

                Nineteen
    Bram Bolling. ~~seventeen~~ years old. A big bugger.
            prize Holstein way.
Handsome in a ~~hillbilly way~~.^ Cocky, tough. First kid in ~~the~~
    town   A hero because of it. You're
~~neighborhood~~ to get a dose of clap.^ Son of the mayor.
lucky to get the mail in a town this size.
hell-raiser, but in love with Merry. An adolescent

Wallace Beery. Has crushed a lot of beer cans in his life.

    Willie, Lucky's dog. Mutt type. Sensitive. Limps

to make his master feel comfortable.

        hill people-- great show of Adam's apple and
    Various ~~██~~
tobacco spit. Mayor, prissy churchwomen, redneck townsfolk,etc.
~~████████████████~~

4

summer '33

Time and place. It's the ▓▓ of '▓ in Gap, West

                                 Didn't have a first

Virginia. A down and out town. Gap was depressed even

picture show, let alone a last.

before the '29 crash. ^   Clapboard houses, more clap

          So ramshackle the attics have dirt floors

than board. ~~Even the house doesn't have holes in them.~~ Only

The kids can't even afford acne. Only the church and the

rectory are in decent repair.

          Al   just

    ~~####~~ Striker's house is ^across the street from Rev.

                       Al's

Cutter's church. ~~#### #######~~ ~~#####~~ house is

particularly derelict--it could panhandle from winos.

~~##############################~~ Shingles blow off.

                the front lawn.

There is a dry well on ~~the right~~ The grassless earth is

               appliances

cluttered with tires ▬▬▬▬▬▬ furniture--things that Al,

          slick   The front porch hangs like th

conned by his own ^voice, has auctioned off to himself.^ The

jaw of an idiot in thought.

land is rocky, unnourishing. Despite this, Lucky has

                   tall   jump   vacant lot

managed to make fifty ^rows of corn ~~spring~~ up in the ^~~####~~

                                     window

on the right, ~~just~~ opposite the rectory. Lucky's ~~####~~

faces the church. At twilight, as the sun sinks, the cross

                 will reach

on the church steeple ~~#######~~ its shadow, over the ~~####~~

lawn, ~~###############################~~ up the front wall of

Al's

~~######~~ house like a sinister, ~~#####~~ three-fingered hand.

5

Plot break-down:

       Sunday   A sell-out house.
Scene 1.^ The people of Gap are in church.^ The choir is
twanging
~~singing~~, "Oh, what a friend we have in Jee-sus." Lucky
limps-hops   his mother.   built-up
~~comes~~ in with ~~Betty-Striker~~ Lucky has a special^shoe~~s~~.
His walk is ungainly, yet rhythmic; the crippled know about
~~he limps~~^Kids snigger. We C.U. on Merry. She's
walking. a Zeffirelli ingenue. She doesn't snigger.
beautiful,^~~#######~~ Rack fade to Bram, singing in the choir
      Merry.   nude, sensual nape.
behind ~~her~~ He's staring at her^~~nude~~ Lust throws his voice
   he goes suddenly soprano and is embarrassed. Mrs. S'
off-key:^~~###~~
face is parched, as though piety, like puking, dehydrated
~~##############################~~ Rev Cutter unloads a sermon on big
the body.   and hepatitis from tattoo parlors.
city evil -- sex and drink~~s~~^ He rattles the congregation.

An old man swallows his tobacco wad.
                    In the vestibule
   The service is over. ~~#################~~Rev. Cutter
      Al   this time. She wears Battered Wife make-up
                   treated.
asks where^~~###~~ is~~#~~^ Mrs. Striker looks ill-~~#######~~^ Rev.
by Revlon.   He has seen her gauzy under-
Cutter gives suggestive comfort.^ As the Strikers cross the
wear on the washline -- a sort of semaphor. Lucky
dusty main street, ~~############~~ a stone hits ~~Lucky~~ in the
back.
~~#####~~ An eight year-old boy has thrown it. Mrs. Striker

admonishes the boy; then winks. For Lucky it's abuse—as

usual. He walks on with awkward dignity.
               An average day in the life of Lucky Striker.
      Montage. ~~##~~
                       gawky, cheerful
   In the cornfield. Building a^~~#############~~ scarecrow.
      With an apron on. Doing dishes, mopping floors,
   Inside.^ ~~###~~
hanging wash.

Reading aloud. Lucky trying to enunciate more
His tendon-bound
clearly.∧ ~~but the~~ tongue frustrates precise speech.
                              She has a vacuum pump.
     Mrs. Striker cupping Lucky./ ~~she cuts his heart too~~
The blood wells out. Lucky is weak, dizzy afterward.
~~gorged with blood. she has a pump with vacuum cups. she~~
Mrs. Striker is aroused -- her revenge against males.
~~does this every day.~~ She would like to bleed A1; emasculate
him.

     Mrs. Striker is out. Lucky has taken his clarinet
With reverence   wild with improvisatio[n]
from its case.∧ Lucky begins to play. Wonderful music,∧flows

from this sad young boy's heart. (We establish "Lucky's
Theme "   has opened
~~■■■■~~ here.) Across the way a window∧~~opens~~ in the rectory.

Merry is listening. She likes what she hears.

     Between each scene -- gradually, irresistibly the

cross' shadow will approach over the lawn. It wants the

house.

     That night. An old Studebaker makes it's own drive-
Scene 2.∧ ~~night. an old Model A Ford drives up~~. It stops
way across the lawn.   They roll like loose change.
by hitting a stack of tires.∧~~in the street rolled head~~
Al
~~■■~~ Striker falls ~~drunk~~ out. He is el blindo.
He has been driving with a catcher's mitt on and a mask.
~~he has two baseball bats with him. they trip him. he gets~~
He tries to enter the house through an old refrigerator door
~~up.~~ ∧The house door comes off its hinges; he throws it down
in the yard. Mistake.   shivery
the porch steps. ~~Lucky~~ We see Lucky in bed ∧~~he shakes~~
                              kewpie
with fear. We see Mrs. Striker. She's all∧dolled up in

7

We don't want to see through. Her breasts
see-through lingerie. ~~she looks grotesque with her saggy~~
are long dugs. now. Al, no sea-legs, staggers toward
~~breasts all in in in in in in to beard staggering past~~ her door. But,
                                   or
~~HJH~~ on purpose *or* by mistake, he ~~gets his past into Lucky's~~
Striker curses. Catcher's mask still on, Al flops into
~~room in is in streets coming in in in fulls into~~ bed next to
        loops
lucky. He ~~throws~~ a hairy arm around Lucky's neck.
Lucky says ,"Oh!" afraid. A signal. Al takes out a ten
~~probably thinks her in a whorehouse with some more lucky~~
dollar bill and tucks it into Lucky's pajama top. He caresses
~~as frightened in in begins to adore the sounds are~~
his son's chest. As though Lucky had breasts. Al starts to
~~threatening~~
snore. The sounds are a threat.

                                             Al's auctioneer
Scene 3. Morning. We hear, Lucky can hear, ~~HJH is tobacco~~
voice. Al is practising his salespitch by auctioning his
~~auctioneering voice as he practises this goes out for some~~
wife off. No takers. The voice seems to come from their
~~time in in the sound is needless and irritating in in in~~
ancient radio. Now Al swaggers into Lucky's room.
~~comes into Lucky's room. He is handsome, but looks~~

~~debauched~~ he has a black eye and two days growth of beard.
He's full of himself. Tells Lucky about the game; how he
            poor   Then he stops. *seen*   *naked*
spiked some *bastard.* He has ~~####~~ Lucky's ^club foot.
He orders Lucky to put a ~~show~~ *Shoe* on. *as a breeder.* Al
It disgusts him; it reflects on his manhood ~~HJH~~
                                             urges *lucky*
has a present for Lucky. A baseball glove. He ~~takes~~ ^ to
        Al   *cheap cussedness*
lay catch. ~~HJH~~ throws the ball hard, lets his ~~viciousness~~
        The ball hits Lucky all over. His thumb is bent
come out. ~~Lucky gets hit by the ball several times his~~
ack; his wind is knocked out.
~~and is hurt~~. Lucky is game enough. He wants to please his

eye and hand don't have the same sheet music.
father, but ^~~he's a dad very good~~ Al makes savage comments

about corn and clarinets. Al is disgusted.

church
Scene 4. A ^square dance. Lucky is there. ~~with his mother~~
Betsy has forced him
to come. She wants to flirt with Rev. Cutter.
~~Rev. Cutter is there~~ Merry is the main event. She moves

~~like~~ like a young doe. All the boys are after her,
is elusive as light. Not a tease, just closer to the m[...]
but she ^~~figures all there is to do is dance~~ Lucky is ~~very~~ shy.
Yet his good foot keeps perfect time.
He can't dance. ^Bram runs into him, pours apple cider
all over Lucky's
~~his~~ one good shirt. ~~Everybody laughs at him but nobody~~

~~laughs who thinks he can be big time.~~ Merry sees this.
walks
She ~~goes~~ over to Lucky. Merry is radiant. ^She tells him
He thought his
how much she enjoys his clarinet. Lucky is astonished. ^He
playing was a private act.
WORD
is tongue-tied in both senses of the word now. Merry goes
guess
off to dance. We ~~see~~ that Lucky is falling in love. ~~It's~~
It's not her beauty; it's the attention Merry has shown him.
~~Nobody has such feelings to him before.~~ ^Rev. Cutter closes the
The eleventh commandment is Thou Shalt Not Ne[...]
dance with a prayer about the evils of lust. ^Afterward Bra[m]
Merry slops
asks if he can walk Merry home. ^~~She pours~~ apple cider on h[...]
walks away
string tie. She apologizes, ^~~but~~ Everyone knows she did

it on purpose. Bram is mortified. Someone will pay for hi[s]

dripping tie.

             afternoon. Al is
Scene 5. Next ~~day, if it is~~ gone again. Lucky sees his mother
    a strip   bra and panties# Sound of a vibrator buzzing.
performing∧in ~~disgraceful lingerie~~ for her own mirror #
Lights go out; the fuse again.
reflection.∧ Lucky is frightened, distraught. He runs out of

the house with his clarinet to a secret spot in the woods
       local   discursive
near the ~~old~~ swimming hole.   He plays beautiful,∧sad melodies.
                         come down on
Suddenly Bram and his gang of boys and girls ~~find~~ Lucky.
    mock him.   decide to   Lucky flashbacks on his
They ~~make fun~~   They∧strip him for laughs.∧ He is all
half-naked mother.
toneless flab. He tries to hide himself. One girl wants
                    wrestle
to see the club foot. They ~~pull~~ the shoe off. This is the
                 crazed
worst stripping of all. Lucky is ~~crimson~~ with embarrassment.
         girl
He hits ~~one of~~ the ~~girls~~ with his clarinet. Bram disarms
        He snaps
him. ~~and he~~ ~~breaks~~ the clarinet over his knee. Then he

throws Lucky's special shoe in the water. The gang leaves.
               wades into retrieve
Weeping, nude, Lucky ~~retrieves~~ the shoe. It is
heavier than ever,
~~soggy~~∧full of mud.

            has gone   love, solace, but the
Scene 6. Lucky ~~goes~~ home. He wants ~~love, comfort, but no one~~
house is vacant.   spiritbroken,
~~is there.~~ Lucky is ~~heartbroken~~ desperate. Willie licks his
             Outside, Lucky   deep well's edge.
face; it isn't enough. ~~He~~   leans over the∧~~edge of the big~~
         swallowing darkness
~~well.~~ Its∧~~emptiness~~ fascinates him. He drops a stone in;
             well   knots
no sound. Lucky takes the∧rope and ~~ties~~ it around his neck.

10

whimpers, sensing death.
He sends Willie away; Willie ~~#############~~ But Merry has

been watching from her window across the street. She rushes

downstairs, almost knocking her father over. ~~###############~~
                                        sheepish
Lucky is standing on the well edge now. He's ~~###########~~
                  as if it were an eccentric kind of cravat.
when Merry appears. But she ignores the rope,∧ She asks Lucky
        stammers.   Where? Well, someplace.
to play for her. He ~~##########~~ His clarinet is gone.∧ He is

too proud to tell her what happened.~~#######~~
                        Lucky
      Merry is curious. She asks ~~######~~ why he talks so funny.

Well -- there's something wrong with his tongue, but his moth
and father don't   in the cornfield
~~#########~~∧believe in doctors. They sit down ~~################~~
                                          see his tongue.
~~######~~ near Lucky's swell scarecrow. Merry wants to∧~~####~~

Lucky is abashed, but he opens him mouth.
            can see
      Merry ~~####~~ that the tendon under his tongue is too
            headstrong
long. Merry is a ~~############~~ young lady. She says, It look

simple, she'll just cut it for him. Lucky is scared. She
              Secretly she's scared, too.
makes a game out of it.∧Merry gets a pair of scissors, heats
                match flame   She laughs: didn't you
them sterile over a ~~#######~~ Lucky trusts her.∧Trusts her
ever play doctor?
assurance. Carefully she snips the flesh. Lucky is brave
    begins to bleed a lot.
but he ~~############~~   For a moment they're both afraid. The
              slows.
the bleeding ~~######~~ Lucky's tongue is free. He talks wildly

so much to say. They hug and laugh, excited by the adventure

Lucky adores Merry. Willie races around them in lunatic circ

Scene 7. Sunday. Outside church. Bram approaches Merry.
   gives her a rustic, courtly, over-rehearsed
He ~~beats a weak courtly flute~~ compliment. Merry explodes.
   slaps   Then again. Then again.
She ~~hits~~ him. /~~[struck]~~ The parishioners are shocked.

Merry has heard what Bram did to Lucky. Bram backs off.
   murder
He glares∧at Lucky. ~~But Lucky has eyes only for Merry.~~

     Late evening. Al drives in drunk again. Lucky wants
Scene 8. ~~It is the same drunk again that later evening.~~∧
to show him his mouth.
He hits Lucky. Willie tries to protect his young master;
     Al.   Al
he nips ~~[struck]~~ ~~[struck]~~ is furious. He ties a rope around Willie's
   drags   Al
neck, ~~hauls~~ him into the car. Lucky begs. ~~[struck]~~ But ~~[struck]~~

drives off to dump Willie on some unknown road miles away.
                      shoves
Lucky runs to his mother. She ~~pushes~~ him off. She's drunk,
too,   hurries
and in her underwear. Lucky ~~runs~~ to his room. He takes
     Al   ever
everything ~~[struck]~~ has∧given him -- glove, bat, fishing gear --
                   his penknife.
and breaks them, cuts them up with ~~[struck]~~ He falls,
   exhausted by anger,
sobbing,∧on his comfortless bed.

                  razz-ma-tazz   Al's
Scene 9. Morning. We hear the ~~[struck]~~ drone of ~~[struck]~~
    jive.   Al
auction ~~[struck]~~ Lucky is out weeding in the cornfield. ~~[struck]~~
   butchered   ·   fishing He's enormously pissed.
finds the ~~[struck]~~ glove, the broken∧pole. ~~[struck]~~
                 He smashes into daylight.
He takes off his belt. ~~[struck]~~
             He is, as expected, afoot.   hopeless
after Lucky. Lucky runs.∧~~[struck]~~ not too fast∧ He takes~~[struck]~~

sanctuary   Al
behind the frail scarecrow. ~~####~~ screams at him, calls him
a bastard, a queer.   his courage freed by Mer[ry]
~~##########~~ Lucky curses back, his tongue,^~~####~~
               They fan themselves for some reason.
Neighbors walking along the road are horrified.^ Rev. Cutte[r]
in the rectory, opens his window to hear better.
~~##################################~~ Al goes at Lucky right throu[gh]
   straw-stuffed, wiry frame.   The scare-
the scarecrow's ^   He gets tangled in it. ~~######~~
crow grins. Its arms seem alive.   Al
~~#########################~~ Abruptly ~~####~~ is stricken. He
   It hits him like a .375 magnum bullet.
has had a heart attack.^ He drops dead across Lucky's feet.

A black crow flaps up; smaller, smaller; gone.

                              A day to rot meat.
Scene 10. At the graveside. A brutally hot day.^ Black
                              Al.
umbrellas are up. Rev. Cutter eulogizes ~~####~~
Father, husband, provider, churchman.
^He makes overt references to sharper-than-a-serpent's-tooth
                    humiliated before the town.
children. Lucky is ~~#########~~^ Merry is ashamed of her
     Already he has done some heavy consoling with the
father.^~~##~~
Widow Striker.   She has to pull nostril hairs out to
~~#######~~   The Widow Striker is trying to weep.^ The pall
get a decent tear   cardboard suitcase
bearers help lower the coffin in. It's so^~~##############~~
cheap~~##~~   Not nailed, stapled.
the bottom starts to rip out.^ They hurry it down, but not
               Al's   He is barefoot.
fast enough. We see one of ~~######~~ legs drop out.^ Neighbors
Shoes too good to waste.   Al's ballteam is
ignore Lucky. They're commiserating with the widow. ^
there, beershot to a man.
Lucky stand in the graveyeard alone~~#~~ afterward. He is
               Not because Al is dead. Because he's glad Al
conscience-stricken.^ ~~####################################~~
is dead.

13

Two days later

Scene 11. ∧Lucky alone. He watches his mother cross to the
                              pastoral consultation.
rectory. She's not dressed for a ~~religious visit~~ ~~She~~
                   walks   The scarecrow is
~~passes~~ Lucky ~~goes~~ into the cornfield. ~~The destroyed scare-~~
wearing Al's belt.
~~crow seems to be starting a family secret~~ Lucky stands, hidden
          The corn is higher than his head..   with him.
between the rows.∧ He starts. Someone is there# ∧ Merry.
                                            great
She kisses him. This scene must be filmed with∧delicacy.
                        She is silent.┼that's vulnerable,
Merry strips down; slowly, naturally∧ She has a body∧~~of some~~
untouched as new snow.   terrified by her beauty; he doesn't
~~instinct~~ Lucky is ~~mouth drops open~~∧ With a mother's care she
want to see her exposed, assailable.   She calms him.
undresses him. They make love. Afterward, for long
                    Slim foot and club foot.
moments, they lie embraced.∧ Then Merry gets up to show Lucky
                     bought
something. She has ~~bought~~ him a new clarinet. They hold

it, dark and firm#. ~~like a#~~ A sword between their bodies.

                              commotion   Rustling
Scene 12. That night. Lucky hears∧~~a sound~~ outside. ~~A loud~~
loud as storm shook trees.   hobbles
~~Listening there~~ He jumps out of bed. He ~~rushes~~ into the
                                  Moonlit eeriness here.
yard#. ~~limping~~ His corn is going down.∧ ~~Lucky races from side~~
We can't see what's happening.
~~to side~~ The stalks snap and give, they fall. He lunges
from one row to another.
~~four people in the field. In the moonlight he~~ He can't make
                  yells Stop! Stop! Please stop! But when he
anything out. He ~~yells for them to stop. When he rushes~~
rushes   section   is crushed down.
to one side, another ~~area~~ of the crop ~~is destroyed.~~ Finally
                              gutted
he stands helpless, weeping, beside the ~~fallen~~ scarecrow.

14

Scene 13: Morning. Lucky alone in the ~~ruined~~ ravaged cornfield.
He hears something. Rev. Cutter's voice ~~coming~~ howling from the
rectory. ~~The man is wild~~ with ~~anger~~ outrage. He calls

Merry a whore. Lucky hears the sound of whipping. Merry
cries out. Lucky rushes ~~#####~~ toward the rectory, stops. Instead
he gets his clarinet. From the window he begins to play a
~~####################################~~
beautiful, loud improvisation. A melody of braveness and
~~################################~~
friendship. The rectory window slams down. A pane breaks.
~~################################~~
Lucky plays still louder. The clarinet seems to talk.
~~################################~~
Clouds come. The cross's handlike shadow hesitates; then

disappears.

Scene 14: Church. Merry comes ~~#####~~ down the aisle in her choir ~~#~~
She can't walk easily. Her limp is very much like his. Sh~~e~~
~~#########~~ Lucky goes into his pew. ~~#########~~
has been hurt. of his hymnal.
~~######~~ A note falls out#^ He hides it. Rev. Cutter's
He seems apprehensive, tired. Lucky
sermon is ~~#####~~y muted.^ ~~#########~~
sees the scarecrow there. Afterward, in the vestibule, Cutt~~er~~
~~#############################~~
shakes Lucky's hand. He can't let it go. It's as though

wanted Lucky to speak. He ignores the Widow Striker's

clownish coquetry.

Home, Lucky opens the note. He readS. "Meet me at the

big sugar maple on the road to Wheeling. Tonight at midnigh~~t~~
codeword
Pack your things. Don't forget Oscar." Oscar is their ^####

15

for the clarinet. Lucky is thrilled. He dances; the club

foot doesn't seem to cumber him. He begins to put his
           wardrobe into a burlap bag.
pathetic ~~wardrobe into a burlap bag.~~

Scene 15. Midnight. Lucky is waiting by the big sugar
                              afraid.
maple. Merry appears. Lucky is ~~worried~~ She has no suitcase.
                       says
They kiss. Lucky ~~thinks~~ they'd better hurry before the Rev.
                         left.
Cutter finds out she's ~~gone~~   Merry doesn't answer. She hands
                                          New York
Lucky a wad of bills. She tells him to go to ~~the big city~~
               great
and become a∧musician. She can't come with him. Lucky is
dismayed, adamant.
~~He is heartbroken~~∧ He won't go without her. She says he must.
                         No, Lucky says, he's a sick
Her place is with Rev. Cutter.∧ ~~but there's another~~
man. Merry nods. All the more reason. But he beat her.
~~Lucky says she told him the truth about~~∧Yes, because she told him
               and the cornfield.
about Lucky∧ Lucky can't believe it. She says she did

wrong, but she doesn't regret it: it was the most
     Their love-making and the beating for it. Because of
wonderful moment in her life.∧ ~~she's decided to make it~~
that she can understand her father now. Lucky pulls at her.
~~up to her father. Lucky keeps. She tells him to be brave~~
She is disappointed in him. There is a high moral force
strength away. She smiles, serious -- the leaving must be
about her which takes his
for his music, not just a childish elopement. Lucky holds her.

She makes him let go. You see, she says, I've been to bed with
        We don't know whether to believe her; we will
Bram, too. Let me do one thing right in my life.∧ Lucky begins
never know.

16

to stammer; his tongue caught again. No, she says, you're
beyond
~~beyond~~ that now. You're beyond me. She kisses him. She

starts back to town.

Scene 16. Lucky alone. He watches her go. Then he picks
                          an involved, splendid
up the clarinet and plays ~~a mournful~~ goodbye. Crying still,

he begins to walk slowly northward.

END

3

(Read to the tune of "Anvil Chorus"—*allegro ma non troppo* and *con molto* clang.)
Wank! Wank! Wank-wa-*wank!*
Wa—"Hooo!"
Wa—"Hooo!"
Wa-*wank!*
"Hooooo!"
It's Granite Man: gaaaahr. Simon has been wanked up: a coming to, not a ready-on-your-mark arousing. Fingers peel off from their squadron leader thumb. Grease/sweat smearing on the desk top (that Martha Washington didn't-use-but-could-have) has all his left earmarks of a brittle sleep there. Simon is eight-count blotto. He has stood a long graveyard shift in the precincts of his crooked adolescence. He will think up yawning: aaaaah. Contact lenses have been in contact one full day and a half: they mix up something like Bettina's starch-plus-water play paste with the W.C. flush machinery in his eyes. Faah-ning, nnng: true grit, pain. Already he has a new, double corneal scar: two dark Messerschmitts that come at him, come at him, out of the sun. His right leg, listening for a separate reveille, is still asleep down there. Simon busts wind: can't sniff it out, the inner himness: Jesus, depressing, life as an unlisted number. His joints are sclerous, multipully. Rear butt-welded to the Chippendale chair that Martha Washington could have sat on, if she had an air-bag ass. And they wonder why our forefathers were stiff and unbending people. A page of *Lucky* hang-glides down on the first draft. Is it good? Oh, grub-fingery Mammon, make it good. Ha, cancel that order, not good: a good film'll play in-flight on Greyhound buses to Scranton. Make it predictable, trite, formulaic: and perfect in ways like that. Wang! A trouncing headache on top of all this. Wa-wang! No. No, somebody must be doing ironwork in the street outside Van Lynxx Manor.

Wang! Wa-wang!

"Hooo! Enough! My behind is got a puncture. Stop!"

Wa-craaack!

"Don't look down! Don't look down! You're a stranger by me."

What now? From that very window out of which once fifth-grade astronomer Simon, taken by a different star system then, had telespied on Mrs. Yuzica piling into her Spandex girdle—hop, hop, hop: solo sack race against time—he can now see the bony wrecker's truck, its rust-fawn-color hook set to give his beautiful van an Italian bum-boost. NUBAR'S BODY SHOP 781-4110. Jesus a/k/a Christ, are his permafrozen assets gonna be impounded in front of a hydrant, across a driveway entrance, on Mon. in a NO Mon. Wed. Fri. zone? Damn nit-picking slimola bung-shoe cops. But not so. His van door waterfalls up. Someone, Nubar, built in the shape of a Goodwill drop box, has jumped down, holding Minnie's hinge-open modesty ajar: holding also: hand sledge, three chisels (one bent) and an acetylene torch. Minnie is on the tailgate in her suburban morning robe. They haggle: apparently no precedent for this kind of body work, and she didn't get an estimate in advance. Nubar has his principles. For that much he'd just as soon solder her back in. Minnie will settle: three tens, Simon would guess, and enough scrap bronze to cast half a Henry Moore. Simon is done for, down: laughing. Wait'll the no-fault people process this one.

Friday is boning up on Simon: the title role: a formidable, opéra bouffe part. Since midnight, with caricaturist fine-hair trowel, the monkey has been—guess what?—aping this representative gesture, that garnished quirk. For instance: the comely trick Simon has of pushing two fingers up one nostril: of chewing wristbone flesh: of peeling callus strips from his foot ball: a stylish repertoire. Friday is on the toy chest which was brought Sunday afternoon out of Simon's warehoused youth. Past-life therapy: Wolff's advice. Toy soldiers, in battalion strength, web-armpitted, web-crotched from a crummy plastic mold. Old bubble wand, yo-yo, kazoo, top, rubber snake, spark wheel, crayon box left in 1959 sunlight, now one fist-big crayon that will draw sixteen flecky colors together. The toy microphone just-like-Dad's. But his most fertile memorabilia lie on an altar-clothed bureau. Kaleidoscope containing elastic band, paper clip, staple: secretarial equipment: to make a little six-sided workaday rose window. The replica SMALLTOWN, POP. 95 village hobby-built before Simon found out that Lionel had chosen another right-of-way—under Stevie Hoffman's Christmas tree. Six or seven curiosa from that famous model railroad embankment mentioned in Part V. Two condoms, both tipless and graham cracker crumbly, about as prophylactic as hope. An archivist's rich surprise—"Tales from the Crypt" —its comic-book binding sprinkled with snip ends of some forgotten haircut. Was he blonder then? And Tinker Toying, still in an architectural form that had pleased eight-year-old Simon: derivative work: derivative of some other him. But not one item, he notices, that you'd play at *with* other children. Simon doesn't fancy this research: the past is past: Simon has looked toward his future so long now, he's nostalgic for it. Let him be in the present, tense. Simon inhales. The smell of lightning bolted through a narrow heaven: only that. Might have fed his nose coke cut with Polident. A run on the sensual data bank.

And Dick Diver free-floats. A stupid British toy, presented by Uncle Arthur on his mid-'50's visit to New York. Simon will scrunch the bulb: air is thrust into Dick's secret swim bladder, just beneath his also floating ribs. The leaden feet drift up. Dick lies water-bedded in his tank: a psychoanalytical position. The helmet face is blind: ears abstract: all supersonic modern: as though evolved in an environment where things breathe through Micronite and do not speak. Simon sends him another dose of air: enough to keep Dick up, above the plastic treasure chest, above the ever-unfed and goofy barracuda. A state of suspended inanimation.

Friday gossips: the noise you make mouthing around a too-big ice cube: chee-chik. For some reason, since about 5 A.M., he has had this tight and black elastic band on his left upper paw. Friday will too often pluck it: using Martha Washington's perhaps personal goose-quill pen for a plectrum. The sound is monotonous: and not a great tone to mono either: splock! mainly. Simon has had enough of that. He picks up a pencil and his own rubber band. Three, two, one—go: they play-off for the mirror championship: a mimer mimed. Friday will soon seem on edge: he has never swung across so willful, mad and thorough a naked aper. One action—splock! splock! splock!—Chinese boxes of mimicry: looking-glass precision. The loser, they know, both man and animal, is he/it who will first, through foolish creative pride, commit a variation. Splang: Friday, beaten in his own ball park, jerks the black band off: a commission resigned. Simon, king of boredom, is already stooping to collate his . . . um, pediscript: footprints all over it. Who will retype this scratchiest of scratch copies: especially page five with the monkey turd on it? Simon bellpulls his desk lamp off. In one day he has remastered the knack of walking hunchbent, adjustment to extreme attic roof slant. As a teen-ager he only came full upright when three or four blocks from Lynxx Manor. Each of six pencils has been chewed pocky, nothing—we all feel it: throwback to al dente breast feeding—more satisfactory than molar give on a new Eberhard Faber. Simon won't reread: he has a favorable last impression. No sense undeluding himself now. He goes for the window again. Its sill is urinal rim low. And carved there: S.L. LOVES—who? whom? An intransitive verb for him anyhow. Simon can't recall her: whomever, she didn't last the carving. Simon will pee out/onto shingles:

long, thick, hard: urine plays in the gutter, ponging. Simon has never taken a leak. He gives. Gives.

"Still waving your pecker in the wind, huh?" Robert Fischer loafs, in his own sphere of influence, beside the desk. Of late, he has put a close tail on sunlight: his burnt face out-reds the acne: unattractive but voluntary at least. The disfiguring we choose is respected: tattooers and lobe piercers count on that.

"At least I don't lie in bed trying t'unload my own Daisy .22."

"Ha. Brought some coffee. Always thinking of you." Simon will lunge for it: appetite his best thank-you. Robert has lit a half-hour cigar: sixth digit, pointer, distraction, sword, smoke screen, stammer-cover. "Finished? This is it, huh? The five-hundred-grand Jew screw?"

"Ahhhhrrm."

"*Lucky?* Bit obvious, don't you think? *Rocky* and all that?"

"Take your rectalgic fingers off it." Simon is a parapet around the desk: all four sides. "If you knew what I've gone through, Bed Rag. Haven't sat in one place for so long since Mother pinned my diapers t'the crib mattress. Writing is work for people who can retract their legs like a DC-10."

"Sy, old fungus." Cigar blow. "Tell me—no bullpiss—between you and me. Is it good?"

"That, Retentive, is a hymn t'plagiarism. It's a Harlem fence's back room: ideas stolen from every film since *Tillie's Punctured Romance*. They won't have to shoot this one, just splice it. It's exactly what Wolff loves: homespun Americana. Which, with his Eastern European background, he thinks is Dr. Pepper served from a samovar. F'Herman, Johnny Cash is what you use in a pay toilet. We go up from here. We go." Simon's voice has begun to scrape thin, high, sissy for him: short on sleep. But Robert has guessed doubt, and he probes for the soft organ: a slip-up.

"It fuckin' well better be good." Simon will just stare at Robert: ten seconds, another ten. The pace, the intensity are royal: yet impassive: hairy blood threads weave through his vision. Robert has dropped under 98.6° F. "Okay. I'm s-sure it is. Okay."

"Sugar in this?"

"Sugar? Well, no. I thought your taste was gone."

"You thought. Listen, just because I can't taste doesn't mean I wanna be ripped off like a blind newsdealer. I needta bust a glucose cap. I been living on air rations."

"I'll get sugar."

"Next time around, Nematoid."

Simon does the baby-bottle test: coffee spilt on his soft inner wrist. Just right. A postcaution really: what could come after third-degree burning? An honorary degree of burning? Friday, poison tester, has one or two sips first. Robert is nauseated, uck. This sort of thing goes with: wash-fruit-before-eating: hold-scissors-point-down-when-you-walk: and put-paper-on-strange-toilet-seats. Simon, in a management position with his shorthanded staff, the body, will administer coffee down. Right eye watches along cheekbone. Left hand napkins chin. He can't depend on his lower lip to accomplish a fluid-tight seal with the cup rim. Simon is weak. He has lost twenty-one pounds: will miss especially the torpid, important sensation of genitals hung under a blown-out stomach. Friday and he share the dregs. In courteous exchange: handle first. A conspiratorial tease: Robert should sense that: two clever, smirking animals ganged up on him.

"People drink out of that, you know."

"He's a liberal. He doesn't mind."

"The niggerlips on him. Apespit. How can you stand it?"

"Keeps me in touch with middle America."

"Why isn't he with whatsisname? Arf? Alf. How'd he get in here with you?"

"They bused him in. Affirmative action. We need a zebra and three pythons on the payroll, too—otherwise the Feds take away our funding." Simon yawns. His breath is awesome: the opening of a three-month-old mass grave. Robert smokes all around himself.

"Did you work right through? The light here's been on since eight P.M. last night."

"Uh. Nine or ten o'clock this morning the desk came up and hit me on the head. I remember thinking, Is this a nap or a concussion? Couldn't't've kept going that long except for six ampules of Bolt that Larry gave me. Also two bennies, one dex, one crank, and a soft yellow jacket. Also a small, white round thing that may have been a collar stud. Hanh. Had so much speed in me, my heart beat a month in six hours. It was space-bar time and not just on the old Royal non-electric. But she's all there. Needs a few days on bread and water, might be some three-syllable words that haven't reached L.A. yet, where the *Little Golden Dictionary* is on every bookshelf, right next to the P.D.R. God. Pass the cigarette and my Louis Vuitton blindfold. Wolff may be on my team, but he's got seventeen uppuckered cutworms in the Accounts Possible Department that'd play 'Good Night, Irene' if I short them one cliché. This is my first big chance. I can be a multinational failure f'once. Not just a hometown flop. Aaaah. Say—James Wong Goldfarb—whyncha scuff out that Al Capone Perfecto Perfecto for now. I hate t'spoil your look—I know you're camouflaged as a fake stucco aluminum hacienda in Anaheim—but I can't smell and it makes me jealous. Also my eyes are raw as sushi."

"Sure. Sorry. Christola. Five hundred grand. You got five hundred grand from Herman Wolff." Robert ups Simon a kittenish knee in the groin. "Come on, tell me how you did it?"

"Uh-uh. I said already. No."

"Wolff hates you. I gotta know. Why can't you tell me?"

"Because, Pathogen, I wouldn't trust you as far as I could throw my back out."

"Really?" Robert is complimented: these are credentials. "Why?"

"Why? Because I may be smell-less and taste-less, you twisted prawn, but I can still hear." Simon is serious. "Give it up, kid: even I can't imitate myself yet. But I know what I'd do if I were you, and I told me what I know about Herman Wolff."

"Well. Can I read the treatment at least?"

"In here. You don't move from this room. And watch out for page five, there's a rather pointed editorial comment." Robert and *Lucky* chest-flop on the bed. "I see they opened your mother's bulkhead. Was any of the crew left alive?"

"Ha. Yeah. Some scene. It was boff-a-minute. You shoulda been there." Robert cackles. "She was scared shitless, which is good because there was no, like, waste disposal. This dumb Armenian I think he was, Nubar, knew from nothing but fenders. He could hardly speak English: he thought at first it was, ha, it was a new kind of seat belt she'd got stuck in. But Lar said, Well, we can't find anyone under Chastity, Removal of, in the Yellow Pages, so he called the AAA. Lar told them, ha, that there was someone trapped in a very small foreign car. Nubar tried the torch first, but it heated her up so bad she nearly went through the skylight. Larry had to throw water on her. Then Nubar went at it with his chisel. She bounced back three feet every time he whonked her, until she got stuck in a corner. And this jerk-magurk Nubar, he finally got mad. He kept saying, 'Your behind is too good for Nubar, heh. I give your behind a too good.' And whank!" Robert has laughed again. Simon, it isn't fair, he realizes that, will find the laugh repugnant. "Oh. By the way, she'll probably tell you something today, if you see her. I think she wants out. Not too soon for me. With Aunt Rose gone and you up here, she's been acting deadly motherous. A pain I can do without."

"Whadja mean? With Rose gone? Gone where?"

"Um. I didn't wanna disturb you. I mean, not while you were working. What could you do, anyway? She left."

"Left? Rose left me? That chapped udder. For where? For what?"

"We don't know. But it's for keeps, I think. She took all her things, except one pair of sneakers and a lot of dirt on her bedsheet."

"No." Simon has sat. "Rose. Old Rose. Well, I guess she's free, white and about forty-five. But why now? She knew about the Wolff deal. She knew I had backing. Or does she know more about the Wolff deal than I do? Why was she at Kyryl's party? For years I expected her t'leave, but not now. Why? I can't figure it. The reason—I can't put my finger on it.

It's like trying t'find an itch in the folds of your scrotum. Rose. Now. Why?"

"Don't get your bowels in an uproar." Robert has crossed one arm, then the other, behind his head. "We can do without her."

"And I brought her from oblivion to Bayside, Queens. The gratitude. Not to mention the hours and hours it took me t'give her instant gratification. Say, can your mother type?"

"Well. Not with her fingers, they're too fat. She had a high school typing course once and got her pinky caught between the M and the N key. They had to dismantle the whole thing."

"Don then. He's slow, but he's got that special male-squaw fussiness. It'll look like a needlepoint sampler made by Charlotte Brontë when he's finished. I want this thing for presentation tomorrow afternoon at the latest."

"Ah." Robert pounds: gives the pillow his head size. "I've got some more news. Ah. Keep calm. Ah. Don is no longer with us either."

"What! Don't tell me he and Larry went with—"

"Hold your heat, Sy. Lar's still in. Solid. I—well, I guarantee it."

"Wait. Read that transcript back t'me slowly. Now . . . Now. First of all: Don left?" Nod. "For good?" Shrug: nod. "And without Larry?"

"Uh-huh."

"Is everything there? Did he walk out with a brown paper bag shaped like a 400-cube diesel engine? Saint Salvage, Don must've gone over that van like four Puerto Ricans and a lug wrench. Discoroma and KY in the gas tank. Does it run?"

"Sure. Calm down. Nothing's gone. I checked. Just a lot of cowboy tack."

"I don't, do not, understand. Now: now when I've got my chest out t'break the tape—Rose and Don. Don left? Don left Larry. After all those years? For God's sake, Robert, they were an institution in downtown Fag-Ho. They were George Burns and Gracie. They were Dagwood and Blondie. Who'll get custody of the butt-plug set? No, I don't mean that. They cared for each other. It was a mystery: I couldn't analyze it, but I respected it. I did. It was about all the domesticity I've ever known. Was there an argument?"

"Oh—of sorts. You better ask Lar."

"Don'll be back."

"Maybe. I don't think so."

"Is Larry all right?"

"He was doing his hair last I saw."

"Look, was it me? Was it something I did? Said? Does Larry blame me?"

"Nope. Your name didn't even come up."

"Don and Rose. Did they go together?"

"No."

"I can't figure it then."

"Listen, we don't need either of them really. I can do Rose's work. Probably most of Don's. We can hire temp men for the heavy stuff. We'd have to anyway. It's one salary instead of two. You just worry about the creative end."

"I see. You've promoted yourself already. Producer, is that it?"

"Hey. Titles don't matter. I just wanna help."

"As the man said when he cut the guillotine rope."

"If that's the way you feel. If—maybe I better leave, too."

"Forget it. I'm in shock, is all." Simon pumps Dick the Diver up: then himself. "Doesn't reflect well on my charisma, does it? Don and Rose. And Minnie next. Can you type?"

"No. But I'll learn."

"Thanks. Not by tomorrow. Ho—but maybe the broad can."

"Which broad?"

"Yeah. My voice is a little high. A-sleeeeep in the dee-eeep. Some oro-tund love lyrics on wry t'go. Ah-hummmmm. Should I be five hundred grand richer? Or still poor? Of course I could offer t'pay her. But that would cheapen the act. Worse, she might take me up on it."

"Who?"

"Be careful with that. It goes at about fifty grand a page. Plus a beach house in Malibu and a Lear jet and—yeah, a wall-to-wall carpet made of breasts."

"Wait—"

But Simon has pushed off: off the Chinese /\/\/\/ screen that has been alleging: THIS ROOM CLOSED TEMPORARILY FOR RENOVATION. Christmas, he's the lead again: thank you, thank you. The upstairs corridor is packing them in: heavy museum traffic. In particular the Episcopal Women of Grace Church College Point: their monthly Queens historical outing. Simon zips his fly up: OPEN TEMPORARILY FOR RELIEF. They are an earnest picture gallery breed: doubled forward at the hip, every hand held PLEASE DON'T TOUCH behind the back. Simon in armpit-less T-shirt, and jeans that display his still-fat bare right buttock under worn horizontal thread-weavings. History in the unmaking here. Friday has brought up his own rear. He will walk on tip-paw, one long arm held fencer-balance style behind: recapitulating, could be, that un-propitious and scary moment when quadruped first aspired to the biped stars. Or some low fruit.

"See."

"A little monkey, see."

"See."

"Now, isn't that comical?"

"Does he live here, you think?"

"Look, Edith."
"Cute."
"Maybe they have a show."
"See."
"It's part of a show, I bet."
"What?"
"The monkey, there."
"See—ugh."
"He did something, don't step in it."
"Dirty animals. Right on the floor."
"I don't care if they have a show, I'm not going."
"Oh! He fell. Oh. That poor workman fell."
"Call someone! He fell down the stairs. Run!"
"I stepped in it. It had to be me. I stepped in it."
"My God. My God."
"He just fell. Just like that. He fell."
Simon has chuted-the-chute, right leg out, left bent underneath. His arm will happen to lodge in the banister struts: stopped there, saved by elbow room between. Simon can't fathom it all, this sudden six-foot spiral drop: his thinking is frivolous, tranced. Thud a-thud: sound has come in late: like the crack from a distant muzzle flash. Women, Episcopalian and afraid, window-shop into/through his fish-eye lens. He sees them red: a slow and succulent red: blood capillaries have cut off credit to his brain. This was—don't tell anyone on the bowling team—this was a faint. Friday starts to groom in his hair. Simon will try a crab, on palms and heels, stomach bellying up. Yes, he can sit. And anticipation of a half-pleasurable kind, the touchiness that comes before we sneeze, has settled in behind his nose. For this moment Simon is unresponsible: hasn't even the long agenda of desire. Until elbow and kneecap and coccyx rebut his claret aloofness: wow—pain, ombudsman of the body, brings a class action suit. He has to rise: a red woman will help him after the fall. Did-you-drop-this-madam, smiling. But subject and verb are turned around: a Latinism: a slurring. Simon can just walk, legs sailor-spread, through the restored kitchen door.

And now—hanh?—his truant nose is cramping up. The earth must feel such pressure/ache before a new wellspring jets through and out. Simon has sawed his arm across. A gusher: trinket-shiny blood spurts down the arm: spurts, spurts again. And he has been swallowing: Christ, could that be blood, too? Simon vomits up: a gargoyle blast. The stone kitchen floor has caught it: looks Aztec sacrificial. Simon is in shock: no bone marrow can amortize a lavish splurge like this for long. God*dam* Wolff and his magic snot syringe. Simon must find a place to sit and cure himself. He slogs left: into the ground-floor bedroom that Bettina had once used to establish her separate residence at home. And where now Mrs. P sleeps alone. There it is, just the ticket, a two-quart ashtray near her bed. Simon retches, pours: he snivels blood in it. A Tiparillo butt will float up. His pants legs are tight, blood-curdled. Clotting will tie his arm hair together. The coagulation has that much force: can almost pinch. Simon strips her pillowcase away: he will jam it, a bandage pack, against his hemorrhaging face. He is in big trouble, he knows that: something has gone wrong with the PCV system. Wooziness: an unsportsmanlike clip behind the knees. He will lie back and flat—only gentlest breathing now —across the bed. His head is hung over: blood-logged, heavy, down.

This is where he came in: so many times. This was the place of letting. Bettina cupped him here, on her bed, pants open and drawn down to his buttocks' décolletage. Simon will point up: left hand crackly with blood crust. See his friends. It'll take your eye a moment to decode them from the cryptic graining: faces in that oak-knotted beam above. A fish. A girl child. An old man. He is nervous. Thub, thub, thub: right now you could take Simon's pulse from his teeth. Yet weakness seems a good barbiturate high: lazy, expansive, fool-headed: without ambition or resolve. And then, better twenty years late than never, it will hit: why Bettina used the pump. To keep her giant son pale, vein-empty: manageable. He laughs. Simon, SOB, has sudden pride in his mother. Yuh, and some abatement is felt: he can still heal. Simon unsticks the pillowcase dressing. It is transfused: a floppy red-on-white carnation. Cheap, dyed, suitable for American Legion buttonholes. He will inhale: he will exhale: tight fit. All at once, despite—because of—his two-decade-old gripe, slow learner Simon will want a female caring-for. He wire-pulls the telephone from its bedstand, down. To dial red.

"Hello?"

"Isssp. Hi, Silken Quiver. Merry. Isssp. How's the complete physical?"

"Who is this, please? Simon?"

"Isssp. Thought you'd like an obscene phone call. The—isssp—heavy breather went for his emphysema checkup. I'm filling in."

"Simon."

"An ort of him. Issp. About two fingers' worth in a dirty shot glass."

"It doesn't sound like you. Have you got a cold?"

"N'. My nostrils fuller blood. Gotta breathe careful."

"What?"

"My. Nostrils are full of blood."

"Why are your nostrils full of blood?"

"Dun ask me. Issp. Just fell down a flight of stairs—isssp—on every part of me 'cept the nose. Then alla sudden my hoot went in for senseless blood-shed. Wait." He swallows. "Wow. I'm a mess. Lurid is the word. An' I'm still collecting residuals. Long-line bra of blood down there. Christ, Mer, I vomited red all over myself."

"Are you serious?"

239

"Issp. Yuh. It's post-op town in here."

"God. There's something wrong. I could tell. I think when you burned your mouth—I don't know, maybe you burned the sinus tissue. Simon, I've said it before, now listen—you've got to see a doctor."

"Nah. Isssp. In nursery school I played first nosebleed in a quartet that included a kid who could turn black from not breathing and one who hadn't had a bowel movement in three months. The Four Tantrums they called us. Isssp. Who was the other kid? Yeah. Ernie Adams. He could get his eyeballs stuck looking at the bridge of his nose. You had to rap him on the side of the head. Like a TV with flop-over."

"Simon—"

"First day I emptied all over Miss Feinbaum—Baumfein?—Feinbaum . . . Issp. All over her best S. Klein markdown frock. Whoosh. I was a projectile bleeder. She gave me an F in Health Habits, the vindictive old trull."

"Simon—"

"Had a few leg-ups went with it, though. Bigger kids, they're squeamish, never hit me in the face. I could turn a game of dodge ball into what looked like second-degree assault. Of course, like bedwetting, it does not well become the adult man. They say little infantile tics return with cancer and cerebral blowout, is that true? Isssp? What they say? About sudden incontinence and the bizarre discharge?"

"Get a pencil. I've got a number I want you to call."

"Hold it, Cone Tips, I haven't told you—isssp—the good news yet. Dateline, Flat on My Spine: the Comeback Kid has money now. M.O.N.E.Y. Um." Sound of swallowing. "Real money. Five hundred thousand stagflated American dollars. I put a touch on the Ark of the Covenant, and no lightning came down from the Big Penthouse overhead. Herman Wolff, you heard of him? Huh?"

"Of course."

"Herman Wolff is behind me, Mer. Herman Wolff. I've got a Jewish angel, and that's the only kind. You don't think all those serabim and cheruphim in the Bible were Methodists, d'you? Hey. Isssp? Aren't you proud of me?"

"Yes, but—"

"And I've just ransacked North Banality for a four-Kleenex screen treatment. Wrote all night. Dogs and little boys. *Crippled* little boys. Country music and small-town life. All that's real good about America like back roads and taped-over baseballs. And a beautiful girl in it named—guess what?—named Merry. It works. Smooth as, isssp, smooth as walking on railway ties in the pitch dark. I'm a new man, a man of sentiment, and I owe it all t'your tempering influence, you should be ashamed of yourself."

238

"679-3331. You have a pencil? It's Monday. Dr. Gobel has hours from—"

"Goebbels? Marvelous. What's the area code for Argentina?"

"Don't exasperate me. Dr. Gobel is a first-rate internist and a very good friend of my father's. If you call him now—"

"Jussa sec. Issp. I'm flat-out here like green baize on a poker table. In a strange room. I sit up t'look for a pen, it'll start the red carpet treatment going again. My idea is better."

"What idea?"

"Isssp. Give me the number in person. Soon's I knit a nice scab, I want t'see you, Mer."

"See? But is that wise?"

"It's two, two-thirty now. I'll be over at four."

"Here? No. No, you can't come here."

"Why not, dammit?"

"Well. I won't be here, is why. I've got to go out."

"Fubis t'that. Christ, one minute she's the angel of the battlefields, next I gotta call her booking agent before I croak."

"Where are you?"

"At home. At the Manor. Where else?"

"That's about twelve blocks from Francis Lewis Park?"

"Ha. Issp. You looked it up in the phone book, like a high school girl with a case on her shop teacher. You do care."

"Francis Lewis Park, you know it?"

"Sure. When I's thirteen Hughie McCorkle useta pay me twenty-five cents t'hold his pants creased when he went behind the VFW monument with Maureen Flynn. One night he said, 'The damn rubber broke, kid. You just had innercourse with Morry Flynn, isn't that right? She was real hot stuff, wasn't she?—or I'll break your arm. She has a mole on her left tit and I'll pay you ten bucks if she comes up a watermelon and you tell the judge.' That's how I lost my virtue, by home delivery."

"I'll meet you outside the kiddie playground at seven."

"Seven? You'll—I'll need more time than that."

"There's something I have to do. I'm sorry. And anyhow it's better if you rest this afternoon."

"Uhhhh. Say, while you were getting horseback riding lessons and learning whether the asparagus fork went on the left—didja father see to it you took typing? I mean, in case he was suddenly disbarred?"

"I can type."

"Oh, good. That's a happy circumstance. Listen, Lambent One, I've gotta have this treatment ready for presentation tomorrow. Would you mind—?" Silence. "Hello?"

"Shit. That's why you called."

"I knew you'd say yes."

"You're a son of a bitch."

"Funny. I just came to the same conclusion. I'm in my mother's old room."

"Shit."

"Merry. Y'gotta bleep out that language. On you it sounds like a *Hustler* centerfold in the Book of Very Common Prayer."

"Oh, shut up, you pompous prig. All you want is someone you can use. Men, that's all I get from men."

"I bleed for you."

"Shall we end this conversation?"

"No, we shalln't." Silence. "Okay. I'm thinking. I'm analyzing this whole phone scene. I'm being honest. Right?" No answer. "Well, it's about fifty-fifty. Fifty, sure I need someone t'type f'me. But fifty I wanted t'see you. They don't give better odds in a Cuban cockfight. I mean that. I'm laying it out."

"Bullshit."

"Seven o'clock."

"Only if you make an appointment with Dr. Gobel."

"Fine. You're on."

"When?"

"Very soon. I'll know better tonight, how I feel. Ooop-hah! Get off me, you."

"Who is it? Who's there with you?"

"A monkey. I got a monkey on my chest. I thought I shut him outa here."

"That's a new one. Have her type your stupid treatment."

"Her? It's a he-monkey, and he can't type. He helped me write it, but he's not smart enough t'type." Phone background hiss. "A monkey, a pet. A spider monkey. You want me t'put him on, for God's sake?" Further hissing. "What is this? Willya for once make up your attitude? You can't hate me and be jealous at the same time."

"Your nose is bleeding and you're in bed with an ape. And you expect me to believe you."

"Well. There's another thing."

"What? A giraffe?"

"I think I prefer your vulgarity t'your wit. Issp." His silence now.

"What other thing?"

"I've lost my sense of smell."

"What?"

"I can't smell. Don't bother with the Tabu tonight. Look at it this way, it'll save you a fortune in Ban and Scope."

"You've got to go see—"

"All right. Maybe I will. Enough about doctors. Just enough. Right? Two of my staff quit on me today. I've got my big chance, I've got money, and I don't want t'fumble in my own end zone. Time is running out. The ball is flat, it doesn't bounce true anymore."

"I'll see you tonight. But, I think—I think it's just out of curiosity. That's all. And I think it'll be for the last time. You understand what I mean."

"The treatment—it's just nine, ten pages."

"You'll get what you want."

"You won't regret this."

"Shut up."

"Okay." Silence. "Did you hang up?"

"No."

"Good."

"Why?"

"Touch me when I see you. Nothing risqué, just my arm, something. Whatever's to hand."

"What're you talking about?"

"I'll see you. An' for Chrissake don't make me sneeze."

"Goodbye, Simon."

"Right. G'bye, Music Box. Love ya. S'long."

Simon lies there. His body has adjourned: is not in session. And, as usually happens through a period of rest, he will get aroused. Stillness, for Simon, is suggestive. Blank-check desire: something to do in an off moment: maybe you crochet or strip old wood instead. In part this response is Merry: he could dominate her, throw himself over her like an obliterating cloak. He can sense that: it'd require only a dance in the right plumage and one week's full, suave attention. In part this response is Friday, who has—uff—been stepping on his groin. Simon rubs gummy clot off his upper lip, his chin: one-eighth of an inch thick. Nosebreath down to 30 percent efficiency, much silting there. Simon is disturbed, on red alert: his hand sweats blood off. But circulation has done an about-face now. His erect member is trap-set, triggered against the denim crotch. Hanh. Has to be an omen of long life: there are cities of children still in him: death couldn't come for anyone this fecund. He digs heels into the hard mattress: spurs it: gallops it. The bed ridden.

Thought-bulb! A finagle-break here. How about this? How about Merry in for Rose, at a much reduced percentage, of course? His hands begin to soft-sell, waving: Middle Eastern and voluble. Then one will touch the furry blue kick-on slipper underbed. Its open toe is rougey with Siren Scarlet #5 nail polish, Mrs. P's. Simon, restless on his back, plucking, gives the slipper a spot of mange. And, atop her bed table: two Tiparillo packs, two elastic wristbands: a photograph behind them. "Bournemouth, 1947" written on it with green ink faded to opalescing yellow-brown. Simon reaches the photograph down. Handsome in a sergeant-major way: he'll grant her that. Mrs. P has a nurse-length white tennis costume on: the racket—no, make that racquet—is held back-handed and at ready. Her forearm muscles ridge out, firm. And, beside her, leaning left-toe-on-right-instep, a dated, jaunty posture that men no longer affect—as Wolff and Wolff II, at another time, had another jauntiness—leaning beside her is some grade of merchant seaman. There are tattoos across his hand. Shorter than she, but equally nerve-fibered and more dangerous: the face, petal-hidden in lapels of his pea jacket, is secretive, picky, mean. They are a match. Simon is curious: he ought to know this woman, his adversary, better than he does. Pull the bottom drawer out. A set of small wrenches. A can of Copenhagen snuff. An aerosol thing to spray on rapists. A, whazzis?, a diaphragm: old age not contraceptive enough. Friday has stolen it from him: has bitten into its rubber cookie shape until he is cross-eyed with exasperation. Friday will throw: what-can't-be-eaten-is-a-cheat. The diaphragm skims: UFO shape: flight-engineered. To hit the door. Which is opening—cheese it, Simon—now.

"Who's this here? What?"

"Mrs. P. I know you're concerned f'me. But don't worry. I'll recover. I'll beat this thing somehow."

"In *my* room. He's in *my* room."

"Don't panic. Right now I feel like a sea gull sucked up by a 707 jet intake, but I'll be okay."

"I just hope it's nothing trivial, is what I hope. I hope you're dying, but not a ruddy chance of that—no. Get out, Simon. Now."

"Please. Don't do anything I'll regret." Simon has sat up: he counts on the spilt gore, her sight of it, to defray a moral expense. "I've been hemorrhaging. Just my sanguine nature, as Bettina used t'tell me. Issp. A bloody fool, hah? You said that."

"Yes. Oh, right. I see. All over my good Marks and Spencer linen. And the coverlet. You've really mucked it about in here, haven't you?"

"Look, it was accidental. I had no place else t'go. It just came over me. Like I hadda pay a cover charge t'live. Blat and I was the Crimson Tide."

"A sign of syphilis, most like."

"Mrs. P—"

"You've had it, Jack. This is fair warning and more than you've a right to. I've just posted a letter to the Landmarks Commission: destruction of public property, unlawful trespass. Better get along out of here and smartish, too, or there'll be a criminal action and you won't half like it, I promise that."

"Mrs. P. I don't understand: why've you always had it in for me? No one else can resist my acid-forming charm." He grins. But the blood on his teeth will make this seem rapacious, sordid. "It's been almost twenty years since I visited you and Arthur in England. Since I swatted your prize roses off with a cricket bat."

"It won't work, that mincing face. I've got one responsibility and that's to Arthur Gordon. I imagine you know: he reckons you're some blighted revelation. It's made him go all odd. Rather like a nigger native come unstuck at seeing an airship for the first time. Don't know whether to worship it or throw a spear. And I daresay you've been taking sharp advantage, haven't you?"

"Whoa. Run that loop again." Simon laughs, isssping. "This is the first I've heard. If old Flash Gordon thinks he's Juliet of the Spirits—geez, you can't blame me. I don't exactly come on like Jim Jones and his purple Kool-Aid vat."

"I can blame you. I do."

"All right. Never argue with a paranoid. Look, we're packing it in here anyway. I've got money now and a heavy backer: five hundred grand. I'll leave things, including Arthur, just the way I found them—in the 17th Century. Just give me until Wednesday, Thursday t'firm my position up."

"Not good enough, mate. You're out—tonight." Mrs. P leans back against the door. Her forearms are still rugged. One knee has been taped, running back style, under pantihose of a varicose vein shade. Simon can stand. He walks toward her: punchy, blood-thin in the equilibrium. Mrs. P has lit a Tiparillo: his nearness now is un-British. Then American Simon will try physical contact: a light hand on her shoulder: not, you know, allowed.

"Mrs. P—"

"Bugger off, you." She has jolted him: heel of palm, up. Hard to find an unblooded place. The baritone voice will go down: indignation slants her toward maleness. "I loathe the sight of you. You and your whore of a mother. I can see her face there, under that stupid leering phiz. The—the murderess she was."

"Murderess? Isn't that a bit extravagant? Mother had her off days, I know—"

"No. No, you don't know and it's a rotten shame. Off days. Oh, yes."

"What don't I know?"

"What I don't mean to tell you."

"I see. But you wanna. Ever so much. It's hard t'resist, I know the feeling. Like amoebic dysentery. What? Oh, Arthur has sworn you t'silence on the Bible. What is it, you old bladderwort? Huh? Say, whyncha have a sex-change operation and become a woman? Huh? Y'go around like y'just had a horseradish douche."

"It won't do. Not with me. You can't make me angry enough."

"Fine. Then tell me for the sheer vulgar satisfaction. I love gossip. Even about myself. Come on." He pauses: stands easy, at parade rest. "No? Well, who gives a donk, anyhow? Want some bloodballs? They're fun to roll between your fingers. Pleasant as pouring hot water on poison ivy boils. Here."

"Bettina had a child in England, did you know that?" She exhales: the smoke will give her security clearance: set her apart. "Did you?"

"No. No, I didn't. Is that true? When?"

"She was fourteen at the time."

"Fourteen. My God. Mother."

"Yes. A bit forward she was. The child was a girl. Amy."

"You mean. You mean I'm a sibling. A step-sibling." Simon has sat: incomplete bed rest. "Amy. Geez, I have a sister. I can't believe this, no one ever said—does she look like me, the poor kid? Kid? She must be forty, forty-five. And all this time I've been carrying on like your typical, store-bought psychotic only child. But I have a sister? Where is she now?"

"In Brampton-Thetford cemetery."

"Oh. Dead. Oh. Oh, well. Easy come, easy go." But Simon has been deflated: a female him, the possibility of it. "When did she die?"

"I—"

"You've gone this far. Anyway, I'll ask Arthur."

"No. Don't get at him about it. I'll tell you: I had it in mind to from the first. It's been enough for Arthur, seeing you again. He's been worrying at it like a terrier. It's brought her back." Mrs. P in a straight chair: square-set, indifferent as figures at Abu Simbel. "A cot death, that's what they let on it was. But they were lying. Bettina smothered her child, one month old if that. And there's others will tell you the same thing. Others that remember."

"Where did it happen? How? You're raising Mother in my estimation, y'realize that? Unless the whole thing's some old libel from *The Police Gazette*. Huh? Hanh."

"She'd come to London with Arthur. She had to. The Gordons Senior went into a perfect gormless funk, their daughter with child. They lived like a pair of andirons, playing lords of the pathetic manor in a village near Thetford. It wasn't the permissive society then. So Arthur, the blessed fool, took her off—her, all of six months gone and with a soul as black as your hat. To a flat near his first curacy. That was St. Jude's on the Cromwell Road. I was on altar guild then. I was—it was me was the godmother. One of them." This isn't for Simon: cheap smoke takes her away: back. "Cor, it was lunacy, as anyone could predict. A fourteen-year-old and him not there half the day to keep a weather eye cocked. You may have your fun, looking at Arthur now, but he had prospects then. He could preach a fine sermon. And he was a gentleman. But he didn't see it, plain as day, that she had her hat set for him. Bettina was in love with Arthur, her own born flesh. No more than a schoolgirl's morbid crush, but dangerous for that. He—Arthur? He never understood women, not now, not then. I knew her for what she was, first crack. After the confinement, even at the baptism, shoddy affair though it was, even then she made . . . advances, was what we called them then."

"At Arthur. She advanced at Arthur? Just fourteen years old. I can see it now, my mother advancing." Simon is enthralled: child fingertips in his mouth. "Bettina. Oh, Bettina."

"She was a feckless slut. She wasn't the worth of him, not his life. She wasn't worth a dish of suet pudding. I hope they've got her on a rack in hell. She killed that child, to spite him—when he ignored what she was set on. She was jealous of the child. The attention he gave it."

"Yah. But can you be sure? Sounds like the blurb from a Gothic paperback t'me. I mean, I'm with you, I want it all to be true, but—"

"I heard her tell him. Herself, the minx. You forget I go back a long time with your twisted family—too long for what it's cost me. The cot was over there and the dead child on it. She was standing where I am with Arthur. I wasn't further off than you are now when she said it. I tell you she gloated, that's the word for it."

"Bet you were all ears, too. The old sound jack plugged in tight. Hanh. Oh, I don't blame you. No. I'd've been taking color transparencies." Simon strides: bed to door: door to bed. "Christ, this is like seeing the gummy underside of a pew. Could I pad it into *Lucky*? But who would believe? I always thought Mother was just your workaday neurotic, though she did have some spectacular moments. But this. This gives her a kind of stature."

"You, of course, would think that." Mrs. P lights another Tiparillo: as if to nerve-block his presence there. "But that wasn't all, enough as it might be. Arthur protected her. He bloody perjured himself to save her from prison. And what did she do to pay him out?"

"I can't guess. Go on."

"Bettina told everyone she met that Arthur—that he was the child's father."

"Bettina! Let's have a hand for the little lady. Bettina. That must've made St. Jude drop his first name."

"Oh, she was quite the Ancient Mariner about it."

"Did they believe her?"

"Not many would. The bishop came out for Arthur. And the congregation. But it did for him, nonetheless. The rector didn't like the notoriety of it. And the pompous ass was jealous. From that day on Arthur's ambition fagged. I think he felt, Bettina and he, they had the same genes. He could go around the bend like her any day and him a priest. He said, 'I can see myself in her.' I told him he was mad to go on about it—"

"His dark side. Right there and visible in her. Hanh. Like Expressionist art. Who was the real father?"

"Does it signify now? She'd drop her knickers for anyone who was equipped. At the last Arthur had to have her committed. It fell square on him, the Gordons Senior were a dead loss. And it ate at him, the decision —though anybody with two eyes could tell there was nothing else for it. You see, after a while she began to strip off and urinate in public. Bettina was locked away for seven years, until she was nearly twenty-two. Did you know that?"

"No. Mother said she went to private school."

"Private it was. And padded."

"God. I wonder if Aldo knew?"

"Not until too late. Not that he wasn't mad as she, in his own way. You come from diseased seed, Simon."

"Thanks. And you have a nice day, too." Simon dwells. "Amy. There but for the grace of God and quick reflexes went I. How did I ever survive? Well, say what you will, Mother was someone special."

"If a whore is special."

"But incest. Of mortal sins the dingiest. A thing like that takes chutzpah. Incest, wow. Her heart musta been made by Krupp."

"I've told you. She never committed incest."

"But she tried. It's not her fault that Arthur didn't respond. Hey, be fair now. You gotta give her an X for effort at least."

"I don't find this amusing."

"Ah. I get it. Dumb Simon. All along it was staring me right in the face. You were jealous of Bettina."

"What?" She laughs: it isn't well achieved. "Me, jealous? Of a degenerate nymphomaniac? Not bloody likely, I think."

"But you were. She was beautiful, I know that. And Arthur—he may have retreated when she advanced, but . . . But he wanted to. For just one moment maybe. That would've been enough, a moment, with a man of his touchy-pious sensibilities. It shook him. That's what he saw in her. That was his dark side."

"Nonsense."

"And you. You and Arthur. You couldn't compete with Bettina, even mad as she was. You—"

"Well. I think that will do nicely for now. You've had your nasty mind titillated quite enough for one day. Don't want to overdo." Mrs. P scuffs ash from her dress lap. "I'll admit this. I had thought the revelation would give you a bad moment or two. But I see that's not possible. You thrive on the perverted. Like mother, like son. At any rate, I want you out by sundown."

"Tough as a Slim Jim, aren't we? Listen, go easy f'once. Can't you and me come t'some compromise? After all, I've just had a death in the family, so t'speak. Give me two days—"

"Not a bob, mate. You're out tonight, you and that great box of a lorry and the poor idiot Jewess you've got tinned up in it. That Punch and

Judy show this morning with the auto-wrecking gang was a right farce."
"You do keep a lidless eye on things, don't you?" Simon rakes blood off
his neck. "I know why your knee is wrapped. You've been praying in
front of keyholes again."
"Oh, that's not required. Not when one has three flaming faggots at it
all day on the back lawn."
"Three? I only register two. And they don't tend t'breed. Or you mean
me? Is that a snide remark in your, thank God, inimitable style?"
"I wouldn't be surprised, what you'd get up to." She crushes her Tip-
arillo down. "They've proselytized the Jewess's son. I all but stepped on
him, with your pretty blond friend. In the rose garden. Mounted. That's
what he was."
"He? Not Robert? You can't mean Robert?"
"I think I've surprised you again."
"Ha. You're kidding."
"Why should I go to the bother?"
"That's right. Why should you? Wait. Oh! Oh!" Simon tears a passion
and his shirt. "Don. I see it now. That's why Don saddled up. Robert.
Robert! He goes from being a Poor Clare for innocence t'playing Gore
Vidal. I told him. I told him. Two things in life: don't smoke in the
refueling area and don't make a queer jealous."
"Well, that's your lookout. Tonight puts a full stop on your ridiculous
panto."
"Shaddup, you old Gladstone bag. I'm thinking."
"Don't you dare speak to me—"
"Speak? I'll Nair your little goatee off. Get this, you cigar-smoking
bull-dagger, I can peep, too. Couple or five days ago I just happened t'be
out there in the kitchen and who—whom, whoom—should I see giving Alf
the Human Doodle Pad a dry organ grind? I saw you, is whom. So don't
Miss Grundy me, you slaked lime." Simon points. "Ha—silence. At your
advanced age. You can put your diaphragm away, that's like locking the
door after the barn is gone. Hey, don't leave. I just started in."
"No, you're more than finished here. At five o'clock I mean to call the
police." Simon will show her such a vigorous middle finger, up, that his
deltoid muscle rips. The door is open. "Right. By the by, a man called
Herman Fox rang up last night. I spoke to him at length about your ex-
alted opinion of the Jews. He didn't leave a message."
"Fox? Wolff. Wolff! Wolff!" The door has shut: Simon alone. "You—
aaaah, aaah, aaah. Calm. Oh, God up there in the big situation room, tell
me it was a bad connection. Aaah. One local call and she runs up five
hundred grand in message units. Aaah. Aaah. Don't choke, Simon. Call
Wolff back. Be confident. Use him like a woman, just pretend it's Merry.
Relax. Ho, Herman, that was my ninety-four-year-old aunt you just
spoke to. Caught her at a bad moment: in the middle of her electroshock

treatment. Jesus. Dial. Make the hand work, even if it doesn't want to. Finger in the tiny hole. Bettina. Mother. You killed the wrong one, you— shut up and dial, Simon. This is your brain talking to your yellow, hankie- waving central nervous system. God, is this how schizophrenia be- gins? Simon, listen: you can do it, you can make anti-Semitism sound like a bachelor of arts degree from Brandeis. You can say—no, don't rehearse it, improvise. You're best at existential moments. Yeah, but suppose your existential Now is an inconsequential Then? Suppose it's all over? Gee, you can't talk in the first person anymore. You're an omniscient ob- server of yourself. He is: Simon is drowning, he. Leaching out into dark and septic drain fields. Do. Do. Action. Dial. Six. Tick-tick-tick. Good boy. Now five. And three. And oh-seven-oh-seven. Pick up, Herman. Pick up. Hello—?"

"You have reached the office of Herman Wolff. Mr. Wolff isn't availa- ble at present. If you wish to leave a message, just wait for the beep and speak distinctly. Mr. Wolff will return your call as soon as his heavy schedule permits. Thank you for calling." Sssssss. Beep! Simon has hung up.

"You know, you know what—it's time t'run. That's all there is to it, running time. Kill this megalosaur's sick body before it can kill you—run. You and me, once around the block full out and last man in gets the carved curbstone. Hanh. Final chance: hang out the collision mats. If it's cancer or heart, let it come now. Up, you. Dig for home, open her wide. Watch, Wolff. Watch, Herman. The whole block, all four sides, and shove it up your thunder tube. I'll run. I'll run."

Yes, he will, and gangway all. A damburst of running: boulders, tree trunks, drowned small children in it. Out the rear patio door, down the drive, right and north. High on one high-rise balcony some indifferent snare drummer will rattle off tempi to pace his feet. It is not a jog: not a sprint: rather his own slovenly and peculiar, labor-intensive striding out. Clots of blood have been grapeshot from each nostril: but they are dry, dead. North on Van Lynxx Place, east on Thirty-ninth Avenue, south on Bowne Street, west on Thirty-ninth Road and back north on Van Lynxx again—the urban rectangle is almost a quarter mile long, wheeled off al- most a quarter century ago by Joey Genese's bike odometer. Cars are braking: suspicion double-clutches them. The slaughter-on-Thirty-ninth- Avenue red shirt has made Simon seem an emergency. He tears at it, runs ragged: rips, splits the shirt apart: violent as a larval shedding. His chest is arrow-hit: pain flies, steel-tipped, in. The left contact lens has gone blind with sweat, blood, tearfulness. Arms grab space just ahead and haul his body to it: swimmer in an unbuoying element. His throat husks for air. Simon might have masturbated, a better distraction from fears that run relay inside, but pleasure would deform the experience, its clarity: his particular sort of Calvinism. Last corner now, right: his van up ahead. He trots, rib cage staved out, lungs on the surface and done rare. There is a snatching up in thigh, in calf. His head, crazed to faintness, pulses, another muscle. But he has broken its wind, lapped it: death.

Simon mounts the stirrup of his van. All biceps pull: leg-weak, greetings from paraplegia land. Wind will ignite chill on his sweat. The cab door has swung wide, blown. Larry is there, half of him: in the copilot seat, flying nose wheel down on four-karat Acapulco gold. He tweezes at one eyebrow with a brass roach clip. Simon is nauseated: a stitch won't let him consummate full breaths. Larry has shouted now, in silence: the blood on Simon is hallucinatory: a caricature of inner savageness. Hand under knee, Simon babies each leg up. The windshield, sensing his tropical flesh, has begun to mist over. Simon doesn't like being near himself: arms and legs are sultry, little people from Calcutta: he is claustrophobic among them. The door slams: decompression in his ear maze, a steep landing approach: he is almost, pop, deaf. Larry has come forward with a wet cloth. He will root Simon up by the forelock: will draw it and its tractable head back: a position for cutting throats. In someone else this familiarity would have been punched off. Yet Simon is docile: the maternal in Larry. He shivers, but it's from physical release: a touch with, let him hope, no erotic consequence.

"Where is it, Sy? I can't see the cut. Is it in your scalp someplace?"

"No. Hahhh. Get my breath. Issa nosebleed. Hahhhummm. I'm all right now."

"So much blood, from a nosebleed? Is that possible? Your pants are covered. And your sneakers even."

"It was like a neon disco fountain. I coulda used a maxi-pad in each nostril."

"You're not hiding something? A fight with? You didn't meet—?" But curiosity has been overruled. "I mean, like that time we were walking over by the docks on Eleventh Avenue and those three rough-trade types tried to jump me. I thought you'd bleed to death."

"That's the trouble with getting hit on the head. It's tough putting a tourniquet on."

"What did he have—a mace?"

"A thong with a spiked ball on it. And gauntlets. And chain mail. All bought right off the rack at Torquemada's basement. You, Ditz, you hadda laugh at him. Never laugh at a two-hundred-pound, solid-metal ponce."

"I'll never forget that sound. Right behind your ear. Oh, my God."

"What about the look on his face, you remember that? When I just kept coming, arms out, like one of the Undead."

"I remember your face. There wasn't one white place, except the teeth and the eyes. A sheet of blood. It poured off your chin."

"I think, y'know, I think he was more scared of himself than he was of me. Swinging that mother: he'd never done it before, I bet. It was just dress-up macho: a kinda medieval body stocking. I could see him wince when he choncked me. After that, hell, he knew he'd haveta kill me or take what I had t'offer. It was daydreamy—my mind was following me by about thirty seconds—watching his teeth break off while I crammed the ball in his mouth. They were all jagged. Ha. You could've punched a music roll out on what was left of his teeth and it woulda played 'Yankee Doodle Dandy.' Geez, when was that—two years ago? Those were the good old days. Things were, uh, simple then." Larry will scrub the underchin, the throat. Any Adam's apple, pressed down, can bring to mind an aspect of crying: long sobs ache there. Simon might go with that suggestion: sentimental for past violence: the romantic cleanness of it. "You sewed me up tight as a third-hand sacksuit. I still—just feel over my ear—it's fat as a softball seam."

"My hands were shaky. You wouldn't go to the emergency room."

"Fags are supposed t'be neat, I thought."

"We only had the basting needle I was going to use on the turkey. Let's not talk about it anymore."

"This is what I get for defending my date. Love is blind."

"Your skin feels hot."

"I just ran a quarter mile: yours would be, too."

"Run? Why? To kill yourself?"

"How'd you guess? I'm not taking anyone along on this expedition unless they can pack wood."

"Your skin is pale, though. I know you, you get all baby pink when you exercise. But maybe it's loss of blood."

"It's hard work, you genital ambiguity. I wrote all night and listen—your sprinkler system'll go off when you read it. Honest. I've outfilched myself. Lar, dove, this is what I promised you. Remember? So many lies ago?" Simon has opened his two hands: Larry puts one in: it is lost between. "We'll shoot on location. Outdoors. West Virginia. Stark stuff. I know how you love a long tracking shot. You can texture it any way you want. Gold. Blue. Lava Light green. I won't even peek in the viewfinder. Surprise me. It's yours. What? Did you say?"

"No. I'm listening. What's it about?"

"A boy. Hey, is there any blood in my ears?"

"Just a little. Specks."

"Must be the running. Feels like when I was a kid and I had this eardrum the size of a grape. Pressure. And the doctor says, 'Just let me look.' Hanh. 'Just let me look.' I've used that line a thousand times since. Then, gaaaauugh, he poked a four-foot toothpick in my ear. A very special kind of pain: a Sunday-go-to-meeting pain. Which reminds me, guess what Mrs. P stuck in my ear this afternoon?"

"Oh, that. Well, you see—"

"She told me—and she's the sort that'd buy season tickets to an abortion clinic, so you can imagine her profiteer's glee—she told me my mother, Bettina, was a murderess. No less than that. I've always been lucky in my role models. Apparently Mother crib-killed an infant stepsister of mine. Amy, by name. For which she spent seven years in the nutcracker suite of some British prison. Can you imagine?"

"A sister? You? I'm interested." Larry lights up: marijuana packed tight and twisty as a firecracker fuse. "Want some?"

"No."

"A toke. You could use it. You're on an edge."

"No. It isn't real if I can't smell it. Lar, you've got a good focal length for the grotesque, in all these years have you ever picked up pulsars of inherited loopiness in me? Beyond the usual blinks and twitches and chin drool?"

"Oh."

"Whaddya mean, 'Oh'?"

"I'm thinking it over. That kind of 'oh.'" He is looking quite pretty, coy: American blond or blonde. Simon hadn't realized. Larry inhales: he will hand-pump his David Bowie slight chest to help it down. Simon has been put on notice: his friend is happy: even, yes, gay. Simon might rule on this: and find it disloyal.

"Well?"

"You're mad as a March hare, of course. But—in my opinion, hon—it's purely an acquired trait, not inherited. And just a bit theatrical."

"Tell me. Should I be comforted by that assessment?"

"A sister would've been so right for you. You have to be the boy you and the girl you all at once. It isn't easy. I always wanted a sister."

"Back to Numero Uno. Let's not go off on a tangent, huh? And I am the thing from which all tangents go. We've got a crowded agenda: me."

"Well, now. You and I, we're not that different."

"You'd like t'see me in garters and black hose. Seamed yet."

"Why not? Let yourself go."

"Larry. I'm tired. I'm the red-eye special in from Hong Kong. Where's Don, huh?"

"Oh, I just remembered, a note came for you. By messenger. Right to the van."

"Don't change the subject. Where's Don?"

"He. God, I've been dreading this. That's why—" He puffs: why.

"So?"

"Don't cross-examine. He left."

"Sit down. Sit there and don't move. Warning: travelers' advisory. I wanna know all the off-screen details."

"Oh gosh. This is awful. You won't believe it."

"Yes, I will. Where the genderless gather, any kind of gamahuching is possible. I hate having t'deal with the limp and the wet."

"Oh, I agree. Oh, yes. Believe me, Sy, I feel just the way you do. We're a driven species. That stupid Thomas Jefferson and his pursuit of happiness. It isn't an inalienable right, it's an inalienable nuisance."

"Let's forget constitutional law for the moment, huh? Open up, you mental preemie."

"Sy. I really, really didn't think I had it in me, at my age. I'm so *set* in my ways. I'm so middle class, so middle America. As the French say, bourgeois gay." Larry holds breath. "I'm in love."

"Uh-huh. Just what we need. You seduced a sixteen-year-old boy. That's statutory breech-loading. They'll have you up on a bum rap, his bum. Fifteen years to life in Attica, whichever comes first."

"Oh? Oh. But he wouldn't." Larry shows an acute, hurt, profile: charming.

"What about Minnie? Or, better, Mr. Minnie?"

"I didn't think of that. Am I in trouble?"

"Worse yet, you played rumble seat in front of Mrs. P. And she just gave me 'til five t'wrap myself in a magic cape and disappear. Worse on worse, Wolff called here and she read him a hangnail sketch of Who's Who in anti-Jew. My entry ran t'ten pages. You just had yourself a five-hundred-grand piece of unconsenting tail. Unless I can convince Wolff he dialed the PLO information office by mistake. Christ, I'm gonna need the whole ways and means committee."

"Wait. *Wait.*"

"I'm waiting. So, Robert? How many passenger miles've you run up on him?"

"Sy, you know me. I'm so passive. Always a bottom, never a top. I eat ten Valium 5's a day. I'd never seduce anyone. I couldn't find them to seduce them. Oh, God. I don't want to give you the wrong impression of Bobby, but—"

"Bobby. It's Bobby now."

"He came into my bunk, Sy. Just like that. We were both surprised. And so tentative, and so apologetic. But after that it was all moss and little yellow flowers."

"I'll kneecap him. I'll elbowcap him. Have you got triple vision? He looks like a Hassidic chinchilla."

"Well, now. Now, that's not true. His body is glossy smooth. And he's so young. I have to teach him everything." Larry hugs himself: competition for Robert there. "Don never listened to me. What Texan can listen? But this is different. And Bobby loves me. Really, his enthusiasm for me is infectious. He makes me love me. I know I'm only thirty-two, and it's early for a mid-life crisis, but he said—and it's true—that Don didn't respect me. We weren't an item, we were a habit. It is true. Don made me have colitis. He was jealous all the time, but he didn't really care."

"No, Lar. Don loved you."

"You're trying to make me feel guilty. That isn't fair."

"Look. I'll confess—Don was about as much fun as a twelve-gauge clyster. But that's because we made him feel insecure. You—you're gorgeous. He couldn't keep up. He had the charisma of a Harold Stassen. Me, I treated him like a church kneeler. Yet—face up—you two made it together for a long time: I admired that. Geez, another blow t'the nuclear family. I mean, Don was totally untrustworthy, but it was a predictable untrustworthiness—which is as close t'honesty as any of us will ever come. On the other hand, Robert—" Simon whistles an unmemorable tune. "Well. Don loved you. And—frankly, Lar—at times you can be a one-child day care center."

"All right. You've made me feel bad enough. He loved me, I suppose. And I—there were good times. But this is better for both of us."

"Yeah? And what about poor me? Where'm I gonna get such cheap labor again? I know. Maybe I'll pick up one of those dominance magazines. 'Submissive male loves severe B and D, will be your live-in maid.' Of course we'd have t'whip him off and on, and that's always an annoyance, but it's hard t'get a good underling these days." Simon with his leg up on the dashboard: feeling full of breath again. "And ten gets you a hundred we haven't heard the last drawl from Don. Uh-uh, puffs of smoke'll be rising from the grassy knoll. Some morning we'll find the van up on milk-bottle crates, all ten tires gone and an anaconda under the hood. I can't believe it. You mean t'tell me he gave up his drilling rights without a Jack Wrangler tantrum?"

"No. There was a dreadful scene. We screamed and screamed: it was two hours of uninterrupted Verdi. Then he broke down and wept. That was just too grim. And then, when I went to give him the ring back—talk about dramatic gestures—it just wouldn't budge off my finger. I had to use soap. I'm sorry for that—the tackiness of it all. But I didn't plan. It was spontaneous. I never thought I'd have the courage or the energy."

"Glad I wasn't the official scorer at that event. Typical. Look for this display wherever bent chanteuses meet."

"But I'm very happy now. I called in to quit the beauty parlor. I've been singing old Neil Sedaka songs all morning." He falls, to the left: being silly: his head on Simon's lap.

"Fool. We may need that money yet." Simon leans forward: writes DEATH in the windshield mist.

"Oh don't throw one of your fits, Sy. You haven't worked at Niko's since last Monday."

"Well. I've been sick. Not as sick as I am now, though. You and Robert, what a double-decker that is."

"And whatever you do, don't talk common sense to me. Mmm. You taste of hunky sweat."

"Don't mention that, huh? Jesus, at least I'll never taste defeat." Simon, thumb and forefinger an old curling iron, plays in the mild blond hair. "But don't underestimate young Mr. Fischer—I advise you. He reminds me of someone these days."

"Yes, isn't it cute? I know Bobby's a little conniver. But he's so transparent about it. I promised to teach him. To let him be my apprentice. But I would have anyhow. Honest. I didn't buy him. And he's not just using me. Sy?"

"Uh?"

"Is there a chance for us? How long do you think it can last?"

"About as long as a Greyhound rest stop. Declare a mistrial now, Lar. Be smart."

"There's the age difference. I can't take him anyplace. But I don't have to think about that yet. And we'll be working soon."

"Minnie hasta think about it."

"Oh fish. I am upset about her. She knows. This isn't exactly a four-bedroom apartment. And she wants to tell you something. It's about us, I guess. No matter what she says, you won't try to make him leave? Say you won't. Poor thing, I like her so much and she's so sore. That ghastly Nubar hit her like she was a crankcase or something. Please defend me. Us. I can't bring it up. But you understand. You and I, we're such strange people."

"Aren't we? God knows—I'm all action, yet I never seem t'do anything, it all happens to me. Ah—this scene from *La Bohème*—could it have had anything t'do with Rose? Her leaving. Is there another confession you want t'make? Look me in the eye, Lar. Come on, closer: I wanna do some iridology."

"Sy, I haven't the tiniest. That just floored me. In fact, she left before Don and I—the day before. Saturday evening. Bobby . . . he wouldn't have done what he did if Rose was around. She hated him. She just wouldn't leave him in peace. But why she left—it escapes me. You can see—everything's gone. Minnie and I and Bobby and Don were out seeing a revival of *400 Blows*. I don't know who'll dye her hair now."

"Rose. My Rose. I'm more afraid of her than I am of Don. She doesn't move, she metastasizes. The minute I met her I felt like a fly in a pitcher plant. Hanh. Even her orgasms, she practiced them in an elocution class. Think, Simon. Why? Why this minute? No. Like King Kong said to Fay Wray, It just doesn't fit. Now? Now of all times? She knew I'd boosted Herman's pocketbook—" Simon has Larry by the neck: playfully: yet it reminds him, this unarmored connecting thing of skin, with what casual pressure he could kill another man. "You. Did she offer something a shegetz cowboy like you couldn't refuse? Does she have a property, and

I don't mean in the Catskills? Are you leaving next? Come on: I recall
a day and so do you. Andy Rabin wanted her t'manage a unit on *Night
of the Martian Lizards*. But only if she brought you along. The time I
made a three-cushion bank shot with her head and she went through
the canvas sink back there. Speak t'me, Lar. Lemme test it on the voice
stress analyzer."

"You're on the wrong track, Sy. There was nothing like that. Trust me.
She just left."

"Hum. And Don. What about him? Rose and him? Was a Morse lamp
seen blinking on the water at night? Had they learned new bridge conventions? One No Simon. Two Clubs. Four No Simon. Game and rubber."

"That's not why Don left. I'm sure of it. I'd bet my life on it. I know
Don. And Rose—believe me—she was never the least interested in Andy
Rabin and his reptile house. You just weren't paying enough attention,
you were after that little bit of fluff. Melnick. Marsha. A woman like
Rose doesn't mind getting beaten up a little. It's better than being ignored
totally. And her orgasms were real: I have perfect pitch in the orgasm
department. She loves you."

"Yeah. So where is she now, that vapor lock? Rose loves me like an
eyeworm loves a cornea. If she—whoa, holding pattern, don't approach.
Hanh. Ha-hanh. Rose was at Wolff's party. On Saturday night. An arm
around his shoulder, when everyone else hadda have a negative GI series
and a note from his dead uncle just t'get in. Wolff! My God." Simon,
trigger-happy, blasts the horn. For one moment, over his aeronautic
dashboard, he is—da-da-da, ba-whoom—Simon on a bomb run. "Got him.
Got him. Never mind secondhand Rose. I've gotta retroact what damage
Mrs. P did. Geez, my cecum is perforating with fear. I tried t'call him
and all I got was this Autoharp recording. Wait for the beep and then
you have thirty seconds t'synopsize *The Brothers Karamazov*. Man, the
number four hitter's up and my curve ball is hanging."

"Why don't you read the message? I think it's from him."

"What?" His lap comes up, a theater seat: Larry's head on it. "Why
dintcha tell me? Where is it? Why dintcha tell me, you parahuman?"

"I did try. I did." Larry has unlocked the glove compartment jaw.
"You're so crazy. You said I was changing the subject. It came this morning. Then Bobby went in to see how you were doing. I thought he'd tell
you."

"I can't open it. It's a telegram from the War Department. I'm missing
in action and hoped dead. Look at this pretentious thing." The envelope
can intimidate. Thick chips of pulp float on its twenty-four-pound-paper
surface. Upper left—H.O.W.—embossed deep as a cattle brand. Simon, it
says, but the writing is more discursive than cursive: a stalky, left
slant/right slant child's hand. Simon will insert his forefinger beneath
the flap. Simon will get another paper cut: painless, sharp as Solingen

steel. Simon holds it away, up to the windshield: more than opaque: solid Beaverboard. "No. No, I can't."

"Come on, you big sissy. I'm all nerves."

"Hanh. You? Suppose this is my unconditional release? Last night I was half a millionaire. Huh. You know, when I was four years old, I licked an entire Volkswagen clean. With my little tongue."

"Simon. Don't talk nonsense. What does that have to do with it?"

"Oh, I dunno. It was the last steady work I had, I guess."

"Open it."

"Okay. Here goes. The envelope, please."

> Dear Simon, Friend:
> I gave a call to your place, the Mansion whatever, at 8 o'clock p.m. yesterday. A female person, certainly a relative, picked up. Such things she said I had to put the receiver under my armpit. Don't worry. I also have had a relative or two like that. My experience is you shouldn't let them answer a phone or appear at the front door, which they always do with the fly open.
> In any case I figured this is not the person to leave a message with. Come tonight (Monday) to Ten Great Ferry. Eleven o'clock. Kyryl wants to meet you, we'll all shake on the big deal. Large possibilities are in the wind. I told K. what you did for me. He cares and is grateful. I look forward.
>
> Your Friend,
> Herman

"It's okay. I can see that. Your ass cheeks just relaxed. You're sitting about three inches lower."

"Yes. Yessss." Simon draws a cross on the windshield; then a star of David, a swastika, a hammer and sickle, a crescent, a National Artists logo. "Have I propitiated everyone? Christ in a canoe, that was close."

"What's he say?"

"Kyryl and him and me, tonight we meet and—uh, lemme think." Simon folds the note: his letter of credit. "That's right, I've gotta see her at seven."

"Her who?"

"Maybe I should cancel. She won't be able t'type it in time. Well, maybe that's better. I'll act it out for them: I'll be six characters in search of a handout. I'll distract them with body-English, they can't read the other kind anyhow. I'll limp like Lucky. I'll flash my merkin like an ingenue. Then I'll hit 'em with the typescript tomorrow, or Wednesday."

"Who's Lucky?"

"We are. You'n me. We're on Wolff's tit like Romulus and Remus.

Plus, with Don out, with Rose gone, we can dip a ladle inta the cash flow any time. Herman loves me. Do something, you old nance. Gimme a fat Carole Lombard kiss."

"Big boy. Mmmmm, there. What is it? Is my breath ickish?"

"No. No. It's just—all in a ten-yard dash, vast waves of German romantic angst've come over me. I guess—I guess success is a little death. Already I'm wondering what I can take t'cure it."

"Aldo and Bettina. They made you feel guilty. They never gave you any validation. You don't think you deserve success."

"But I do, don't I? At least as much as any other thimblerigging fraud. Don't I? Pick a hand, any hand. Go on, pick one. Ha. Empty, you lose." Simon turns the wheel, sideswipe. "Wow, that was a near-miss. Imagine if we were moving. Why do I—?"

"Calm down."

"Why do I want it, all this film flam? Now it'll start again—actors, editors, tech men, bad weather—the usual backbreaking course load. Plus Wolff and Kyryl on my neck like an artistic surcharge. If I don't like it, why do I do it? Huh, Lar? Does fame and a phone on the restaurant table mean that much? I'm not patient enough t'lay in a Jacuzzi. Is it all in the spermatic cord? Is it just the retained earnings of lust? But I can get my kielbasa peeled any time. What am I trying t'prove then?"

"You've got talent, Sy. Great talent. You have to use it. And it uses you."

"Heh? Is that really the reason? Don't pour the emollient cream on, because I'm just tired enough t'believe you. Will I ever make a film worth opening in a Port-O-San? Do I really have great talent? Huh, do I?"

"Sure."

"Sure, he says. Are you bored with the subject?"

"You have. I said so."

"Boy, y'won't win a Clio f'that commercial. I shoulda never asked you t'be honest."

"Well, I think so. I do. But—in this business—it's hard to tell. There are so many people involved."

"You mean—those awards I won—I couldn't have won them without you."

"I never said that, Sy. I never meant it either."

"Well, who knows, maybe it's true. Where are my ideas? What am I trying to say? If I have great talent, how would you characterize it? In a caption."

"Stop it. All film is derivative to some extent."

"Derivative? I don't even have anything to derive from. I'll tellya what my talent is. My talent is still being alive, after years and years of dropping midden heaps on people. It's a wonder someone hasn't made me do the floorless jig by now. A sudden—gaggg—neck lift. I should be dead."

"Yes. I've wondered about that, too. You live a charmed life."

"Well. Enough of this sebum. Suppose I take a walk. Hey, Lar, maybe you shoulda left with Don and Rose."

"Oh, stop being silly. I love you. Most of all—you. Go inside and change your clothes. You can't take a walk looking like that."

"Yeah. Better do that. I'm wearing fatigues of blood. My mother killed my sister, maybe I'm just jealous she got more attention than I did."

"Oh. And while you're back there, please—say something nice about me to Minnie. Yes?"

"I'll say something nice to Minnie."

If he can find her. Damn dark as a mole's lunch in here. The van is incensed with dimness: smoky, shifting fumes: brown-on-gray-on-black. A metaphor picked from his dead nose. Simon asks: Is smell the aide-de-camp of sight? Trying to have a great idea. But he is only the imagist, the frame matcher. Dark as trout in deep rooms of a stream. Dark as double bassoon sounds. Dark as. Dark as an association yet unmade. His eyes, crossed with weariness and abuse, don't iris open: the place is lightfast. Simon will walk: shadowy, a stagehand between scenes. Ah: the van floor is slanted left: things run down to Minnie: to her gravity. He screws in a small-wattage bulb. Don and Rose have left space: the van is emptier, improved: two down. Simon tugs a bunk curtain back. Lord—his hands worship, up, spread—the Federal Reserve of nakedness down there. Minnie is stupendously bare: a ship to sail on: strange landfalls, exotic merchandise, oh, the sheer seaworthiness of her. Simon has knelt. He now stimulates her right breast: with one finger, clockwise. The areola, large and brown, a cornbread heel, goes about its silent office: contractile, poking up in flesh points like rubber cement. Then the left breast, untouched, will shut its petal: out of nervous sympathy. He can admire. Each nipple is a pushpin head: stuck in soft cork. What nursing Robert must have had: not the continental breakfast Bettina was. Simon is touched by the good-scout alacrity of these skin parts. He will wake her. Just the hairs on his third forefinger joint brushed, hardly felt, against Minnie's lower lip. They instigate a dream kiss: her mouth pops.

"Ssssp? Mr. Lynxx? It's you in the dark. Oh. My hip. And also the other one."

"Don't move. How are you?"

"Like a slice flank steak. What a schallumping I got from that Armenian dreck. First I can't convince him to start, then I can't convince him to stop. He gave me a miscarriage, if I ever get pregnant again, it'll last."

"Ha. Good line. I'll use it someday." Tucked around Minnie's abdomen there is a diaper of greenish verdigris. Deft, speculative, his finger will rim her buxom navel. "So that's what your private sector looks like. Now I know how Pizarro felt. Alone, with his Inca in the great golden room. Treasure. We could open a store with this. A wholesale chain."

"Please, Mr. Lynxx. Whatever you do, don't get in a man's way with me. My tookus would fall off under you."

"Don't worry. Native beaters couldn't get it up right now." The finger is gone. "I only touched for good luck. To ground myself."

"I apologize for the stink in here. It was a while since I could practice the seven rules of female hygiene."

"Don't tease me. Your woman smell must be a hormone rainbow. So much of sex is in the old sinus cavity. Dogs would know that. But my nose is made of Nerf right now."

"Robert told me. Did this thing with your nose happen from the fire?"

"From a long story. Uh-uh—" Simon's finger across her mouth. "Mention the word 'doctor' and I'll call Nubar to make your ass a shut-in again."

"Mr. Lynxx. I need a word with you."

"Sure. I'm available." He has sat: bedside-mannerly. "Go ahead."

"A minute. I've been practicing this talk, but with you it's like speaking at a wild Arab person. Such a man I've never run across before."

"You and me both. I need a translator t'talk to myself. Sometimes a bodyguard."

"Look. I went at this like a schnook. You don't jump into a new world with maybes and a thing for chastity. If I was honest, I should have given myself to you first day, from head to toe. Now look what happens, I'm an invalid." She has her hand on his nude chest: it smoothes, reflective. "This is not the place for me. For you, yes. For even Robert—I don't know. But, you shouldn't be angry, I've made a decision. As soon as I can walk I'm going back to the bushes. I'm not a jazzy person enough. God knows what's happening on the TV soaps since I'm here. It couldn't be more than what's going on with me." She considers that. "So, a neighbor will fill me in. I'll get my excitement from the 'Eyewitness News.' And maybe a husband will forgive. Do I have your all-clear to get out while the getting is good?"

"I'll miss you. You were an endless source of frustration." Then Minnie is weeping. "Let's talk about the real problem. Robert, huh? You want guarantees for him?"

"Did I say anything? Did one word of reproach come out of my mouth? No. No." She has covered her face with the pillow. Simon waits. The voice is distant, burry: over an intercom. "I can't give my blessing. You see that? Maybe this is what has to be. Larry is good, but from where comes my grandchildren? Tell me that?"

"Minnie, Robert is a blank check right now. All men walk on the queer side once or twice in a lifetime: or they think about it anyway. It's part of a rounded education. The trick is not t'take it seriously. It doesn't pinch off the vesicles. You'll have grandchildren. It could be worse. Larry could be a shiksa."

"Don't make fun."

"I'm not. Honest. I know you're upset."

"He can be so intense." Minnie has risen. Her breasts stagger, tumble down: with such importance, such sudden deadfalling weight, that Simon, an athlete's response, will half move to catch. "You should have seen him in his playpen. With blocks he was making an Empire State. Any hobby he took up, he did it like a full professor."

"Robert's young. This'll pass. The Second World War was won on the playing fields of Eton, and in the locker rooms of Eton everyone was making a fairy ring. England didn't skip a generation."

"From history I know kishkes, but what his father would do—that I can tell you. Rose could stop him, but she's gone now like the wind. I want to stay, but I'm only a buttinsky here. He won't listen. And what good am I, with my eyes shut, afraid to see what already I've heard? You understand what I'm saying?"

"It's very understandable."

"I'm not a bad mother, to leave? He won't come with me. And to send his father after him I haven't the heart."

"Go home, Minele. Yeah. I wouldn't be surprised, that's why Robert took the primrose path. T'crass you outa here. In part, anyhow. I haven't talked t'him, but I'm a pensioned-off son myself. I would've gone steady with a Rhode Island red, if it would've made my mother dissolve like an embolism."

"What's wrong with a mother?"

"Nothing. Never anything. That's the catch seventy-four. Mothers are perfect and they wiped kack from your tiny papoose and they shook you around a lot when you had colic. Who can deal, man-to-man over drinks, with someone who slopped up your infantile let-loose? My mother, I just found out—well, that story should be told on a moonless night. But you could be a murderer and still, t'your son, you could say, 'Don't put your feet up on the couch, it's not polite.' Robert doesn't want much. He just wants you to, oh, die. So probably he's killing your grandchildren in him for spite. It'll go away if you do."

"Is this what love does, you're telling me?"

"The Chinese definition of beauty, so I've heard, is 'love touched by death.' If so, mother love is very beautiful."

"He'll get over this? If I leave?"

"In time, I think. Especially if you tell him, before you go, that you're proud he's a homosexual and doing his part for ZPG. My son the nosegay. Say you want him t'be the the most famous fly-boy since Eddie Ricken-backer. That should do it. Meanwhile, fade out."

"I don't know. I don't know."

"Try it. And, if y'get sad seeing his little empty, unwetted bed, you can adopt me." Simon weighs a breastful in one hand. "I'd love t'be weaned again."

"Listen, Mr. Smart Mouth. You have a responsibility in this. I'm expecting action from you. And reports—I've got here the address of a friend where you can write. I'm making you the parent now."

"Not s'fast. I'm no alma mater."

"Don't use bullshit words on me, Mr. Lynxx."

"Eh?"

"I said—no bullshit."

"You rehearsed that."

"He comes out wrong, I'll be here to kill you. With a knife. Don't smile."

"That's not a smile, that's fear. It so happens I believe you."

"Then promise."

"I promise."

"Robert is a smart boy, isn't he?"

"Brilliant. Even crafty."

"And special. One in a million."

"Like hypergonadism."

"I give permission to hit him. He could use that. Whack him a good one now and then."

"I'll hit him."

"But not in his head."

"The coroner won't find a mark."

Simon, digger, has yanked out an artifact. Chron. approx.: 1956–1959. The wire bone of a sparkler: corroded, bent, still crumbly with burnt-down magnesium. Simon waves it: his old, insipid happy birthday salute to America the Explosive. Each Fourth Aldo bought him one box of ten, while he himself reveled elsewhere with belligerent, emphatic ash cans and cherry bombs. Here, beyond the chapel, before the orchard, where his cornfield had once stood at muster, six- and seven- and eight-year-old Simon, phantoms overlapping, would windmill sparkler one-through-ten: obediently: hot prickles against his bare wrist. In the holidaylight they had a washed-out aspect: his vapid, sunshine patriotism. Yet Simon lit, waved: lit, waved: to no audience but the nation's indifferent spirit. And at night, as he lay in bed, Thirty-ninth Road would relieve itself with ta-blams that buffeted the chest, like some old man punching a gas pocket up. Ta-blams that would rip any beer can inside out and give it tin ruffle edges. Aldo, in another yard, flattering teen-age children with his great firepower. Aldo Lynxx, radio person, esteemed all noise: still in the golden age of sound.

By August Simon's corn had tasseled: each ear an adolescent: surprised by its pubic silk. And Aldo would again acknowledge his sudden, late-summer paternity. Simon can recall him best from behind: bent forward in the garden: just medicine-ball nates: legs beneath too shanky and over-tasked. Reaping where he had not sown. There were pinto bean freckles across his upper back that would bloat and get murkier in sun: paramecia stained. Once each afternoon, on average, Aldo fell: taken down by his unbalanced stomach, to drop front first, pureeing green pepper and tomato under him. Simon could absorb these losses: only in August/September were Aldo and he that subtle thing, a fatherson. Besides, it was the growing he loved, not the eating: in those days at least. And how—it impoverishes memory—*how* Aldo could eat fresh corn: put in boiling water thirty seconds after the ear was wrenched off, before sugar could metabolize to starch. His flat incisor teeth had evolved for corn: specialists in herbivore. Aldo would gnaw left/right, arms stiff as a typewriter carriage, from margin to margin, ding! And return, food secretarial. Bettina cut the kernels off: because a hot cob smirched her red and line-drawn mouth. Beefsteak tomato, eggplant, cucumber, pepper, watermelon: zucchini so immoderate you might commit murder with one. Fatherhood seems still to Simon, not a relationship, but a short season of the year.

This season: September. It's a prime day: commodious, high-ceilinged, a day of tall french doors. Bright and warm, rational: yet elegiac. The sky knows it may not perform so well tomorrow or again. Simon has been sitting this half hour on a TV set: pitched last week from eleven flights up: traumatic therapy for a stuck horizontal hold. His garden has been vegetating: high grass, burdock, goldenrod, milkweed: here and there young trees of paradise, that undesirable alien, mover-in to any careless middle-class block. Music above: John Lennon: seemly theme-singing for Simon's sentimental backpack trip. If he squints, the high-rise wall at either side will appear evanescent, done in gouache on paper. Friday is around: watching, anxious: given to come-follow-me dashes at the orchard. Simon has ignored Friday. Right now Simon is a revisionist autobiographer of himself. His Quaker gray childhood, on second thought, had adventure in it: risky as a crocodile bird's inter-molar feeding. Crib killer: madwoman. Since you bring it up, Simon can recollect a cast he was cemented in from left wrist to clavicle. At what age? Three? Two? Why? And years ago he had found a bony, serious orthopedic brace in the cellar: its opening infant-wide. Too, there are scars on his kidney: old, raised no more, beneath the finger touch, than a corporate seal on paper. And his stepsister. Though dead, she stands for fable, plus a thirty-three point three, three, three, three, percent increase in immediate family. Just the thing to tell Wolff tonight: Herman loves a missing-person relative. Chee-chik: Friday has pointed again to the orchard where five derelict apple trees—one dead, four effectively sterile—hunch, gibbous near a gate on Bowne Street. Simon will fence him away: the TV aerial, épée supple, thrust home. Friday distracts him: the present is anachronistic here.

Bettina obsessed outward: around and through a ten-block compass. At PS 204, at South Bayside Junior High, her name and sexual liner notes were publicized in that choicest marketing space—on the wall above boys'-room urinals. CALL BA 8-4107 FOR A CHEEP FEEL. Also occasional verse:

IF YOUR DONG IS FULL OF KINKS
GET IT BLOWN STRAIT BY MRS. LINKS

MY SHIT SMELLS, YOUR SHIT STINKS
A ROSE IS A ROSE TO BETTINA LINKS.

And, in the long summer-off, they came. Glandular, chunky, sneaker-rotting boys of twelve and thirteen: to stake out the Manor patio. Unremunerative employment that: twice or so every week Bettina would appear, wearing B-cup bra and shorts, to harvest her basil plant and stock Aldo's bird feeder with strychnine. If Simon were outside, they'd push a call-your-mother nickel through the fence. Pointless, he kept telling them: Bettina never came for Simon, indoors or out: even on that day when Aldo and his snowman went together to a wild, gully-washing death. Yet, for some time, until contemporary girls had requisitioned the government issue gear of their sex, six- and seven-year-old Simon was little-brother intimate with eighth-grade male children. They would bring Simon home, often before he'd gone ten feet, hoping to catch Bettina nude at her front door.

"Here he is, Mrs. Lynxx, I found him on Fortieth Avenue."

"Yes, but I sent him there to buy some fags. Now he'll have to start all over again."

Little Simon was an unwary pander: he procured for the inner eye. Porky Serafin, who drank paregoric (which gave him a binding high), and Vito Manuche, who had acne even on his feet, would bribe Simon with egg creams and bike-handle rides to tell them, in detail, what Bettina did alone. It made Simon feel prodigious: as though he owned some powerful fetish: the complete Topps baseball card collection, say. Around him their faces were a drowned gray-blue: taut, blown-up smooth, red under the lid: faces of children too long in a chlorinated pool. He couldn't comprehend, except over-literally ("box," "slit," "lips"), their crude, intense questioning, but he could affirm with his tongue-bound "yeth." Yeth, Bettina used on her "crack" a candlestick, a full economy-size Ipana tube, his Mr. Marvel Atomic Squirt Machine Gun, the legs of Victorian furniture. Whatever: Simon was, yeth, complaisant. Now and again he would deliver a pornographic, yet strangely formal love letter, written by committee, to "Dear Mrs. Linx." There was no RSVP on Bettina's face. She would settle, like soil, into a stillness that he never felt obliged or qualified to intrude upon. Eyes open, but duller than light off ceramic tile: set on some unassuming object: her match pad, her Welsh trivet, a ceiling corner. The kind of concentration that only saints or those advanced in dementia praecox can sustain.

Maleness came with a certain warranty: payable on request. Manuche-Serafin believed it: that an Older Woman would appear one day to rehearse them in love's long, depraving strokes. It was what became of the tooth fairy when you grew up. But why his mother had been appointed by public referendum to this salaryless post, Simon couldn't imagine. Her beauty, perhaps: perhaps her knowing, sardonic Englishness. Or her nugatory career in regional theater. Maybe—it was possible, their hatred knew no Geneva conventionalities—Aldo had dashed off that bathroom graffiti while lecturing at PS 204 on "Radio, Your Career?" Or maybe—the thought is an hour old—her insanity sent out wide-band goatish CB waves. Yet, to his knowledge, Bettina had given no minor child either tea or sympathy. But then Simon was a boy who wore casts on unremembered broken bones.

Oh, he'll buy it: Bettina an infanticide. True, the style—crib suffocation —sounds prosy, imitative, without *ton:* worse than that: impromptu. The fulfillment should have come in premeditation and an antic, garnished staging. But, let him be just, she was raw talent then. Aldo, Simon can suppose, bought it, too: he must have known her blotter record. Through the latest period of their cold war ménage, Aldo prepared his own food and slept alone behind defense apparatus so intricate (including one time lock device bought at a bank distress sale) that he had to keep chamber pots for quick night relief. And each morning Aldo would look under his car hood: still, yet, it has come back to Simon here, that July afternoon when Aldo's lawn mower had blown up. Not an extravagant blast: sufficient, though, to leave Aldo sitting on the hedge, drive wheel and gearshift in hand, both shoe soles concussed off. And Arthur: there's a poser for you. What in Arthur, stout and furry, could have engaged Bettina's predacious rut? Well, incest: well, the priesthood: defilement, blood and spirit, killed with a single stone: promising workshop debut for any probationer of lust. Simon wants to know Bettina in love, but his lines are down now: Arthur is paralytic, knelt: straining through the paddock turn of a twelve-furlong meditation: in Van Lynxx Chapel. The ceramic-glazy Gordon eyes are his, too. And for once, or again, Simon did not feel qualified to intrude. At last he can countenance his heritage:

with a twining, cog-loose genius plausible in it. Only the mad / Only the mad / Only the mad / Deserve the fair.

All of a fleetness, Simon is glad. He lapses time back: to that long-gone waver of sparklers here. And can stand beside him, the poor sap shafted from Article One. Tears bead: it is fatigue and stress and sweet, kind self-love. Simon has cried only at the histories of great men dead without coin to place on their eyes. And at supreme art misunderstood in its narrow age. And at laconic male heroism: how he has sobbed when Jose Ferrer, Cyrano, tosses up his wood-plane nose to say, "My . . . white . . . plume." A couple is salsa-ing on the third-floor balcony left: four children run around and through them, in an abstract dance hard as child's play to learn. Simon on the fields of his youth, cropped away, cropless, will enjoy them: he does not condescend from below. He can breathe again. He has written well. There is a lovely girl at his disposal. And Minnie has just fathered Robert on him. He will teach: he will be a parent. Perhaps, yes, he could do worse than marry soon. There are no other Lynxxes left. What, what would it be like to cover a woman with purpose? To rush separate half and separate half together for that one moment when sperm and egg are just life sparked-off, sexless, biasless, in the rude astonishment of being.

Simon has risen. He will stand, standoffish: an artist's conception of himself. At some more appreciative time he might be commemorated so in bronze. SIMON LYNXX. HIS EYE WAS THE EYE OF AMERICA. Tears assemble in that national eye. Weep, Simon: weep for yourself—anyhow, it's an expedient knack: next to guitar playing, women are undone best by men who can cry. But Friday has taken this portraiture for a go-ahead. He waves, over-here, catch-me, swathed in foot-high grass: gone, seen, gone. Simon, withdrawn, does follow: made outlaw by genius: a melodrama walking. Friday has monkeyed around/up the nearest apple tree trunk: it swings there, head down. Chee-chik! Chee-chik! Chee-chik! Chee-chik! Simon once read Albert Payson Terhune in this tree, in its gazebo-like, leaf-tenting crown: when joint of bole and branch fit joint of hip and thigh. Simon kicks grass ahead of him to—haaaah! Ambush! Ground alert! Down, down. Simon will sprawl, rifle over forearm. Uh-oh. See there, Alf is lying propped against the trunk. Uh-oh. Simon, thanks anyway, doesn't need such brawling, crabbed companionship just now. Imitate a hydrangea: creep back. Yet somewhere, pineally, he knows. There is a cream-dense bird dropping at Alf's mid-forehead: the kind of mark Krishna Kids paint on. Alf is watching Simon: ironical, patient. They are both aloof. Yet Alf doesn't register Friday loud above. Well, whaddya know and hmmm. Alf, the unilluminated manuscript, is dead.

Simon will now couch himself: sociable: head on hand on elbow: straw in his mouth: *Déjeuner sur l'Herbe*. He has ever been at ease with the great: and death seems to have an old-money charm: cultivated, accommodating. Boy, did Alf go out with flair: giving the hairy bird no less. Middle right finger points up, held in place against his sternum: a farewell fooot at life. His old blue seabag pillows one arm: luggage to be sent on under separate cover. All this is, well, punctual: it clicks with Simon's mood: sentientious, prophetic, thrilling. Simon has leaned near: two living men would not come so close. With finger and thumb he reads the nude stomach, pressing hard vellum skin flat. A bestiary: eagle, lion, bull, snake, griffin, toad, shark, mosquito: the magic of Pleistocene hunters: no human picture here. Alf is wearing a tunic of driven-in ink: naked he came to the world, scribbled-on he will go out. His last tattoo: this one bugle-blown. Simon sits up. He will hold a buttercup under Alf's chin. Yellow shine there: dead men have still their preference. And below—where his jugular is now a long, stunned worm—initials: M.P. Through them—arrow or blowtorch flame or Malay kris—in any case, a savage cancellation mark. Friday is down. He has turned out the one loincloth pocket: self-made executor of Alf's will. Simon can't accept: a tooth-marked Baby Ruth bar. The scene is bucolic: blue jay and grass. Also one apple: the entire produce, through a summer, of this sun- and fluid-powered plant. Yet, overhead, over-heard, city-slick music will offer counterpoint. Simon has to like the values: this is real as film.

"Lookit him. Hanh. I hadda press agent once with the same go-get-em attitude. Couldn't book me into a greenhouse. What's it all about, Alfie? When you told the girls, Come see my etchings, they didn't have t'go far, did they? You, kid—you with the prehensile behind—watch this. I saw it done in a Renoir film." Simon has raised, veed, his first and second fingers. Dexterously, with tact, he will flick Alf's eyelids down: silent, smooth as a cadmium switch. Alf sleeps. Then—wonk!—right lid up. Wonk! left. Rise and shine. Press gently down again: wonk! wonk! Push stupid things, unnh: double wonk! "Look at that. It worked for the Frog. Harder than getting the bedroom shade t'stay put." Friday sputters: this false-animate trick of rigor mortis has a familiar Alf-willfulness to it. "Okay. Okay. I'll go shake Arthur out of his continuing, twenty-eight-part revelation. It's his job. There might be union trouble." Simon looks down. "Hang tight, Alf. Great scene. Cut. Print. Wrap. Gee, if there's a resurrection of the body, they'll need a night and day shift cartoonist on your case."

They've been sitting at it, Arthur and he, through a quarter hour now. A silent, inadvertent wake: more like a failed picnic rather. So still that robins have stood, confident, beside them. The old man is hung over from meditation: eye grit of it in his vision. The black clerical jacket lies across Alf's chest: Arthur had made a quick, prudish shroud of it. Had made and had said, "Well, Alf. Well. Now you've really done it, haven't you?" That stumped Simon: unreasonable criticism, he would have thought, in any civil man-to-corpse conversation: death spoken about as a kind of bumbling carelessness. And Simon can sense from Arthur— paramount above all other emotions—a resentment, an annoyance. After- noon itself has one foot in the grave: random coolnesses rise up: there might be a limestone cave exhaling underneath. Arthur is compressed in the lotus position: an over-ripe flower: his short legs won't inter-petal well. Simon has been clawing at, pulping the windfall apple: late break- fast: pinches of mush, beak-fed with thumb and forefinger deep/behind the tongue: he is a mother bird in his own feeding. Friday, orphan, sits on one shoulder. Simon will be quiet: the way we are around people rapt in fussy, minor operations: people who count change or dig a splinter out.

"Alf," Arthur says. "Who would have thought it? I mean, of us all— Alf? Not him. Never. He looked to be immortal, vicious little cove that he was. Because of that very thing, his viciousness. And now." Arthur has been eating grass: he spits up. "Like Nebuchadnezzar. Gone completely off my chump. Oh, I knew it well enough, what I was about. A damned fool's errand. Pacing myself, the blasted impudence of it. Pacing myself. I did the same at Cambridge cramming for my tripos in Greats. With such careful diligence. Yes, and I got a 2.2 for all my trouble. What you Americans would call a gentleman's C. But for a spiritual pole vaulting like this . . . No, there are no trots. No old exam copies. Nor ways of a gentleman, either."

"Huh? Sounds like your mind's been redistricted. I don't understand." But Simon is patient. This talky preamble: a prisoner will break down after such turbid, first-come-first-served associations. Simon can wait. Arthur—Simon has it planned—will tell him about Bettina today.

"No, I suspect only the young are powerful enough, or certain enough, to be humbled. There has to be something left over. To jettison, if you will. Ah, and this. This puts a frost on it, once and for all."

"What you want is the Serbian delegation. No capiche."

"Look here, it's simple, you don't do it on the layaway. Haven't I told you that before? It isn't a fridge or an annuity. What we have to give is given in the prime." Arthur slaps his thigh: no, can't even hurt himself. "Fiercely. One has to be tall, in the neighborhood of small things, to pull the lightning down. It requires, I should almost say, an athlete's condi- tioning. My intentions were correct. But in fact—if you like the unpretty truth—I'm a bit of a stick. Stiff. No good. No good at all. Or too good. Not very interesting at any rate."

"Uh-huh."

"You don't go there. You break in. You kick the bloody gates down."

"Hey. Watch your treble-control knob. Hell, it's only a corpse. He's taking it better than you are."

"Now look here." Arthur points at Alf: a disciplinary action. "Caught him on the hop. Yet you saw his finger, Simon. You wouldn't miss out a thing like that, not you. He had time for that. Or the presence of mind. He was a bad hat, the worst, an utter rotter—still, you see, I have to wonder. In the end. With that finger. Didn't he have better odds? He—I mean, He—He's always been fascinated by the hugely unregenerate. Not the ninety and nine." Arthur laughs. "If it weren't theologically unsound, I'd say it was rather a fault with Him. This wanting a challenge."

"Arthur. Alf was hauling seventy-five at least. I was reading his chest t'pass the time: he's got tattoos by Currier and Ives on him. He's dead. It's not what you'd call untimely."

"D'you realize who that is?"

"Who? No. You mean we finally found Jimmy Hoffa?"

"Alf is. Was. Alfred Poole." Arthur has unlatched a sandal: his feet are swollen: spotted white. "Mrs. P's husband. That Poole."

"Hanh. I'll be a snake's footprint. The kitchen. Alf and her. I slandered the old adhesion. Of course—geez, I thought we called her Mrs. the way you call a whorehouse manager Madam. T'improve the tone."

"And now I shall have to marry her."

"Shall you?" Simon is entertained: Arthur's seriousness.

"Yes. Bathetic, isn't it? I thought he'd live longer: those wiry types do, as a rule. And she's a woman—you'll hold this in strictest confidence—she's a woman of strong drives. Even in her maturity."

"Uncle. Since we're dispensing comfort like two hookers in a price war—take this from me. There's nothing you haveta do. Except eat. Even that not so much, I find."

"Ah, well. You don't know all the absurd niceties. The history." Arthur has pulled up a grove of arm hair: skin rises, pointy: fake gooseflesh. "There's no help for it. I have to."

"She's pregnant? She needs someone t'help with the two A.M. feeding?"

"Oh, no. Lord, no. Nothing like that. Her desires are intact, but she's well past that, I daresay. And we haven't had contact since—ah, well. No. I can't go into it. It would involve some unsavory matters of fact."

"Wait." Simon has one hand across his forehead. "Wait. My tout in the spirit world is calling. Collect, as usual. Aaaah. The ground fog has risen—it's, it's . . . it's 'Hollywood Squares.' No. Wait. For $6.98 I can get a recording of Fats Domino's Greatest Hits. If I act now. Wait. We get a lot of interference from the Chrysler Building. I'm not on cable yet."

"Simon—"

"Wait. Twist the contrast dial. Yes. There's a crib. And an infant. Amy. Amy is her name. And Bettina is in the big filing cabinet, under U for Unglued."

"She told you, Mrs. P."

"With a flannel board and slides and running commentary."

"That was wrong of her." Arthur has placed two fingers, the two that bless, on Simon's knee. "I'm sorry. She can be like that. I don't at all expect you to understand. She's had a deuced bad time of it. Have you known for long?"

"At least two hours."

"It's my mistake. I should've been the one. She probably put the worst possible construction on it. It must have been a nasty shock for you. But she'll do that, you know. Take things into her own hands."

"No. I hold you responsible. It's one thing t'hoist my inheritance. But a man's past is—it's material for a screenplay at least. I deserved t'know."

"Yes. I suppose you did. But, remember, it was my past as well. And my sister's, may she rest in peace."

"Oh, righto. Uncle Arthur was sparing Uncle Arthur, not Nephew Simon. Rest in peace. My tassel, rest in peace. You know her, she's cleared hell out by now. It looks like a government office building after four P.M. It's you wants the RIP. After all, you both took the same primal flume ride out inta the world. Must be a worry, that."

"Got your knife into me, you think?"

"Well. If the chemise fits, wear it."

"I remember often enough, thanks all the same. I promise you that, Simon."

"So, keeper of the tribal record, I wanna hear." Simon clacks thumb and forefinger: an abusive sound. "Shall I help? The way I see it Mrs. Poole, your girlfriend, had a crosstown rival she couldn't cope with. Bettina."

"I wouldn't put it that way. And she wasn't Mrs. P then. She didn't meet Alf Poole until many years after. No, you haven't got it the right way."

"Well, what way then? What way? I'm bilge-sick of your goddam British reticence. You've got permanent resident status, so act like an American. Gossip, f'God's sake."

"Keep your voice down. And try a more civil tone. I'm making allowances for your distracted state and our relationship. But I won't be bullied."

"So. Go on."

"Do I have to review it all again?" The question isn't asked of Simon. Arthur swallows: shows sluggish tongue. "I was young. We were having a—a liaison."

"You and Bettina."

"No. Good grief, man. No. Never that. I swear it before Jesus Christ. She was a child."

"Yeah, like Brooke Shields. You couldn't tell her puberty from her menopause. A child with child."

"Wait. Did Mrs. P say that? About Bettina and me?"

"No." Simon sighs. "No, she defended your honor like it was the Spirit of Camp David. It's Bettina's ghost she's after."

"I can't say I blame her. Well, no—I do. A bit. There has been time enough for charity. It was altogether a beastly mess. In those days an affair—if the woman were respectable—it meant marriage. In those days, my God, if a check bounced, you had to resign from your club. Ruined. I might as well be a Polynesian for all you can understand it. That time. And I intended to marry her. I surely intended it." Arthur listens: as if to polygraph his voice. "Then Bettina came down to London, with Amy almost due. Bettina was very acute. I reckon the stress made her even more so. Right off she gauged what the terms of our relationship were—mine and Mrs. P's. It gave her moral support—immoral, I suppose you could say. After all, I was a priest. It took the wind out of me: I couldn't very well make her a sermon on continence. I didn't want to, I loved her. But I was hamstrung. I have enormous capacity for guilt. And virtually none at all for enjoyment. Right there, you see—I wasn't much of a Christian. The lack of joy. But you don't care about that." Arthur looks up: correct, Simon doesn't. "Well. At the first, I think it was just a matter of attention. So many hours given her, so many hours given Mrs. P. But Mrs. P—women can be like that—Mrs. P indicated that she had the upper hand."

"In bed?"

"Yes. Oh, she shouldn't have. But she was in a compromising position —and quite stupid, quite awkward in her fear. There were social differences between us. Cambridge. And the Gordons were a county family. We had a bit of land. Then, at any rate. She was of very decent middle-class stock—but tradespeople. Furniture. Enough difference to get her wind up. She should have trusted me more. She shouldn't have let Bettina put her hook in. For all she was eight months with illegitimate child, Bettina had airs. She let on that Mrs. P wouldn't make the mark. It wasn't, you see, a sexual thing between us, between brother and sister—it was social. It had to do with class. Mrs. P won't believe that. She can't yet, for her self-respect. Of course, what happened later—by then Bettina had gone quite off her . . . off. Can we let it lie now?"

"For the moment. For the moment." Simon throws a stalk of dry grass: it will hurtle spear-efficient: with the poise and accuracy that a javelin can bear. Simon is patient: timing this. Then abruptly, fingers long in mouth, he will whistle. But his tongue, his cheeks, are unresponsive, scarred. The sound is loud: yet more an animal's shout.

"What? What?"

"She killed it? The child. Did she kill it or not? Don't hedge. I've got a witness here. Did Bettina kill her child? Answer me. I have a right t'know."

"God, that hellish noise. You scared me."

"Did she? Did she kill my sister?"

"Ahhhh." Arthur looks at the chapel. "It's not a thing to be spoken of."

"She did then. Hot ding. How'd I scrape through? Penal battalions on the Eastern Front had a better chance. There I was, complacent, soaking up mother love. Like Mr. Magoo stepping over open mine shafts. What?" Arthur has flopped forward: onto hands and knees: a grotesque pose, that of the legless begging.

"You see, it was my very fairness that led me to be unfair. Do you see? If I were going to lock her away—my own flesh and blood—then I owed Bettina that much. Not to marry hugger-mugger so soon as the doors were shut behind her. Do you see what I mean? It would've seemed I'd done it just for that—to get on about my sexual business undisturbed. Can you understand?"

"Yeah. Better than you think."

"What's that mean?"

"That you didn't love the old piece of asbestos tile anymore. Mrs. P, I mean. Or maybe you never did. But the British haveta hire Henry James t'write a moral Mishnah so they can excuse themselves. You wanted out."

"Oh, no. No." Arthur can't close his mouth.

"Think it over a bit. It'll grow on you."

"It couldn't have been like that. I'd remember. No."

"Back up. Sit down. You embarrass me and it takes a lot t'do that. You look like an incompetent pack animal. Try t'manage some civility."

"I won't believe what you say."

"Unk, you got your hong konged. And after that Mrs. P had all the attraction of a wooden magnet. There's nothing like a good orgasm t'make a man wanna eat Chinese alone."

"I tell you—it was a different time then."

"Between man and broad the time never changes. Lustless is listless. So Mrs. P relieved her gallbladder on you?"

"She was hurt. Stunned. I—well, she had acted badly toward Bettina—"

"Stop blaming Mrs. P. You wanted sick leave with pay. It was you. What did she say?"

"She didn't. She just went off. To Scotland at first. Then around. I didn't see her again until a decade later. In 1948 it was. Bettina had gone to the States. Mrs. P had married Alf. And what a wretched match that was. Him a pub crawler and a common bully. Had up twice for picking pockets. He was in the Merchant Marine and the Navy during the war, in the brig mostly, I suspect. He used to beat her just as a matter of course."

"How about that, Alf? Defend yourself." Simon listens. "He said, 'De mortuis nil nisi bonum.'"

"I pleaded with her to divorce him. Doesn't that prove my love for her? But she wouldn't—not to marry me. It was my own stickish sense of fairness turned back on me. I was then rector of a church with all of eight families in it. A complete washout. The rectory wasn't fit for a decent woman. Actually Bettina could have made a go of it, that's another social difference. For all her pretensions. But the merchant class, they put great store in the look of things. It's their security."

"Besides, Alf was better in bed."

"What? Did she tell you that?"

"Did she have to? You probably think 'oh' or 'aha' is an ejaculation. Sperm like those pasteboard communion wafers. Anyhow, women of that sort need t'have a good bash in the stash. T'be beaten up. They gotta lose —nine, ten and out—before they let themselves have an orgasm. I know."

"Perhaps you do. It hardly matters now. Alf was away a lot. He came back every now and again. He caught me once having tea with her. He hit me."

"And you enjoyed that. A spiritual come. Don't tell me about your capacity for enjoyment."

"You're a very cruel young man."

"Like mother, like son: t'quote Mrs. P."

"But Bettina wasn't—I haven't. No. Well. Mrs. P has been a great support and a great friend. And now I'll marry her."

"Uh-huh." Friday has been collecting sticks. There is a stack, nest-shaped, pyre-shaped, close to Simon's leg. "Okay. Enough therapy for you. Back to the prosecution. About my mother. Multiple-choice questions, circle the answer that seems most outrageous."

"Wait. Do promise me one thing at least. That we'll be friends. You won't cut me off."

"What's the lanolin treatment for?"

"I've felt this moment, here—it coincides, connects. You know. There's a verse in St. John of—"

"Uh-uh. I never touch the Bible. It gives me reader's cramp. Don't spoil a mediocre situation. I'm feeling good. I've got cash. My brain is full of bait-and-switch scams. I don't haveta eat. I don't smoke or chew anymore. I'm growing."

"Growing? Yes? How?" Arthur has moved toward Simon: walking, sort of, on his buttocks. "How d'you mean? I'd like to know."

"Ha—that reminds me—friends that we are now. The old pre-op transsexual in there gave me an ultimatum this morning. Out by five P.M. or she'll buzz the fuzz and make sure my next film opens in a Lighthouse for the Blind."

"Oh, that." Arthur disparages with one hand. "Not to worry. This—Alf —this event will jolly her up, you'll see. Shall we take him in now? It is rather a morbid conference we're having."

"*Zitzenzie, Mein Herr.* You don't hear him complaining, d'you? Him or the flies. My question first: about Bettina."

"What more could there be?"

"Bettina mad. What was she like in the cootie closet? Describe it for me. Use your hands and feet. Did she go soft like so much floating island? Did she talk t'tiny, invisible civil servants from the Home Office? Did she pick the paisleys off her paisley carpet? Did she make a pass at you?—out of mere class solidarity of course."

"No. I won't beat that horse again. Absolutely not. It's gratuitous and inhuman."

"You will." Simon jabs Arthur with a twig: under his left big toenail. "It's my birthright. As your fiancée, the English Channel, says so cheerfully—I come from diseased seed. How diseased is what I wanna know. Suppose I build a child myself someday. Will he wear booties until he's forty-five?"

"Diseased seed?"

"Not that I mind it—a sound, rational madness can be mistaken for brilliance. But I gotta know what kind: more than just name, rank and padded-cell number. Was Bettina's insanity generic or did they give it an expensive brand name?"

"Diseased seed?" Arthur laughs: but his face is white. "You? Bettina? That's perfect nonsense. Mrs. P doesn't know a thing about it."

"About what?"

"That you—wait up here, Simon. Are you having me on? Bettina wrote me. She said that you knew. That you'd taken it very well."

"What did I take well? I'm not taking this who's-on-first? routine very well at all. Say it."

"Ah—"

"What, dammit?"

"You were adopted, Simon."

"What!"

"Don't—not so very loud."

"What? I whaaat?" Simon bucks up, swirling, hazardous, wing-broken: a wagon wheel come loose. Alf will slump over: dead again. Friday has rolled off. Simon is standing, fists wild and jabby, above Arthur: he won't break clean. "No. No way. Uh-uh. It can't be. It can't. You're lying, you priestly function. You wanna protect me. I've gotta know the truth. Now."

"Don't—"

"Now!"

"It is the truth."

"No. Oh, no." Simon looks: behind, overhead, around: hare pursued by owls. Then he will stare: at one hand, at his feet. "See. I look like them. See: my nose and chin—Bettina's. My size—his. My voice, listen to it. Aldo. In the dark I can't tell him from me. I'm growing into him. I know that. It can't be true. It can't."

"I agree. The resemblance is extraordinary. Perhaps—I always thought —well, environment, something of that sort."

"What! What? Whaaat!" Simon has taken the tree on: hugs it, bearish. A leaf will fall. "Just when I'm getting close, there's nothing. The box is empty. You gotta be lying. Or. Or. Or she lied t'you. That's it. She lied t'you."

"No."

"How can you be sure? Hunh? Hunh? Bettina told me Sleeping Beauty lay in a coma for years until someone cut off her life support. I believed her. She told me Hansel and Gretel ended up as sauerbraten. I believed her. How can you know?"

"Because, Simon, I was there. No—stop, hear me out." Arthur flattens grass: as though the story needed a smooth place to lie on. "You were adopted in England. Bettina had had a miscarriage or an abortion—I was never clear which—just after she married Aldo. Then, for two or three years, she was sterile. So they decided on adoption. Bettina and Aldo came here—I mean, to England—for six months. I suspect she wanted the child to be British. More hers than Aldo's, in a manner of speaking. And she wanted you to seem her natural child. They had it timed that way. For their return. Perhaps the sterility struck her as an omen—Amy having her revenge. Bettina—well, she was susceptible to false pregnancies. Often. Her menstrual cycle was capricious. Psychosomatic, I have no doubt. At any rate, they came to me. They needed a clergyman's recommendation, but it would've taken a good deal more than that—Bettina's past history didn't inspire confidence. I tried: albeit with only half a heart. After all, I knew . . . But, of course, no respectable agency would countenance it." He tamps grass: recollecting. "Yes. I'd thought they'd written it off as a bad go. I didn't see Bettina or Aldo for two months. Then, on Boxing Day it was, she rang me up. They were staying at the St. James Hotel in London. Bettina had a surprise for me, she said. I was to come right away, Aldo had air tickets for New York the next morning. I presume there was some spite in it: I hadn't helped enough, she knew that. But I must say Bettina was quite dotty with joy. She even—her brassiere was padded out—" He smiles. "So, there you were. In a bassinet. And the bassinet got up with a little Christmas stocking at the foot. It jogged me back—to that other time. In London with Amy. I'd say you were no more than a fortnight old. But a big child. Big even then. Eleven pounds I think she said."

"Where?" Simon is quiet. "Where did I come from?"

"I haven't a clue. I never did want to know, frankly. There has always been a black market in babies. This was—oh—five years after the war. We were still on short rations—powdered milk and all that. Aldo had money. He could arrange things. You were arranged. Think of it this way: you got a decent bargain. Your natural mother probably didn't have a pin. Or a husband."

"That's the truth?"

"Yes. And all I know of it. I swear to you."

"Fraud! Aaaargh! They gouged me. They gouged me. Aaaah!" Simon is in a fight with the tree: half up it: tearing branches down. "She leeched my blood and I wasn't even her son. I had rights. I had rights. Why didn't someone protect me? She charged me back rent on her womb. How many times, how many times did she tell me about the pain of it—childbirth? She said I ruined her for another child. With my size. Aaaah! Aaaah! And I believed her. I wasted my God-given Oedipus complex on her. With my size. I might just as well have fucked her eyes out. Oh, why didn't I? She was just another broad. And they even made me look like them."

"Shut up, you! Shut up. I won't listen to your self-indulgent raving." Simon is rigid: fisted: lip-bitten. "She was perfectly right not to tell you, not then. It was a loving act. And she wanted to believe it."

"A stocking-stuffer, that's all I was. A rich man's gift to his bimbo, for her conspicuous consumption. This isn't mine—none of it. I'm not the last Van Lynxx—I'm nothing. I don't even have a birthday."

"I should never—"

"And I let those two extortionists get away with it. I let them die a natural death. He hit me until I slipped in my own nose blood. And I felt guilty. I. I. I felt guilty. My father. He bought me like a slab of meat. It was bondage. It was motherfucking bondage."

"Stop it! Just stop. People are looking down."

"Ohhh. I'm hurt. I hurt all over. Who am I? Who is my mother?"

"You'll never know. Resign yourself to that, Simon."

"Then every woman. It's incest. Merry. Minnie. Rose. God, Mrs. Armistead. Every woman could be. A sister. A mother. I'll breed on myself."

"Simon. Get a hold of yourself. Please. Take Alf. We'll go inside."

"Yes. Alf. Come, Alf." But Simon waits: stooped. "You."

"What is it?"

"You're not even my uncle."

"No. Not in actual fact. I suppose."

"Well, I'll tell you—just as a friend. They broke my heart a thousand times."

"All parents do. The real. The adopted. Let's go inside. You're shivering."

"Ah, well. Ah, yes. Come, Alf. Up. You're dead and an embarrassment. We have to go inside now. We don't belong here."

He cuddles Alf: right arm under back: left arm under knee joints.

Simon, anticipating dead weight, is set for a difficult squat lift: but Alf
will surge up, as though in his own less ponderous gravity. Simon over-
balances backward: heel edge and heel edge and heel edge: and erect, in
control. Uncle Arthur, then Friday form a recessional behind. At Van
Lynxx Chapel they win respect from the community above. Salsa music
is rearranged: to a jivy dirge: these people are nodding acquaintances of
death. And Simon must stop: it is required. He introduces the body:
right, pause: left, pause. Alf feels hollowed out: a decorative vessel.
Arthur can't breathe: afraid of some mad desecration. But Simon will
walk nobly: memories from his high school graduation: through the
elitist graveyard, along the garden path, across the patio. So, once, Simon
carried Merry: live persons, by contrast, are untoward cargo: resistant,
shiftful, without trust: weight rolls around in them—here, there—like the
metal ball in a plastic jumping bean. To the kitchen, which isn't his,
Simon's, either now.

Mrs. P will open up shop at once. Linen snapped off the long table: a
rubber groundsheet on. Simon might suppose she has been in training
for this event: sudden death drills—bong, bong, bong—at 3 A.M. The
loincloth is gone: torn away, a calendar page. Alf lies nude, deadpan,
trivial: and slightly doubled up—some suggestion of the apple tree trunk
in that. Tattooing imposes a death-by-fire, charred look. Mrs. P has lit
up: Simon guesses there is an odor already. Arthur, fiancé by default, has
been abridged by her presence: just background now: left hand diddling
on the mantelshelf. Mrs. P swabs Alf down, swipes at him: the big, foot-
square motion she would use on a wall. "Little bastard," Mrs. P says. She
has taken the obscene middle finger and—crack!—broken it to politeness.
Simon winces: an uncompromising censorship. Mrs. P has begun to dress
Alf: his one suit is Second World War mufti, but well kept or never
worn. This dressing has a familiarness, a facility. Through that long marriage Alf has often been, drunk and senseless, her plaything: a doll.
Eleven minutes by the tall clock. There is dust on his face: she puffs it
off, spit in her curt breath. Then she will coat each lower lid with Super
Glue. Down: hold: stick: the eyes are out.

"This was my husband. I suppose Arthur has told you that already."

"Yes, he did. Ah, my condolences. Also my apologies—for what I said.
I mean, about you and him in the kitchen—"

"Shove it up your arse, mate."

"Margaret, in God's name—"

"And as for you: you'd best call Dr. McManus. We'll need a death
certificate. And the funeral people at Flynn and Martingale. Their number is in the address file on my bureau. Ask for Peter."

"Yes."

"Peter. Do it now."

"I was going to."

"Then do. Don't gawk there as if your precious presence were a comfort. For once, don't be a priest. Be useful." Arthur will have to exit. Mrs. P has poured herself black coffee. She stands, judgmental—north, south, east, west—at each side of the table: Alf as primitive art. She sips. "A stupid, stupid man. He was. And of course you cross-questioned Arthur about Bettina."

"We spoke."

"He didn't controvert it. He didn't dare do that."

"No."

"I hope you're proud of her?"

"I am. Now." It will be his last pledge of allegiance. "Thanks to you."

"Don't mention it. This, what you see here, is the sum of my last thirty-odd years. This and him, in there, your uncle." She stares at Simon: a bold looking. "Not much in all. Between them, not much. I haven't had great satisfaction. Eh? You think me bitter? Is that it?"

"I don't think a lot, Mrs. P. I plan sometimes. I act sometimes. But I don't think a lot."

"Go away, Simon."

"I will. If—though . . . if I could have a small grace period."

"Grace? I'm fag-tired of that word."

"A little time then."

"Oh—if it matters."

"Thank you. I'll go upstairs now."

"Wait. Arthur: did you find him at prayer?"

"Yes."

"Ah, indeed. He must be feeling very sorry for himself just now." She exhales. "I'll drag him down."

"I don't think so."

"Yes, I will. Or I'll die trying." She has set her coffee mug on Alf's chest: an assertion. "The monkey seems to have chosen you for his new master. I'll arrange to get it placed in a testing lab, if you want. There's a market for monkeys."

"No. No. In my line of work it's always good t'have a second opinion."

"Right, then. You were going upstairs?"

"I was. I am."

Simon, you, he, I—wheee! on the up and up. A flight he has taken before: sixteen spiral steps of it. The loose fifth stair tread will bitch, as it did once, though with less shrillness then, about a ninety- or a seventy- or a fifty-pound Simon sent to his room. Sent for sulking, rejoicing, idling, running, messing, forgetting, not answering, answering, answering back, laughing, crying, sneezing, coughing, belching, farting, listening, interrupting, shouting, whispering, and now for carrying a corpse across the threshold without wiping his feet. They have had a heavy caseload: these stairs: childhood spent in one sort or another of recidivism. A newel post, big plumb-bob shape, will help him to the safe upper landing. He—who?—has taken air in: breath is full of side stitches and giddiness. He does not think a lot: he does not think: this lost and foundling: leader of an impersonality cult. Sight has become pressureful: it asks, like some racial subgroup, for self-determination. He will snip one contact lens out. Tension relief has projected down from his eye-strings, along his bead-telling spine: a first belt of Wild Turkey can do that. He must sleep in whoever's room it is. So just fold back the Chinese screen—OPEN FOR RENOVATION—and,

Rats, Robert—his fostered, foisted child—is still waiting there. The chair will hop, its old wood scrawks alarm, but otherwise Robert has disciplined himself: uh-oh, some sort of confrontation arriving ASAP. Robert's heels are on the desk: he has taken office. New, inch-thick, crepe soles on his feet: they depreciate his other parts: the way cartoon people are drawn: all shoe and head. Simon's optic nerve has given the sack to his shortsighted, unproductive left eye: his right (microscope users learn this) is going it alone. Could Robert look someday like him: can an egg, its genetic intentions, be thwarted so? Robert is memorizing Simon: Simon, the text, the drama. Robert, chin tilted back in still-warm cool—saying, by that pose, Wherever-I-am-it's-the-first-class-section-I-make-rooms—Robert is, thus tilted, exceptionally unhandsome. Draw your attention to: a hoggish underview of his nostrils: a broken-out, untanned throat. To throttling, grappling, grasping fingers: the well-known hand wash: a characteristic habit, but characteristic of someone else. Robert nods Simon to the other chair, hospitable. There will be trouble: and with Simon's compliments. He is watching Robert, head askance, to focus his good eye front and center: behold Polyphemus, monocular, man-eating, here. A strand of pot smoke attaches Robert to the ceiling: Irish courage inhaled.

"Where y'been? Hanh, Sy? I've been cooling my heels in here since one o'clock."

"That's what you're paid for, little proto-man."

"Sure. Hey, sure. I know my place—behind the elephant with a big broom. Sit down, you look beat. Man, how can anyone stand that spicorico music all day? They even played 'Pushin' Up the Daisies' just now."

"Yeah. It was the Dead Man's Tango. Alf just passed on t'the next local stop. I found him dead in the orchard. Thumbin' a ride with the wrong finger."

"Alf is dead? No kidding?"

"Go on down. I need this room." Simon jerks aside: something has hooked his leg: Thank God It's Just Friday. "Beat it. Mrs. P's in the kitchen now, preparing him like an oven-stuffer roaster. Go on, you Jews never get t'see a good laying out. Coffin's always closed so some mortician can pocket the teeth and the gold mezuzah. Go."

"Sy, please. Sit down. We need t'talk."

"Look, all afternoon I been talking—like a man who's just done solitary f'ten years. I've got an important appointment tonight—two of them. I wanna nap. So flit off, like the good arch support you are."

"Sy, please. I think we really better talk first. This, *Lucky*—ha-ha—it's a piece of shit. It sucks. We gotta have a conference." Simon's eyes dilate: terribly, malformedly: the left, the one without the lens, is vein-shot: a perfect goggle. "Whoa. Hold on. Don't have a stroke. I know you worked your butt off on this. And I think there are things—maybe a lot of things—we can still save. But we've gotta talk before Wolff barfs all over you."

"Give. Me. It."

"But you'll die out there. They'll cut you up. Can't you see, for Chrissake. S'crap, crap, crap. Scarecrows and corn. And not just on the cob. It's strictly from *Ladies' Home Journal—*"

"Get out of my—just get out of here."

"And all that religious sing-along. Churches and crosses. Is Herman Wolff gonna pay good money for that? And, anyhow, what'd—what d'you know about being Christian? You're an atheist, you told me that yourself. You—it's you told me. This is phony, is what I'm saying, can't you see that?"

"Shut up, Robert."

"I mean—what it is, it's not *you*. You're the interesting thing. The youness. It's not—"

"I said, shut up. Warning, Robert. Warning. Don't tinkle your chemical arrogance on me. You're supposed t'be afraid of me, remember? That's our working arrangement."

"Right. And I am. I am. But I'm also afraid *for* you. Can't I be that? Look, could be it's the pot—otherwise I wouldn't say this. But I'd still think it. They'll laugh at you, Sy. I don't want that. And you'll piss all our money away. I don't want that either. I mean, do you? Just be open to suggestion."

"I said, shut up."

"Sy, gosh. You won't—"

"That does it. Roll out!"

"What? Hi—yike!"

It's a movie-set crash: picturesque: accomplished with penstroke grace. Just latch one foot under a rung and, ufff!, lift. The desk goes over, backwards: dictionary, vase, inkwell, bottle of Schlitz, ashtray, Robert. His crepe soles high-kick up, up. The chair, aslant already, will upset itself: domino theorizing here. Robert has flipped: a regulation 360° somersault. He sprawls now, sliding, caught under the bed. Marijuana will make it seem largo-elegant, a minute long. Simon walks on the debris, at Robert. Spit is fizzing out of his mouth. Robert stands in time to be shoulder-jolted, six feet back, against the wall. A lithograph of Croton Reservoir in 1867 slides down, hits, leaks from its frame. Friday has tried to climb Robert like Iwo Jima: Simon throws him away. This one, Robert, is all his: property of Simon Who?

"Listen, you freshman fag, just because someone's been filling your privy purse, doesn't mean you're an *artiste*." Simon in close. He has Robert under the armpits: hung to dry: crucifixion style against the wall. Robert can't feel: his hands seem fingertipless, buzzy.

"So you know about Larry. So you know. I don't care. God, you don't think I like it, do you?"

"You love it. It's the first power you've ever had: playing Lolita-in-jockey-shorts. Oh, do it. Do it. But don't play Who's-got-the-reticule? with Larry's head. Larry's too important. Don't think you can swish in here like Susan Hayward and run my film company with your spindly backside. I won't let it happen. Not after all I've done for you."

"What? What've you done? Aside from trying to fuck my mother."

"You—" Simon has let Robert down: hands free to hit him. "If you're jealous, just keep it to yourself."

"Jealous. Trying, I said. Trying. You couldn't even make it with my dim-witted ma. Right? Right, Mr. Stud? Oh, you're pathetic." There is a brackish challenge in Robert's face. The face has said, Kill me. And Simon is nauseated—will he have to? Will he have to murder this child, for his own sake, for Robert's pride's sake? "Pathetic. You're pathetic."

"Shut up. Shut up."

"No. No, I'm gonna tell you for your own good. You're nothing without Larry. Why'd you think Rose and Don left? Because you're nothing. That five hundred grand is a big joke. Wolff gave it to Larry, not you. To buy him: you don't think Wolff wanted an original screenplay by Simon Lynxx, do you? About imaginary kids growing corn and having their tongues cut loose. And Rose and Don, they were going to take Larry. That's why I did it for you. To save what's left of your last chance."

"Larry. You don't know a thing about Larry. The others—but Larry would never have left me."

"He was going. He'd be gone right now. He stayed because of me."

"That's not how he described it, my raw-kneed little friend. And just an hour ago."

"He—he told you what I told him to tell you. For some stupid reason I—no, we—didn't want you embarrassed. But now—after this scene—now, just get away from me. I'm taking a walk. I've had enough of your bullying. Go on, show *Lucky* to Wolff. Maybe he'll let you sell popcorn in one of his theaters."

"Hold on. Not so fast." It isn't the insult: it's the leaving. Simon can't bear to be left.

"Let go. Get out of my way."

"What? Going down to fuck your mother goodbye?"

And Robert has hit him. To both their surprises. A nice overhand chop that will catch Simon in talk: tongue between incisor teeth. Simon is stung, open, off-stride: he could be hit again: a left hook might take him out. But Robert has already covered up: forearms high, a peekaboo defense, something very like prayer. It must come. Simon, in tongue pain, in anger, in frustration—perhaps more decisive yet: in doubt—Simon will go to town. A rabid, unscientific, herky-jerky mix of punches. At rib and kidney and neck: it is a northeaster blowing over Robert: a wild, destructive kind of weather. The expelled snorts—huh! a-huh! a-huh! a-huh! —are more terrible to Robert than the hurt. Simon right-uppercuts: an elbow struck: Robert will skid left along the wall and down. Simon is over him: automatic now: worn: doing menial labor. He sets his target up: keeping Robert afoot by the shirt-throat. Then a left, a left, a left, a left—this has become dogmatic persecution, not fury—against, against, against and against Robert's stomach. The belt buckle will slash his fist open; anyone else would need stitches there.

"Hit. Me. Unh. Go on. Go. On."

"I am. Oh, I am. I am." The shirt-throat rips: Simon will grab skin instead. "What happened to your stutter? Hanh? Hanh? What happened to it?" A left. "Where'd it go so fast?" A left. "Huh—maybe we can knock it out of you." A left.

"Please. Enough."

"Stutter! Stut-ter!"

"Enough."

"No, not enough. Stutter!" Simon has gone to the head: despite Minnie, his promise. A backhand slap: a forehand slap. The glasses leap off, rigid as some pre-Wright Brothers air machine. Robert is weeping. "Stutter! Stutter! Say you're sorry."

"S-stop. I—I'm so-ohry."

"More. I want to hear more."

"Um. Whatem-em ore? Please."

"I'm your father now. Minnie said so. She's leaving and she made me your father. You don't talk smart t'me. You don't hit your father."

"Oh. Oh, kay."

"Fag. Fag! Why'd you do it? You'll kill Larry—he thinks you're in love with him. But you're just using him."

"I—aaah." He cries. "Don't hit. I. I thought. Wuh, what you. You would do. Do. If, aaah." Robert speaks in the trough after each sob. "If—uh, a-uh—if h-he was leaving."

"No."

"Yes-ss. Y'would. Uh-uhhh. You would."

"Well, the damage is done now." Simon has sat on his bed. Robert kneels against it: hand under belly: trussing himself down there. His glasses, arms crossed under them, a little director's chair, look up from the floor. Simon can feel thawing: blood breaks from one nostril. "You can't be me, Robert."

"I so-ommm day. I will. I'll buh. Buh. Be better."

"Better than me? At being me? No one can do that, not even me. I've exhausted the possibilities. And why bother, anyhow? Huh? Oh, shit. My nose is bleeding again."

"Did-di do that?"

"What? Ah, yeah. Cheap shot, I wasn't ready."

"So—gaaap." Robert belches, from air sobbed in. "Much b'loood. I'll—I get—uhhh. A towel."

"No. Did I hurt you? In the face? Don't let your mother see I hurt you. Let her go away thinking we're friends."

"Oak. O-kay. Bu'we are, huh?"

"True." Simon lies back: shirt to nose. "Between man and man there can be no real friendship until punches have been exchanged. It's a get-ting-to-know."

"Wuh-what I said. Ah'bout *Lucky*—"

"Forget it. You could be right. You could be wrong. No one knows. Corn and tied-up tongues: I didn't believe it myself. But let's see."

"Wheel. Make it."

"I shouldn't have tried with your mother. I admit that. It was beneath me. Or it would have been if she ever was. Beneath me. I shoulda tried with my own mother. Maybe I have. Or maybe Mrs. P is my mother. Only Friday knows for sure."

"Simon. I'm—n'not a fag. I, Im-ean. I don't think." He cries: a freeing cry. "I don't like it. Uh-uh-uh: oh, gee. It hurts. Me. When h-he . . . Y'know."

"Okay. Nuts, your ear is bleeding. I'll catch hell from Minnie. Come up on the bed and rest."

"I'm. All right down, here."

"Come."

So, Simon carries Robert up to him.

2

"Wheee—

"We—

"Cramm. Jam.

"Well, said the hanged man, that brought me up short.

"Indeed. You are stuck tight as a pimp's pointy shoe. Push, unh. Stuck two-fifths down my best favorite slide in Francis Lewis Park. Alone. Waiting—with hope in his heart—t'unbatten Merry's wet and fur-lined hatch. Uh-up. Simon, you're packed in like weather stripping. Here, where—used t'be—his four-year-old glutei minimi would ssshush down to Bettina, who . . . if I can recall without too much prejudice . . . caught you maybe once in five times. Oh, Foster Mother. Oh, Dry Nurse. The blood-grated kneecaps I got trusting in your store-bought parenthood. A .200 fielding average you had, Bettina, for this poor merchandise, me. Han?

"Christ, think. What grammatical person are you in now? Now.

"The omniscient observer—right? Isn't it? The unjudgmental camera lens. But would an omniscient talk aloud to himself? Itself? I mean, knowing what will be said. And won't.

"It comes down to this . . . or something like it: Do you be, Simon—me? Uh-huh. Have a court reporter read that back while I type the committal papers up. Do you be comma Simon dash me. Question mark.

"It's no self-defrost, not easy—to separate these uncertain forms of address. The old shell game. But with an old pea under every shell.

"Yet simple comma Simon . . . what it is—I am the object of your thought. If (and however) I am, he is. Or me. Or, among friends, you are.

"STOP WIRE MONEY STOP LOVE . . . Hum, be prudent now . . . Shape whole, globular words. Just loud enough so it doesn't play table tennis—pock-a-pock—inside your mind. I think inflammation of the nermis that way lies. Da-dum. Keep the fat lips moving. Stay outside. Be a spokesman for the brain.

"Yes, yes—I know this. Contrary to popular mechanics, I AM, the pure BE, is hardest to pull off . . . even for him.

"For Simon, you mean.

"Num. Once . . . I once thought Simon had an ego so huge it was state-supported. Awn. I-ness, your royal. Yet ego, like three pair in seven stud, looks like a lock, but is a second-tit sucker more often than not.

"And—awn. Ah. Being so overtired, plus loss of nose blood—has the effect of good Connecticut-grown pot. The mind associates . . . with known criminals. Drawing freehand . . . Get wary, Simon. You almost thought that. Aloud. Say it aloud. Madness. There are no businessman's rates in that roach motel.

"I despise abstract thought.

"Yet, wait . . . There's something in this, as the man said when he broke his tooth on an olive pit. Hanh? Is this the actual perception of To Be? Well? Say three states of objectivity coexisting side-by-side-by-side. The I, the you, the Simon-him. Sleeping together like kids in a tar-paper shack. Or is it three states of subjectivity . . . ? Toward the object, me? Me.

"But it's true. I've always felt that. Simon has never had a fixed POV. Toward him.

"Or are we—no, God, for humane reasons, don't make it plural, too.

"Three.

"Still . . . the notorious Three-in-One of legend is singularly plural. Yesss . . . How does God speak in plenary sessions of the Trinity . . . ? Awn? By inter-office memo, probably.

"From the Desk of—

"From Our Desk?

"Three's a crowd said the Holy Ghost.

"Speak. Say it aloud. Don't just think. That scares me . . . like when someone repeats, repeats everything you say. When I was a sapless kid, they did that t'me. Can I play? Can I play? I can hit the ball. I can hit the ball. My name is Simon. My name is Simon. Meaningful monologues for two those were.

"Then again, though . . . I ask you, where is the audience? Um . . . awn. In the performer? In the perceiver? Do the Rolling Stones make sound in a vacant hall? Does an audience applaud itself? Congratulations to us for being here. Being moved by this. Do we entertain thoughts, like a USO tour? Or they us?

"Or, even more to the point—how am all three of us gonna get out of this o-gauge slide? Push. Uh-up. Together now. Houston, we have lift-off. And down.

"Remember. Little Simon talked like this a lot. And they told him the

Good Humor man knew, and would come one day t'truck him off. All smoky in dry ice. Ha.

"I waited. He never came. I was disappointed.

"Pathetic frip. Me, then. If I . . . No. Shall we not, in retrospective sympathy, take the three and drag-rope them back through the past. To the railroad-track vanishing point. Where sane and insane are mother-daughter look-alikes. Hagggg, Jesus. A set of three for every instant of consciousness. Imagine.

"No don't—kick. Pump. Make the swing go. Manic. Depressive. Up, manic. Depressive. Pump the swing, Simon.

"But did he have . . . ? Hum—little Simon, that is . . . or does he have . . . a right to exist back then? Now? After the Freedom of My Information Act got passed this afternoon? Can he be the same? Can the present, oh, overhaul . . . in both senses . . . what was?

"Think now . . . Am I, is he, that hero of myth? Left exposed to perish on a mountainside . . . early form of planned parenthood . . . because his existence will threaten the peace of the state? Are there scars where your infant Achilles tendons were pierced and roped together? To be discovered later by upper-middle-class shepherds? And used as a tax exemption?

"Pump up. Oooh, man. You are weak. Do not break the nose clot.

"Red Flag. Hanh? That's the Fourth Person, isn't it? Public Simon. Created by a committee of the three—yet never clearly perceived by us. Or even seen. Defaming ethnic groups. In a gorilla suit. Because, numerous as we seem t'be getting, we are not a public.

"Ha, pump. Be physical for squiff's sake. Too much of this and the cranium is Three Mile Island.

"But what did she call him? She-who-exposed-you-on-the-open-market? Ech? Anh?

"Naming. Is that a fourth person thing? Can I-you-he be nameless? Just be. Go on, try to conceive of it. Beeep-beep, coming through. Is a chair a chair, if I call it a table? Sure, I guess, but it's not a *satisfied* chair. Hoop. And she, what did she call you? My Trouble? My Little Indiscretion? The-Thing-in-My-Womb? It?

"Or maybe George.

"How many shots at abortion were there? One for each person? Sitting in a hot bath t'boil us out. Eating ergot. Stirring the recipes of old midwives. Did we, three musketeers, thrust and parry en garde against a bent coat hanger? Did we cushion ourselves, in fetal position, as she fell on purpose down the staircase? The Thing thinks. George thinks? Did she ride horses to gallop me brainless? Is it any wonder he has a fine, firmed-up paranoia? People have been trying t'kill you. But I'm alive. Let us take a walk through the playground before it gets too dark.

"Lo. Who were these people? B.T., L.S., C.M., D.K., H.B., R.R. A lost race of carvers, that's his initial reaction. Eh. Time machine: remember, at this very picnic table, yellow jackets would squat on your peanut-butter-and-(always-grape)-jelly-sandwich. Until I wept from hunger. And sting fear. DINO LOVES LUCIE. Didn't he, though? RAT LOVES PINKIE. DOM LOVES DOT. CARL LOVES JOYCE B. After Joyce A. Just before Joyce C. TIM LOVES . . . someone. Someone worn illegible by twenty years and elbows-on-the-table.

"Merry, I want you t'meet—

"My sandbox. You're the first woman I've ever shown it to. You cannot know me until you know how I dug. The sand splashed. Against the sun it made sandbows, if such a thing can be. To Simon Little it could be. I was Sam Spade. I was the Army Corps of Engineers. Yah-yah. Talk it up. That kinda sentimental stuff. Got to fold in some human interest. Women love men who're in touch with their past. Especially when their present, like mine, is Krakatoa South of Douglaston.

"The question remains—ten-four, repeat and copy . . . (Hey, he's talking inta his fist, just like Simon the Fabulous Skull-Damaged Child useta do, remember? Eeee-yummm. Eee-yummm. Zero at twelve o'clock high. Blat-crack! God, God, God. There's fuel all over the Plexiglas. I'm blind and my stick won't answer anymore. Jesus—I'll never see the Pulaski Skyway again, guys. Jag! Jag! Ba-spizzzz. Crackle on the airwaves. Ace Lynxx has bought his farm. Prime real estate, too. If you've got a bathysphere t'commute with.)

"The question remains—why are you here? Nah—not 'Why are you on this earth plane?' Nothing so simple as that. Why are you locked in this ferdinging playground, at such an hour, when Simon should be sending up snore flak in preparation for Herman Wolff tonight?

"Between you and me—and this is dead serious (I'm getting annoyed) —why did he have t'do it? Call Merry, that is.

"The treatment . . . ?

"Prack that one. Don't believe him. Norty's receptionist could've typed it up.

"Oh, Merry—let me off: I've got a note from my urologist. As the male sturgeon said, 'What's caviar t'you, is just prostate trouble t'me.' I'm tired, Merry.

"Think of it—the ergs involved. We could invent a cure for cystic fibrosis, go to Betelgeuse, make a car that ran on what's left in the bottom of beer glasses—if it weren't for the work units shot on women.

"Huff. It comes t'my omniscience now—da, da, de, *dum*—that . . . take away sex . . . take away even the she-thinks-I'm-attractive subsexual male validation . . . take that away, and Tiger Lynxx has never invested one hour in a woman that didn't, awn, bore him t'fructose.

"God, if they weren't sexually permeable every day of the month—if they were bitches, say, in heat just now and then—men would've gassed

them long ago. No. Kept them in breeding pens. Women are—the word is
. . . t'put a kind construction on it . . . uninteresting.

"Awn . . .

"Nuh, worsen at. Women alone have *feelings*, we're supposta believe.
Da-da-de-dada, feee-lings. By which is meant, they schlump around in a
mental housedress all day and appreciate hell out of themselves. Otherwise called compassion . . . or sincerity . . . or being-into-the-real-me.
Which emotion no man, ever, can clamp his booster cable onto the poles
of—somehow. Or so they think. Female authenticity, dontcha see. Stems
from the pompous and insipid undulations of giving birth. Ah, *giving* . . . ? Why? Mmmmph. How come you *take* a dump but you *give*
birth—same effort and general IQ required. Women take birth. Bettina
did. And, yah, they have about as much real feeling as—oh, the organ
music between periods at a hockey game. No flooze has ever felt the
sweet honesty of a street fight. Sock: here's my best chop, now try yours.
Lord, that is *feeling*. Unperverted by Barbara Cartland or Rollo May.
Clean. Genuine. Unlike the Fu Manchu negotiations that go into getting
your teapot poured in bed. Fact . . . women are . . . well—a kind of unsuccessful fag.

"Ho. Unsuccessful fag.

"A well-lathed, Wildean phrase.

"And accurate enough.

"Gimme a male molt for companionship any time. They've got enough
manpower left for sarky wit, for imagination—and the biker-gear fruits
can take a punch. Also give: with metal grommets. Awn. Besides, since
they clothe and make up and hairstyle and interior-decorate for women—
all's you end up seducing in a woman is a pook's dress dummy anyhow.
Oh, authentic . . . women. With eyeliner so thick you could land a
Cessna twin engine on it. Or the 'authentic' natural look: frescoed tight
in some French flipside's chi-chi blue jeans. A woman with pants on is
like an organ grinder's chimp wearing a suit. You hand it a dime out of
embarrassment.

"And still, still the Prince of Pong persists. Like a rattlesnake with its
head lopped off. Hissless. Floppy. Squirming t'bite. Why?

"Got the Protestant Hump Ethic, I guess.

"No, man. Why, man? Why are we harassing Merry? She's okay. Huh?
Answer me, you micro-mind. Could be maybe the one time I feel strung
in tune is—is when stalked by the reproductive demi-urge. Nah. Merry
could use her time t'better profit. Take up law, sew ashtrays. Simon
doesn't reproduce. I am The Last.

"Up, climb. Safer if I . . . see Merry . . . before . . . she sees me. Up
on—unnnh . . . the jungle gym of childhood. (Jesus, his voice sounds off
mike and on reverb.) To the top . . . unnnh, where's my Sherpa guide?
This way I can still skulk off. One more rung. And up. Just don't bleed.

Hah. Uh-hahh. My head feels like the Orient Local: full of third-class passengers with live chickens under their overcoats. Here.

"Ahab in his crow's nest, looking for the Great White Tail.

"Why?

"To kill it, of course. Her.

"Now you're talking sense. Women gotta be killed. Over and over again. What was that fabulous monster—the more you sliced it in half, the more monster you got? Hanh. Those were days of low labor costs. Bettina, mother, is it all you? Chopped up fine through the world?

"Love, they sing. And sharing. But how can you share with a hole? Hanh? Yet—mark me—emptiness sucks fullness into it. By some sexual physics. To feed: that thing is a mouth. Emptiness has no creativity of its own: it hasta scrounge. Hup. Uh-huh. Now you're on, Ace. And when I am siphoned into that emptiness—I am, for one moment, fe-male. Thoughtless, imageless: a dull stirrer of the universe's turgid amniotic fluid. Even on top, hammering into the void. Even then. Especially then. Especially when killing, we are unsexed. It is their piddling three-second victory.

"Hey. She's late I think.

"Your honor, they tease us into killing them. My client pleads innocent by reason of a temporary and recurrent insanity. Uh, all women want t'be raped. Yes, your honor, I realize that sounds a bit Paleolithic and not to be found in *Ms.* magazine. But may I make a distinction? Thank you—ah. See, women don't want t'be raped by blacks and Chicanos and penniless flower children: but that has *nichts* and *nada* t'do with female dignity—it's just class prejudice. Women want t'be raped by Warren Beatty or Burt Reynolds or any one-headed male with $40,000 per annum after taxes. Ha? War between the sexes? No, your honor, with all due respect —t'run a decent war y'gotta have some equality between the warriors. Anything less is a massacre . . . No, women just commit suicide: again, again, again. My client has been the unwitting accomplice in five hundred self-immolations. And they're *grateful*. It's the only way they can duck into the VIP section t'some small significance. Through losing. Being beaten. Having their soil turned violently. Children are born of an enduring masochism. The life-urge is murder.

"Hum. And well.

"I'm impressed, Simon.

"But, yes. He believes that. It's true.

"Yuh. And . . . and in reprisal for these little deaths, they hold the male child hostage . . . ha. Breast-feeding guilt. Egging on lust. Until father and son go at it: in the corner, on the ropes, thumb in eye: and maleness is subdivided against itself. To the point even of war, that Esalen training for nations. Say Aaaah, Simon. Stick a finger down your flame-thrown throat. Gup: a wet belch. I almost lost it then. The truth shall make you nauseous. Consider it. Aldo and he might have wrist-wrestled and pulled big punches and been a small stag gathering to-gether. But for—but think of something else. Oh, it comes to me in Maui-size rollers: blond, tan Tab Hunter types could surf on them. Crude as I am—I don't relish tossing meat to such a hate as this. Hate gives her honor. It's like having a baby tyrannosaurus imprinted on me. Change the subject, Simon.

"Or the object.

"To what?

"Oh, um. Well. Crane the camera up. Intercut here: an overhead shot. Hanh? This place doesn't smell. It once did, in September. How? Of a useful dying. But how? And remember the taste of iron jungle gym bars licked? Remember? No. You can't. He says it was an acid taste: like juice kept too long in an open can. And what taste is that?

"As a solipsist I create a lousy universe. Deprived. You wonder why the inhabitants complain? Why they rush with torches at the castle?

"Let me take this man's pulse. No second hand, no watch—but feel that tiny drumfire—fast as an over-tuned tappet. I live with the torridness of insects. Cut you open, they'll find the organs of a seventy-year-old child.

"She's late.

"So nu? Let's suppose she doesn't show. How would Simon take that? Huh? Gimme an honest reading: slip your fat thumb off the scale.

"Aaaah.

"Hurry up.

"I'm thinking.

"Yes?

"Aaaah. Okay. I've got it: relief. I'd be relieved.

"Thasso? Hunh. You *are* tired, man.

"But they always show. Like death. They always have . . . Or. Wait.

"What?

"I'd be relieved. Yet, you know, uneasy. Too.

"Uneasy? Why?

"*Because*, dammit. You know why. Speak aloud, Simon. I can't know Why unless you tell me. And I won't listen 'til you vocalize it out, why? It . . . Because the brain lives, bagged, in the scrotum. And the scrotum, boned, in the brain. Listen. Oh. It's, if I can't cork the little hole—I, we, we're superstitious—then I can't surprise the metaphor, produce the image. Art is erectile tissue.

"And—oh-ho, yes—they know that. Our superstition. They disable us with it: the threat of impotence. Look at him. Can't get it up, can't get it up, can't get it up. That's the mansnare. Because copulation—they know, we know—is a symbol of art. The most trivial creativity. The creativity of baboons scratching on a rock. It lessens man—to a feral, instinctive pocket of sperm. Huh—women depend on that. See . . . See—most of all they fear Man-the-Artist, Man-the-Thinker. Those two, gee, they might not be interested in womanslaughter. The endless, net-profitless killing. Those two delinquents might forget t'blurt out children someday.

"And that . . .

"Aha!

"That's where the first person is. Goes. The I Am. The inherent Be.

"Of course. That's it. Men are he. Men are you. Men see themselves as they suppose—hope?—women do. As an object. A drone in mating garb. And that—that's the fourth person, twice removed. Man, the-dancer-of-sex. A persona. A decoy on the pond. Of wood.

"And still, knowing this, he is uneasy. If the flag isn't up, we can't claim the land. If Merry doesn't arrive. If Simon can't . . . Hah. Touch . . . diddle with yourself. Movement: it's alive. Come up. Come up. Give him his comeuppance. Prove his mind.

"It's an incantation. He asked her t'this place for magic. If you lay pipe in Merry, it'll mean good luck. A fruitful harvest. With Wolff. Seed in her will be seed in him. An old wives' tale. But those old wives . . . they knew.

"Knew what?

"Their old husbands.

"Spout ho. Wrench that silver dollar out of the mast.

"She's here. And on a bicycle.

"And I'm relieved.

"Aaaah. Aaaah. Watch her ride: ass high . . . some jock kicking a thirty-to-one shot home. Oh, gosh. So clean and healthy a dung beetle like Simon would famish on her. Circling in the street now. On the lookout for you. She thinks you've stood her up. And is she relieved? Pretty calf muscles stretched, erased, stretched, erased. Pedal, pedal, pedal.

"Now, for your viewing pleasure, the Accident, the Indiscretion, will invert that image. Poof. Let those legs pedal-push at heaven. Plaid skirt fallen back: an umbrella disemboweled by the wind. Me latched in place and digging for first.

"Give her credit. She doesn't dress like a man.

"Uh-oh, unsaddled. Chaining fierce bike t'the fence. Hanh . . . Let's slither down. Bonko, unn. He cracks his elbow—some slithering. Pain can make you feel relevant, too. Ssssh. But it can. We know, but not so loud. Walk.

"There's time yet—

"Step silently—

"To call it off—

"Across the playground—

"And vanish—

"To the fence—

"Dum-da-dum. Simon, Last Mohican, you're quiet as an Indy qualifier in these brittle leaves.

"Sit. Sit on the bench, Merry. Let him observe you. Simon puts an eye, voyeur-wise, to one of a thousand diamond holes in this mesh fence.

"Can she sense you looking?

"Does Simon want it?

"Simon, awn, wants.

"Count—thirteen, fourteen, fifteen brush strokes through brown hair. Is she humming? Or practicing some prologue t'the night? He observes her, the thing does: nameless and without origin. Hanh. Now some pointillist makeup on the forehead. You can pick up her excitement: it's on all frequencies.

"Note. Hah. She can't pose her arms. Both flailed back over the bench rail: prow first, like a ship's figurehead. A sales pitch for the old Siamese outlet on her chest. Mmmm. We detect some insecurity there. Not much for a drowning man to grab. About the size of boiled gnocchi. Must give a rave: shape, texture, proportion. If we can find them.

"Here comes someone. A male. We, Merry and Simon, watch him. No. It isn't us—too short. We'd know us anywhere. See, at the last moment she pulled both arms across her milk pods. Tut-tut. Her courage failed.

"And now a couple walking past, toward that two-foot-deep lake. She watches them. Ah, woman. Capital W—I know what you're after. Don Juan that you are. To break him down: capture and crib his sperm. Oh, how she loves their walking together. Bumping. Making a joint fist. The girlishness of lovers.

"Watch. The Thing's ghastly mouth has flopped open. The Unspeakable will speak.

"Pssst, Merry. Pssst.

"Spring-bok! Did you see?—her compact high-mileage body went one-two. Hanh. Like a concert pee-anist alerted to play. Upright, at tea: a cucumber-sandwich earnestness about her. Can you screw me? No, it's *may* you screw me. Conjugate the verb t'conjugate, Miss . . . what's your last name? Har. Must try t'remember, Simon, really. It shows a certain seriousness.

"Duck. Peel out. She's looking at the fence.

"No. Double take. She's staring up. At the treetop. I'll be a Polish admiral, she thinks you're up the tree.

"And, frankly, Simon—who would put it past you?

"Down, Merry. Here. Hey, you—you. Blind Purveyor of the Species—can't you smell, as a fat wildebeest could, the lion downwind?

"Don't I stink of your hot, little death?

"Or is the wildebeest staked out? Docile. A last meal for the wild-maned assassin?

"Yo. Merry. You with the corrective corneas on. Here."

"Where? Who is it?"

"Who? Who? she says. I'm a rapist working on spec. I got your name from Consumer Reports. Under V for victim."

"Simon."

"In person. Ah—I mean, if that's possible."

"What? Where? It's getting dark."

"I'm inside the fence, Durf. Here. I'll rattle my cage.

("Observe, Simon. Merry can't not run t'you. They come. They all come. Oh, prance, you unbroken filly. Make the leaves shush and rattle. Hanh. She wants t'be demure, t'be old-fashioned as polio. But she can't.

"Note. Famous-maker's pocketbook gives her a hard hip-check. Butt. Butt. Oh, and those Park Avenue cheekbones, they slope like script esses. My left finger through the mesh will chuck at her mouth. Lord, I had forgotten. Even at rest her lips make a moue. Now, with the other hand execute a chess move. Knight to Queen Six: two down, one diagonal. Some droll love play.)

"Checkmate.

("Our hands French-kiss through the wire mouth. My finger tongues the palate of her palm.")

"Simon. I'm a little late."

"Don't blame me. I toldja t'get fitted with a rubber washer."

"No, I mean—"

"I know whatcha mean. You dint wanna seem too eager. No, you hadda jump-start your Schwinn."

"What're you doing in there? It's locked."

"They gave me a legal-aid lawyer. This is his idea of plea bargaining.

("Clammy palm. Her circulation's torpid as gluten flour. Hah. Simon, the clotting factor. Let's see if we can balance our forefingernails edge t'edge. Good, she knows that game. If you meet a girl whose nail edge fits into yours—it's love. Lucky my edges are ragged as a perforated stamp. Uh. Time check: figure you've got an hour and a half. Not much room for foreplay. Haveta settle for threeplay, I guess.

"Strange, isn't it? How the ionized field of female I-want-you can cancel all unsightly fears.

"Except one. Except one. Except that one.")

"So? Are you coming out of there?"

"No. You're coming in. Walk t'the left. Down and around t'Fifty-second Road. Weird y'should pick this joint. I'm its alumni association. I remember Frannie Lynch told her father she got knocked up from a dirty seesaw here. Coulda been true."

"The gates on Fifty-second are locked, Simon."

"Walk. I can get you inta anything."

"That's what I'm afraid of."

"Come."

Their hands trail together on the fence: electricity as in boyhood games of metal tag. And at the double gate Simon will put on a show: and boast. Preparation: uh—aaah-ap: an inhale soccer ball large: air so oppressive in its diplomatic, scentless neutrality that he might almost black out. But then—booost. Sullenly, with a grinding demurral, each two-hundred-pound gate pole is jacked up: out of/from its six-inch pit in the cement. A space has given way. Size five Merry will jiggle through. To be hugged up. His palms seat the spread of her taut, defensive butt: they hoist. Amazement outpolls her certain primness: his strength, so much male force, can goad and irk. Now her shoulder has come even with his nose: are there, Simon, perfumes invisible about? One red sandal has stepped off. That bare sole is somehow galling. The shoeless are disadvantaged: and quickly overtaken. Merry, a tenderfoot here, knows.

"Your ass is hard as shuffleboard discs. Relax it."

"I think you'd better put me down. Please."

"Can I push you on the swing then? Hanh?"

"Yes. Just put me down. I don't like being helpless. It makes me feel impotent and angry. All right?"

"So stern we are. All right."

Having felt her up, Simon feels her down. They step back: they model for each other then. It is well to point out here that Merry and Simon have met just twice. Recollection summarizes: the master tape is short-lived and weak: it cannot often reproduce a face. And a face pestered by memory will disband its features: nose, ear, eye shadow, teeth: to an inadequate paraphrase. So now they are surprised. She, by the tasteful, planar nose: by a little boy woundable expression around his brown and, well, pug eyes. Effrontery, lewdness, much attractive turmoil has been her synopsis of him. He, by the good yoke-wide breadth at her shoulder: also by a self-making and combative ridge from chin to neck. Too available, weak with progesterone, was his abridgment of her. Both are, generally speaking, pleased. She will downcast her eyes: to direct feet while they scuff out a nest in the late-September leaf trash: maternal enterprise. Simon is clued in: grossness, Doctor, has been contraindicated here. He will take—a may-I-please-if-it-wouldn't-seem-etc.? in his head-shift—he will gently take her hand. They couple and walk. Arms are stiff: formal, unintroduced. Their reciprocal grasp knocks, clapper-like, between.

"You a swinger, hah?"

"I *double entend* you. No."

"Dooble, yourself. Have a seat, my little cherrystone. Not that one, that one's held together by a Charleston Chew."

"Wait now. Wait 'til I'm ready."

"Pull out the blocks. Contact. Extinguish all smoking materials. You are about t'be swung. Oh, *swung*. The Pleiades will duck. Gravity will doubt its jurisdiction. Aaaah—"

"Wuh-aaate!"

The amplitude of that first arc awes her: it is vast and true. Chain saws her hand. Now Simon has gone up, as for a two-hand jump shot, catching the seat edge with his long fingernails. Scimitar swish! Merry whoops: she has given in: her legs pump: they collaborate. With a shove from Simon so dynamic that the streetlights in all Bayside go on.

"Careful!"

"I've—"

Out/back.

"Never—"

Out/back.

"Lost a—"

Out/back.

"Swinger—"

Out/back.

"Yet."

"Eeee—it's gooood, Goddd!"

They let the cat die under her. For Simon this is sudden Tibet: a mountainous, air-famished land. He hacks at breath. The effort disbursed in such magnificent shoving has put him over budget now. Simon will lash himself—arm on top of arm, a clove hitch—to the swing pole. Park lamps glare green—overtime photosynthesis—in tree-branch fretwork above. Maple-leaf shadow has blemished Merry's cheek: is she angry?: is she taking umbrage? And, in turn, the cobra rise of her cigarette smoke, projected, campfire big, lazes up one brick rest-room wall. Simon must squat: he dips down for a thicker oxygen mix. Her cheek has grooved, maybe coy, maybe regretful, on the swing chain. One foot has written longhand in sand: then longhand erased. Her toes, in bondage to their sandal thonging, are extremely sensuous. Simon is aroused, but can't arise. He would like to ravish Merry, her behind up/over the seat, swung in/out, an energy-saving apparatus.

"Simon."

"Ah-uh. Heek. Mmm-breath."

"I brought you a present."

"A present. Y'shunta. What is it? Huh? Something useful I hope, like a new lint filter f'my tongue."

"See? I just hope you can handle all this emotion." Merry has unflapped her leather bag. "I made it myself, so try to be receptive."

"What is it? A tie? Oh, how offbeat and kinky. I haven't worn a tie since my last arraignment."

"It's not a tie. Get up, come under the light, I want to see it on you.

Rise. Show some polite interest." Simon, hand over hand, bell-ropes himself up on the swing pole. "It's a belt. Macramé."

"Macramé? Where'd you learn? I hear they have adult extension courses for children now."

"Ssssh. Don't slouch." She is posing him. "I've noticed your pants tend to droop."

"What? Me? Droop? Listen, my tailor did the wardrobe for *This Was Burlesque*. Droop, hanh." Merry will rotate him: will tunnel the belt through his blue-jean loops. "Don't get me dizzy, I feel like Wake Island as it is."

"Let your stomach out."

"Out of where? That's all you're gonna get."

"My Lord, you've really lost weight. I'll have to make another notch. But there—do you like it? I like it." She waits. "Well? Do you?"

"Hold on. I usually dress in a body bag, I haveta think."

"Think."

"It's sublime. Especially the color. I haven't seen a red like that since Carmen Miranda's lips died. Now I can hold my *cabeza* up high with all the other *maricóns* in Spanish Harlem." Merry has worked her tongue out: but she is—but what did she expect?—hurt. "Naw. Gee. Ignore my Wallace Beery suave. The Duke of Derision is really very moved. And you musta thatched this together just for me. Dimmesdale, your priest-lover, couldn't wear it—unless he's a cardinal. Sinner. Gosh, Mer-maid. And I didn't knit you anything. I'm crotch-fallen with contrite."

"Don't worry. I didn't figure you for a gift-giver. Somehow."

"Well, I allus think my presence is door money enough. But why, hah? Captain Craft, using his own mercenary self as an archetype, sniffs some posterior motive. Hanh? Y'wanna be in moom pitchers, lady?"

"No. Just foolishness. I didn't think you got many presents. Somehow." She scarfs her hair back/up: in the aloof, high lamplight it will seem metallic: a centurion's helmet, bronzed, protective at her forehead and nape. "Just foolishness. It's the last time, though."

"Awwwwww. Aww. Aww." He reels her, one arm taken up fistful by fistful, into a spinal-brace hug. "You're right. You're right. The last present I had was when little Nancy Shellenbacker gave me erysipelas." Simon kisses Merry: his lower lip will seem blown, loutish against her.

"Your mouth. It feels—" Censure: start again. "That's why you're losing weight. You can't eat, can you? You have scar tissue there. It's in your throat, too, isn't it?"

"Hey, man. That's nice. You just went stiff as a Prussian orderly." He has unlocked his embrace: given her leave to go: milking it a bit. "My lips, huh? Repulsive, huh? Like kissing a closestool. Jesus, and my breath is probably a defoliant, huh?"

"No. I didn't smell your breath. Let me check." Merry is eager: on tiptoe. "Breathe out."

"Hey. Push off. What are you, a carrion eagle? Christ—Miss Sordid—you outboor even me." He cups one hand over his mouth. "Haaah. Haah. Huh, I forgot. The pilot light blew out on my smeller. Not that I could ever get t'windward of my own breath. Haah! See, when you breathe out, you can't jam her into reverse gear fast enough."

"Never mind that. This is serious. Are you taking vitamins? Protein? Your skin looks awful, sallow. It's in rags around your eyes."

"You're a real image-builder, aren't you? Listen, I've had a full day of crisis training—and it worked. My crises got bigger and bigger."

"You've been hemorrhaging? Just from the nose? Or the mouth, too?"

"The nose. The nose. Hell, think of it this way—"

"Hush. What have you eaten today?"

"Ah, crow. A lot of crow. And some humble pie."

"Food, Simon. What?"

"Oh, I can't remember. Robert made me coffee this morning. Ah—and . . . maybe something else this afternoon. Are there any grease spots on my shirt?"

"Let me get this straight. You don't want to eat? Or you can't? Which is it?"

"Well. A little of each. I do get hungry. But it doesn't possess me the way it used to. I useta eat up t'my wrists. Hey, I was overweight, I can afford t'cannibalize myself."

"Does your mouth hurt?"

"No. It doesn't feel at all. Like I picked it up with a potholder."

"As if you had Novocain?"

"Dunno, never had it. My teeth're so perfect they look false. But it's a hassle. It's real casework, eating. I haveta watch my mouth so it doesn't gnaw half my head away."

"And now you can't smell at all?"

"Sometimes I smell a no-smell. Like what a sunlamp smells like."

"Look. You're not stupid. Even you can guess how serious this is. You're injured, Simon. You've got to go see Dr. Gobel. Or, if not him—I haven't any stake in him—someone else who's qualified." Simon dishes her hand up: for a Mantovani kiss.

"All I need, my little bicuspid, is a skin pop of tenderness." His voice has its damper pedal on: long chords. "I was a child conceived with the lights out."

"Don't change the subject."

"Change? This *is* the subject."

"Here it comes."

"It comes. Oh, it comes. Walk with me and my new *Men's Wear Daily* belt. I wanna make some castles in the sand."

"Damn. I thought you were more intelligent. A doctor could—hey, don't pull like that. At least about your own body, I thought you had some common sense."

"Me? I'm just a night effect, fulla distortion. I'm a player t'be named later. A drinking song. An improper fraction. Sense? Watch your step. There's two. Down. Here."

"Why? Where?"

Simon, host, will do the courtesies: Merry, my boyhood sandbox: old sandbox, friend, say hello t'Merry here. It is rink-shaped, icehouse solid: a good child-confiner: and culvert-dank now—wheeee! Simon—last one in is a sigmoid—has belly-flopped on his back: to form sand snow angels there. His body can trust: it is drunkard-supple and not hurt. Simon lies flat, chain-gang-dressed by a striping shadow from the iron railwork around. He will coax Merry in. She misgives: is this a romantic prank? The sand looks smutty: embossed with child footprinting (and, she doesn't doubt, adhesive child debris). But Simon can make Merry aware of her constrainedness: for him she'd like to be a hail-fellow soul. Merry picks off her left sandal: then her right. Holding both in one hand, a pair of unfilled scales, Justice—female and pretty much blind—will step down. With encouragement from Simon. There are dry leaves, edge-up in the sand, that feel razory as a tin-can rim. She has no purchase, traction: her fine toes claw: forget a quick escape. Is this some ant lion's sandy trap: will she be sucked or suckered in?

"Ugh. Clammy. And there's lumps in it."

"Just a buried Pamper or two. Calm your tracts, Merino. Listen, out Big Sur way, you'd pay a C note per hour for sandbox therapy like this. You'd be wallowing nude with some Werner Blowhard type, peeing on yourself and regressing like the tide off Laguna Shoals." Well, Merry has sat: and grit infiltrates her skirt at once. "See. Hanh. No expense was spared t'trivialize this evening. One—a Bird's Eye juice can for making turrets. Two—a pound Maxwell House can for the castle keep. And three —a milk carton bottom for the serfs' Dive City. You be Helmsley, I'll be Spear."

"Oh, fun."

"You sound blighted with pleasure." Merry's hand, a sneak thief, is in her bag: furtive, fast: as though purse-snatching herself. "I saw that. Uh-uh. No smoking. If I can't enjoy it, nobody can. I'm self-considerate that way."

"All right. Ow." Simon has sloshed water between them: cold simulates pain. "My feet."

"Hey, Dimpiss, all's you can make with dry sand is a surfer movie. Slosh it around. Knead. As Sergeant Preston useta say, 'Mush.'" He passes her the coffee can. "Then pack. Tight as an underaged prossie.

You put up the castle. I'll put up some inefficiency apartments. Leave out the dog turds, they have no consistency."

"Uh, Simon."

"Whassamatter, you lose your play faculty?"

"I think so. It's kind of dark in here."

"Creativity is play. Sex is play. In this outfit we play."

"If I must."

"A little incidental music while we build. Need a sound track t'cover the lousy visuals. Ah. In this very pit dwelling I gave Deirdre Feibleman a schmeck of sand that reinfected her stye. In return she gave me a scratch with her pinky nail that took like a cowpox vaccination. I still have it. Da-de-dum, the way we were, de-dum. Those were bright, king-fisher days. I lost a red shovel in here—a Stradivarius for burrowing—we probably could still exhume it. Hey. Hanh. Come on, Goldbrick. Pack it. *Tight* I said. What is this, the Ashcan School of architecture? You work like some Mafia capo throwing up a low-rent hambone hutch."

"I'm trying."

"Very. See that rest room, looks like a Bauhaus Indian hogan? That's where Simon the Kid eye-dropped on his first extramural sex. Dino and Lucie. My primal experience was very secondary. I thought she had ring-worm on her back, but it was only her vertebrae were rubbed scabby by the concrete in front of the urinals. Hahhhh, yes . . . Dig and scoop and gouge and cram. Dino'd boost me through that fanlight over the MENS door—I was seven or eight . . . at just this time of twilight when Fat Ganuche, the parkie, went home with his thermos of Sicilian purple—*mise en* bathtub *au château*. Then I'd drop down and open the door from inside. How many kids played pipe cleaner in there for the first time you'd need a certified public abacus t'count. Not me. When it came t'getting screwed Lad Simon was a prohibitive underdog. Dig. Churn. Ram. But there must be children around today, prenatally influenced, who think of mother when they hear a men's-room toilet stall slam shut."

"Charming."

"How did it go, you remember? One o'clock, two o'clock, three o'clock —rock! Hey, Ilioc, and this is the jock and I'm on the scene with my record machine. In return for my first-story work Dino'd let me sit in his '49 Buick and go rhum-rhum. He wanted t'be a DJ and thought Simon, through Aldo, was not-what-you-knew-but-who-you-knew. Ha. Miscal-culation. Where is Dino now? God, he must be thirty-seven, thirty-eight, getting his DA hair-transplanted. Does this recent change in your mythic past, huh, avert his future?"

"My past? Who're you talking to?"

"Simon saw the silhouette of Lucie's legs up and heard a lot of melo-orgasmic simpering. What did he make of it? Mix. Dredge. Grub and daub. And, you think now—can it be?—that Dino slapped Lucie once because her passion made him fall out onto the ceramic tile. Was it good for me, too?"

"Simon. Wait." She will interrupt his hand. "What's going on?"

"Huh? Am I building on your property line? I'll give you an easement."

"Ssssh. You sound just a little disoriented, that's all. Manic. Stop digging for a minute—please, I'm scared. Are you talking to me or to yourself? Or is there someone else in the dark here with us now?"

"Ahm." Simon is stopped. "Well. This could kill my reputation as an anti-intellectual." His hand bulldozes: aimless heavy equipment. "Well. Can I trust you? What I say will go no further than these four, uh, railings here?"

"Yes. But what?"

"Before—give me that coffee can—before, when I was waiting here . . . this may sound like dermabrasion of the mind, but—I thought . . . Suppose, just suppose, the human personality was really three subheads instead of a Roman Numeral One. Not the Id and the Ego and D'Artagnan, whatever Freud had on his pushcart . . . but . . . hanh . . . Am I, I? Or am I, You—You, Simon? Or He, He-Simon? I mean, what is the state of my being? What person am I in? Any of the above? Or two? Or all three at once like a club sandwich? Not t'mention Simon the cabaret and street-corner personality—a guy even I hardly know. Huh? Do you ever feel that way? Or do I not express myself well t'the layman?"

"I—"

"Y'see. I talk t'myself a lot. And sometimes I don't know how t'get my own attention."

"Your state of being?"

"Yuh. That."

"It sounds like Heidegger. Have you been reading Heidegger?"

"High-digger?"

"Martin Heidegger." Merry tonks a can with her nail. "D'you know German?"

"Do you?"

"I can function in it."

"A functional German. So?"

"Heidegger coined a word, *Da-sein*. It means, oh, being-there. Existence. My being-there is my *Da-sein*. Your *Da-sein* is your being-there. *Da-sein* is pretty much always your own particular *Da-sein*. As differentiated from the being of *vorhanden*, inanimate things. Or *zuhanden*, utensils made by man."

"Oh. Well, I'll just dig. In that case I'll take my little *zuhanden* and dig. Jesus, *Deutschland über Alles* t'you, too."

"At any rate: all modern concepts of being—existentialism and so on —derive from Heidegger's *Da-sein*, which is concerned with its own special aptitude for being-in-the-world. Quickly then, before you turn off. We, the sentient human beings, go into a state of *verfallen*-ness—too much concern with the world, the *vorhanden*. Distraction from our actual and potential being. All men experience it. And with it we experience dread. Not fear—fear is fear of some specific thing. Dread—well, even you know the German word, Heidegger made it commonplace—*Angst*. That is: we suddenly discover that we are in an eerie state of thrown-ness or *Befindlichkeit*. Thrown like dice into a there or here. It seems random and terrible. Un-understandable."

"I think I preferred Deirdre Feibleman."

"Ah-ha, *you* started this." A minute: a handful: she lets sand run out. "*Verfallen* man, thrown into there-ness, will feel dread and, through it, will arrive at an essential perception—his Being-toward-the-end. Death. The one thing he can be certain of. Mortality is crucial to the awakened *Da-sein*. Being-toward-the-end is a mode of existence which Being must assume and acknowledge as soon as it truly *is*."

"*Ja. Ja.*" Simon has a finger between Merry's toes: he will rasp, in/out. "Does that arouse you? I took a course in foot reflexology."

"No. So, what it sounds like—your fragmentation of self into I-you-he—it sounds like a perception of *verfallen*-ness. A natural step, through *Angst*, to Being-Toward-Death. To Being."

"I despise abstract thought."

"Apparently, though, you've been indulging in it."

"I'd much rather suck on your nipples."

"Infantilism—in more senses than one."

"Ah, what say we forget I ever opened this pot of stale *Kartoffelklösse*? Huh? Being-Toward-Death is a fat waste of being, you ask me. All three of me. It might give Young Werther and his band of madcap mourners a Teutonic high but t'me, thanks, it's just a lotta coal-gasification."

"It's *you*, though. Anyone can see that. If ever there was a man who courted death, expected death, it's you."

"Sure. I put a personal in *Cadavers' Exchange* every month."

"It *is* you."

"Merry, I seethe. I'm the fecund silting Nile. I'm a sea of nourishing krill. I'm—I'm germs. I infest. I'm the things that grow on an old shower curtain."

"Sorry. That's bull. You want someone t'kill you. Oh, but someone important. You're very picky. A star. A headliner. Someone you can take down with you."

"Cut. Hold it right there, my—"

"Too bad you're not famous enough to be assassinated. Just murdered."

"Warning: high explosive. Lay off trying t'understand me. I don't think it's wise."

"Oh? Does it threaten you?"

"Merry, dear. Dear, nothing you say can threaten me."

"How acid. Why, then?"

"It's just, my little Seed Pearl . . . it's just you can't fuck what you un-derstand."

"Ah. Such *sportif* language all of a sudden."

"Or you don't wanna fuck it. Right now I'm trying very hard not t'un-derstand you—for at least another week or so. It'll be difficult, but—I don't see much future for us otherwise. I bore so easily."

"Do you? Then—ha!" Merry is invading: on her knees, impetuous: an aimed stumble. She swats, shoves, beats at his sand neighborhood: she thrashes it. The architecture is disheveled under her: grains will no longer cohere. Merry has been laughing. She cannot see Simon's fist reach back: to cock itself. "Do. You. Understand this? Too? Huh, Dr. Death?"

"D'you understand this?" His arm is down now: on safety. Still, it trembles. "D'you understand how close you came? Huh, Merry? Don't do that again. Ever. I advise you."

"Ooooh. So much anger coming up."

"No—just contempt."

"Anger or fear. Take your pick. But not contempt. You don't hit what you contemn. Shall we go now?" Merry stands: sand will sprinkle off her skirt. "Where is this screen treatment I contracted to type up?"

"In my van."

"That's the hideous thing I passed on Fifty-second Road? Lynxx Pro-ductions? Well, let's go get it. Recess period is over."

"There's no need. It was just an excuse."

"To see me?"

"Whatever."

"You mean there isn't a big movie deal after all? No five hundred grand? I thought as much."

"There is. I exaggerate sometimes, I don't lie."

"Excuse me, but I have trouble believing it. How would you get that kind of money?"

"I told you, Herman Wolff."

"Why? Out of a clear sky like that?"

"Why? It's simple. I conned two very gullible darkies inta mugging Wolff last week. So, while they were selling him a war bond, I jumped in t'save him like Cowboy Bob and the Three Mesquiteers. I know it's not an accepted business practice, but Wolff was five hundred grand on the grateful side."

"A likely story."

"I told you once. Once is enough. I don't lie."

"Seriously?"

"Seriously. Can you think of anything more serious than that? Ha, I can't. You could deliver that information to a certain Italian restaurant in Red Hook and my skin'd be an ironing-board cover the next day. Twenty-four-hour service. Wolff has friends."

"God. I suppose I have to believe you. Most of it. God, well—" She pokes sand from between her toes. "And you're not a Being-Toward-Death. Oh, no."

"No." Simon hurls his coffee can swingward: it hits, rolls, hits: the sound of persecution. "I'm a Being-Toward-Calculated-Risk. Listen, poor man's rich girl, only outrages—howls—get any air time in this society. I useta walk around in a gorilla suit. It assured me of some notoriety and a seat in the subway. I go. I go. I get close t'impact before I jerk the nose up, but I jerk it up. I'm no suicide. I despise suicides. I'm not through with the things of the world. I'm an impulse buyer. I'm who they invented supply-side economics for. I want it all. Including, yes, you."

"Not me. My body."

"Well, I wouldn't wanna break up the set."

"Uh-huh. By the way, Simon, I'm not mad. There's a lot of truth in what you said—about fucking. About *fucking*. Making love is something else again. But your intentions are so obvious, so perfunctory—they, well, they bore me. For all the marvelous verbal life."

"No. Moth crystals t'that. It isn't true. I don't bore you. I excite you."

"Right." Merry thinks. "It isn't true." She has smiled: even in the selective light he can see that. "Missed your chance. You might've made time."

"I still will. You're in love with me, remember?"

"You insist on that?"

"Yup."

"Does it matter? Even if I were, don't you think I have self-will enough to break away? I've done it before. I'll do it again."

"Sure. I think you could. But, gee, why? Why would anyone wanna break away from me?"

"Because unrequited love—presuming I loved—is rather a humiliation. And I don't think you'd ever love me."

"I'm interested, though. And not just in the obtuse angle your legs could make. What—with all this German pedantry—whaddya do for a living?"

"I work."

"Oh. You just work. Play it real close t'the chest, dontcha?"

"Small cup size."

"Ha. I wonder how much of this is real. How much is for effect. But you must wonder the same of me. You remind me of a woman who once was my mother."

"Once? How many have you had?"

"Ah. Do me a favor, huh?"

"What now?"

"Pull up some sand and sit again. I've had a depressing day—revelation after revelation. I feel like the pin boy on a target range. The body count is way up. I'd like t'spread my misery around. I ask you this friend-to-friend. We'll go back to our nice predator-prey relationship later on."

"Can't we talk someplace else?"

"Look, think of all the typing you got out of. Sit." Merry comes down: they are knee to knee. "Besides, this is the proper place. The story should be told in this place. It has the shape of a menstrual cramp."

"Well?"

"I found out today that my mother murdered my baby sister. I didn't even know I had one, a sister. Wait: I mean my sister was a baby. This happened before I was born."

"Mmmm."

"That's all you can say? Mmmm? Murder and you can't even get a vowel sound out? Who'd you serve under last, Lieutenant Calley?"

"Go on."

"It's hard t'impress some people. Must be all the violence on TV."

"This is Bettina, the one with the peccary?"

"Peccary? Oh, yeah. Her."

"Go on."

"Uh. Furthermore and hence: Bettina did this after trying unsuccessfully t'seduce her brother."

"Who writes your material, Sophocles?"

"Merry. Hey."

"Mmmm."

"It's true."

"Who told you?"

"My uncle—"

"The coy seducee?" Simon nods. "Is he reliable?"

"He's a priest, f'God's sake."

"Is that a guarantee of anything?"

"Leave the worldly cynicism t'me, huh? Anyhow, his housekeeper told me first. I hadda dredge it outa him. They got my mother off on a plea of temporary insanity. She spent seven temporary years in the crazy kiln before I was born."

"Oh, dear. That is unfortunate."

"Wait: bad news, good news. The good news is she wasn't really my mother. I was adopted."

"Hold on. All this is a little hard to digest."

"For you? Imagine for me. And all in one day—like the classical uni-
ties. You ask why I'm addressing myself as three different people. I
don't even know my birthday. My zodiac sign. This'll kill my cocktail
party conversation."

"Who was?"

"Was what?"

"Your mother."

"Oh. No one knows. According to Uncle Arthur, I was a drug on the
baby black market. Reduced f'quick sale."

"You never suspected this?"

"Suspected? She said she was in labor sixty-five hours. The pain was
terrible. She once—oh, Christ, I've never told anybody about this—she
once showed me her . . ."

"What?"

"Her wound, she called it. Made with my brutish baby size. Ragged
flesh lips, all shrivelly, brown. Like pieces of beef in a Chinese meal. She
said I did it. I was five years old then. Five is not old enough for that. I
didn't even know what it was."

"Well. Goodness. That is—that is a strange way to express love."

"No, she hated me. And I see why now: because I wasn't hers. Merry,
you don't know how Bettina competed with other women. That other
woman, my real mother—ah see!" Simon slaps his face. "Bettina kept
cupping me, for blood. Like in the Middle Ages. She said it was good for
my health. I get it now: it was that other woman. Her blood. Bettina was
sucking my real mother outa me. God. God, of course. That was it. That.
That was—"

"Hey, Big Boy. Come on. Take it easy."

"All the tie-ins, I'm starting t'see them now. Ho. Ho, Jesus. Look.
Look, maybe if I coulda once talked t'her person t'person. Like said—like
said, right, okay, Bettina—you know. Okay, you wanted a kid so y'could
pretend you were a woman. And, okay, me too. I wanted something.
Room and board and a place t'weep. But I thought she was my mother.
That thing intervened: that place where I'd been so clumsy. My zipless
birth. I dreamed of open doorways and—and gaping. Gaping. I thought,
Jesus, I thought she needed surgery."

"All right. That's enough. Let's get out of this place. It isn't good for
you." She touches his cheek: to distract him. "You need a shave."

"I been up thirty-six hours. My lenses feel like emery wheels. I'm
sorry." He shakes his head. "I shouldn't be talking like this: in the past
imperfect tense. It's not your problem. Man, I need a long wet spell.
That isn't all today. There was the carnage of my nose. And half my staff
went over the hill: the cowards. The other half is playing 'You goose me,
I'll goose you.' And—oh, I almost forgot—I spent the afternoon preparing
an old man's corpse for burial."

"What? How's that?"

"I'll tell you later. For now—what I have in mind—let's make out. Hanh?" Pause. "Huh?" Pause. "Please."

"Make out? What would this making out entail?"

"Gee. Whaddya want, an environmental impact statement? I'd like t'touch you a lot. Is that strange?"

"A lot? I don't trust the sound of it." She gets up. "Well, not here. Not even a little here. Someone will see us."

"I don't mind. I'm prouda the way you look. You've got a natural-shoulder body."

"Fine. But not here. Let's sit for a while in your truck. I'll go that far."

"Van. No. No, we can't."

"Why?"

"Ah, there's a guy inside, Nubar the auto wrecker. He's doing some body work. We wouldn't be alone."

"I don't mind. I may need witnesses."

"I do. What is it, my lips? My lips disgust you? Say it. I might as well know."

"Nonsense. Your lips are fine."

"Then come. The Grand Dragon of Grab says come."

"Where?"

"I have everything in control. This is my park, remember? Don't worry." He jerks at her hand: she doesn't like his urgency.

"Hey."

"Sorry."

"Where are we going?"

"Come. I'll show you. Come."

"Don't pull. I'm not your luggage."

"Well, get a move on then. Up. I'll skip and prance for you. I'll shake it on out. I'll be that old taxi dancer, Pan. Hup. Hup. And a da, da— d'jum."

Simon the hoofer is all around: a vaudevillian faun. Sand pings Merry's calf. She is spooked by him: in the strange curvature of darkness he seems shook and flung about. Is Simon dancing, she would like to know, or is he being danced? If the latter, then who (what?) could partner him in such a sizable, sandblasting step: this cakewalk, fandango, mazurka, saraband, reel? It seems profane and hazardous and . . . *see,* Simon has barked her shin: the same damn one. He won't notice: instead he urges her along/out, as though pain were a place to be left behind. Up, across the park asphalt: mother and her flagrant, huge son. Over to a structure, an industrial plaything, designed for children by bureaucrats of fun. That is: ten fifteen-foot-long-by-thirty-six-inch-wide cement-lined pipes: five set on five: O's in a double bank. Painted red, yellow, orange:

modern colors: colors of progressive recreation: of frolic standardized
and brought up to date. Infants creep through these, recapitulating other
culverts they have known. Simon will sit, sniveling breath in—short of
choreography now—on the upper middle pipe lip edge. His body has a
viscid smell: tarrish: three or four coats of odor. Merry, just behind, is
limping: resentment divulged by body speech. A square of cellophane
has stuck around her lollipop toe. Sandals hang down from one wrist,
pigeon-heeled.

"Here, my little plate of forcemeat."

"Here? Here what?"

"In here. In. Take romance where you find it. Don't haggle. Just keep
your eyes on the swinging watch chain and lie back."

"What d'you mean?" Simon thumbs behind his shoulder. "In that? In
that big sewer pipe? Why? What's in there?"

"Nag, nag, nag. Gee, Mer, d'you know how much a studio apartment
with kitchenette goes for today? At least this is rent-controlled. Relax,
huh? Life is a term policy: we're none of us getting any less fledged."

"In that? In a concrete pipe? You jest, surely. I hope."

"Merry, Joyride . . . I can see no one has told you. This. In there—"
He will whisper. "It's Where Love Has Gone."

"Simon—"

"Let me see your hand."

"Why?"

"No. The right one."

"The right?"

Ha, fell for it: Simon has given Merry a whirl: hand up and over her
head, his best 1956 jitterbug spin. Now her behind is flush against Simon's high-seated groin. Merry will say, "Nuh," preamble to some sore-
head complaint. "Nuh," again: Simon has hiked her up, palms beneath
rib cage, and onto his lap. No event so presumptuous or startling but that
great adroitness—for one moment at least—can make it seem credible.
Leaning them both back, glib of movement as a floating dock, Simon
dollies her on his raised pelvis, up. And crab style: into the pipe. One
inept shift, one lid-flick of indecision—a finger bent, dress material
snagged on concrete—and his illusion would perish. She might scream:
she might even slap him. But Simon-be-quick will carry it and her off:
crawling prone—on upside-down all fours—he has hand-trucked Merry
eight feet deep. She is taken in.

"Simon. Stop. Let me out. It's dark. It's dark. Where does this go?"

"I dunno, but I think we just found Bridey Murphy."

"Don't talk that way. I can't see your voice. You're scaring me."

"It goes at least another six feet, Miss Yellow Stripe."

"It's cold. I smell old beer. What're you doing?" She elbows him: not
in anger, in the crankiness of fear. "Oh, you have a knife. Oh, God."

"That's my new macramé belt buckle, Ditz. Relax, you'll hurt yourself —not t'mention me. There isn't room for the luxury of panic in here."

"That's it. I'm scared of narrow places. Uh. I can't sit up."

"Aha. You guessed my strategy."

"Please. Let me out. You don't have to do this: I wasn't resisting you. Be nice. Come on."

"Sssssh. Unfratch yourself. I'll set my voice on soothe. I'll be the George Melachrino Strings." His tone is grace-noted: a parliament of echoes will embellish it. "You don't haveta appease me."

"Well, what d'you expect? This is unfair. I'm not comfortable. I'm disoriented. This isn't the way you want me. I'm no good to you this way. I need my own space."

"Gee, greedy. I'm halfway up the curved wall as it is. Hanh? You must be hell t'sleep with. Probably the kind that swipes the sheets off at night."

"Is it you? Your voice sounds different. Are you crazy? Is that it? Are you schizophrenic?"

"Yuh. But both of me want the same thing. We're just trying t'figure out who gets sloppy seconds. I score women on the rebound from myself."

"Ow. It's hard and cold. The floor is rough."

"Rough? Hang on, all that has been taken care of. This is a full-service seduction. Unh. Heave your butt up."

"Why? What're you going t'do?"

"Wow, you can sure make your behind into a fist when you're nervous. Up. Up."

"What? What is it? A blanket?"

"Yuh. Sheer serendipity. I found it. Maybe this is a disused civil defense shelter. Capacity One."

"Uck. Take it away. It's probably full of lice."

"No, it isn't. Up, I said."

"It is."

"No, Marrow Meat. I hate to kill the spontaneity of the moment—but this is a clean blanket."

"How can you tell? You can't tell. It's black in here."

"Because, in a flurry of lust and cunning, I put it here."

"You? You what?"

"I—"

"I heard you. Bastard. A little overconfident, weren't we?"

"Oh, no. I'd never take you for granted. Never. Would you like a ham and cheese sandwich?"

"My God, he packed a lunch. My God." Laughter, his, has been muzzle-loaded in the smooth-bore pipe: it goes off. "Funny am I? I'll teach you what's funny, mister."

"Don't be mad. It's okay, Mer. Y'can go if you wanna. Any time."

"I'm not mad, you jackass. I'm scared to death." Merry is silent: a gauging, suspicious hand on his chest. They lie side by side: like wet laundry come to rest in the tumbler bottom of a washing machine.

"Well. Huh. You wouldn't let us use your kip. I am at present homeless as a citizen of Mu. This cement roomette is cheap and the concierge doesn't care what goes on. Anyhow, for your information, I just went through here on my hands and knees with a whisk broom. I wouldn't do that for just anyone—" She jogs him. "What?"

"You don't really have a ham and cheese sandwich?"

"Aw, gosh. You got me there. I was fibbing."

"Ha, I knew it."

"Why 'Ha'?"

"Because you made me hungry."

"Perhaps I could interest you in a piece of tongue."

"Down, Fido." She deflects his face: by the nose. "I'm being thoughtful."

"Don't. Thought is the enemy of a deep-dish orgasm."

"Shut up. This is ridiculous. What would they say? What would anyone say? What would I say—if I weren't here already. Lord, what's come over you, Merry Allen?"

"Well, you're lying intimately, albeit a bit crampedly, in a giant flue. With an attractive and somewhat compost-minded young man. You're being gracious and good-humored about it. Angels are preparing your reward."

"TOT FINDS FOOLISH WOMAN DEAD IN PLAYGROUND PIPE."

"Listen: the offense hasn't rested yet. We like each other, huh? You're as close t'me as the fur on the roof of a leper's mouth. We belong together, like black and blue." Simon kisses her: by rough triangulation. "I hope that was your cheek." His hand swoops around: but her body is tight, arm-bound, reefed. "Nothing. Here I am in the exact-change lane with a hundred-dollar bill again. Huh, Merry? How come you've got a flak suit on? Huh? Hello there. Merry?"

"Mmmm."

"Come on. Let the snow cover melt."

"Uh-huh."

"Relax."

"Uh-huh."

"Great. I'm getting along like a Solarcaine salesman in Harlem."

"Is it any wonder? Is it any wonder I'm uptight? You always throw me on the defensive. You can never play it straight, it's gimmick after gimmick. Just when we're having a—God forbid—serious conversation and you might come off as—God forbid—a human being, then you have to do something smart-ass and physical. Appear in blackface disguise. Hit me in the leg. Or—now we're in a stupid—what is this?—storm drain."

"Hey, don't spit out what you haven't tasted." Simon will kiss Merry's hand: back and front, side, finger interstices, thumb pad, wrist: mostly to check out the radium watch dial there. Quarter past nine: cutting it close with Wolff. "I was a kid, I used t'come here—sometimes all ten pipes were occupied. You hadda book in advance and slip five bucks t'the real estate agent. And it wasn't easy t'maintain the proper, oh, tone. You'd get your wad t'the end of the runway, flaps up, and some ten-year-old jerk'd flash a match and yell, 'Ya-ya-ya, I can see your wee-wee.' Or roll a basketball in that'd wonk your broad on the head. I mean, when you said, 'Did you come, too, dear?' three people would answer. It's a little dicey here, sure—sex should be. Hell, does it always have t'be on a Sealy Posturepedic in the apostle's position with petroleum jelly on the night table? Bor-ring. I'd rather go out to JFK and read old luggage X rays. Think of it: we're screwing the whole Parks Department. The day you hit the age of consent, Mer, didn't it take some juice out of the old hairy squeezer? A bang like this has t'be swiped."

"Bang? Excuse me? What bang? Which bang?" Simon, in darkness, gives himself the finger. "Maybe you know something I don't know?"

"Too quick, huh? Ejaculatio praecox of the mouth?"

"I think. I just think."

"But. But. I don't wanna beat around your bush either. I need you. As well as want. I haven't put my non-dairy creamer in anyone f'months. I talk big, I don't like t'admit it—but you're all I got goin' for me. And that's an awful lot. I'm lucky t'have met you. I get lonely." His voice is mink-lined: they both enjoy listening to it. The text does not receive a close reading. "Don't let me down, Mer. Let's polish our stomachs. Put some rosin on my bow."

"Simon—"

"You won't regret it."

"I'm sure you're very deft."

"Deft? I WANNA GET LAID!"

The pipe is a bullhorn for him. One hundred feet away two Canada geese, laying over on their autumn milk run south, are struck awake by Simon's peevishness. They taxi out, oaring, across Francis Lewis Pond, up, and northeast toward the Whitestone Bridge. In reply a wino has told his dead daughter that it is night-night time. Some leaves fall: though Simon can't be given credit for that. And Merry will laugh, laugh —ho, laugh—convulsed by Simon's exasperation and a bright thought-picture of Caliban with his whisk broom, manual-laboring. Then the laughter has become almost tetanic: hurtful: echoes take shorthand and read it back. Simon had better be concerned: humor is a specific against sexual heat. Her feet reach up to the pipe's vault: they clop out heel-fire there. Simon, who got a B+ from Miss Drinan in "Uses Spare Time Well" has used it to open one blouse button. Then another, then three: she doesn't monitor the pilferage. Laughter has demoralized her early-warning system. Simon is close: in for a pre-emptive strike. He caresses her bare, roof-kicking calf and thigh: new hair, recently Neeted, will sprinkle his palm. Time to restore order here. Both geese, having aborted, barge into the pond. And are already asleep.

"Leave us not wet our little polling place with mirth."

"But—oh, I can't help it. You're a ridiculous man. Can't you see that?" Merry has her Marlboro pack out. The lit match gets a candid of Simon: all teeth and frustration.

"A pre-coital cigarette, I trust?"

"Phah." She laughs again: out of air, just lung room enough for a hee-heeh-heeh: and some choking.

"Serves you right."

"Oh, Simon, you should see yourself."

"Laugh. But in a minute it gets very serious."

"Ah. Oh, my. You expect me—after all that talk about how you can't fuck what you understand—you expect me . . . ? Nerve is your strong suit."

"Search and seizure, that's what'll be f'you. Hanh. I'll break your kiosk door down."

"You intend to rape me, sir?"

"If it'll solve any problems of guilt and free will you have."

"I believe you're semi-serious."

"It's been a long day."

"But I want you to woo me. It's so much fun."

"Darling, that isn't the golden fleece you have down there: it's just an old brown scalp doily. This is our third date: the stockholders need a better rate of return."

"That isn't very attractive."

"Tenderness, honor, affection. The real you. ERA. A strong commitment. Respect for your needs as a woman. Erica Jong. Gloria Steinem. The Feldenkrais Method. Creative lust. We shall overcome. Give peace a chance. The joy of inner fear. Carlos Casteneda and how t'find orgasm with Shiatsu. Have I left anything out?"

"Funny. But not fun. I don't like this anymore. Hey."

"Time's up. Now for some tongue and groove action."

"Hey! No fair. Gimme back. Oh, Jesus."

Simon has raked the cigarette away: such hand props steal focus and distract. Holding it up, where Merry must see the genial, hot fag tip, he rubs it out against his palm. For a moment she can smell Simon on fire. He takes receipt of pain: a character reference. Merry has said, "Oh, damn you," this morbid grandstanding offends her. But Simon is a fool for work now. He will shift Merry, palletized on the blanket, down and under him: moving men use their thick rugs so. And his hand has driven a salient high/along her thigh, where never-yet-shaved feathery hairs curl.

"Oh, boy. Here comes Ham Hands."

"Quiet." He is bossy with her. "No more jokes. Enough."

"What d'you think you're doing?" The skirt hem has come up. "Simon, wait—"

"No. I'm going to take you now."

"Take? Oh, yes? Oh!"

Slip: Simon has a shifty finger in: so that he won't lose his place. With another digit he will tap out three bars of a favorite melody on her mons veneris. This is the key to his great success in bed: music. Simon has learned that all women share one secret sensual tune: more or less, "Old MacDonald's Farm" played at various tempi and with feeling. Merry hasn't fought off his hand: neither, though, has she sung Eee-I, eee-I, oh. Her arrowing breasts are taut and pleated under crepy bra stuff. Simon unglues a cup: the areola under it is knotty like raw planed wood. In passing Simon can eavesdrop on her skittish heart. One, two unbuckle his shoes. Spring-soled, they clop down the pipe length. Simon has un-zipped, balancing with left arm and right leg: while one finger still strums Here a quack, there a quack, everywhere a quack-quack. Adroitness and more adroitness, Simon: he is as light-footed in the pipe as a horizontal chimney sweep. Cement begins warming: condensation must soon bead on it. Sex seems, to Simon, pretty much the business of getting undressed in a Pullman car upper. Now, nude from the waist down, he will settle on her: pelvis atop pelvis, big molars biting down. Her flesh is hot, dry: a sick dog's nose.

"Simon—"

"Too late. Hang on—don't rest umbrellas on the moving staircase."

"No—wait." She has a good swatch of his hair. "Please."

"Sorry. This car doesn't brake for humans."

Then softly: "Please."

"Jesus, what now?"

"I'll do it. I don't care what they say. Who do they think I am?"

"Sure. The sons of bitches. Eh? Who?"

"For spite, first. First, that. Out of sheer, oh, impatience. Not out of lust. To make a point."

"Thanks."

"No. No. Nothing personal. I just didn't want you to think it was rape. Well, it is—or we're both raping me. That strange me down there. Who wants it. Who wants it, no matter what I say. I'll take half the respon-sibility. Who've I been kidding, anyhow?"

"That's what I—"

"Shut up. You talk too much. Hurry before I change my mind."

"I hurry. Yas'm I hurry. I fetch it t'you good."

Simon, with the side of his finger, reopens her carefully: as you would work pliable caulk into a joint. He picks up the hoedown sensual tune where it broke off. Merry is speaking to a third person, not present: she doesn't hum along. Her right leg has risen, hospitable. Panty crotch fabric gives slack room enough. Simon the filler, the replenisher, is primed: he hunches over Merry, ceiling zero in here: pelvis low, cocked. Three, two, one and—no, kill it. Merry's hand has meddled with him. A controversial move: to guide, to experience, to cooperate, what? Merry touches his length. Simon is both irked and teased: too many cooks down there. He will bribe her hand away by caressing it. Desire, like a hot lavage, is massy under his tailbone: buttocks clutch, so gluteal, to drive the thrust and—eee-I!—Merry has turned away. Sudden, fetal, on her side, leg down. Simon misses everything. He is deflected off her right hipbone and into the concrete wall.

"Christ—damn you—I almost lopped it off."

"Wait."

"Wait? Uh-uh. I've waited long enough: this isn't an erection, it's fossilized. God, I bet I'm bleeding. It's grated like a carrot. I'll look real snappy with a Band-Aid on. Lay flat: and signal next time when you're gonna turn."

"No. You don't have a protector."

"A who?"

"A con. You know. A condom."

"What? Whaddya mean? I haven't worn a rubber since 1954. Rubbers went out with Nehru jackets and the Studebaker. This is the permissive age, Sandra Dee—wake up. Don't you take the pill?"

"No. No, I don't."

"Well, why not? You're a woman, aren't you? Who's your gynecologist, Doctor No?"

"I'm sorry, I just don't." She is whining: well aware of it: and displeased with herself. "I don't do this very often. You do. You're the expert. I thought you'd be protected."

"Me? Me? A woman your age has certain responsibilities, dammit. This—gross negligence, that's what it is. You misrepresented yourself, you —you female quack."

"Simon, I would. But I'm scared. I just can't get pregnant. I can't, that's all."

"Mer. Take it easy. Look." Simon is all come-let-us-reason-together now. "These days even I could get an abortion. It's a civil right, like rural free delivery. Barbie dolls come with a little toy plastic curettage kit."

"No."

"I'll withdraw. I'll drip my seed all over Francis Lewis Park. I'll light matches under my scrotum. Huh? Hey, rhythm. What time of your month is it? I've got a thermometer in my van, we'll play Vatican roulette."

"I'm sorry. I'm too afraid."

"It isn't fair. It just isn't fair. I ache. The Messiah comes more often than I do."

"I wanted it." She feels: shoulder, elbow, arm: to his hand. "I wasn't cockteasing. We'll do it, I promise. But now, just hold me, and—oh!"

Whap! A flashbulb has hurled silks of light at them: Simon is dazzle-blind. Merry's concise bosom will develop on his retina: her breast meat dark, each nipple pale. Whap! And whap! again. A shutter is snipping, garden-shear noise, at the pipe's foot end. And another whap! Simon and Merry are a matter of record now. She will retreat, up the pipe, away: short-hopping her nude breasts on one bounce, catch. Simon (it is instinctive) will attack: a human gutterball, bucking, rolling, tha-thoncking down the pipe. Whap! Simon is out in time to see Merry on camera, skirt up, bra around neck like a set of discarded earphones. Her helplessness is sensual. Merry's hands are up/about/over, to censor chest and groin, whap-whap-whap! disco-fast strobing here. The photographer has her rigged out in glare. He is sidestepping, new angle after new angle: a photo essay: in the round: professional work. A small man who should be on horseback, pixie feet that turn in to prod flanks, widespread at the crotch. He has gone bald along a straight line: the opposite of a Mohawk haircut. His cigar is wet, slithery: it hints at fellatio in his mouth. Merry has crouched, beaten down by so much light: this double exposure. She blinkers her face: it is, after all, the essential nude flesh. Whap! Whap! Simon, barefooting it toward her around the pipe emplacement, will get more white silk draped over him, point-blank—and a portrait of his naked lower self. Merry sobs. Mr. Bald has split, leaving a spume of radiance behind him. In tepid pursuit Simon steps over one flash ghost, around another and—broach—no, not through number three, which is the very solid jungle gym pole.

"Ow, nuts. Stop. Slow down and think, Simon. Gotta think this out."

Keen, tense as a hoodwinked falcon, Simon inspects the piebald night. He can be patient. His eyes reminisce over a lifetime of corneal scar tissue: not much information there. Lids drop: Simon will let himself go blind. Now he just listens in profile: one ear on directional pickup. There is, he has remembered, no exit from Francis Lewis Playground. Mr. Bald must still be on the premises. Merry has become silent. Simon's own breath is irascible, coarse: weariness has body-slammed him. Yet Simon would like to rumble, man: fighting is more effective than a cold shower anyway. The poor sleepless geese have been scrambled again: they be-beep overhead: big fear in a small pond. And—ho?—hear that? Clong.

And one more: clong. Wrench, clong. The fence has taken human weight fifteen yards to his left. Simon is fifteen-yard-dashing at it—aaaah, curses, missed by a hand length. Against the overcast and city-lit sky he can see Mr. Bald. They observe each other: Mr. Bald observes downward, leg straddling, mounted atop the fence. He will cock a snook at Simon with his murky cigar: give-my-regards-to-Bayside: smile, *Auf Wiedersehen.*

A-a-a-and Simon says *Guten Abend* Hello! Up the ten-foot fence in one spectacular moon-surface leap. Mr. Bald is staggered: reaction time much too slow. Never did he think a man this large could move so suddenly. Simon's bare toes seize diamond wire mesh and drive, scale, vault upward—one arm will rise a full yard *above* the fence ridge. Mr. Bald has ditched: body overboard. But, big snatch, Simon's right hand will grab the shoulder padding of a gray $29.95 trenchcoat. And—clasp!—left hand down for reinforcement. A howl from Simon at this point: half war cry, half asthmatic wheeze: solar plexus has belly-whopped hard across the fence ridge. Mr. Bald's cigar, bitten, is unraveling. The strength, the strength: he hangs in harness like a treed paratrooper: hung from Simon. They have a dialogue of plosive hisses. Simon will do some savage moving and shaking: disciplinary action: the fence clanks its chain. But his left hand has cramped: all good things must end. First, though, a thieving finger will deploy itself beneath the camera-bag strap.

"Lemme down, you big mug. Lay off. Hey, my neck. Stop."

"I'll knock it out of you, Sink Trap. I'll teach you t'flash in my pan." Simon moves and shakes some more. "Who set you up? Who wants my picture? Was it Wolff, huh? Was it Kyryl?"

"You? Jesus. Who cares about you, Tarzan? It's her they want."

"What?" And Simon has let go. Mr. Bald hits, stooped, a sprint-swimmer takeoff position. He will start to run.

"So long, schmuck."

"You forgot something, schmuck." Simon, a Humpty-Dumpty, has seated himself up there. The camera is twirling on its strap.

"Oh, no. Fuckin' cocksucker. That's mine. That's mine. You crook, give it back." He will make measly jumps up: more symbolic than efficient. "Hey, be a sport, gimme a break. I'm only a workin' stiff. I'm just doin' a job. Don't break my chops."

"Her picture? Why?"

"Gimme it back and I'll tellya."

"Ho-ho. I've heard that one."

"Come on. Whaddyou care? What skin's it off your back?"

"Why her?"

"I dunno. That's the truth. They just told me t'get the goods on her."

"Who's they?"

"Aw, shit. You know I can't tell you that. I'm supposta be discreet, for God's sake."

"Discreet? What was that bright particular moment back there? That feast of lights? Stick a lamp up my coulee, will you?"

"Hey. I can expose your shots. I don't need them. Here, gimme."

"Oh, I'll give you. Oh, I'll give you."

"No. Please!"

"Freeze frame. And. Wipe!" Simon lambastes the camera, frail aperture first, against a steel fence support.

"Awwww-Christ. You mother. You fuckin' motherfuck." And reprise: bash: this time the strobe light hails glass down on Mr. Bald. Destruction can be remedial. Simon needs it: Merry, after all, has left much to be desired. Again, way overhead and down: crash. The camera case is divvied up: fifty-fifty, a photo finish. "I'll kill you, I'll kill."

"No, you won't, you liver spot, you little clonic spasm. Here I come."

"Wait. Listen—it's just a camera."

"I'm coming for teeth and balls. I'm after gums. Hanh. Hi-aahh!" Simon throws a nice head-fake: as if climbing down, after. Mr. Bald is on his mark, set, already gone: one shoe off, toward the corner of Fifty-second Road and Bayside Avenue. Humpty-Dumpty reseats himself: ten feet up. On his nude rear, chill, anesthetic metal will give a midi-length paralysis. Simon is thinner: there are ribs. His strained left hand can't grip: it fidgets in a separate palsy. Yes, she has made him jealous: he crumples the film of her. Simon, star, is not your best supporting actor. A stoplight clicks green to red on carless Bayside Avenue. The geese again return from wherever wild geese must go. Leaves tremble like a leaf. Here is September. A playmate wind will push the empty swings.

"In the glove compartment. I think there's a bottle."

"Here?"

"Try further over. Pull the maps out."

"I see it."

Her lit cigarette tip is thrilled by breath: full-blown: a white-orange of forges in the dimness. It will jigger: her lips, he would surmise, are shaking. Simon, driver-seated, is bum-nude still. Just now he trudged this way down a suburban street: barefoot, pants over shoulder: too done in for blue-collar propriety. The pint bottle of Wild Turkey is passed and her fingers encounter his. An incidental touch, yet—for that reason—somehow evocative. He can be at ease here: their interacting (Simon couldn't think of a better compliment) seems almost male-to-male. The relationship has grown older than this half hour: forced by dismaying circumstance: they are veterans together. Merry, head down, low profile, is round-shouldered against the door: all set to eject. Her blouse has been misbuttoned and one breast appears gone. The hair is insubordinate: brunette scribble. Simon knows where that sad, weak sound has been coming from: from his own throat, remote and pneumonic wheeze.

As if the skin were a pocket edge. Simon pulls his lower lip out: to drain bourbon in.

"Is he gone? D'you think he's gone?"

"Sure-sure."

"How can you tell?"

"Haaaahh. Felt that hit my stomach with golf shoes on. M'urph. Tasted like a glass of cipher, though. My damn inner bouquet is really wilted." Merry shuffles, bent down: a GI advancing behind low cover. "Relax. Don't rock the bus. You're messing with the artificial horizon in my head." She kneels: for an extended moment she will observe the entrance to Francis Lewis Park in his sideview mirror. "He isn't around, Mer. Last I saw he was running like a Soviet nylon."

"The prick. It wasn't fair. What am I going to do now?"

"Sit, I hope. I can't keep adjusting my head t'see you. Huh. Breathe. Man, I'm run-over. Wasted. Haaa: breathe. How'd you get in here, anyway?"

"The door was open. Isn't it all right? I thought if I went back to my bike he might be waiting. Didn't you say someone was working in here?"

"Work? Oh, yes. Man, I don't have the Hi-Fli Bounce Back that I useta have. He must've knocked off."

"God. Oh, God. It happened, Merry. You pushed your luck. And now see." She claps her hands: the sound is substantial, encouraging: company. She will clap again. "It happened. My. My. My. Just like I knew it would. Well, it's all over. The shit has hit the fan."

"To coin a phrase. Here. Vaccine against remorse."

"No. I don't drink much, thanks."

"This isn't the moment for temperance. Even Carrie Nation'd drink—if someone'd just taken a snapshot of her with both bluestockings off. Here." Merry doesn't reach. "Well? Go ahead. I'm not contagious."

"It isn't that."

"Then drink."

"You're right. This is the time." She swills: quickly, neck back: with both eyes shut, so that no one can see her. "Brrrr. Foul stuff." But she will set 'em up again. "Still foul. Well, it'll distract me, I guess. I guess. Are you okay? You seem cramped together. Like you were trying to ignore a pain."

"No. It's just the egg on my face setting up. M'urph." Simon sends the bottle back. Merry will take another, a facile, hit. "I asked the inquiring photographer back there why he wanted my picture."

"What did he say?"

"Never mind that lard. You know very well what he said. Miss-Birdlime-Wouldn't-Melt-in-My-Mouth."

"Uh-huh."

"Uh-huh?"

"No. So what did he say?"

"He said he wanted *your* picture, Merry. Not mine. No demand for autographed glossies of Simon. Like t'tell me about it?"

"Not really." She sips. "No, not really. But I suppose it's time. Oh God. You won't hold it against me? You won't do a whole comedy routine? You're so bigoted. Could you try to understand?"

"I think I understand already."

"You do? No, I don't think you do." A Marlboro has been lit. "You should've seen me go up that fence. Fear is a wonderful incentive, like an upper. I flew. I showed everything going over. Ha." She waits. "Don't change the subject, huh? Well, what's done is done, I suppose. In black and white." A laugh. "Or in color? D'you think I'm in glorious Technicolor? Oh, my Lord."

"What's done is done, yeah. But I undid it." Simon drops the film roll in her lap.

"Huh? What's this? Is it? Is it? Oh—oh, you spectacular man."

"Hey." Her hug is reckless, upsetting: Simon almost falls off. Merry has knelt, head against his thigh: a disciple's pose.

"Oh, wow—saved. Wow. I thought it was curtains. This calls for a drink."

"Hold on, that's just a pint. Save some f'me. I've got serious oral ravaging t'do yet t'night."

"How did you manage it? How? How?"

"I'm always prepared—unlike some people I know."

"Don't worry. I'll take pills. I'll get fitted for whatever you want. We'll fuck."

"Come on, Merry. Don't use that word."

"What word—fuck?"

"Enough, sssssh. It's the last time I offer you a drink."

"But not in the park. Not in a public place. I couldn't go through that again. We'll—make woosie alone."

"Make woosie? I'd rather not. What a horrible-sounding thing. Like sex between two people with surgical stockings on. Whoa. Watch it: your gratitude is getting a little coltish."

"Did you hurt him? You must have. He didn't return this out of kindness."

"Let's say I turned his head a bit. I got his full attention." Merry has sat in Simon's lap: her elbow will cause a short beep. "So?"

"A nice kiss. I'm gonna give you a nice kiss."

"Stop it. You're not all that drunk. I'm still waiting f'my accounts receivable. What was he after?"

"Is your lip better? This van is something else. I thought you had a real fly-by-night setup, but—"

"Cut it out, Merry. Listen, I risk life and ligament for your—the least y'could do is tell me why."

"Oh, it's a long, stupid story. You've got an appointment in a few minutes. It can wait: it'll mean y'have t'see me again. Listen, I have a question?"

"Wha?"

"D'you like my breasts? Even if they're small?"

"All right, enougha this bubble dancing." Simon covers her mouth. "How many y'got?"

"Two. Like anyone else."

"Not breasts, you partial eclipse. Kids. How many y'got?"

"Huh?"

"Okay. Stop me if I'm wrong. You want custody. Or you want t'keep custody, eh? Your ex is trying t'prove you're an unsafe mother. Not a princely type, I don't think, hiring that chili-bowl t'do a photo spread of us in fragrant delicto. Am I warm?" Merry has her head on his shoulder. "But that's okay, Slipware—it's nothing t'me. Not the first time I've been an illegitimate step-parent. In the Army, down South, I dated a divorcy with four kids. Always a blue Chevy pickup followed us. Even in bed she wore dark glasses and a red wig: in case someone came outa the cupboard and said, 'Smile.' Am I right so far?"

"Gee. It sounds real plausible."

"I'm right."

"No, you're not. I wonder, though, if I'd be better off—being divorced with two kids."

"Two? That's why I can't visit you at the apartment, I knew it. The kids're there. It's all falling inta place. Boys or girls?" Merry has sighed. "I see, hermaphrodites. Huh? Gosh, Mer, he hasn't got a pop fly's chance. You're the mother. Unless you've really been opening the secret game preserve, which—from recent frustrating experience—I don't think you have. Lemme see your stretch marks, Mem-sahib. I love stretch marks."

"Hum?"

"What?"

"I don't know. 'Old MacDonald Had a Farm' is going through my head for some reason. And on this farm he had some chicks. Simon, you're wrong. I have no children."

"Listen, I'm good with kids. I could be a great father one or two days a month. I've thought about it recently."

"If you knew what a coward I am. Oh, Jee-sus. If you knew."

"So much retaining wall and so little t'retain. Y'got this big stake in being mysterious."

"Oh, yes. Let me be, huh? Mmm, that stuff hit me like a hammer. I'll probably throw up. Will you take me back, drop me near my place? I'll come back for my bike tomorrow."

"Yeah. I gotta get a move on, anyway."

"Will I see you again? In spite of this? You won't just disappear? I know what the female competition in New York is like."

"Ssssh. Kiss me one for the road, my mouth is protected." Merry leads, working carefully inside his burnt upper lip. They try to be considerate: it is a disappointing kiss. Then she will lie, totally still, against his chest. She seems intangible to him, despite the touching: probably her lack of smell.

"Some things need doing yet. Y'know. I want to have respect for myself. Before—ha—I can lose it again with you. Cows, pigs? What did Old MacDonald have? If you knew how terrified I am of boring you. It's like I'm in school again."

"Scooch over t'the other seat, I'll start my mighty engine. Your poor husband, doing it with a rubber on all that time. Maybe he had grounds."

America, the van says. His control console is serious-minded: full of that national love for quick information: like the news coming on. A power transference has been patched through: Simon rallies. The engine, in idle, will gag once or twice: then, imperturbable again, it is beautifully orotund: an on-key, sonorous base vocal line. Simon can focus and aim his rearview TV screen: sixteen inches of hindsight. The indicator system has reported in: there are more than three dozen spry lights—red, yellow, green, blinking, steady—and one digital computer readout for MPH, MPG, RPM, Est. ETA, Air Pressure, AMP. They, he and the machine, compete, collaborate: switches rebut lights. Merry has caught him being unfaithful and is jealous: these are loves no woman can cut in on. To her it would all appear energy-extravagant: a jingoistic, arrogant enterprise. Simon, ready, beeps: blowing his horn.

"A bit much, isn't it? Don't tell me you need all those lights."

"Ha. No, not when I'm just cruising around. But when we film I can run an entire light and audio mix off this board. By remote if I want to. There's nothing like the Lynxxmobile anywhere. It does everything but impersonations and charity benefits. I designed it myself three years ago, cost me a hundred fifty-five grand. I've been offered twice that since."

"Must be expensive to run. How many miles per gallon?"

"Gallons per mile, my dear."

"Well, it's pretty."

"Yeah, isn't it? Wonder if I'll ever make a film half so satisfying. Hold on. Yank the gantry away: five, four, three, two, one. Raummm: let's lay a batch."

A fluent pickup: as though inertia could be stored, and this start were the smooth perpetuation of his last ride. Merry is gay. Even uphill the

van seems to coast. She has been made a passenger by it: someone between and on leave: at ease, sojourning in Queens. Vibration through the
cab floor is tonic. Her feet curl, then arch open: cats on their backs.

"Mmm. What's that word in music? Glissando. Gliss-an-do. Smooth as
a Cadillac."

"Cadillac? That's all she can think of, Cadillac. Snore. Where'd you
get your great sense of fashion—from a handout copy of *Muhammad
Speaks*? Cadillac. I bet you think a Princess telephone is the height of
bon ton."

"Don't complain about the conversation. You're lucky I can stand
up."

"Seems that's all you do at the critical disjuncture. Hanh. Me and the
Knothole Gang, gonna haveta do it upright, I guess. Sex with you is like
playing gin rummy with a snake. It's a long time between shuffles."

"God, d'you talk this much when you're fff—making love?"

"No, Glory Hole. No, I'm quiet then. The pleasure of it awes me silent.
It's worth trying, just for that."

"I'm tempted."

"Hey! Look who's here."

"It's him! Him! Him!"

Sssssh, Merry. Simon can see. Six car lengths ahead the door of a gray
Ford Pinto has wingspread out. Mr. Bald is on tap again, his second-
chance camera up and framing. Readily, with no brake touch, Simon
steers blue murder right at him. And Mr. Bald (hit-run death much
magnified in his viewfinder) will pull out first, will Fosbury flop across
the Pinto trunk, head over ripple-soled heel and sock-holed heel—one last
(whap!) art shot taken of unphotogenic Bayside sky—then pancake,
down. Simon's face is grillwork now: intense: with crackerjack finesse he
has snagged the Pinto door on his bumper: a neat half inch of 30 m.p.h.
touch. Pebbly glass sounds pelt behind: the door is unsocketed like a
cold chicken wing: Simon hurrahs. It would be apropos here to dun
Merry for praise, but he and his triumph are alone. The inner van door,
between cab and bunk room, is just a hand width open. Toppling back,
Merry has gone through. Light of a low-budget wattage pries into the
cab.

"That was inopportune, wasn't it? Now she'll meet Minnie in her cor-
rosion-colored negligee. Charmed, I'm sure." Simon roots nostril hair out:
a sign of resignation: his contact lenses go into halftone, teary, then they
flick clean. "Think, Simon, think. You lied. I lied. She'll want an explanation and the plain truth is *Rashomon* to everyone. Jesus, why does my future always look like next year at Marienbad? Why can't I live out a nice
Monogram gangster flick with dialogue and death that makes sense? Just
watch. Here comes some absurdist conversation written by Resnais and
Antonioni. The *nouvelle vague* breaks on poor, old Jones Beach. Beat the

red light, van, beat it. Ah, Northern Boulevard: my homeland, where Marty still can't plan a decent weekend. Doris Day, I've been unfaithful, but let me ride in your station wagon with all the kids just once more. I promise I'll never use a jump cut or a sound bridge again. It'll just be your face in frame, and you can smile. Oh, smile." The bourbon is done for: he spills much. "*La Douchey Vita*, will I ever earn enough t'be really bored? I talk, I talk and even my echo has a contrary opinion. I'm too tired for this next take, but here she comes."

"Simon?"

"Hear that? The question mark. What'd I tell you? My name is now an accusation."

"I can't hear what you're saying." The cab door clacks behind her.

"All clear, I said. Steichen of the scum-board is gone. Y'shoulda seen him pull the chicken switch. He got a great picture of his own feet—while they were trying t'walk over his head. Marvelous composition."

"Simon. There's a woman back there named Minnie."

"Ah? Mmm. She introduced herself?"

"Yes, she did. She said, 'Pardon my condition if I don't rise. Hello there and welcome. Are you joining us tonight?' A rather thought-provoking statement—I mean, when you consider that she was totally stark naked."

"That's a bedroom back there. When you barge into someone's boudoir, y'can't expect soup and fish. Mer, Minnie is a member of my production staff."

"I'm sure. And what does she produce?"

"Yes." Simon has to regroup. "Well, she's in charge of—well, continuity. On and off."

"I thought you said your staff had quit."

"Not all. I didn't say all. Not Minnie—that's the continuity she's in charge of. Still being here. Mer, look, I'm tired, so don't have your grand climacteric all over me."

"I'm not upset. Don't flatter yourself. I'm not even shocked. She has a very nice, a very, shall we say, *complete* body. I'll give her that."

"You had time to notice?"

"Oh, yes. She offered me a sandwich. Matjes herring on rye."

"Sounds good. I'd ask you t'go back and get me one—but I guess this isn't a dinner flight. And I guess you're not in a fly-me frame of mind, huh? Damn." Simon beeps: a proxy scream. "Look at that. Why's there traffic at this time of night? Must be an accident. Is that a police flasher on the left? Talk about flashing, better put my pants back on."

"Her breasts are a lot bigger than mine. And quite firm, considering her age. I don't blame you."

"You don't? Oh, you don't, do you? Listen, Warm Front, between me and Minnie there isn't even a static cling, so don't go into false labor, huh? She's a JAP, a Jewish American Prude. It's her son, Robert, if you wanna know. He's indentured himself t'me. She's just here because the apron strings don't reach down from Westchester County."

"You expect me to swallow that?" Merry's arms fold over her chest: in a mechanical way: like windshield wipers stopping. She has stood directly behind him. "You expect me?"

"Oh, God, no. Nothing so outlandish as simple trust. Hanh. No one ever believes me. And, frankly, I don't give a tank-town whistle stop whether you do or not."

"You can let me out here."

"Spare me the coloratura emotion. We're just north of nowhere. I can't even open the door here, traffic's like a walk-in closet, I'm halfway across the white line as it is. Let's have Minnie out here, she'll tell you."

"Thank you, no. I'm sure she's trained to back up anything you say. I'd rather not be made a fool of. She's a woman who's been around, I can tell that."

"Oh, Christ. A shopping mall or two, that's all Minnie's been around. I'm innocent, I tell you. Why does my reputation precede me by half a mile, while my experience is back somewhere fixing a flat?"

"You mean—come on—you mean you've let all that very available flesh go untouched? Like St. Anthony on wheels?"

"I have not had intimate relations with Minnie Fischer."

"What a failure, poor Simon. You're resistible after all. A likely story."

"Leave off the arch tone, like you just found a gonococcus in your soup and I'm the chef. Last time I stand you a drink."

"The fact is: One—you told me there was a man called Nubar or Numar doing repairs in here, that's why we had to crawl down a drainpipe t'make out. Right?"

"Yes. Right."

"You lied."

"Yes, I did. I didn't wanna disturb Minnie. Nubar was making repairs on her this afternoon, she had a chastity belt on—and . . . and let's not pursue that line of thought."

"Let's not. Please, let's not. The fact is: Two, you said—I quote—'but you're all I've got going for me.'"

"Well, you are. You are. And, given that fact, looks like I'm in pretty bad shape."

"Bullshit. Well. Oh, well. I don't blame anyone but myself. I knew what you were. You were even kind enough t'tell me. But I thought I could make you see something better. It's the historical weakness of women. Thank God—thank God—you didn't succeed back there. Now, if you please, I'll get out."

"It's an accident. I think she's dead."

"Where?"

"Across the Boulevard, on the sidewalk. Under the movie marquee. Heart attack, I guess."

"Oh. And I've been drinking. It must be on my breath."

A squad car is canted up: left front wheel on the curb lip. Simon, theatergoer, will stand to look: good sight lines from his cab. APOCALYPSE NOW. The woman lies supine. Though it is night, her indolent sprawl—coat beneath head, footwear off, inner thigh and arm turned out —might suggest mad sunbathing. And now a policeman has begun to batter her: hard, voluptuous, double-fisted thuds on the breast. She will shimmy and buck: it is the peevish resistance of a loafing child. MARLON BRANDO. Ring on ring, as tree trunks form, a small crowd has grown to watch this gross mismatch. Simon can identify the husband. He lurks, no doom by association for him, ten feet away. At each breast-thud he will nod: yes and yes, give it to her again. He has been holding a red pocketbook—not by the strap, that might show familiarity with pocketbooks—but ball-carrier style. ROBERT DUVALL. He has two tickets in his hand. He will never forgive her, her alive or her remembered, for the sensual intimacy of this beating: a man mounted across her groin in public. AND MARTIN SHEEN. Simon would like to collect it on film: for its unsentimental value. But a vain and fastidious ambulance, the ranking vehicle, has started to harass cars behind him. Policemen give Simon that vulgar, official move-along hand jerk. His van passes by.

"She probably said, 'You never take me anyplace.' Well, it ain't Biarritz, but he took her. For good. I wonder, will they give him a refund at the box office? Will he ever try t'see that flick again? Is he figuring how long he can postpone telling his mistress—is he afraid he'll haveta marry her now? He was composing himself t'be uncomposed, didja see that, Mer? Zang, and we're gone into the place of undifferentiated molecules. That cop, Christ how he was banging at her. If she wakes up, her boobs'll be behind her like water wings." Simon has tried to adjust his rearview TV screen: not enough lateral play. He can only see a young woman running toward the crowd. "He'll go home and in her bottom bureau drawer—under a dildo vibrator—he'll find love letters from someone else. Maybe a woman. He'll find spare teeth and realize she wore bridgework. And a little wiglet t'cover the thin spot he never noticed. And— because he's a sport—he'll bring them t'the funeral director in a little brown bag. Along with a dress he once bought her that she refused t'wear. Hah. He'll never haveta eat tuna fish casserole again, which he hated for fifteen years. Or lift the toilet seat. He'll wonder how much soap you put in a washing machine. He won't be able t'get the blanket and sheet made tight. He'll miss things. Oh, he'll miss things. But not her —he never knew her. It was like that with Bettina. I remember. Hah, but he can be proud of one thing. In death, on a Monday night, his wife

outdrew Francis Ford Coppola, that fat pasta fangool. Hah. Huh, Mer?"
Simon swivels around: alone again. Her exit made through the far cab
door and during his big monologue. "Yeah. And you'll never know me either. No, you stubborn bitch. You stubborn pretty bitch. You go try and
get a refund f'your injured sensibilities. Wolff—here I come. You understand me, dontcha, Herman? We've bayed over the same corpses: there's
good fellowship in that."

He accelerates, but the light has gone red. Simon will honk at it. His
speedometer waits at o.

1

This was all water. Tonight, three hundred years ago, the Dutch brig *Rijswijk* stood at anchor on Great Ferry Street: where now there is a NO PARKING sign. Simon, false scion of patroons, can't know that. His van has backed onto a warehouse loading ramp. The engine suspires: is quiet. Without that high-compression sound, Simon will feel good-forsaken. Murk from the Hudson wads shapes in gray: as if, fragile, they had been packed for shipment elsewhere. Across Great Ferry at #25—Est. 1837—Roman goddess caryatids shoulder up an old market-hall façade: hard-working pagan women, turned out from the pantheon, led here in captive triumph by 19th Century Protestant mercantilism. They are noseless: erosion has given them harelips: cheekbone structure is worn like the stoop of a Gothic cathedral. Breasts are eaten around: a coin clipper might have been at them. Simon would rather not perform this evening. Great Ferry, silent, has the ambiance of a theater on its dark night. One contact lens is grating: raw, dry from too many things seen. Knuckle in, rough, Simon will rub: will hurt the pain. Then—to hell with it—he honks. For companionship and to advertise that Simon Van Lynxx, LIMITED ENGAGEMENT, is appearing solo and without much rehearsal in LUCKY tonight.

Westward and riverward he can make out glare from the wide bay window of Ten Great Ferry: a cat's eye seen side-on: protrusive, flicker-lit with green-gold and movement, very keen to hunt. Watching it, Simon could become irresolute. That derisive eye isn't fooled: it knows stagecraft and all popular illusion. Simon will have to rub the magic lamp for it: and baffle description. He rolls his manuscript of *Lucky* tight: into a paper truncheon. The pages are grimy, finger-smutted: each, left flat, will curl up, snap, like a long wood shaving—you can't put *Lucky* down. Kyryl's window has dilated: the room is circling on its axis. Just a block away, Simon: not far. In one quarter hour the *Rijswijk's* pin-

nace rowed that distance: from Ten Great Ferry to his van. Four men
and a boy disembarked here: they came to get New World water. In
some coextensive time plane, maybe, they are still disembarking. The
pinnace ducks and shifts, deprived of their weight. It is shallow outside
#25. Gray forms march off: they interpenetrate van, lamppost, caryatid,
market hall. And Kyryl, from his marvelous window, might see tall rigging ride past. All this is not reason to be afraid: no ghosts are more
genial than the ghosts of commerce.

"Minnie?"

"Yoo-hoo, come in."

"Yoo-hoo, yourself. Come out here." Pod and pod: Minnie is walking,
feet very separate, the way a hurried armchair would. Then there are
Eastern European oiks of pain, each with an implicit question addressed
to God Himself. The inner cab door is open. Minnie stands, timid, more
hidden than attired in a blue nightgown. And one leg up, as though she
were horseshoeing herself.

"A busted toenail. I'm learning the movie business with my feet in the
dark. So—what happened to Flushing? Where are we?"

"Great Ferry Street, on the lower West Side. Where sex is always a
fielder's choice. See that self-glorifying light there, up the block? On the
left, second story. I'm going up there now t'pump the great Herman
Wolff out like a flooded basement. Lock up good when I leave. It's a bad
neighborhood. Remember, your virtue is lying somewhere with a bunch
of rusted transmissions tonight."

"I remember, believe me. I'm wearing a Playtex of aches."

"Okay. I'm off."

"Wait. Did I do a dumb trick, Mr. Lynxx? I see she's not here. A very
classy girl. Right from Fifth Avenue and still in the box. What's her
name?"

"Merry Goy."

"She was flummoxed, I could tell—to find me lying there in my happy
birthday outfit. Say it, be honest: was she upset? To me she was polite as
Amy Vanderbilt, but she wouldn't eat. Did she get off before her stop because of me?"

"Yeah, she flunked. She kinda lost her limber in the clutch. Not too
much wet strength under pressure, huh? Thumb went right through. She
disappointed me."

"Don't be so tough. What girl wouldn't have questions—with a naked
goulash in the back seat. Is it—is it serious between you?"

"Nah. About as serious as jewelry rash. I'll take two Cortaids and sleep
it off."

"I think you like her. I think."

"Ech. I put in a little time, yes. That's all I managed t'put in, by the
way. Another scoreless inning for the Big Bopper. Let it go."

"It isn't over, is it? I'll think it's my fault, from not keeping my night-gown on. What did you say by explanation?"

"I explained that you were my mistress. It was almost true, wasn't it? Hanh?"

"Pah. You're a botcher on purpose. That isn't the way to get her."

"Who says I want her? Anyhow, you'd be amazed." Simon is ripping at his hair with a comb: small knots pop. "Money will come t'money. A successful male is like the scene of a crime. The more women crowd around, the more women push in t'see. Well, I've had enough with Miss Merry Allen. She's one of those women who're so terribly deep and sensitive they turn inta pure DNA all over you."

"Mr. Lynxx, I know I'm speaking from out of school, but I think you need a woman like that."

"Thanks, I can do without a *shatchen* right now. Don't *hock a tchainik* at me, Minnie."

"Who's *hocking*? *Hock*—you speak almost like a native."

"Why not? I've lived long enough in this client state of Greater Zion. Do I—ah . . . smell? Give a sniff."

"Um."

"Um?"

"Um means you'll be with men and men don't pay attention."

"No. And after the trail *Lucky* lays down, I'll probably smell like L'Heure Bleu."

"*Lucky?* You're wrong. *Lucky* is very good."

"You read it? Whaddya think? You think it's good? Huh? Say something middle-class and encouraging. Say it isn't a garbage trove. You liked *Lucky?* Hanh? This line for ticket holders only."

"It made me cry. It's the you that I always thought was in you . . . if— if I make myself clear. The real person."

"Jesus, yeah, him. Let that gibbering dunce out and it's time for the nitwit net. The real me. Uh-boy. I changed my name and P.O. Box years ago t'hide from him. But you like it? Hanh. Huh? Really? Not because you don't wanna walk back t'Bayside? Huh? You notice my great self-assurance. Huh?"

"The scene in the corn is beautiful. And also at the end."

"But—but . . . Would you shell out $5.00 at Cinema East t'see it?"

"Are you kidding, Mr. Lynxx? To see a movie my son was working on—"

"Oh, great. I've written a film for one woman. I shoulda made poor Lucky into the Vienna Boys Choir with a club foot. Some advance sale we'll have. I hope you see it twice, so we can double our grosses."

"Ssssh. That was stupid of me to say. I'd like it even without Robert. It's good. It touches the heart. Better than that thing with the mule, what you were doing before."

"Christ, yeah, it's gotta be better than the mule. The mule didn't even have a mother. Well. Well, I'm tired."

"It's no wonder, you go like a dreidel."

"Time's up. *Sieg Heil* and a kiss. Let me double-dribble your left tit for luck."

"Mmmm. Don't worry. You'll do fine with Mr. Wolff."

"Listen. My Patton-like spearhead advance may bog down into a big, fat *Sitzkrieg*. I could be a while up there. If I'm not down by dawn, don't worry. Or call the Anti-Defamation League, they always know where I am."

"Just be honest. Say what you feel. It's a good movie story."

"Be honest? That's kinda subtle, isn't it? Well. Into the night. Ungently. Clank."

Fibers of dry lightning knot overhead. Merely an electrodynamic reflex: Manhattan discharging itself for the night. Simon moves toward Ten Great Ferry. Lightning again: for one shutter-crack the street seems a Mathew Brady caught by naive magnesium flare: grained, black on white, solemn: more public archive than photograph. Information has been given that HIRAM SHROUT & SON, FINE BREWERS, 1861 are no longer at 22 Great Ferry. The structure, a brownstone front, is still substantial, burgherish: posed, hand on lapel, like Grant's general staff before Spotsylvania. Bas-relief crenellation beneath each cornice: loopholes: a mock portcullis carved with some ingenuity above the main double door. As though beer were in need of defense. Eight tread-chipped steps gimp up, at a right angle, to the bandstand-square loading dock. Simon can go back in his mind: such grandiloquent barrels rolled out: imagine the full wood booming over cement. He is late, but perished workplaces please and get him curious. Anyhow, better take a leak.

The twelve-foot-high loading-bay door, of oak and splendid casters, has been sold off for debt. How it must have slid shut at quitting time in, say, 1872: with what a railroad yard sound. Now there are only three transverse boards and one diagonal: a farm gate design. Not for protection: to distinguish that which is in from that which is out. Simon, out, peeps in. By lackluster streetlight he can guess at the wooden housing for a ten-thousand-gallon vat. Mixer-arm apparatus, evidently of no scrap value, hangs down: forlorn: like the catcher in a trapeze act who has just missed. Would any odor be left: is beer smell, too, in Chapter Eleven? The vat, worth its weight of iron or brass, has been dismantled: cut apart with a torch. Simon will unzip and, by so doing, will intend no disrespect to Hiram Shrout, his heirs or assigns. Simon, in fact, is moved: even despondent: fatigue, mostly, has made him sentimental. But he does know one thing—he won't fool himself—it is not by art or film or even by the nagging media that Americans touch (we are essentially, proudly illiterate of ear and eye)—it is by cordial trade. This has been our nature: we make things for each other. A bill of lading is our best literature. We learn to write so that receipts may be signed. And it is time to go. Simon, all out, will open fire, open water—between board and board—at the vat hole: ten thousand gallons to come up with on short notice. A rat, splattered, has run off. Simon doesn't reach.

Then it's "I'm a Yankee Doodle Dandy," George M. Cohanning his way down the eight-step flight. Heel and toe, scuff: strut, strut, strut. Get down, Wolff and Kyryl, pull the hole in after you: here comes an entire goddam *opera*. Da, di-da-d'ja: away. Simon is galloping consumption. One shoe has picked up a thumbtack: tappety—tip, tap, toe: it ticks vivacious racket off. Simon is approaching: over there, over there. Sidewise up the street, elbow down and elbow out. Ja, d'ja, oh-jah! The screen treatment, wound stiff, is his Donald O'Connor top-hat-toffing cane. 18 Great Ferry, 16, 14: he and his shadow getting closer. Light has browned out in the bay window above: it seems less alert or less truthful: a shiny, vapid lobster stalk eye. Simon tiger-rags: for him, confidence is an idea associated with rhythm and athletic hoopla. Teeth line up: d'ja bursts through their exact clench. Simon is chipper again. That brewery meditation has put a head on him: or perhaps it was the bladder relief. He is up for Wolff now—14 Great Ferry, 12—he'll take center stage at the top of a secret inner dance finale if this. Arm around his throat. Would go away.

This. Terrific arm is aroung. His throggh.

"Huck. Eguh m'winpipe. Hugg." The arm has him crooked. Simon arches to it: a cruel swayback. The vomit mechanism has tripped: a gorge rises and is caught. He could choke on the trash of burnt membrane in his throat. Think, Simon. Microdots fizzgig across his vision: an alarmist vein has swollen blue over one eye. This is serious: of vital importance. Better be affable and coy here. No sense giving a backers' preview of his own strength: not now: not breath-taken and bent like a big croissant. But the necklock, won over by his quick meekness, has loosened its belt. Simon can speak-exhale, can just. The words that come will be laryngitic and deaf-mute-slurred. "Liss'n. Huck. Whoog-ever. Hugg-ah. Three bugs 'n change, huck, in leffand hip. Guhp-hip pogget. Taige. It."

"Mmmm. Mmmm." Mmm? Mmm, what? Simon hates an inarticulate enemy. They are neck and neck: this palooka, he judges, is tall, also no piece of doll furniture to shift around. Ah, well. Every day another challenge for the Kid: high noon in Dodge City at all hours.

"Ag-up. Taige. Huh?" The arm is conscientious and very firm: a small rafter. Developed muscles are heard in it: they grind. Simon has been arched further back now: he would gladly go along, gladly even go down, but for some snub object, like a dull table corner, that has been key punching his lower vertebrae. "Taige. Hugg. J'gimme receipt. For taxes, unh."

"Mmm? Mm!"

"Whag?"

"Hole him." Another voice: to his left, down and beyond eye reach. Simon is outnumbered: so much for the romance of single combat.

"Mm!"

"Hole him, I said. Can't get this thing on. Stupid's stuck." Some technical hang-up, it would seem. New York, New York: even mugged you run into featherbedding and ineptitude. Simon, stood up, waits: irritable now, an inconvenienced citizen: he'll kill it here, he'll peak too soon for Wolff: damn. And now he feels hungry: his stomach is yelling. Maybe they'll take him hostage: that'd solve the room-and-board problem for a while.

"Mm! Mm!" Uh-oh: Mr. Arm has gotten crabby, too. That now-not-so-blunt instrument is tapping out the word "quadraplegia" on his spine.

"Man, I'm comin'."

"Huck. Whassa holdup, this holdup? Sutthigg Igan do t'hep? Hug I'm in a—daaaow!"

He has been hit. Daaow: again. Bolo punches up in the gut. They are manageable, yet surprising and wind-expensive. More to come: Simon tightens, consolidates his midriff for it. Still, he has been unsettled. This isn't your naive, straightforward intent-to-rob. Principles of some sort are involved: and idealism, as we all know, can be dangerous. Guh: a lower blow, between decks. But his abdomen is turtle egg leathery now: Simon more than stomachs it. The aggressor wrist has cracked: with pain and . . . and—Jesus Jokester—Ball Peen is standing there. No: ha, no: B.P. has capon-stuffed his head into a pair of pantihose. Both shriveling, wind-socky legs hang down: a long beige rabbit ear on each shoulder. His palatial Afro has been snooded up in the left thigh: conical, like Mrs. Katzenjammer's cartoon hairdo. Simon, if he didn't have to ration air, would break up.

"Beeep-eee!"

"No, I'm not!" Ball Peen is scandalized. He had thought himself unknowable: nose squelched against cheek, lips deploying all over, half blind in queen-size L'eggs. For the sake of his stolen identity, Ball Peen will unwrap a big one now.

"Hoop! Huck. Sledge, lemme talk, dammit!" A roar through flat larynx: ferocious enough to bring out the habitual deference in Sledge. "What is this, an Actors' Studio project? Hanh? Huh. I said I'd give you both good parts. Now call off Primo Carnera here before you break a wrist hitting me. Jee-sus."

"We gotta, Simon. Gotta clean your whole shelf, man. Oh, man. Gotta fram you good. No use talkin', y'diggit? No use—we don't wanna, it's a thing has t'be done."

"Come on. You look like a three-month embryo in that thing. Or a human moussaka. Take it off. Let's talk." But Ball Peen has rushed him. Foot up, Simon tables his motion: a Thai boxer kick in the hip. Yet gently: Simon still doesn't believe. Ball Peen has fallen: in getting up he will step on one of his L'eggs: and fall again. The left bunny ear has become an elephant trunk, flopping straight down. Sledge inclines Simon back further over that hard thing: could it be a gun muzzle? Yes, Sledge is beginning to concern Simon. Not for his strength or even for his obscure weapon: because, Simon feels it, the man is scared.

"Wait. Listen, you blowhead dinges, lay off. I got a big appointment with Herman Wolff and I'm late already."

"You ain't late, Simon. This is *it*, man. *This* is it."

"Hanh?"

"This, man—this is your fuckin' big appointment with Wolff."

"What?"

"Oh, man. Man, I am sorry. He found my VISA card in his cuff. He damn found it—when we beat up on him Friday night last."

"Your what? You left your card?" Simon can't keep it down: he cracks, giggling, full of spittle. "Oh, no. Oh, no. Your VISA card? Why dincha wear one of those convention tags on your lapel: HELLO! My Name Is BALL PEEN."

"Don't laugh. Don't laugh, man. We in big trouble."

"Why? Is he running up a bill on you at Korvettes?"

"Stop it. You don't see—"

"Leggo, Sledge. Absurdist moments like this y'haveta enjoy. All my fine-fingered trip wires, my pitfalls covered with pine boughs: and Mighty Moke here leaves his VISA card behind. What idiot bank'd extend you credit? Leggo, Sledge."

"He can't. He can't. Dontcha hear me, Wolff's gonna file a big one on us, we don't work you over good. He's gonna bust us for assault with a deadly weapon. We'll get seven to twenny-five."

"What deadly weapon? Your lack of intelligence?"

"That's what he tole us. If Wolff says he saw a gun, who they gonna believe? Huh? Huh, man?"

"Calm your corpus. He won't. He's bluffing. Look, use that bloated grit you call a brain. Hanh, we'll whipsaw him. I'll bandage myself up like a smoked ham. I'll limp and put my arm in a sling. Larry can paint concussions on—and fake stitches so I look like a yard-sale remnant. Everyone'll be happy and you can stop drinking cough syrup. Leggo my neck, Sledge."

"No." Ball Peen has shook his head. And now blanching light hoses them down: as if a nightclub act were set to begin. Ball Peen's elephant man shadow is ten feet high and climbing on the gray brick wall. "See? I tole you. It's too late, man. It's gotta go down."

"Him? Is that him?" The Cadillac headlights publicize and point.

They stream from a vacant lot across Great Ferry. Sledge has cramped him again, Simon inhales: just breath enough left for his battle cry. Wolff, impatient, will tap the high-beam button: bright, brighter, bright, brighter, bright. Their shadows skip back/forth: like a single object seen, blink, by right eye and then left.

"It ain't gonna hurt. Don't fight us and it ain't gonna hurt."

"Wait. Lemme talk t'him. I'll take the blame. It was a joke, f'God's sake. No one got hurt. I can explain anything, B.P., you know that. I could sell shaving cream t'the Hassidim."

"Nossir. I been afraid of you, Simon—but that man . . . you seen his eyes: that man is death. You maybe might get off, but us poor black boys, we gonna be left t'suck nothin' but piss."

"Wait—"

"No!" The shadow-play elephant has leaped. There is one silhouette now, struggling, a turmoil out of which forms want to be born. Ball Peen has slugged Simon groggy in the ear. Simon ducks aside. And this time Sledge is hit by friendly fire.

"Mmmm!"

"Well, shit, Sledge—lemme at him."

"Aaaaaaaarghh!"

And a black squall, Simon, a holocaust, Simon: Simon has cut loose. Heel stamped down on Sledge's metatarsal arch, quick turn inside the slackening choke-hold, then—hi-yaaaah!—with both fists straight up: so close that a thumbnail will catch his own chin. Sledge's jaw has chomped shut: his bite is excellent and parings of tongue snip off. Bright, brighter: the Cadillac light frets. Sledge has skidded ten feet back on his coccyx: left hand out, as though at the guide rope of a luge sled. But Ball Peen will take fifteen yards for clipping: a cheap cross-body block from the rear. Simon's knees yield. He has gone down in a slovenly, legless way: latitude and reach are crabbed with Ball Peen slung across his calves. Now Sledge, on hand, on knee, is crawling toward him. Somehow feminine: blood has lipsticked his mouth. They are in four-point stances, two opposing linemen. And there it is, the blunt instrument: Christ unmighty, a stupid bathroom faucet screwed onto one foot of pipe. Sledge is kneeling up, this jester's weapon in his right hand: absurd, yet mace-swing-heavy: what a bathetic way to go. Simon can't maneuver: it is, he knows, end game and time to settle up. Sledge bashes. He bashes in anger and in pain, a two-hand baseball cut, remorseless. The sound behind Simon's left ear is terrible: is not a sound at all. The unsound of famished, sucking vacuums in outer space. Simon has been opened up.

"Stop! No, Sledge—no, don't hit him again. Oh, shit. We done enough, that fuckin' Jew. Get up, man. It's enough. We gotta get outa here. We gotta run."

Simon in the lurch: up. A stupid, incautious reflex: the reflex leg-broken horses have. He will stagger: then, incredibly, stand aright and still. One hand rises up: Simon, alone on the field, is calling for a fair catch. Dip-uh: feet splay to amend his balance. Simon reaches back, left hand a damage party, but he cannot somehow touch the wound. Blood is spattering down behind him, loud as female urine. The Cadillac's lights are out. Simon can appreciate that veiling courtesy: he isn't himself just now. The rich engine has throbbed awake. There will be dark motion and a fastidious turn-signal blink: go left, uptown. And Simon says,

"I'm hurt."

And suddenly it comes—wirewalking, whirling, tumbling, barreling, bowling, backflipping, juggling, harebrained, insane—a grotesque super-consciousness. All the buffoons and jackanapes of wit: simile and simile for simile, they clown it up: the freaks that human fancy, unconstrained, will make. Simon can't not free-associate: each idea or thing is the pyramid top for an explosive geometrical progression down of ideas and things. Parallel, equivalence, symbol, trope: they have no end, they have no art. The metaphor-making is dissolute and mechanical: automatic, pre-assembled: it comes and comes and comes: it does not omit, select, forget. Simon has screamed across Great Ferry: screamed at the pain pressure of a total and idiot imagination. Where nothing will be done with: where the implications of everything in everything—image to image to image—are misshapen and obligatory, fierce.

"Stop. Stop. it. Stop my head."

He wants unconsciousness: there is too much to imagine. Garbage can near the wall. Simon, dying of perception, clumps toward it: a strenuous approach. His hands grasp the empty can rim, yet they miss. He has seen them there, yet they interpenetrate what *there* is. Simon leans forward on them: he doesn't fall. His hands, passing through, hold him up. They hold him up and pass through. Holding.

through.

4

His hand has been commissioned: to hold an empty glass. This is high-tech work: exacting: there are fine data retrieval systems in the flesh. Simon will pant and crack sweat: very concentrated here. Hi: his right arm jerks up from the hospital bed, gangly as something on a rope. It is eager but fuddled: and separate. Simon has had eight days to evaluate his personnel: slow reacquaintance with each limb. They are a pickup squad of parts: the ensemble work is gone. They just run errands for him now: like some child with a note it cannot read. Simon, impresario and straw boss for his body, is watching from the prompter's box: to cue in muscle: to restage a tendon's curl. Scene One, "Glass," Take Number Sixty-seven or Seventy-six, whichever: he has been doing this mi-fa-sol for the right arm since lunch. His wrist pivots: thumb and forefinger spread to appraise width. They push, they butt the glass: they hook around. An accomplishment: when you remember that, since one week ago Monday, Simon's hand and Simon have felt nothing at all.

Then, oh, down. The bed is gone again: he falls. Drops, plunges through it: sinks: in a monotonous surprise, down. Freefall, deadfall, giddy. The avalanche of a single paper sheet. Down: through. He has no presence: he is neither here nor there: Simon, in the hospital, can't place himself. And has to look: to find his body lying familiar and prodigious ahead of him: make it, by visual evidence, be. This time at least he didn't flail out the way new skaters do: arm and leg wild for balance. That first brainsick Tuesday afternoon he vomited: swam, airless and very near death, in chunks of his own retch: with garbled howling, enormously afraid. The glass clinks: apprentice work and humdrum, but he must stay engrossed: there are so many intangibles now. Move the hand: watch the mattress. And today, and worse, gravity seems just a prejudice: since morning it has been possible for him to fall up, to fall aslant: like an idle floater in the eye. It isn't merely that skin nerve ends are out of touch: rather it is as if an encircling neutral ambiance, a bubble, a repellent magnetism, had isolated him. He has no weight: he is ambivalent in space. He who loathed abstract thought and threw his weight around.

The glass has risen: off, from, over a bedside table. Secret pulley systems in his elbow pay slack out: swivel, then extend. Simon, crane jockey, stops the glass above his naked breast: *skoal*. A toast to the hospital room. This is success, but success qualified: he still can't look away. We hold objects by registering, in an offhand manner, their slight friction on the skin. Simon has no record of friction here: everything is asymptotic to him: it approaches but will never arrive. Simon, in his solvent bed, must consult the hearsay proof of sight. For example: he can see that his grasp is overwrought: the thumbnail has been squeezed ash-blond. It is an implement, his hand, cunning enough yet rudimentary: like the primitive steel mandibles that shift radioactive waste around. Up, down: tilt: pour nothing out. In this last week Simon has let three or four hundred glasses fall. Left, right: hoist. And one he simply crushed.

"Rahhh. Rahhhhaaaah!"

"Hang tough, Packard. Go with it, baby. Ride that sucker out."

But Packard, in the other bed, gets morphine and cannot sense this word-applause. His long rahhhaaaah is surly: a sort of bleacher catcall. Simon has come to relish it: more a male territorial threat than the expression of six months' spark-gap-leaping pain. Now Packard will convulse again: a powerful spastic: acting on misinformation from the facetious yellow tumor in his brain. Packard's spine has curved up like a Japanese footbridge. Left hand is belt high and rigid, open against the crib rail: the hand of a ready gunfighter. Badda-badda-bah: heels give his mattress a good larruping here. The bed has ridden forward one half inch: it'll be a foot ahead of Simon's by dinnertime. They are quite the pair, Packard and he. Contemporary, robust: matriculating in the same weight class. Packard, Simon has been told, played cornerback for money once. His nose has been beaten down: level with the cheekbone, almost Chinese tight. His left front tooth is out. The skull has been shaved for brain-tapping so often—back and top and side—that there are five or six different degrees of croppedness in his crew cut. Raaaah-uh? Simon can't help him: the electric agony is closed-circuit stuff. Pain self-involves: this afternoon has been a comatose and snarly one for Packard. Simon, practice, practice, will return to his handiwork. But the glass isn't there.

"Christ. Where'd it go now? Gotta keep the pinky hooked underneath, Simon. I told you that. Hanh. C'mon, you fat acromegaloid, get in the game. Sheesh, I'll be ready for the Special Olympics by check-out time. Uh. Here it is. Down here. A glass in my armpit and why not? Your hand moves like an armpit, doesn't it?"

"Errahhh. Rahhh."

"You can say that again. Jesus, Packard, what're we gonna do? I can't feel anything and you feel too much. Huh? Maybe I could give you a transfusion of bland."

"Rrr."

"Uh-huh. Y'know what these physical ABC's just reminded me of? My father—Aldo—he sent me t'acting class once. How old could I've been? Eight or something. My mother's idea really. Madame Zamara's Academy of Dramatic Arts: registered in Panama, I think it was. Well, y'know what I did there for sixteen weeks?"

"Rgah."

"Nope. Not even warm. I did just what I'm doing now. Hanh. For sixteen subsimian weeks I picked up a glass and put it down again. A Welch's jelly glass, what they useta call Polish Anchor Hocking. I'll never forget it."

"Rrrung."

"No. Be serious, Packard. 'Hold the glass, Simon,' she'd say. 'I am holding it, Madame,' I would say. 'No, you're not.' 'But it's in my hand, Madame. Can't you see?' 'It may be in your hand, but it has no weight. It has no character. It has no *history*. What have your fingers done? Yes and why? Of course you haven't the slightest idea. You're an insensitive boy. Your glass bores me.' Well, it wasn't exactly Seven Flags over Puerto Rico t'me either. Or t'the other twenty kids in class, all of whom were rolling their snot into peaballs by this time, outa boredom. 'Now pick it up again, shall we? And shall we try to feel it this time?'"

"Rah . . . uhhhhrt."

"Up 'n down. Up 'n down. I mean, Packard, until then—I mean acting t'me was just a series of big leers pitched at the front row. That glass, it went with me everywhere, like the fourth leg on a tripod. People useta drop nickels in it. Believe me, it was a big event when Madame put water in the glass: it was a damn *premiere*. 'Now pick it up and drink, Simon. No—I do not believe you are drinking. Class, do you believe Simon is drinking?' Nooooh, they'd all groan, the little tuft-hunters—like they couldn't wait t'give her a pedicure with their tongues. Fifteen times I did it on that tiny stage. Until finally I hadda say, 'Madame, if I'm not drinking, how come I gotta go t'the bathroom now?' 'Go, *piss*,' she says like some ancient sub-deb. And Freddie Shimkus, who, at age eight, was already playing Hamlet while I was getting the bloat, says, 'I bet you won't believe his dork either when he pulls it out.'"

"R'guun. Gahr."

"I know. I know. But be patient. Talking like this helps me t'concentrate on the damn mattress. Which—hah—tends t'disappear like the Murphy bed in an Abbott and Costello routine, if I'm not careful."

"Raaaah!"

"Wow. Scared me that time. They really put a stop payment on your brain today. Christ, when I figure the street value of what goes into your left buttock—we could be rich, Packard, you poor candle end. Huh. Where was I in my two-man soliloquy? Oh. Anyhow, comes Parent Day at Madame Zamara's, and I've really been promoted. Postgraduate work. I'm doing knife and fork. Tough. Jacket slipped on and off. The famous Briefcase Act: lift first with nothing in it, then full of jewels, then loaded with TNT. But I'm last on the program and Aldo has really shot the cuffs of his mind by that time. He's got one hand on his crotch, the way he always did when anyone but him was talking f'more than six minutes. Mind you, this is the first time he ever visited me, except maybe twice in the hospital. And what happens—my classmates are doing whiz-bang method interpretations from *Our Town* and *Streetcar* and Aldo hasta watch me—his son . . . well, he's made this big trip t'watch me do essentially what I do at home, in the bathroom, at dinner. But I did try, Packard. I tried t'feel and be specific and make imaginative choices and there was even some polite applause. The kind a horse gets when it counts t'three. And then I hear my father say, 'Fifteen bucks an hour to tie his shoelaces in public. What is he, an actor or a retarded child?' "

"Rrrr."

"No. No, actually, Aldo had a point. At that frantic rate I was never gonna get t'play Stanley Kowalski. Let alone King Lear. My range as an actor was my arm length, pretty much. Hanh. But that's what'll happen when they type you as just a knife and fork and shoelace man."

"Rahhhh."

"And now I can't even do that. Shoelaces, my God. I don't wanna think about it. T'me now shoelaces are like doing a mouse vasectomy with gloves on. I'm a wipe-out: even the Right to Life people're willing t'make an exception in my case. Hanh. Huh, Packard? Packard, listen: I wouldn't say this t'anyone else—but you and I . . . I mean, I can tell from your wilted snoot that you've caught some ninety-millimeter fist artillery in your day—and shoved up from the floor again. That never fazed me. Y'know what I mean? Hunh? When you cock someone with your best daisy-puller and he just blinks. And it's his turn t'make anchovy paste outa you. I wouldn't tell this t'anyone else, but I'm scared reekless, Packard. It's true. I admit it. I'm not ashamed. Packard, when I close my eyes, it's like I'm in Allah's great asshole. I can't get a fix on myself. I'm not there. I've lost the owner's manual t'my head. I'm . . . I'm afraid of the dark, buddy—isn't that a fine dish of Filipino rations? Jesus, I'm afraid t'shut my eyes and you're afraid t'wake up. We'll never meet, Packard. We'll miss each other coming and going. Huh? Huh. Why is my hand still up in the air like one of those drink holders you stick in the lawn? Bastard. Watch. I'm going back t'Madame's sense-memory class. Got some aggression t'get rid of. Watch."

"H'rrrarh."

"Not yet, Packard. I appreciate your support, but wait for the idiot card. I haven't done it yet.".

New play: hut-hut-hut. Simon, signal caller, barks an inaudible out. Hand and wrist are in the set position: tight, waiting for a center snap. Spontaneous once, now they respond only to ideas—not to native stimuli. And when let out on their own recognizance they will tic and blurt: answering wrong numbers in the cerebellum. Simon has phrased a telex: my-right-hand-down-and-crush-the-hospital-menu. His wrist pushes against—what? Oh. Forgot to impower and inform the elbow: details, his autonomous nervous system swamped with paperwork. Down, downness: his hand. Fingers close and crumple: they ball the menu up. This slow action might remind Simon of Ricky Spellman's toy coal bucket. It stood just one scaled-down block away from his American Flyer RICKYTOWN DEPOT: quick to drop and bite on a hill of Bokar coffee grounds. Upness, clenchedness: then, spread the word, shoulder to elbow to wrist to swift finger release. Ha, throwing is an elegant enterprise: why did he never study its sweet uncoil? Simon has hurled the menu ball. It will flutter left, a girl-toss, inaccurate. And—just to see is sickening—his hand, ungoverned, has hit Simon's crotch on the follow-through: thuck. Yell: yell out of habit. One monster blast to his gonads and no pain. None of that kidney-sucking, doubling ache which is both penance and certification for a male. Dead there: the crotch an unembellished U.

"Rah."

"Rahhh!"

"Rahhah."

"Rahhhhahhhhah!"

And bitter, berserk in the heart, Simon has shut his eyes.

Gone.

Ga-ohhhhn.

He is lying face down: he is lying face up: Simon has no face. Shot out and ga-ohn: a tramp missile at escape velocity: the wild sperm's first rush re-enacted for him here. Yet, as well, as clearly, contracting on himself, an inner infinite spiral, to some point with no dimension or hope. At the moment of blindness his knees were flexed up: and now up, up, they come with a mad inertia. God, his legs, God, are inside his head: they kick a tantrum there. Simon is hovering, aghast, in blank parentheses: out of any context and shapeless. Nose, ears have been sloughed off: the smooth face is somewhere on his chest, grotesque. He flails around to touch, then to touch just a fingertip, to touch touch. Ga-ohn: nothing with noise. Noise: yes, he and Packard are in a duet and they howl. But the rrahhhh! has no direction: it seems to circle at him with an untrackable Doppler effect. Simon is dense: caved in on: then diffuse, a spray: atomized apart, yet imploding back. He is all ambiguous and inexact: turned inside out, through the void, like a fantastic pocket lining: gone.

"Look! Lookit the van! Maaaa, look!"

"Rrrrm."

"Oh, shit. Shit, no more. Please, God: I can't take any more of that. All right? All right? Shit, I'm afraid."

Eye-peeled Simon shinnies, shimmies up the bed: out of sight he has been almost out of mind. Fear sweat-glosses him over: that skeletal sound you hear is hard teeth snacking. With one foot he will knock the single sheet down. Half hidden by it, untouching, he seemed an amputee: a torso murder: a repugnant stump of him. Simon counts heads: arm, stomach, mattress, ceiling, bed table, door: the visual ideas that define him—Simon-in-space. He is here, evident: he can authenticate it. Simon folds arm over arm up, in view, across his breast. Danceless bare feet draw together: framed, too, by the eye. This has become his stock pose. He doesn't, like a mother with four intractable children, trust his extremities. But for urine-antiqued jockey underwear, and the front-open hospital gown, Simon is nude. Chest flesh hops to a double-quick beat: his seeable pulse: a countercurrent in the long swell made by startled breath. That first day, at that first perception of sightlessness beyond mere sightlessness, Simon went into cardiac arrest. An intern had to hit him: and shoot adrenaline through. Simon doesn't know this: but fear has placed his heart at risk.

"Jesus. Jesus, make it go away. What is this, what's happening t'me? Huh? Hah? A joke's a joke: enough. Hanh. Are they right, is it all in my porous mind? I saw my van: I saw it perfect. You know, Packard? You know what I'm saying? Huh? I mean the way it was before I built it. The way I planned it, all beautiful. Before. But it was there and I saw it. And—oh, boy. And now I haveta come up with something else. To remember. Get something ready, Simon, before the sun calls it a day. Christ, just let them keep light around me. That's all I ask—ah. Ah. Breathe out. Ah, but suppose the bulb on my night lamp goes kerblooey? Suppose some jolthead at Con Edison fuses a whole substation? Think of something else t'remember. What?"

"Rrrrah."

"No. See: I can remember things, Packard. If I try, if I concentrate—even in that slipping, sliding fun-house infinity, in that goddam black flushing crapper. Or. Shit, how t'explain it? It's not like remembering, it's more intense: more like I'm on weird tea or Mexican buttons. But it can jerk the craziness up short. If I remember, if I zoom in on something, it gets my gyroscope working again. Like—just now I saw my van, every part of it. And Uncle Arthur's face this morning: every part. His nose and the inside of his nose and the pores. Y'can't do that: I know it's impossible. Sure. Okay, so maybe I'm just imagining, whatever. I mean I useta remember in camera angles. One take after the next. You focus on one place at a time. Huh? Gotta think of something new. If I lose control, if I let my mind run out—it's like a fishing line with something big and dark and deranged on the end. And yank: seeya later, Charlie, send the charter boat home without me. But—but the funny thing is, is I can only remember it once. No matter what it is. Why? Maybe I burn it out like a flashcube in there. Out there. I've already used you, Packard. You came out very well: your head with all the holes drilled in it—it seemed t'make sense. Which it doesn't. I mean, you should be dead, Packard: you know that, don't you? Oh, baby. I don't blame them. I'm not expressing myself well, am I? Shit, did I piss in my pants again? Uh-no. I don't think. I'll use the urine bottle next. I'll remember that. Okay. Urine bottle, urine bottle. Remind me, Packard."

"Rrrr."

"Shees, you know. It's like someone's tryin' t'extradite me. Well, they won't. No. I'll fight it. I'll get a mouthpiece. No."

"R."

"Uh-uh. No . . ."

Minutes elapse: Simon and Packard save their breath. For best effect pain, fear also, require a certain pacing: deliberate pauses, some suspense. Afternoon has become irresolute: poised at the top of its circle, set to trade one momentum for another and wheel down. Simon is under surveillance. Tentatively, like a twelve-year-old girl unsure of her sensual worth, his left nipple has come erect. Quite big: larger than he can recall: a nut and bolt screwed down. Simon will watch: to wonder what major obsolescence is implicit here, in men's breasts: what miscalculation of the evolving human tribe? He tweaks it: or is seen to tweak. His fingernail has grown out, has mitered itself: matronly in shape now: must ask a nurse to clip them all short. And how do women touch, removed as they are from honest sensation by such a horny point? On him the hospital gown, with its groin-length décolletage, is mini-hemmed and out of style. Simon causes one leg to go up: a curvy, svelte thing. He has lost weight, down eighteen pounds: they have threatened him with an intravenous meal: but eating is gaffer work and doesn't attract him anymore. Simon, spiteful, will raise both legs just one inch up: and hold: a difficult calisthenic act. Yet yesterday he did it for three hours. His body, though unresponsive, cannot oppose him. This is not exercise, it is an image, a picture of exercise: pain and fatigue do not relate to abstractions. In a way, diminished so, he is superhuman.

"Hey, lookit. Watch, time me. See, my legs're so stupid they don't know they're dropping off. It's eerie, huh? Useta be, thirty seconds, a minute—I couldn't do this inch-up exercise for more than that. Now I'm the most powerful invalid since FDR. I could be a fakir: I could play rich kids' birthday parties. Simon the Sufi, poke a sharp curtain rod in his eye, burn his taper at both ends: he can't feel, he can't itch, he can't—shall we be frank?—Simon, he . . . shit, I can't get it up anymore. Huh, Packard? It's a no-show, nothing. Packard, didja hear what I said? I can't get it up."

"Nnnnuung. Rahhhgh."

"Oh, I get a hard-on now and then, the way you'd get a wart. I look down and there it is, like a coat hook or a knickknack from Niagara Falls. Someone else's. Christ, you know what that's like? You know, Packard? I've tried, I've made the old friction test and there's nothing but gross absenteeism: I can't even rub myself the wrong way. Little Johnny doesn't wanna come out t'play. Some sorry state of affairs, huh? Affairs. God, no more overnights based on the double-occupancy rate. It ain't funny, McGee. No. I mean—you know—I try t'keep a stiff upper lip, which is about all I can keep stiff—but I'm kinda bitter. In fact—put this under your hat with all the other little holes—I could cry. I wouldn't mind it, I wouldn't mind crying. You understand, don't you, you're a guy. I miss it. There was always that. No matter how bad things got, there was always that. In the night. Even alone. And now— Hey? Get off! Dammit, what's this now?"

A loose strip of bandage. It slides down from his head, across one eye: milky, vague as reminiscence, sheer. For that instant Simon thinks he is monocular: he is impaired. He will swipe at it and—fupp—take a flat slap on the jaw. Vision heels over, head aside. The bandage ribbon has curled back around his shoulder: a thin ponytail. Simon recovers, hauls neck muscles in: he is irascible, yet wary of brain injuring. Dr. Cox has shown him the gauze pack, hemispherical, large above and behind his left ear, like an outer brain lobe. Simon is bald now: looking, by his own estimation, eminent and forceful. Hair, all these years, has been a weak modifier: a distraction on him. Why didn't he try it before, this impressive persona? Impressive, too, the staple-taut blue sutures and his fracture. On an X ray it is K-shaped: strike three if you're scoring. Yet electroencephalograms report normal traffic: an ongoing barter of impulse and galvanic wave. Dr. Cox is very optimistic: also, he suspects Simon has been malingering.

"Wow. Clocko, wow. Where'd that come from? Hanh? Sneak-punched myself, shit. Shit, this is getting hairy. I'm just swaying here, Packard, like I'm in the fast lane on a rope bridge: my right hand doesn't know what my left hand is doing and neither of them tells me anything. Uh. Careful: watch that trapdoor in the mattress. Maybe I should sleep: sleeping isn't bad. At least when I dream I'm someplace. I have fingers and toes. If it wasn't for that damn half second—that half second when I wake up, if I don't open my eyes and get situated right away. Listen, Packard, all this is strictly off the record: whatever you do, don't tell my uncle when he comes in. He really yanks my tiller with that by-the-light-of-burning-martyrs look all over his rood screen. Huh. I mean, he comes in here like a tourist, dammit. I think he's got this idea I can go inta the big vacuum tube and do his meditating for him. Like we were a tag team in some cosmic wrestling match."

"Neeef. Neee—hff."

"That's a new sound. Nice, old buddy: work on it and leave your answering service number. Uh-oh. Did I? Did I? No. Jazzus, Packard, I can't push the beef tree up, but I sure can piss like a shot waterbed. Uh. I am not popular with nurses. Refresh my memory, eh? What's that little arabesque we do so carelessly, that pinching in the prostate we all do when we wanna stop a wee-wee? You know? I remember how it looked, sort of, from the outside, that reflex. An up-tightening in my behind. But I'm just guessing. I can't feel inside so good. Goddam, God freakin' damn, my skull has a flue in it and I'm dangling in space like a stupid Boston fern. D'you think this'll affect my status in the National Guard? Huh, Packard?"

"Raaaghh. Pppp."

"Not interested, eh? Poor jerk, why don't they just let you die?"

In response Packard will start to gnaw. This is the worst number on his misfiring brain's program: it has a knavish and lizard pitch. Hissing, smacking: little bites of a corn-on-the-cob sort that grind: that fret tooth enamel down. None of Packard's visitors can tolerate the gnaw for long: they stand up better against his competitive rahhhhh. Simon has checked the guest list out: big men for whom a physical doing—handshake or punch—is articulate enough. But here they pause at the bed foot, decorous and unsure, as though Packard lay in state: topcoat bent over arms that hang crossed, waist high: rocking from ball of toe to ball of heel. Then they nod or smile or throw a salute up: they seem foolish and hurt, left out: in an odd, distant relationship with their friend. These are frank men and they hold Packard disloyal: someone who has found new company in a more exclusive neighborhood. Where he is getting stronger each day. Convulsions are a dynamic exercise: they keep Packard in shape for pain. His biceps are gorgeous: wide and shiny. Now or then Simon will hear the locked vertebrae unchain: prack, p-prack: like a thawing stream. But Simon, out of cussedness, intends to put up with Packard. Packard has been moved into the room for his annoyance value. Dr. Cox wants a recantation from Simon: wants him vexed to sanity.

Must be almost 3 P.M.: Simon has calculated the sunlight. Time doesn't occur to him now: he is without a dateline. Hours and their normal sequence seem neither ahead nor behind: but rather at his right elbow, running alongside: ever-present: pacing him. Light has slumped across a bombastic flower wreath near the windowsill: it is canted back on three green wire legs: about the width of an archery target. Simon is pleased for once to be without smell. A spray of flatulent lilies has been blowing at him from the green center. They are servile and stupid, grown apparently for their weight like cattle: so large they remind him of the old RCA His Master's Voice logo. Simon is discomfited: he'd have to drop dead before the wreath felt at home in here. And on a red ribbon banner: FOR ONE REAL COOL CAT, FROM HIS TWO SOUL BROTHERS. GET WELL SOON. Bought probably on the VISA charge card.

"Good afternoon, Mr. Lynxx."

"Huh? Oh, Peggy."

"How d'you feel today?"

"I don't."

"I know that, Mr. Lynxx. I didn't forget. I meant—oh, wow—you know what I meant. Like, how are you?"

"For someone who needs a federal matching grant t'move his left arm, all right."

"Uh-huh."

"Uh-huh."

Pegeen, the nurse's aide, is hanging loose again: child idle: wrist on his bed footrail, as you might test water in an infant's bath. Pegeen has the large teeth of Celtic people. Wide freckle stains, like peanut butter on gray rye bread, smutch her forearm. Paprika hair, frazzling, split end over split end, has been drawn back through a single barrette that is tight and large as mousetraps with their dead. Each afternoon now she has ambushed his semi-privacy: stealing around on blue Adidases. The sort of girl who could talk all night under a 75¢ MINIMUM AT TABLE sign: and then ask for more cream in her one cup. Simon will try to be limber: to unbind his body. Pegeen has a way of not-glancing at his nude stomach that makes Simon feel exploited: some visual gigolo. But this is only her on-short-notice parental rebellion: the best she can manage: brought up with severe Catholicism, Pegeen has gone in for bedpan porn because Mr. O'Connell won't let her see R-rated films or date Tony "Ham" Prosciutto.

Gaaarh: a bit of Packard grousing. Pegeen will grant him deference: will listen and concur. Packard's condition is what they call guarded: important, precious. Simon, on the other hand, seems a mere dauber, a patient without portfolio, unclassifiable. He is bashful: uncertain. There are probably old male stinks on him: of crotch and pit. His oafish hand/eye coordination must be distasteful: slow and over-detailed: like a drunk explaining life. Simon is vulnerable here: abashed to know it. Given youth, given normal agility, even this adolescent girl could overpower him: and do her naive will.

"Uh-huh."

"Uh."

"You're a big star now, Mr. Lynxx. Everyone on the floor is talking about your case. Uh-huh. It's very rare."

"Yeah. I bet. Cox isn't gonna give me tenure here. He didn't like the pilot film. He wants me transferred t'the wet sheet wing."

"Oh, wow—I guess that means something, but it's way over my head. Did the morning nurse put your contact lenses in?"

"Yuh."

"Let's see, what else? You get Valiums, right?"

"I get them but I don't take them. I toldja that."

"You should take your medicine, Mr. Lynxx."

"Valiums are for people who're nervous for no reason. My nervousness is very reasonable. My arms and legs are void where prohibited, which is just about every place."

"Well, I just try t'keep up on things. Uh-huh. I want t'be a nurse, if I don't get t'be an actress first. I like to study people for their characters, you know. I'm very inner-directed, Mr. Lynxx. When you have five brothers and two sisters—oh, boy—you learn to be motivated."

"What d'you little O'Connells call yourselves, the Rhythm Eight?"

"We don't sing. Oh? It's some kind of joke."

"Forget it."

"No, I'll think about it. I know you have a very clever mind, Mr. Lynxx. Some of the things you said that first day—oh, wow. It was like algebra. And I thought you'd break the straps. You talked one word right after another, just like Spanish or Chinese. And it was like a whole bunch of people were talking. Uh-huh. Did you see *The Exorcist*? I wish I had: but I know the story. Uh-huh. I'm glad you've got a priest."

"That's not a priest, that's my uncle. My foster uncle. Let's not make small talk, huh? Why dontcha go someplace and chew a whole lot of gum?"

"Oh, sure." Peggy smiles. "We don't have to talk. I know you're real busy, uh-huh. Is your urine thing full?"

"My thing is fine."

"Gosh, I don't believe it, you're so shy. I changed all my five brothers. No big deal. When you've seen one you've seen them all."

"As Eve said to Adam."

"Did she? I can't tell when you're pulling my leg."

"That makes two of us."

"Huh?"

She mooches, languid and coy, toward his pillow: a child abuser. One hand has been resting on her abdomen: where the rhythm is. Chubby, promiscuous freckles drift, bacterial, like oil in water. Her bustline is tumid: it promises slush funds of flesh. Rahhhh: man to man, Packard has warned Simon. The leg that Simon can see is provocative: her ankle bracelet around it, flashing through pantihose, suggests warm slavery.

Simon will stare aside: he has had failure dreams already, penis melted, wax runoff down one thigh. Pegeen is straightening his bed-table top: a warrant to pry.

"What is it, Peggy? What d'you want?"

"Just making neat. Can I do anything else for you?"

"Climb in." But his voice is immature, broken: and fatuous.

"Oh, wow. I don't think that's on your chart, Mr. Lynxx." The nose has pleated itself: four sniffy wrinkles. But her face is blank: the kind of face that should be inside an Irish nun's coif. "No. I don't think it'd be good for you. Uh-uh. Uh-huh. Anyway. And anyway I'd want someone who could feel me."

"Oh? Such grown-up bitchiness, Peggy."

"Well, it isn't nice to tease and talk dirty. Is it? Uh-huh."

"I'm sorry."

"Oh, don't worry. I'm used to it. And I know you didn't mean it: it's the sickest people who say things like that. I had a man talk fresh to me and he died the next day. Maybe it was the last thing he said: oh, wow. I mean, imagine having that on your mind last thing. When you meet God."

"Okay. Thanks. Your conversation's scenic as a New Jersey tank farm. I said I was sorry."

"Uh-huh. Sure, no hard feelings. Have you had any visitors today?"

"If you mean Robert, he should be in any minute."

"Oh, Robert. Well." Pegeen touches her lipstick. "Well, better do some work. See ya. You, too, Mr. Packard."

"Onnnnnnnnn." And Mr. Packard pipes her overboard. "Onnnn."

"Jesus, what was that noise? Eh, Packard? The last of the big band sounds? Oh, mother. Oh, Christ. Didja hear me? Didja hear your old roomie? Climb in, I said. I really said that. I was Mr. Small Curd, wasn't I? But—well. Well, I tellya. She unnerves me, that Irish water spaniel. Imagine me: me who's jumped into more beds than Bernadette Castro. I never realized how scary sex can be when your two-by-four is one-by-one. Jesus, and I useta be The Home of the Whopper. Jesus. I guess that's what women felt, when I useta go at them, all hands, like Mussolini after Ethiopia. Climb in, he said. Simon Lynxx said. Oh, gag. A disgrace. I was bluffing with a very small pair and she knew it. That damn condescending uh-huh of hers. Oh, Aldo. Kill the snowman, kill him, you had the right idea. I'm miserable. How'm I gonna cure this? Huh, Packard? Maybe if I hired those two spigot murderers t'whack me on the other side of my head . . . what? Whoo. Bang. What was that noise? Steam coming up, I guess. Is it cold in here? The nurse this morning said —what time have you got, October? Just think, I'm stuck from here t'everlasting Tuesday in the same weather. No more seasons for Simon: his body has retired to a co-op in Key Biscayne. Uh, better try an' piss.

Cox wants t'put a catheter in: that'd really hold me on a short leash. Hanh—up. See. Lookit my ankle now."

It is empurpled in the joint: plum color: grown clubbish with swelling. Yesterday again Simon fell twice: fell to no particular moment or place of impact, though noise beat around him in the hospital corridor. Walking is feasible: when both legs and his wooden cane are supervised by sight: forward progress made in clusters of movement, stop, as you might shift an easel, stop. Simon has put his ankle aside: what he can't see won't hurt him. The urine bottle, glancing off thigh and thigh, is piloted down/into his ferry-slip crotch: docked at groin. A well-thought-out vessel: flat underside and wide oral neck: it waits, throat tilted, like a glass held ready for draft beer. Time to weed his member out. This will be speculative work: he can't tell flesh from cloth. Memories rise to the top of his deck and are dealt out. At age eleven, with Aldo just dead, Simon became quite bladder-wild during sleep: dream of shipwreck, dream of deluge, sunk. For almost one year he had to turn down any overnight excursion. Bettina was understanding: her kindness, in fact, had fierce gusto to it. She bought Simon a diaper wardrobe and plastic underwear. Very large: from some fetishist jobber, he would guess in retrospect. Sixth-grade Simon crackled to sit: he was heard arriving. Other children thought he had extra, strange joints that could pop: knuckles at the hip. Now, for privacy, he will build a roofed-over pavilion with the sheet. Set: go: Simon looses abdomen, thigh, thigh, then that flat, desert isthmus between scrotum and behind: each an abstract idea of relaxing. It isn't easy to find the decisive muscle. "Sssss," from Packard, helpful coaching. The fluid clatter on metal alarms Simon. He will say, "Aaaaah," but he doesn't identify relief. And—on camera, smile—Robert has been observing him.

"Can't keep your hands off it, can you? Huh?"

"Jesus, hide the silver amalgam in your mouth. It's the *Apprenticeship of Duddy Kravitz*."

"How're you doing, uh?"

"I'm making potty in the right place. The last drop goes clank."

"Finished? Let me, I'll take it."

"I can manage."

"I know. I got it." Simon has difficulty threading himself back through the placket flap: he bends a lot, S-shape. Robert will try not to watch: but his eyes self-propel. Simon is a curio: and big.

"How much's in there?"

"Oh. Half a quart, maybe more."

"Half a quart. Go down, Noah, chance of flooding in poor drainage areas tonight. My bladder must've been inflated like the prime lending rate and I couldn't even tell."

"No sensation yet?" Robert has stood the bottle on its end. "Huh, Champ?"

"Let's say I've played my last game of touch football. This is some budget discount disease: its symptoms are no symptoms at all. But don't take my name off the letterhead yet, Mr. Rising Expectations. I can walk. After a fashion, like a two-legged daddy longlegs, but I can walk. I learn fast and it doesn't hurt when I fall down. Well. Oh, well. My, my: what have we here? Cashmere, today? You look like someone's ex-mistress."

"I, I find jealousy unattractive. Admit it, I look good."

"Uh."

"Well, I look better than I did. Right?"

Robert skims a chair forward. The measure is temperate and decorous: headwaiters seat women so. But Robert will stand: to take off, to dismantle rather, gray gloves and a vicuña overcoat. Hot stuff: he sweats with New York chic. An amulet of very ecumenical mysticism—ankh and mandala and Freemason tool—is hanging down on old gold. Robert pets, subdues the cashmere sweater front beneath it. Simon has noted a new orchestral tact in hand and head: large gestures, not entirely precise, yet whole. The aplomb, Simon can't help but think, of an Eighth Avenue shoeshine artist: buffing cloths whip-cracked and fast. Robert would like praise. He has come up in the world: at least an inch or three on Gucci elevated feet. The walking stick, beside Simon's cane, is class-conscious, smug. Robert would appear to be a derivative thing: close quotes around him. Hair, composed and allocated by Larry, has the structural firmness of beaten egg white: delicate, air-full, slick, not bad: in high wind Robert will look persecuted now. Down payments have been taken on a sort of mustache: blocked out in very low relief with wax and liner. The theory is legitimate: his lips, indeed, are thinner this way: set for fine pronunciation. Also, Robert has gone tan: which, in autumn, in New York, makes him seem an envoy from some more exclusive place.

"Sit down. I'd rather you didn't lean over the casket like that."

"I. Ha, I can't."

"Why? Your creases might shatter?"

"No. This'll make you laugh. I've been going to one of those instant-tanning parlors, you know. Yesterday was the first time, uh—first time I took my pants off in the booth. Ha. My ass is red like a baboon's. And—oh, man—is it sore. Ha. But my skin looks good, doesn't it?"

"Yeah. Like someone hennaed your face."

"Come on, break down: be, be honest. I'm looking sharp and you know it. I mean, *compared*. And it gives me more confidence. You notice I don't hardly stutter at all. Larry gave me a good tip on that: he said to look away when I'm talking to someone. Just a little. So I don't get distracted and psyched out."

"Oh. I thought you'd caught wall-eye."

"All I need now is to get rid of these. All my life it's like I've been behind bars with them on. How long did it take, getting used to your contact lenses?"

"About an hour. But I was kinda determined. I put them in with masking tape."

"Maybe I'll try. And how about my hair? Simon, look—see the back. I even look good from the back. I used to hate myself from the back. You said it yourself: there's a reason why fags do our hair and design our shoes."

"Money, that's the reason. Fag was one of the twelve tribes of Israel. And, by the by, you've got some crust referring t'fags as 'them.'"

"Cut it out." Robert glances around: to the door.

"She isn't here, don't worry. Anh, so you're being kept."

"Don't say that. This, these things—they're a loan. I'll pay Larry back."

"Yeah, well—if that's a loan, just don't show your collateral in public."

"Oh. Mr. Scruples now."

"Not me. I admire a self-procured man."

"Hey, no kidding. I think you sound a whole lot better today. It's like old times when you start getting on my case. A week ago, that Wednesday afternoon, you scared me something awful. I thought sure you were down for the count. I mean, Jesus, you were talking about death and goodbye. And—and you spoke normal, like the rest of us do, without that gahr-ahr stuff in your voice that you bully people with. Your voice was gentle: it made me sick to my stomach. Larry started crying in the elevator down. But now. Now you're your ugly self again."

"I'm coming home on Friday."

"Cox said that? He told us—"

"I said it. I feel artificial in here, like an induced birth. Rest isn't good for me, it makes me tired."

"Are you sure? I mean, your skull isn't healed yet."

"They won't do anything for me over the weekend—except run up a fat bill I can't afford. It's get out or atrophy. Uh. Cox talks about a catheter. And intravenous hamburgers. Thank you, I'm pulling out before they turn me into the moral equivalent of a floor lamp."

"But maybe he's right. If you can't eat—"

"I eat. I can eat if I watch my mouth and tongue in the mirror. Be ready about two o'clock and don't keep me waiting."

"Well. I'll bring the van."

"No—Arthur's gonna take his car. Watching you drive the van I'd relapse all over myself."

"Arthur. Oh, gee. He's a drag. All that religion shit—"

"Don't give me a hard time, Fruit Compote. What is it? Y'don't want me back maybe? Having too much fun being me while I'm away? Is that it, you little meat substitute? Huh?"

"You know, sometimes—sometimes, Simon. Well, if that's the way you want t'think—fine. All I can say—you'll be sorry for it."

"I will?"

"Yeah. Oh, boy. That talk stinks. It stinks, you know. Here we've been working just so we'll be ready when you get back. Not that you'd appreciate it. I told Larry—I told him. But. Oh, well."

"Working on what?"

"To get *Lucky* set, that's what. So you can start as soon as you're feeling up to it."

"*Lucky?* I thought you said *Lucky* was a reject from Rain-out Theatre. About as exciting as a test of the emergency broadcast system. If I recall your critical asides."

"Well." Robert's hands move: to forehead, arm, mouth: a third-base coach. Gestures of the old Robert: small and hurried. "We've been looking at it. We shifted some scenes around. You know, laid in some dialogue. It was a rough draft, right? I mean, you hadn't set anything, right? And it's looking better. It has a feel to it. Listen—Larry is committed: committed enough to put up seed money. You'd be surprised how much he has socked away. He bought Krugerrands at about $100 an ounce and sold them for $700. We can start. Huh. Look, Simon: even if you don't trust me, you've gotta know how Lar feels about you. And we all need to work. We've all been going stir crazy. I figure—what d'you think?—I figure we hit the road as soon as you can and drive. South. West Virginia, someplace real. Away from the city anyhow. Where we can start fresh. How does that sound?"

"I see. Shifted some scenes around, did you?"

"You're not glad. I knew you wouldn't be. I said to Larry. You know—your problem is: I mean, everything is dog eat dog t'you. You won't believe people care for, for you. Larry says it's because of your parents. I don't know. I didn't have anything to do with your parents. I, I just don't think you're being fair."

"Maybe not. Well. I'll look at it."

"That's better. Gee: you had me worried. Your eye is still great. And nobody can hit you hard enough t'shut your mouth. We can do it, the three of us."

"I guess. I guess if I can direct my arms and legs I can direct a film. It's just—I've been laying here like a sodded lawn in Rockland County—it's different."

"I figure we—"

"Three of us, did you say? Has Minnie gone?"

"Thank God. Boy, she was a mess—ever since she found you on Great Ferry Street. She would've come in. But seeing you like this, it would—well, at home she had trouble even carving a turkey."

"I wanted t'thank her. Cox says she probably saved my life. I was losing a lotta blood."

"The thing that blows my mind, she had no clothes on. She saw them unload on you and she just started running down the block. With a wrench or something in her hand. Naked. My mother running naked in New York. Wow. Police come up with anything?"

"No."

"Two niggers, huh?"

"As I recall."

"That's not much t'go on in New York. Shit, I'd—I'd put them all in a gas oven. Funny, though—"

"What?"

"Somehow I didn't think anyone could take you."

"Sorry t'disappoint, hope you didn't have any money on it."

"It's like one day when my f-father, when he got pulled over for speeding. He started to shake. I saw his hands shake. And his voice—his voice got crappy and humble. It's a shock, you know. To see that."

"Rahhhhh—" Packard drubs the mattress. Robert, nervous in cashmere, will reach for his new mustache: and smear a corner of it.

"God, how can you stand that?"

"If he can, I can."

"Sounds like goddam Wolfman. Hey, what am I doing? I forgot: and it's all I was thinking of when I came in here. You got a letter from Wolff this morning."

"Who?"

"Herman Wolff, dummy. It came by special messenger t'the van. Here. Open it."

"No. You do it. I haven't practiced envelopes yet."

"You don't sound too interested."

"I don't, do I?" Robert has slashed the flap. "No. You can read it."

"Hey."

"Um?"

"Hey, wait. Hot damn. Listen to this. Let's see. 'Dear Simon:' He's got some fancy handwriting, but it's all in print. He prints like a kid does. Uh. 'Dear Simon: I hear by the grapevine that you've had an unfortunate mix-up with dark elements in the city and are hurt now in the head. This grieves me. I wonder what our society'—he spelled that wrong—'what our society is coming to. Some people, I won't say who, are no more civilized than Fort Apaches. You're a tough luck person, which is so often true of the very talented. Too much talent can be a hardship and this is why I've always tried to avoid it myself.' What's he mean by that?"

"Just what he says."

"Yeah? Well. But here's the good part. 'I don't think Lynxx Productions has a Blue Cross, so I have arranged with Dr. Cox that all your bills come to the above. This should save you worry. Also, I have told him that Herman Wolff takes a personal interest here and you should get the full VIP. I know from doctors: they need a little poke or they treat you like a towel rack.' New paragraph. 'Get well full speed ahead. When you're feeling A-1, we'll talk film again. I have plans for working together. As ever, Your Friend, Herman Wolff.' " Robert pops the sheet with his forefinger. "Well, what d'you think of that? Something, huh? You gotta admit he's being pretty white. He must really care for you. See, what'd I say? Boy, looks like that avenue is still open. We thought, with you sick, maybe he'd cop out on the half million. And Wolff can make things a lot easier, can't he? I mean—I don't know the film distribution system, how it works, but from what Larry told me, we'd need help. Herman Wolff, huh. Say something, Champ."

"The rich can afford t'make collect calls. The rest of us gotta scrounge for a dime."

"What's that supposed to mean?"

"All in all, I prefer West Virginia."

"Oh, Jesus. I know—it's your crazy pride. Well, I'm not proud and neither is Larry. If you don't wanna deal with Wolff, we will."

"I know you will. Be my guest."

"Shit. Are you mad at me? For God's sake, what is it? I've done everything I can. I've kept the shop going and still you don't trust me."

"Talent is dangerous like Wolff said. I know that. It has nothing t'do with trust, Robert."

"You—you have much more talent than I'll ever have."

"Yeah, I do, but not for standing up. Forgive me, I miss the little things: like being able t'pick my nose without putting an eye out."

"God. I never thought I'd see it. You're feeling sorry for yourself."

"That I can still feel. Don't take it away from me."

"Hi, Bobby."

"Oh, hello. It's Miss O'Connell. How're you this afternoon?"

"Bobby? Bobby? Did she say Bobby?"

"That's my name, Simon. Robert-Bobby, right? Come on in, Miss O'Connell."

"I'm not interrupting? I wish you'd call me Peggy. Uh-huh: well. Well, I've done some work on your suggestions."

"Good. Good. Getting rid of that body tension we talked about?"

"Gosh, I'm trying. But—oh, wow—it isn't easy. My hands are so dumb. They're real rats. They make me wanna scream."

"Take a step or two. Imagine we're not here. Go on."

Peggy will open herself: one arm out, the other arm out: like a studio card with no message inside. The barrette trap on her hair has been sprung, though not soon enough to save its prey. Simon can see second-coated lipstick: of a wet adobe thickness and sheen. Robert has his

thumb up, apparently to catch light readings on her russet flesh. Robert
is in active agreement with himself: nod, recheck, verify, prove, yes.
Now tap-tap: his foot has cadence and a one-two, one-two, one: musical
byplay between them, their cue. Peggy organizes herself into a short vignette. There is loneliness here: a paperback romance: much passion in
arrears. Moonlight and wind have been put up for the night: and a
branch striking gabled wood. Hands wide, fingers wide, groin wide,
Peggy will execute a pigeonwing. Circle, circle, circle—oh, bush. The asi-
nine floral wreath has horned in and for a moment they samba together:
caught: woman and undergrowth. Then it trudges off alone, two-step-
ping on three legs. Peggy is rattled: she steps with half a lily in one
hand: her normal question-mark hunch has returned, the way air bubbles do under wet wallpapering. But Robert is supportive, gracious. He
comes forward: he will pull tension from her arms, jerk-jerk, as if they
were let-out kite string. Simon could take up his bed and, a miracle of
disgust, walk.

"That stupid wreath. Oh, nuts. I flopped."

"Hey, hey. It was good. I saw a big improvement there, at least until
you lost concentration. No kidding. You really let all the arm and hand
tenseness go. Couldn't you feel it?"

"Well. I guess. You think? Oh, wow—it's hard when you've been a
Catholic from birth. Bobby is a film director, Mr. Lynxx."

"She, she—" Robert laughs. "Well, she wormed it out of me. Mr.
Lynxx knows that, Peggy. He taught me everything I know."

"Yeah. With a disposable nurser kit."

"Ha. Mr. Lynxx is a brilliant director himself, Peggy. You should see
him at work." Robert lights a dark Balkan Sobranie cigarette: the smoke
is devious and Slavic: it haggles around him. And his gold cigarette case
has a monogram: the wrong monogram: CCK: personalized for some
other person. "Yes. Have a look at this. We've got a letter here from Herman Wolff offering to back our next film. You better take good care of
Mr. Lynxx, Peggy. He's an important man. And influential."

"Ignore Robert. He just got his personality capped."

"Is it true? Bobby says there's a part for me. If, if only I can learn to
be, whatchamacallit, freer with my darn body."

"Well now. What I meant, Simon—seriously. All those kids in Lucky's
class. She's just the right age. And she has a natural look. Wouldn't all
that red hair look good on film?" Robert has turned toward the bed: a
story conference. Tongue swabs up/over the two front teeth. Simon, odd,
Simon can't remember seeing those teeth before. The mouth, in his
mind's file copy of it, was red and chapped: a suckling thing. "Don't you
think? It's a possibility, isn't it? Of course I haven't promised anything.
Peggy understands that."

"There's always a part for those who can learn t'be freer with their bodies."

"Is Bobby a genius like he says, like a young Orson Weld?"

"Orson Weld? You mean Tuesday Weld's uncle? Is that who you meant, Robert?"

"Oh, you know, Simon—exact comparisons are almost impossible t'make. I was—it was just a for-instance. Everyone has different talents, of course. Wouldn't you say?" Robert beats down the price of his brazenness with a self-renouncing gesture: palm up and out. Yet he doesn't seem particularly ashamed: also, it's clear that he will expect Simon to chip in with fan mail: man and man colluding: doctors at a malpractice trial. But Simon, in masculine heresy, has nipped his mouth shut: tight as metal roof flashing. He divulges only an impartial mmmmph. "Right, Simon? Welles, Picasso—who can put a finger on genius? Wouldn't you say?" Robert is suddenly overbearing: too present, too life-blooded: and all head like a Toby jug.

"He is. A genius, Peggy. Hanh. Most of all Robert has a special way with cameramen. He knows just how t'approach them. So what if someone steps on his hand now and then."

"Flatterer." Robert laughs. He is—why?—delighted.

"Rahhhhhahgg."

"See. Even old Packard thinks so. That's his certificate of compliance. Or his reggae beat. Something supportive, anyhow."

"Well, a girl can't be too careful. Men are only after one thing, you know. Uh-huh." Peggy is thoughtful: as though unable to recall quite what that one thing might be. "By the way, I looked in my TV movie guide book for the last film Bobby made. But I couldn't find it. *Clap?* Did I get the title right?"

"*Clap?*"

"Ah, Simon—Simon will tell you it's playing on the Coast right now. We don't want t'release it in New York until Christmas."

"Robert—"

"We haven't sold it to TV."

"Robert—"

"We're holding out for a fat price up front."

"Robert. Ahem. I don't mind dancing with a corpse, but when the corpse starts t'lead—"

"Peggy, will you excuse us? Mr. Lynxx and I have t'discuss some location shots."

"Uh-huh. Five o'clock, like you said? When I get off?"

"Five, five." Robert sounds out his new appointment book. "Okay. Right. But it'll have t'be just a quarter hour."

"See you. Oh, wow. They think I'm going crazy here. I do my exercises in the ladies' room. See you, Mr. Lynxx. I'm sure glad you picked my floor to get sick on. Bye."

They confront each other now. Simon's mouth will moralize—eel-lipped and snide. Robert is silent on advice of counsel. Simon has had his finer sensibilities affronted: not by the intent, by the style. Yet he is nearly forceless and must get used to that: his best effects—anger, scorn, menace especially—are as much physical as spoken: a matter of pre-empted space around him: the jostling tyranny that mobs have. And— and drop! Down, down he goes: wallowing, tumbling, decadent. The mattress has given way: it does a stem turn, breaks apart like shot skeet. The bed is unmade under him. He has been careless, caught in a fool's-mate of staring with Robert. It is touch and go, gone. Simon will look, look, look: the floor leader for his dispersed limbs. And, by default, Robert can think that his impudence has won.

"Stay! Stay there. Hup. Stay."

"Are you all right? Are you gonna vomit? Should I call a nurse?"

"Call a nurse? Ung. Call the rewrite shed. Jesus. Jee-sus. I can't believe—where'd you get that Hollywood Talent Scout routine, from the Museum of Primitive Art? Christ. The same guy who thought up that line thought up dish night at the Nickelodeon."

"Oh, don't give me a hard time. Ha. I know it's gross, you know it's gross, but I'm having fun for a change."

"Uh. Za-so? Yeah, but think of those around you, Mat-burn. Two flies dropped dead while you were smarming all over her. And he asks if I'm gonna vomit."

"So. So—you wore a gorilla suit once. I've seen it. The show must go on."

"Go. Just don't use me as a trade reference."

"Okay. I admit—I shouldn't have told Peggy I did *Clap*. That was dumb. But, well, you've kinda disowned it. I thought you'd take the whole thing as a joke and go along."

"It was. I did. It's the waste that gives me a moral hematoma. Huh, Peggy. Peggy O'Connell. When it comes to body language she'd need a Berlitz course. Her face is a medley relay for blotches. And as for brains —listen, she failed scratch and sniff in first grade. Come on, Robert."

"Come on, yourself. At, at my age. Don't. I mean, don't tell me you didn't do the same thing."

"Never. If I'd stooped that low, I'd still look like Lon Chaney swinging from a bell rope. That kinda corned beef and cabbage, you just flip them on their bellies then stuff a fin in their sweatsocks when you're done."

"Jesus. You went all white. And that big vein in your neck is jumping. Hey. What's the big fuss? Calm down." Robert will smile. "First he tells me I'm a fag, then he bitches because I'm scoring a piece of poon."

"Poon? There hasn't been any poon since 1954. Poon is extinct. They built a dam and flooded out its breeding ground. I had the last piece my-self."

"That's what you say. I just found out it's easy—after what I went through up there, up home, up in high school. It's easy and I want my share."

"And what would you do with it? Hanh? Haah? You think it comes with a little slip of paper saying INSPECTED BY #11? Parts and labor alone'll kill you. Listen t'me, since you've plagiarized the rest of my résumé already. Listen, I've dunked my cruller often enough t'know: never stopgap a woman who can't give you man-hours on the side. Like your treacherous Aunt Rose. Otherwise, believe me, it isn't worth the worn mucous membrane. God, in fact, the whole damn skin dance's a big service for the dead. In fact it doesn't mean cassowary shit."

"Yeah. Well, I think it means you can't get it hard anymore."

"An! Angh!" Simon is up and big: a Donnybrook by himself. He fights the air in front of Robert, "Annngh."

"Wait! Stop it. Lemme ex—"

"You contemptible male slut. You think I can't take you anymore and maybe I can't. But, by God—" Loud cross-purposed dispatches go to arm and spine: they downpour in him. "Oh, by God—by God I'm coming for you now."

"You'll fall. You'll fall. Stop. I'll run away. I'll go. I don't wanna fight."

"You snot. I told you that when I was half outa my mind with fear. When I was helpless, when I didn't know what I was saying. And you dare, you cunt, t'rub my face in it."

"Rahhhhhh!"

"I'm sorry. Please. I apologize. I stink. I'm ashamed of myself. I stink."

"Oh. The bed. Hold it. Hold!"

"What? What should I do?"

"There. I see. I see. I am where I am. Oh, Christ."

Simon's face is separate: lifted off like a fingerprint: above. The mouth has been made wide: but no breaths are heard. Is there something with them here? Young Robert, shaken, loathes Simon for his macabre infirmity now. The face is rigid, unblinking, unblinked: suspenseful: the way we wait when noises fall in an uncharted dark. Simon must be reso-lute: with no rest. Robert is jittery: he can grasp the phrase "a rapt at-tention" here. Sunlight has chosen this time to crack and unyolk itself behind apartment walls. Simon is watching his right knee: Robert and Simon together watch. Hairs on it, performing for some atmospheric master, begin to shape a tranced, slow whorl. They coil and uncoil: rise: they feel around. Robert wants out: the room is immanent. But Simon has deputed a hand to mediate. The whorl is broken: hairs accredit fa-miliar electricity on his palm: they fall, asleep. Simon swallows. Simon

swallows. His tongue will stay out, foolish and forgetful: the way a dozing cat's might.

"Say something, huh? Simon? Don't—you look dead like that, Christ.
Your tongue—put, put your tongue back in. It's hanging out. It's just
hanging there."

"Um."

"Thank God. Shit. I was afraid you'd bite it off. It scared me. Are you
all right? Huh? Hanh? Look, I'm sorry for what I said—you got me defensive. I wish you could hit me. I really wish you could."

"Robert. I noticed your teeth today. You know, f'the first time."

"Oh, boy. I said I was sorry. Don't lay this trip on me."

"No. No. Your real teeth. Ah, the things you'll eat. The appetite you'll
have. I'm getting off easy. I know you now, when you're still young."

"Simon. Don't rip me. Don't pull me down. I'm getting it together.
Just a little. I've had a pissy life. You know what that's like. I've never
been free. It's all new. I'll make mistakes."

"Mistakes, no. They won't be mistakes. Well, have it. Have your time."

"Hey, we need each other. You know about me and I know about you.
And you'll get better." Robert has a hand on the mattress: Simon's thigh,
ignorant, will cover it. "Don't let this SOB get you down. We'll pull
through."

"And Larry?"

"And Larry. I'm keeping his fire lit. He's happy. You should see him."

"How old are you?"

"What? Lay off—you, you know how old I am."

"Larry," Simon wonders. "Y'know, I don't think you are a fag. So. So, I
try t'figure—would I have done that at your age? Would I? It seems t'me,
it seems like I had t'learn it all. I was slow. It never came naturally."

"You taught me. I'm your protégé."

"No," Simon laughs. "No, you won't dish that off on me. I'm honored
and all. Yes. But it's the difference between genius and hard application.
You're a natural. Me? The most I ever was—ha. The most I ever was, was
a fair technician."

"Well, well. Good to hear you laughing for a bit. Eh? Do I interrupt?"

Uncle Arthur has incidental music in his throat: ahs, himms, little
replies to nothing. The mannerism of one who has long been a visitor by
profession: whose peculiar trade it is to make other people feel at home
when they are at home: yet who, for a lifetime, through his mere clerical
presence, has spoiled all true sociability somewhat: Uncle Arthur is
among them, is—how could he not be?—a priest there. Robert feels
judged: he will tug at his wide-spectrum amulet. Arthur, he sees, doesn't
look well: febrile, haggard, footsore in the mind: this week he has
shagged too many foul pops for Simon. There is a distinction between
loyal follower and hunter-down, but Arthur can't yet reconcile the two.

Hair has dropped out: or, more correctly, has become brittle like grass from another season and blown off. Off the wool-gathered forearm, too: by whole square inches: as though his hairline had not receded but was in full rout, head to toe. And he is thinner: on a fast of excitement. The time has gotten ominous: Simon's disabilities are Arthur's portents. The two of them have not, nor ever will, reach an accommodation in this dispute. Simon doesn't intend to turn state's evidence: even with such wide and kind immunity.

So Arthur has contrived a sort of obvious, rattletrap spying: that Simon might give himself away with honor and, so to speak, in privacy: that Arthur might secure proof without gross entrapment. There is, they both know, a tape recorder in the portfolio under his left arm: ON now, taking idle minutes for them. Arthur, volunteered by zeal, has become the stenographer to a manifestation. He shams indifference indifferently: the way an actor will yawn in his dressing room. It is often foolish: cloak and dagger of the spirit. Yet Simon, when not resentful or pettish or afraid, can feel gratitude. Surely he has never been loved so before: he is Arthur's grand passion: a fine November fling. Some coquettishness, yes, has been indulged in on either side, but they are essentially of the same generation now: they do not kiss and tell: the courtship is urbane. Here, under his right arm, Arthur hugs a quart of chocolate-swirl ice cream and, by volume at least, not quite as much Thomas à Kempis.

"Dew I interrupt?" Robert will be currish. "Look what the service elevator brought up. Your confessor."

"Lo, Arthur."

"*Simon.*" The tone is impulsive: like automatic writing: Arthur must learn to make light of. "And the impetuous Robert. Ho: ice cream here. It'll go down like clouds. Bought at a supermart. One counter and one tradesperson and all the inventory, I daresay, of a soldier's kit bag, but still a supermart. Ah, America the extra-beautiful. Well: chocolate swirl's what's going today. How's that sound? Rather elegant, I thought. Must say I allowed personal preference to sway my judgment a touch."

"He can't taste."

"True. Nonetheless, he has to eat. And I do wish you wouldn't hop it down my throat at the slightest, Robert. We both want the best for Simon."

"I dunno. I see your kind at accidents a lot."

"Enough, botha you. Stop this custody battle. Thanks, Arthur, I'll have some chocolate swirl. I better. What they'll drop-feed in my arm won't have *Appellation Contrôlée* written on it, I don't think."

"Coming up."

"Robert, push the chair around for Uncle Arthur, since your precious behind's been t'Barbados in a foil-lined box."

"Thank you, Robert. And, by the by, you look very smart today, Savile Row."

"Yeah? Well, you look like Death Row. I mean, doesn't wearing black get you down after a while?"

"The religious life, my young friend, is a continuous battle: against atheism and cat hair. Against sin and lint. Also, in my particular case, against monkey fur. On the other hand I'm never overdressed: it balances out. Here we go, Simon."

Arthur has pried the carton lid off: thin hinges of chocolate pull away from it. The lid must be placed, dry side down, on a certain radiator ledge: there are rubrics, evidently, that stipulate this. Fresh handkerchief linen is unfolded next. The teaspoon has been poking, bowl up, from Arthur's vest pocket: a medal given for some unspecified worth. Arthur wipes, cleans, cleanses even. Then, his own tongue out and lightly bitten, he will scrape across. Simon has never seen his once-uncle prepare the Eucharist, but he might guess, from this High Church dessert course, that it would be meticulous theater at least. Robert, looking down, despises Simon for his passivity here. He is cynical about it: a ruse, he would hope, to get valet service out of Arthur. And, in his own anti-ritual, Robert will set the urine flask on Arthur's Bible, left behind one Sunday ago. Arthur doesn't notice, but would understand: his line of business is cutthroat: there are deceptive claims and false fire sales. Simon, meanwhile, has been accenting the silence: click-beetle noise fretted between thumb and middle finger. After much practice he is adept at this: it can be informative, a bulletin from his extremities. Spoon: below the puddled surface, chocolate swirl has an appetizing grain: rough like that of sawn wallboard. Simon is expectant. Jaw and lower lip drop: so ordered by the puppet regime that runs his body now.

"Which would you rather: the swirly parts or the vanilla? Eh? The swirlies do seem somewhat more glutenous and difficult."

"Vanilla. Like the rest of my life."

"This is bullshit. I mean, why don't you let Simon try and eat it by himself? We can't spoon-feed him from here to eternity."

"We won't have to, not by a long chalk."

"I think you want him like this. You want him t'be a cripple. So you can give him last rites twice a day."

"Oh, sod that. Really, Robert." Arthur feeds. With one foot he will nudge the bugged portfolio closer. Simon, from bad previous experience, bibs one hand under his chin. "Tell me. Is this raging prejudice of yours the effect of an unfortunate anti-Christian upbringing? Or is it wholly personal? I'd rather it were personal, by the way."

"For one. I don't like the phony way you talk."

"Ah. I'm English, you see. Try to think of me as English. Not as an American with pretentious diction."

"Guh. Lemme—ssssswip—catch up on swallowing."

"Sorry about that."

"God, I never thought I'd see the day."

"Shut up, Robert. Huh? Don't talk with my mouth full."

"Okay. All right. Why should I care, if you don't? Hanh? Huh? But, tell me—did you practice walking today, huh? Did you? I bet you didn't."

"Think I'll cadge this swirly piece myself, Simon. If that's all right with you. Mmmm."

"Arthur? Y'remember the game Bettina useta play with me? This is the engine, bite. This is the coal car, bite. T'make me finish my dinner? I never wanted t'eat the engineer. I was a good kid. I had ideals. But Bettina ate engineers all the time."

"Yes. Mmmm. Oh, right." Arthur doesn't recall. He bumps *The Imitation of Christ* toward Simon: with careful insouciance. As a bad chess player might advance his rook pawn first. "Ah. Yes, Bettina. Say, I don't suppose a priest has been round and about here yet?"

"Nnnn."

"Inexcusable, I think." But Arthur is gratified: he has the right of first refusal on Simon: a frozen option. "Shameful. Someone gone missing on the job probably. Just as a matter of course this hospital should be covered. I don't know what they do at the diocese—beyond gay weddings and the ordination of a female priesthood."

"Hold. N'more now. Uh. Take a look up m'nose. Think I been doing the elephant trick."

"No. All clear."

"Sure? I can't tell. All I need's t'start sneezing fudge now. I'd get some funny G'bless-yous."

"Let it alone, that's my considered opinion. You may not be able to feel—and I'm certain that's bloody disorienting—but it works, you know. I've been keeping an eye out. They seem perfectly in order, your swallows. From the outside, no one would guess. You needn't be so sensitive, really." Arthur has set the carton aside. His fingers interlock: like a half-shuffled card deck. "Look here. Item of new business. You'll need to settle up accounts on Friday and I imagine they charge the earth here. Well. I have a small insurance policy. I intend to cash it in. Please don't refuse. You'd be my beneficiary in either case."

"We don't need your charity." Robert has sent a ground wave of spite through the mattress to Arthur's knit hands. "We don't need it, thank you. Herman Wolff, who happens t'be a Jew, is picking up the tab. For everything. For the best medical care. See. He wrote t'Simon this afternoon. So you can stop passing the hat."

"Truly? Herman Wolff? Well, that is good news: absolutely. I'm delighted, Robert. And not a man to do things on the cheap either, from what I've heard. Wolff must be a fine person. Eh, Simon?"

"It's the Jewish law. An eye for an eye, a check for your head."

"What's that supposed t'mean? Hanh?"

"Yes, Simon. What?"

"Nothing. Kill that line. Herman's nice. You're nice. Even Robert. Everyone's nice."

Rahhhhhh-ahhhhr-ahr: Packard spreads a banner howl. His cry is in the second person and they are each addressed. Arthur feeds himself swirl: Robert's youth has a setback. Simon, alone, will look. Packard's feet lift and separate: as if into a gynecological stirrup brace. They hold there. Oh, Simon thinks, there is heavy voltage in a human brain. The yell has begun to spurt: like vein blood through a weak ligature. The crib rail can't last: his fist, bandleader smart, is bashing it. Arthur and Robert are devastated: monotony has caught and overtaken horror: has become horror of a more wounding sort: the thought that even dreadful pain might be just boredom, elevated. Packard flings his pelvic basin up: and up: in a regular, an obstetrical beat: the sensuality of it is repulsive. He screams. And then, without distinct transition, seamlessly, the howl will draw down: to a snore. Packard is delivered of whatever: and can sleep.

"Shit." Robert has been angered by his own fright. "Shit. Is that what God does? Huh? Is that the kind of thing?"

"Don't be such a Tartar, Robert. This isn't quite the moment. Not for yet another of our little theological set-tos. Tomorrow, perhaps."

"Why not now? Not now because you haven't got an answer? Hunh?" Robert gives Arthur the middle finger, up: it is peremptorily not seen. "Well. Well, I don't want any part of it. Your God sucks."

"I'm used to profanity. It's the first sign of an insecure mind. Beyond that—is there anything of substance that you might wish to say?"

"Well. Tell me. Does your God take responsibility for that?"

"For Packard? Indeed, He does. Who else will? Will you? A God that let His own Son be crucified for the sake of man: I should think He had a healthy respect for pain. And, yes, He takes responsibility. Not blame. Where is the blame here? He takes responsibility as well for your youthful preening, for your—whatever else it is you do. But not blame."

"Oh, screw it. You can talk your jolly-what bull 'til the dogs come home. Simon—what about you? What d'you think?"

"Me?"

"Yeah."

"About what?"

"About this—about Packard."

"I'm trine t'remember when he had his last morphine fix. But time's giving me trouble of late. I think he may be overdue. Other than that—I draw a blank."

"No comment, huh. Well, I'm cutting out. I'm not gonna sit here and listen to a lot of religious tallyho. Yesterday was enough. I'll see you to-morrow."

"Sure. Uh. Listen, if you turn any of the Ould Sod, use a muck fork." But Robert has gone: without his walking stick. "Hey. Hanh. Look. So new at being himself, he left some of it behind. I won't forget my cane, though. Something'll remind me. Like a sudden floor."

"Simon. What'd you think of that: what Robert said? Packard's scream took the mickey out of him a bit—he got flustered. Normal enough and I wasn't offended in the slightest. But, you know, there's something in what he said."

"Mmmm?"

"Don't you think?"

"About what?"

"Well, Packard. Or, say, your own injury. It's a decent enough question. The unfairness, I mean. Don't you ever ask, 'Why me?' Or, to put it the way Robert did, 'Is that what God does?' Don't you get angry sometimes?"

"I could garrote myself with frustration. If I could find my hands. This is what they call the ultimate barrier-free environment. Boring and vague. It's like living in the 'Checkers' speech."

"Yes. But, I mean . . . angry at the unfairness of it all?"

"Is it unfair?"

"Oh, come now. There are young men, no better or worse than you: they're fit and healthy. You don't mean to tell me that—that you think you deserve this?"

"No. Do I?"

"Of course not—"

"Arthur. Arthur. Arthur." Simon laughs. "Trying t'do me like a Dober-man pinscher would: you old stern chaser, you. What a missionary."

"Well. The devil's advocate, you know."

"Y'mean the devil needs a lousy court-appointed lawyer?"

"I'm that bad?"

"Just kinda obvious: like a shoplifter in a granite quarry. Hanh. It goes like so. If I get angry at this—angry that I'm the speaking likeness of a beanbag chair in no one's living room right now—then, well, then I have t'be angry *at* something. Right? Then you opine how there are matters that only God and the Trilateral Commission know the real truth about. Then—font!—we're talking about God: the spirit everyone loves t'hate. Point to Mr. Gordon. But I'm not angry. I don't see the purpose in anger."

"You're not an atheist, either. I'd bet that at Ladbrooke's."

"I'm not. True."

"Ah. Well, would you call yourself an agnostic?"

"No. An agnostic is somebody who—if I recall—thinks the truth about

God can't be known one way or another. But he takes the trouble t'think that. I don't think about it at all. There are more important questions: like where my left ankle went just now."

"Simon. You used to rag me: to make fun of my priesthood. Didn't you? I've always felt it showed a—well, a certain earnestness of loathing. I've set great store by it."

"I know. It was thoughtless of me, leading you on that way. I have a confession t'make. I was—gee, I was being insincere. I ravage everyone. But ravaging a priest, hanh—it kinda shamed me. It's so trite. Ravaging a seven-foot spade at the Harlem Hallelujah Club, now that's what I call a high-principled ravaging. With you I was just making a duty call: didn't wantcha t'feel neglected. Look, face it. God is—oh—a lunar module and I'm a Bushman. I know how t'get ants out of an anthill with a stick and eat them. Lunar modules I don't even have the vocabulary for. And I'm busy anyhow: I've gotta sharpen my ant stick."

"You can't be that naive. I won't credit it."

"I'm not naive. I just couldn't care less. How can I get it across? Hanh? Okay. Have you heard of the Jeanette MacDonald fan club?"

"Can't say that I have."

"Know who she was at least?"

"I think—an actress."

"Uh. Does it trouble you—I mean, that you never think about Jeanette MacDonald?"

"No."

"Well, God's got the same, uh, Doriden effect on me."

"But Jeanette MacDonald exists, you admit that."

"Well. She died maybe fifteen years ago. You wanna take that line of reasoning any further?"

"No."

"Rrrrrgah."

"See, it's unanimous. Push some more vanilla in. And try t'get it behind my tongue."

"Is there nothing to be done for him? That shriek before. I've been among the sick often enough, but that—that was the hound of hell."

"Yup. Old Packard can really make a stump speech when he's in the right mood. It's quadraphonic rage." Simon has swallowed: he is proud of Packard, of them. "But I don't think he feels very much. The nurses keep him well stoned—for their own sakes. We've talked a coupla times: a sentence or two. He doesn't know what yardline he's on. But he keeps lining up."

"That can't continue."

"Nah. You'd be surprised. Packard's strong as an Armenian's breath. He could last years. He could work up the AAU record for hospital bills."

"Open. There. Nerve-wracking for you, I should think."

"Nuh. He comes in handy. Packard's no snooze alarm, thank God. When he yells general quarters, you move. Which is what I need. I need t'be reminded that I'm here. That I'm anywhere and quick. Packy's saved me from stepping off the big curb more than once. And he expresses my feelings for me: I just wish I had his command of the language. Eh? Did I shrug then?"

"No."

"Could've sworn. Meant to. Jeez, I can't even be offhand without an effort. Anyhow, I wouldn't give Cox the satisfaction, him with his fifty-buck 'How are we today?s' He takes my pulse, I want a receipt. They'd all like me out of here. My symptoms're making them set up a new file folder. Enough of Packard and Cox hopes I'll go inta mental receivership and crack."

"You want that, though. You want out."

"Yes. Please. Friday."

"Well, I'll come for you. The Martha Washington room is yours. I have my misgivings, but I'll come."

"Listen, I've gotta split. Hanh. Cox wants a fat referral fee from the dingbat dorm. Functionally, he says, there's nothing wrong with me. Except that I don't function. You could say the same of a cadaver, come t'think. My skull crack is replastering itself: the EEG gets my call letters right. I'm fully operational flat on my back. Yesterday, get this, he dropped a lit match on my chest. Ooops, so sorry. Hanh. Bought a pack of Camels just t'make it look good. Naturally I jumped and half punched myself loopy doing it. I mean, what would you do if you saw a lit match on your chest? But I *saw* it. I didn't feel it, I saw it. Aha, he says. Aha. He thinks I'm trying t'beat the draft or something. But—"

"But?"

"Baby, I am one sick pup."

"Or—"

"Never mind 'or.' You're another one wants a fat referral fee. I did a play once: I had to fall backward off a five-foot rostrum. Trust us, the director said, I'll have two guys ready t'catch you. They were there maybe nine times outa ten. But that tenth: it was a show-stopper, lemme tell you. That's how I feel now: nervous and just a bit cynical. It's the night the bed fell every minute here. Watch—" He has sat up: shoulders just an inch or two above the backrest. "See that. If memory serves, this is a very uncomfortable position, yet it feels fine. Only way I can tell I'm straining is the difference in my stomach muscles: they're tight here and here. But I've gotta see them. With an overcoat and mittens on I'm just a floating head." Simon will slap his chest: inexactly. "Oh, they got me good. They hurt me."

"I know." Arthur feeds quickly. Not just nourishment: a way to buy equal time. "I believe you. Absolutely. But to give Beelzebub his due, I can understand Cox as well. What you've got isn't exactly covered by the rules of Queen's evidence: it's off-pattern. In human experience, I daresay, there is no precedent. Cox may think you're a wanker, shiftless: that's because he can't empathize. Open up again. Good. Now if—if you could only word it right: you've got a very descriptive intelligence— maybe then he'd come round to our side. For instance, go on a bit about what it's like when your eyes are shut. The explosion, the spiral in, all the rest of the boiling. Metaphor, you know. It's your forte."

"Mmm-wip. Arthur—"

"Now don't get in a foam. I'm not being morbid. It's damned important. I wouldn't pursue it if I weren't dead certain of that."

"I told you on Friday. I'm not talking about it anymore."

"Well." Arthur spoons silence in. "Let me talk about it then. Nod if I strike a nerve. Yes, ahm. I think this—what you have here—I think this is the dark night of the soul."

Swallow.

"Have you come across that phrase? No. Don't answer. It isn't likely. But in Christian mysticism, in all the literature—depending on how you count—the dark night, well, it's the fourth stage. And the most excruciating. The terrible attempt to silence the sensual faculties and drop into an absolute blackness of unknowing. A total letting go. But, sod it all—" Arthur is perplexed: he begins to feed himself. "But there are preliminary stages. Conversion. Purification. You seem, at the very least, to have given those a complete miss."

"Mmmm. Forget it. Two smudges knocked me into a lower-income bracket, that's all. Remember?"

"Perhaps, but—" Arthur stares at Simon. "If we take the phenomenon as a whole, the fire in your mouth, the—"

"Oh, shut up. Is the tape recorder going, huh? Are you gonna write a book for St. Vanity Press? Or am I an item for *News of the World*? Right next t'the article on a cancer cure from fried garbanzos and the picture of a two-legged dog that operates his own wheelchair in Liverpool? Arthur. You know what your dank underside of the soul is? I'll tell you: it's madness. Madness, that's what. Five minutes of it and I'd be a lip-flicking moron. They say you're an empty golf bag if the brain doesn't get oxygen f'five minutes. Well—it's the same with imagery. Without input the mind starts t'make luncheon loaf of itself. I. Don't. Want. That. And I don't wanna talk about it. Can you understand?"

"Yes, but—"

"Wait. This mystical swoon—aren't you supposed t'want it?"

"Yes."

"Well, I don't. I refuse it. And if I refuse it, it doesn't mean rock wool. And I'll tell you another thing."

"What?"

"You want me t'die."

"I—what?"

"Don't you? Think about it. We're friends here. Be honest."

"Ballocks. That's pure drivel. You're strong as a water buffalo, you'll laugh this off."

"Objection—the witness isn't being responsive." Simon smiles: not unpleasantly. "You didn't answer my question, Squire. I didn't ask whether or not I'd live. I fully intend t'live. Oh, yes. But you—the cloistered you—you want me t'die."

"No. Never. I do not." Arthur has gone into a child's cross-my-heart. "I swear not. Why? Where did you get such a swinish idea?"

"Never mind the disclaimers. Just let's look at this thing from a dramaturge's standpoint. Hanh? I mean, it loses artistic shape if I get better. Here he is, Simon—the same loutish bush pilot, the same slobbering geek —and no punitive damages. Geez, what's the point? Huh? And meanwhile, where is ex-uncle Arthur? He's married t'that old panty shield, Mrs. P. He hasta duck out on the sly t'do his church meditations, like some unfaithful bounder. Uh-uh. The third act won't play—"

"Please stop."

"You know what? I will. Because, well—well, somehow I know your murderous intentions are honorable. And I know you care f'me. But, my friend, it ain't gonna work. No, sir. Young Simon's gonna flail his way outa this water trap. And y'can print that in thirty-point type."

"Good. I'm glad t'hear you say it. I am. At times here I've thought your morale had gone down."

"No. It's just that I love life and I hate not being good at it anymore. Lookit this mastiff's body—even now, even in this very slack season— y'can tell it was made t'ravish the land. T'breathe contrails out. And I'm gonna make a comeback. I'm gonna rip hot meat off bones again. I'm gonna wade in swinging like a storm center and connect and get cold packed and feel that sweet pain again. I'm gonna rope calf and make cervixes groan. I am what I am: the goddam friggin' origin of species. Hah. So go home and transcribe that off your little Panasonic."

"Simon—"

"Ah. Here's Dr. Strange-glove himself. Still splitting fees with the dissection room, Cox? C'mon in. I can afford your presence now, I just won a Guggenheim Fellowship t'be sick."

Dr. Cox is something made, Simon has fantasized, of drops: a long, tallowy accretion: stalagmites are built and built upon so. No hand movement will extend outside his shoulder line: in impression, then, every item of clothing seems a sleeveless cape on him. He is six foot: spareness, though, overestimates that. The bowler-shaped skull has gone bald at top: but long fringes of hair sweep around it and down: a woman in a cheap stole. Each hand is upright now at the elbow: as though surgical gloves had just been put on. He has not affirmed Simon's welcome: which is fine: Simon's body will need time and library science to catalogue itself. Cox has become reflective near Packard: very still: a high, draped piece of furniture, hat rack or grandfather clock. Packard is also quiet: he won't countersign the moment. Cox's fingers argue: they group the way they would to hold a pair of shears. Then he nods: it is an entire diagnosis. Cox has crossed to Simon. Without preface or consent, he reweaves the head bandage: gifted, swift work. Inside the cloak of his self-containment Cox butters left hand with right: a housefly washing up. Arthur must rise: medicine has its Introits and Offertories, too.

"Good afternoon, Dr. Cox. Well—I see it's gone four o'clock. I'll nip down and get lunch, Simon." Cox's hands approve. "Eh. One thing you learn as a priest—the cheapest meals are in a hospital kaffe. I'll have a nurse put this in the fridge. Right. Well. I'll be on my way."

"Yes."

"Good day."

"Yes. How are you, Simon?"

"Is he gone?"

"He is gone. Why?"

"Cox, it happened again. My hearing switched off again last night. For ten, fifteen seconds. Pop-blip. Both ears, no transmission, nothing. Like I'd driven into the Holland Tunnel with my radio on. Jesus, Cox, that's the third time since last Friday. What's it mean? What's going on?"

"I've looked over the new X rays. You're healing quite nicely."

"Hey, Cox. Don't stick a fingerstall up my behind. Didja hear? Christ, I went deaf as a bench mark last night and you say I'm healing quite nicely. Hanh. Talk t'me like I was a person, not like I was a—a condition."

"I heard you, Simon. Now. The other symptoms? They remain stable?"

"Yeah. Yeah, stable. Good God, I'm a lame-duck administration in this body and he wants t'know if my instability is stable. Whose side are you on?"

"Calm down."

"Okay. Let me explain myself. I do not—repeat—I do not wanna go deaf. My personnel pool is limited enough as it is. Please do something about it. Please, huh? Give me some hope."

"Simon, I've told you. There is no known somatic cause." Cox's hands receive communion: right palm flat over left. "You have a slightly fractured skull. For the last fifteen years we've understood the brain and its functions pretty well. The areas of function at least. Believe me, there is no relationship whatever between the affected part and this massive loss of sensation. If you'd been hit from above—but even then I'd be skeptical. You shouldn't feel—or not feel—the way you do. What else can I say?"

"You think I'm winging it, huh? You don't believe me?"

"On the contrary. Your fear is authentic and more than persuasive. You have no motive for inventing this: none, at any rate, that I can discern. Even quite painful stimuli evoke no response in the neuroanatomy. This, apparently, is real to you."

"Apparently, huh? Listen—like I said, I'm still checking myself out on Friday. A tennis pro'd be more use t'me than you've been. I'm going."

"And, again, I advise strongly against it. Patience, my friend. For one, you can barely walk—a fall, another cranial injury . . . well. Moreover— with this absence of sensation—I can't even be certain that your digestive tract is absorbing sufficient nourishment. Note, for instance, that the saliva production in your mouth is well below norm: without incentive the glands are becoming lazy. They might even begin to atrophy. Give us another two or three weeks: otherwise I'm afraid that I can't assume any responsibility. Nor can this institution."

"Stay? Why? What're you doing f'me? I feel so little I couldn't get stuck on flypaper."

"Well." Cox's hands screen: as you might hold a lit match in wind. "We've discussed this before—to very little effect. Nonetheless."

"Dr. Abraham?"

"He'd still like to meet you."

"You think I've got bubbles in my catch basin. Hah. Once I get inta Dr. Abraham's bosom, it's the last anyone'll see of me. I know."

"Listen to yourself. Does that sound like the assessment of a balanced mind? This isn't Gulag. We aren't your enemies. You're an abrasive person, Simon—but people seem to like you. This morning I received a call from Herman Wolff—*the* Herman Wolff. I was both surprised and, yes, impressed. I admit it. Wolff is convinced that you're a genius. He went on at some length. Of course I'm no judge of film art, but it served to reinforce my opinion."

"What opinion?"

"I've gone over this with Dr. Abraham. Informally, you understand."

"Informally. Yeah, that means you can't figure out a way t'bill me for it."

"Please. You do get tiresome."

"So?"

"I would much rather this weren't done secondhand." Cox is irresolute: a humor, Simon thinks, that has not often invested him. "Well. Since there is almost no likelihood of a firsthand meeting—"

"Say it. You're gonna say it anyhow."

"It has to do with the experiences you've described to me. Particularly those that occur when you have no visual reference."

"Which experience?"

"The images. The ones that appear with extraordinary clarity—super-extraordinary clarity—and then cannot be repeated. The faces. The everyday objects. Heightened—if I understand your meaning—to the level of, well . . . to an almost hallucinogenic intensity. You described that, did you not?"

"Uh-huh."

"Evidently—and this is Dr. Abraham's surmise—when sightless you enter into a spontaneous and immediate hypnagogic state: the twilight period between sleep and wakefulness. It is the moment or condition—some suggest—when insights of great scientific or mathematical or artistic genius appear. The perfect sonata. The exact equation. It is sudden and brilliant: beyond conscious control. It can't be re-experienced, though it is available, in some degree, to memory. It is also, in some of its manifestations, untrustworthy. St. Theresa, Dr. Abraham hypothesizes, was thrown into hypnagogic moments of vision by her terrific pain. A pain which has often been considered psychosomatic: but that is another matter, I won't judge it. On less speculative grounds: it is a phenomenon most commonly associated in clinical study, as far as we can tell, with various forms of autism."

"Autism? Oh, great. First he calls me Einstein and then he calls me a Mongoloid. Talk about your mixed reviews."

"Think a moment, Simon. You may see giant ants on the wall—that is probably madness. You may see the Virgin Mary—that is a category I am not prepared to deal with. You may understand $e=mc^2$. Now . . ." Cox's hands cup perfectly: Simon, in childhood, held a frog like that. "Now. Three hundred years ago the giant ant and the Theory of Relativity enjoyed about the same level of popular acceptance. With an edge, perhaps, to the ant. It is the state I'm talking about, not the product. Subject matter is drawn from the physical world and transformed. A woman becomes the idealized virgin. Certain deviations in the orbit of Mercury become a theory of relativity. Tibetans train a lifetime to achieve what you seem to have stumbled on: I don't wonder it frightens you. It would me. An autistic mind is hermetic: it takes from—but will make no concession to—the real world. It is imagination pure and horrifying. Pure and exalting. You might learn to control it. Or you might go insane."

"You're trying t'scare me."

"No. I merely suggest—take it or leave it—that you'd be better off under constant observation just now. Dr. Abraham is both a neurosurgeon and a psychiatrist. Beyond that, he has lived in the East. You interest him: very few people do, by the way. I certainly don't, if that's any satisfaction to you. As for scaring, it's not me you're scared of now."

"Look. Okay. I appreciate your informal time and all. But I can handle it. Okay?"

"But can you? Wouldn't it be more, shall we say, economical, to sort out *all* your problems at once. In controlled, safe circumstances? In one place?"

"All? What's all, Cox?"

"I've spoken to your uncle. He tells me that you had a rather disagreeable shock recently. News that might easily nonplus anyone. Just several hours before the 'accident' in fact."

"I heard it. I heard you put quotation marks around 'accident' again."

"Nonsense. No. Of course not. News about your dead mother? Is that right?"

"Don't try t'draw me out, huh? We're not in a singles bar. If Arthur told you anything, he told you everything. Arthur belongs to the holistic school of gossip. So my mother, so what?"

"So what? Come now. In one afternoon you learn, first, that your mother was not your mother. That your real mother is unknown and probably never will be known. Parenthetically I mention that all this is true of your father as well: but, for some reason, that fact doesn't seem to hold as much significance. Moreover, you learn that your adoptive mother was insane: to the extent of child murder. Quite a Book of Revelations, I'd say. Mmmm?" Cox thumb-wrestles himself: impartial: neither hand is a favorite. "Your relationship with Bettina Lynxx, as I assess it, was very close."

"I hated her."

"Yes. You see, that's precisely it. Hate and fear excite a thrilling, even a sensual, kind of intimacy. I put myself in your place and I'm astonished. Rev. Gordon says you took it badly. You screamed. You expressed anger. I'm not surprised. That's a bit much for anyone to assimilate—let alone in a few hours."

"I took it pretty damn well, I think. I took her death even better."

"Whistling in the dark. But suppose. Suppose—" One thumb has pinned the other: there is no compassion or sporting grace: it suffers underneath. "She might come back, Simon. Suppose she comes back, what then?"

"Huh?"

"In one of your hypnagogic moments. The transcendent false mother. The transcendent child murderer. Here."

"Cox—"

"Hate and fear, absolute. Huge, shining: a Virgin Mary of your terror. You and she. In the infinite darkness. The intimate darkness. Do you really want to be alone then?"

"Jesus, Cox. Stop." Simon has turned away from him: deliberately, stupidly: as one would roll a carpet. And there is urine now in his crotch.

"I will. It isn't pretty. But, well—you may want it. You may want just that. Who am I to interfere? There may be unfinished business between you. No. No, you can't turn your back on that. You haven't got a back anymore. Or so you tell me."

"My mouth—"

"Yes? What about it?"

"My mouth is real. You told me that. You saw the scar tissue. You saw it."

"Certainly. Yet you did that to yourself, didn't you? A strange mistake: confusing gasoline for salad oil. And even if it were an accident—no quotation marks—you have to ask, I have to ask, are there any true accidents? Or—if it were the most innocent, motiveless event—did that loss of one sense serve as the key trauma? The suggestion? After all Herman Wolff himself vouches for it—you have a remarkable associative mind. She drove your father to a fatal coronary, isn't that so?"

"Christ, where'd you get all this Snocane? Out of a Viennese fortune cookie? Cox, two members of the disadvantaged lobby hit me with half a kitchen sink. Did I imagine that?"

"Did you imagine your deafness?"

"No. Cox, listen: I appreciate your spirit rapping. But if something comes for me out of the dark and narrow house, if I gotta make old acquaintance unforgot, then I'll do it without Dr. Abraham. He isn't family. You underestimate me, Doctor. I'm scared bungless, but I'm not afraid. You understand that? And I want out of here."

"Think it over until Friday. I'll leave now."

"Do that. Oh. Wait: one thing."

"What?"

"Wolff. Make him squeal. Take a pound of flesh: do a breast reduction on him. Send Wolff your top billing."

"Grateful, aren't we? Goodbye, Simon."

"Yeah, I think it is."

Simon misses Cox at once. By himself: he'll have to be alone for both of them: for Packard and for Simon: a double solitaire. Prank-playing night is one time zone closer now: Simon has almost had his day. He would stir at this point: but what is *to stir*—that nondescript reflex of unease—how do you purposely act it out? Along one thigh tics signal: blinka-plip: his ankle has bent back without leave: shifting for itself. And—behind you, look—a fist: left hand has shut up, half cocked to blind-shot his jaw. Simon, as all old tyrants are, is shaky on the throne, they know their time. These signs and preparations hint a mutiny: scheming in malcontent flesh. His big body, that trumped-up republic of patient jungle and Indian fear, that Central American place, is restive at last. What if the whole thing rioted: what if, in a zany coup, it took his capital? Suppose they, the peon limbs, rose to dance—d'ja—alone: and left his wallflower mind outcast? Suppose—

—enough. The head. In that direction an unmarked burial lies. Ripe time he did some walking work. Since Friday, as creeper infants will, Simon has begun to repattern himself: left leg, see, stop: right leg, see, stop: armswing, armswing, to keep the torso above and abreast. It is not his usual panther lope: it is how the aged scuff about in flat slipper backs. Eeeesh-eee: Packard has a scream impediment: he lisps out roar. Now Simon, with study, will drop each leg over the side: just so one might drop a rope ladder to climb down on. He has got thin. The kneecap looks like a square machine stud hammered in. Warn Cue #11: feet are both level: aligned, let us hope, by the floor. Right hand must brace here to push and—Packard, did you say? A word: a lucky hit? Simon holds: has he been spoken to? Did Packard talk or did he, in that random spill of noise, chance on language? But the face has turned: unmistakably turned, not thrown there by a spasm's joke. Packard is stark-staring: yet the eyes articulate. Caw, he will say. Then—*heil!* his left arm swats up, half a sudden salute: hand snagged by railing and by sheet. It is, the hand, a personality. The fingers spread in linen and are: one bent kite, one stuck parasol, one broken Chinese fan: many hurt, webbed things of strut and cloth that cannot open full. And Packard has said,

"Calll."

"What? The nurse?"

"Calll."

"Sure, sure. Hang on. Shit, the lazy bitches, I knew it was time. I knew you were overdue."

"Calll."

"It's okay. All right. Hang on."

The call bell, made like a venetian blind tassel, clips under his pillow ear. Simon has flung one hand at it, but the arm is ropy: a bowline cast just short. Let her out: more play this time: fingers knot a half hitch around the cord, tighten and reel in. Packard is constricting: stiff: caught by the python of himself. He snarls, slurs that snarl: phlegm puddled down in the throat will lend his gibberish a rung and stately tone. Yet Simon can translate: still, now—as in a dialect of a dialect of a forgotten tongue—there is articulation enough. The word Please. No difficult first consonant: vowels dilated: the ess sound spat out: Please. And, buzz, Simon is mad. This medical oversight, this unnecessary consciousness, outrages him. Buzzzz: the bell machine has cracked apart beneath his rash thumb-press: plastic hangnails split away from it. Down a hall someone outside the magistracy of pain will say, "So who did she go out with last night?"

It is the hand he, Simon, won't allow. One finger has torn linen and hatched out: blood specks touch white up. Packard, in whom there is no structural fatigue, will bend a metal rail: to snap it at the solder line. His pinky, snagged there, crooks back: almost a knuckle in reverse. Simon has stood, feet wide apart. He isn't tall any longer: he is just high now:

and afraid up above. Quickly he superintends both feet: gets a walking start: right hand seen, watched, perceived on his bed table for propulsion, for support. And, swing, across the ten-foot aisle between. A glass falls: the shattering is germane. Packard has constructed his acrobatic bridge again: he spans the bed. Simon can examine Packard's bare navel, drawn to a slit by stress. Also the tongue: it suckers up/against palate: like a poultice packed on. That tiny under-ligament—the hinge of speech —seems fine wire. It may pop. And then Packard would wolf himself down.

"Hold on. Let me get your hand out of there. Nurse!"

"Eees. Eees."

"She'll come, nurse! Don't crap out on me, Packard, help me find your hand. Come on, baby. Come on. You'll break it. Nurse! I! Need! A fucking nurse!"

Simon has raked sheet off Packard's hand. They scratch each other: one in many fast convulsions: one in a spree of clumsiness. Loose, Packard's hand will up-start: with such wild leverage that the bed rail is capsized aslant. Simon has been taken: fingers are pinned against steel. And Packard, of a hunter-gatherer tribe, has shut his own hand in triumph over them. Simon can hear bone: his knuckles pile up: the flesh above is zinc white now. But Packard's bridge has fallen down: aggravation centered in that he-man grip. Simon would like to feel: this, anyhow, must be an eventful communication, male with male. His fingertips are madder red: they stash blood away. Packard has good sport here: pleasure and distraction. It is a nice arrangement. Packard won't let Simon fall: and Simon won't begrudge him his dulled hand.

3

The man-who-empties-bedpans will cross himself again. In his home-land an eye has great agency: it can glare the womb dry and stunt all good luck. See, Simon is asleep: with lids far open, in a chair just beside the bed: as though he were visiting himself. The contact lenses seem in-grown and cataracted now. There is no intelligent light behind: Simon doesn't look alive. Since Tuesday he has developed a whitish, translucent film—an expression of mucus—that will droop at command over his sight: like the false eyelid in sick cats: a way to doze and still be aware. The man-who-empties is disturbed, yet drawn, yet girlishly afraid. He has been in this room alone before: to frighten himself, homesick for that old-time superstition. Simon hasn't properly sat: he is, instead, a big lump sum settled on the chair: a Halloween guy made by rural children for their front-porch swing. The man will sneak out before long: no sense in exasperating a special providence. But he feels brave to have been so near: feels modern, American even, suddenly naturalized. It is something he will tell the wife about: for he has dignity and likes to romanticize his work.

Mid-Friday afternoon. Packard has been taken away: to shout in an-other town. Simon's cane is snagged on a chair arm. His suitcase, terrier size, will stay at one knee. The dressing has worn Simon out. Not physi-cally: hand and foot are without advocate or recourse: they do what they are told. Worn, rather, by small business administration, by hotel porter work. The shoe tongue is a dumb trivia question: so, too, the belt loop and the fly and the mysterious sleeve that he has nothing up. Of six buttons on his age-yellow white shirt, only one has been mated with a hole: the rest are still in their bachelorhood. Shirt material flourishes at his right blazer jacket arm cuff. Left arm shirting, though, has piled up inside: to wrap a blousy tourniquet at the elbow line. Simon can't know, but his left hand, blood-budget-slashed, is asleep on its own. The gold tie has been hung like a eucharistic stole over shoulder and nape. This is all teen-age wear: clothing scrounged by Mrs. P from some basement trunk at Van Lynxx Manor: they smell of mildew and the unquiet 1960's. Yet they fit well: he has been starved back to adolescence now. One high school shoe is off: the other on, but not bound down. Shoelaces are unaccommodating. Never in his life—why?—did Simon watch hand and hand collaborate to assemble a bow. Try that yourself: cross, recross and under, loop, then loop in the air. It's a difficult pantomime: memory in the finger, not the mind.

But his socks made Simon weep. They lie, disciplined, on the pavement outside: a twelve-story jump through abundant rain. One sock: one hour. Again and again he rolled it. Stretched it slowly with the thumb and forefinger of each hand—stretched it into an open oval. For half a moment he dared do no more. He waited on the ebb and flow of his concentration. Then, breath exploding in gasps, he wrenched the right knee up to his chin. Locked it there and patiently, toe by toe, began to insert his foot. The cursed toes wouldn't go in. The black opening wavered from left to right, down, then up. He could hear sinews crumbling in his thigh. He began to pant. But it was too late. Attention cracked and the knee joint gave way: the lower leg sprang forward. Little toe caught on the oval's edge—the sock leaped from his hands. Again. Again. Now the window is open. A rough draft of October, unfelt but thready with rain, has reached in.

He twitches: along the forearm, on shin, on cheek: as if a ghost were tapping memos out. Sleep has been finicky. Simon dreams the dreams of a watchmaker now: mote extracted, seed put in, half second set ahead or back: his subconscious is exact. Thumb plus ring-fingernail tweeze: they re-enact some super-cerebral dexterity, but miss. It is pleasant to oversee the body's minute domestic enterprise. Peace, like glaze on old tile, will attend that. Throwback to the animal time when cleanliness meant safety: no scent clue left for a predator smell. It is why our dying, in their last day, pluck and preen deathbed sheets so conscientiously: they don't want to be followed out of life. Here are a few dream chores for Simon: roll and lift sunburn crust to molt it off: chapped lips, they have a shiny plate surface that can be broken away: bend, pinch tight sideburn hair, listen while it crackles club soda sound: find where soil has lain, mouse-dirt shapes, in a navel, then press them out. And that narcotic third-grade shop class afternoon where he discovered first the wonder of Duco Cement: coat, recoat fingertips, until they have warm frostbite. Carefully strip each: the pliable caps, often a whole glue thimble, are stamped with fingerprint intaglio. Ah, layering: lamination to the bone: bone another set of laminations: there is slow math in it and harmony. Simon will dream: film-maker, film-taker: wish fulfillment: to be obsessed by matters no more dense or significant than callus and sweat.

Knocking: rap, rap—*rap*—rapp. Long, long—*short*—long, as locomotives warn a hick-town railroad gate. The hospital duty priest is unwilling, also somewhat hard-bitten: a long day and not much spiritual commission in this door-to-door approach. Simon does not hear. A six-by-eight card has been conferred with again: PACKARD, WALTER, EPISCO-PALIAN, ROOM 1203, yes. Simon's shoulders are turned doorward: his new skinhead and that Easter Island topknot of bandage can just be seen above the chair top. A rain gust has spanked in: outpatient maple leaves paste their duck feet on glass. The priest will rap just once more: drumming business up. A depressed market here: street clothing and luggage mean convalescence, the enemy of sudden faith. Still, his room is mean. Rainwater has begun to depend like little teats from windowsill and radiator top. PACKARD, ROOM 1203, is directly under the weather. Wind will flap his collar wing. The priest feels compunction: which is goodness of a venial sort.

"Mr. Packard? Mr. Packard, would you like me to close the window?" Simon's cane falls. The priest, wary—is this a death?—has come near his chair. "Are you all right?"

"Annnh?" Simon squints: he can't understand what there is to be seen.

"Mr. Packard?" Simon has become a blinking idiot. Left eye, right eye, alternately: his new practice, to sideslip even that one telegraph-key beat of inner darkness. Eye phlegm clears from his contact vision.

"Arthur?"

"No? No. Oh, God!" The priest has seen him. And her hand is up against her throat.

"Bettina, there?" Vision is still fur-bearing and double: a hazed split screen. "Where's your Joan Crawford picture hat at least, eh? They said you'd look bigger than a life annuity. They said you'd be a spectacle and an eternal hot spot on my negative. Huh? I used to call you when the big kids gave me a belly burn. And now you come."

"Simon. Your head. Don't you recognize me? I'm Merry."

"Aha. Are you now?" He is crafty: but his vision has been wiped. "Hold it. Halt. This is Checkpoint Charlie. I've had some dreams and some things in between. Pardon. My mind is like chipped beef with freezer burn on it. Merry, eh?"

"Yes."

"Then, if you're Merry, why does she look like Jesus Christ as played by Jeffrey Hunter? Huh?"

"You mean my clericals? Because I'm a priest."

"Oh. Uh-huh. Of course. I useta wear a gorilla suit myself. Now I have no hair, you see. And a white turban like Madame Blavatsky's hired avatar. Not too original, I admit. Going to the ball as Mother Cabrini is better. Much better. You wow me, kid: I didn't think you had the light-seeking bluff for it."

"Let's not talk about me. The bandage. What've they done to you?" She kneels: her right hand is on the suitcase latch. "You look awful. I mean—thin, thinner. But you're going home. You must be better, huh? Was it serious? Have you been here long? Oh, I thought you'd given me the heave-ho. I went around my apartment sitting you in chairs and talking. I have a whole set speech, very logical, with four-letter words. Dammit, Simon, why didn't you have someone call me? I'd have come right over. That wasn't kind."

"Wait. Wait. Not so swift, you lesser primate of the Church, we have certain procedures here." Simon will need to correct for drift: to establish his true axis in space. With one hand he guides Merry back: so that he can look down and be sure of his two-leggedness. Against her black dickey front an abstract cross hangs; Jesus crucified, expressing Cubist pain. "Okay, I'm in a chair. That's clear enough. No set change during intermission. Huh. Be patient. Your new wardrobe is a bit disorienting: like spending Christmas Day in West Palm Beach."

"Tell me what happened."

"Aha. Aha, as Dr. Cox would say. What happened is now an unsolicited manuscript at *Cosmopolitan en Espagnol*. It wouldn't interest you. Nuh." Simon will shrug successfully: and then pause while a shoulder is trued off. "Boring. Instead, why don't you go out t'Roosevelt Raceway and wait for valet parking in the rain?"

"You fought with someone."

"Me? When I fight, it's a blast oven, it's a half-track coming. TV's pick up interference like there was a new power drill in the neighborhood. Hum. Merry, uh. You could do me a big favor. You could leave."

"But why? We're friends, aren't we? We're at least that I thought." She picks up his hand and is immediately uncomfortable with it. The palm has sprawled like a fresh kill: no wire-drawn reflexes move.

"What? Oh. You've. Got my hand." Simon is just making out a receipt: for the traffic department. But she can't understand that and, to Merry, his intonation is bizarre.

"Tell me. Why won't you?"

"It's like this—I'd rather not give you the satisfaction."

"Oh, give it. Go on. Do—it's good to give people satisfaction." She laughs. Her face is lovely: nervous and clear: her face is—can a face be? —naked. They are the same age and now Simon holds youth against her. "Tell me. I'll find out anyway."

"You won't find out the truth. They'll say I was—God—mugged. No. It was Wolff."

"Herman Wolff? How? He's an old man."

"Remember? I sicked two half-steppin' boogs on him. You expressed concern at the time. Well, in an Old Testament spirit, he sicked them back on me. Only, when they collapsed my cruet with twelve inches of cold-water sink line, Wolff didn't rush in and say, 'Shalom.'"

"Your cruet?"

"They fractured my skull. It has a little logo on it now. Here. A letter K, as in kaput."

"That son of a bitch."

"It's nothing a little Plastic Wood won't cure. Listen, they jumped me. They're my friends, otherwise I'd've liquidated their assets but good. They surprised me. They hit me when I was most vulnerable, when I was talking: it isn't polite t'interrupt. Huh—you remember what I did t'that mohunk in the park?"

"Never mind that—did they get him?"

"Who?"

"The police. Wolff."

"The police? I didn't tell the police."

"What? Why not? That's armed assault with intent to kill. You're not going to let him get away with it?"

"Oh, man. Never involve a broad: women can't understand. Huh. Watch: imagine: laugh. There's Young Simon paddling in deep water with his plywood shark fin up. I mean, nothing's more pathetic than amateur evil. Then—glash—real fin, real teeth: a few bubbles and silence. The straight-faced ocean smooths things over, bye. Uh. I can't bitch. Wolff got me by the prairie oysters fair and square. It was welcome t'the bigs, rookie. Hanh, Mer. After what I pulled on him, you didn't expect Wolff t'give me Most Favored Nation status, didja?"

"Bullshit. You didn't fracture his skull." Merry has stood: and, to assert her intention, she rattles the window down. "If you don't tell, I will."

"Uh-uh, you won't. I'll call you a perjuress in court. Besides, don't you see, Ball Peen and Sledge didn't mean it. I'm sure of that: if they'd meant it, they'd probably've hit each other in the cronkite. They're innocent and stuck in the middle, between two culture lags."

"Oh—it's all stupid macho, isn't it? That's why wars start."

"Hey. There's nothing a matter with macho: it's got right and wrong, and a lotta handsome ceremony. Nun-uh: it's the men who can't fight—the connivers, the highbinders, the women-men—who start wars. Let it loose, take some deep breaths like you're doing Lamaze. I'm fine. My thought bowl is splicing itself up. Uncle Arthur'll be here with his car any minute. I'll be playing pinochle with Helen Keller by Tuesday. Wait—" Simon pokes at her clerical collar. His action is not well judged: the impact on Merry's throat will make her go hoarse. "Hold on. That Sunday black hanging in your john at the apartment. And, you know, I figured you were giving a priest some horizontal absolution. Wait a sec. Is that carnival dress-up, or is it a real work shirt?"

"No. I don't want to get into that. Not now. You're changing the subject."

"You—you changed the subject in your dressing room. It's at least as worthy of a medical prognosis as my no-longer-lowbrow head. Huh? Are you?"

"I'm a priest. I've said that."

"Nosso easy, Virgin George. This isn't like confessing you've got type O blood. Lemme put it in the most churlish light I can. Ah. You—you whose pubic hair catches like Velcro, you whose loamy inner thighs have known my damp eel trail—whose nipples I've grabbed like June bugs— *you're* a priest? I mean, what kinda priest? Were you ordained or did you send away? A priest like my uncle is a priest?"

"He's an Episcopalian, did you tell me? Yes. Like your uncle. There are a lot of us now. Women in the priesthood, that is."

"I mean, you raise up bread and wine and—zap—the great I Should hot-wires it? You pray and He makes an immediate prepaid drop shipment? Hah, gosh: I'm throaty with wonder. You can marry people into sickness and death? You put a watermark on little non-consenting babies? You can do all that?"

"I repeat—I'm a priest."

"You even get paid for it?"

"Not much."

"St. Scagliola, what an engaging shakedown. I'm spiral-bound in admiration. You probably useta sell real estate on Love Canal. Hey, since when've you been wearing this strange scrub suit?"

"Try to rephrase the question. And your tone."

"How long've you been a priest?"

"About three years. No, that can't be right. I was ordained—let's see, two years ago last Easter. Yes? It seems longer. Simon, now that we've got that out of your system, let's not talk about it anymore."

"Oh, but let's. Let's." Simon is nodding, nodding: a seizure of affirmations. His fitfulness will disturb Merry: the head is teetering: over-committed to motion. "Boy, what a press kit that must've made. I bet your clipping service was swamped. TV and radio: popular song. Gee, hell, that's where women have it over men: they can get coverage on the old coaxial cable just by joining the Detroit fire department. Huh. Hey, could I become a nun?"

"A monk you mean."

"Why not a nun? Well? If you can become a priest, why can't I become a nun? Why can't I express the secret broad in me?"

"Ah—"

"Gotcha there. Caught you being sexist. Hanh. I know all the liberal consciousness-raising flackery by heart. I been around militant dykes and other dry-fly fishermen all my working life. Time, hold: let me plot a juky lecture circuit. See. I become a mother inferior, then I buy an electric mandolin and renounce my nun-ness and make platinum records singing 'Jesus Loves the Weak and Weird' with an all-smoke gospel band. I'd get fifteen of 'Sixty Minutes.' Phil Donahue would profitably insult me. 'Real People,' too: I'd have the biggest build-up since Kohoutek. I'd last at least a nanosecond in the public eye."

"Oh, Lord. I don't think I can take much more of this. I knew you'd carry on this way, I knew it."

"I could wear—ah. Ah."

"Simon? Are you all right?"

"Um. Ah. Aaaah."

"Jesus, your face went almost blue, then. Are you faint?"

"Nuh. Am I—out of breath? So much talk. I talk t'keep. Myself busy." He pauses. "Not sure when. Lungs're empty. Aaah."

"Well. Please, let's stop it. That's a good idea, huh? You're not supposed to get excited, I'm sure. That's what they always tell me. Don't excite them. I walk in on a dying woman and they say, 'Don't excite her.'"

"Ah." Simon's chest is on schedule now: he can see and count: crest, crestfallen, crest. "Aha. Recharged again. Lessee if I can shame you out of here."

"Shit, I need a cigarette." Merry is up and near the window. "I can't handle your cynicism without a cigarette."

"Cynical? Who's being cynical? I'm not the one dressed up like the protagonist of a funeral."

"Dressed up? I am not dressed up." She can't get the Marlboro going: matches, carried flat in a vest pocket, are rain and sweat damp: they slide, they do not scratch. Simon will take advantage of her lull: to station hands and feet in the general delivery zone. "You don't understand yet. This isn't some masquerade. I believe in it, Simon. I've made quite a few sacrifices for it. I believe very strongly, my friend. You won't get my goat."

"Aha. I see. Scusa. You really believe?"

"Yes. I do."

"No doubt that's why you told me about it the first day we met. And repeatedly thereafter. You were gravel-blind with conviction."

"Goddam. I knew you'd throw that in my face. Stupid matches. Damn. Well, I walked into that one, didn't I?"

"Hey. It's me has the grievance. I almost committed adultery with God's own jane. Not that I blame you two-timing Him. Those omnipresent guys, they get around. St. Joseph wasn't the first."

"Fine. Have your way." Merry is smoking. "I should have told you. I should've witnessed. I was wrong not to. But I knew full well what your cheap reaction would be. Voilà. All the cute sniggering. Ho-humm, so predictable." She has her back to Simon: smoke, like a gray-pawed kitten arching, sits low above one shoulder. "I knew it would turn you off and—and, right or wrong, I'm tired of turning men off. It's a bit unfair. A male priest can date: it doesn't automatically turn a woman off. And it's accepted. Whole church altar guilds get together to—to *procure* the right woman for a priest. They love it. In two years now, the only contact I've had is with other priests. The singles scene isn't quite suitable, you know. For me." The kitten has blown its fur up: in fear, in self-persuasion of courage. "And, to be forthright—to be even a little bitchy—male priests are kind of wet. I mean, they're good people, but—you know what I mean. I mean wet: what I said in the first place. Wet. Let it out, Merry. Christians, in fact, as a subset—well, the Church is where they have to take you in. Isn't that a wonderfully spiteful thing to say? Yes. True, though. It's such a pleasure: talking to an atheist. Ha."

"But. Lissen a minute, just because you dress like a very low mass—that would've turned me on. Not off."

"Yes. Probably. I thought about that." Merry has faced him. She powers abrasive smoke into her chest: the cough is a circumlocution. "Yes, but marriage. Anything serious. You wouldn't have married a priest."

"Hey, Veal-Soft, when we were lying in the drainpipe—your legs were wide as a carriage entrance. You weren't keeping yourself for a marital transfer payment. Uh-uh."

"Shut up."

"Mmmm."

"Well?"

"You told me t'shut up."

"Don't rub it in, that's all. Be a gentleman about it. Want a puff?" Simon says no. Merry will sit, a patient, on the bed. "Can I talk for one uninterrupted minute?"

"Sure. Take two."

"This is the way I've worked it out in my mind. At night: talking to you while you sat on my kitchen chair. And, believe me, I'm aware of the contradictions. No one is more aware. But you'll just have to accept them. So?"

"So I'm not interrupting, much as you'd like me to."

"Great. One: I am a Christian. By that I mean the whole shtick—not just what you put down under 'Religion' on the census form. I believe in Christ: the resurrected Son of God. That Christ. I believe in the sacraments. In my sinfulness and my possible salvation. Got that?" No response. "I knew this would bore you. As Christian to atheist I should have witnessed—but then you would've gone away, wouldn't you? And then what good would I have done? Does that sound like a rationalization?" Simon is silent. "Yes, all right. And I am—I am attracted to you physically." She inhales. "I'm very attracted." She inhales. "Well.

That seemed to stir the audience deeply. Well. I guess we both have a secret. I won't tell about Wolff, if you won't tell about me. So?"

"So?"

"You can talk now. Is it cold in here? What're you thinking?"

"I'm thinking your hair is splendid. In that blackout curtain you've got on, most women'd look about as sexy as Milton Eisenhower in a peignoir. I am chiefly amazed."

"Thank you. I do appreciate the compliment. But. Anything else?"

"Only: that I'm not responsible for your guilts. I came in late. I can't be their foster family."

"Fair enough. And I'm not asking you to be."

"Yes, you are. Hum. You want me t'be a bender f'you. Six Bloody Marys, a hung head and what'd-I-do-last-night? Maybe I'm a little at fault. Maybe I gave you the idea: that I was irresistible, that I'd work like Liquid Wrench on your tight joint n'matter what. But I'm resistible. Hah, yes. You can't get a contact binge from my lust and drive. And plead non compos mentis after."

"Did I? Have I been doing that?"

"And see: I book what you say about faith. Swell, everyone should have an outside interest or two. But—hanh—why a clergyperson? That's not faith, that's promotional material. Huh?" Simon is, indeed, curious. "Was it the power? D'you feel switched on when you dress that way? Ah, like I useta wear white when I played handball: it made my serve into a particle of matter, or at least I thought. D'you wear rubber soles so your handshake won't anodize people?"

"Power. Wait. Let me give it a square try." First and second finger bobby-pin her hair up: out: on each side: leaves of a draw-top table. She cannot think well with her hair down: it is like onlookers. "Yes. I suppose. I do feel power sometimes, sure. But there's good power, God power. Pride is another thing." Head back, she will train her sight along swept cheekbones: the swan pose that is his favorite. "No. I feel both, to be honest. But that's not why I went into it. I think."

"Think? That's some credo, huh. Here I stand. I shall return. Give me liberty or give me death. I think. That kinda attitude didn't filch Lazarus outa his shroud, always presuming he wasn't waiting in there with a week's supply of liverwurst and a thermos. You've wanted this for a long time? Did you dress your doll in cassocks? Did you play rectory instead of house? Huh. I mean, is this more than a summer vocation?"

"Actually. Strange you should ask that. Actually I wanted to be an astronomer or a physicist. But I wasn't encouraged, my professors kept saying my math wasn't good enough."

"So, you became a feminist, which is what women do when their math isn't good enough."

"Yes. I did." Her hair has fallen: a face guard. "I am that. I am a feminist. And I'm not sure my math wasn't good enough. Anyhow, I believe a woman has as much right to be a priest as any man. I warn you, don't get me started on that. Give me the arguments from St. Paul and I'll answer them one after another."

"Uh-uh. Y'won't get any arguments from me. I go along: 'cept I don't think either part of speech—male or female—should be a priest. I know people too well. I think I'm moral as anyone, maybe a little louder—and that, believe me, is no vote of confidence f'human nature. Eh, even my old uncle: and he's too empty-marrowed t'do a sin unless he jobbed it out. Even him: he just spends his released time meditating and tryin' t'jilt death at the altar. It's all bald follicles. You're both equal: you're both unhappy."

"Oh, no." She has set off another match. "I'm not unhappy. I'm just fucked up at the moment. There's a difference."

"Bet you didn't use that grisly language until you got God-sodden. A stylistic reaction, huh? Until then you were someone who called a thumbtack a drawing pin. And we can date your best horny from two Easters ago."

"Ha." She laughs. "How smart-ass. Marvelous what can be deduced from personal nastiness. No. It's just a test. A passage. I'll get through it." She touches each breast. "Look. I've been under pressure. I get hate mail. People spit at me: nice old people, the kind that knit afghans for a penny social. That photographer. He was hired by a redneck Christian conservative in the New Anglican and Triassic split-off church. They want some compromising evidence on me. To embarrass the bishop and force me to quit. It's like the KGB. You haven't seen me at my cheerful best. This is a bad period. I'll surface yet. I'll be better company. I can be a lot of fun. Stick around and try."

It is an advance. And Simon, silent, rages against his own mouth roof: sucking there, distraught: vexed by this tasteless suit of hers. He will have to look away: at the mattress where Packard halooed and sang out pain: he craves the strange bed-fellowship of another sick male here. Her beauty is so obvious, so much a repeated slogan—no mole or cast or disproportionment—that she can appear both ravishing and commonplace. He could shut her out, he might have done that, but for the clericals and their peculiar consequence. They dramatize her: they bait his perverse sense. Abruptly she has that special fascination of a sacrilege: fascination he could live without now, when his body has become soluble even in air, and the vigor which can carry high over thresholds is gone. Why did he not enter her back then: or at least, in good light, verify those breasts: why didn't he get that obligation cleared up before? He peers down at his idiot fly: half open, a railroad switch. Shirttail and underwear, like some young rupture, press out. Still, as she is sitting there, lap drawn up, each bare knee to support a small clamshell elbow point, drawn up also in the prolonged mystery of apostolic succession and female rut, ah, Simon wants. Simon wants. Simonwants. Such outraged desire he has not felt since he was that princeling despot we all once were: an infant child, to whom the breast, by royal privilege, is due. And Merry, selfish, slow and autobiographical, has been saying, what?

". . . that, well, they made me feel like I was Jackie Robinson. Together: my father and the bishop were in the same fraternity at Princeton. He—the bishop—enjoys having someone on tap to memorialize and celebrate his youthful sins. Such as they were. In fact, if truth be told, he was kind of a prude. An undergraduate prude." She smokes, she screens herself. "But, God, they flattered me. The bishop always let it be known that Merry Allen was spiritually precocious and set apart. At age four or five I had the knack of speaking in ellipses: leaving just enough out of a sentence to make it seem profound. I can still do that: and he does, too. But somehow it's harder for both of us now." Merry has been picking her lip: she can afford to be unattractive and is aware of that. "He never patronized me, though: nor did my father. I swam in it: what child wouldn't? It spoiled me for boys my own age: and I guess that was a stratagem, too. Ultimately, bringing me into the priesthood—it was a way of making all three of us men. I got initiated into the frat, so you might say. But I see a certain unpleasant pragmatism now. It was a way, too, of cutting my mother out. Mother is—ah, yes—Mother is a natural bore: curtains and tasteful bric-a-brac and no dust anywhere. She realizes what she is: maybe, if she had married someone else, it would've been different. Her math might have been good enough, you know what I mean? Oh, I'm at fault as well: I accept that. And today I'm closer to her than my father: cheerful boringness can give off a sort of peace. But the bishop went along with my father: consoled him for his suburban, married martyrdom. And excused, by implication, certain—certain other things my father did in certain other cities. Still, the man is immensely attractive. Still, I've seen him in a bathing suit around our pool—and even then he looks like a bishop, every pale inch. But I also watch him more closely now. I watch him, say, pretend to get drunk with innocent company. They love him for it. Yet he's always alert. It's a trick: he's just eavesdropping on them. He's capable of that. And sometimes I wonder—as far as I'm concerned, me, Merry Allen—what else he is or has been capable of.

"It's weird. You know—" She doesn't look at Simon: afraid to see that he isn't listening. "Though I've always had faith, my spirituality—the thing that has set me apart, if you will—came through science. Being amazed by an equation. Or paleontology. Or curved space. Then, in the late sixties, we all got Eastern religion: thirteen-year-old children were reading *Siddhartha* or that Arab Rod McKuen, Kahlil Gibran. The idea of becoming a priest did seem intriguing. I was isolated from rock 'n' roll and the bishop made it sound like a crusade. I'm not naturally brave, not a boat rocker, but he covered all my doubt with his authority. And the first year or so was exciting. A wonderful turmoil. I appeared on panel shows. I spoke at conferences. I even had a little short-lived syndicated column." She lights up: for the fifth time. "I'm a better priest than most men: it has cost me more. But I don't do much now. No parish wants me, though the bishop could have forced me on one or two. Parish life anyhow doesn't interest me. It may be God's work: keeping the alto in a choir from strangling the soprano over one wrong note. But if it's God's work, then let Him do it. I edit a newspaper for the diocese. I'm on six commissions. I cover a hospital when the regular man is on vacation. The bishop and I pretend to get drunk together once a month—and cause a little gossip. That's what the photographer really wants, me and the bishop in bed. Fat chance: sexuality is irrelevant to him and I got over that crush when I was sixteen. He feels, I sense it, a little guilty about me: because I bore him now—certainly me the Priest, and probably me Merry Allen. He's into more radical things. He'd like to sell off all the diocesan property and give it to the poor. Make his Ford Camper into a cathedral and park it in some ghetto. Maybe he's right: maybe he bores me, too. Mind you, I don't intend to quit on it: I'm not a quitter. My bravery is suspect, but not my stubbornness. I just need some time to reevaluate. I think—what you said about a bender is true enough. In part I was using you for that. A bioenergetic weekend. Ha. Also, I've never disappointed him and it's certainly overdue. Make him feel less guilty. And me, more my own woman. Yes? Huh? Did you say something?"

"Damn, I said. I said, damn. Damn it, I almost screwed a priest."

"Well, my friend, be of good cheer. You still can."

She is off the bed: so impulsively, so full of impulse, that by equal-and-opposite push it will trundle six inches away. Her new cigarette has been dropped on the sheet edge: a fuse twenty seconds from mattress fire. Simon is jostled. Her kiss touches down, where? The hand, which has flanked his neck, which is an epaulette on his left shoulder—did it go right through him? Simon feels enfiladed by Merry: she is mobbing him. Jesus, on the silver chain, will slide below her breast: like a broken mountaineer, rappelling over broad rock outcrops, down. The artery in her throat is quick: assigned to blushing. Why does everyone else seem more alive? Simon will block her: forearm up and hard as a nightstick in crowd control. Merry, bewildered, balance overset, has fallen back: the heel of her left low shoe snaps off.

"Shit. You're so clumsy. Look what you made me do."

"Go away, Merry. Leave."

"Oh, come off it, Simon. I didn't mean that. I wasn't really mad."

"Now." He gives her his quick thumb: to the showers. "Take your traveling passion play and beat it."

"Fine. Just fine. I open myself up to you like that and then you throw me out. How chivalrous. Does it give you great pleasure, humiliating women? Boy, I must say, you really are a first-rate crud."

"Visiting hours are over as of now. So long. Go say a wide-band novena for me."

"Wait. Hey, you can't just leave it like that. May I know why, is that too much to ask?" Merry's chin has gone in/down: against her throat. She is white: the blushing spent and no change left. "Tell me. Is it because of what I am?"

"You'd like that: then you could be the suffering servant's suffering servant. But no. It's because—I've told you this—I've never met a woman who didn't bore me to a soap dish."

"Crap. That's crap. I haven't had time to bore you yet. And I don't. I know I don't. Right now I interest you. In fact, in fact—I can sense it— something about me frightens you. Yes, that's it. You'd never give up the chance for a free lay otherwise. What is it, huh? Is it because I'm more intelligent than you are?"

"Yes. Now go."

"No." Merry can't agree. "No. It's not that. You wouldn't have said yes if it was."

"Look. Just shake dust off the one heel you've got left and go. We can do without each other. As for sex—you can always return t'private practice."

"Simon—"

"I'm about as useful t'you as fly ash. And you'd just be a dewclaw on me. We have nothing in common, Candy Tuft."

"Yes, we do." Her hair is shook umber: she smirks. "We're both good-looking, you and I. I think that's very important. What's more important than that?" Merry has the detached heel in her palm. It might be some fast and African animal's small hoof. She will use it as a trade-in now for his tolerance of her. Left foot up, nails finding nail holes: hopscotch. "You notice I limp. I never told you: but one of my legs is shorter than the other. Reason for my left leaning." The heel is fumbled: it bounces: hockey puckish. "Oh, well. I think we'd make a striking pair. Me with one built-down shoe and you with your snazzy global head."

"Stop. I don't want this."

"Oh? What is it you don't want?"

"You. To embarrass yourself. To be pathetic. I didn't ask for that. Just go. Just leave me by myself."

"Pathetic. Do you find it so? Well, at least I'm trying." She blinks fast. "Understand: I don't intend to cry yet. I mean t'save that for last— build to an impressive coda. Just give me a little time, a little room. All things have their proper form. And, besides, I have a great deal invested in you."

"Such as?"

"Such as I just got fitted with an IUD, you bastard. In Newark, New Jersey, so no one would know. I borrowed a wedding ring. I wore sunglasses and I spoke in a Spanish accent."

"It was fitted f'you, not f'me. You'll find other uses for it."

"Wait. Why've you been looking at me like that? It isn't just to stare me down. I thought it was. What am I missing? Jesus—you haven't blinked. You don't blink anymore, except one eye—"

"Merry, go—"

"What else? And what else?" She is looking at him: as at a puzzle where faces are hidden in leaf cover. "I know. I'm a jerk—your hands. You haven't moved your hands, at least not the way you used to. That's it. Oh, my God: there's something wrong. You're hurt. They really hurt you."

"Let it alone, Merry. Back off."

"Hush. Hush a minute. I'm thinking. Are you in pain, is that it?" She has pulled up his suitcase: they sit at the same height. "Christ, lover, look what you've done to me. I can't see beyond my own self-congratulating misery. I'm appalled at myself. I thought this, your eyes, your slouch in the chair, I thought it was some judgmental pose. I thought—and the cane. You haven't danced for me. It's something very serious, isn't it? My hand is shaking, see. I want to know and I don't want to know. It was all bullshit, wasn't it? You aren't healed at all. Simon: your eyes. They're raw and dry. What—"

"Look out, your stupid cigarette."

"Ow-frig!" Merry is brushing, blowing: ashes of sheet sootfall. "Jesus, some hospital chaplain. They'll name a burn center after me. I can cover it with the blanket. It's only a small hole. See. They'll never notice unless you blow the whistle on me. There."

"I want you t'go. I can handle this on my own."

"Uh-uh. I'm sure you can. But, uh-uh." She is upright, standing his ground. "Uh-uh, I feel like an—"

"Wait." He has section-bossed one hand up. "I'll put it differently. Please go. Please respect my wishes in this. I can't run away from you: be decent about it, Merry."

"But why? What is there that you can't tell me?"

"After I go. I know you. You'll question the nurses and you'll find out. But let it be after I've gone. Okay?"

"And where will you go, Nepal? Dar es Salaam? I'll find you anyway. Might as well have it out now."

"I won't tell you. Now go."

"Won't? Won't, because why? I'll grill you like they do in a police station. Ha. Because why? Ha." Simon has turned away. But she will duck around the chair: across his vision scope, impertinent. He can't shift fast enough: he can't close his eyes. She is the present: she is terrible in his sight. "Come on. I won't be put off. Because why? Come on."

"Because—you jackal, you dirty bloodsucker—because. I'm. Impotent. And because your fucking body is a rebuke t'me. Shit! Shit on you. Now get out!"

"Sure. Impotent. I've heard that one before."

"Shut up! Shut your filthy manikin's mouth."

"Jesus. Is it true? Jesus, is it? Go on, hit me if you want to."

"I can't. I can't." Simon is almost blind with rage now and must be careful. "I wanna strangle you. I wanna cut the flesh from your cheeks and your eyes. But I can't."

"Ssssh. Sssssh. Please. Calm down. Your face is going blue again. Breathe."

"Ah. I've lost all feeling. I can't feel anything. Any. Thing."

"Touch?" She has acquired his hand again. "Do you feel that?"

"Merry. This isn't like your leg going t'sleep. Ah. Ah. I can't even walk unless I babysit each foot. I don't. Know. Where. They are. Got it? My feet. Ah. I haveta sit to pee the way you do. I shuffle like a Geisha girl. Hanh. When you kissed me, Jesus, it was like that scene in *Invasion of the Body Snatchers* when Kevin McCarthy kisses the girl and there's nothing and he knows the pod people've got her. Ah. I don't exist in space anymore. I've got no weight. No place. It's musical chairs and I'm out. As far as I know, I could be sitting on a barstool in Washington Heights. Huh? Didn't you feel it?"

"No. Well, maybe. No I didn't. I was thinking of myself. I guess I felt myself."

"You wondered, perhaps, why I didn't rise t'greet you? Why I've been sitting here like a sprung davenport? You didn't miss the usual Italianate gestures? None of that crossed your self-fondling mind, did it?"

"Stop. It did. But the bandages, the fracture. You've been recuperating. I thought you were tired. It made sense. And you said—"

"Tired? Baby, I'm all broken down. I've gotta watch everything—ah. Watch my hand. Watch even my breath. The transition team can't handle it yet. My body is a press gang and there's only one guard. Hanh. Oh, yes. Yes, and as for the morsel you're interested in—if I didn't stock-check every ten minutes, my voice'd go up an octave. I'll never make sheet lightning again, Merry, or stuff your plump little ballot box."

"It can't be that bad, can it? Surely they can do something."

"They did something. They dealt me this losing hand from a cold deck. When I walk on stage they cover me with a black follow-spot. I don't exist. This thing I'm sitting in, it could be the chair of East Asian studies at Oberlin, I can't be sure."

"But—"

"Enough. You got a drag on that for me?"

"Oh, sure. Here." Merry, imprudent, has tendered Simon her sixth cigarette: passes it over, playing into his hand.

"Not so suave. Between my fingers. This offering is not valid without a formal prospectus. Careful. I've got some visiting rights, but my hand is a ward of the court."

"Got it?"

"Yeah. Excuse the showboating, but one atrocity is worth a thousand words."

"What?"

"Observe." He has huffed the ash vivid: this with an apprentice's swank: new to his trade. "Good." Motor-minded, fuss-budgety, Simon will aim the cigarette point: at his right cheek. It is ground out there, sparking, bent dead. Merry can smell discharges from his face. Then she is all about the chair: swatting, fanning, a unanimous show of hands. Simon has slumped down. His right shoulder caught beneath the chair arm: hanging there in effigy of himself.

"You stupid prick."

"Pull me up."

"Jesus. Jesus, you just missed your eye."

"Pull me. Up!"

"You did it before. I remember: in the drainpipe."

"It hurt then. Oh, it hurt then. Pull me up, quick. I can't feel with my legs."

"Oh, shit." Simon is thrashing, great shakes, uncertain what his feet have accomplished on the floor. Merry will approach. He can't right himself: he is on his beam ends. The chair has been clacking like a loom. "Oh, shit." She is demoralized. And this time he, they, will both detect revulsion in her speech.

"Don't just stand there. Pull me up." She has Simon beneath the armpits by now: jimmying his unhelpful torso left/right, as one would uproot stone in a frozen field. "Thanks so much for the lift. You can go now. The tent show is closed. And I'm soon t'have a major motion sickness."

"I—I was surprised. I didn't mean to say it like that."

"No?"

"It just—came out."

"Indeed it did. You should've seen your little patrician bitch's nose furrow up."

"Please, Simon."

"You found me repulsive. Like a thing with its spine cut out. I don't blame you. I'm a dogfish the whole lab class's been working on. Get out. Leave."

"I won't, you can't make me. Oh, God." She has shut her eyes. "I'm sorry. It's just a dumb phrase. Children always say it."

"Go. Huh, please? You're—well, frankly, you're torturing me."

"Yes, I know I am. I realize that now. Forgive me. I should have left. Left, found out what was wrong and come back. That was the right way to do it. But my instincts deserted me. I thought I could cute it out. And I was insecure: I thought—I couldn't help thinking—it was just a gimmick to get rid of me."

"And now—now, after the disgust—comes the pleasure. He's down to size. Down to size! Down to size! Lying flat in his own sitzmark. We're equal now: oh, yes. I'm a defective and you're a woman."

"I love you."

"Damn, I'm tired. What time is it? Why don't they come?"

"Simon, somehow, some way, we'll beat this thing. Give me a minute. I'm still shaky. Let me organize myself into committees."

"A cause. The burnt-out priest has found a cause. Aha. This is the lowest point in my life: for the first time I'm attractive t'rich liberals, just like the NAACP. I must really be sick. God, stop looking at me like you were a suffragette and I was the vote. They've handed me a section eight. I can never rejoin my unit again."

"Take a second. Wait." Merry walks to the bed: her limp is a small exoneration. "Let me brush my hair. I think better that way." Simon gazes out: acute yet dull, as a burning glass is. He can spot blue apertures to the west. This will depress him. Rain and sun are indifferent: changes, however, make him feel unprogressive: out of date. Merry has been slashing with a pocket brush: high, salt-over-the-shoulder swipes that make her scalp move. "May I ask? What do your doctors say?"

"They think—or they hope—that I'm wacko. I'm my own precedent and I'm ruining their point spread. They say it's autism or hysteria: they say I've got a power surge for Bettina's ghost. No one seems t'remember that my head was trumped by a low spade: that's too simple. They want me committed t'see if I salute on Mothering Sunday. Hah—but you can be sure of one thing."

"What?"

"Simon, he scared."

"Yes. So am I."

"I've lost my hearing three or four times."

"What?"

"I haveta sleep with my eyes open. Otherwise: I don't need t'tell you, you've got an imagination, otherwise I'm just a jumping-off place for the black country. Last gas before the abyss. But you're a priest, right?"

"Yes?"

"Then I claim privilege of the confessional. What I said is between you and me. I hear my uncle in the corridor."

"You mean—wait—you can't go yet."

"Listen. Get out while the getting is good. I don't need pity and you could do without a two-hundred-pound Waldorf salad."

"No."

"Merry, pay attention. I shriek at night. I wet my bed. Long strings of drool surprise me. I am not attractive. I am not the man you fell in love with. Put me in the prayer pool if you want, but keep away. I'm managing. I've got both elbows on the mortality table, but with men I can manage. With you—you take my dignity away. Leave me that."

"Dr. Gobel can—"

"No-no. This is something else. This is something else."

"Well, Merry Allen. The bishop's precious fool herself: fancy meeting you here. No demonstrations in favor of Christian pederasty to stage-manage this afternoon?"

"Oh, great. Just what I needed."

Their eyes make citizen's arrests. Simon will be a thing in litigation between them, but both are off-balance and not trial-ready yet. Arthur can imagine that his yellow slicker and wet pink plastic rain bonnet, bow-tied under chin, are less than conclusive evidence: so, too, the driving goggles; so, too, the fingertip-open driving gloves. He might, in fact, be a priest out of Beatrix Potter. Merry, not well-heeled, has an uncertain deportment: she will seem to teeter, fall back, tip: someone on loose beach sand when carpets of wave are pulled out underneath. Her skin is extra-fleshy, red: not jurisprudent: over-exposure to emotion and Simon. Both would prefer venue changes here. Robert, for instance, might disorder the court. Merry, it is obvious, has surprised Robert: clerical black, on a sharp woman, may tease out his exciting, new ambivalences: to gender: to love: to power in uniform. Robert has one arm around the large small of Peggy's back: a sponsoring pose. But Simon, their contested will, is insusceptible: busy at this moment checking his passenger list: arm and leg and all aboard. His body must be repacked after each stop, like a salesman's sample kit. Arthur has thrown one glove down: Merry, responding, will knock both shoes off. They are arraigned, in session now. Robert, observer, is lifting Peggy's better breast, her left: as you might lift the head of a wounded man to give him drink.

"Let's cut, huh? Let's get a move on. Robert, grab my duffel. God, being in this hole—I'd rather watch a hand of bananas turn brown, one by one. In Passaic. Huh. Gimme a boost up, Uncle. What took you so long, dammit? I been waiting 'n waiting, lodged in this chair like a fat ovarian cyst."

"Not just yet, Simon. You, young lady." Arthur has accused: his goggles make Merry appear hazardous to the eye: as direct sunlight might be or arc welding. "What're you about in here, may I ask?"

"About? I'm covering for the regular man—priest. I'm making rounds. What does it look like I'm doing?"

"Don't take it personal, Merry. Uncle can't help sounding like a takeout from Arthur Treacher's."

"Merry, is it? Simon, d'you know this person well?"

"Yah. Yah. She's an old friend. Listen, Uncle, we gotta flit. Cox may drop in any minute and decide I should be hooked to a rubber placenta."

"An old friend? You don't mean to say—you can't mean. Oh, good God. You and she haven't—"

"No. Merry and I haven't been doing an inside job together. No, far's I know she's still got the sticker price on. If someone's been lining her corner pocket, it isn't me."

"Never mind that. I don't care a pin for that. What I mean is—you haven't been worshipping with her all this while? You haven't been sending me up that way?"

"Worshipping?" Simon's expression is a split ticket: as much amusement as impatience. "Worshipping? Me? Jesus. When they make the highlight film of my life, I just hope this conversation isn't in it."

"Rev. Gordon, I believe." Merry has taken one nylon step toward him. "I can assure you that Simon remains a pristine atheist. Just the way you left him."

"I certainly hope. That is, I mean: I hope he hasn't been duped by your appalling revised version of the faith. Perverts, inverts, anyone but converts—eh, what? God forbid Christianity should interfere with anyone's system of belief. An atheist is just your cuppa, yes. After all, we must be ecumenical. Even to the point of utter paganism."

"Oh? And I suppose that elegant fossil, the C of E, is a hotbed of faith? God the gerontophile. You can convert and bury all in one neat service—convenient. It's a tourist religion. Churches with marvelous architecture and no congregation. I've been to England. A priest there is a curator of monuments, no more than that. You've got more Japanese with Nikons than believers."

"Why, the cheek—"

"Hey, hey." Simon is on overload: he can't watch them both. "Cut it out, you two ayatollahs. We're wasting time. T'me this's all a concerto for dog whistle."

"Well, he started it."

"Oh, innocent. Yes, Ms. Allen. I did. And, while I'm at it, allow me to acquaint you with several facts, right-o." Uncle Arthur has kicked his yellow slicker hem, walking forward: in position now between Merry and Simon. Simon is perplexed: he has never seen his uncle in such a Hunnish state. Water is dripping from the plastic widow's peak: as though it had been wrung out of him. "You're in the wrong pew, my dear. Simon is my nephew. He is now in perfectly competent and loving hands. We do not need any five-bob-a-look sensation mongering on your part."

"Uncle—"

"Simon, I don't mean to sound harsh. It isn't my nature, you know that. But if you realized how much agony this pigheaded young woman and others like her have caused honest Christians. Look. Got up like a socking great male impersonator, she is."

"Well, Uncle, you look a bit like Henny-Penny yourself today."

"Simon's my friend. I'm concerned for him. I don't—"

"Indeed. Not concerned enough to do up his shoelaces, though. Can't expect that of a dedicated revolutionary. Nothing quite so practical." Arthur kneels. "How are you, Simon?"

"The same. A little bored with all this religious overbite. How comes it you're dressed à la Barney Oldfield?"

"It gives me a small measure of confidence behind the wheel."

"And, let me tell you, he needs it." Robert is doing wash-my-ear-and-brush-my-teeth: circular motion with one finger near his head, then point at Arthur. "The man is a lunatic. He climbs in through the car window. No kidding. He hasta stand on a wooden crate t'do this. A wooden crate which he pulls in after him with a long bent wire. Wait'll you see."

"Well, both my front doors are on the kibosh."

"Then he tries t'hit potholes."

"Only when the radio won't come ín. The radio needs a bit of a whack now and then."

"Get ready for disaster. Hey, Simon, good news, though. Wolff wants t'see you at Ten Great Ferry tomorrow night."

"Robert, I thought we agreed not to mention that just yet. It's somewhat premature. We're all grateful to Mr. Wolff, but I do think at this moment that Simon's health is the prime consideration."

"He has t'go. It's important. Huh, Simon?" But Simon is watching Arthur align his shirtfront. Almost scholarly work: to squeeze each button through as if he were pressing the thumb index on an encyclopedia. Simon has relaxed: when last did someone dress him? "I'll drive you downtown. Kyryl's gonna be there, too. I think it'd be good for me t'meet Wolff and Kyryl. Get my feet wet. What d'you say, hanh?"

"Robert. I useta be a meat eater. Right now I'm low man on the food chain. I'm what the algae eat, if they eat. We'll see, Robert. Uncle. Now: it's time. Let's try 'n raise the *Titanic*."

"Alley-oop." Arthur has lent Simon an arm and shoulder up: buttressed him in place. "There. You look splendid."

"Okay. Back off. Cane, please. Thank you. Hooops. Almost wiped out then. What I need is a kickstand, so I can prop myself up like a flooded-out Honda. Here we go."

"Are you sure?"

"No. But I'm going. One small step for a man, one giant pain in the duff for everybody else." Simon is scrawling triangles with his cane tip. He has become an astute geometrician: there are configurations that will defray balance: and more that will not take his weight. Sweat blisters break: suppurate down. Step and step: for one second, he will falter right. Merry has his arm. "Damn. I move like a two-hundred-pound bag of Hamburger Helper. Hey?"

"Give way, you." Arthur hauls in on the other arm: they have Simon extended between them, out to dry. "Let go of him, I say."

"Wait. Botha you—"

"I'm just trying to help, can't you understand that?" Merry has made gains: more Simon on her side of the line. His cane is weak on its pin: and will fall. "See. Look what you've done now."

"Both. Of. You. Hey, watch out, careful, Christ, hold it, don't fight, wait, wait. Are you crazy? The big top's coming down. Lemme alone!" They do. "No! Hold me up!" They do. "Man, that was close. I've lost the memory yarn in my legs. Let go one at a time. And take it slow. What is this anyway, a proxy fight? Uncle, you first. And then hand me the cane."

"No, Simon. Not until she does. I won't have it. I can't let her interfere now."

"Reverend, I promise you—I don't give a goddam about Simon's soul. It's his body I care about."

"I'm sure you do."

"Yes, and you should, too."

"Mother, now I know what life as a cleft palate feels like. Cut it out, you two woodwinds. Hanh? Please. Please? Robert, if you can get your hand offa Peggy's minimizing bra for a moment and stop laughing—pick my cane up, huh? I'm a walking schism is what I am and I'm gonna land on my postprandium f'my trouble. Huh? What'd he say now?"

" 'Let the woman learn in silence with all subjection. Suffer not a woman to teach, nor to usurp authority over the man, but to be in silence. For Adam was not deceived, but the woman being deceived was in the transgression.' "

"St. Paul was a neurotic."

"Oh, yes. Quite. The fifth gospel of St. Sigmund. I forgot. Did you read it in the original Hebrew? Neurotic. Anything that doesn't titillate your self-serving ego is neurotic, I presume."

"St. Paul—"

"Shut up, Merry."

"St. Paul—"

"Shut up, Uncle. Whatever St. Paul was, he was Mr. Mental Health compared t'the two of you. Robert, help me. Look at this, I'm trying not t'fall on my Canal Zone and they're busy arguing about how many angels can sit on the head of a cabin cruiser."

"All right." Merry has relinquished her interest in him. Arthur, the principal shareholder now, tilts left with Simon. "That was stupid. I'm sorry."

"Robert, my cane. Uncle—you let go, too."

"Can you manage?"

"Listen, children. I will probably fall down a great deal: ignore it the way you would a dowager's belch. Remember, it doesn't hurt and I'm loose as someone on Methaqualone injections. Forward. Goodbye, Peggy: it was a pleasure being part of your late adolescence. And if that nurse comes in t'ask if I've voided today—tell her, Yes. Yes, indeed."

"Oh, I'll see you tomorrow afternoon, Mr. Lynxx. Bobby's giving me a screen test."

"He is, is he? Written or oral?"

"Simon, I didn't think you'd mind."

"No-no, this is just the time: when we're out of film. Let her play Godot: especially his great entrance scene." Simon is triangulating: he has a course now. "Y'know, I useta fight gravity when I walked. I hate laws. And it reminded me of Aldo for some reason. But now I have no weight. I'm like an astronaut on the moon: it's not a bad sensation: I'm kinda hovering. I'm that famous lead balloon that people talk about. Merry, you there?"

"Yes."

"S'long, Flavor Bud."

"Is that it? Is that all?"

"Yah. I think. Don't take an Alpine slide over it. I'd like t'have raised the pot and seen your hole card. I'd like t'have cross-pollinated with you and maybe even had dinner in a good Szechuan restaurant. But my Long Tom won't fire and there're other irreconcilable similarities. Wishya the best, Lamb Chop of God. Let's move, Arthur, Robert, before I go splat on my Great Divide and ruin that nice exit speech."

Simon leans toward the door. And his feet, invited as an afterthought, come along.

2

Pop

"—that, *that,* I could have done without, believe me. But, no, instead she—" Norty Sollivan has cut his throat again—

Pop-hsssp.

—and Simon is deaf for the third or fourth time today.

An interval. Pop.

"—father of his grandchildren. Right?"

"Uh-huh."

"Uh-huh? Are you listening? Eh, Simon? Shit, old bar-buddy, I can't get over how wrecked you look. Knock-knock, hello? I don't wanna rub it in, but you got that crazy hemp-head nigger stare again. Like you had bifocals on. Like I'm down here and you're up there being very far-sighted or something. Maybe I'm dead already, huh? And you can't see me. Huh? Zip and zip." Norty has slashed both wrists, a fingernail slit across each: underneath, where they're fat as cold cuts. Slow Roman death yet kosher enough. Beard growth of Monday is still there. Rug remnants from his crew cut, several almost one half inch round, were worn off on the pillow last night: scalp, a shining dime of it here and there, will flash through. Anxiety plus recurrent suicide have somehow untanned him: he is without complexion at all. That, too, tires Simon out. "Listen, f'me it's been combat training with live ammo every day. I never needed to believe in an angry father God. I had Herman and with Herman every day was Yom Kippur. He led me out of Egypt into poodle shit, Simon. He saw I got manna, but he gave like it was *shalach monoth:* charity for the crippled-up. He wouldn't admit it, that he needed me. Oh-ho, it was no office party with mistletoe for me—I mean, to take that hawkwoman, that daughter, off his hands. I did him a favor. If it wasn't for me—listen, even the greediest chiselers stopped dead in their tracks at the thought of living with Adele. Now she's gone home to him. Most of all he can't forgive me that. No, now he—"

Pop.

Simon, quite casual, hit or miss, raps on his mastoid with the wooden cane head. Rap and rap: raps, that is, where a mastoid ought to live: within earshot of it anyhow. No pickup, he's still off the air: a shoddy connection someplace. Simon is almost accustomed to this: this moment of silence (in memory, in spite?) about five times each day. Like Arthur and his 1956 Buick radio, he has been rushing to hit the special pothole of sound. Rap: then he will stop. Given the gist of Norton's complaint, Simon is probably better off deaf. Moreover, this fourth affliction has been, to him, humiliating: as a bloody show in women might be. He has tried to keep his tics of hard-hearing on the quiet, auricular: they shame him. There isn't much left: men with one finger don't gladly shake hands.

Eleven to eleven: Wolff and Kyryl, the effrontery of it, have kept him waiting nineteen minutes here tonight. Simon doesn't approximate that: since Wednesday he has worn his old Omega watch, banded by time like a migrant bird. Duration and sense of touch are, in some high percussive way, dependent on each other. Simon, whose pulse, unfelt now, was his private chronometer and almanac, can no longer beat the separate seconds out: they measure an elsewhere, a different place. He would leave Ten Great Ferry, but the walk up, all those delegated hand-foot tasks, have left his will overdrawn: it has no credit line. Simon just watches. Nort is committing low-comic hara-kiri: both hands on the Samurai blade to pry drawer after drawer of his stomach bureau out: with a narrative line that won't lip-read well. It isn't Saturday night: it is a week from Saturday night. Simon, you see, has kept Wolff and Kyryl waiting, too. He dunks his head: hearing did seem, once upon, to be a clear blood that ran best downhill. But no sound effect will come. And Nort, in a suicide break, has caped Simon with his muscle-built right arm: from shoulder to shoulder, seen. How heavy, how incumbent on him that device of friendship once was. Now it is volatile, more impression than act. A bizarre disablement, this, that can make Norty seem suave.

Pssh. Op.

"—know I'm hugging him."

"What?" Christ, sound is loud. And dear. "What?"

"You don't hear me?"

"I hear you fine. So?"

"So, look. Look at that, my old army pal has a cane. Son of a bitch. Some job he did on you. Throw an arm around my best sidekick—how many roadside hookshops have we closed, huh?—throw an arm around him and he doesn't even feel. I could be in an isolation booth. But, if it gives you any joy, which it probably won't, Herman went to temple last Saturday. After you said you couldn't come here. You threw a scare into him. The rabbi was scared, too. He thought Herman was looking for a film location: couldn't be any other reason, hah?" Norty, hand to head, discharges a pistol: at fingertip-blank range. He will flop back against the couch: eyes roll up white. "Oh, shit. Oh, yes. I'd have given a month's salary—which I'm unlikely to collect after November 1—to've seen that *meshugaas*. Herman Wolff mugged by lunatic coons. Herman with kaka in his pants. Everyone knows. You saw him the way only his mother saw him. And her he'd knock on the head, too, if you could hire a hit man for the dead. Huh?"

"Yeah. Right."

But Simon, by listening carefully, has not heard. Children around him make vagrant noise: they are, to Simon, like voice parts of a lucid motet: whine and laugh orchestrated, shriek in nice arrangement. Only silence can be dissonant. It is bedtime for the commune at Ten Great Ferry. Kyryl's rotating gallery floor has wound down. His SEM tooth plaque statue seems just furniture: stately and impractical: like the idiot firstborn of royal blood, honored yet shut away. Motherhood and child-hood are promiscuous here: parentage is a joint venture, eclectic as Kyryl's other art. Simon can account for at least eighteen people: six women, twelve children. A two-year-old will stagger past him with no cane. Unbonded pairs kneel to retrieve play gear: cap gun, Matchbox car fleet, a Lego set, small airport and small shopping center, one arc of Lionel track. Such things, remarkable, snap and clatter and tink. Simon is eavesdropping in plain sight, tapping their wire: his acoustics are punc-tual now. Five children of self-dressing age chant a vesper prayer:

> "Now he lays him down to sleep
> He prays Our Lord his soul to keep.
> If he should die before he wakes,
> That's the way the cookie breaks."

Simon has auditioned them. At the couch's end, five feet away, a woman is breast-feeding: one child clipped on each teat. She gushes: they pilfer her. Simon, he could swear, can hear lactation. Her breasts are illus-trious, glassy-full: yet no more sexual to him than the egg-packed stom-ach of a queen wasp. Mouths smack and gnaw: smack and guh-naw, he has said it aloud. Oh, onomatopoeia: chime, flute, trill. Even the words for sound are sonorous. His vision is rocked. Norty shakes him again.

"Hey. You there?"

"Norty. Come out with it. What is it you want?"

"Want? Want? Is that the way to talk? You and me, hey, remember that night you were so smashed you drove us both into Caribou Lake? Lucky it was a convertible or I coulda been another Mary Jo Ko-whatsis. Huh? And come to think of it, she's in better shape."

"All I have nostalgia for now, Norty, is my behind. I'm flying standby over thin air. My life is one long dump taken with the seat up. Too many surprises. So, like I say, what is it you want? Why're you here?"

"Because, kid—I'm whispering now—because they want me to soften you up. Or at least find out which way your wind is blowing. The reason I haven't been fired outright from NA is they think I might have some influence with you. Little do they know what a prick you are. Listen: Herman is afraid of a damage suit or even criminal charges. You have him right where I want him. He's ready to forgive and forget and pay for the privilege. Me, I'm finished. I have no illusions about that. When he's done settling with you—poof—Herman presses the squelch button and I'm gone. Dead. I mail a letter to myself and it comes back marked Undeliverable. Shot while trying to escape. Dead." Norty hangs himself by the neck until bored: head at a fantastic angle, much tongue out. "She wants divorce. She left. She left me and took the kids. One mistake. Just one. Georgette sent me a love letter, to my house—to my *home*— what mistress is such a jerk? Quick, without even reading it, I ripped the sucker in a million pieces. Flush. Right down the basement john. I know my wife: she smells the mail. Even a Spencer's Gift Catalogue, a letter from the congressman: God help me if there's perfume on it. So I flushed and I ran. Did I know my son, the young scientist, had dropped a ton of Play-Doh in to see if it floats? Play-Doh don't float, Simon. It sits there. The john did nothing. It backed up like a storm sewer in Far Rockaway, and, before I know what hit me, my wife is in there drying out pieces of Georgette. A few sentences were missing, but she got the storyboard. Jesus, Miss Upper East Side on her knees sifting through the shitter. Disgusting. And they say I have no class. Right away she's on the phone to Herman. Dead. I'm a no deposit, no return at NA. The cleaning woman hasn't emptied my basket since Monday. The lock on the executive bathroom has been changed. Huh? I suppose, with all your trouble, you couldn't care less?"

"No. Not much. I'm sorry."

"I didn't think so. Oh, boy. Oh, boy. My downfall will be much applauded around town. Toasts will be drunk. I shouldn't be selfish, I should think of all the pleasure I'm giving—gluggg." Norty's hand has risen: to chin, to mouth, to nose, a water level. "The alimony. Oh, boy. They'll need a deep-water port to bring it in. Shiffman, Wolff's lawyer, is in stitches when I call him up. Outraged she was: heart-smashed, humiliated. A cruel affront to her womanhood. Not cruel enough, though, that she didn't forget to take my bankbook and the safety-deposit key. I'm dead. I'm an open sandwich. They'd lower the curtain, but maybe you and me—they can't be sure."

A Superball has rolled dead against Simon's heel: bounce, some backspin, stop. In a moment he is lonely for sport: for the surprise of unknown competition and reflex: an event that always gave him more pleasure than deliberate art. There was syntax and metaphor in the body spontaneous, sung: baseline jumper, crosscourt handball smash, straight right over dropped left hand. Simon will try to play the Superball as it lays: pitch shot with his cane tip. Miss, miss, miss, miss, shank. Five over par and—flaaaaange, ah, dah-ownnn: barrel-roll, veeeer. The couch is gone from under him. Simon, eye concentration lost, will fall, will fall. He is rotating now, thrown clay. Look, look, look: see the SEM sculpture, see Norty, see her left breast: run a visual surveyor's chain from each to each to each. Wow: upright and seated again, What? Who? A girl child, rabid with toothpaste, kisses Simon good night. She is catholic about her parentage, it might include him or it might not. Nonetheless, Simon can tell. Even here, in this dollhouse of pop grotesque, with the aberrant and the radical-freak, Simon still has frightened her. His bandages are off. White skin is showing: so much of it, so high and thick, that he might be scalp-wigged in the manner of clowns. Scar tissue, rare, a New York cut, must seem like boot-lacing there. His lips are big and glazy-brown: the color of jellied madrilene: macabre. Simon has had 96 hours' cockpit time on his new feet: he can move with rule-book efficiency enough. But the eyes have had it. They are morbid, gibbous: hairy with blood threads: they may hatch. Simon has been dreaming through his eyes. Even the subconscious him is a watcher-from-inside.

"—what's left for me? Sure, I could always get a job like my uncle, Hymie the Measurer. Never missed a day in thirty years. The depression squeezed him dry, but Hymie was a fighter, he didn't give up. He bought two POLICE LINE sawhorses, a yardstick, some chalk, one of those tape things you pull out and a green uniform with hooks so he could snap a whole tool kit on. Also a sign that said CAUTION—BUREAU OF MEASUREMENT. Rain or shine he would be on the job. A busy neighborhood? It didn't bother Hymie. Fifth Avenue, Flatbush Avenue, Northern Boulevard: he liked pressure. And, listen, he got respect. Eight A.M. he would set up, right in the middle of the fast lane. Nobody bothered him: he was the only man in the city who gave a full day's work. It was always his idea—he could wear you down with this brainstorm—it was his idea that we didn't know how big or how little things were. So, with the chalk he drew lines. The middle of Broadway, it didn't matter. Cops knew him: they would direct traffic around. And every night Hymie would mail a registered letter to the mayor, I have carbons somewhere: 'Do you realize, Your Honor, that the sewer on 59th and Madison is exactly four feet six inches from the pedestrian crosswalk and consists of a grating with seventy-two holes, each three inches square?' My aunt would pack him a lunch and a kiss goodbye. After 1929 his brain went sour: he wanted job security. No pension or benefits, no pay envelope even, but job security he had plenty of. 'And,' he would say to me, 'and I'm my own boss.' There was some kind of beauty in it, don't you think? Yeah. Beauty. But it was also fortunate that Aunt Mitzie was a high-class waitress six days a week."

"What's this all about, Norty?"

"I'm not ready to be a measurer yet, Simon. That much of a romantic I'm not. I know it sounds small-minded, but I still wanna bust chops and make waiters sweat. Is that unreasonable? To have my Porsche brought round at three P.M.? A picture of me in the Sunday People Section in return for leaking personal dirt from NA? Huh? To give a private interview and general fitting session to some model-turned-starlet now and then? You can understand what I'm getting at: of all people, you. These are daily requirements like potassium in the system. And listen—it's the craziest thing—all I need right now is one good word from you. In there. When you go in there."

"From me? You're insane. I'm on Simon Weisenthal's hit parade."

"No. No. Can't you see?" Norty is distressed: his hands strangle each other: they have a suicide pact. "I told you already, jerk. I'm on the schneid, but you could be a big filmmaker by midnight tonight. The fix is in. I get it at NA: people are asking for your phone number, what hooch you drink. You'll never need toilet paper again. That was a three- to five-million-dollar schmeck you got."

"Aaaah," a yawn. Simon has rapped the floor with his cane. Three hard knocks: let the performance begin. "Why're they keeping me? Is Rose in there? I've heard that Rose is with him now."

"Her. By any other name she'd stink the joint up as much. She sold Herman the Williamsburg Bridge and he bought it. You haven't heard? She's his new relative: he may have lost a son-in-law, but he gained a niece. Didn't you notice the resemblance, ha?"

"What?"

"Look, I don't mind taking three or four giant steps downward. It isn't I want to stay at NA. That'd be the iron sweat box without even visiting hours for my own mind. I'd need a court order to get exhumed. But you. For this film you've gotta have an associate producer. Okay, all right—I'm asking too much. A production assistant, someone in publicity—"

"Norty—"

"Please. Let me get it all out. You know what he can do. When he's finished I'll be the whole Hollywood Ten. Okay: so there were times when I didn't stick up for you when I should have. But I was scared. I'm a desperate man now. You've never had it, Simon. You don't know what happens in the belly when you lose it. All I'm crapping since Monday is mucus and water, just mucus and water. I can't even shit. In this business a person without a past still has a future. I'm about to have a very bad past."

"Norty—"

"We've shared the same dose of clap, Simon. We've punched the same people. You always said I drank like a goy—and I thought, for you, that was a great compliment. Just tell him to go easy on me. Just tell him you want me on the job with you. He'll listen." Simon bangs his cane. "You want to say something? I can tell. Go ahead, say it. Feel free to speak."

"Words fail me."

"You? Come on. That's not the Simon I know."

"I've been out of touch. For some time now."

"Simon—"

"I'm feeling around and, y'know, all I come up with is a mild distaste. What you say—I hear it, but it's scrambled. It doesn't print out on my screen. I remember hearing that some African tribe, when a woman ran away from her husband—they put a white-hot coal behind her knee and tied her ankle t'her thigh until the coal burned through the ligaments. And I thought, now that's pretty severe. I felt disgust, but not enough t'write Kurt Waldheim. After all, it didn't have anything t'do with me. It was their way of making a point: t'each his own. Live and let live, that's why they call it the Third World, I guess. And, sure, it wasn't my knee. What I mean is: you disgust me, Norty, my good friend, but not too much."

"Oh, boy." Norty has jammed hands under his own rib cage: as if to roll it up like a venetian blind. "Oh, boy. I didn't expect that. Not from you. Disgust. Is it my manner? Is it because I'm whining? I might as well find out, now's as good a time as any. Other people have expressed the same opinion. Now you—you could be attractive, yet you always repelled people. It was hard work, but you made a point of it. With me it was second nature. From birth. So. I disgust you."

"Norty. This place is Mondo Ersatz. It's piss from an artificial kidney. Get out, friend. Cut your losses and run. I know a couple of guys'll give you a good shot in the head."

"Zen I never understood."

"Get out. Get a decent job. Lift things. Push them. Whatever. It stinks in here. I know that and I can't even smell. They don't bury their dead deep enough. They never know when they'll want a snack."

"Sure. You're probably right on the nose. But I'm one of the dead already and what else can I do? When Herman cuts you off, even the candy machines in the lobby say OUT. I'll get stuck with kid payments enough to keep a whole Boys Town running."

"How long have I been here? Why is he making me wait?"

"I'm not trained, Simon. I'm trained to be a son-in-law and order people around. You don't see that job listed in the New York *Times*."

"Norty. Just once more. Listen to me: we were always small-timers. A couple guys with a cardboard carton hustling bucks at three-card monte on Forty-second and Seventh. We never had what it takes. We were in the wrong business."

"I know, I know, but—"

"Go in, Norty. Tell him I'm not waiting any longer."

"I can't. Not without a promise. I'm scared. I haven't saved a cent. I'll be nothing."

"Jesus—"

"Promise me—lie to me, but promise. Promise, if you get money for the big film, you'll clear it with Herman. You'll give me a job."

"I promise."

"You're lying. But, no: don't tell me. Don't tell me. That's my good buddy. That's my special friend. I knew you'd come through." Norty has his hand on Simon's biceps: tight as a sphygmomanometer. "Gee, I just wish you didn't look so thin. We gotta put some weight on you."

"Tell him."

"Sure. Sure. Now. I'll go. They've got some nerve, to keep you waiting."

Simon has wet himself again. Urine stain takes the right-hand fork, down his leg. Trouser material is deep navy blue: a tactful color: chosen by Arthur with just such misadventures in mind. An automobile key ring —KWIK PIK USED CAR SERVICE—trails from the zipper fly tab: for e-z finger grip. Simon can recall the discomfort he should be feeling: wet swimsuit on under his pants through a two-hour school-bus ride back from Candlewood Lake: no, he doesn't miss that. Negligently Simon will slipcover his tweed jacket skirt across groin and soaking leg. Arthur has also bought Simon warm slide-on moccasins. And his new shirt is zipper-down-the-front: ASTORIA BUICK on that tab. He ought to sell ad space like a minor-league outfield wall. But shirt collars faze Simon: they force him to blink. Last Monday he almost vanished without trace in a turtleneck: head through to some other, illogical universe and time. Arthur cut the sweater off. At least, unlike an amputee, he has no commemorative ache in arm or leg. These are already implements, not limbs: the life instinct, unsentimental, has adjusted. Movement rides a visual Star Route: delivering advice to that windlass shoulder, that derrick knee. He has special affection for objects now and a common interest. Animal, vegetable, mineral: which would the answer be, were he, "Simon," the question? Fingers wickerwork together above his crotch: the cane reined in tight between them. All ready at a moment's noticing.

"Careful. Watch."

The woman, heavily papoosed, backs toward Simon. Under long nightgown hem, her big bare heel is shapeful as a beanbag-ashtray base. Simon will recruit his left hand: order it up to sustain a collision, though there are no impacts for him now. He can read the ID bracelet on her wrist: AILEEN F106. Aileen F106 bends at knee and hip. For half a shake, while unharnessing, long black hair will shower her backpacked child. It wakes. The front-lit wall is prurient: her substantial nude buttock cheek crouches, heaves into sight through sheer rayon. What a goodly mother: what a secure fortress and hiding place. Simon, with delicacy, will dispatch his glance elsewhere. The metal and blue canvas child carrier, half unshouldered, hangs like a bosun's chair. Aileen has smiled at him: he grins, but cannot recapitulate the subtlety and intonation of a smile. They share couch space. Canvas turns inside out with her child. It is drowsing: a one-stoplight town on Sunday afternoon. Aileen has thumbed open the Pamper: to read and construe a healthy brunette bowel movement there.

"Oh, I'm sorry. I'm used to it, the stink. That wasn't very polite."

"Not at all. It doesn't bother me at all."

"No?" She laughs. Her face is liberal: flat-cheekboned. She has a bosom, not breasts: they are one rich thing. The kind of body seen carved on old carousels. "No? Uh-huh. Well, if you don't mind this, either you've got one beaut of a head cold or you're the man I've been looking for since I first started looking, which is too long ago. But I guess you've been snapped up already. You've got kids of your own, I bet."

"Ah."

"I'm right, huh?"

"Kids? Yeah. Who hasn't?"

"Kids and roaches, you can't figure how they got in." She laughs. "Hey, would you mind keeping an eyeball on this one? Be a second, while I get another poop catcher. Y'don't haveta entertain him, just don't let him roll off the edge."

"Yes, but, I'm—"

"It's just down the hall. I'll run. I'm running. Hang in there."

"But—"

How did this happen? Simon, with his premature child, is rattled: is suffering from sudden full-nest syndrome. How in hell to pick the infant up if it falls—he has no carrying capacity left. Simon will moon-land one conscientious finger on the bare-boned chest, child support, as you might pin down cord before tying off a package knot. There is protest and reflex. New hands flap around, sweeping the field for tangible evidence. Both grip his finger. Simon recalls how they used to choose up in baseball, fist atop fist on a bat. Though unfelt, he can tell that the grasp is already veteran: want, take: first- and secondhand information. Once his palm, too, could hear like a snake's tongue: all matter has characteristic vibrancy. Simon bends. And, upside down, his cowface is stimulating. The nude child has begun to squirm: gums champ. It, he won't forget this occasion: nineteen years from now, reading *Moby Dick*, that whale of a forehead will loom again: pallid, hairless, ocean-eyed: personally archetypical. In a freshman literature class, for one April moment, old disquiet will make him breathe out and start. The primal fear of Simon: and of covering whiteness, upside down.

But now a plastic baby bottle has distracted Simon. Why didn't Arthur think of that? He can dispense with glasses that no longer dispense at all. Self-conscious, embarrassed by silence, as most men are with children, Simon will sing what Aldo had sung before: sung not to Simon, to that faceless, competitive sibling, his radio audience: "Come little leaves said the wind one day / come o'er the meadow with me and play: da-da, de-duh"—hum a snatch, *snatch.* Simon hooks the nippled bottle up. With gawky stealth he will squeeze it at his mouth. Milk has gone in. The child watches: judging, yet not judgmental. Its eyes, also, are over-tasked: they play pepper, ricochet. There is so much to be indexed: movement: color on big flat flash cards: the wonderful "in front" and "be-hind" of depth perception: most important, how to ignore what will not be me-related. It yawns. And Simon, cradle robber, is off the bottle just in time.

"Haven't you seen one of those before?"

"No. Just looking. What?"

"It's got a little plastic liner bag inside, collapses so there's always a vacuum. See. God bless the guy who thought it up. No more air bubbles. Cuts down on burping and that echy wet belch, you know what I mean, the one that oozes down your shoulder blade. Great invention. Uh, you can take your finger off now. You're pressing kinda hard. It's not a tiger you're holding down."

"My finger? Oh."

"This kid's okay. Some of them here, wow. Play us off one against the other like riverboat gamblers. Real manipulation." She has unscrewed a tube of salve. "The one I had last Wednesday—"

"This isn't your child?"

"Nope."

"Who's the mother?"

"I dunno. Who knows? Kyryl's supposed to—but sometimes I think he isn't all that interested. He takes them away when they're born and mixes them up. Borrows here and there. He can really hide a card in the deck. This could be mine, I wouldn't know except that my last—and I mean my *last*—was two years ago."

"Simon! You're on deck." Norty is waving a come-ahead from the Bronze Room door.

"And the father? Is it Kyryl?"

"Kyryl? Man, Kyryl makes it *only* with himself—in front of the mirror. And we're the mirror. A very flattering mirror, you bet."

"Then it doesn't have a mother or father?"

"Well, it has lots of them. Kyryl says that's better. Art can't progress unless we have a new set of neuroses: the Oedipus complex is dead. I dunno. Good or bad? Ask the kid in fifteen years."

"Hey, Simon."

"They're calling you." She is apprehensive.

"And you don't miss your child?"

"Well, there are days. And then there are other days. Dig it?" She laughs. "Hell, any mother'd tell you the same thing. The little bastards can get to me. This way I don't have any guilt. And he won't either. He won't forget Mother's Day and have a heavy trip laid on. I guess it depends what you wanna leave behind when you kick the big bucket."

"What d'you want?"

"Me, I'm into Navajo sand painting. I think I can be a great Navajo sand painter. Not that I'm a Navajo, of course, but—"

"Yoo-hoo, Simon."

"Better not keep him waiting."

"Why?"

"It isn't worth it. No, sir. Believe me it is not."

"Ah, well. Those bottles—can you get them at Woolworth's like?"

"Sure, why? You gonna have another kid?"

"No. I've got one already."

"This age?"

"No. Yes. Maybe a little younger, give or take."

"Simon!"

"I'll go. I'll get up now and go."

So this, at last, is the great Bronze Room: a nine-day wonder in pop art for almost thirty years. It has been cast whole: from the largest single mold ever shaped and broken. Bronze: floor, wall, chair, table, lamp, book, bookcase, window, windowpane: pencil and manuscript page, ashtray and butt on the bronze desk: bronze. A seamless place in which no object can be moved. Yet the paint is exquisitely persuasive: *trompe le doigt*. Dark mahogany-grained panelling: azure drapes: one tulip in its long-stemmed bowl. A Persian carpet is gold and green and amber, bronze thread over bronze thread, woven with paint. Bronze sunlight—the permanent cast from life of 1 P.M., May 15, 1942—has been painted glaring through bronze glass aslant. It is a spiteful attack on sanity: people, left alone here, have thrown up. All substances, under color, are one substance: they are hollow and go bonk when hit by a duped fist. As though the atomic stuffs from which everything was made had given away their trick of valence and modulation: difference is gone, or is known for what it always must have been—a superficial hoax: the same dull matter arranged, rearranged. Young Kyryl brought this to Ten Great Ferry in 1952: Simon can recall hearing that. On a flatbed truck since adapted to coax Atlas missiles into place. It was his entire *oeuvre* then: a decade spent and 80,000 pounds of metal. That weight is present. Simon, who has been passing duty-free through the planet's gravitational tug, will sense it. Weight without texture. The place is appropriate to his state of mind. He feels at home: a nomad in another desert now.

"Sit. Sit." Wolff is hospitable for someone else. "Pull up a chair, not that you can pull anything up in this crazy-genius room. The trash can, look, it has metal paper garbage in it. I forgot and almost broke my hand throwing a Kleenex out."

They are lime-lit for him: Wolff behind the bronze desk, under a Florida-tan baby spot: Kyryl washed bland by salmon-pink gels. Kyryl is sitting, socket loose, on the high bronze/pine dunce's stool. Head and body have an aquatic temperament: modified, as it were, to take advantage of undertows or the slack tidal shift that might be left in some half-dead estuary. Simon has begun to walk ahead. His cane clonks on parquet, clonks on thick rug: it is like moving inside a misconceived bell. He can't see clearly. A white spotlight has been assigned to him: it follows or it leads. There is, in all this commonplace furniture, in that violent 1942 spring sunlight, the troubled, shoddy stillness of an Edward Hopper painting: where color will denote affliction or loneliness, not various joy. But, to his right, surreal, goldfish are roiling in bronze sediment and their own sloughed-off scales. The pond might be five foot square: hardly one foot full. Fish thrash to conceal their fins: under and under each other, the way a mob would retreat inward on itself when fired at. They plop: water smacks of fish. That sound will agitate him throughout.

"Hello, Simon."

Three chairs confront the desk: they seem to hold a closed hearing about it. Each is grain-scoop shape: the scoop bowl set upright on its handle. Rose has been sitting in her lesser light just there. She smiles: the hello first spoken above is repeated for effect. An eyesore, Simon will peer down at her. But Rose, in keeping with the room's theme, is brazen. He can perceive no remorse. She has contrived, rather, a comprehensive accusation. Of what, what-dammit?, Simon would like to know: unprofitable time spent? a compromising liaison? or the sexual pleasure that she once acknowledged with bit, blunt fingernails dug in along his back-rib flesh? Clipboard and yellow pad square her lap. The sneakers have been left off. She is wearing a high-top leather buttoned shoe. The dress has puff sleeves and long hobble skirting. Alone, on another chair, yet able to occupy it as a person would, is her wide, veiled equestrienne hat. Rose's scarce hair has been taken up: the bun tense, a crossbow wound to fire. She appears in restraint, bound by convention: doing time maybe, some other time than this. Simon has sat. His scoop is padded with a kind of metal shaving: he has seen such on the floor beneath lathes. Fish splatter beneath their low combat ceiling: the heavy slap of chops licked.

"Norty, you can make a guest disappearance: so long. And pick up a crippling disease while you're out." The door has gonged shut: a sound of either cathedrals or prisons, Simon can't decide. "Bum. Skirt-chaser.

After all I did for him, he gave my only child a breakdown. Under a nurse's care she is, around the $30 per hour clock. Not only was he playing loose and fast but—this I just found out—he passed her a case of crabs. My daughter is so innocent she called the termite people in. But you can't understand, you have no children yet. Adele's unhappiness is my unhappiness: believe me, she sees to that. Well. But, well. This isn't why we're here." Wolff tries to lift the pencil: but it is just pencil color, not a pencil, and won't come up. "I keep forgetting. Well, do we need an introduction? Kyryl you know, as who in the world doesn't? And my niece, Rose, is an ex-employee of your own Lynxx Productions."

"She's your which? My hearing isn't so good—not t'mention my gross credulity."

"Uncle Herman, I don't think we should go into it with Simon. He has a skeptical mind, and this is, you know, *family*."

"Why not? A surprise, Simon? To me as well. The nicest I've had since my wife told me she was pregnant after twelve years of doing my best three times a week. Rose is the only child of my lost brother. You may remember, we spoke about him on that night which is better left forgotten now."

"*Uncle* Herman? Come on, everybody, is this the real world, or is it a segment of 'Mr. Rogers' Neighborhood'? Spare me, huh? If you're his niece, Rose, I'm Jesus' bastard get."

"I knew he'd—"

"Herman, check your money clip, she's got all the attachments on her little Hoover. Swopp! and gone. You think I yanked your beerpull, wait'll she starts tending bar around here. Rose doesn't believe in the two-party system."

"Hah, you don't think I wasn't suspicious, also, at first? Research has gone into this, Simon. There are documents and photographs. I'm not such a fool."

"Where certain parts of Brooklyn're concerned, you've got a negative number upstairs. If I could smell, this whole thing'd stink like a broiled umbrella."

"Simon—" Rose has been taking the temperature of her bun with a ball-point pen: normal apparently. "Let bygones be bygones. We've shared a lot. It was fun. Now, for some crazy reason, you feel I've screwed you. But how? Think about it. There was never any contract between us. And, look at things this way, I'll be better able to help you now. We all want to help you. That's why my uncle asked you to come. Right?" Wolff nods. "See? How are you?"

"Let's say my feelings are hurt. Herman, this is none of my business. You want Rose t'be your network affiliate, fine. Meanwhile, what's up? What can I do for you? You're a busy man, uncle and father, and I'm up well past my bedtime, which is twenty-four hours a day of late."

"Watch, Rose. He's going to make it hard on me. He's going to pull teeth. I can hear it in his voice—"

"Ahhhhh." Kyryl has inhaled through one nostril: his atomizer dispenses strange relief. Wolff is waiting.

"Yes, Kyryl?"

"Mmmm?"

"You wanted to say?"

"Nothing. I said nothing."

"Where were we?" The inhale has distracted Wolff. Simon is irate: no one man's breath should be so determinative.

"You asked me down here. I could've seen *Pather Panchali* twice in the time it took me t'dress. Now what?"

"Right." Wolff tamps his forehead with a handkerchief. "Simon, I'm beside myself. Believe me, things weren't supposed to turn out this way. With you so hurt. But that's what happens when you hire blacks."

"They did okay when I used them."

"With a VISA card left behind? You call that okay? If I could tell you the maids my wife went through. So. So. It's water under the bridge. So." Wolff will ask for corroboration. "Look, Rose. He's coming along, isn't he? And without the hair now he reminds me of someone. Handsome, a mature young man, a world beater."

"The picture's been retouched, Herman. I'm a mock-up of me: it's orientation day every morning. Someone's riding gain on my amplifier: the needle doesn't move at all. I'm a wreck. It'd get me down, if I could remember which way down was."

"Please don't rub it in. I'm heartbroken."

"Is that what your EKG says? Look, you nearly killed me, don't bore me t'death. What's on your mind? I haveta go home and put name tapes on my hands."

"Okay. Businesslike you want, businesslike it'll be." Wolff has made a victory sign. "Two things. One, first, about medical care, not a worry. From the bills I've had, your blood type must be Chivas Regal. Ha. But that's fine, I can stand it. For as long as you need help."

"Great. I've saluted, you can dismiss the color guard. Next item."

"Sure. Next item. I made a promise to you that night. It stands, even despite—can I say?—despite your somewhat unethical procedures. Kyryl has agreed. Correct?" Wolff would like Kyryl to underwrite him. But Kyryl, high on his stool, will neither move nor speak. It is a luxury, Simon thinks, that famous people alone can afford: the rest of us must answer: or at least display life. "See. What did I tell you? We're behind Simon Lynxx one hundred percent. The money has been cleared. It's already in your name: you can begin drawing tomorrow. No, Monday. Three million dollars. Well? Three million and more if you need. For the film." Simon will turn to his right: goldfish, packed like sardines, make jelly of their water. "Sure, you're a bandit, but I like that. What you did to me Nixon wouldn't do, still it took chutzpah. And I learned from it. So. So, crime pays."

"No." Simon will begin to rise: will set that irksome business on foot.

"No?" Wolff is grinning. "A three-million-dollar no?"

"Three million. What does that mean t'you, Herman? A tax write-off? A decimal point moved? Three million is what goes up Kyryl's left nostril in a year. I can't accept that as compensation. I was a great feeler once. I could grope the globe. Give me the shape of a breast in my hand and I might consider it. But no. No millions."

"I half expected this."

"You can fully expect it. I'm going."

"Wait." The desk bongs.

"Yes?"

"It's Jewish money, is that it—eh, Mr. Big *Petzelle?* For you, Jewish money has germs on it."

"Gosh, no, Herman. I've always been an equal opportunity opportunist, you know that."

"Still, there's a difference between us, that's how you see it, no? You're big and you drink and you throw things away. You make noise and you're poor. All this somehow makes you an American and a gentleman, which I somehow can't carry off: that's what you think, right? You sneer at a Jew."

"Uh-uh. Let's get it straight, I want this business t'be clear, especially now. I'll tell you how I feel about Jews. I have an almost superstitious awe. And I'm afraid. That. That, and I'm jealous. I've been alone: as far as I can tell, a Jew is never alone. But sneer, uh-uh, I'm not that dumb."

"Well, Mr. American gentleman—"

"I don't think you're listening."

"I hear, Mr. Son of the American Revolution. I also hear the latest about your mother and father."

"Oh? What about them?"

"That they weren't. You're not a Van anything—with a manor house back to George Washington. They weren't your mother and father. You're a nothing."

"Thank you, Rose, for the update. So?"

"So." Wolff smiles. "So, *kveller,* you could be Jewish. It's possible. Did you think of that?"

"Not much. About as much as I thought of myself as an American gentleman. But you thought that: that's how you still see me, apparently. Hanh, it's funny. I'll have to think about that. I'd never have guessed."

"Listen. The year before you were born I was six months in and out of England. I had a percentage of Castle Films. I got around with the ladies."

"A married man, too. Poor Carlotta. Did you import a case of crabs?"

"Schmuck. You miss the point."

"No, I don't. You're saying I could be your illegitimate son."

"It's possible, isn't it? Why not? You can't be sure. You'll never be sure. Would you then sneer at yourself?"

"No. Rose and I would be first cousins. Gee, I could have my own documents and photographs. Are you offering to acknowledge me, Herman?"

"I'm saying—"

"Never mind, I accept. Simon Van Wolff. Why not? If you're not my father, you're probably like him. Only shorter. Hanh, I'm honored. I've been rootless long enough. I accept."

"You're making fun."

"Hell, no. I respect you. I'm afraid of you. What more should a good son feel?"

"Then it's on, we can shake."

"Oh, you mean the money. I see: my portion. No, but I'll get bar mitzvahed. I'll have a second briss: I wouldn't feel the pain. I've got a local anesthetic all over. But not the money."

"Why? Why?" Wolff shakes his head. "The gentleman from no place is still talking, I see."

"No."

"Then why the big *tzimmes* over a little money? Take. Look, if it would make you feel more at home, if you don't want to be indebted—I could leave it around and you could break into my apartment. Huh, bandit?"

"Thanks but no thanks, I don't steal from family."

"Simon." Wolff has stood up: the spotlight will open and follow him. Fish boil like french fries in deep fat. Simon, chair-borne, unable-bodied, is defenseless: Wolff could kill him now. "Then why did you come here tonight? You could guess what was up."

"I almost didn't, you know. I almost didn't come, but then—after all— like some kid I hadda go and endanger myself. Fifty bucks, three million, whatever it was, I hadda see if it'd still jerk my cord. The temptation. And maybe it kinda appealed t'my melodramatic side, too. I mean, if I dropped out of the running here, in the Fiction Factory itself, where all sleazy dreams come true. Hanh? Also—also I guess I wanted t'meet you again. See if you had changed. That is, if the way I perceived you would change—when I didn't want anything. And I like you better this way. It becomes you, Herman. It becomes us both. Does that answer you? I really gotta go. I've taken up enough of your time."

"This is all fine and dandy, these reflections on life. But we're missing the important point—"

"Those fish are dying. Why isn't there more water? Herman, ask the Shaman of Sham why he doesn't put more water in his pond."

"Simon—"

"Ask him, g'wan."

"Ah—" Wolff is tentative: as we are when waking sleepers up. "Ah, Kyryl. For some reason my friend here seems to be concerned about the fish, of all things. Could you fill him in on that?"

"Nnnnnnnnn." Kyryl has a buzz on: the small amplifier grazes his raw larynx. "There's a leak we can't seem to locate. But the pond is never empty. We pour water in from time to time. They're quite alive—and this keeps them active. They'd bore me otherwise." It is a voice that should be listened to through hearing aids: the bronze, not the air, has brought it. "Will that be all, nnnnnn? My throat hurts."

"Right. That's all."

"Kyryl, while you've got the engine running—back me up in this. We're not seeing the forest for the trees. It isn't me. It isn't you, Simon. It's the film. You don't have a right to refuse. You don't have the *right*. I know your work, you're on the way to being a brilliant director. You have something special to give, something that—"

"Oh, go blow it out a shofar, Herman. Spare me that at least. I'm not brilliant. Sometimes, on a fair day, I can see a cloud that looks like a whale. Who could care less? I haven't got one idea worth two sixes in a crap game. And, Jesus, it's so much work. I'm tired. Just lucky I never had success, I'm not used to your standard of living. From here on in all I wanna do is get well. Right now even Mr. Bill'd feel sorry for me." Simon is on his own three feet: the light above him has gone dim. "Fuck film. Fuck the damned *image*. We're all of us fakes. Especially that coiled copperhead on the stool. My tooth kack isn't art. Uh-uh. No. No, sir." Simon has projected a triangle away from the desk. "Soon he'll figure out how t'market his own excrement. After all, it's just a matter of packaging. He'll sit on the thunder mug and get rich."

"Nnnnnnnn-ah."

"Yeah, Kyryl? What?"

"It's in the works, how did you guess?"

"Cuff links and bracelets and paperweights. Signed and set in Lucite. Maybe you could get Marlon Brando and Barbra Streisand t'take a laxative."

"There are many possibilities. The field is wide open."

"The art world'll wait on your regularity, I'm sure."

"Simon." Wolff has raised a hand. "Think things over, there still is time. You'll regret."

"Probably. But not enough. Anyhow: mucho grassy-ass f'giving me the chance t'kiss so many clams g'bye at one time. It's the high point in a career of nickel-dime bunko work. Rose, if it won't give you an attack of dysmenorrhea, do me a favor and open the door."

"You can't press charges. You haven't got a leg to stand on."

"You noticed? Please, Herman"—Simon has given Wolff his back—
"don't disappoint me. I've had a lousy experience rating with fathers as
it is."

"Nnnnn-zzahrr." The amplifier will peak: there is distortion. "Mr.
Lynxx. I want you to know that I don't approve. This has been made too
easy for you. I don't approve and I don't understand."

"Funny. I thought you would, of all people. I don't understand either.
What's more, I don't intend to."

"No?"

"No. And get this: I'm not even curious."

"How clever. You're cleverer than I thought. But you bore me already.
I'm turning the switch off now."

"Herman, I'll say *shivah* for you when the time comes. Or you for me,
huh? Whichever is first. G'night gentlemen."

Bronze-slam behind. Simon will rear up and, uh, lurch: full of crazy
angles in his high-stepping, like a Baltimore chop. Left foot, right foot,
cane: left foot, right foot, cane: it'll be tough to fill his shoes: right foot,
cane, left foot, right. Drool has fizzed out: he can't deputize a hand for
the mop-up action now. Simon is fishtailing: he bears off, ungainly as a
spinnaker in adverse wind. He has no hull balance: he can't locate his secret keel. And there are thirty feet of this pitch-toss walking still ahead:
past the SEM sculpture, to an EXIT door: feet, feet, feet, Simon knows
why they are called that. How come he didn't ask Rose or Wolff to con-
voy him out and down? Pride, yike, goeth before a complete folderoo.
Left, right, cane-left, right, left, cane-miss, left, cane, right: Simon can no
longer sight-read the prose of his movement. Too fast: this has happened
before. His upper body weight overshoots its chassis: headlong, at full
tilt. He will fall. But where? Against some wall, over the couch, into molecules of tooth plaque or?—good God—there's a woman on his narrow air
corridor. He might, with such linebacker momentum, blast her through
the wall into downtown So-Ho west.

"Look out, lookout, loooogout, bee-beep!"

But she doesn't hear. Her back is to him, attention on a full-length mirror and—mommy—see the swell woman-curving of that full-length spine.
Can bodies be aquiline? Well, this one is. She has designer-label legs:
rangy and high, they glassblow out into a blue tulip behind: that iliac is
sacro, man. On another day her nearness would have healed Simon: or
thrown him into violent remission at least. Yet here he is now, rumbling
down on her like a damn *incident*. Bee-beep. Hooga-hoo. Her blond
head, in the babushka, won't look around. At Ten Great Kyryl madcap
noise, scream and bang, are vernacular: the truly self-involved don't let
such things distract them. Twelve feet to impact. She has button-opened
the white blouse: as if to flash herself. Pose and pose: in sexual dead
heat with the mirror. And about to be bounced through her looking glass

by this human falling-rock zone, this cannonball local, by Simon. His one chance is Kyryl's eight-foot, all-aluminum statue of a tonsil. Left arm might snag it: might yet stop him the way trip cables on an aircraft carrier would. Coming in, coming in: the woman kisses her reflected lip. Simon, a basket case out of its basket, is bearing down—chump! Aluminum sproing. Hung upright, safe, still, on a tonsil. And now—now—she turns around.

"Oh, huh. Hi. You all right?"

"Shure. Just leaning on this iron glottis, if that's what it is. I'm fine."

"Hey. Hey, you're the doctor. You're him. Like, your hair is all gone, but I remember you. Jesus jodhpurs. You're the doctor. Right here. I turn around and, poof, you're right here."

"We've met?" Her face is gorgeous but trivial: a platitude of beauty. And she seems shorter than whoever she was before. "I can't place—"

"Hey, it's Annie. Old Annie-me. Don't you remember? We were gonna do sex at Herman Wolff's party, but then we got off the subject. Oh, jeepers. I've wanted t'thank you. I've wanted and wanted. Hey, this is super, that you're here. I mean, you're right here."

"Annie? Wait, let me guess—upstairs, in the room with all the funny circus heads." Simon would like to beat it: this woman, her curving, menaces him. "Well, good t'see you again, I—"

"Doctor, you know, it's crazy, wild, I never got your name. Oh, parsley: it's parsley. No one but no one seemed t'have the vaguest—the even slightest—when I described you. I asked all around. Zero. Just zero. And I hadda thank you. Hell, hey, all you did was save my life."

"Oh?" Simon has smiled. "Save my life" means nothing to him: in this part of the world they say it often.

"Sure. Take a quick look-see."

"No, don't—"

"Hey, look." She has spread her blouse apart again. "Why wontcha look? What is it, cripes? Didn't they do a good job? Huh, don't gimme the heebie-jeebies. Tell me: look."

"Ohh." He has seen. Her nude chest glints: it is only that now, a chest. Two shallow pools have been inset where once her fine breasts passed the time at ease. They bounce light off: dishes of prime reddish earthenware. The scar tissue is lacquered: older than his, but still very fresh. "What? What is this? Please—I don't understand—why're you showing me this?"

"Because, ninny. Because he said—if it hadn't been for you—he said just a couple weeks maybe it would've meta, meta. Meta, phooey. I can never get that dumb word off my roller right."

"Metastasized?"

"Bingo, that's it. I had two fat cancers, I was Tumor Town, just like you said back there when you examined me. I was a dead doornail. The big C had it in for little A. Headed right for my nodes, wherever they are, Christ knows and don't tell me. They sound bad." Her hands circle, palm out, one over each empty dish: like a slow Charleston dancer. "Anyhow, it was crappola for dumb old Ann."

"Oh, no. Oh, Jesus God, No. You didn't—"

"Men make such a boring fuss over tits, dontcha think? Holy-cannoli, y'know, I hardly miss them."

"But they were beautiful. I remember them: God, I just remembered them. My mouth. Jesus, my stupid big mouth—"

"What's the matter with it? You just went pale like you're gonna throw up. Does your mouth hurt? It looks funny, I didn't wanna say, does it hurt?"

"Yes. But you—"

"Well, anyway, Kyryl says boobs are out this year. Lucky for me, huh? And now"—she clicks finger against thumb—"now, just like that, I've got a whole persona. Before, oh. Before—maybe I told you—I couldn't get my act together. I was laying around trying t'look sexy or mysterious. Like parsley. Parsley on a filet mignon, Kyryl said. Old anonymous Annie. Listen, whoo-hoo, I'll never be famous for my brains. Oh, brother—" She has rolled eyes up as though to stare into her head. "Now I'm someone special. The other girls're jealous. Kyryl's creating a whole new fashion line around me. It's called the Sleek Cylinder look. I've done a centerfold for his magazine *Prosthesis*—"

"Wait—"

"And I'm gonna have a feature part in his movie *Mutation*. With that wild black guy who has a horn sticking out of his head. Maybe you heard, the guy Kyryl discovered when he was down in the Caribbean last year."

"Annie, wait. I've got to ask you something—"

"So, see—let me just finish—not only did you save my soup, but you made me a star, too. A stah. I'm on a dynamite high now all the time. Though, to tell you, back then I had a pretty good scare. Oh, little Annie's knees were going chitty-chitty, bang-bang, you bet. Hell, I'm only nineteen—they say I'm eighteen, but I'm only nineteen—I hadn't figured out what life was, never mind dealing with the slow death scene. But it's all okay now, and I've only got a little soreness when I raise my arms. They call me Sleek now. That's Kyryl's idea. Just Sleek. But you can still call me Annie. What was it you wanted t'ask?"

"You said *he*. *He* said it would've metastasized. Who is he?"

"Kyryl, who else?"

"Yes. But wasn't there a doctor?"

"There was you."

"Right. But besides me?"

"Oh, sure. Kyryl's personal surgeon did the operating. He's the best around. He did Kyryl's throat."

"Did he examine you?"

"Well, I guess. It happened so fast. Like, I was in the hospital that night. Two hours after you gave me the bad news. I didn't really see him until after. But he's very nice and I had my own private room."

"You—did you feel the lumps?"

"Oh, wowsie, all I felt was lumps. Even my fingertips, I thought they were lumps. Or I couldn't feel anything at all. It was time for the big red zombie pills."

"Annie. Did you ask for a second opinion?"

"Why? I had you and Kyryl, wasn't that enough?"

"I think—yes, it was."

"You know, they say a lot of bitchy things about Kyryl, but he was with me from start t'finish—right in the operating room. Before that, I'd been signed up here for six, seven months and I couldn't get the right time a day from him. But he's not the cold fish you hear about. He cares. He paid for everything and he was the one who insisted the surgeon carve me up like this, all smooth—not with the old-fashioned scars. It was, well, he said, 'Since we have to do it, we might's well make you into a work of art.' And he did."

"Annie, I'm—" Simon has to breathe. "I'm glad it worked out all right. I'm glad."

"But you've got a scar, too. On your head. And you didn't need a cane before."

"No."

"Were you in an accident?"

"At least one."

"Automobile?"

"Yes."

"Man, driving. No one's gonna get me behind a wheel. Was it serious? You all right?"

"I'm getting there."

"That's great." She has a smile. "Then you understand what I mean. About it being good t'be alive. People around here are so *shallow*. You know what?"

"What?"

"I'm gonna pop you a great big kiss. You mind? I feel like doing it. You mind?"

"No, I don't mind."

"I'll be careful. I can tell your mouth's banged up. Me, I hate people who kiss you like they were eating a spare rib." Her arms have circled him: slow, Magellan-like. Simon can see it coming and they kiss: the sense memory is there. Her brave, new butchered chest lies, must be lying, against him. "Nice, huh? That was nice. But you're tired: your eyes are teary and red. Hey, want a snort of coke? I get all I need now and it's not chalk dust, uh-uh."

"No, thanks."

"Hold on. You know my name and I still don't know yours. I'm kissing you and I don't even know your name. What would my poor dead mother in Kansas say?"

"It's Cox. Dr. Cox."

"Dr. Cox, promise me. Promise now. If there's ever anything I can do for you. Just ever. Will you tell me?"

"I promise. And, well, you know—you know there is one little thing."

"What?"

"It's a long flight of stairs down. Just that far, down to the street. If you'd put your arm under mine."

1

"Quick!"

"I'm trying, dammit! Dammit, get back!"

"F'Chrissake, Merry, let me in!"

"Stop it! Don't push against the door! I can't move it if you push."

"Let me in!"

"Please, Simon. Please! Listen to me—"

"Lemme-innnnn!"

"Take your hand out! Take it out, I tell you—the goddam chain won't unhook."

"Lemme-innnnn!"

"D'you hear me? The chain won't unhook! It won't unhook with your hand in there."

"Lemme-innnnn!"

"Forgive me. Shit! Shit, forgive me this."

"Nohhh! Don't close it, Merry—nohhhh!"

She will have to break his hand now. There is no nicer choice. It has seized the opening: it pincers, hooks. First a simple C clamp on her door: then, by cunning yet uncanny changes, a probe, a fin, a palp, a long sucker mouth. She can't relate this dangerous and lurid reach to Simon: he, whose hands once sang a patter tune. If it should catch her arm, they might both die: half in, half out. The door is shattering. With his other hand Simon clubs. The peephole has lost vision: gouged out, rolling between her feet. Paint will fall in splinter groups from burst wood. Outside, the landing is almost dark: a 75-watt bulb snitched by Mr. Wong in 5E, third time this week. Simon is coming through: Merry can't let him get a foot in the door. His hand has bent back: nearly reversed, unrecognizable: a palm full of knuckles. Wood and blood grime fatten beneath each fingernail. She sees disorganized matter only: not an intelligent limb, ambassador for the self. And that perception will make her mean act easier. She hacks down: a three-pound marble ash-tray down, again down: chopping Simon off her door. Greenstick frac-tures pen-and-ink the wristbone. Simon has lost his grip. He howls: not with pain. This is a denatured cry: sheer toneless loud soprano, as if he had been beaten toward androgyny. But her door can close. Simon is cast, for one moment, into the Wong-made outer darkness.

"No! No!"

"Hold on. The chain—"

"No! Ay-cantseee!"

"There. Don't—ah, owww!"

She has been thrown by him again: abruptly back: boarded up be-tween swung door and wall. The knob is in her wind: she can't inhale. Simon hulks: sidesaddle on himself, doddery, like some premature and lame experiment of a man. He has gone ten feet into her living room by now. Perfect teeth browse on air and grind. The left fist, great door clouter, stays cocked near his temple: he doesn't know enough to fetch it down. Urine has been spilling from a crotch rip: it carpet-bombs. Simon is agog with sight. To him, all things project the human body: or a body part. Chair arm and table leg, of course: clock face, minute hand: these terms we use casually enough. But here her odalisque couch is lounging. Lamps have pinched waist, bustline and summer hat. The room itself can look-out-on. Simon's world is full of hidden people: is super-animate. Merry has shouldered the door off. She won't shut it, though: she needs access behind. Singsong respiration: his lungs are back-ordered with breath: he can't talk. But the lip and tongue make prattle. She has seen faces this vehement, this opinionated, only among insane men. It is not rage, nor fear: rather it is, she feels, a dreadful sociability: endless and indiscriminate fellowship with his dumb environment around. As though Simon could no longer separate what is personal, what is addressed peculiarly to him, from the whole of insensate being. Chairs exist and walls for his particular inveiglement. Merry doesn't think she is equipped. Simon has the mind of a wild pantheist just now.

"Don't come near me, you hear?"

"Hahhhh."

"I'll run. If you take one step toward me, I'll run. I'm scared and I'll run."

"Hahhhh."

"Put your fist down. Put it down now."

"Haaaah." He has put it down.

"Simon."

"Haaa. Take it. Easy. Ah-haaaa. Don't be afraid."

"Well, what is it—why'd you try and break my door down like that? What am I supposed to think? The noise—most women would've called a cop by now. I think I did pretty well considering." She has seen: his wrist joint is flat, disassembled: blood sweats out. "I was terrified, dammit. You wouldn't stop, you wouldn't listen. Jesus, why'd you make me do that? I said, I told you your hand was stuck."

"I lost my airspeed, kid. There was hardly any light out there. Haaa. I'll go quietly from here on in. Come around front so's I can see you. I'm not sure I can turn."

"I don't know. I don't know, Simon."

"Merry. Haaaa. I couldn't hurt you: the chain of command doesn't work anymore. I'm a cob of myself."

"Okay." She comes. "Here I am."

"Still the princess. Come near, Hamster. Haaa. Don't back away like I was a controlled substance. You don't trust me yet? Or do I smell that bad? Shame. What would Jesus say?"

"Why don't you sit?"

"I don't think I'm recommended for upholstery. Paint comes off where I sit. God-golightly. It was—haaa—you don't know what it was like out there. Deep space. Just deep space. I could only see my toes with light from under your door. Haaa. And so many stairs up. I carried myself. Remember the guy who once carried you up here? He left. He left my employ. What do they expect? Huh. I can't watch everything. Watch, watch, watch. That little crack of light on my shoes: that was the goddam first principle of the universe."

"Sit." She has taken his hand: the left. "Don't talk so much. You're talking too much."

"Ah, little tufted duck, you shoulda been there: they japped my wonderful van tonight. It's a total, gone the way of canasta and other once-fashionable things. Oh, I attract 'em. I'm just a bear pit. Haaa. Sledge-hammers, linoleum knives, even a blowtorch. The Westchester Hell's Angels went rumbling tonight. They did a scalp dance on me. No book value, not even burial insurance, and I met a woman named Annie with breasts that shined like silver serving bowls. Only they weren't there and I think it's my fault. Maybe she had her chest on inside out: what's the opposite of a breast?—you like that kinda question, I recall. Jesus, its eyes were poked out. Haaa. I'm in pain, Mer: I loved that big bus. It was my only blood kin. Robert is through with me, even him, the one regular sycophant I had, he's still standing on Great Ferry Street like Scarlett O'Hara, cursing the sunset. God help him. Oh—oh and I've been a three-millionaire tonight. From rags to riches to utter stark nudity in half an hour. I can't think: my mind's a non-conductor. I'm jammed in the projection booth, with one camera lens left. My home street home, my moving split level, they split it up on me."

"Okay. Come, sit. I don't understand what you're saying, it's all jumbled up. Come. Help me get you down. Come, Simon. You need a rest, you're not making any sense."

"I know. I know. And I'm just reporting fact. Does that tell you something about the visible world, huh? I'm not even hallucinating yet: that'll come later. Zip-zop. Whoop. Looks like I really hammertoed my wrist on the staircase somewhere. I know. I know. I'm bouncing around the old cloud chamber, I just lifted off from Peenemünde—wait. Dr. Cox gave me tranks. Haa. Frisk my shirt pocket. Arthur put them there, he said."

"All right." She has balanced Simon: he sags here and there. Funny what you think of: she can never buy a Christmas tree that's full all around either. "I have it. They're big."

"They better 'be. Gotta get off Rocky Mountain time. Speed trap ahead: I'm traveling at warp ten tonight. I've got no total bases. They field-stripped me back there, the pricks. Gimme a pill."

"Sit first. Come over to the couch."

"Put a paper down. I'm not storm-tight. Hey, Mer, I need a sanitary belt now. How d'ya like that? Oh, they want me t'change my tune, but I won't."

"Sit. It's all right, never mind the couch."

"Put a goddam paper down. Shees, I know what's alamode and what's not. I shoulda come in through the mud room. Put some paper down. I need a desk pad for my ass."

"Well. Are you sure—can I leave you like this? Can you stand? Brace yourself on the couch, like—there, like that."

"You got fish in the tank. Lookit that. And a lot of water. It useta be empty."

"Yes. Hold on. I'm coming back."

Simon leans over himself: as you would to vomit or to bite a runny food. His left hand has grasped the couch arm at, more or less, its elbow place. For one moment Simon will imagine that he is paramour to this chubby, idle thing. Eee-run-uppp: water makes a glassful sound in the kitchen. Simon is perplexed: Merry shouldn't be wearing Gloria Vanderbilt denim plus a bulk-knit sweater just now. He had banked on the collar and her black olive-drab: some warranty of concern or Christian social service: a vested interest at least. In this state he can't earn love: he has a *cordon* un*sanitaire* around him: is sad and insecure. Tropical fish steer with one linoleum-knife fin: how they gash tires and pour a padded bucket seat out. He wouldn't mind crying: they've hit him where he lived after all. Simon looks. There is a small Zenith TV on her white-draped table: antenna ears listen for an electronic confidence. Simon will smile at it: he has been ingratiating himself with objects of late. And—what, oh—Merry has come back. She flaps the Episcopal *New Yorker* open: not sufficient dressing, Simon would judge, for his wound of incontinence. She will arrange it on her couch: uncenterfolded. Then tap-tap: the way you persuade cats to jump up.

54

"Not thick enough. I'll perc right through that flyleaf. Haven't you got something more substantial, like Webster's *Unabridged*?"

"Oh, just sit, dammit. I'm catching vertigo from you and the couch is Salvation Army anyhow. Come on." She knees his damp thigh around: impatient and rough. Simon—huh?—is sitting. The paper snaps like a new wood fire underneath him. "Your lip is bleeding."

"Is it? That's the least. Am I all the way down?" She nods. "Now, where was I? Am I? I presume there's a back on this thing somewhere."

"You're leaning against it already."

"Christ, I've bemired myself but good. I'm sorry."

"Don't be. And, somehow, I don't think you are. Part of you enjoys it. I mean—if you're going t'be sick, might as well be sick in some sensational, one-of-its-kind way."

"Yeah, I'm a conversation piece now. Like a Fabergé turd. Haaa. Y'got a pill f'me?"

"Okay. Here. Why didn't you take one before this?"

"Uh. Pride. And I couldn't get my finger in the pocket. They hook on things: essentially, I find, we have too many fingers. Right now I'd flunk a childproof cap. You shoulda seen the cabbie: he was pretty disgruntled. I couldn't open the door. Not often you get stuck taking a wet cripple t'Queens. Robert gave him a twenty, but—let's just say his next fare'll have an absorbing experience. Lordy, lookit my wrist. I'm probably suffering great pain from that."

"It says two when needed."

"Four when very much needed."

"I don't know."

"This is four on a scale of four."

"All right." Simon catches Nike sneaker flash.

"Where'd you go? Huh? We need more light in here, Mer. Put on more lights. Edison was a great man. Merry? There you are. Listen: don't do that, enter the same way you exit, huh?"

"Okay." She has a glass. "Open up."

"Throw them way back, like you'd feed an alligator. And don't pour too fast. I've been choking."

"I won't. Open. Aaaaah. Good boy." She massages his gullet: to inspire the swallow reflex.

"I've gotta tell you about my van. About the Bush King and his brother. And Annie who—" She has patched a hand across his mouth: the lips feel like tough glycerine.

"First. Will you help me to get your pants off? Just nod yes or no." Simon nods yes. "Let the medicine work. I can see the pulse in your neck. It must be one-twenty at least. No need to talk yet. Collect your thoughts. We've got all night." She has set his mouth free: on parole.

"I must stink."

"No more than usual."

"Oh."

There are molars of windshield glass in his moccasin. The right heel has bled circumspectly: behind his back. Sweater sleeve up at each elbow—as though she meant to grope in water—Merry will disconnect the belt and then zip down. A lug nut drops out. Simon is, she might have guessed it, no one to mess with: his slops are there, a compost bottomland: yet Merry will farm it. Her cigarette has been lit: incense and fumigant, they both know that. Simon is disgraced: his body volunteers embarrassment in a shying away of hip and groin. Merry, nonetheless, yanks down: stuck. Simon must try to arch up, the way a hundred women, compliant, have done for him. No luck: his feet are unseen: they won't bond to the floor. He gasps, inept: a primipara in this kind of labor. Merry, though, is good for the short haul. She lifts, one shin beneath either armpit: she has made a handbarrow of him. The pants come down/off. They take one sheet of diocesan gossip with them. The genitals, last to lose weight, are still prosperous and thick. Simon will look away: snubbing his own soiled nakedness. But he has seen her hand: there seems to be peanut butter on it.

"You were saying? Go on."

"Jesus, Mer. Jesus, I'm sick with shame. This is terrible. I shouldn't've come. I shouldn't've laid this dead mouse at your door." He blows himself to a long exhale. "Well, one thing it proved: you must be a priest. I wouldn't do what you're doing now for anyone."

"I'm a little more than professionally concerned."

"I haven't eaten anything, honest. Not hardly. I don't see how—where all those toilet articles came from. I don't see how it could happen."

"Can you lift the right leg?—good, hold it. Now down. I better go get some equipment. Tell me about your van. I still don't understand."

"See, Wolff and Kyryl invited me down t'Ten Great Ferry. They offered three million zircons f'my busted cue ball. Poll tax, y'might say. So's I could make my film."

"Louder."

"So's I could make my film. Three million's a lotta whip-out, but still. Still, may their expensive Mexican grass be forever doused with paraquat." Simon is laughing: four-on-one, the pills have begun to use their milligram weight. "Three million. Man, if those two brown spots'd killed me, I coulda been a billionaire."

From the kitchen: "Of course you turned it down."

"Of course. They don't call me Goldfinger for nothing. I dunno. I try t'be Dick Turpin and I end up as poor old cross-eyed Ben. Every damn time."

"Rather a grandish gesture." Merry is in front of him: her entrances are full, slow now. She has the red bathrobe. Also warm water in her best roasting pan and a roll of Bounty towels.

"Uh. *You* think so. Ha, y'shoulda seen Robert when I relayed the news. His top lifted off like a German beer stein. He took his belt and, get this, he started t'whip me with it like a plantation overseer flogging Butterfly McQueen. I bet that really hurt."

"So that's what they are: there're welts all along your thigh. See. Frankly, Simon, I didn't like the look of your Mr. Robert. That cinches it. The little rat."

"Be magnanimous. I thought it showed get up and go. Y'haveta put it in perspective: this was just after I told him there was a hundred percent deductible on my van insurance and we're standing like rival fakirs on a lawn of broken glass. Jesus. My marvelous van. My patrimony. I could've sold it and endowed a land grant college. Now I've got nothing."

"But how? Who did it? Wolff?"

"No, no. The Bush Brothers. They commuted all the way down from Middlebrow-on-the-Hudson or some pitch-and-putt Westchester burg like that—t'do this: t'give me a sudden sunken garden."

"The who?"

"Oh, of course, you don't know. Robert's father and his uncle, who's Rose's husband by a previous marriage. They're big in sod and humus. They landscape breezeways or something. How'd they get here, I wonder, by the Saw Mill River, by Amtrak bar car? Anyhow, I'm a casualty of green backlash. I got sandbagged by a Moral Majority of one."

"But why?"

"Why? T'redeem Robert from the dropout drug culture, y'know: as if I had scat enough t'buy uncut calamine lotion. Hanh. And t'revenge themselves on me f'turning Minnie into a 44-inch hippie. Minnie's Robert's mother, did I mention her? Oh sure, sure, she offered you a late naked lunch that night. It's so G.D. ironic. I swear, Mer, I've swum upstream in a lotta birth canals, but all I ever got from Minnie was rust blight. She wore a triple-gauge chastity belt. Honest. Okay, I admit there were moments with her when I was hell-bent for erection, but I woulda needed a punch press. And for that, for that, you're a priest, why don't they punish me for the sins I commit? What kinda accounts payable system're they using anyhow? Minnie was—"

"And Rose?"

"There y'go. Just like a woman. F'Chrissake, quit while you're on a streak. Rose was Rose. Her body was like a sexual Nautilus machine. Anyhow she left her husband two years before I came along—'cause, she said, all he wanted t'fertilize was the azaleas. More-besides, she's Wolff's niece now. He stuck her on the family tree like a hammock hook. Breathe—haaa—in/out. Robert says they were really beered up: with softball team T-shirts on. Praise Jesus, there's nothing like a bourgeois vigilante in his mid-life pinch with a blowtorch and a Skotch Kooler full of Bud, coming down hard on something subversive and foreign like, oh, Swiss chard. Ye-God, imagine what those Sunday Slo-pitch boo-hoos would've done t'me if I wasn't upstairs with Wolff. Probably beat me t'death with Danish modern furniture or the leg of a mock-Colonial captain's chair. Or with rolled-up *TV Guides*. The final Scarsdale Diet. I can't get a running fix on all this. Robert and Min, they just came one day, unannounced, like spinsterhood. I gave them shelter. And for that my home gets entered in a demolition derby. Is that fair? I mean, is it?"

"The bastards. No, I don't think it's fair." She has started to wipe him dry: not with paper now, with her own good terry-cloth towel. She holds it like a receiving blanket under his wide pelvis. "Simon, I'm so sorry. Your van was terrific: all those blinking little lights on the dashboard. It reminded me of Christmas."

"They dropped down through my roof. Broke my skylight, just sledged the skull in. Robert was sacked out: for him it was Masada, or so he tells me. They wanted t'drag him back to Landscape Land and have him deprogrammed. Christ, they must think I'm a brigadier in the Moonies, either that or I'm the Abominable Dr. Phibes. His nose was bleeding and one cheek looked like blood sausage. But he managed t'get away. Lucky they weren't in film, they didn't know the best things t'maul. What was glass, what was thin and would make an expressive noise, that they smashed. Then they set the engine on fire. The cab and the whole mouth part of it is charred. But they were pressed for time: hadda catch the 12:15 back t'Croton-Vapid, I guess. Robert got in the back and used my big foam extinguisher before the gas tank went like a prolapsed uterus. The kid did good. I give him credit. There might even be salvage. Maybe the Movieola, but not much else. I leave it to Robert, my last will and testament. Shit, it was a scene from *Pork Chop Hill*. I couldn't go inside. Make funny faces, don't let me cry, I can't see when I cry. That was me. People knew me when I drove by: it was my Harlem yellow pander-truck. Jesus, there's nothing left. I'm just a check stub now."

"Did you call the police? Did Robert?" She has draped the red bathrobe over Simon. "I'm sick of all this violence. It has to stop."

"Don't worry. God help them. And God help Robert. I never hated my father as much as he hates his. I thought I did, I thought. But, so far as hating goes, I'm a business management trainee by comparison. It's ugly, Mer. I never hit my father—and he wasn't even my father. Robert hit his in the neck with a metal light brace: that's how he got away. Well, the police will come and legal costs'll run them a mess of forsythia, I guess. But I wasn't a witness, I can't testify. Robert wanted me t'lie, t'say I saw it. But lying is hard work. All I'm fit for now is a job as track walker on the Third Avenue El."

"And what about Annie?"

"Annie? Wha? Hey, how'd you come t'know Annie?"

"You told me about her. Just a few minutes ago."

"Yes, maybe. I was saying things then. What was it I told you?"

"Something about her breasts, I do believe. You weren't too lucid. But I might as well know the whole story. I mean, don't you think? Since"— she has picked up the roasting pan—"since I've been such a good sport. Just a little quid pro quo, huh? Who is she?"

"Oh, hiss and boo. Come on, Mer—I'm Mr. Wilt now. My line of fire is bent. Don't push the other-woman thing. I'm not looking for a harem these days, I'm looking for a ground crew."

"Yes? So why won't you tell me about her?"

"Because. Because, when I think it over, it's not a story you dine out on. Except alone. I don't think it'd make me more attractive t'the buying public somehow."

"Come on. After this? I've seen you at your worst, *mi amigo*."

"Listen, my worst is high-key stuff. Murder, acts of international terrorism, cow rape: I mean, y'might take a philosophical attitude toward them. They dare: they're free-form events. But this was a frat-house prank: and a waste of soft, round things. Not up t'my usual gross tonnage, just second-division ball. Let it alone, huh, Mer? I'm dealing with it. I am."

"You got someone pregnant?"

"Ha. No. I'd be glad of that. The way my South Pole's thawed out now."

"What then? What could this Byzantine crime be?" Her smile is an invoice. Terms: payable on receipt. "Mind you, I'm not jealous, I can—"

Pop. Hssp.

"—it's just that I've been left with the dirty end. I can't help envying another time and other people. Even your parents. Women, men, who knew you when—"

Pop

"Merry. Hello, there. Speak to me."

"What d'you mean? What is this now?"

"Huh? Huh? Don't play tricks."

"What tricks? What's happening?"

"Jesus, not again. I think I can't hear. Oh, shit, no—my hearing just shut down again."

"That's convenient. That's a convenient ploy. You just don't want to talk about this Annie."

"Hello? Are you hearing me? I can't hear me. I can't hear my voice. Help. Can you hear it? Please, do something. Acknowledge my voice. Don't tell me—oh, Christ—don't tell me I'm mute, too."

"I can hear you."

"Is that a yes?" She nods. "Yes? How do I sound? Is there fear in my voice? Do I sound like a coward? Can you hear that?"

Merry shrugs.

"Jesus, at least I was a voice. God, I was that. Even when it got dark, I was a voice: I'd know it anywhere. Not good. This is not good." Simon drubs his head: punch and punch. "Not good. No, not good."

"Stop it. Don't do that."

"My arm? Leggo my arm. Don't get on top of me. I can't see. Back off."

"Are you joking, Simon? Is this the truth? Is it really happening?"

"What am I gonna do? Operator! Operator! If I hit it maybe, or lean down like when you come out of a swimming pool. No. The line is down, Jesus. I can hear myself think, but I don't wanna think."

"Keep talking. Go on." She has made hand moves inward: as you direct a truck back to the loading bay. "Don't worry about it. Keep talking. There's something I have to do."

"Your lips're moving too fast. I can't read them. Wait—first put some more lights on. It's happened before, so don't panic. Oboy, don't panic. Listen, make a circle with your hand if you want me louder, and cut your throat if I'm blowing the amplifier out." But Merry is gone. "Huh? Where are you? Where'd you go? Don't leave. They've disconnected me. Christ, my head's in an egg cozy—Merry! Merry! Am I screaming? Am I screaming? Merry!"

But Merry, behind him, tiptoeing high, at the top of a TEST YOUR STRENGTH amusement park mallet swing, has dashed her big Haviland platter down—a-whammmm! Chunks backfire: they slide or roll or coin-toss: they are flip, quite unlike their best company selves. And yet, when settled, they still have a peculiar quiet chic: not chips, verse rather, iambic foot and assonance, the debris of sonnet-making. Who, after all, but those certain elite would break Haviland—Grandma Allen's last gift— just to prove a point? Merry will kneel on porcelain. The crash has evoked a petulant mop handle's banging from Mr. Guttman below: but from Simon not a fidget, nor a misdrawn breath. Merry, sure, has doubted him: you might, too. But she concedes the infidelity and will request forgiveness from a higher-up. Be fair: it is to her credit that this was an extravagant, an heirloom, act of doubt—not, as might easily have been, the Tarpon Springs ashtray or some empty fruit juice jar—instead her one piece of flatware that can accommodate a twelve-pound roasted bird. Simon is shouting. Merry dashes around the couch. He has been struck all of a heap. The bathrobe is half off: more sarong now. Merry window-dresses him: upright, rearticulated. And, while so doing, she can touch his forehead, sternum, left pap, right: blessing him the way a pickpocket might. Then, with one hand on her hip, one to censure a false yawn—conversationally, oh so idly—she will say, "Have mercy upon you, pardon and deliver you from all your sins, confirm and strengthen you in all goodness and bring you to everlasting life, through Jesus Christ our Lord. And the blessing of God almighty, the Father, the Son and the Holy Ghost, be with you always—" ho-hum, yawn and amen. Simon has nodded. Deaf, he is a good listener finally.

"Hey, Star Shell, don't wander off like that. Huh, please? Raise your hand and I'll give you a home-room pass. Huh? Remember, we're not on speaking terms just now. Sit. Sit, where I can see you. Show some staying power." Merry has sat. "Oboy, speed. A lotta speed. I'm in the jet stream. Can you hear me? Nod bigger. Yeah, that's it. Oboy, cracked the sound barrier again. Jaaah, someone lowered the sonic boom. People in Teaneck're ringing the newsroom. Crockery is rattling. How long since I fell on deaf ears? Five minutes? Ten? Longer?" Merry will display six fingers. "Yeah? That's a long take f'my fixed-focus camera. The longest it's been so far, I think. Oboy, one card t'draw for a full house. It's all over but the shouting and even that I'll haveta read off the monitor."

"No. Don't talk like that."

"Whassay? Uh. Y'know, Mer. While doing this bad remake of *Johnny Belinda* I've had a brainflight or two. Hanh. Hearing is a much underrated job skill. Those so, so serious people who ask all the time: which would you rather lose, your hearing or your sight or—I dunno—two arms and a hand? And most everyone'd say, hearing. Me, too, I guess. After all, the world is full of mike feedback and overload and call-in talk shows. Still. Still, you know what deafness is?"

Head shake.

"It's a life without straight men. No setups. No topical material on the readout. Y'can't lampoon silence or impersonate the air. I need interplay, Mer: I'm gonna starve. My mind'll bite its leg off in the trap. I'm an embassy in a nation where no one's asking for asylum. Hah. On the plus side, of course, it's pretty hard t'insult me either. Me?"

Pop

"Hey, *me*. Ho hey! Yaaaaggh! Testing one, two, three."

"What is it?"

"I heard. I hear. I can hear my raucous voice. I've got audio and, boy, am I loud. Why dintcha jam a mute in my horn? Speak, say something, y'been put through. Quick. Say hi t'your mother in Piscataway. Hurry, before they stick the acoustical tile up again. I could rejoin the silent service any minute now. Quick."

"Uh—I." She thumps a cushion. "Say what? Damn. Damn. It's the same when I make a long-distance call, I can never think what t'say. I choke."

"Well, while we got this trunk line open, I wanna tell you—" Simon's neck is set-screwed: he doesn't dare rewire the connection. "I mean, I wanna ask. That is. Y'know why I'm here, don't you?"

"Yes. Sure. You need me. Why else?"

"Uh. Does that give you razor burn? Does it make you feel like a piece of business reply mail?"

"No."

"My heart is a lousy hunter, kid."

"Simon, sure, I'd prefer it if you had come on other terms. But I'm satisfied. And I'm pleased—even surprised—by your trust. Before, what you let me do: it wouldn't be easy for any man."

"Your voice is nice. I like you, Merry. And it's not just because I've got the scare strap buckled on right now. Honest. I liked you so much I almost didn't see you again. Back then. Y'know what I mean?"

"I think I do."

"Ah. Then. Ah, can I stay here?"

"Yes."

"Just a while: just for a few reels. I'm not a man anymore, the drive shaft is bent, but maybe I can still make you laugh. And I won't raise your consumer price index. I eat like a bird: a stuffed owl."

"You don't have to entertain."

"Y'see, Arthur's putting me through my spin cycle. He has a kinda greenhouse effect on my mind: he watches me so close I've got powder burns from it. I mean, he's been great: of all my many non-relatives he's the best. I love him, but I'd also like him t'wash up on a hard beach somewhere. He thinks I'm St. Senseless, a prodigy, an apostle t'the numb —whatever. He has people in t'see me: even, peg this now, even an exorcist. Who dispossessed me of some urine but not much else. I try t'be civil: Lord knows I'm not the most convenient visiting fireman. I need more than a guest towel and clean sheets. I try, but—well . . . Arthur has his own worm holes, I understand that. Age seventy, a good man, a good priest and still no commercial endorsements from God. Heck, as far as I can see, he has it made in suede. If there was a heaven, he'd get in on a moral grant-in-aid."

"I know." Merry is lighting a cigarette. "I've had him on the phone four times since Tuesday."

"Arthur? You have? He didn't tell me."

"Yes. We're cautious friends now." She will smile. "Well, to be frank, he tolerates me for your sake."

"Huh, that was a real duel of half-wits, your little twosome in the hospital. I've never known Arthur t'leap down from the forest canopy like that. You musta really hit his flashpoint. Ordinarily I'd rank Arthur somewhere between Gelusil and a glacial deposit f'passion. Well, it's all religious wheel static far's I'm concerned."

"Arthur's devoted to you."

"Yeah." Simon laughs. "P. T. Barnum was devoted t'Gargantua. I'm an attraction. I'll help sell out the whole Sunday subscription series."

"No. Be fair. It's more than that and you know it."

"Maybe. Maybe. And you, your Effeminence? Whadda you think this indisposition of mine is?"

"The test question, huh?"

"So?"

"I think there's something very wrong with you. The physical you. I think we've got to do everything humanly possible to get you well."

"Hit the shift lock, baby, and type it out in caps. I'm gonna spike this thing. Arthur figures it's all for his personal instruction—like I'm a home study course. Some guff, huh? With Arthur—y'know, with him I sometimes pretend t'be deaf."

"I'll make an appointment with Dr. Gobel tomorrow."

"No."

"But—"

"No. The animal's going off. To a quiet place he knows. It's in the crease where the road map folds, where your finger can't follow it anymore. He's gonna heal himself there."

"I don't understand."

"Right now, Mer, there's only one thing I trust. This great body of mine. We've ridden together: it's always carried me before. The lung and the heart and the muscle. I'm still strong. God, I'm stronger now than I've ever been. I could lift this couch and you on it. Don't tell me that isn't health. I trust it as far as I could throw you. And, oh, I can throw."

"But that—that sounds like superstition."

"Sure. The only one that's true. My mind has cancer, Merry."

"Cancer?"

"Cancer of the impressions. Cancer of the consciousness. Mad, malign cell growth. Uh-uh, I know where imagination leads. I can't pick up a paper clip but it's attached t'all the others in the jar. No more of that. No more." He has scared her. Once Aunt Phyllis gave Merry a puzzle: the plastic box held two metal balls. She was four: she found it hard. You had to shake and tilt until one ball settled in each of a blind clown's eyes. And she can see that now: Simon's small pupils rolling. "I'm afraid, little oyster cracker. But I'm not afraid of death: please make that distinction. It's just—in the last two weeks or so—I've seen things."

"What things?"

"Ha, no. Objection: prosecution is leading the witness no place fast. Uh-uh. I won't think about it. If I do, it'll be time t'sing the National Anthem and sign off. The body, Mer. That's my answer. The beast and me. We're gonna work out together: gonna build the tissue back up. I'll enjoy the competition. And it'll teach me. We're only looking for a few good men."

"All right. Whatever you think is best. I'll go along with it."

"You're a fine woman, Merry Allen. Y'know—hey. I notice y'got a real TV now. Once there was just a blank screen here. Bit of an affectation I thought."

"Yes. I was kind of a jerk back then, wasn't I? Now I like to know what the weather might be tomorrow."

"Ha. Makes sense."

"I watch all the time now. Even the commericals."

Pop-hssssssp. Last pop.

"Yes," Simon says. "Ah, yes."

"It's interesting: TV and me. I was afraid of it—that it would be stupid. And that it would make me think less of the people who watched it. And, you know, it is stupid. And, you know, that's a big relief." She laughs. "Who can tell? My body may go up into the hills with yours. If I can follow the track you leave. I'm not as strong as you are, but—do you think it's possible?"

Simon nods.

"Simon, for my sake, not for yours, for my fear, not for yours—will you let me recite something? Something, don't throw a tantrum, from the New Testament? Not because I need to convert you or get the job of witnessing off my chest: because I want comfort now. And because I think it fits somehow, with the trip you're talking about. I don't care if you believe in my God: that's His problem, not mine. Let me say it because we're both afraid, we two animals, and it's dark outside. May I?"

Simon nods.

"I've got it by heart. It's from St. Matthew." She has prepared her throat. "It goes: 'Take no thought for your life, what ye shall eat, or what ye shall drink: nor yet for your body, what ye shall put on. Is not the life more than the meat, and the body more than raiment? Behold the fowls of the air: for they sow not, neither do they reap: nor gather into barns: yet your heavenly Father feedeth them. Are ye not much better than they?' "

Simon nods.

" 'Which of you by taking thought can add one cubit unto his stature? And why take ye thought for raiment? Consider the lilies of the field, how they grow: they toil not, neither do they spin: and yet I say unto you, that even Solomon in all his glory was not arrayed like one of these.' " Merry is passionate: a sensual flush has scarfed her neck. Fish, free, cut sharp corners in their tank. " 'Wherefore, if God so clothe the grass of the field, which today is and tomorrow is cast into the oven, shall he not much more clothe you, O ye of little faith? Therefore take no thought saying, What shall we eat? Or what—' "

Simon nods.

" 'Or what'—what? Oh, my God—you can't hear. I see it in your eyes. You're deaf again. You haven't heard anything."

44

Simon nods.

"You're not there. You've gotten away."

Simon nods. Then, to be gracious, because he is a guest and she has shown him great courtesy, he will smile.

I

1

Simon.

Simon.

Simon—you'll forgive him, the deaf seem rude among us—Simon is on a dig again. Claw up dirt, catch it, raise—aaaar-um, sprocket wheel around and dump: the fifth hole he has exhumed tonight, todawn. His sandhog immigrant hands dredge and pry. Scrape, haul: lean on the pick: wait. Yet, after a while, they will obey that non-union overseer in his head. Above Simon, above Van Lynxx Manor, the balconies high-rise: they have been shut for the season, each like a small lakefront property. Collapsible furniture bound wrist to foot with tarp around it. Screens stacked triple mesh. A dolphin-form infant wading pool: some father's breath of last June gone out of it. Simon has no audience: the dress circle is closed. But, to his left, arm over arm over arm, with extra monkey suppleness, Friday trembles: a sidewalk superintendent on the grass. Simon has valued his inhuman patience and companionship. 38 degrees F in Central Park, where New York weather is kept and interviewed. Slim ice feathers preen around the birdbath: summer, held in six-month time deposit, is ready to be rolled over now. And Simon has on one cotton shirt, plus Bermuda shorts and a kind of bedroom footwear. His bare skin long ago stopped piling gooseflesh up. Yet every other minute or so he will be jounced by a nostalgic shiver. Then dirt splashes: his production schedule is set back. But these boat people, his hands, can make it up on cheap overtime labor. If you allow for circumstance and drawback and hitch, Simon is at peace. The sun has risen: full in its youth as a Mozart. No expense spared on this, his first wedding day.

He sits efficiently: each leg outcurved around the hole. Hand and hand have a close private-eye tail on them. He lies within easy reach of himself. Ho, in digging, Simon might be excavator to the carriage trade. Fine commission work: abstract and portraiture and public monument. Of all men, of Kyryl even, he alone could shovel a Calder mobile out. But these five are just numbered reproductions: derivative of his early self. One foot in diameter, one foot deep at their inverted beehive apices. With the signature SVL. Simon will try not to abuse his right wrist: that, Dr. Gobel told him, is a little maraca full of bone chips. So far he has disinterred no archaeological evidence, except for one Coke bottle cap, bent, pre-twist-off era. C. 1950–55 he would date it: an old pause that refreshed. Not in museum condition: rust-charred: probably fecund with the seeds of tetanus. Simon has set it aside: a bequest. The find does imply some advanced and thirsty civilization here, then. One cap, however, is not decisive. Simon must be skeptical. He has heard of intrusive burials: what else, after all, were Aldo and Bettina in his own shallow site?

The grass is arthritic: gray and lame-kneed with new frost. It has about it that particular bentness of an insect leg. Lilac bushes bundle up: clothed by Arthur in flannel, in burlap, like Radcliffe women tailgating before game time. Autumn is still a close split decision: soil one inch down has late-summering worms and can be broken. Simon doesn't mind: he is at constant room temperature here. Aldo's bronze Spirit of Radio has a rimy-white jockstrap on, where underage sunlight hasn't thought yet to peer. Each gravestone is in strict confidence: cold shoulder beside cold shoulder. And Van Lynxx Chapel, with all that west-fallen morning shadow tent-pegged down, seems on a retreat: the big, unfriendly loner that he knew in childhood. Simon sneezes. Friday, alarmed, will bounce a gesundheit: bouncing can warm, he must do more of it. Next Simon has to yawn: nice science that: try holding your eyes full open through a yawn. But these automata are promising: they mean that the night desk of his body is still on call. A large terrace spotlight shines: outshone now. It has been on, over Van Lynxx Garden, since 3 A.M. When Simon's personal and comprehensive blindness arrived once for a moment, then for a moment once again, in his lamplit upper room.

Sing horror: sing out. Simon has been broken in to it: has consorted with that Grand Terror long enough and knows the high society, the exact knife and fork placement of it. These will never dazzle him again. No, nor will the inexhaustible, electric fire-throwing arc that human fear can inscribe. To be unpresent: to be without place or rank: in rankless place. To be merely hypothetical, a fair assumption, he who was hard news wherever he went. Damn it, damn the snobbery, the *pride*, of crass perfection: Simon jeers at it. Roundness, rounding yet more: the sovereign pious luminescent curve: that monotone harmony of sphere and sphere—no more, at bottom, than the right circles traveled in. He can jeer because, for all that insolent and preposterous wholeness, it will never be *art*. Will never *want* to be art. Absolute beauty is beauty-the-less: sad for its old finishedness and with no dramatic tension there. Simon—Simon—can do better: because he can still do worse. He is Adam-who-might-fall: the first promising artist. Yes, Simon will scream: and his screaming, soon, will be perfect as well. He will bend like light of its own ludicrous sublime velocity. But having dwelt in it, he will not dwell on it. Why should he? There are no possibilities left in that genre. Simon, you may have remarked, is not often of a philosophical turn. To measure and suppose: to record: to speak revelation and surprise: that would be a concession. Simon is impossible: he can yet want. A breast piques him. And running water. Or, praise it, this inconsistent soil. Some perverse and flawed activity: the digging, say, of holes not quite similar here. He is an heir presumptuous: it must come to him and offer terms. He may accept, but let them realize—let them never forget—that this isn't perfect round benevolence but an arrant imposition. Oh him: Him: a man with better uses for his free and foolish time. Simon would like whoever knows to know that.

9 A.M. Reports of shale encountered. Depth: moderate. Width: unknown. Decision: proceed. A fifteen-minute exercise, for which Simon has been specially job-classified. He can recall how once his fingertips would dent and burn, jacking up some fatuous, sullen stone. He will rock it left/right, as you might gearshift a car out of snow: but the stone holds its ground. His right thumb is variously inept: like the grown-out bill on a rooster. Close work: and difficult. Yet at last the shale swatch has come loose. Disappointment again: why is resistance always greater than size or worth? Simon will dry-clean his specimen. Ah-ho: he has been preceded. Three incomplete fossils, shell-shape, fingerprint one side. He can surmise: what offset plate of dead calcium is this? Spirifer remains most likely: common, if memory will hold, in paleozoic strata. They denote a stolid Mississippian bivalve culture here 300 million years ago: not what you'd consider drawing room company, but sophisticated enough. Nine-year-old Simon, Junior Paleontologist, could wonder: 300 million, a three with—how many?—eight zeros after it: ooooooooh! But that is gone: wonder. He has spun, time out of mind, and seen. There is only a single day, so immense that it Rolldexes all time on one wheel. What waste: so many amazements lost for the final, redundant surprise. Anyway Aldo, in a rebuff to crabgrass, had out-of-state shale dumped near: intrusive burial again, no doubt. Simon will set Coke cap and fossil, contemporaries, side by side.

A breeze has scraped itself together: dragging back to sea after the night's shore leave. There is stir and crackle. Simon would love to hear all that. But silence has tone and perfect pitch: if he will hum along, it can be a mantra: a repeat of the pause between chord and chord that is restful: definite. He has looked up. Maple leaves flip over, read cursorily by a skimming cold gust: they rush to decorate his shirt with some October badge. From the hole's rim sand is whisked. Perilous: a tear in either eye might blind. This is no time for sentiment or grit. Arthur has bought him a pair of horn-rims, shatterproof and bulky, but they downframe sight to 35 mm. They have no life: they hang from his nose like the rat guard on a hawser. So Simon, willful, still wears contact lensing: his sight unseen. Moreover, it is—is it not?—a day to look one's best on. And he will try. His hair, which had begun to resprout unevenly, a field of maiden claimers leaving the gate, is shaven again. Rubbed scalp can pick up sun and return it. Friday runs alee of him: windbreaker Simon. Now the monkey will sneeze. It has had poor luck in masters.

A coat is on him: Harris tweed, resolute as the never-twilit Empire once was. Merry's arms come around to snare him in cold comfort. Dirt is wind-sown: he has dropped everything for her. She stands out front—they can seldom indulge in a profile now—one leg on either side of the half-built hole. Merry dumbshows exasperation. This, beyond all else, is most bitter to Simon: that he has made her unbeautiful so often: a yawping deaf-mute to his stupid inner silence. Simon will smile. He would still her lovely face: those moron leers: that coarse overplaying. A Magic Slate has been clipped on her belt. Yet Merry doesn't use it here. She requires of her love, at the least, super-verbal communication. Why can't he hear *that*? Simon, buffoon, has formed one tasteful soil patty for her: a craftsman's best gift. But this isn't decent packing earth and it will disintegrate. His eyes are worn: like the thumb of a carpet cutter. Somehow or other he will kill them off, too: she can guess that. Merry, meanwhile, has reviewed his five holes, the terrace light: and done a simple time-labor equation in her mind. She is distraught. She kicks dirt toward Van Lynxx Chapel.

"Hi there, Pollen Basket. Uh-oh. Uh-*oh*, Simon. She's giving you that pained look, like she had a frozen tampon in. I've been bad and inconsiderate again, huh? What? Is it bigger than a breadline?" Merry taps her watch. "Time. Do the numbers, I've been somewhat counterclockwise recently. Uh . . . five fingers and four fingers: nine. It's nine o'clock and you . . . three fingers and four fingers . . . you hauled in at seven. Uh-huh. Not so fast: remember I just had a brain bypass operation. Yes? You did what—?" Merry stirs. "You cooked. Good. And snip-snip. Something with scissors. Next word. Then—" Fingers walk up. "Then you went t'my bedroom. Ho, surprise. Anger, also. Concern. Then fear. Empty. Mr. Simon, he gone. I got it, you thought I'd finally dissipated myself completely: like a black belch in Yankee Stadium. Here it was your wedding day and the groom had turned into some kind of hovering clear consommé."

"Oh, you asshole."

"I saw what you said. I may be deaf but I'm not a complete shower clog yet. Y'can't talk behind my back in front of me. Not yet, at least." Merry will give him the finger: with liturgical grace, as though it were a benefaction. "Hey. You're doing great. All's you need now is one of those little cards they drop on your knee in a restaurant. 'Hi, there. Sorry t'ruin your digestion, but I'm a deaf-mute and I'm working my way through elocution school—'" Merry is silent: rather, she doesn't move. "Okay. Enough. You look beautiful: like some astral wonder that only occurs once in seventy years. I just wish we didn't have t'go through all this facial fretwork. Jesus, even your nose has frown lines now. Your cheeks'll get box-pleated next. Hanh. We look like two Russian dissidents in a roomful of bugged borscht. If I don't understand, use the slate. Is my voice on replay, can you hear?" Merry has nodded. "Some clotheshorse of a morning, huh? How'd it go with Mom and Dad last night?" Merry has acceded. She prints with the blunt red wooden stick. Simon is proud of her handwriting: Smith girls write this way. Her letter i is dotted with a circle: class.

JERK, ITS 38° OUT. Some cellophane will tear: at the k in "jerk." This is the sixth Magic Slate she has gone through since Wednesday.

"So? Y'getting cold feet?"

HOW LONG HAVE YOU BEEN HERE?

"Until now at least. Time enough t'play five holes without a club. Hanh. I couldn't get the snore door open, even with Dr. G's four-pound Seconals. Nervous, I guess. Felt like the guy who starred in *I Was a Male War Bride*. All my three-way bulbs were three-way on. I was flopped out there like prosciutto on a melon." His arms are open: to indicate the way do-nothing ham would lie. Friday has interpreted this as beckoning. He will climb onto Simon's chest. "Then it came. Or it went. Ga-gaaaah. I hit the long coal seam. Hanh. Twice. I got blind twice. They sent me a tear sheet from the big black book. I don't think it was for more'n a minute, but in that kinda desert the mountains can seem very close. You shoulda heard me scream. I shoulda heard me scream."

WAS IT VERY BAD?

"Oh, Rational Velvet, I dunno. I mean, what happens when terror, when pure abject funk becomes standard—like bulk mail or a check-off privilege? Mind you, it's no flying circus out there, but it isn't like the first time anymore—that much I do know. And somehow I've got a feeling that they've shot their cheekful. In a sense it makes me brave: when you know the worst, when you know that nothing is what it is, then— then there's only one thing left that can scare you."

"What? Wait." WHAT?

"Hope. They'd haveta give me that. And my guess is, they've gone too far."

WHY DO YOU SAY THEY?

"Oh, it. It, then. I say 'they' because I've never met the one anything that could take me in a clean fight. Don't ask anymore, Bride of Frankenstein. That's why I didn't wake Arthur last night. He would've asked what everyone wore and what wine they served with the vichyssoise and did I sign the guest book? And I really can't answer that. Any more than the clay man could explain when some bored child squashes him and jams him back inta the lump. What I was then and what I am now and what I'll be next time around. And will there be clay? I liked it so much better at your place."

WELL GO BACK. THERE JUST WASNT ROOM ENOUGH FOR A WEDDING.

"Poor Merry. Cart horses get a better groom."

IM SORRY I WASNT HERE LAST NIGHT.

"Why? What good could you've done? Held my transparent hand? Got a lawyer t'protect my air rights? No. I haveta go through this hazing alone."

MINDS, YOU KNOW. THERE MUST BE ANOTHER CONNECTION.

"Perhaps. Right now, since my senses gave up their group practice, I'm not sure of anything. I'm just glad they invented kneeling buses."

"Let's go in. In." She has pointed: then a palm is raised. "Up."

"Okay. Bug off, Igor." Friday jumps. Simon, stunt man for himself, will lie back flat: his best standpoint. Drum-sound: give him a rousing, if silent, hand: hours of fall-guy practice have gone into this. Arm around arm on his chest: otherwise they tend to catch, like table legs fitting through a doorway. Now, on his mark: one complete Van Lynxx snaproll and, whomp, face down. Merry has opted to look at the chapel. Push up, then squat. What you see may appear simple: in fact it might be Simon's crowning achievement. He will rise, knee wobble and trick, as one acrobat would balance on the neck of another. This is something, enough: a man has stood up. "All right. I'm on my stalks. Yo, Merry. You can look now, I didn't flop."

I WAS LOOKING.

"Nah, y'weren't. Y'look at me like it was part of giving the United Way."

"That isn't fair." THAT ISNT FAIR.

"This isn't fair. Listen, Royal Jelly, you can still hop a fast eastbound t'Ronkonkoma and leave me barely standing at the altar. I'll forgive you. I might even prefer it that way. I'm afraid of you. Of your body and you." She kisses him: her chin is soiled by it. "I had no right t'propose then. In sickness or in sickness: some choice you had."

I DIDNT HESITATE, DID I?

"True. And neither did Arthur. He knew Mrs. P'd give him a bundle for Britain right up the bumber-chute, if he did. Poor sap." They move: she is ready to support him. But Simon has made great strides in walk- ing: he will no longer use a cane, except for affectation. "The two of us guys on the same day. I can't believe he agreed t'let you perform the service."

IT WAS HIS IDEA.

"Maybe he thinks, you being female and a clerical error, it won't count."

YES, MAYBE. I WAS SURPRISED.

"Not half so surprised as Mr. and Mrs. Allen were, I bet. Hanh. Imag- ine getting a six-foot-three-inch disability clause for your son-in-law. Jesus, eight years of much higher education and what? Their precious daughter is now qualified t'wed the flesh-and-blood likeness of a cat's scratching post."

DONT UNDERESTIMATE THEM. THEY TOOK IT VERY WELL. AND THEYRE COMING, SO BE ON YOUR BEST BEHAVIOR.

"Hoo-boy, me? Just t'make an obscene gesture I need three tech re- hearsals and a week in New Haven." But Simon is anxious: he would like to pass their inspection. "I see it now. When they ask if there's any reason why these two shouldn't be joined asunder, your dad'll come for- ward with a piano wire and do me like a Japanese sentry. Christ, I can picture how last night went for you. Mom. Dad. Ah—I'm getting married. I would've eloped and saved you the trouble of buying a silver mint dish, but he probably would've fallen through the ladder. See, he's deaf. Wait: it gets better. He can't taste, touch or smell anything either. Slip him a little extra and he'll go blind, too. It was love at last sight. Huh-hanh. I can imagine they had substantial arguments against. Then again, I'm the ideal rector's husband: no imputation of lust. Our wedding night'll be sensuous as a return receipt. Talk about premature ejaculation: I had mine five weeks ago."

"Ssssh. Keep moving."

"Though I do, y'know. I do lust. That's the dumb pissant thing about it. The old swarm spores're still alive and clamoring: they want little Simons t'be. Hanh. What got me with sex was—it never put a stop-order in. There is no climax, Mer. God, I remember whole mislaid weekends when I wanted the woman under me t'go bang, like one of those inflata- ble Judy dolls. Y'know, the kind that frustrated shut-ins mail off $29.95 for. I wanted there t'be just a rind left, a few party balloon shreds of plastic. But she was always still down there: and I'd needta retool again. God, we are driven: the screws're put on. Now, now I haven't even got a starter kit and I still want you. I've been terrorized: I've seen circles that had corners on them and light so frazzling black that it left no shadow and no thing t'make a shadow with—and still I wanna touch that splendid part of you: the part where back of thigh—in a moment of sheer, wild ingenuity—rises up and decides, just decides, t'become a shiny buttock cheek. I want that. Did anyone ever tell you you have the behind of a cute Puerto Rican delivery boy?"

I WANT YOU TOO.

"Ah. Ah. Well, I guess—I guess that's as it should be. Let's not talk about it anymore."

WE COULD MAKE BABIES. THERE ARE WAYS.

"By public carrier, full freight allowed? My mailing tube doesn't work anymore."

THERE ARE WAYS.

"Oh, I'd be a model father. I could be the backstop in Little League practice. Let's not talk about it, huh?"

"Zip. Gone."

"More important, what'll we do for petrodollars? Guess I could hire myself out as an object lesson for small children who won't eat their cauliflower. What's all that? God, you talk a lot."

THE BISHOPS COMING. HES VERY EXCITED. ALSO—IM SORRY—SOME PEOPLE FROM THE PRESS.

"Heck, why not? Sell the serial rights. 'She-Priest Marries Incredible Nerve-Deaf Man.' We're an item, kid. Right up there with the guy who plays tennis while hooked to his kidney dialysis machine. Or 'Noted Psychic Predicts Earthquake Will Turn California into a Long, Thin Hot Tub.' Some're just great and some have greatness jammed down their throats." Simon's feet till the gravel. Friday has gone for a ride on him: hands catch at one Bermuda-short leg: feet are in one slipper: as children used to hitch a ride on the back of buses. "Have you told Bishop Whatsis you're unfrocking yourself?"

NO.

"I wish you wouldn't hang it up. You had a great career in white-collar crime ahead of you. Huh, Mer? I've got no prejudice either way. And it does kinda mean you have t'be nice t'me. Somehow the old Backfire Bomber feels in need of reassurance. Visit the widows and the afflicted and those who're sputtering out like jack-o'-lanterns. Don't quit for my sake. There's some sort of resolution on the way. Ha. Guess who's coming t'dinner? Soon. Soon."

STOP IT. YOUVE GOT A LONG LIFE AHEAD OF YOU.

"A day like this is already a long life. Don't wish it on me."

STOP TALKING LIKE THAT. STOP.

"Okay. I just wantcha t'know—I'm ready for the big earth bath. It doesn't scare me. Huh. Can you hear?"

IM YOUR WIFE NOW. THATS ALL I WANT TO HEAR.

"Bless you, but will the diaper service understand?"

AS LONG AS THERES YOUR VOICE. YOUR IMAGINATION. ITS ENOUGH.

"Ah, but deafness. I'm lost in my own private prop wash. Once I could answer anyone, now there are no questions. Hey, Mer: it's getting t'be a big in-joke. In me. I'm playing a tough town with the wrong material. There aren't even hecklers. I mean, who wants a stand-up comedian who keeps keeling over? I could—I could become a bitter person, given a little time. Given a little time. You might learn t'dislike me."

I RENTED A TUX. LETS CLEAN YOU UP AND TRY IT ON.

"Some transition there. The editor's marks were all over that one: a real flair cut. In other words: shaddap, Simon. I'm not the only one with an aptitude for providential deafness here. A tux. Say-hey, I haven't worn black tie since Norty's marriage of inconvenience. And what an evil *nudnicker* that ceremony was. Nort stomped on the wineglass and—*mazeltov*—put fourteen stitches in his foot. Uh?"

THE TUX. WE CAN TALK INSIDE.

"This tux. Uh: what about my dripolator? I'd hate t'leave the next groom with a corroded zipper. I mean, he might not be able t'get his marriage portion out. I should use a relief tube like the astronauts did: the past is hard enough t'forget, especially when it's orbiting around you." Friday has swung down: his stop on the line. Merry will shunt him aside with her foot: jealousy can extend that far. "No. No. Be kind. If he'd had a decent lawyer at the Monkey Trial that coulda been us down there. Friday and me, we've seen some long nights through together: a coupla unhousebroken miscues. He doesn't ask questions and he always agrees with me. Anyhow, I've learned patience from him, Mer. Animals can wait, you know. They don't invest in futures. There's no closing date or past-due notice. No minutes t'post time. It's kinda admirable, I find. Old Simon the plodder. Even in sex, you know, I was a career officer, but now—"

"Inside. Come on." Merry, well, she pushes him. Simon has noticed some strong-arming in the last week.

"Hold on. Hold on. There it is: Aldo's old barbecue. Merry, you remembered, you're a real fair ball—down the line for extra bases. Thank you. Dammit, thanks." She is pleased by his pleasure: yet somehow resentful of a father and a family that, though dead, though illegitimate, knew him better than she will. "Steak in the afternoon. Noodle salad. A half keg of beer. That's what Johnson meant by the Great Society. What happier way t'celebrate the hot-splice of two lives? For me, Soft Wear, no ring or holy hand-pass can bless like friendly words spoken with a full mouth. Did Niko bring the meat? The good meat from Carney's on Tenth Avenue? And—and all the others, are they coming? Even, you know—"

ALL.

"My foster father's ghost will rise in briquet smoke around us. His blood might not have been mine, but his cholesterol level was. God, he

could eat. And I thank him for that: that I was never ashamed t'use my
fingers. Take him all in all, I won't see a glutton like that again."
    MOVE. YOULL MAKE YOURSELF SICK OUT HERE.
    "Sick? Hey, careful, don't shove. Huh? My take-up reel doesn't take up
so fast anymore."
    "Move, you big windbag, we're late."
    "What say?"
    WERE LATE. MOVE.
    There is energy in marrying. Beyond one french door, across an en-
tresol, through Van Lynxx kitchen, the power attends on him. By coming
in, by just that, he has made an entrance here. What new status can this
be? His walk is a progress. Three unfamiliar men in uniform, three unfamiliar women, hand-sign good luck and shape well-wishing ear Braille
with their mouths: for one day nubile Simon will be catered to. He
stops: by now his feet have a standing order. Van Lynxx kitchen itself,
which boy-Simon had thought too hulking for an era of Frosted Flake
and breakfast nook, will appear in proportion at last: brought back from
that time when strep throat meant probable extinction and large families
alone could outnumber death. The long, dour pre-1700 table is sanguine.
Steak meat has been bricklaid around it: and excerpts of a salad yet to
be compiled: and bread you could pillow down on. The ox-length fireplace has flames that pennant up: blown like parade bunting: dark since
Larry and he filmed *Hearth* in there. Colonial museumware is at hand,
not on display. The room looks current. And Simon, marrying-kind, has
done this: it is a virtue, a dint, gone out. He will slide, click, through the
turnstile of his home: where once he was a tourist and where—this ritual
day aside—all people have thenceforward been. But are other homes that
different? Don't they, in their kind, ask a cover charge and minimum?
    Well, look: it's that high-stepping friend of his again. The staircase:
Simon's chute, trace and cataract: his best companionway. Probably nowhere has he made more impression than on this swift, sloped oak banister, with a boyhood-adolescence of buffing up and buffing down. It was
his cane then: or the safe contour and grab for a misjudged speed. Simon
rubs: will sketch, at least, some fair copy of rubbing there. The newel
post has budged in its socket: ha, do they guess, those who travel here to
commemorate America, that a child of their own unremarkable generation did this? Did age history with his weight and stupid vigor, as much
as war or the republic's long weather? Simon, period piece, will climb:
two feet on each tread. The banister has offered an arm. Merry, just
behind, is agile: in such ball-of-foot readiness infielders wait. But riser
and spiral have a feel for him: they anticipate the way man and wife
who have slept double-bed years together can. And, just then, just here,
Simon would like those others to be around: Aldo and Bettina. They

would have had each a place in this defined ceremony: places they never did locate in his undefined life. Simon will hold open house now: a posthumous invitation. They might have given him away: he, for certain, will give them away. There: so: it is done.

"Open my bedroom door. Hanh, say—say, I thought it was bad luck, us seeing each other beforehand. Though, I guess, your luck can't get much worse. As I look back, there's no value-added tax due on my life."

"Go in."

"What a mess. Didn't think a room could come down with toxic shock syndrome, did you?"

UGH.

"You can write that again."

The floor is gridlock and fallen muss. Simon hasn't had time or finger-wit enough to put his childish store away: still bubble wand, yo-yo, kaleidoscope, spark wheel, rubber snake, kazoo, hoop, top and idiotic crayon blob: unstructured play. His plastic soldiery is all outpost and no regiment to warn. Tinker Toy housing starts are way off. Dick Diver is at the bottom of his tank, which has leaked out to watermark scattered screen-treatment ms. Merry, whoo, inhales: one habit she must break. There is an accident of his around: but where? And, with it, ten or twelve gray monkey turds sit: like cement plopping under a street scaffold. They are identical: this is more than regularity, it is digestive mannerism. The wax-wood mock-up of George Washington has been disciplined: face against one wall. It in some hide-and-seek game. Martha's yellow skull—why wigless today?—has rolled dead, a big cue-ball follow shot. Urine bottle, pill bottle, spittoon-made-bedpan: cane and bandaging and oxygen pack: this is a room that has no manhood or middle age in it. Merry will begin to restore their restored 1684 marriage bed. She squints. Simon, with Robert, has lit the scene himself. There are a dozen light cues, all on TEN full: bulb, Kleig, voluptuous flood. No shadow cut out by one can dodge overlapping wash from the next. Darkness won't abduct his vision at any place. Yet the design is indirect: glare can't blind-spot him either. At 9:45 A.M. all this cross-firing brilliance seems misspent: as if the day, though solvent, had taken a second mortgage on itself.

READY?

"Hey, listen, Mer. If ever you wanna fool around, don't guilt-out because of me. I'll understand. Shit, let's not kid ourselves, huh? After a while it's not gonna be a Club Med tour—you know, hauling me around like a big Winnebago every place. One thing in my favor. I might've used the prone pressure method a lot, but I never was the jealous sort. I never begrudged anyone else his own fondue fork."

LAY OFF THE PIMPING AND SELF PITY. WE HAVENT TIME.

"No, wait. I only mean, with me bottled in bond this way, it isn't fair t'all that rich cropland of yours. I just thought: you're a coupla dozen drinks behind. You should have as much chance t'catch the gleet as I did."

20 GUESTS DOWNSTAIRS ALREADY. A. IS GIVING A TOUR TO COVER FOR US. SO SHADDAP.

"Okay. One thing, though. Dress me, but don't make me look in a mirror. I can't relate t'what I see there anymore. The diagram doesn't fit the wiring and my plugboard starts giving wake-up calls t'the wrong room."

"Uh-huh. I'm nodding."

"And, about the press—no flashbulbs, f'Chrissake. If I catch one in the glimmer, I'll turn into screaming plant food before the after-image is gone."

"Taken care of. Here. Look over here." She points. "See? The tux. Pretty, huh?"

"Uh-oh. There it is. Some poor first violinist is sitting around in his shorts right now. Gee, I could go from church t'managing a Loew's flagship theater in that. Do we have to? Yes, Simon, we obviously do."

His tuxedo, more than a mere formality, hangs down. With the bag of full-dress riveting: stud, link, clip. They both feel it, a servant's presence, and are inhibited. Well, he will try: not quite through with costume yet. Merry strips off his shirt: one hole in the chest has left an iron-on patch of digging filth. Clods drop when his belt is opened: sound, damn her mind, of dirt thrown by a three-day widow, in. She will wash his face with cloths dipped at the china table basin: behind ear, behind ear, along nape: a clean breast is made and that thick meat-cut over each kidney place. Merry can be rough: she has often rubbed horses down. Intent, her mouth will thin: as women grimace when putting eyeliner on. Now both hands are set to steep in the bowl: it is almost full and, eureka, a principle: water will slop out. His fingers brawl: they are irreconcilable and cannot make a hand. Merry has to bargain with them one by one, careful, somewhat out of countenance around the swollen wrist. Still not groomed. She inserts her nail beneath his nail, twist up and scrape: USE COIN TO OPEN LID. And, that not thorough enough, Merry will suck the dirt out: fingertip after marrow-bone fingertip: clean. She must talk then: strike up an acquaintance with herself. Simon finds it charming, whatever has been said. Yet he should know that, in just a little while, she will require other fellowship: people who can answer her good voice and mind. For the first time in his life Simon is poor company.

"Stop. Come on, don't. You embarrass me, Mer, giving head t'my hands like that."

JUST YOU DONT EMBARRASS ME TODAY. HOWD YOU GET SO DAMN FILTHY?

"Dirt was my core curriculum in college. I'm sorry. But I needed t'grubstake myself last night: there was nothing else. I'm land-poor and t'dig has always been a kinda teething ring f'me, it soothes."

OKAY. FEET NEXT. ALSO SOME BAN.

"Like Herman said, what's anybody smelled that's worth smelling nowadays? Black tie and rubber undies: I'll feel like Guy Lombardo and the new year all at the same time." Merry has sat him. "You wearing your priestliness?"

Nod.

"Gee, how'll they tell us apart? Some pair. Black and white like a cheap docu-drama. Or like two monks from the Order of First-Nighters. But shouldn't you wear white? After all, we're virgins of each other." Merry doesn't respond: she has been at his feet, shelling each toe from its pod. "Hey, I didn't see. Let Arthur do that. Don't you do it." Merry stands: then she will write at length. "What y'got there? A pre-nuptial agreement?"

SIT AND READ THIS LETTER WHILE I DRESS YOU. DONT— REPEAT—DONT MAKE ANY UNCONSIDERED MOVES. THERE WAS ALSO A NOTE ON VERY EXPENSIVE PERFUMED STATIONERY SAYING THAT A CERTAIN WOMAN WOULD NEVER FORGIVE YOU FOR MARRYING ME.

"Who? Who? Lemme see."

I TORE IT UP. BUT IT WAS SIGNED SOMETHING ARMISTEAD. SHE CALLED YOU RAMON. I WONT ASK QUESTIONS. THE PAST IS PAST.

"Oh, boy. Not like that past was past."

LETS NOT DISCUSS IT.

"Thank God. You'd never, I mean—"

SHUT UP AND READ. GOT TO FIGURE THESE DUMB STUDS OUT.

"A letter? Who can it be from? Oh, Jees. Hey, Jees, it's from Minnie."

> Dear Simon, Mr. Lynxx:
> In your life I've been like a stupid slow leak. Who would blame it if already you pushed this letter in the garbage can? I'm ashamed. I'm ashamed. We expect from black people what my hoodlum husband and his brother did to your wonderful van. (They received inside word from a *certain* party—it wasn't my Robert.) You got hung up for a sheep not a lamb, Mr. Lynxx, and I'm heartbroken. Believe me, a second shot at you I would snap up like nobody's business. You're a gentleman and also you have a beautiful build.
> Enclosed you should find three hundred dollars, which

I got up from advertising the SONY Trinitron in Buy-Lines. (Please keep this under your hat, since my dimwit husband thinks it was stolen—and my cousin, the insurance man, is putting a claim in.) Three hundred, I know, is a piddle at Jones Beach to make up for your damage and sorrow. By the grapevine (collect) Robert told me they smashed things like in a head-on. I will always have fond memories of your super movie van and the happy time we had in it. More cash will come by mail. Right now I'm looking at the dining room set or maybe Mr. Tough Customer's chain saw and four snow tires from the garage. But I have to stay low for a while.

Robert also tells me you're layed up with pins and needles all over from that terrible bash in the head—still this doesn't stop you getting married on Saturday. Such an amazing man! Hercules would lose to you. I'm pleased as punch (though *very* jealous). Marriage is just the ticket, please don't judge by me. For God's sake have children, without Robert I might as well be an azalea. You're a great genius and your kids will be little sharpers. As for the head, rest, eat, make a little love. *Everything will be all right.* This is Minnie speaking, so you got the word.

Robert also lets on that Rose has been hired as Mr. Herman Wolff's niece and is getting big money to make films. What a farfel! I knew her father and if she's related to Herman Wolff I'm the Pope's bimbo. I'm sorry she snitched Larry away from you but could be it's for the best. (A mother's crazy heart is talking, so forgive.) Robert has an Irisher girl for his steady now, which is better than being queer. At least I think. But looks like you were right about the playing fields of World War II. (See, I can remember.)

My husband, Mr. Gorilla, spits on the Karistan carpet when our child's name is mentioned. This, as you can guess, gives me heartache. I've lost two pounds already. Robert is fatherless now and I'm depending on you. (Is this too much to ask? I hope not.) Just keep an eye peeled for what he's up to here and there. He wants to be a big help on Lucky and he will be, you watch. He admires you and is trying to imitate you in every possible way.

Dear Simon, my secret love, I think about you every day. (With no afternoon programming, you can believe me.) It's ho-hum up here when it isn't yell and pound the table time. Maybe I'll run away from home again some day,

Yours with Kisses
Minnie

"Did you read this?" Head shake. "Y'gotta. Minnie's a Formula One person, take it from me."

I TOOK HER $300 INSTEAD. ROBERT SAID I SHOULD. AND WE CAN USE IT. RISE—I WANT TO PULL YOUR PANTS UP.

"Okay. Stand back. Whup, almost got stove-in there. My drift indicator's off a bit. Well, well, from up here I look like what the TV critics would call a familiar format show. A boiled shirt for a boiled mind. Are you pleased? Huh?"

"Good. Fine. I'm very happy. Oh, yes, indeed. Clothes do make the man—and they had one hell of an assignment here. All you need now is a little Pledge for the top of your head. Yes."

"What say? I couldn't read that. Huh, co-maker of my respectability?"

EXCELLENT. LISTEN. MRS. P IS OUTSIDE. SHE HAS SOMETHING TO TELL YOU. DONT—DONT—LAUGH WHEN SHE COMES IN. SHE LOOKS LIKE MISS HAVISHAM.

"Don't laugh, got it. Next page."

THEN ARTHUR WILL BE IN.

"Oh, grand. He'll wet his finger and try t'play my mind like it was a glass harmonica. He still thinks I'm the UPI stringer from Saturn or someplace."

IVE GOT TO COMB MY HAIR AND RUN OVER THE SERVICE. IVE NEVER DONE IT BEFORE.

"How'll I know what t'say and when?" His left eye has misted. Mucus forms around some grit: a quick pearl. "Damn." One blink. "There."

I HAVE IT WRITTEN DOWN ON SLATES. I BOUGHT 96 OF THEM, SO YOULL BE ABLE TO TALK WITH EVERYONE. THE BISHOP WILL GIVE A HOMILY.

"Whazzat?"

ITS SUPPOSED TO BE SHORTER THAN A SERMON BUT ISNT. BE GOOD. DONT YAWN OR APPLAUD. IM GOING.

"Wait. Didja ever get that medical work-up from Dr. Gobel?"

Nod.

"Well? So?"

THERES NOTHING WRONG WITH YOU.

"I see."

THAT HE CAN FIND.

"Wonderful. I say it's a lockout and everyone else says it's a strike. And you? What d'you think of Dr. Gobel's non-assessment?"

I THINK ITS A MYSTERY. BYE. ILL BE BACK SOON. DONT
FALL AND DONT LET THAT DAMN MONKEY CLIMB ON YOUR
TUX.

"Hold it. One thing. Merry, when it happens, pop my lenses—will
you?"

NOTHINGS GOING TO HAPPEN.

"Mer, there's none of us has a no-cut contract here."

NOTHINGS GOING TO HAPPEN.

"If—if—it happens then. Will you pop them? They've made my eyes
tired for so long. I want my video discs t'rest. Promise that."

Nod.

"Who goes first? Us or them?"

US. I DONT WANT YOU TO HAVE SECOND THOUGHTS.

"No chance. But, Mer, there is something I haveta say now: something
you haveta be clear on. It's in me. It's not in you, Lord knows. But I
want you t'understand just how I feel about you, since this is probably
the last time we'll be alone before, before you really commit yourself.
I—" Her hand is across his mouth.

YOU WANT TO BE HONEST?

"Yes, I—" Across his mouth again.

DONT BOTHER. HONESTY IS AN OVERRATED VIRTUE. LOVE
YOU, BYE NOW.

"Merry—"

But Merry has beaten his long rap, out: replaced at once, on the bedroom doorsill, by a very liberal enlargement of Mrs. P. Simon won't
laugh: laughter, anyhow, isn't agreeable without sound. Yet he might:
Mrs. P has a Tiparillo caught on her lower lip and on her head—God, can
it be? It can—Martha Washington's wig. To go with the twenty-seven-
pound "Robe à l'Anglaise in Green and Yellow Muslin over Dark Blue
Satin Petticoat, White Fichu, English, 1781." Stripped, museum card and
all, from one of the Van Lynxx costume manikins. No trouble in your
"something borrowed" department here. And now she comes, ssssh-pow-
pow, punting great hem after great hem in front of her, to Simon for his
rubber-stamp kiss. At which delicate flesh transmission the foot-high
powdery wig will slip sideward and down. Not much cheek room: Simon
almost overshoots: he hasn't proper clearance for a runway this short.
And beneath yellow, yellowing, cuff silk there is still her leather wrist-
band: marriage as match—also set and game. She has a slate held up: the
first of many prepared statements that Simon will read today.

YOU LOOK SIMPLY SPLENDID. This written endorsement doesn't
quite convince Simon: printed, as it was, ten minutes ago and in another
room. But he will accept and read on. CONGRATULATIONS TO
BOTH OF US. I HOPE YOU FEEL WELL TODAY.

"I'm hitting on all two cylinders. Merry and I, we'll just have our wooden wedding early, that's all. But you, you look more than simply splendid. You look very complexly splendid." If not attractive, at least filled out. "That's a memorable, ah, concept you have on."

"Yes, I think so. Bloody great job of work, if you must know, but worth it in the end. Arthur thinks I'm off my head, but I say you want something special on a day like this, might otherwise just go bum-stark. The Landmarks people got a bit doggish about us—private wedding on public soil, you know. Thought I'd keep up the historic side, might soothe the Lords Lieutenant of Antiquity. But I must say your bishop put them straight. Seems to know everyone in this cannibal kingdom they call a city, that one does. I'll give 'em a ring, he says—rings everybody. And they listen."

Simon has nodded.

"Oh, of course, you can't hear."

"What?"

"You can't hear!"

"No need t'shout. Just write it down."

"All I've just said? Nonsense, I can't possibly write all that down. It'd take days. You want a secretary, mate."

"What?"

"It'd take days! To write!"

"Huh? Gosh, I guess you're just as nervous as I am."

"I— Hold on. Hold on. Got to follow the bloody regs here, I can see that. Hold on." IVE WAITED SO LONG FOR THIS MOMENT. "Really is deaf, I suppose. Now if you'd asked me about it yesterday, Lying doggo, I would have said. Just lying doggo." ARTHUR AND I HAVE BEEN. "It's like a wretched steno exam." STAR-CROSSED LOVERS. "Or like talking to some slant-eyes wog."

"He's a lucky man."

"More?" AND YOUR BRIDE IS AN EXQUISITE YOUNG PERSON. "Doesn't know what she's signed on for. Might just as well marry a parched leg of mutton."

"Thank you."

"You're welcome to it. Oh, look now, almost made me forget what I came for." MAY I ASK A FAVOR? "All this jiggery-pokery. Gets you talking to yourself like a complete nutter."

"Shoot."

"Shoot? I would." WILL YOU GIVE ME AWAY? IM IN A STRANGE LAND. "That's nicely put, dear, if I do say so."

"I'd be honored. We're compatriots: I'm in a strange land myself."

"We've had our little set-tos, Simon, but—"

"What?"

"Oh, blast the man and his never-ending whats. What? What? What?" THANK YOU. "All I hope, yobbo, is it won't give your mother any satisfaction while they're turning her spit in hell." WEVE HAD OUR BAD MOMENTS. "Not that she was his rightful mum: the poor crippled bastard staring at me like a dutch door." BUT IVE ALWAYS BEEN FOND OF YOU. "Bastard and cripple. Bastard and cripple! Can't hear a thing. Not half sexy this: like putting through a dirty phone call, when no one knows who you are at the other end." ALMOST AS THE SON I WANTED TO HAVE. "Isn't that right? Isn't that fuckin' right, Simon?"

"Thanks for putting up with me."

"It was a damn nuisance, you great slob."

"Nonetheless, the great slob thanks you."

"What? What?" The Tiparillo has broken in her hand. "You've been hearing me? You've been hearing all this time. I knew it. I knew it."

"Calm down. I can lip-read a word or two. Just enough t'avoid a complete verbal rape."

"Damned eavesdropper. Some filthy nerve. Well, I'll cover my mouth from here on in, you can be sure."

"Have you got a cough?"

"No, I haven't. Peeking at my lips like that. Indecent, I'd say it was."

"We understand each other, you and I. And today you're in your glory —so much so that you even have a little patience f'me. Just a little." He smiles well. "Am I right?"

"Oh, you'll do."

"Shall we shake?"

"Fair enough. He's married to me now, not to you. And there's an end to it."

"Whatever."

"Yes." WELL ARTHUR TOLD ME TO HURRY IT ALONG. HE WANTS TO HAVE A WORD.

"Okay."

"Arthur! Arthur, you can come in now."

"Uncle."

Arthur is on a siding: flagged down there until the satin-muslin train of his wife-to-be can yank freight through. Simon's floor is neat wherever she was: the big democratic hem has cow-caught Tinker Toy building material, paper, six plastic men on dawn patrol, a yo-yo and some monkey poo. Arthur will watch her, sweeping, sweep out. He looks photoreduced: worn: as if body part and body part were gathering in a last dull herd instinct. His white tongue is out. Arthur has a how-to problem: how to finger-read RECORD—not FAST FORWARD or PLAY or REVERSE—on the Japanese tape machine under his side pocket flap. Simon waits: this prelim is well established between them. The microphone, another corsage, flowers near his white carnation. Push: Arthur has selected (my-mother-said-to-pick-this-one) and wahhr-rahrm!—in his pocket Luciano Pavarotti sings an aria about terrible revenge. The sound is staggering: Arthur will do a four-step fox-trot away, old-fashioned bewilderment: and apologize. But Simon doesn't hear either the infraction or the excuse. Arthur, in his calf-love of things senseless and ideal, has become an engaging fool: more likable, at least, than the meditative uncle was. Now he comes, fast forward and lapel ahead, to Simon here.

"Well, it's the recording angel. Congratulations."

YOU LOOK SMASHING AND WELL.

"Sell short, it's just a technical rally. Kind of what makes a corpse rise from deep water after a month. Are we on the air?"

"Eh, what?"

"Don't feed me that snow broth, Philbrick. You've got more hookups there than a bookie's wire room." Arthur will present his foolscap pad: six long yellow pages in outline form: with a space at each heading for Yes____, No____, Other____. "And what's this here? A little SAT? A screenplay based on the Baltimore Catechism?"

JUST A FEW QUESTIONS. THATS ALL. NO RUSH. CHECK THEM OVER LATER.

"A few. It looks like *Summa Theologica*. Arthur, I can't read small print, I get like carsick. I need t'look around: since I went deaf everything's been on sight draft. My head's got a high-pass filter on it."

WE HAVE TO BE QUICK. THE BISHOPS DOWNSTAIRS. ALL 7 FEET OF HIM. I RESENT IT. CANONICALLY YOU DONT FALL WITHIN HIS JURISDICTION.

"I don't? I fall in everybody else's."

MERRY SAYS YOU HAD ANOTHER BLACKOUT LAST NIGHT.

"That nark. I'll get her."

WAS IT ANY DIFFERENT?

"When you haven't seen one, you haven't seen them all."

IT CANT BE JUST THAT. "Damn, I wish you could hear. I can't write fast enough." Arthur seems tired. Wearisome this: keeping a secret that no one will listen to. WHAT WAS THE LAST IMAGE YOU SAW?

"Friday taking a shot from my Coke bottle. And he wiped the mouth off first."

COULD YOU KEEP CONTROL THROUGHOUT? OR DID YOUR MIND LET GO?

"It let go. Oh, yes."

AND WHAT WAS THERE THEN?

"Well, Perrier water. A lot of Perrier water. Universal Perrier water. Pretty dull. Worse than that: it was shabby genteel."

BUT WHAT FORM DID IT TAKE?

"Arthur, you're trying t'wrap orange juice with rubber bands. It doesn't work."

STOP THINKING IN PHYSICAL TERMS.

"Me? You're the material witness. Didn't you ask me what form it took? Listen, there is no metaphor for nothing except more nothing. It's the end of all art and glory, is what it is. It's drab as Phisohex or any other absolute. It's boring, my friend: it's endless Cincinnati. Give it Stanley Kubrick, De Niro, Hoffman and forty million dollars and still you don't have a property."

DO YOU EVER HEAR? ARE THERE WORDS THAT COME TO YOU?

"Sure, out of the void a deep voice says, 'Now this may look like an ordinary handkerchief—' What d'you want me t'tell you, Arthur? That we're in *The Song of Bernadette* and Linda Darnell really is the Virgin Mary? No. No, sorry. This is not a religious experience."

HOW CAN YOU BE CERTAIN?

"Oh? How? Say then, is insanity a religious experience?"

IT COULD BE.

"Could. So could smelling a rose be. People have thought that. You sound like some kid repairing sandals in a commune. No. Uh-uh. If madness is revelation, then God must be mad. And besides that He's working for scale here."

BUT A HIGHER CONSCIOUSNESS COULD SEEM INSANE TO—

"To a lower consciousness, which I am right now? Aha. Then how could I understand it, huh? And if my consciousness is raised, if I go bat-eared and start drinking my space medicine straight, how could I explain it t'you? C'mon, Arthur, we've gone over this before. It doesn't work. I've got no interest in higher truth and I hope it has no interest in me. All I want is t'get well and slug a handball and poke some quack now and then. That's it: that's all."

PAUL WAS STRUCK BLIND ON THE ROAD TO—

"Wait now. Let's rewind that. Let me hand you some supposes. Suppose Paul got up and said, 'Damn mule. Fell off and gave myself a good concussion.' Suppose he hadn't been a superstitious Pharisee who believed in burning animals like religion was a cook-out? Suppose he said, 'Must be a clot pressing on something. I'm blind and I hear voices. Better go check in for a week at Columbia Presbyterian.' Hanh? Suppose he said that instead of writing all those noodgy letters? My question is, what would God have done then? Excused him from class? Or left him blind out of spite? I mean, it worked with Paul, but by that time, how many people were walking around Palestine with white canes wondering what hit them?"

IN THE BOOK OF JOB—

"Don't put me in the same card file as Job. He believed in God, he got what he deserved. But not me, I'm innocent."

BUT— *MMM* Simon has scratched his thumbnail on the plastic cover.

"No buts. The time has run out on buts. Just tell me this: if there was a God, would He be man enough t'admit it when He got the wrong direct object."

"You won't let me write—"

"What if, say, Moses, with other things on his mind, had walked past the burning bush? Just walked past? Hanh? I mean, he'd been around, he might've known that surface petroleum could catch fire: that what he was looking at wasn't God but early OPEC. What if it didn't intrigue him: what if it wasn't a good enough act? We're supposed t'be impressed by a lot of flimsy, made-for-TV miracles—"

THEN YOU EXPLAIN WHY YOUVE LOST YOUR HEARING AND YO—

"No! Oh, no." Simon will knock the slate down. "End of conversation. I'm not responsible, I don't have t'explain anything. Someone, you, some-one—someone, dammit—owes *me!* An explanation."

"Don't get excited, don't. You'll fall."

"What? What?"

"I'm sure—sure—that God is speaking to you. And to me, through you. And to all the world, through you." Arthur stamps his foot. "But maybe you're right. Maybe He made a mistake. Maybe He picked the wrong man and you'll roast in hell, blind, deaf and dumb."

"Why're you yelling?"

"How d'you know I'm yelling, eh? How—yes, how—you who believe only what your senses report? There's no more sound for you: or for all the universe. Isn't that right?"

"What?"

"Nothing. Nothing. Just nothing."

"Hey, Arthur. This is dumb. It's our wedding day. That's a miracle, isn't it? I never thought any woman'd stick her prize flag in me."

"Simon—"

"Never talk religion or politics, that's what they say, isn't it?"

"Simon—"

"All I want is peace, Arthur. Give the poor jerk a little peace."

"Simon—"

"Didja buy Friday a bow tie, like I asked you to?"

Nod.

"Then let's just relish the day, huh? Find my hand and shake it. We're lucky men. We don't deserve what we're getting."

"I certainly don't."

"What?" Arthur has retrieved the slate.

SHE MAY TRY TO KEEP ME AWAY FROM YOU.
"Who, Merry? Nah."
MRS. P.
"She's Mrs. G now, remind her of that. Be a man, Arthur, kick some ass. Now shake."
"Yes. Yes. Congratulations."
"Listen. You've been a real chief these last weeks. I'm grateful. But Merry is coming up soon. Can you give me two or three bachelor minutes alone?"
YES. IM SORRY. THIS WAS THE WRONG TIME.
"No perspiration, man. Seeya in church."
Simon walks literally: doing the legwork for himself: step after pre-designed step, to a low bureau top. With one hand he can brush the now final draft of *Lucky* off: it will fall into a trash basket, below. His contact-lens holder is there: prepared. To what purpose? And he might answer, To what purpose do suicides on a high bridge so often remove their footwear before leaping down? Life, that habit, is not easily kicked. Hahhh: must clear his throat: a guesswork undertaking without sound or inner feel. But Dr. Gobel has told Simon to try: phlegm could otherwise collect in the coughless, untickled trachea and strangle him. Hahhh, hahhhh, Simon says. He has already put the letter in an open drawer. Then his ice-tong grasp will pick and close: to lift Bettina's small ring box out. BGL: and scoring around its latch, where an irritable fingernail has scraped years away. Her wedding band is dime wide: an heirloom, worn by Van Lynxx women since before the nation was, and not much prized by Bettina. He assays it. Gold, or some alloy, has been corroded: eaten at by her acid body flux. Salts of Bettina, salts of Merry. Simon can drop the ring in his breast pocket. He will require help to pluck it out again, but this at least he has done himself: he has participated and is glad. In his own house now he feels homesick. Unlike Aldo to pass up a barbecue. Oh, how he would have fed Merry this afternoon. But Aldo wasn't his father and—who can tell?—his true parents may be here: leaning from a high-rise balcony, delivering catered three-bean salad: with sweatsuit on or miter. They are a large contingent: the possible. In that way he is well-connected. Simon clears his throat again.
"Hahhhh. Huk? Hungaaah!"
Something has just come up. His vision zags: one long whiplash spasm is scaling him, out. A real dock walloper: complete, from hip to stem of head. Simon will almost unbalance, but elbow and hand on the bureau, that heavy armload, guy him upright yet. He has, aha, vomited: neatly, in a single dice-cup throw. Nerveless, blond fluids dissipate across the knitted bureau cloth: Simon didn't think he had it in him still. And—pan back, look—what should that be? He can distinguish a white, flat length of animal in the mess. It lies vermiculate, S and U and ampersand and

unbound loop: broken here, broken again: square-sectioned like a miniature, torn roll of stamps. The worm has no life now: but its form is complex and exotic: in a way, refined. Simon would touch if that were possible: he can't make head nor tail of it. Parts—out of their element,
him—are drying already: they warp and glint: tiny as a kitten's first
teeth, strung. Simon is fascinated: however primitive, natural functions
delight him. He will look again. One thing is sure and it impugns his cordial temperament: here Simon has been an ungenerous host.

"Hi there, little fella. Well. Well, just look at you now. Kinda short rations belowdecks, was it, huh? See, I didn't know I was eating f'two. Or
six. Or how many you are. Gosh, isn't that amazing? All those tiny parts.
In me. Hanh. Right *in* me. Coulda put you down as a dependent. But we
sorta miscarried here I guess."

And, in this game of quick turnovers, Simon is a sudden optimist. He
will heal after all: the entrails, look, have augured well. He may yet run
once more and hear wind from his own momentum coming toward. It
was this thing, then, that shot toxin through him: that made a four-
course eating of his faculties. He can see the contagion, the serpent mystery, stranded in S and U and necklace break. An adroit moocher—
HABITAT LYNXX—has scrounged off him: in his row-house abdominal
way. Simon will stand straight. Now (it isn't beyond thought) he might
still pass as husband and man: not just the barnacle dragged on her sleek
racing hull. Simon, who carries no weight, is empty, high and rare. The
bureau cloth can be folded in half, like so, to hide. He will tell Merry,
but not this afternoon: it isn't an item to announce with the banns: taste-
less, he has enough taste left. You don't let the bride know—listen, dear—
that her spouse of today is someone, well, with worms. Simon has curved
his mouth and blown air through. In shape to whistle. Minnie, whose excellent flesh reminded him of harvest and bull market days, hit it on the
black. *Everything will be all right.* He should have guessed.

YOU LOOK HAPPY.

"Oh, hi. Am I whistling?"

SORT OF. LUCKY YOU CANT HEAR. WERE ON.

"There's no business like show business. I'm ready, lead ahead."

"Wait, let me wipe your chin off. There's some white gook on it. Have
you been eating?"

"Huh?"

"Never mind." LAST CHANCE. YOU SURE YOU WANT THIS? ITS
MARRIAGE, REMEMBER? VERY SERIOUS BUSINESS.

"Downy furrow, I'm wedded to the idea. Shall we advance? Arm in
arm. It's time you made me an honest man."

Simon, né not Lynxx, of questionable descent, descends: buffing the
wooden banister again. Arthur and Mrs. P take precedence under him:
age before disability. Mrs. P is menacing their rite of narrow passage.

18

Her stiff, bone-set gown has destinations known to itself alone: it might
arrive separately and somewhere else. On each new step she will disappear into cloth: décolletage around her chin, like a Mae West floating
up. Simon, right now, seems the more accomplished walker. Arthur has
gotten down at heel for her twice already: to release hem from sneaker
sole. She is not dressed: pavilioned rather. But Simon, behind with
Merry, doesn't notice: he has been counting his house.

Around, left and into the main entryway, right and into a parlor, ahead
and back through Van Lynxx kitchen, there are whole parade sidewalks
of them: boosted, on chair, on table, craning. More than one hundred,
Simon would judge. A network TV camera crew. Frequent priests. Robert. Yes, those two mung beans, Ball Peen and Sledge. Wolff with a yarmulke on. Niko plus three waitresses. Unmistakably a bishop. Unmistakably poor Mr. and Mrs. Allen. Staff from NA—Bill Marcus, Art
McArthur, hmm, Harold Gluck—people who ordinarily wouldn't speak to
him in their, or his, right senses. Conscripted by Herman: shotgun wedding guests. Friday, above, on a wrought-iron chandelier, wearing black
tie and tail. Then the Great Ferry delegation. Polly. Bella Chicago. June
the Prune and Chloe Speed. No Annie, thank God. Eduardo. Vampira
and the Salem Girl. Alice Yawn. Little Zipper, with one eye already on
the episcopal crotch. Each is a college bowl game float: in his or her
What am I? twenty questions self. Several, too, that he can't place: who,
like Simon, have often subsisted week by week on open bars and free
chive dip. He is a cause for feeding: good. Most have Magic Slates: Robert, best boy and best man, will raise his, APPLAUSE. From their palm
speed, Simon guesses that the reception is earnest. Splendid: he has just
gotten an ovation for standing. Well, why not? There are accomplishments and there are *accomplishments*. And Aldo thought he'd never
amount to anything.

SPEECH
SIMON SPEECH
SAY SOMETHING
SPEECH

"Thank you. Thank you. Please stop—please, there's nothing more futile than applause for a deaf man. Testing, testing, is this loud enough?"
YES from Robert. "You all look t'me like an old Vitascope crowd scene.
Right now I'm what we in the industry call a mute print: someone put a
very dynamic noise suppressor on my track. Well. Well, unaccustomed as
I am to public reticence, this is a special moment. I think everyone I've
ever insulted is here: we honor each other. It just goes t'show, there is no
more intimate relationship than that of dumper and dumped upon. I see
that you've got your sentiments printed out like mass cards. I appreciate
it, especially since I know that everyone in the film game or the pop art
flack is illiterate." HEY YOU. WERE THE ONES SHOULD BE DEAF.

"Look at that, I'm still getting brickbats. Is this a wedding or an inquest? Hanh? Don't answer, let me introduce my bride by a future marriage, Merry Allen—press your fat noses t'the glass and yearn. Lush as drawn butter, isn't she? And this is my uncle Arthur and his bride, Margaret. Be kind t'them and keep your hands in your pockets, Zipper. Now. Now, I'll try t'get around t'everyone, but please remember—I'm not a raw egg. Don't be concerned if I fall down. I've spent sixty hours in a Link trainer learning how t'walk. I'm about as mobile as one of those forty thousand cheap desk sets that NA sends out each Christmas—in an attempt never, never t'show a net profit. God forbid, some poor actor or screenwriter should get his percentage. When I was on bourbon street and I took a nose dive, you just stood me up and propped me in a corner. Let the old customs prevail. There is food. I bring you steak. Eat. I'm not a religious man, but I do think that no ceremony can be certified true and correct unless people have eaten over it. Again—all of you. Thanks for coming. I'm moved. Do feel free to say snide and heinous things t'me. I won't hear. And we'll all respect each other the more for it. You may applaud again. Merry?"

"Yes?"

"Innerduce me t'your parents, who, I think, are just about ready t'give you plane fare t'Reno as a wedding gift."

"Don't worry. Come."

Ah, this must be a sandy-haired man. Such people thrive no doubt: we mention them often enough. Novels, for instance, are full of sandy-haired men. But never, until Mr. Allen and now, could Simon imagine what that term meant. Beneath the light desert boot brown top, a sort of valuable grit—like crushed shell in Hyannisport walks—would seem to have been carefully underlaid: more rough coating than hair: a surface to deter graffiti with. Mr. Allen is slim and—can you say this of men?—flat-chested: wearing Scotch-tape-color eyeglass frames to emend the myopia he and Merry have. A powerful, quiet swing vote: someone to sit just behind board chairmen: one of those meek who will inherit the earth and then subdivide it. With a tan portfolio even here: lest, at any moment, from home to marriage to home again, he be left alone and not totally preoccupied beside his wife. Who is crying. Tears have congested her. They appear not mournful but infectious. Yet the good features survive that. Her skin is skintight. Hair, long and dense with proteins and—by a discreet synthetic process—still wonderfully brunette. Millrace cheekbones: a recumbent and accessible mouth. Merry, the prognosis is, will age well.

"How'dja do, sir? I'd say, 'You're not losing a daughter, you're gaining a son'—but that's probably what's got you worried right now."

HAPPY TO MEET YOU, SIMON. YOU'RE WELCOME TO OUR FAMILY.

"Thanks. That's very kind. Thanks, I appreciate it." Simon has a hand out. Mr. Allen will shake and—ha, knuckle pain—his skin is turning sandy, too, now. Mr. Allen had expected a cripple, but not such a loud, strong cripple. His Princeton class ring is, good grief, bent. "And Mrs. Allen. Let me bank-shot a kiss on you. Hold still, I gotta play the angles here. There. Did I reach?"

"Yes. Yes, you did. My face is a mess. You must excuse my face. I think crying is foolish, but I do it all the time. Does that make me foolish? James thinks it does, I know, but it was a surprise, we never, you see—"

"Mother. Your slate."

"Oh, yes. What did I write?" BE GOOD TO OUR LITTLE GIRL. "Is that all? I thought there was more, James says—"

"Good? She's my prime meridian, my Boardwalk and Park Place, my second growth. My living wage, my drug of preference, my inner circle and my outer limit. She taught me gentleness. You wouldn't believe it, but once I was loud and boorish: fire inspectors useta cite me as a violation. Now I'm reformed, thanks t'Merry and, through her, thanks t'you. I only wish I'd had such parents." Simon will lean forward: to, he hopes, whisper. "Listen, I can imagine how you feel. Don't think I can't. I brought a dog with mange home once when I was seven: there are parallels. From your welcome I can measure the length and breadth of your generosity. And your love for Merry."

IF THERES ANYTHING YOU NEED, JUST ASK. I HAVE FRIENDS AT THE MAYO CLINIC.

"Thanks, Mr. Allen. I might take you up on that. Though, from recent evidence, I may just need a good exterminator. What?"

BALL PEEN AND S., ROBERT TELLS ME, ARE SCARED TO STAY. YOU BETTER GO REASSURE THEM. "Mother, Father, please excuse us. Simon has so many friends here. We'll talk at the reception."

Merry has guide-dogged Simon away. Her father and mother are, she knows, bashful people: under a best circumstance it isn't easy to be articulate with Simon: now dialogue crosses in the mail. People shut and open around: pushing them forward, valve, valve, thrombi along a vein. Simon can be rash: there is, be thankful for that, no room to fall down in. Bella Chicago has just absolved a priest of his wallet: June the Prune is shooting up: brides make her sentimental. Niko will present a steak for grading. Meat, its thousand textures: Simon would panel his room with raw sirloin. He orders a kiss-to-go from each waitress. Merry has been waving Ball Peen and Sledge in, near. Ball Peen is doubtful: his black, round Korean face looks like the bottom of a wok. He will come, then slow: to get behind Sledge, who will slow: to get behind Ball Peen, who will slow. But, at that moment and on purpose, Simon falls: they must catch him. His embrace is strong as star gravity: three heads grind. Ball

Peen has a two-hundred-word paragraph of extenuation written on his slate. In one place, poked by remorse, the wooden stylus went—plastic hole—through. Simon can see parentheses and a footnote asterisk. Ball Peen is pointing. But, clumsily, with stunned thumb and forefinger, Simon will pinch the double sheet: and, zip up, magic: Ball Peen has a clean slate.

"Ah, t'hell with it. That'll teach you t'buy on credit. Anyhow, it was me, wasn't it, who wanted t'swim behind the big minelayer?"

BUT YOU CANT FEEL OR—

"Never mind, man couldn't think past his Skinner box until he invented the zero. Listen, I still show up on the extinction meter. I'm a little eye-minded right now, but something tells me I'm gonna get well again."

SIMON WE—

"Forget it. So the pilot fish got eaten. It happens. It's been like freshman week at San Quentin, but I'm job-trained now. In that thrift shop you call a mind, let go. You and Sledge and me, all the food we've made together: that's a loyal order of something, isn't it? Gotta be. Let's forgive left and right. Home free all, huh?" They nod. "And I won't have t'hear about that honky fox Desdemona again. Where'd Robert go, what's he up to?"

Robert is up to crying: weepy as a cold basement wall in August might be: or a sore. Merry and Simon both know this. The just-fit contact lenses have made him an aquifer. Robert will never wear them at ease, but he will wear them: oh, he will. Even in this watered-down version Robert has a new courtly way. The tux more than suits him: it and his aluminum-foil tan are an ensemble. This won't be his last time in full dress: Robert will spend a life seeking, composing formal occasions for himself. Simon can remember that child, scarcely extra-uterine, on the top bunk of his van one long month ago. Simon stumbles: the right leg has missed floor, caught a crab: too intent. There is something offensive but necessary about Robert: like a bubblenest, full of frogs to come, in slow pondwater. He need not be responsible for it. Robert, here, will introduce them to his wedding date. She is black and seemly, with airline wings over a tourist-class breast. Robert has one hand on the place that could be buttock, could be hip: her crupper. A place of transitions and interesting restlessness.

THIS IS CHARLENE.

"Gladda meecha. Robert looks like a pressed duck, doesn't he? I know, I know, you always cry at weddings."

ILL GET USED TO THESE S.O.B.'S. "Excuse us, Merry. Can I have a private word with Simon, huh?" She will step back, but not gladly.

HOW ABOUT CHARLENE? IVE FLOWN HER.

"How. Dead-stick? I hope you were careful. Anything could develop

14

in a darkroom like that." Robert laughs: his teeth again. "Great, kid. This'll really perforate the Bulb Baron's watering can. Send him a wedding snap. You've got an instinct for the old vagus nerve, which, despite the marvelous rant, I never had. You'll go places, Robert—just make sure you can come back again. And watch your own carotids."

SORRY ABOUT LAR. ROSE MADE HIM AN OFFER HE COULDNT REFUSE. AT LEAST IM OFF THE PREP H.

"Yeah. Well, don't forget your mother. I may seem like something only a radiotelescope could find, but I can still pinch heads. Y'hear me?"

OKAY. OKAY. READ THIS.

"So much? Can't it wait? No? All right, hold me up."

NORTY BOUGHT THE VAN. HES GOING TO BE AN INDE-PENDENT PRODUCER WHICH MEANS HES GOT NO PLACE ELSE TO LIVE. HE HAD THE WHOLE FRONT END REBUILT. YOU SHOULD SEE. ITS ALL FULL OF HIS CORNY SUITS AND A COMPLETE BARBELL SET. I GOT $25,000. ALSO A LOT OF PAPER MORE VALUABLE THAN KLEENEX. BUT NOT MUCH.

"Huh? $25,000. For that wreck?"

I THREW LUCKY IN.

"He bought *Lucky*? But why?"

"Wait. I knew you'd ask. I've got it written out. I'm proud of this." I HAD A LETTER OF INTENT MADE UP. THEN I FORGED WOLFFS NAME ON IT. A MR. SHIFFMAN WAS VERY HELPFUL WITH THE LEGAL END—ROSE PUT ME ON TO HIM. WHEN WE WERE DICKERING FOR THE VAN, I LET NORTY SEE IT. BY, HA, MISTAKE. SUDDENLY HE THOUGHT IT WAS A HOT PROPERTY. WHEN HE GOES TO WOLFF WITH THE RIGHTS HELL GET A MIDDLE FINGER. I HAD TO SIGN YOUR NAME HERE AND THERE, I THOUGHT YOU WOULDNT MIND. IM GIVING MERRY $20,000 TO DEPOSIT FOR YOU. ITS MY WEDDING PRESENT. TELL ME, HOW DID THAT ASSHOLE SURVIVE SO LONG?

"He. I don't know. He was, he is, my friend. $20,000? Where is he? Didn't he come?"

CALLED. VAN BROKE DOWN ON THE L.I.E. CRACKED UN-DERCARRIAGE LIKE A GRUMMAN BUS. SENDS HIS CONGRATS.

"Jesus, Robert, $20,000. I can't do that to—"

"Next slate." WILL YOU SAY A FEW WORDS TO CHICK FER-RARI FROM WBOX-TV? HUMAN INTEREST. THEYRE HOT TO DO A SEGMENT OF "THURSDAY MAGAZINE" ON YOU. FER-RARI WANTS WEDDING FOOTAGE AND THEN IF THAT WORKS OUT HELL ARRANGE AN INTERVIEW AT HOME. IT WONT HURT WHEN WE START PRODUCTION AGAIN.

"Wait, Robert, I—"

GOOD. "Mr. Ferrari, we're ready. You can set up here."

"Robert—" Merry has come between. "Set what up? I don't like the way you're rubbing your hands."

"A little TV interview. Stand next t'Simon, Merry."

"Oh? A little interview? And who gave you permission to produce our wedding? We haven't got time right now."

"Three minutes? Sure we've got three minutes. Hanh, Merry? Simon's gonna have the recognition he deserves. Stand there."

"No."

"Merry, this is network TV. There might be a doctor out there who can help Simon. Did you think of that, huh? No, you didn't. Right there. Put an arm around."

"Robert, you're exploiting this—"

"No, I'm not. No, I'm not. Lay off, Merry, that isn't fair. Simon understands. This is the way things are done. Hi, Mr. Ferrari. We're ready any time. May I introduce the bride, Rev. Merry Allen? And this, of course, is Simon Lynxx, winner of two Golden Reels for Best Short Subject. It's all yours."

"Hot up the light, Charlie. How d'you do, Mr. Lynxx? I know he can't hear. I'm being pleasant anyhow, he sees that. Good angle, Charlie? Robert—that's your name?—ask some of those Mardi Gras jerk-offs to move out of the background. Pleased to meet you, Rev. Allen, I admire your courage a whole lot. It's what the people who watch 'Thursday Magazine' really go for. How much tape d'we have, Kim? About five? No, don't change batteries now. Okay, give me a cue. Does he know what's going on? I've got cards here printed up—I'll do a simulcast voice-over while he's reading them. We want t'move it along pretty quick. Pace. It's all pace. We've got sixteen percent of the audience, Rev. Allen, and like I say they really go for courage, but they're in a hurry. Count down, Kim. Take a level on me. 'Thursday Magazine' goes to a unique wedding and bla-bla-bla. Okay? Ride on him, though. He talks pretty loud, I think. Give me a roll."

"Two, one. Roll it, Chick."

MR. LYNXX, IS IT TRUE THAT YOU'VE LOST ALL YOUR SENSES EXCEPT SIGHT?

"Yeah. And if your flunky doesn't angle his friggin' light, I'll lose that, too."

"Cut. Move the light, Charlie. Let's start again. I can't bleep a deaf man. The audience likes t'think handicapped people are happy and full of sweet, wholesome sentiments. They don't like handicapped people t'get angry. It makes them uncomfortable. Me, I dig it. If I was handicapped, I'd throw bombs. If I had hands. Give me another roll."

"Two, one. Take it."

"We're with Simon Lynxx: victim of a rare disorder. Simon can't taste,

smell, feel or hear. We're with him on his wedding day." THIS MUST
BE A PRETTY DARN TERRIFYING SENSATION. WOULD YOU
MIND TELLING OUR TV AUDIENCE WHAT ITS LIKE?

"Well, first they could lean over and turn the sound knob off. Then
they could cover themselves with twelve layers of attic insulation and
go hang-gliding for a week off a cliff in San Berdoo."

WHAT CAUSED IT?

"I was free-basing Nyquil and—wham!"

"Uh-huh. I see. Well." THIS IS REV. MERRY ALLEN, SIMON'S
BRIDE-TO-BE. REV. ALLEN, WHAT PERSUADED YOU TO
MARRY A MAN IN THIS CONDITION?

"I—"

"I'll answer that, Merry. Give me the microphone a minute. I want
t'show the audience how a hand without feeling works. Take a close-up
on this."

"Well. All right."

"Lay it in my palm."

"Like so?"

"Now, rrr, chug-chug, I bring my other hand up and—"

"Yow!"

"Hey!" Simon—arch—has trimly curved the microphone: letter C for
Crumple Up. There is an internal wound: raw sparks hop and rocket.
Kim, on audio, is yelping: the earphones have plenty to squawk about.
"Hey! Hey, stop!"

"Here, Chick, now you can talk around corners."

"He broke it! Hey, Fischer, you told me this guy'd be cooperative.
That's a fuckin' eight-hundred-dollar mike he screwed up."

"Listen, I'll explain, Mr. Ferrari—"

"I don't care if he's deaf, he'll hear from my lawyers."

"Robert Fischer, this is your fault—"

"Merry, take Simon over to Herman. Please. Please? Mr. Ferrari, it
was an accident. He can't control his strength."

"Bullshit. Look at this thing, it looks like a goddamn boomerang. If I
threw it, it'd come back to me. He knew what he was doing. The man's a
menace. I don't wanna be around if he ever gets well."

"Mr. Ferrari—"

"Hey? Hanh? I can't hear, remember? What's going on? Where're you
taking me, Merry? Guess I blew that interview, huh? But I didn't like the
tone of his pencil. I didn't want you t'haveta answer that. Wait. Not so
fast—oh. Oh, it's Herman. Gosh, I'm glad you could come."

"So, still breaking things, I see."

"Huh?"

STILL BREAKING THINGS? Wolff has found his niche: in the Colonial fireplace: HEADROOM 5'3" yarmulke included. He is holding a poker. Flames are behind him. In afternoon sun they seem wan and redundant: like the headlights of a funeral cortege.

"Merry, I wantcha t'meet my foster father. Just last month we spent a few decades in Brooklyn together. Herman, this is my fiancée."

"How do you do? Only for him would I enter a goyish place of worship. On Shabbas, no less."

"I've heard a lot about you."

"From him, I can imagine what. But he's a genius, one in a million. You know why I say that, pretty lady? Because I can't predict him. Listen, I'm not where I am today from artistic sensitivity. It's people I know. But this one—he's a slippery eel. Who can tell with him, from one day to the next?"

"Hey, you two. Is this confidential or can I approach the bench, too?"

MAZELTOV. KYRYL COULDNT COME. HIS MOTHER TOOK A TURN FOR THE WORSE.

"You mean she recovered?"

YOUR BOY ROBERT IS A LITTLE SHARKER. I DIDNT KNOW WHEN I GOT A NIECE I WOULD ALSO COME IN FOR SUCH A GRAND-NEPHEW. I HOPE TO DROP DEAD BEFORE HE GETS UP FULL STEAM. IT WAS A LULU HOW HE FINISHED NORTY OFF WITHOUT MY HAVING TO RAISE A FINGER.

"Herman. As a favor t'me, as a wedding gift, let up on Norty."

SORRY. ITS OUT OF MY HANDS.

"Look, I'm gonna give him the money back. I can't take it, not like that. But you'll just crush his motile cells some other way. I'm saying, Please. Please, Herman. He isn't worth your time."

BELIEVE ME. NORTY, TOO, HAD RESPONSIBILITIES. HE KNEW WHAT HE WAS DOING. YOU THINK IM GOD IVE GOT A SAY-SO IN EVERYTHING. ITS OUT OF MY HANDS.

"The great man. It was always out of your hands, wasn't it? Merry, let me say a word to Herman alone."

ILL BRING THE BISHOP OVER. WEVE GOT TO GET GOING.

"Herman—"

SO, WHAT IS IT, BIG CHEESE? AN INSULT? OR MAYBE KNOCK ME IN THE FIREPLACE?

"I wanna tell you. I just found it out—you didn't even cause this. It was something else. Something in my stomach. It must've affected the whole nervous system. I couldn't blame you if I wanted to. Even that: it was out of your hands."

YOURE MAKING THIS UP.

"No. I'm gonna get well, Herman. I'm gonna sack this thing. I know it. Then all you'll have on your conscience is the blue baby films you've made. You and me, we're clear."

DOCTORS HAVE SAID THIS?
"I say. I know."
IM HAPPY.
"Me, too. Gimme a smooch, Herman. On the cheek, lean up. Thanks. This is my great day. Like any other middle-class jerk, I'm getting married."
"You won't be well, my friend. No." Wolff is smiling: pleasant. "Look at your eyes, any fool can see. You're already half dead. Just a craziness is keeping you alive now. And madman willpower. Who can deal with stubbornness like that? Who can talk sense to it? You're making a getaway, whether you like it or not. Take luck where you find it, Simon Lynxx. Take your dumb luck and go. I'm tired. I need a rest."
"Eh, what? I can't hear. But you're smiling."
MY SINCERE WISHES. THERES A RELIGIOUS PERSON STANDING BEHIND YOU. TRY TO TURN AROUND.
It is a very large bishop. One low ceiling beam has bent the twin artichoke leaves of his miter down. Six foot seven Simon might guess: no celebrant elevates a higher host. Thin, beautifully gaunt: firm like the artful power forward he once was: lane blocker, rebounder, tipper-in: Simon, even Simon well, wouldn't want to drive a baseline against this man. Merry's bishop can still play schoolyard full-court: defender of the faith in a 3-2 zone: it is his best and most effective outreach to black communities. Bella Chicago has just reintroduced herself. In all regalia he is casual: these people are known to him by name or pseudonym. He has been at Ten Great Ferry often and endorsed it: indeed, seeing Simon here, the bishop, who has no dismissive eye for costume, will remember a certain gorilla suit. In New York there are many weird apostolates. Pot and incense mist his cathedral. He has marched with all relevant minority groups, the Episcopal minority aside. And, this June, he will publish an abortion mass: taken, with nice liturgical rhythm, from services for baptism, child burial and the churching of women. Merry has presented Simon now. The bishop is affable: low church way up there. He chain-smokes in Jesus' name: so that he can ask awed five-foot-six-inch laymen for a light and, by this passing of fire, make them feel necessary to God. His lungs are black with Christian fellowship.
MY BLESSING. THIS IS AN HISTORIC MOMENT FOR THE CHURCH. OUR FIRST DOUBLE INTERSEXUAL WEDDING WITHIN THE CLERGY.
"That's nothing. At the reception we all put our car keys in a shoe box and pair off. I hope you drive." The bishop is laughing: he patronizes smut.
I LIKE YOUR SPIRIT. CHEERFULNESS IS THE ESSENTIAL CHRISTIAN VIRTUE.

"Yeah. I remember. Adolf had some great parties in the bunker."

ARTHUR HAS TOLD ME ABOUT SIGNS AND WONDERS. I HOPE YOU HAVENT GONE AND COMMITTED A MIRACLE. IT WOULD BE AN ENORMOUS SETBACK FOR THE FAITH. ID HAVE A LOT OF EXPLAINING TO DO.

"Don't worry. The only miracle is they can find training pants my size. I'm no Lazarus: I won't miss a bed check."

"Who here is Simon Lynxx? Huh?" A workman has appeared. Over his denim heart Simon can read "The Gentle Movers." "Huh? I'm double-parked outside."

"This is he."

"I got a delivery for you, where d'you want it put?"

"Eh?"

"He can't hear."

"I got a delivery!"

"It's no good, my friend, he's deaf."

"Well, Jesus, I'm not delivering a phonograph. He's gotta sign for it. I can't take it back." The man is nervous: noise and overdressing have irritated him. "Huh? I got one ticket today as it is." Merry will intercede.

HE HAS THIS BIG CRATE FOR YOU.

"Too soon. Much as I love cheap funerals, too soon."

FROM KYRYL.

"Uh-oh. How big is big?"

20 × 20, FEET. AN ARTWORK HE SAYS.

"Probably one of my own corns blown up t'the size of Long Island Sound. Your Reverence?"

Nod.

"How'd you like an original sculpture for your narthex by the great Kyryl himself?"

REALLY? ID LOVE IT. BUT WONT YOU LOOK FIRST?

"Nah, it might be a good likeness. Going, going, gone t'the man in the pointy hat."

ARE YOU SURE? AN ORIGINAL KYRYL AND A WEDDING PRESENT AT THAT.

"It's okay. Half the people I know are original Kyryls." Simon has turned to the mover. "Gentle friend, be patient with me. Before you unload the damn thing, deliver it withersoever this impressive person tells you to. He's a bishop and a big tipper. I'm sure he'll make it worth your time."

"I can't just— A bishop? Hey, I'm sorry. I mean, how's I t'know? Everybody here's got a Halloween getup on. Jesus, and I said, Jesus—"

"No problem." The bishop has taken out his pen and a cigarette. "No problem at all. Got a light? Thanks."

"Enough!" Simon, he trusts, is shouting. "Gee, I never commanded

8

perfect silence before. I feel like the Star-Spangled Banner. Ball Peen, Sledge: yes, you. Open the french doors. This has gone on long enough: Hymen has fallen insteps from dancing, the bridal wine is poured, my carnation is wilting and all such righteous blare as that. Let's get it on the road, huh? Besides, you dog ticks, you spongers, we can't *eat* until I'm married off. Move! I want to be a pair. I want!"

And this is the order of their going:

Arthur and Mrs. P
Simon and Merry
The bishop
Mr. and Mrs. Allen
A spider monkey
Robert and Charlene
Ball Peen and Sledge
Niko and waitresses
The same spider monkey
Herman Wolff
Representatives from NA
A mass of clergy

Various mummers, clowns, male and female impersonators, emblems, logos, trademarks, charades, mises en scène, pageants, masques, harlequinades and tableaux vivantes.

A spoilsport wind has come up now. Mrs. P can't shorten sail: she will yaw off to starboard, aside. Arthur, close-hauling muslin, must put her helm over and make some way. The bishop has ground another pastoral butt out: his miter, blown, is mitered and aslant. Friday out-rides, rushing like scandal from van to rear to van again. Mr. and Mrs. Allen are miscast: they came as they were and that wasn't quite enough. Herman Wolff futzes with his yarmulke: it, Harold Gluck can't believe, it actually has a warm earflap on either side that will pull down. Tears blind Robert: Here—one big, congratulatory gust has said—is mud in your eye. And, from that spot where long ago a wise mule followed his own peculiar star to Bethlehem, Chick Ferrari et al. are putting the procession on videotape. Simon gets his wish: a film, though silent, has been made at last. Merry vanishes: into her flare-back, bursting, resplendent hair. The wind is a light comedian. It has dragged smoke over them from Aldo's barbecue: a member of the wedding. For just one half frame Simon can't see. Then it will be clear to him.

Their gait is gentle, slow: they rather promenade. Mrs. P's hem has rustled a harvest home of autumn leaf-fall up: she is shin deep in old foliage and cannot hurry on. Simon, careful ground observer, walks quite well: an intellectual act: he must stand, if anyone ever has, to reason. Through Van Lynxx Garden, where his night-long digging could seem a little foxhole defense. Through Van Lynxx Cemetery: last resting place of strange blood. From behind one cumulous boll the sun has made spot checks: yes, indeed, they are a gala crew. Doors above have opened for them: there is interest and good welcome here. Left, from balcony 7M, a solo trumpeter begins to take off on the Wedding March: in salsa transposition. She, merry, will wave up. Past Aldo's Spirit of Radio and, by unrapid transit, toward the hijacked Florentine chapel: that other unwilling orphan taken in. And, from apartment 15D on high, a handful of Uncle Ben's rice is tossed. The ingrate wind will blow it back. Again: once again. Then the whole damn box for ballast, not a missile but a gift, flung end over end, emptying as it falls. And emptied now.

0

O,

Grace, the lawless, break in now. Haphazard, peradventure, at random, by chance: arbitrary as all things with great license are: steal. From the poor to the rich (so it must be): in neither fairness nor reason: last come, first served. Fixer of elections, thug of the spirit, kidnapper, felon: You that cherish passion most, watch Simon dance. Da-dja-dja, deedah and *jah*: replete at last, No Vacancy, Occupied, Sold Out. Big steps, mad steps, da-dja: steps that only a wild, outlaw lover could sound music for. Gall to gall, nerve to nerve, cheek to cheek—dance: he has suckered You in. You who made the sun out of obstinacy: and stars from a bountiful arrogance. Grace, soul-tease, flirt here: be sweet, be senseless: charm him. He has steadied Your promiscuous will to his: you are a handsome pair. Take his empty hand now and, O, together dance.

On the bed blind Simon hums: a thin, fine reed blown through: inner ear noise, the sort we imbue quiet seashells with: listening itself can be a sound. His inch-deep breath will not retune or modulate this theme. Merry feels it in diapering him: he has reached a certain pitch. The legs are up: lax, but, to her eye, hamstrung still with latent nimbleness and strut. Along one elbow intravenous liquid ticks: her new way of fixing time. The mouth has been sprung shut and will not release. She knows, she knew, how much of him was spoken: his own herald and oral tradition: she misses that. It is the eighth day after darkening. They have made his room neat. Fragrances are around that can start girlhood in her again: Simon has been a kind of pomander here. Thoughtful, good Friday is sitting by his chest. Simon won't be drawn out: there are no antic games in him, nor anything worth a nice imitation. But the animal can wait. Furry arm across furry arm, Arthur drowses in his upright chair: Simon has grass-widowed the now Mrs. G. A tape recorder is on: the hum of inactivity in Simon will erase the hum of blank Mylar. More than one hundred cassettes have taken his faint dictation: each with a catalogue date: they stack up poorly against the wall and Arthur's huge expectation. Though amicable, Arthur and she don't often talk. Merry prefers service: he has begun to guess that they are overheard. There is something in Simon beyond, behind unconsciousness: maybe a super-ironic stealth. Merry, done, has put the ankles down. Let loose, Simon will tend to ball up: curved at hand, at knee, at neck: as quicksilver globs seek other quicksilver globs out and join. His pulse is forty. The just-vital sign of someone going to sleep in blizzards at last.

But Friday ran that other afternoon. And a mouse died of shock. Roaches, so usually aloof, began to swarm out in sunlight from the kitchen wood: their native self-reliance given up. No one or creature could long bear new-blinded Simon's loathsome howl. Then, that afternoon, his pulse was one-twenty, one-thirty, one-sixty and beyond human invoicing: a foot-to-floor acceleration of the blood. His heart, she thought, must flame out or flap itself apart. Veinwork hemorrhaged in the eye-white: jag, jag: one abrupt red web. His face spread, as if under pressure of innumerable, secret G's. Merry saw all the perfect teeth: a dog's snarl-show of threat. The spine vaulted: arms and legs swam circling back: so we thrash for balance on a narrow place. Arthur and Merry could imagine wind against him: swift atmospheres re-entered: immobile, he fell earthward in a little room. It gave them fear of heights: they crouched low. And, soon after, the cat-screech came out: kaaaaaghht-ahhhrthh: whether fear or defiance was ascendant in him, Simon hissed or Simon spat. They held, so to speak, each other's ears: they embraced in another, far room. Pardon them this: and excuse, yes, their repulsion. How, after all, do you comfort at parsecs something that has rescinded matter and gone quite through? Yet the time was not immoderate: perhaps a half hour by her judging. For him, though, for him without relativity or end, it was the duration. They found Simon in a dead man's float. Face down, light, planing: on the floor. Finger wide, knee wide, eye, oh, wide. From blown-up corneal tissue his contact lenses had popped off. Something less for her to do. And he hummed.

Snow falls, fills outside. Merry will watch for some while. Depressions in Van Lynxx Garden have been rounded off to the nearest whole digit. There is boutique neatness around: a sort of enormous bed-making done. The birdbath has brimmed with snow: so, too, Aldo's twenty-seven-point-five-gallon barbecue. In each hole that Simon dug on his marriage eve Arthur has planted a hale evergreen. Meanwhile, at places Merry cannot see, and wouldn't mark if seen, this is happening: An eleven-story apartment house has been built where once the Avon Lady never called. On girl children of twelve or thirteen breasts thrust up overnight: responsive to the deep hydraulic force in puberty. Fish will dive down: gas tanks are siphoned into. Herman Wolff is wearing a warm homburg hat over his concave skull. Vesicles replenish their store: women are pregnant. A puma has taken up East Side residence in the room used by certain chicken leopards before. Our universe is unnoticeably larger. Madmen will put on Porky Pig's head. Melted snow has seeped through rotten planking to flood an ancient beer vat shell. Below her, crafty and explosive seeds hide in furrow and crevice and pot. This isn't all: all will be more. But Merry, with her unrequited, her glossed-over love, can't think of such things yet.

Simon is humming: on the beam. Merry will wipe new eyeglasses to look at him. Even slack, his great, ungrudging nakedness might arouse her still. The chest and abdomen are model. He could afford all substance lost: there was this second, better nudity under that. She can see, in his child-crouch, a standing broad jumper's vigorous flex implied. And she has to smile: at the body's resurrection he need not be ashamed. Diligent yet, she will tuck a sheet around. Then, sitting beside Simon in her red dress, Merry sleeps. Robert, last week, thought she looked beautiful: he was off to the Coast in a country that has more than one. So they, Arthur and she, are alone. A few minutes or an ounce of glucose, however you choose to reckon time, must pass, must go in. Snow is falling. Men eat on a lunch break. Noon. Listen: the humming has broken off. Arthur's tape machine will register that: but it can't be interested. Friday only notices. This, or something like it, has happened to him before. He blinks: he touches Simon as he would touch a female of his race. For one moment here the face might seem mankindly and evolved: but that, we know, is just an old illusion. With subhuman grace Friday swings across the bed: to settle, unremarked, in her red lap. He is a pragmatist: he has learned to have masters. Merry will do for now.

And Paradise, a china shop, Simon thunders in.

DALKEY ARCHIVE PAPERBACKS

FELIPE ALFAU, *Chromos.*
  Locos.
  Sentimental Songs.
ALAN ANSEN,
  Contact Highs: Selected Poems 1957-1987.
DJUNA BARNES, *Ladies Almanack.*
  Ryder.
JOHN BARTH, *LETTERS.*
  Sabbatical.
ANDREI BITOV, *Pushkin House.*
ROGER BOYLAN, *Killoyle.*
CHRISTINE BROOKE-ROSE, *Amalgamemnon.*
GERALD BURNS, *Shorter Poems.*
MICHEL BUTOR,
  Portrait of the Artist as a Young Ape.
JULIETA CAMPOS, *The Fear of Losing Eurydice.*
ANNE CARSON, *Eros the Bittersweet.*
LOUIS-FERDINAND CÉLINE, *Castle to Castle.*
  North.
  Rigadoon.
HUGO CHARTERIS, *The Tide Is Right.*
JEROME CHARYN, *The Tar Baby.*
EMILY HOLMES COLEMAN, *The Shutter of Snow.*
ROBERT COOVER, *A Night at the Movies.*
STANLEY CRAWFORD,
  Some Instructions to My Wife.
RENÉ CREVEL, *Putting My Foot in It.*
RALPH CUSACK, *Cadenza.*
SUSAN DAITCH, *Storytown.*
PETER DIMOCK,
  A Short Rhetoric for Leaving the Family.
COLEMAN DOWELL, *Island People.*
  Too Much Flesh and Jabez.
RIKKI DUCORNET, *The Fountains of Neptune.*
  The Jade Cabinet.
  Phosphor in Dreamland.
  The Stain.

WILLIAM EASTLAKE, *Lyric of the Circle Heart.*
STANLEY ELKIN, *The Dick Gibson Show.*
ANNIE ERNAUX, *Cleaned Out.*
LAUREN FAIRBANKS, *Muzzle Thyself.*
  Sister Carrie.
LESLIE A. FIEDLER,
  Love and Death in the American Novel.
RONALD FIRBANK, *Complete Short Stories.*
FORD MADOX FORD, *The March of Literature.*
JANICE GALLOWAY, *Foreign Parts.*
  The Trick Is to Keep Breathing.
WILLIAM H. GASS,
  Willie Masters' Lonesome Wife.
C. S. GISCOMBE, *Giscome Road.*
  Here.
KAREN ELIZABETH GORDON, *The Red Shoes.*
GEOFFREY GREEN, ET AL, *The Vineland Papers.*
PATRICK GRAINVILLE, *The Cave of Heaven.*
JOHN HAWKES, *Whistlejacket.*
ALDOUS HUXLEY, *Antic Hay.*
  Point Counter Point.
  Those Barren Leaves.
  Time Must Have a Stop.
TADEUSZ KONWICKI, *The Polish Complex.*
EWA KURYLUK, *Century 21.*
OSMAN LINS,
  The Queen of the Prisons of Greece.
ALF MAC LOCHLAINN,
  The Corpus in the Library.
  Out of Focus.
D. KEITH MANO, *Take Five.*
BEN MARCUS, *The Age of Wire and String.*
DAVID MARKSON, *Collected Poems.*
  Reader's Block.
  Springer's Progress.
  Wittgenstein's Mistress.
CARL R. MARTIN, *Genii Over Salzburg.*

Visit our website at www.cas.ilstu.edu/english/dalkey/dalkey.html

DALKEY ARCHIVE PAPERBACKS

Visit our website at www.cas.ilstu.edu/english/dalkey/dalkey.html

Dalkey Archive Press

ISU Campus Box 4241, Normal, IL 61790–4241

fax (309) 438–7422